BIRTH MARK

Bill Rowe

Peter Cooper

PUBLISHED BY VIVISPHERE PUBLISHING, INC.

Copyright © 1998 by Bill Rowe and Peter Cooper

All rights reserved under International and Pan-American Copyright Conventions. Published in the United States by Vivisphere Publishing, Inc..

http://www.vivisphere.com/

ISBN 1-892323-00-1

Library of Congress Catalogue Number 98-85443

Manufactured in the United States of America

The book is set in Adobe Apollo, a face designed by Adrian Frutiger in 1961 for the Monotype Corporation. Designed and typeset in the foothills of the Adirondacks by the folks at *Syllables*.

Cover design by
CRESCENT HILL GRAPHICS
Brooklyn, New York

To our darling Jess

Prologue

Each memory has purpose. We remember with each conscious and unconscious aspect of our being. Not all these recollections rise to the surface. And, knowingly or not, we bring almost everything of significance with us.

Like refugees from a war-zone of the past, we arrive in the present and march into the future, carrying essential goods and baggage from our past lives, hoping to take advantage of the freely-chosen, fresh opportunities thought likely to present themselves in the life we are about to live.

This manuscript does not ask your acceptance as proof of reincarnation, but it is hoped that the reader will grow from exposure to one certain truth: The Cosmic implications of cause and inevitable effect—the eternal, entangling webs spun by unresolved karma—as set forth in this tale and as they affect every individual life.

I know not what the future holds. But what I do know of my many pasts has shone forth from illuminating fragments—brilliant bits and pieces of splendid and sometimes terrifying parchment-memory—unearthed in various, far-flung ancient clay pots. These discoveries, disinterred by some magnificent and mysterious archeology, have brought significant lessons from the past and were induced either by unknown, subconscious intention, or by fear and the desperate instinct to survive. Most have involved brushes, skirmishes, even collisions with spirits previously known.

It is my hope that some grace or higher Consciousness has come to me from each remembered encounter, where righting a previous wrong by a freely-given act of kindness may have occasionally resulted in a balancing or a forgiveness.

It is also hoped that you will sense the spirit that survives and will live on, eternally.

There is no greater wish for my manuscript than that future generations who read it, understand that in striving to balance a checkered past, I, an ordinary, flawed human being, have tried to live rightly. After all, of each individual, God asks not Sainthood—only personal decency and responsible virtue.

Let the reader not misunderstand: I bear no responsibility for good character or lack thereof in other people, nor for the failures or successes in their lives—only for my own. Our sole responsibilities are *to* each other—not *for* each other.

It is my final desire that we meet again, to embrace in the glowing light of our individual souls, as seen through the much brighter eyes of our future incarnations. For you are all my brothers and sisters, my children, my mothers and fathers, my lovers and beloved.

I shall miss each of you...until we do meet again.

Doug MacBrayne,
APRIL, 2002

CHAPTER ONE

LONDON, 1664

His hunger for words blocked out the cold, the dank misery of the room, masked even the ache of an empty stomach, but not the shame. Phineas put down his nib and closed his eyes, not sure whether he could once again face the chill streets, with that relentless acrid fog, made heavy and foul by the smoke that poured from every hearth in London.

Well, almost every hearth. Not all households could afford coal, nor did many occupants have the canniness to steal wood enough to encourage a small flame.

Phineas grabbed his hat, started for the door, then leaned against the jamb, ear alert for any sound of movement in the hallway. Mrs. Grimsby should pay him to stay in that small sty of a room. After all, what other flats in this part of town could boast a Cambridge graduate among their tenants? Cripes, she could raise everyone else's rent just for the chance to hear his conversation, alone.

Satisfied she wasn't lurking about the hallway, Phineas pushed through the door and started out.

"Mr. Davies!" A paralyzing screech, not a call.

"Halloo, Mrs. Grimsby." Phineas waved over his shoulder. "No time to chat at the moment, I'm off to an appointment."

"Your rent is late, Mr. Davies."

He stopped to give her a shallow smile.

"I know, Mrs. Grimsby. I expect to receive my stipend this evening."

"Stipend?" She cackled, wiped a slur of phlegm from her mouth with a dirty sleeve. "Is that what you call sticking your hand out to strangers in Picadilly?"

"Mrs. Grimsby—"

"Ah, none of yer guff. Me father told me never trust an 'educated' man for regular rent. He's up in 'eaven, laughin' at me now, over the likes of you."

"Mrs. Grimsby, I assure you—"

"And I assure you, Mr. Davies, you'll be in the street if I don't have my rent on the morrow."

Phineas fled, the ratty tail of his coat flapping behind him. As he entered the market square, the orange-and-green-striped tilts fluttering from some of the stalls drew his attention to the smell of the food on display and to his hunger. Well aware that strangers gawked at his convulsive, spastic progress across the rough cobblestones, he slipped into a dark alley. Blinded by the sudden darkness, he tripped over a small furry ball that yelped as if in mortal pain.

Reaching over from where he'd fallen, Phineas tried to gather the tiny black-and-tan mongrel pup to him. The creature spun in circles, dragging its hind foot. His own leg aching from the spill, Phineas finally stretched out enough to grab the mutt, lifted it to his breast.

"There, there," he murmured. The pup shivered, more frightened than hurt, but didn't squirm to escape. Phineas smiled. "You like the warm, don't you?"

The pup worked its way into the opening in his jacket, was soon at Phineas' neck, nursing on the dry skin. Phineas chuckled, leaned against the wall, sighed for what felt like the first time in weeks. He stroked the puppy, tears welling in his eyes. He reached into his pocket, pulled out a thin scrap of cloth. Two coins rattled to the cobblestones. He quickly retrieved them, wiped his eyes, then folded the coins back into his kerchief.

"Ah, pup. If I could take care of myself better, I might be able to take care of you, as well."

The creature was now working its way up into Phineas' long blond hair. One of its paws caught in several strands near the back, yanking painfully on the livid, red birthmark, spread like an inkspill on the back of his head. Carefully, Phineas pulled the dog down to his chest.

In the dark, to his left, he heard the low growl of another dog, probably the mother. Creakily, he rose, carried the pup over to an emaciated bitch lying amidst the rubble. She looked up slowly. Phineas noticed the thin froth at her jaw. Suddenly her growl deepened.

"It's okay, mum. Your pup is here now."

But her attention was behind him. Phineas turned to see a huge, glowering man with a dark, curly beard split at the chin. Dressed in rags, he held his hands behind him.

"Her pup wandered off," Phineas said, meekly. "I was bringing it back."

The man nodded. Phineas straightened painfully, started to hobble past. There was a brief flurry, the man's arms moved quickly. A brilliant explosion went off in Phineas' head. Sparks burst, cascading behind his eyes—fleeting streaks of starry light, meteor trails which smeared, then faded to total blackness.

❧

EN ROUTE: ST. ANDREWS, SCOTLAND,
NOVEMBER, 1969

Felicity stared at the Scottish countryside, a postcard framed by the oval window of the chartered Gulfstream II. The hills and glens were carpeted with various shades of brown, beige and faint traces of green. A ribbon of dark gray tarmac roller-coasted down the middle of the patchwork quilt landscape.

"We're almost there, baby." She patted her stomach, and wondered whether she was carrying a boy or a girl. Would its hair be blonde like hers, dark like Peter's, or maybe even a redhead? She giggled at that.

A slight bump from the tires hitting the pavement made her close her eyes. Why was flying so tiring? All you did was sit. No, this had nothing to do with travel. Since she had discovered she was pregnant six months earlier, she had been weak. She was so tired that she'd resisted when Peter suggested they come to Scotland to hire a nanny.

"Couldn't we find someone here?" Felicity had asked. "Why not an American nanny? Why go all the way to Scotland?"

He shook his head. "This baby will be heir to the Douglas-MacBrayne family fortune and is descended from a long line of Scots. Where else would we find someone relatively unspoiled by modern materialism? Someone with good, old Scottish self-reliance, honesty, thrift and truthfulness—not to mention faith?"

Felicity stared at him. As much as she loved her husband, she was not blind to his shortcomings. Raised amid wealth, he was extravagant with himself, could be ruthless in business and was possibly the most unspiritual person she had ever met. There was no reason even to discuss faith.

After all, when they bought their first Mercedes, they didn't fly to Germany to pick it out. They hadn't gone to Italy for the marble in the living room, or to China for the silk draperies. "I don't dispute the advantages of such a nanny, but why couldn't we do it through an agency?" she'd asked.

Peter had assumed the look of false patience he wore whenever she questioned one of his "decisions."

"Do you really want to bring someone we haven't even met over here to care for our baby?" He ran his hand through his short, black hair, lowered his eyes. "Besides, as long as we're there, I thought I might play some golf at St. Andrews."

"Darling, couldn't you do that after the baby is born? The doctors ordered—"

"The doctors gave the okay. I talked to them myself. Besides, while we're there I can do some research on my ancestry."

She should have known. Peter never had just one reason for his actions. This was less about a nanny for their child than his two obsessions: golf and his lineage. His ancestry fixation started with a wedding gift from her father: an elaborate leather-bound, gilt-edged book, tracing her family's direct descent from many important crowned heads in Europe—Charlemagne, Alfred the Great and Anne of Russia, to mention only a few. The magnificent book was replete with pages of hand-painted heraldry in full color, with names, dates and certified historical references.

Nothing more might have come of the gift, if Peter hadn't overheard a drunken, distant cousin at the wedding.

"That Peter's a clever one, isn't he? All that money couldn't buy a respectable lineage, so he married into a family that had one."

Liquor-talk, not worth a moment's consternation, but it had branded itself deep inside Peter and altered his whole attitude toward their relationship. Oh, he was still considerate and loving on the outside, but something within had become blocked off from her.

She loved Peter with all her heart and didn't care a whit about such things. She wondered if she ever be able to show him that ancestry didn't matter.

"What about that firm in Massachusetts? I thought they were working..."

"There are some things that require firsthand checking—" He swallowed hard several times, his Adam's apple jerking his bowtie up and down. For a moment, Felicity feared the giant moth might actually take flight. Maybe if he finally found what he was searching for, he wouldn't suffer so. She stretched out her hand, a white dove of peace.

"Then let's go to Scotland and hire the best damn nanny they have."

Now Peter held her hand as Felicity disembarked carefully from the private jet. Maybe he had been right about making the trip. Although she was tired, the Scottish autumn air was bracing, laden as it was with its exotic, restorative dew.

She remained outside the long limousine to stretch her cramped legs, idly watching the luggage being transferred.

"Darling, where are your clubs?"

"Damn, I must have left them at home." Peter blushed, recovered quickly. "I guess I'll just have to buy a new set when we get to St. Andrews."

She watched him limp around to the other side of the car. He had never intended to bring them. She wished she didn't know him so well. Even the smallest white lie showed up as clearly as a shackle on his right ankle.

High on a hill near The Law, in the west central part of Dundee, the first glint of the rising sun cast a rosy glow over the city's glistening slate roofs. Most house windows were shuttered, or closed against the first light by heavy curtains. Not those at 1441 Pentland Crescent, where light blue, floral-patterned curtains fluttered in the brisk breeze blowing down the River Tay.

Fiona McLean blinked awake, smiled at the feeble, newborn sun and stretched her arms from under the light coverlet. It was barely five-thirty, but Fiona happily reached across to the small table by her bed and grabbed her book. The first hour of daylight belonged to her. The rest belonged to whomsoever she worked for, but she derived her greatest pleasure from reading several chapters of the latest mystery before starting her day.

It was a secret habit, confined to her bedroom, which she had shared with only one person during her forty-five years alive.

Five years previously, she met and, after a short courtship, married childless widower Tom Ogilvie, an engineer at the local Timex factory. His brother, employed by the City, helped the newlyweds rent a two-bedroom Council house on Balgay Hill.

As giddy as teenagers, Tom and Fiona even planned to convert the extra bedroom into the perfect nursery. Fiona ordered fabric to make curtains and coverlets. Tom sanded and refinished the floors, painted all the rooms, and even installed a new tub in the bathroom. Together, they bought much of the furniture at an estate sale.

Fiona's happiness turned to horror on their six-month anniversary: Tom collapsed, helping the delivery man carry a large, secondhand sideboard up to their flat. He was pronounced dead on arrival at Dundee Royal Infirmary. A massive cerebral hemorrhage had made Fiona a widow.

Once the sharp pains of grief subsided, Fiona became resigned to the bitter possibility that God intended she remain childless. How she had hoped to have her own child, instead of always caring for someone else's. It had taken her thirty years to find and marry Tom; she was unlikely to find another suitable husband before time would catch up with her child-bearing abilities.

The conclusion was inescapable. As a professional Nanny, the only children she would have would always belong to others.

Fiona turned another page and looked at her wrist where she wore Tom's wedding present—an electric Timex wrist watch, bought on "special offer" at the company's quarterly, in-house sale. Unable to afford a diamond ring, he'd refused to borrow money for anything and gave her a simple silver one instead. Fiona did not mind. She approved of his thrift. The ring told the world she was married and the watch was the loveliest she ever owned.

After the funeral, Fiona Ogilvie had her maiden name legally restored. There had been two Mrs. Tom Ogilvies but only one nanny named Fiona McLean.

Now, as the city slumbered below, Fiona heard two herring-gulls squawk past the windows of her fourth floor flat, noisily pursuing a third, en route from the harbor to its aerie.

Half awake, a sudden emotion overwhelmed her: A hunch. Something special, important would happen. Dark, soulful eyes now wide, Fiona threw off her blanket, walked to the window and looked past the city, over the silvery River Tay to the hills of the Kingdom of Fife. During the night, a knife-edged cold front had passed, scraping yesterday's pelting rain and unstable, humid air away to the North Sea.

"We may have seen the best o' the day, just; but the sleep is still on me." She said aloud in the Gaelic manner, the language of her parents. "There's still twa hours, afore the alarum'll go off."

She tossed the book on the bed. Before marriage, she had read romance novels, calling them her "husband research." That part of her education was complete—she'd earned a true Bachelor's Degree. Now she consumed mysteries every morning. Not even her flat mate, Kate Cameron, another nanny, knew what she did in those early hours.

Kate was fifteen years younger, but their mutual profession made sharing the flat easier. Except for the occasional holiday trip together, they rarely saw each other. Any dinners shared were congenial—two aunts discussing the foibles and misadventures of their charges.

At least until Kate had found herself unemployed the previous month. Unlike Fiona, Kate had gone to Seymour Lodge, the "Nanny University." They had referred her several times, though a proper position had not yet materialized. She barely kept up her end of the finances by working part-time here and there. Weekends were spent with her mother, Maggie, and a red-headed boyfriend named Sandy.

Fiona sighed. She, too, would be looking for steady work, now that Commander McGhee and his wife had been transferred south to Portsmouth. She closed her eyes to shut our the vision of their little Willie, crying his eyes out, clinging to Fiona's leg, begging her to come with them.

For twenty-eight years, the same scene had played out time and time again. How she wished she could care for a babe—just once—from birth and stay with it through... through what? To the end? Fiona shuddered.

"Ach, you've become a silly old woman, Fiona McLean," she grumbled, dragging her feet from under the covers.

Maybe this way was better. She could love them all she liked and although giving them up was painful, it could never compare with the pain of watching them grow up and leave home. And she rarely had to witness the angry teenage years. Watching their sweet faces grow into hardened pre-adulthood. Ach, those terrible clothes and awful music. No, she had them at the right age. Before their clay hardened. And none had ever died. What must a mother go through if...?

She quickly accomplished her toilet and went out to the kitchen to start the kettle boiling. For a moment she considered returning to her mystery. That Agatha Christie could sure spin a tale. But Fiona was determined not to undermine her schedule during this period of unemployment. Might as well have a look at the morning paper.

She poured hot water over the bags in the teapot and glanced at the front page under the column headed "Domestic Help Wanted." Not one advert for a nanny.

Sleepy-eyed Kate wandered in. "Morning, Fiona. Is there enough for two in the pot?"

"Aye, lass. Sit yourself down. I'll get ye a cuppa."

"Bless you."

Fiona walked to the stove.

"You're a bit late this morning, aren't you?" Kate asked through a yawn.

"Yesterday was my last with the Commander's family. Looks like we'll be having breakfast together for awhile."

Kate nodded. "If things don't get better, I may have to drag Sandy to the altar and be done with it."

Kate was lucky, if worse came to worst, she could always move in with her mother, but Fiona didn't want to suggest that: Jobs were hard enough to find, good roommates, nearly impossible. Anyway, Mother Cameron was given to strange dreams and premonitions that could be unnerving.

Fiona poured Kate's tea. "Why doesn't Sandy just propose? You've been going together a long time."

"Too long." Kate said. "He says he won't marry until he can afford to support a wife properly."

"So that's why he gives all those free rides in his taxi." Fiona laughed, looked at the paper again and felt a sudden unusual chill. That corner of the room had unaccountably become icy cold. Halfway down the back page, at which she seldom looked, there it was—out of place, a last-minute advert.

> NANNY REQUIRED IN AMERICA
> Mature, responsible lady.
> To care for infant in the United States.
> Long term position.
> Excellent pay and working conditions.
> All expenses paid.
> Contact Courier Box #4144

She wanted to laugh out loud, then looked over the top of the paper at Kate. An evil thought crossed her mind: All she had to do was fold up the paper, keep it with her. Kate might never find out. Fiona shook her head. Evil thoughts acted upon, lead to evil deeds.

"Kate, dear."

"Yes?"

"Would you ever consider taking a job in another country?"

Kate looked up. "I suppose it depends on the country. Don't think I'd want anyplace really foreign. Like India, or the Middle East. You know, non-Christian."

"But what about Sandy and your mum?"

"Me mum can take care of herself. As for Sandy, maybe it would teach him a lesson were I to go away. Serve him right for taking me for granted."

Fiona handed the newspaper across to her. "Look on the last page."

Kate read, her eyes opening wide. She glanced up.

"Would you be applyin'?

Fiona nodded.

"And... you wouldn't mind if I did as well?"

Fiona smiled. "Why do you think I showed it to you?"

"I sure am tired of those part-time jobs." Kate read the advert again. "Tell you what. I was going to start mixing the Christmas cake. We can make it together, now; but wouldn't it be better if we could get Widow MacGillivray's recipe?"

"I don't think she'll give it to us, you know how she is about her precious recipes. I'll ask her when I go downstairs later."

"If she doesn't give it to you, we'll use mine."

"And whoever lands the job..."

"The other gets the cake."

The two women shook hands, then hugged, laughing.

Felicity awoke with a start. A deep pain stabbed her chest. She had trouble breathing. Tried to sit up.

"Oh, God. Please don't do this. Not yet."

Disoriented, she looked around the room. It took a moment before she remembered she was at the Rusacks in St. Andrews. She willed her body to relax. Slowly, the panic subsided. She placed both hands on her swollen middle.

"Don't be in such a hurry, baby. It's not time yet."

The moment passed, the pain left and Felicity smiled. It was a rare baby who would begin obeying so early.

Peter tapped lightly on the door and peeked in.

"Feel up to a little work?"

"Depends on what you have in mind. I don't think I could dig a ditch."

He held up several envelopes. "The first replies to our ad."

She shifted in bed and sat up. "If you could order some juice and toast, I'll be ready by the time they bring it."

Peter and Felicity took turns reading the resumes to each other. They put one aside for future reference. Signed "Fiona McLean," postmarked "Dundee," it had been posted at 21:00 the previous evening.

A hundred applications came over the next two days. They spent the middle of the week sorting out the most promising.

"Maybe we should have engaged an employment agency," Peter said, looking over the letters spread on the table.

They finally selected the five best. After checking all the references, Peter then wrote identical letters asking each to telephone for an interview at The Rusacks on Sunday.

"That gives us a free day on Saturday," Felicity said. "I suppose you planned it so we'd have tomorrow off?"

"I hoped it would work out that way."

"When's your tee-time?"

"Nine o'clock," came the sheepish reply.

Luckily for the golfers, Saturday brought clear skies and warm weather. Felicity felt cooped up and decided on a stroll. A taxi pulled to the curb just as she reached the front door of the hotel.

She walked toward the cab, hesitated and for a moment considered returning to the room. Peter would be unhappy if he discovered she'd gone out without him, but she had no intention of spending every minute looking out the window at the golf course and the sea.

The cabbie motioned her inside and Felicity flipped a coin in her mind. Heads, she'd go exploring. Another gesture from the driver and Felicity opened the door.

"Where to, Lass?"

"I... I'm not sure."

The driver smiled. "American, eh?"

"Yes."

"Shopping, seeing the sights, or a spot of tea?"

"What would you recommend for a first-time visitor?" She looked at the driver's identification card posted on the back of the seat. "Alexander Potts."

"On a sunny day like today, I'd recommend a walk round the Abbey."

"That sounds lovely, Mr. Potts."

"Call me Sandy."

"Okay, Sandy." Felicity giggled. "But on the other hand a walk might be too strenuous. You see, I'm going to have a baby."

"Bless you both," Sandy said.

"Thank you."

"If you're up to it, there's a woman who bides not far away, near the village of Lumbo," he turned, put his elbow on the top of the seat. "Old Maggie's got what we call the second sight. All the local women havin' babies go see her for good luck and mebbe a peek at the future."

"I... I'm not sure. That's not—" As soon as she said not, Felicity felt a little jump in her middle and put a hand on her stomach.

"Ah, 'tis a rare opportunity, lass, if she'll see you."

"Could we telephone her?"

"Sorry, she's not on the phone. Besides it's really not too far to Lumbo."

Another kick convinced Felicity that Sandy was right, although she knew Peter would disapprove. Maybe she wouldn't tell him.

"Okay, what the heck."

Sandy chattered away, guiding the taxi through the narrow streets. He seemed to know everyone's business, describing the major and minor soap opera tragedies and infidelities of the families that lived in various houses along the way. Finally, they pulled up in front of a ramshackle cottage.

"You go ahead on in, I'll wait outside."

"I don't want you to miss another fare."

"I have a standing rule, ma'am; pregnant women from other countries always get free waiting-time."

"Why, thank you, Sandy, I'm sure it won't take long."

Sandy leaned back and put his cap over his eyes as if to nap. "You just take your time, mum."

Felicity opened the creaky gate and picked her way along the rough stone path to the door. The cottage looked as if the door was the only thing keeping it from crumbling. She tapped lightly. No answer. She tapped again, harder.

"Who's that bangin'?" The cat-scratch voice made Felicity want to run away.

"Maggie?"

"What ye want?"

"I, uh, I was told you could tell me about my baby."

The sound of slow shuffling feet came close to the other side of the door.

"You pregnant?"

"Yes, ma'am."

The door opened. A gnarled hand reached into the bright sunlight, grabbed her arm and towed her inside.

The woman didn't turn around, just pulled Felicity toward a table. The room was stifling hot. A peat fire glowed at the bottom of the black, cast-iron stove that seemed to take up most of the space in the tiny kitchen. The hand let go and motioned her to sit at the table. Maggie still didn't turn around, but shuffled toward the stove.

At the table, Felicity folded her hands and looked at an untouched cup of coffee. A cigarette had burned to its cork tip in the ashtray, with two inches of ash intact, a long, dead slug. Close by, unnaturally bright false teeth grinned menacingly.

Felicity took her hands off the table, leaned back and tried to relax.

Maggie put a steaming mug in front of her and snatched the grinning teeth from the table. In one quick motion, she sucked them into her wrinkled, pink maw.

Tangled strands of dyed black hair tumbled from the untidy bun on top of the old hag's head, while her newly-toothed lower jaw moved irregularly up, down and sideways, occasionally almost touching her long, crooked nose. Finally, the dentures found their proper place. She turned full-faced to Felicity, who caught her breath.

Three ugly, hairy warts on the crone's deeply lined, weathered face mesmerized Felicity. Surely she was in the presence of a witch.

"Got a bun in the oven, eh, dearie?"

"Y-yes."

"Drink your tea whilst I see what the wee thing's got to say for itself."

Felicity lifted her cup, sniffed at the rising vapors. If Maggie were a witch, what might this concoction be?

"It's only Lipton's, dearie. And no bat wings. They're out of season." She cackled what might have been laughter and wiped her mouth.

A tiny sip confirmed the brew as genuine. Felicity blushed and looked closer at Maggie. The body and face were historic, but the eyes were young, clear as the blue sky outside.

"What's your name?"

Felicity told her, then found herself blurting out all kinds of information she never expected to share: her fears about the trip, Peter's insecure lineage. How she hoped the baby would repair their faltering relationship. She stopped short of telling Maggie about her physical condition and what that might mean to the baby's chance of going full-term. She pushed that thought deeper and took a long sip of tea.

"Ah, darlin', every new babe is a miracle of possibilities. This boy you're gonna bear will be healthy, smarter than paint. He'll have a special kind of love and hope inside him—which he'll get from you—that comes along very rare." Maggie paused, seemed to nod her head, a bird bobbing at water. "He'll have his troubles, to be sure, the special ones always do. But there's powerful spirits around him. They'll help him find his way."

"Even if...?"

She looked into Maggie's clear, blue eyes, which glistened as large tears slowly formed. A sudden peace swept through Felicity. No reason for it, except perhaps the comfort that someone else seemed to know.

"Yes, dearie. Even if..."

"Are you crazy?" Already limping from a bad round of golf, Peter shook a funny-looking club at the ceiling.

When Felicity first entered the room and saw the ancient putter in Peter's hand, she hoped to avoid the scene which unfolded. He had smiled, told her that he had wound up renting a set of clubs in order to save money and buy the ancient putter. Handmade, it had been used by Old Tom Morris, the famous Scottish pro and club-maker. Peter couldn't get over the fact that Old Tom had won the British Open with it. Felicity was sure she was out of the woods, until the cab driver came to the room to return her shawl, left in the taxi.

Peter had become more enraged than she had ever seen him, his bowtie nearly taking flight.

"Bad enough that you go out without me, but why on earth did you have to see some witch about our child?"

"She's not a witch. She just tells women things about their children. She was perfectly charming and completely harmless."

"There's nothing harmless about it. Goddammit, Felicity. I got enough of this crap from my grandmother and my father, without you springing it on me, too."

"Grandma Sarah seemed to do okay with her crystal ball. Didn't she attribute the success of the business to it? And Grumpy didn't do too badly, did..."

"My father was and is a fool. All he ever did was get drunk and play with fast women and bet on slow horses. If it hadn't been for those two charlatans, my mother might still—"

He stopped abruptly, turned and hurried from the room. Felicity went over to the bed and lay down, exhausted. She had come home with such energy, only to see it smothered by Peter's anger. She might even have fibbed about where she'd been, but he'd caught her off guard by already being in the suite when she returned.

She closed her eyes and willed her heart to slow its arduous beating. Her mistake had added yet another layer of brick to the wall between them. But Peter had almost slipped, almost let out whatever he'd been carrying around since his mother's death.

Felicity could not see what going to a psychic had to do with her mother-in-law's death a year earlier. Victoria had suffered a heart attack. She'd been rushed to the hospital. Felicity had waited outside while Peter went in to see her. Grumpy had arrived a half hour later, but when he'd tried to go inside, his own son had angrily ordered him out of the room.

Felicity had never figured out why Peter and his mother had been so close. Grumpy had always been gregarious and personable—thus the childhood nickname—whereas Victoria had invariably been tight-lipped and unapproachable. Peter, however, was devoted to her and took her side in every argument with his father.

Out in the hospital hallway, Grumpy had been gray and shaken. Felicity remembered the first time Peter introduced her to his parents. Watching them during dinner, she couldn't imagine how Grumpy and Victoria had gotten together in the first place. When she later asked Grumpy about their courtship, a mystical gleam came into his eye, but evaporated in a moment.

"People change," he said with a shrug. "I thought she didn't care about money and she thought I did. When we discovered we were both wrong, our marriage went kaflooey."

Meanwhile, Peter refused to leave his mother's side. Twelve hours later, Victoria died. Peter was overcome with grief. He wouldn't talk, wouldn't eat. He had snubbed his father at the wake, refused even to look at him at the funeral. Back at the house, all he could do was sit at the piano playing the same funereal lament, over and over. Finally, he closed the piano lid, went upstairs to shower and left for the office without a word.

Three days later, a newspaper article reported that Grumpy had retired and Peter had taken over as head of Douglas Industries. When Felicity asked him what happened, he refused to discuss it.

Since then Grumpy had been traveling around the world. His only communications were postcards or short letters—all addressed to Felicity.

Now, it seemed she had inadvertently reopened her husband's old wound.

Birthmark

By the middle of Sunday afternoon, the interviews were finished. Typically all business, Peter had made a spreadsheet. Across the top were the names of the five finalists. The left margin listed the characteristics he thought most important to the job. Faced with Peter's cold efficiency, Felicity had agreed with his evaluations, although she still smarted from their argument.

Three of the ladies had already been dismissed, but Fiona McLean and a Miss Kate Cameron, their brollies, purses and raincoats in hand, had been asked to wait in a little study off the sitting room.

"Miss McLean seems a bit more solid," Felicity said.

Peter pointed to Fiona's rating on the chart. As Felicity looked, she felt a sharp twinge.

"If we choose Miss McLean, we probably won't have to worry about a husband or a boyfriend, Peter," said Felicity, brushing a loose strand of hair from her eyes.

"On the other hand, Miss Cameron is younger, seems to have more energy," Peter countered.

"Younger and prettier," said Felicity, risking a small joke.

"You know better than that."

She swallowed hard and studied the chart, then spoke with an unsteady voice. "The only other major difference seems to be that Miss Cameron received a diploma from this Seymour Lodge."

"That would seem to give her the edge, don't you think?"

Felicity's instinct said that Fiona McLean was the nanny for her baby, but the intense feeling seemed to stem from her conversation with Maggie. She would never be able to justify her choice based on a hunch, especially when Peter seemed to be leaning analytically toward Miss Cameron.

"Why don't we give the lodge a call?" Peter said. "If she rated high in her class, that might help us make the decision."

"They wouldn't be open on Sunday, would they?"

"I'll just give them a try."

Peter opened the cabinet under the telephone, got the phone book and dialed the number. To Felicity's surprise, Peter began talking to someone. Two minutes later he hung up and faced her.

"Well, I guess that's it, darling. They said Miss Cameron was one of the best students they'd ever had. These last two ladies are so close on everything else, I guess the diploma has to count for something."

"I guess," Felicity said.

"You don't seem overly enthusiastic, darling."

"It's just that I had a strong emotional response in Miss McLean's favor."

"I thought so. But we can't ever let emotions rule over logic in our decisions." He came close, put his hand on her arm. "We can't lose with either one, why not have the best?"

She couldn't disagree, not without sailing into dangerous waters again.

"That's it, then." Peter leaned over and kissed her on the cheek. "I'll get Miss McLean."

Felicity felt a slight pull when the woman entered the room.

"I'm sorry, Miss McLean," Peter said. "As you can imagine, it was a terribly difficult decision, but Miss Cameron's diploma from the nursing school made the difference."

Miss McLean nodded, a hint of misery in her dark soulful eyes. Felicity felt another tug, stronger this time. She nearly reached for Peter to tell him she had changed her mind.

"I wish ye the best of luck, Mr. and Mrs. MacBrayne," Miss McLean said, extending her hand. "It's been lovely meeting you."

"I'm sure you'll find another position soon," Felicity said.

Miss McLean forced a smile. "After the babe is born, ask Kate to tell you about the Christmas cake."

꽃

The oven scones were beginning to smoke. Maggie sat at the table, eyes glazed, staring out at the late January, leaden sky. Across from her, Sandy sat with a similar expression, his hand wrapped around a half-empty tin of ale.

"My Kate, goin' off to 'merica in four days," Maggie muttered.

"She's my Kate too, Mrs. Cameron."

Her stare sharpened. "You bloody idiot. If'n you'd told me she was going to apply to be that 'merican woman's nanny, I could have steered her in another direction."

"How was I to know?" He took a mighty swig from the tin, nearly finishing it, slammed it on the table. "Now she's going for good. I even asked her ta marry me."

"What'd she say?"

"She laughed. Said if I couldn't afford to marry her yesterday, I couldn't today either."

"If you'd asked before, as ye should've, she wouldn't be leaving."

"Yah, well, if you're such a great witch, why couldn't you see this woulda happened when you saw that 'merican woman?"

Maggie's hand waved an arthritic dance. "I just tell the mothers what they want to hear. I larned the patter from the gypsies."

"Why, you old faker."

"A lot a good it done me." She sniffled, wiped her nose on her sleeve. "Now our Kate'll be winging across the Atlantic, wavin' goodbye to both of us."

Sandy staggered to his feet.

"Where're you off to?"

"Got to get up early to put in my picks for the football pool."

"A fat lotta good that'll do ya."

"Worth a try. Besides, all the strongest teams in the league are playing the weakest. I'm gonna play them all to win."

"Won't everybody else?"

"Sure, but winning will still be worth a few hundred, maybe a thousand quid. That could be enough…"

"Ach, get away from me with your dreamin'."

She barely acknowledged his departure. Had to think. Something was amiss, out of whack. She didn't want to tell Sandy, but when the woman was in her kitchen, Maggie was sure she had seen something.

Unfortunately, what she saw would also mean that Kate might stay in America until long after Maggie was gone. That meant she'd never see any grandchildren. Damn that Sandy, pinning all his hopes on a stupid football pool.

She pushed the newspaper off the table in disgust. It fell open on the floor. She glanced down. The football listing page stared up at her. She staggered to her old rocking chair, sat down, closed her eyes and nodded off.

Several hours later she sat up and shook her head. Her eyelids fluttered and her eyes cleared, focused. A sharp, uncanny chill filled the air, despite the heat from the stove.

"If you're such a great witch…" echoed in her mind. She looked around, pulled her tattered black wrapper over her skinny shoulders.

"Witch, witch, witch."

Her eyes bugged in terror and she looked around. No one was in the room, but the voice was clear as a bell.

"Witch, witch, witch."

The chilly draft fluttered the newspaper on the floor. She hobbled over, picked it up and looked at the football listing.

"Witch, witch, witch."

"What? Blast ya. What?"

She scanned the page again. What had Sandy said? All the strongest teams were playing the weakest. She crooked a finger and went down the list of town names. Then she saw it. Four teams on the underdog side. Of course! She laughed and danced despite her creaking bones.

"Ipswich, Bromwich, Norwich and Greenwich."

Grimacing with arthritic pain, she put on her slippers, grabbed her purse and headed for the door, where she stopped, hurried back to the kitchen, pulled the batch of smoking scones from the oven and threw them in the trash bin. Then she limped outside to the cobble-stoned street.

Maggie stumbled three houses down and banged on the door of a cottage almost identical to her own. "Wake up, Sandy!" she called, quite out of breath. "Wake up, damn ye."

In a moment or so, the door opened. He stared out at her.

"What's the matter, Mrs. Cameron?" He rubbed his head, looked over his shoulder at the clock. "Whatever's the matter wi' you? Do you know what time it is?"

"Ipswich, Bromwich, Norwich, and Greenwich."

He rolled his eyes. "You're giving me a geography lesson at one in the morning?"

"No, you great lummox. It's a sign, I tell you. It's a sign that'll save our lass, Kate."

"I still don't get it."

"Look at the names." She waved the newspaper at him. "Wich. Wich. Wich. Wich."

Sandy stared the paper. "But that's not how they're all pronounced."

"First thing in the morn, Sandy me lad," she reached up and pinched his nose, "you are going to buy that friggin' ticket."

❦

Fiona pried the lid off the cake tin. Who needed Mrs. MacGillivray, anyway? Fiona closed her eyes and let the aroma of rum fill her nostrils. Then cut a slice and took a large bite.

"Ach." She hurried to the sink, spat it out. The cake had somehow gone off. What had they done wrong? When Mrs. MacGillivray passes away, she'll surely take her grand recipe with her; then, the knowledge will have to be relearned. "Ach, such a waste."

"Did you say something, Fiona?" Kate called from her bedroom. "I'll be right out, I'm almost packed."

"No, just talking to myself."

She rinsed her mouth, raised up, closed her eyes and was overcome by a sudden dizziness. She opened her eyes, but the vertigo remained. She felt suddenly outside herself, looking through a large rectangular window down at white-capped, dark green waves dancing through a wafting mist. Across from her sat a handsome, blond-haired young man. He looked familiar but she couldn't place him.

Dark gray, bluish hills rose from the water when she again looked through the window. Above the cliffs an irregular shape appeared, vanished, then reappeared. Enshrouded by the fog, its outline resembled an ancient castle or fort.

Not the kind to suffer hallucinations, Fiona shook her head to clear the cobwebs. True, she had been upset about the American nanny job. In fact—but this was foolishness. In the corner of the living room stood a brass box where they kept the week's newspapers. All she had to do was go through the "Domestic Help Wanted" columns and begin sending out letters. But she couldn't. Every time she tried, her hand would begin to shake and she would find herself walking into the bedroom to lie down. Where did this lethargy come from? Could she be ill?

No, it was the image of Felicity Douglas-MacBrayne that kept rising in her mind. There had been a connection between them, a piece of news in her eyes that she couldn't tell anyone, but was there for Fiona alone to interpret. That baby was Fiona's to take care of, of that she was positive.

But, if that were the case, how come they had chosen Kate?

"Ah, Fiona. Don't be such a bloody fool. 'Tis your imagination and nothing more," she said aloud as she walked over to the stack of papers. "It's time to get yourself another position, and fast."

Just as she picked up the top newspaper, there was a rapping at the front door.

"Who is it?"

"Sandy. I've got to talk to Kate."

Fiona opened the door.

"Is Kate still here?"

"In her bedroom."

"Thank you."

Sandy brushed by her. Fiona couldn't make out the words, but she put her hands to her chest as the voices grew louder. Sandy was obviously making one last pitch for Kate's hand. Fiona closed her eyes and said a little prayer. Suddenly, a sharp cry came from the other room. Fiona rushed to the door.

"Are ye okay, Kate?"

Sandy opened the door, a cat having-eaten-the-mouse grin on his face. Kate sat stunned, on her bed.

"What's the matter, girl?"

"Looks like I get what's left of the Christmas cake, after all," Kate said, still dazed.

"How's that?"

Kate handed an envelope to Fiona, who looked over to Sandy for an explanation.

"Ipswich, Bromwich, Norwich and Greenwich."

Inside the envelope was a check for two hundred thousand pounds—and an ornate, silver engagement ring.

"It was me mum's," Sandy said shyly.

In the rear of the limousine, Fiona surveyed the landscape of this place the Americans had named New Jersey. Although late January, thus far the winter must have been mild, as there was little evidence of snow. The shadows cast by the setting sun seemed to slide off the sand hills to her left instead of catching in the ancient, craggy crannies as they did at home.

The car swung through a huge, wrought iron gate. Giant figures had been trimmed out of the ancient privet-hedge which surrounded the property. She could recognize the shapes, although they were without their green spring clothing. A large crocodile, jaws open wide, gazed hungrily at its prey: the one-handed Captain Hook braced to defend himself.

Fiona looked at the gate. On one side stood the sculpted figure of Dorothy Darling, on the other, Peter Pan—arms raised in joyful greeting to all who entered.

"What a lovely, gentle touch for such an imposing estate," Fiona said.

"Typical of the missus," the chauffeur replied. "She has a knack."

As they drove on, she noticed a small sand-bunker and the outline of a putting green. To her left, a row of shrubbery barely hid what must be an orchard of fruit trees, then a pair of gardens. Vegetables and flowers, no doubt. As they approached the house, Fiona saw a large canvas rectangle, the swimming pool, covered for the winter.

"Lord a'mighty," she said softly.

"Ma'am?" said the driver.

"This is a house fit for royalty, to be sure."

"Yes, ma'am."

In front of the house, she saw a truck at the side of the driveway. Two men struggled to unload large cardboard boxes.

"What are they doing?" Fiona asked.

"Ah, the missus ordered a new washer and drier. They redid a whole room, new wiring and the lot, just to make things easier after the baby's born."

The car stopped and Fiona stepped out, taking a deep breath. Peter MacBrayne met her at the front door.

"Miss McLean, I'm so happy you're here."

"Pleased to be here, sir. But if you don't mind my saying, in Scotland my name is pronounced McLayne—rhymes with your own."

"Sorry, Miss McLean."

"Thank you." She smiled. "How's the missus?"

"Always tired. In fact, napping at the moment." He took Fiona by the arm. "And she'll be very happy to know you've arrived. Why don't you freshen up and we'll have dinner together."

The chauffeur carried the luggage upstairs, Fiona following. Her room was next to the nursery. She couldn't resist taking a quick peek inside. Each of the four walls was painted with a different scene from Peter Pan. Above the crib was a panoply of stars. Tinkerbell hovered just above where the baby would lay its head.

"It's good to have the protection of faeries," she said softly.

"Ma'am?" the chauffeur said.

"Nothing." She grinned. "Just a bit of jet lag makin' me tongue loose."

After he left, she closed the door and sat on the bed.

"Well, Fiona old girl, I don't know how this all came about but it's a far sight better than inedible Christmas cake."

Walking was difficult, but Felicity was determined to see everything in order before the baby came. Today was one of the few good days. She would not spend it in bed. She stopped at the secretary-table, gazed at the Hospital Ball invitation. Nice artwork. She hated missing the annual fund-raiser—her favorite charity. She'd chaired the committee five years in a row. Not this year. She had another engagement.

She walked slowly to the dining room. Peter was absorbed in the business section of the paper.

"Good morning, Peter."

He looked up. "Felicity, you're supposed to stay in bed."

"I'm having a good day." She sat across from him. "Besides, I want to talk."

"But I would have come up."

"No. I have something important to tell you and, for once in our married life, I'm not going to take 'no' for an answer."

"What are you—?"

"We both know the doctors have been concerned throughout my pregnancy." She picked up a fork and doodled an invisible pattern on the tablecloth. "I just want it understood that if there is ever any question of my life or the baby's, I want my child to have the chance to live the life God has given it."

"Felicity—"

"Hear me out. If that means I have to go, well, then that's how I want it."

The pain and fear in his eyes was so startling, Felicity caught her breath. For just a moment she glimpsed the real Peter through a sudden gap in the wall.

"Don't be so melodramatic."

"I have to." She smiled, not wanting him to raise the barrier again so soon. "One of us has to be practical."

Normally, that kind of statement would have brought disbelief or argument, but Peter appeared stunned that she thought she might actually die.

"Now, for the name: If it's a boy, I want him named Peter Douglas-MacBrayne IV, after you. Though he should be called Doug, to prevent confusion."

Peter stared at her, speechless.

"And if it's a girl, she will be called Sarah Douglas-MacBrayne—after your grandmother." Felicity reached across and took his hand. "But call her Sarah, or Sally, not Doug, okay?"

This time he smiled. She patted his hand and stood.

"Now I'm going to check the new utility room, then I promise to go right to bed." She stopped in the doorway and turned. "Peter—"

He looked up. There had been so many misunderstandings, but they all seemed insignificant now.

"You know I love you."

He grimaced. She could see the battle he was fighting inside. Finally he nodded.

In the hallway, she heard Fiona speaking with the cook and decided she would ask her for help up the stairs. She felt drained, but wanted to make sure the workmen had finished the laundry room to her specifications. She patted her tummy.

"Come on, baby. Let's go make sure there'll be plenty of clean diapers for you."

The new utility room gleamed, sanitary and efficient. White walls, chrome fixtures, and the new washer and dryer. She looked behind the dryer and smiled. Not a trace of where the electrician had installed the new, high-voltage circuit.

A brief cloudiness partly covered her eyes and Felicity leaned against the dryer to steady herself. A sudden spark, a massive jolt. She screamed, covered her stomach and fell.

When she awoke, she felt trouble swirling all around her. She looked up into a large round mirror to see herself lying on a shiny, antiseptic table. The bright light on her fair hair created a halo effect; the royal, bluish blood in the tiny veins of her neck resembled faint watermarks on fine writing paper.

She sensed the desperation of the team of doctors and nurses crowded around her in the tense, stifling atmosphere. Silent, straining professional chins dripped worry into face masks. Expensive medical nerves jangled, noiselessly. The spotless room stank of antiseptic.

Barely conscious, Felicity could not fully comprehend the distress signals flying in every corner: Dials, gauges throbbed.

"Blood pressure, low and dropping!"

Iridescent green computer-lines spelled out unhappy messages. "Heartbeat, faint."

Electronic bleeps sounded their alarms, stabbing the jittery delivery-room staff.

She groaned as the chief of obstetrics injected a heart-revitalizing drug, with little effect.

"Quick!" he yelled. "Another!"

The second injection worked, but only for a brief moment.

Beneath the tumult, Felicity struggled with an old memory: A different doctor stood above her then ten-year-old frame, talking to her mother about the disease that had caught her—diphtheria.

"Even if she recovers, her heart has been severely damaged. I'm afraid there's nothing further we can do."

A calm came over her. She felt herself being lifted from the dark emptiness that surrounded her, by a bright, firefly-like being. Tinkerbell? A ray of warm, smiling light engulfed Felicity. Ever since her mother first read her the story, she had always wanted to visit Never-Never Land.

The pain and fever that had captured her was far away. From the tunnel, she thought she could see the island where Peter Pan and the others would be waiting.

Close your eyes and make a wish.

She did. She wanted to have a baby someday, so she could read it the story as its mother. As soon as this wish came to her mind, she felt a whooshing sensation.

She opened her eyes and cried out with fleeting unhappiness, back in her diseased body. The doctor dropped his pen, stared at her open-mouthed, then rushed to her side.

For several minutes the doctor and nurses worked to stabilize her. Afterwards, fully aware, she saw him tear up the form he had filled out. She could barely make out the first word at the top: DEATH.

"What was that?" she asked in a small whisper.

"Just a form."

"A prescription?"

He stared at her. "Something like that."

"Why did you tear it up?"

"You won't be needing it now, thank God."

Suddenly, a new tidal wave of pain crashed through her chest, breaking through the anesthetic. Felicity could feel her heart galloping around the cavity in her chest, struggling to keep its rhythm. Just as it would catch, another convulsion would knock it out of synch. She tried to remember the calm of her childhood, that safe tunnel from which she had rebounded back to life. She couldn't find it. Her energy dropped. The pain engulfed her.

Her eyes opened briefly, caught a glimpse of her own Peter being hustled out of the room. He stopped in the doorway, mouthed the words she realized he hadn't had the courage to say that morning.

I love you.

A stabbing pain shook her body—she was being torn apart. Hot waves pushed her away from her body until, from nowhere, a hand caught her, pulled her into a safe embrace. A presence only, she was carried up, out of the body on the table, just as the doctors were making a large incision in her middle. She could feel the force of a bright light but kept her attention focused below, where she saw a small, red creature plucked, separated from the mother that used to be her.

She heard a dim cry and the presence that guided her chuckled.

"Who are you?" she asked wordlessly. "Where are you taking me?"

"Home." A voice whispered deep within her.
"Who are you?" She asked again.
There was a soft caress against her cheek. A kiss? A breeze?
Then she moved toward the light on her own, willing and free. She called again.
"Who are you?"
The voice wrote the answer over and over in the clouds: "Alzar. Alzar. Alzar."

Prudence Peabody watched the Head Nurse take the infant to a nearby table, where she quickly placed its right foot on an open ink pad. She gently pressed the boy's inked foot on the upper right corner of the Birth Certificate.

"Carter, get over here," a doctor shouted.

The nurse handed the baby to Peabody, leaving a slight trail of blood across her crisp, pink Nurse's Aid uniform.

"Take over, Peabody."

Prudence looked at the baby in her arms, started to smile, then realized she would have to do the APGAR—a new system of scoring an infant's physical condition, one minute after birth. She looked around for some assistance, but the entire delivery-room staff was frantic in its attempt to save Felicity.

Prudence brushed a lock of red hair under her pink cap. She picked up the APGAR Form to record the baby's Pulse "Just over 100." She noted his Respiratory Effort "Good." Muscle Tone "Active Motion." Reflex Irritability "Coughed once, then sneezed." Finally, Color "Completely pink."

At the bottom of the form, Prudence saw one more task to perform. She carried the baby to the padded, delivery-room scale, removed the infant's blanket, laid the little boy down gently, to be weighed. A flailing, tiny arm struck the exposed edge of the metal pan.

Fresh from the warmth and peaceful comfort of his mother's womb, he let out a loud yell. His tiny hands and feet waved and kicked helplessly. Patiently, Prudence penned "8 lbs, 1 oz" on the line marked, "Birth Weight." She quickly rewrapped the baby in the warm blanket and picked him up, tenderly.

When it became apparent nothing more could be done for Felicity, Nurse Carter returned, exhaustion and pain creased her face. She looked at the APGAR.

"Well, young man, that's an astonishing score for one who arrived under such terrible circumstances. You'll not be needing any pinking-up at all."

Things had settled considerably by the time Dr. Fussinbacke, Chief of Birth Records, strutted into the maternity area, stroking his carefully-groomed goatee.

He grabbed the "Birth Certificate, State of New Jersey." It was blank except for the boy's sole print. He called for the Douglas-MacBrayne baby. Prudence timidly brought the boy and stood, holding him quietly.

There was a note from the Chief of Staff pinned to the Certificate: "Instructions from the family: If female, name it 'Sarah.' If male: 'Peter Douglas-MacBrayne IV.'"

Dr. Fussinbacke began by carefully recording the boy's name. Everything went smoothly until he got to item 22: "Birth weight_____, (Confirm infant's weight recorded on Modified APGAR.)"

"Where's the APGAR, Miss?" His fingers drummed impatiently.

"Here you are, Sir," replied Prudence. "I'm sorry. I guess I should have had it on the table."

"You know the protocol, don't you?"

"It's my first time. With all the confusion and—"

"Carter?" He looked around, couldn't find the head nurse. "Don't you realize that this is the MacBrayne family? They founded this hospital, there can be no mistakes."

He removed the blanket and reweighed the infant.

"What's your name, Miss?" he said.

"Prudence Peabody, Sir."

"Well, Miss Peabody, you got it wrong."

Startled, Prudence looked at the scale. The baby's weight stood at eight pounds, two ounces—a gain of one full ounce!

"But Sir, I know I recorded it correctly a little while ago. It's gone up!"

"That's impossible! Or did you give it something to eat?"

"No, sir."

"All you Nurse's Aides are impossibly sloppy!"

"But I double-checked it, sir—"

"Don't lie to me, Peabody. Consider yourself on report." He glanced at the rest of the form. "For God's sake, even Superman couldn't get a 'ten' on an APGAR."

"I told you this was my first—"

"Carter, come here."

The head nurse hurried over. "Yes, doctor?"

"How could you possibly assign the MacBrayne baby APGAR to someone who has never done one before?"

"Doctor, a little black girl got hit by a car today and required emergency surgery before she died. Everyone else was busy here trying to save the mother's life."

The Doctor snorted, took out his pen and drew a thick line through Miss Peabody's "1 oz." Then he wrote "2 oz." alongside, underlining it heavily. He gave Prudence a scathing glance, continued filling out the Birth Certificate.

Near the bottom, he came to item 46, "Congenital Anomalies." Dr. Fussinbacke carefully examined the baby, then wrote, "None." After he filled in the last couple of items, he signed the Certificate with a flourish, turned to Prudence.

"You may want to reconsider your career choice, Miss Peabody."

The Doctor jammed his pen in his pocket, strode away. Tears in her eyes, Prudence waited to be reprimanded by Nurse Carter. But the older woman just sighed and rewrapped the baby, with tender, loving hands.

"I'm sorry if I messed up."

Carter handed the baby to Prudence with a wan smile. "You didn't, my dear. He's just an asshole."

Miss Peabody placed a beaded identification bracelet around the boy's tiny wrist. All the beads were blue, except for 19, which were white with black lettering:

"P. DOUGLAS MACBRAYNE IV"

"That's a pretty impressive name for such a tiny lad," she said, on the way to the nursery.

Five hours later, it was time to weigh and bathe all the infants. When Doug's turn came, Prudence picked him out of his bassinet, took him to the bathing room, where she removed his blanket and put him on the delicate scale. She winced a little as the indicator stopped at just under eight pounds, two ounces.

"I don't know how I could have missed it," she said, chucking him lightly under the chin.

Smiling, Doug MacBrayne gurgled as she poured the warm, soapy water over him. When she turned him over to bathe his back and bottom, she let out a little yell.

"Nurse Carter, come here."

"What?" Prudence pointed.

A purplish-red blemish had appeared behind the baby's right ear. The two nurses stared in disbelief at the port-wine stain about the size of a quarter.

"In forty years of nursing I've never seen anything quite like this," she said. "Sometimes a birthmark will get missed because it's too faint. You can't see it until the baby calms down. But this must have popped out when no one was looking."

She went to the office, pulled out Doug's Birth Certificate, found the word "None" in Dr. Fussinbacke's choleric hand.

"Prudence."

"Yes?"

"Would you like to call the good doctor back down, or shall I?"

"For what?"

She pointed to the birth certificate.

"We have to ask him how he missed this birthmark—on such an important baby as little MacBrayne, over there. He can't say this is our sloppiness."

"You call."

Red-faced and flustered, Fussinbacke took cover by claiming he knew of cases where similar birthmarks appeared days, or even longer after delivery.

The two nurses just smiled as he walked away.

"Just think, he was going to put me on report over something as insignificant as an ounce." Prudence sighed. "Though I swear to God that's what the scale read."

"Most doctors are assholes. Better get used to it, dear." Carter put her hand on the young aide's shoulder. "But this should help you remember that an ounce of prevention is worth a pound of cure."

"Yes ma'am."

Carter shook her head. "Prudence, that was a joke."

"What are you playing?" Fiona asked Peter, who was slumped on the organ bench at the far side of the small hospital chapel.

"Rachmaninoff's Prelude in C sharp minor," he said, glancing idly at a young black couple, huddled together at the rear, sobbing quietly. "Fiona?"

"Yes, sir?"

"It's just not fair."

"Aye, sir. She was a sweet lass."

"A sweet lass." He tried to smile, tears welled in his eyes.

Fiona sat with her hands in her lap. Suddenly chilled, she turned to see if someone had walked in, then buttoned her sweater. The door remained closed.

"Fiona?"

"Aye, sir."

"I—I'm not the easiest man in the world—to get along with, I mean."

He did not look for confirmation and Fiona restrained her nod of assent.

"Felicity understood, seemed to love me anyway, always."

"That she did, sir."

"Yes, that she did." Again the tears threatened, but he fought them. "What I'm trying to say is—you might want to reconsider taking this job—"

Fiona started to speak. He held up his hand.

"This baby is going to need to know that someone will always be there, for a long, long time—besides me, that is." He looked at her, looked away. "So, I would understand if you didn't want that responsi—"

A nurse walked in, carrying something small wrapped in a blanket. She stopped in the doorway, looked at the two of them.

"Normally, we would keep a baby in the clinic, but under the circumstances..."

Their prayers and grief interrupted, the black couple rose as one, looked first at the newborn baby, then meaningfully at each other and quietly left the chapel.

Fiona got up, walked over, took the baby in her arms and looked down into its face. Two eyes peered straight up at her, a shadow of a grin curled across the mouth, followed by a small burp.

"Well, wee one, you're either a boy or a badly-mannered little girl." She walked over to Peter.

"He's a him, all right," the nurse said.

"A boy?" Peter gazed down at his son. "Douglas. Hi, Dougie."

"Mr. MacBrayne, I swear on your dead wife's heart that this wee lad will never want from love, affection and care from me. And you can be as difficult as you like. I'll not leave him." She looked him square in the eyes. "But swear to me—in the same manner—that you'll never make me leave him."

"I swear, to you and to Felicity."

"And another promise, while we're at it?"

Peter frowned, shrugged his shoulders. "Go on."

"I've held scores of babes in my day, Mr. MacBrayne. I can tell a great many things aboot them from the very first." She held Dougie upright so Peter could see his face better. "This is not a boy who'll ever need spanking or hitting. A word of repair is all he'll ever need."

"I'll do my best."

Fiona's dark, soulful eyes sparked. "Promise."

"Okay, I promise."

Fiona nodded, turned to the nurse.

"Now, show me where the wee one will be sleeping tonight. I want to make sure that everything is—"

"I assure you, he will get the finest care."

"Show me."

"But it's against the rules for anyone but the family—"

"Take me there now, or we're leaving with Dougie this very minute."

The nurse looked at Peter.

He smiled, nodded his assent. "Show her."

As they walked down the hallway, Fiona peeked several times at the little face looking up at her from the blanket. His eyes stared straight at her and her alone.

"I'm sorry about your mother, Dougie," she whispered. "But I'll do my best on her behalf, and yours."

Behind her, she could hear the soft, haunting sounds of the organ, as Peter played out his grief in the chapel. Her steps remained firm, but a small tear trickled down her cheek.

CHAPTER TWO

CHRISTMAS 1975

The pop of the flash startled Doug, who was barely visible in a sea of wrapping paper. He grinned at Fiona, who had taken another picture for posterity. Peter sat across the room, arms folded over his chest, watching Doug open his gifts. After five increasingly tense, dismal Christmases, Fiona knew that Doug's appreciation would never meet his father's expectations. She turned the camera on Peter. The viewfinder caught a diving eyebrow, an Adam's apple all awobble and an accountant's glint that seemed to shift another dark, imagined hurt from one side of the ledger to the other. She put the camera down.

Doug picked up a box wrapped in tartan Christmas paper. He shook it, undid the paper at the seams with the same care with which it had been wrapped and removed the box. Then lifted the lid and peeked inside. His joyous grin quickly diminished to a cautious smile as he saw the expression on his father's face.

"It's... great, Nanny. Did you make it?"

Fiona nodded.

"What is it?" Peter asked from across the room.

"Nanny knitted me a sweater, Daddy. All by herself." Doug held it up. "Go ahead, touch it. It's so soft!"

"Real Irish wool, Fiona?" Peter rubbed it between his fingers.

"Scottish, if you please, sir."

He nodded. "Must have taken you quite a long time."

She shrugged, glanced over to check for any hint of threat in the statement—he expected her to devote her time to Doug, but not her love.

"I did a little each night before going to sleep. Knitting is my cure for insomnia."

Doug giggled, covered his face with the sweater to keep from laughing out loud.

"And just what's so funny, young man?" Fiona asked.

"Is snoring another cure for insomnia?" He held the sweater up in mock protection.

"Very funny." Fiona tried not to laugh but did. "I guess I'll have to give up my afternoon naps if you're going to tattle on me."

"What's the design on the front of the sweater?" Peter asked.

"That's a Mull rainbow."

"What's a mull?" Doug asked.

"Mull is a Scottish island."

Peter shrugged. "Funny, I've been to Scotland three times and never heard of it."

Doug turned the sweater around. "Are Mull rainbows different from regular ones?"

"I've heard the ancient Celts thought rainbows were symbols of eternal life. And there's so many of them on Mull today, the locals pay hardly any mind." She sighed, began to describe the herds of dark, white-topped thunderheads parading from the Gulf Stream over the island. The sun always seemed to be at the proper angle to extract beautiful rainbow colors from the myriad, bright diamond-drops, cascading earthward, to form huge, vaguely circular prismatic swathes, in vivid contrast to a menacing, dark background. Sometimes the clouds appeared as an invading army of giants marching forth from the Atlantic displaying their multicolored standards—different intensities, sizes and shapes—poodles, elephants, even an occasional god.

"I think I saw some of that in—" Peter said.

Fiona nodded. "I'm sure you did."

She couldn't help notice the increasingly obvious difference between father and son. Whereas Doug soaked up the stories and adventures of others, Peter stayed at the periphery, looking for opportunities to interject some aspect of himself into every conversation. She could see it building with each word she spoke. Almost certain he was about to interrupt again, she shifted gears.

"Now Dougie, enough about Mull." She pointed to the tree. "Besides, I believe there's one more present under there for you."

She cast a cheery grin toward Peter and watched Doug wade through the paper ocean. He held up the package and shook it, trying to guess its contents. A funny glint held court in his eyes for a moment, then faded.

"Who's that from?" Peter asked.

"Your father, sir. It arrived yesterday."

"Grumpy!" Doug began tearing off the paper. "Where is he this time?"

"I believe it was postmarked Beijing."

"Wow!" Doug stared at the mahogany frame with silver rods and rows of obsidian counters. "An abacus."

He quietly flicked the small counters, adding up numbers and multiplying, as if he'd been using one for years. He completely disregarded the train set, model cars, two pairs of thick-padded boxing gloves and other gifts from his father. Peter, jealous and red-faced, tried to take the abacus away.

"Stop tinkering with that. You don't know how to use it anyway."

"Yes I do, Dad."

"Don't lie to me."

"I'm not lying. Try me."

"Okay, smart boy. What's... twenty-five times thirty-two?"

Doug flicked the beads, laughed. "Eight hundred. Ask me a hard one. That was too easy."

It took a moment for Peter to do the same calculation, then his face darkened.

"Who taught you how to use one of those?"

"I don't know. Just knew how. From before, I guess."

"Before? That's a load of rubbish. Impossible."

Doug's eyes turned funny, then clouded over. He shrugged.

"What do you mean before?"

Doug collapsed inside himself, tears formed in his eyes.

"What's the matter with him?" Peter asked Fiona, then turned to the boy. "Why can't you answer me?"

Tears poured from Doug's eyes. He looked into his lap and mumbled.

"What did you say?"

Panicking, Doug sniffled louder.

"What did you say, crybaby?"

Doug jerked his head upward. "Why do you have to be such an autocrat?"

"Auto...?" Stunned, Peter asked, "And where did you hear that word?"

"I don't remember, Dad. It just popped into my head—

"Before? Before. You're beginning to sound like your nutty grandmother, Sarah." Peter turned and grabbed the boxing gloves from the pile of presents. "Well, if you're going to call people names, you'd better learn to back it up."

Doug stole a glance at Fiona but she had no help to offer him. He picked up the gloves his father threw at him and slowly put them on, his tiny arms thin sticks stuck in leather-covered cotton.

Peter got on his knees, lifted his gloves.

"Okay, let's have at it."

Fiona gasped. Would Peter break his promise to her?

"I don't want to hit you, Daddy."

"Come on, put something behind it."

Doug hit at his father's gloves, little dabs.

"Come on, cry baby."

At the taunt, Doug waded in swinging both arms. His right hit Peter's Adam's apple, the left connected smack on the nose. Blood spurted. Peter wiped his face with one glove and held the boy by the throat with the other.

Frustrated, Doug flailed the air until Fiona saved him and took him out of the room.

"That's not fair," he yelled over her shoulder. "You said you wanted a real fight."

On the way to Doug's bedroom, Fiona heard Peter call the cook for a bag of ice and worked hard to keep a straight face. In the bathroom she rinsed out a washcloth to cool Doug's forehead, then plopped him on the bed where all the struggle went out of him.

"Now you just lay there, slugger." She caressed his cheek then frowned. "Are you sure there's no Irish blood in you?"

"Well, Dad's Scottish, just like you."

"I was just funnin' you, Dougie." She pinched his cheek. "Though from the way you were using that abacus, I wouldn't be at all surprised if you didn't have some Chinese accountant's blood in you, as well."

"It's no big deal." He put his hands behind his head. "I didn't mean to make Dad angry, it just felt good using it again."

Fiona patted his arm. She had run out of words. The little boy frightened her almost as much as he frightened his father. Irrational? To be sure, but there it was.

"Why don't you take a little nap and we'll have dinner together. Maybe everything will be all right by then."

"Sure, Nanny."

She closed the door and went downstairs. She could hear Peter on the telephone in his office.

"I don't care, get Jenkins to contact Larrabee's Toy Store and have the owner meet me there in an hour—That's right. And if he won't do it, find someone who will."

She tapped on the open door. Peter looked up, motioned her inside.

"And don't forget about the photographer." He hung up. "Yes, Fiona?"

"I was wondering what time you want dinner."

He shook his head. "Not tonight. You and Doug go ahead without me."

"On Christmas? Surely—"

"Can't be helped."

Fiona's anger rose as Peter took the bag of ice from his desktop and applied it to his nose, then turned his chair away from her. She walked out, retrieved the abacus and marched upstairs. She peeked into Doug's room and smiled when she saw his drowsy wave. Then she placed the abacus in the crook of his arm and tiptoed out.

Doug sensed a faint movement next to him, then felt the room begin to chill. Part dream, part awake, he heard a kind of music—no notes—just a throbbing that seemed to shake his entire body. He struggled to stay awake but the vibrations took over. The music reached a crescendo, the bedroom disappeared and he felt the warm air of springtime, heard birds singing. He barely felt the sharp stones on the path. Surprised, he looked down at his bare feet, callused from walking without shoes.

His sister was to be married. This would be his first visit home after ten years of study in the monastery. He fought to hold on to the calm he'd been taught, the centering of his insides, that would keep excitement at bay. His master had encouraged him to face his mother and father.

"Lin Feng, it's important to keep your detachment from the old emotions that trap everyone," the master had said. "The need for love and approval. The remembered fear of childhood mistakes."

Lin Feng's hand went to the back of his head, feeling the large purplish disfigurement that had brought tears to his mother's eyes each time she saw it. How long had it taken him to accept the fact that she would never look at him directly?

How could he explain the peace he had found in the monastery? His father had also been ashamed of Lin Feng, ashamed of his son's deformed head. Locked in his room, out of view, his only solace had been the manipulation of the abacus. This had been his only hope: to become useful to his father in the family business.

Instead, he had been sent to the monastery at the beginning of his fifteenth year, rather than go through the useless charade of finding a bride.

Now he realized that his father's shame had given him a new life, an inner freedom he might never have experienced in the ordinary world.

He gathered his saffron robe onto his right arm and stopped, his attention arrested by a nightingale partially hidden by bushes to his left. He heard the rolling wheels of a carriage slow behind him but he did not turn around.

"Would you ride with us?" A male voice.

He turned toward the ornate carriage and bowed.

"Thank you, but I am used to walking."

The man smiled. "Please indulge me. A man about to be married needs every favor the Buddha will bestow."

The mockery in the man's voice was alien. Ten years in the monastery had made Lin Feng forget how careless the laity could be with the Enlightened One's name. Lin Feng stared at the man. Could he be the one his sister would marry?

"Have neither pity nor scorn for those who know not enough to follow the Buddha," his master had told him. "You alone, are responsible for your soul."

He bowed again, then entered the cart.

"Good. Good." The man said, moving his considerable bulk a little to one side.

The face before Lin Feng was round as the moon. The clothes spoke of prosperity. The silk reminded of his childhood, his sister. He tried to remember her face. She would look quite different from the six-year-old girl he remembered, already arrogant, tears streaming down her face as she sat on her bed, commanding him not to leave.

"But who will tell me stories, Lin Feng?" She pulled the two black braids from behind her neck.

"You will not need made-up tales very much longer, Mei Li. Soon, you will start your lessons."

Her little-girl lips extended in such a pout, Lin Feng thought he would laugh.

"Who will rub my legs when my feet ache so?"

"One of the servants."

Mei Li had turned her face to the pillow and sobbed. Lin Feng reached over and gingerly caressed the slender bamboo shafts of her legs. She was right. Only he had pity for the selfish little girl, with cotton and silk wrapped tightly about her feet. Only he came to soothe her when the ache of her growing bones collided with this ancient tradition of the rich.

His pity was such that after she fell asleep, he would carefully loosen the silk and cotton, releasing her feet from their bondage.

He glanced again at the man next to him. Would he put up with her demands? Would he tell her tales? Would he rub her legs when they ached?

"You say you are to marry today?"

"Yes." The man popped a small sweet into his mouth.

"Then it is a good day."

The man shrugged. "Our families do business together. This is just one more transaction."

Lin Feng could not stop his rising eyebrows. The man laughed.

"The idea shocked me too, my friend." Another sweet flew into his mouth. "But sometimes one must make sacrifices for the sake of a family business."

"Sacrifices?"

The man leaned over, his sugary breath barely hiding his nervous aroma.

"She is ugly beyond belief, but her father is rich and will forgive my family's debts."

Lin Feng kept his face immobile. What could have happened to the little girl he left behind? She had been such a beautiful child: skin like porcelain; perfect features. Could such a doll have grown so crookedly to warrant this description?

"Time absorbs beauty," the master taught him. "And beauty absorbs time. Be not fooled by either."

The carriage slowed in front of Lin Feng's childhood home. He climbed out and thanked the man for his courtesy.

"Pray for me, brother," the man said.

Lin Feng bowed and watched them pull into the path that led to the house. He walked a few yards up the road and turned into a grove that led to the rear entrance. He hesitated.

"I have been in the monastery too long," he said to a squirrel.

He lowered himself to the ground and assumed the lotus position, feeling the need to meditate, to center his feelings before going inside.

A hand brushed his shoulder. Doug looked into Nanny's face. Not yet alert, he nearly dropped the abacus. Stared at it.

"It's time for dinner, Doug," Fiona said.

He fell on his pillow and let out a long sigh.

"Are you okay?"

"I had a dream."

"Scary?"

He shook his head. "No, it had something to do with the abacus, but...."

"Can you remember it?"

He shrugged. "It wasn't very exciting. I was just kind of going home, remembering stuff."

"Here in Douglasville?"

"No. I don't—I was wearing funny clothes."

"Well, come on downstairs. Dinner's ready."

"Great." He jumped off the bed. "Is Dad still mad?"

"He went out. Said to start without him."

Doug nodded and walked downstairs hand-in-hand with Nanny.

Halfway through the turkey and trimmings, they heard Peter's Bentley in the driveway. Doug jumped up but Fiona restrained him.

"Just go on eating. He'll be right in." She brushed a few bread crumbs from his new sweater.

A moment later Peter stood at the dining room doorway.

"Fiona, Doug, I need your help."

Doug wiped his mouth and rushed from the table. He followed his father into the living room and stopped.

All his presents were back in their boxes.

"Help me carry these to the car," Peter said.

Doug looked at Fiona. She bit her lip, then nodded.

They ferried the packages to the car. Peter motioned them in. They entered without a word.

In ten minutes, they parked behind a small van in front of the Douglasville Orphanage. A man was unloading packages wrapped in Christmas paper.

"Mr. MacBrayne, what—?" Fiona raised her eyebrows.

"It's time Doug learned a thing or two." He climbed out and smiled just as a man with a flash camera aimed and shot.

Stunned, Doug and Fiona followed Peter to the entrance where they were met by a stern-looking, short, round woman in a gray, starched uniform.

"This way, Mr. MacBrayne." She looked at Doug. "Is this your son?"

"Yes, it is."

Doug clung to Fiona. She squeezed his hand as they followed a few paces behind the matron and his father.

"Please don't let Dad make me come here to live," he whispered, his voice quaking. "I promise to do better. I'll try not to make him mad anymore."

Just as Fiona started to answer, a young boy careered around the corner and nearly bumped into the matron. She grabbed him by the sleeve.

"James Ulysses Lyden, you know the rules about running in the hall." She spun him around, peered at the multi-colored stains on his shirt. "So. You've been painting again, haven't you?"

Panic-stricken, the young boy's jaw dropped. "Sorry, Matron."

"Sorry's no good after you break the rules. Go to your room. We'll discuss this later."

"But, Matron—"

"To your room. Now."

She cuffed him on the ear, the boy yelled and ran around the corner that had been his undoing. He glanced sideways at Doug and stuck out his tongue, then disappeared, his hand first straightening his hair, then covering the side of his stinging head.

Doug started to stick his tongue out in return but stopped when he saw tears in the boy's eyes.

The matron led the way to the auditorium, where some twenty children of various ages sat quietly. A small Christmas tree stood at the far end next to two tables loaded with boxes.

"Children, this Christmas we are very honored to have Mr. Peter Douglas-MacBrayne and his family as our guests. Mr. MacBrayne has arranged a gift for each of you. You will now come up, one at a time, select your gift and thank Mr. MacBrayne properly."

Each child walked up, took a box from the table and thanked Peter. The girls curtseyed and the boys bowed. All the while, the photographer snapped pictures. Doug saw the children watching him and couldn't help blushing without quite knowing why he was so embarrassed. When the last boy walked off with his present, Peter cleared his throat.

"It's a pleasure to bring presents to children who are so appreciative. I hope you enjoy your toys. And Merry Christmas to all."

The matron signaled the children to applaud, then ushered the guests to their car.

"If you'd given us more warning, Mr. MacBrayne, we would have had some refreshments prepared, made a proper reception for you."

"That's not necessary, Miss Groebnick. Just seeing their happy faces was party enough in itself."

"What about that boy Jimmy?" Doug asked. "Will he get a present too?"

The matron frowned. "Jimmy knows what happens when he breaks the rules."

"But it's Christmas—"

"Then maybe he'll remember next time he thinks about ruining his clothes with those paints of his." Her brittle face looked as if even a slight smile would crack it. "The other children know they're lucky just to have a roof over their heads."

A hundred questions ran through Doug's mind, but one look at Nanny told him he should remain silent. During the ride home he thought about his dream and the abacus. His father kept looking at him in the mirror, glaring at the new sweater.

Doug had tried to appreciate whatever his father bought him, but the presents never seemed appropriate. How was it that Grumpy could know from so far away and Dad couldn't from so close? Still, something good had come out of the fight with his father: Doug liked giving those gifts to the orphans. He sure didn't need them. He would talk to Nanny in the morning about making sure Jimmy Lyden got some kind of gift.

Even though Nanny was a pretty good substitute, Doug had sometimes felt badly about not having a real mother and, although his father seemed angry much of the time, it would probably be much worse having no parents at all.

True, it would be fun to have lots of kids around all the time but he was certainly glad his father hadn't made him stay in the orphanage.

He snuggled up against Nanny who wrapped her arm around his shoulders. He would have lots of friends when he started school in the fall. At least Nanny said so, and she was never wrong.

SEPTEMBER, 1976

The Bentley moved slowly around the semi-circle that fronted the school. Fiona squeezed Doug's hand.

"It'll be fun, laddie. You'll see."

He nodded.

She straightened the strap on his knapsack.

"Look at all those kids." He pushed his nose against the window.

"Everyone one of them waiting to become your friend."

He took a deep breath as the limo stopped. Fiona reached across to open the door. She resisted an urge to lick her finger and flatten the slight cowlick atop his head.

"You'll do just fine, Dougie. Just remember to report to room 6B."

He turned, gave her a big hug. "Thank you, Nanny. I won't forget."

Then he was gone, launched like a moon shot, legs flying up the concrete steps. She thought for a moment he might stop at the big double doors and wave, but he was swallowed up in the stream of eager girls.

She got in the car and sank into the plush upholstery.

"Where next, Miss McLean? To the grocery?"

"Y-yes." Her voice was thick with honey-like grief. Was this what it would be like every time he took another step toward growing up? How did mothers stand it? She dabbed at her eyes. How awful it felt.

"C-could we go to the park for a few minutes, first?"

The chauffeur's gaze met hers in the mirror. He nodded, looked back to the road. She dabbed at her eyes with a handkerchief.

"Sure, Miss McLean. No sense rushing anywhere on such a lovely day, is there?"

She shook her head. No sense rushing at all.

There were so many kids, Doug thought his chest might burst from the excitement. He recognized some of them from the park, others from brief passings in stores.

A group of children were gathered in front of 6B. He walked happily toward them, carried on a magic carpet of expectation. This was his classroom, these would be his classmates.

"Hi," he said to a boy in a blue-striped shirt.

The boy tilted his head. Didn't smile. Several others turned, stared at Doug.

"What's the matter?"

"Door's locked."

Doug reached over and tried the knob. It wouldn't turn. Overhead, a bell rang and the hall began to empty.

"What are we going to do now?" A girl in a green dress with white frills slumped her shoulders. "My mommy's already left with the car."

"Someone'll show up," Doug said.

"But what if they don't? Does that mean we don't get to start school?" The girl's blonde hair was set in big round curls that bounced when she spoke.

"I'll get someone from the office." Doug looked for it down the hall.

"We don't need a teacher to get in."

Doug turned to see who had spoken. The boy moved through the crowd toward the locked door. He wore a tan shirt and slightly frayed blue jeans. There was paint on the shirt. Doug smiled.

"Hello, Jimmy." Doug stuck out his hand. "Nice to see you again."

Jimmy frowned through a suspicious glare and seemed to remember where they'd met. He swept past, reached into his back pocket and slipped something into the jamb. The lock sprang and the door swung open. He turned to face the class.

"No sweat."

He walked in, surveyed the room and selected a desk in the back of the room by a window. The others trooped in after him. There was a brief jostling for the desks in the rear. Doug selected one near the front and put his knapsack under the seat. He pulled out his notebook and sat sideways watching the others, not looking at Jimmy.

He couldn't figure out why Jimmy had snubbed him. Some of the paint on the boy's shirt had probably come from the watercolor set Doug had insisted Nanny buy for him last Christmas. Surely he couldn't be angry about that. Doug had just put his chin in his hands to think things over when a folded, paper airplane whizzed past his ear. The class bubbled with laughter.

Doug swung around in his seat. Jimmy sat staring at the ceiling, hands behind his head. Moments later another creased Doug's ear. He grabbed at it but missed, got out of his seat and picked it up. Doug was about to launch it in Jimmy's direction when he heard a throat being cleared just inside the door.

"I suggest you flatten that aircraft into its original shape, young man. We'll have none of that foolishness in this class."

Doug looked up to see a tall, skinny woman. He blushed and returned to his seat. The teacher unloaded some books onto her desk and faced the class.

"My name is Miss Stipple. I'm from the art department. Your regular teacher became ill yesterday; I'll be filling in until she recovers."

Miss Stipple scanned the class, reminding Doug of a picture he'd seen of a vulture. The children shrank like mice to escape her gaze. She settled again on Doug.

"Your name, sir?"

"Doug MacBrayne, ma'am."

"Well, Mr. MacBrayne, I'd like you to put your name at the top of this sheet of paper, then pass it back so each of the students can sign in, as well."

Doug did as asked then passed it to the student behind him. After several minutes, a girl from the front on the other side of the room, took the paper to Miss Stipple. She counted the students, then the names on the page.

"There seems to be someone missing. When I call your name, please stand up."

She went down the list. Soon everyone was standing but Jimmy.

"What's your name?"

"Jimmy Lyden."

"Why didn't you put your name down?"

He looked straight at her. "I can't write."

She frowned. "How old are you?"

He mumbled.

"Speak up, Mr. Lyden."

"Six and a half, ma'am."

"And how is it, Mr. Lyden, that you are nearly seven years old and still don't know how to write your name?"

His shoulders moved but he didn't speak.

"Answer me, Mr. Lyden."

"The letters don't stick in my brain." He blushed. "They don't make no sense."

Several children giggled. The vulture's head swung back, then forward. Her sweeping gaze silenced them.

"They don't make any sense." Her beak bobbed upward. "Repeat after me, they don't make any sense."

Jimmy did so.

"That's better." She shuffled the papers on the desk. "Normally, you would have a few days of regular classes, then take some tests to check your reading and math skills. But because Mrs. Plotnick is ill, we'll do the testing now. Regular classes will begin on her return."

The class groaned. Tests already? Miss Stipple silenced them with a sharp glance and handed out the test.

"Remember, just do your best. Answer the questions you know. There's no penalty for not knowing something. You're here to learn, we just want to find out what you already know."

Doug nearly laughed when he saw the questions. Pictures next to simple three and four letter words. Multiple choice. The arithmetic problems were unbelievably easy. He completed the test, put his pencil down and thought a minute.

Suddenly a light went on. He raised his hand. Miss Stipple walked over.

"Yes, Mr. MacBrayne?"

"Do these tests tell what grade a person belongs in?"

"What do you mean?"

"Well, if a student got a perfect score on this test, could they maybe go right to second grade?"

"Maybe."

"And is there a test for each grade?"

"There is. All the way through the twelfth grade."

"Thank you."

Doug grinned. It would be the perfect present for Nanny. He doodled on his paper. Monday, first grade; Tuesday, second grade; Wednesday, third grade. Take one test each day, he would be finished school in twelve days. He laughed a little, which brought a warning stare from Miss Stipple.

He looked around the room. The other children were chewing on pencils, fingers, pulling at their chins—all seeming to be searching for answers. Only Jimmy had his head up like Doug. Their eyes met for a moment but Jimmy looked away, out the window. When Doug turned around, Miss Stipple was glaring at him.

"If you're finished, face the front and stop bothering the other children, Mr. MacBrayne."

He blushed and put his head in his hands. He'd better pay closer attention. He felt like a mouse and she was now a cat that needed a bell. This made him smile, but he hid it in his fingers, watching her.

His thoughts drifted forward beyond the twelve days. He and Nanny were halfway around the world on a huge cruise ship when suddenly a fly buzzed at Doug's face. Another attacked, then another, shattering his daydream. He looked around. The children in the classroom were all staring at him. Arms crossed, Miss Stipple stood directly in front of him.

"I'm glad you've decided to rejoin the class, Mr. MacBrayne. Perhaps you would be so kind as to collect the papers for me."

Doug did as he was told and, with a smile, placed his on top and gave the stack to the teacher who simply snatched them away.

"All right, children, you'll go outside for recess then we'll have a bite of lunch. You may now leave the room in an orderly fashion."

Doug followed the other students. Halfway down the hall his feet went out from under him. He grabbed for the radiator to steady himself, but went down. A loud clanging sounded above him. He looked up to see a small red box with Fire Alarm written in bold red letters. The glass window had been smashed.

Miss Stipple hurried into the hall and stopped in front of him, hands on her hips.

"Mr. MacBrayne?"

"I..." He saw Jimmy slip behind her. "I... guess I tripped. I didn't mean to—"

"Go outside, children." The teacher waved the others on. Glared at Doug. "This is a most inauspicious beginning to your school career, Mr. MacBrayne."

"It was an accident." He wanted to add that someone tripped him, but the look on her face said she wouldn't believe him. "I'm sorry, ma'am."

"Outside, now."

Doug stayed near the fence that surrounded the asphalt playground. All the happy energy that had carried him into the school was gone. He ached to be home with Fiona. Maybe he could convince her he wasn't ready for school. That would save him from Miss Stipple's anger. He crouched, grabbed his elbows.

Several children pointed at him, laughing.

A large brown rubber ball bounced off the side of his head. He got up, whirled and kicked it. Jimmy stood ten feet away staring at Doug, that same funny smile on his face.

Doug's mounting rage felt almost as intense as when he'd fought his father. He balled his fists and went for Jimmy, who stiffened, put up his dukes. Doug waded in and started flailing his fists, left and right. Jimmy grabbed him around the waist, wrestling him to the ground.

The other children shouted, "Fight, fight!"

Kicking and swinging, Doug tried to push Jimmy off. With a mighty heave, he rolled on top and put his knees on Jimmy's arms. He reached back to take a mighty swing but his arm was stopped.

"That's enough, Mr. MacBrayne."

Doug looked up, startled.

"You're going to the principal's office, young man."

Chastened, Doug stumbled to his feet. Miss Stipple grabbed his hand in her claw, marched him into the school.

Fiona put the paperback down and stretched. The unaccustomed luxury was seductive. She couldn't remember the last time she'd just sat like this late in the morning with her feet up. Recently Doug had seemed to gain ever more strength and energy. She might not have been able to keep up if school hadn't come along. Twenty minutes of sniffling in the park had taken the thorn of

Doug's absence out of her heart. She knew Doug would flourish in school. He was ready. Apparently she was too.

The telephone rang and she got up to answer it.

"MacBrayne residence."

"Mrs. MacBrayne?"

"No, this is Miss McLean, the nanny. Can I help you?"

"There's been some trouble here at school."

"Trouble? My God, is Doug all right?"

"He's fine. But we need someone to come for him right away."

"What's the problem?"

"We can discuss that when you get here."

"Tell me now, for God's sake."

"Well, he'll be staying at home for a few days."

"Why?"

"He's been suspended..."

Fiona looked at the phone, put it to her ear. "You are talking about Doug MacBrayne?"

"That's correct."

"Why is he being suspended?"

"For fighting. He viciously attacked and beat another student."

"Doug—?"

"Please come to the school, Miss McLean."

Doug and Fiona sat across from each other at the dinner table. He jumped when he heard the car door slam out in the drive and the front door bang open. His head bobbed in time with his father's angry footsteps. He cringed when they stopped at the dining room entrance.

Doug looked at his father. After several moments of icy silence, Doug lowered his head.

"You, go to your room."

"But he hasn't eaten, sir." Fiona said.

"Doug, go to your room Right now."

"Yes, sir."

Doug folded his napkin and put it beside his clean plate. His legs wobbled as he walked past his father, half expecting a slap on the back of his head. The tears began as he stopped at the foot of the stairs but he stifled his sobs. The last thing he wanted to hear was another "cry baby."

Fiona started to rise.

"Stay," Peter said. "I want to talk to you."

"Yes, sir."

Peter paced around the table, his limp so severe he finally had to grab the back of a chair to steady himself. Fiona folded her hands in her lap.

"This is absolutely unacceptable behavior. He shamed me. The family name."

"The other boy started it."

"I heard it differently," Peter said, knuckles white. "I heard he charged the boy—one of the orphans, I might add—and began throwing punches."

"The other boy started it in the classroom, sir."

Peter waved her off. "Doesn't matter. According to the principal, Doug would have been suspended for a week, maybe even expelled, if I hadn't intervened."

"You—?"

"Yes, me." He pulled the chair out and sat. "Doug will be in school tomorrow, but I want you to make sure there's no recurrence of this trouble."

"Trouble?" Fiona started. "Doug's the most well-behaved—"

"Miss McLean, I believe it's time you took off the rose-colored glasses and started acting like a proper Nanny."

"Mr. MacBrayne, I resent that. It's—"

"And I resent your not doing your job properly." Peter's bowtie bobbed uncontrollably. "On the first day of school he acts like a hooligan. If you had taught him proper respect for others, instead of letting him wrap you around his little finger..."

Fiona fought for control, her heart pounding. She wanted to slap his face but held off. It was there in his eye: a deliberate challenge. He wanted an excuse to fire her, despite the promise he made in the hospital chapel. He was almost gloating at what he perceived as her failure to prepare Doug for school.

"He would have been advanced to the second grade if it weren't for this episode," Peter said.

"What?"

"His test results warranted it, but they said he was obviously socially immature and would be kept in first, until he demonstrated more self-discipline. Besides, this will give Doug an opportunity to make it up to that poor boy."

Fiona heard something at the door, realized Doug had been listening. She quickly looked at Peter but he hadn't noticed.

"Doug already told me he'd apologize. He feels bad about losing his temper."

"He'll do better than apologize. I've arranged it."

"What?"

"It's going to be up to Doug to teach the boy he beat up how to read."

With that, Peter limped from the room.

❧

Fiona hid the wrapped sandwich in her knitting bag together with a small carton of milk. She slipped up the stairs and peeked into Doug's room. He lay staring at the ceiling, hands behind his head on the pillow.

"Doug?"

"Yes, Nanny." There was no life in his voice.

"I've brought you something to eat. You must be hungry."

Doug's head drooped, he picked at the satin edge of the blanket. "Did Dad say it was okay?"

"He didn't say it wasn't." She sat next to him. "Come on, you must eat."

He sat up, unwrapped the sandwich and took a small bite. It looked as if the effort to chew was beyond him. He handed it to her.

"I'm sorry, Nanny. I'm just not hungry."

"But you must eat, Dougie. You have school tomorrow."

"Not going."

"Of course you are."

He shook his head.

"Why not? Just because of a little smidgen of trouble?"

"It's not a smidgen. It was a lot." He rolled over, away from her. "Besides, now everything's ruined."

"What's ruined?"

"I was going to surprise you."

"How?"

He explained that according to his calculations, he would take a test for each grade and be finished school in twelve days. Then they would take a trip around the world.

"Now I'll be stuck in first grade forever."

"You can't give up after just one day, Dougie. Remember the Little Train that Could?"

He rolled his eyes. She patted his arm.

"Well, it is a silly story, but I know a better one."

"A story won't help."

"Ah, that may be true, laddie but—" She sighed. "—I never thought the day would come when you wouldn't want to hear one of my tales of Scotland."

"Sorry." He closed his eyes.

"No, you're right. Willie Whitelaw's sail-train wouldn't interest a big, grown-up boy like you."

"Sail-train?" One eye opened.

She started to leave. "Sleep tight, Doug."

His hand snaked out and grabbed at her skirt. "What's a sail-train?"

"I suppose if you ate the rest of your sandwich and drank this milk, it wouldn't hurt to tell you the story at the same time."

"Okay." Doug reached for his sandwich and took a bite, chewing big to show Fiona.

"Well, back in about 1830, some of the very first railway tracks anywhere were laid out in Scotland, between my home town, Newtyle, and the great port of Dundee.

"They built the railway to take produce from the fertile Valley of Strathmore to the big city of Dundee, and to bring imported coal and lime back to the vale—with the occasional passenger, of course. Landowners in the valley and merchants in the city financed it."

She opened the carton of milk and handed it to Doug.

"The first train, if you could call it that, consisted of a single carriage with specially-flanged wheels, to keep the newfangled contraption on the tracks. The rails were secured upon square, stone blocks, far enough apart so a horse could walk on the path between them, pulling the carriage along the level stretches.

"The designers installed steam-powered winches at the tops of hills, where they knew a horse couldn't handle the load. At these places, ropes were wound round the winches to haul the carriage up the incline or to lower it down the other side.

"One of the early horse-drivers, perhaps the very first, was a Mr. William Whitelaw. Willie had always dreamed of being a sailor, but suffered from a terrible seasickness. He gazed out at the ships in the estuary and almost wished he could go with them. But he was quite content driving the train back and forth.

"There's hardly a day in Scotland when the wind doesn't howl. Well, our Willie had a lot of trouble with the wind ripping at the cargo-covers. These were old, canvas wagon-sheets, intended to keep the rain out, and to keep light materials, especially grain, from blowing away. During a typically windy trip, he often stopped his horse five or six times to re-secure those covers. He thought this a terrible waste of time."

Doug nodded, nearly finished with the first half of his sandwich.

"Now Willie was a very clever man, a typically thrifty, ingenious Scot. One day, when he was tying down the canvas, he looked out over the estuary and saw a ship trim her sails to catch the wind and begin to push out into the sea. That's when he got the idea."

Doug's face was all screwed up making delighted pictures in his head. Fiona grinned, knew she had him.

"Willie realized he could turn a disadvantage into an advantage: One evening, he attached a pole at the front of the carriage, fashioned a sail out of a wagon-sheet and next day, when the wind favored, he hoisted his canvas and set it, much as the mariners did, out in the estuary."

Doug wiped milk from his mouth with his pajama sleeve and Fiona gave him an eyebrow.

"Did it work? The sail, I mean?" He asked.

"It worked so well that the poor horse was forced to gallop along behind the carriage and soon became exhausted. He couldn't keep up. So Willie built and attached a rear platform. With the proper wind, he would unhitch the horse, lead him onto the platform and hitch him there. Then Willie'd get on board, unfurl the sail and let her rip."

"Wow. So he did get to sail after all." Eyes wide, Doug had pulled his knees up to his chest.

"There was this long stretch of magnificent grain fields, a few miles north of Dundee, where the roadbed was relatively level. Just before harvest time, people would gather from miles around to watch Willie's wind-carriage smoothly clickety-clacking along the tracks, at almost twenty miles an hour, seeming to sail right over the brown waves of grain. What a sight it was, to see Willie Whitelaw standing at the front, with the horse on the rear platform. Some said you could even see the horse smiling, such was his enjoyment of being relieved of his duties.

"Man and horse continued their sailing for two years, until they installed a brand new, Carmichael steam locomotive to haul the carriage over the entire route. When that happened, everyone was sad to see the wind had finally been knocked out of Willie's sails!"

Finished, Fiona looked at Doug. There was a tiny smile on his face.

"Thanks, Nanny," he whispered.

She tucked in his covers and caressed his forehead. "Think you can sail to school tomorrow?"

"I guess. But having to stay in first grade is going to be really boring."

"True enough. But think of yourself as the horse on the platform, saving your strength for when the wind dies down and you have to pull again."

He squinted at her. "You're pretty smart, you know that, Nanny?"

"That's right, darling. And do you know why?"

"Why?"

"Because I went through first grade twice."

At school next day, Doug was quiet, attentive, and on guard. He made sure he knew where both Miss Stipple and Jimmy were at all times, having attached a mental bell around each of their necks. The class work was so simple, he split off part of his attention and made up his own arithmetic problems, then answered them. When he tired of that, he would picture himself at the rear of the sail-train, watching the Scottish landscape as it whirled by.

After recess and lunch, Doug and Jimmy were given a far corner of the classroom for the writing lesson, while the rest of the class worked on individual projects.

"It won't do any good, you know," Jimmy said. "I don't see things the way other people do."

"Can't hurt to try. Say a word, I'll spell out the letters and you write them down. You do know the letters, don't you?"

"I know them one-by-one. It's when they get strung together that my brain stops."

"Okay, give me a word."

"Car."

Doug slowly spelled the word letter-by-letter and Jimmy appeared to be writing them down.

"Let's see how you did."

Jimmy handed him his tablet. Doug was surprised to see a very lifelike picture of a car.

"Why didn't you write the letters like I said?"

"I did."

"This is a picture."

"Look closer."

Sure enough, each of the letters was incorporated in the drawing.

"That's how I see things."

"I don't understand." Doug scratched his head. "Can you do this with any word?"

"If I see a picture, yes. Sometimes it's hard."

"How about 'go'."

Jimmy sketched the G inside the O, which was tilted as if rushing along. Doug tried several other words: apple, camera, school, cat. shirt, deer. Each time Jimmy produced a cartoon using the letters. When he was finished, he tore off the page and handed it to Doug, who laughed.

"What's so funny?"

"You really do know how to spell."

"No I don't."

"Yes, you do." Doug pointed to the pictures. "I didn't say the letters one-by-one. But you got each of them right in every picture."

Jimmy's face grew red. "Look, you tell anyone and I'll get you."

"But why don't you want anyone to know you can write? That's not a crime."

"I just don't."

"But they expect me to teach you. I'll look bad if—"

"You won't get in no trouble. Your father's rich. He runs the town. You get anything you want. I do things my way."

His hand shot across and pushed Doug, who toppled from his chair. When Miss Stipple looked over, Jimmy was studiously drawing.

"What's going on?"

Doug looked up from the floor. "I...I just leaned back and my chair fell over."

"In the future, keep all four legs on the ground and that won't happen." She reached down and righted the chair. "Come join the others, it's rest time."

Doug went to his desk and put his chin in his hands. He stared at the drawings Jimmy had produced. The picture of a running deer caught his attention. He started to feel dizzy and closed his eyes to fend off the vibrations.

"This hunter touch you for luck." Tehuti said, as he reached over to rub the large red mass, protruding from the back of Ashna's bobbing head. "We hunt for meat at light of day."

Ashna grunted and continued chipping at the new lamp he was making. His mouth watered from the memory of deer flesh. He had already seen the herd.

He waited until Tehuti climbed onto his four-leg and rode away, then lurched to his half-stance for walking. His right arm hung lower than his left because of the twist in his spine but he used the arm to lift his right leg for each step. He crashed through the underbrush to the secret opening in the hillside. He looked around to make sure no one watched and stooped to collect the colors he would need: berries, different clays, chalk, even his own blood when necessary to make the images.

Sweat poured down his face despite the chilly day. The hunters always touched his deformed head for luck, in hope of a successful hunt, but only Ashna knew the truth. The deer taste came to his mouth again and he wiped drool from his lips. He could be stoned for making the pictures, but knew the making of the images stole power from the animal being depicted—the intended prey. They could touch his head all they wanted, but they would eat, only after he stole the animal's speed and power in color.

This was his knowing.

"Ashna?"

He turned. Huva approached with a bowl of food.

"No follow," he growled, waving his arm.

"Food. Eat." She held the bowl out to him, lowered her dark, soulful eyes.

He took the bowl from her slender hands. She had been given to him in mockery: this straight-haired, skinny girl, stolen from a clan three mountains away. Tehuti had gargled with laughter when he handed her to him in front of all the others. Ugly girl. Ugly man. Everyone laughed when Tehuti laughed, even Ashna's brother, Hamar.

Tehuti rode the four-leg. He was as different from the others in his beauty and strength as Ashna was in his twisted deformities. Tehuti used the power of the four-leg to make him faster. Ashna secretly used the power of the paintings.

"Brother Hamar look for Ashna," Huva said, sneaking a glance toward the side of the hill where Ashna was headed. "Come now."

Ashna frowned. Made the sign of the sun behind the mountain: "Tonight."

Huva tried to pull him back, but he shook her off. Made the sign again. He saw the fear she tried to keep from her eyes. He growled, handed her the empty bowl.

"Go."

His anger softened when she lowered her head.

"Huva."

She looked up and he made the sign of man-and-woman and then the sun behind the mountain. She nodded, a light in her eye.

He waited until she was gone to continue his descent. Hamar would also want to touch his head before the hunt. Ashna would have liked to show his brother the truth about this "luck," but did not want to endanger his life. Before Tehuti came, every clan had one-who-draws-pictures to help with the hunt. But Tehuti forbad the drawings upon his ascension to power, saying they were old, tired magic. Anyone caught painting would die.

Ashna would keep his secret the way Tehuti concealed his power over the four-leg. Maybe if Huva gave him a baby, Ashna would show the boy how to steal an animal's power by drawing it in the cave, but only when the boy was old enough to understand the necessity of secrecy. Certainly not until it was almost time for Ashna to go to the dirt—to his grave. If there were no baby, he would show his brother Hamar. But only then.

This magic was too powerful for more than one person to know.

He pushed the underbrush away from the small opening. One look around convinced him he was alone. Inside, he took out his small lamp and filled it with dried moss. Two strikes of the black rock and a spark caught. He waited until the moss was completely red then poured the fat inside. The soft glow barely lit the entrance. He walked deeper into the cave and pushed several rocks away from a hidden passage. Images from ancestral hunts danced on the walls, in the flickering light. He could taste them. Auroch, long-tusked boars, mammoths—every kind of food that walked.

A mere handful of water was all he would need to paint the deer. He took the flat rock he used to mix his pigments and squashed several berries. Squinting, leaning to one side, he dipped his finger in the paint and moved it across the wall, eventually making four images which would mean extra food—a great feast.

Finished, he wiped his hands in the dirt and put his new lamp next to the flat rock. The cold of the cave made his legs ache. He scrabbled out into the twilight. He was no more than a few trees down the mountain when he heard a twig snap. He whirled, but saw no one. Nevertheless, the hairs below the red bulge at the back of his head bristled. He growled. There was no further sound, so he continued to his hearth, felt himself rising at the thought of doing man-and-woman with Huva.

Tehuti's joke had turned into a blessing for Ashna, but he could never reveal that irony. So he kept his soft heart for her hidden in front of the others, and she kept her dark, soulful eyes hidden from everyone but him.

If another ever saw her inner beauty, they would take her. He wouldn't let that happen. She and his brother were the only things he cared about in life. Them and the paintings in the cave. If Tehuti knew about any of it, he would take everything away.

This Ashna knew.

When Doug opened his eyes, he saw the girl in the next aisle staring at him. Her smile seemed to tickle at his eyes.

"My name is Sally," she whispered.

"I'm Doug," he said.

"I know." She giggled. "The teacher keeps saying your name."

Doug sighed. Maybe first grade wouldn't be so bad after all. Sally smiled again. Suddenly, something wet hit him on the back of the head.

"Yipes!" His hand felt for the missile which had stuck. He tried to pull it away, but it clung to his hair.

"Do you have a problem, Mr. MacBrayne?"

"No, ma'am."

He removed as much of the gum as he could. He never turned around to see who had thrown it. He didn't need to.

Chapter Three

February, 1980

Fiona poured two eye-dots of pancake batter into the little frying pan, then a thin nose-line between them, hooking it slightly. A smiling, crescent mouth finished her Picasso-like design. She then covered it with a layer that filled the entire pan.

Fiona knew she was being silly. After all, Doug would be ten years old in twenty-four hours, and probably considered himself too mature for this. But she just wasn't ready to let him grow up so quickly.

Two minutes later she flipped the pancake, reached for a plate.

"Breakfast is ready, Dougie. Are you at the table?"

"Yes, Nanny," he called through the door.

"Then close your eyes." She slid the pancake on the plate and went into the dining room.

"It's a happy-face pancake!" Doug shouted, his hands over his eyes.

"You peeked."

"Did not."

"Then how did you know?" she said.

"Well, whenever you cook breakfast, that's almost always what you make."

"Hmpf."

"Besides," he grinned, pointing to the middle of the table, "why else would syrup be here?"

"You just eat your breakfast, Mr. Smarty-pants, and leave me to the newspaper and me tea."

She opened the front section and pretended to read, then lowered it to peek over the top. He was grinning at her.

"What's so funny?"

"You are, when you pretend to be mad at me."

"Angry. There's a difference between anger and madness."

"Oh yeah, Irk and Quirk."

She raised the paper again to hide her smile. When was she going to learn not to get into word play with him? As her mum used to say, "Never go into a battle of wits half-armed."

"Nanny, is Dad going to be home tomorrow? It is Saturday."

"I'm not sure, Dougie." The expectation in his eyes hurt her. "He's been terribly busy at work."

He shrugged and began eating his pancake. She was glad he didn't pursue the subject. When the boy was smaller, it was easier to mask his father's absence from birthday celebrations. The older MacBrayne was incapable of hiding his resentment over the thought that his son's birth had caused his wife's death.

Footsteps sounded upstairs and Fiona quickly straightened and refolded the newspaper, then dashed to the pantry where she ironed it flat.

It just wouldn't do for anyone to read Mr. Peter Douglas-MacBrayne III's morning chronicle, before he did. The man himself strode into the breakfast room just as Fiona returned from the pantry, waving the newspaper behind her to cool it. "Good morning, sir."

"Good morning, Dad," Doug said.

"Mor'gm," Peter said, glancing at the paper, then at his son. He pointed to a loose thread on Doug's shirt. "Explain how you lost that button."

"I don't know, sir." Doug said, lifting his arm to look, then back at his father. "Sorry, I mean, Dad."

Fiona understood Peter's resentment and frustration, and thought to intervene, but he spoke first.

"I think addressing me as Sir would be most appropriate, from now on. It'll prepare you for later in life."

"But, Dad, I don't think…"

"Don't tell on yourself. If you don't think, you shouldn't speak."

Tears welled in the boy's eyes.

"Have you finished your breakfast?"

"Y-yes, sir."

"Then you are dismissed. Take your plate to the kitchen."

Doug left the table. Fiona followed. She opened the cupboard and brought out a small tin box, took out a button and a threaded needle.

"I'm sorry I didn't notice before your father did, Doug."

"It's okay, Nanny."

"Give me your shirt and fetch your school bag."

He raised his arms, swam out of his shirt and started toward the dining room door, then thought better of it and went around the other way.

Fiona cursed softly as the needle stuck her thumb. Soothing it in her mouth, she noticed the partially-eaten pancake on the counter and shuddered.

The eyes stared out in floury innocence, but the smile was half-eaten away.

☙

Maybe it was time to put up a new slogan. THE UNIVERSE WASN'T MADE FOR YOU, YOU WERE MADE FOR THE UNIVERSE, was starting to annoy him. Lots of things at the Sarah Douglas Foundation for Psychic Research were starting to annoy him: Dr. Armen Ramis, the Director, was breathing down his neck, demanding more budget cuts; the electro-encephalograph was stuck on schizophrenic and the manufacturer said it would be out for sixty days. Now even some clients were starting to get on his nerves. If he knew what he wanted to do on sabbatical, he would have taken it a year or two earlier.

He glanced up at the wall behind him, at the framed copy of Lincoln's Gettysburg Address. He might have hung a picture of the sixteenth American president, but he got enough comments about looking exactly like Lincoln without inviting more.

Set me free, Mr. Lincoln, he thought. Get me out of here.

And yet he loved this crazy outfit, chartered by and named in the fifties for an eccentric capitalist. The Sarah Douglas Foundation was not as well known as the Cayce Institute and other big-name paranormal research centers, but they had developed a good database on psychic phenomena and worked directly with people—ordinary or not—investigating the role played by such phenomena in their lives.

"Dr. Avisson?" She crossed her legs on the sofa. Plenty of leg, not enough underwear. "Or can I call you Abraham yet?"

She said the last part of his name as if ordering a sandwich at a deli. He shook his head. "Please, Mrs. Clark, if you don't mind—"

"But I do mind." Her lipstick was reddish brown, the color of spoiled apples. "My Reiki instructor says I have to get rid of my subservience to authority before I can advance to the next level."

"Calling me Doctor Avisson isn't being subservient. That's just my title, my function in your life."

"So I should call Larry 'husband?'" Her rotten apple lips formed into a well-practiced pout.

The pout had begat magazine covers, the covers landed her a rich lawyer, but Avisson was determined it wasn't going to violate his rules of professional etiquette. He wondered if the son she doted on had the same pout. Her leg lifted even higher—she must have been a high school cheerleader, probably college, too.

"Tell me about your latest dreams." Avisson used his notepad to block the glare from her upper thighs.

"I didn't journal them this week."

"Why not?"

Her sigh was a whale, spouting at the surface. "Larry was between cases this week."

"Meaning."

"Meaning—" She stretched, leaving no doubt she'd left her brassiere at home. "—I didn't need to dream about having sex with a stranger. Meaning I could use the stranger who calls himself my husband only at cocktail parties."

"Were you able to use any of the kundalini exercises? Open up your fifth chakra?"

"With old pump and dump? I don't think so."

Avisson put down his pad, rubbed his eyes. "You know, we could have canceled this appointment and met when you had some material you wanted to go over."

"But Doctor Avisson." She rolled over, half off the sofa—a bad imitation of a B-grade, French porno-flick. "You don't understand. Larry returns to the courtroom next week."

"Yes."

"And I wanted to see you," she got up and drifted toward him, "so I could fix your face in my mind—" She put one hand on either side of his chair, leaned over until her lips were inches from his. A mixture of cigarette and mint washed against his mouth and nose in waves, timed with her breathing.

"My next subject will be here in—"

"No, Doctor Avisson, you don't understand." Her designer fingernails brushed under his chin. "You're *my* next subject."

"Mrs. Clark, I don't think—"

"Oh, but you will, Doctor. That's one thing you will do, this week." She snatched her purse from the sofa and sauntered toward the door, hips swaying. She turned, wearing an even more dangerous version of the pout. "And I promise to be a good girl this week. I'll write in my journal, faithfully every morning." She lowered her voice. "I don't want you to miss one little detail of my dreams, Doctor Avisson."

She was gone.

Avisson slumped in his chair, willing the mint vapors away from his memory. Part of him knew she was just mocking him with her antics. Another part mocked him for not taking up her challenge. She would probably back down if he did. But there'd be hell to pay if she didn't.

Maybe if he applied for his sabbatical now, he could go early.

❦

Doug placed a small chunk of lead on one side of the scale and a similar-sized piece of feldspar on the other. The lead hung lower.

"But they're the same size," Sally said. "How can one be heavier than the other?"

"I think Mr. Smithers said—"

"That the specific gravity of different rocks determines their relative weight," interrupted a stern, loud voice addressing the entire class.

Doug jumped in his chair and Sally giggled. Smithers continued his stork-like stalk around the science lab.

"Whereas the weights of each type of rock are interesting, their physical properties are even more so. From the beginning of recorded history, when flint was used to start fires, Mankind has taken substances from rocks to make everything from metal for cars to crystals for lasers."

Sally leaned over to whisper in Doug's ear. Smithers stopped talking and extended a claw-like finger in their direction.

"Not to mention how important diamonds are to young lovers." The teacher craned his neck around the room to silence the snickering coming from the far corner by the window.

Doug knew what the intermittent giggles were about: another cartoon would soon be making the rounds. He tried to concentrate on weighing the next series of rocks but every whisper and rustle of paper distracted him. He knew a copy of the cartoon would show up in his locker, or be slipped into his bookbag by the end of day.

Jimmy Lyden liked making fun of him in these harsh, satirical sketches labeled "The Tales of Dougie-Poo." And the joke was not complete unless the subject knew why everyone was laughing.

Doug glanced over at Mr. Smithers, not sure whether he was truly hard of hearing or only eccentric. He wished a teacher would confiscate just one cartoon, so they would know what was being done. Heck, they intercepted love notes and shushed all laughter mocking other students, whereas every barb aimed at Doug not only hit the target, but spread from classroom to classroom faster than a fire drill.

If he hadn't been the brunt of the humor, he might have been more appreciative of Jimmy's skill: Doug as a bee during a spelling contest, misspelling the word honey; Doug in the family limousine, giving the finger to a bunch of kids riding the school bus; Doug being served a sumptuous lunch by a butler, while the other children stood in the cafeteria line to receive blobs of unnatural, blue glop.

He returned to the list of weights. It would probably be awhile before the new cartoon appeared.

A folded piece of paper fluttered to his feet. He checked to see if Mr. Smithers was looking, then bent to pick it up. He rolled his eyes. The direct approach. Not very subtle. What was it this time? He unfolded the paper, squinting. No cartoon. Just a simple message:

> Happy Birthday
> If you want your present
> meet me outside the gym after school.
> A secret friend

He spun around. No one was peeking at him, or grinning. No sign or signal as to who wrote the note. Even Jimmy seemed intent on his experiment—though Doug was sure there would be more art work on the pages than actual weights. Besides, Jimmy wouldn't print anything so directly. His hieroglyphic calligraphy had become an accepted phenomenon. The teachers recognized he was unmoved by any threat of low grades and had simply promoted him along with the other students.

Doug looked at the note again then slipped it into his pocket. If only it were real. He hoped someone did want to be his friend. But five years of harassment, of being the rich kid, the butt of every joke Jimmy and the others could dream up, had made him wary. No way he'd be at the gym after school.

He glanced over at Sally, who had turned away. He remembered the smile she gave him the very first day of kindergarten. Every time she displayed any sign of friendship, something bad happened. Now with Smithers' crack about the diamond, she had suffered a public humiliation. Who could blame her for putting as much space between herself and Doug as she could?

The wind threatened to send him off the road. Grumpy fought the steering wheel, pulled to the side. On rainy days he appreciated the extra height of his Volkswagen camper. He spied a rutted path leading to a small clearing and headed for it. The windstorm showed little sign of abating and this was as good a time as any to stop. He maneuvered the camper around the deepest ruts and avoided most of the rocks.

Czechoslovakia. Funny how every country seems the same when you've been on the road for so long. Oh sure, the food and language, the faces and dress of the natives—all different, but the land itself, the trees and streams, rocks and hills, had their own kind of similarity.

He was tired of wandering, but had not yet found what he sought. What was he looking for? Could he recognize the answer when he wasn't even sure of the question?

He ran his hand along the small shelf that held the artifacts gathered during his travels: Kokopelli, Buddha, Shiva, a Mayan calendar wheel, a miniature Muzzah, a Jewish phylactery, a Russian Orthodox Cross. How Peter would mock him if he saw this shrine; he'd probably never appreciate its meaning.

Nor would his son ever understand how desperately sorry Grumpy was that Victoria had found out about his affair with Molly. Would Peter ever comprehend the thirst for passion and simple human joy that drives a man into another woman's arms? Probably not, Peter was Victoria's son, after all.

So what was Grumpy looking for now? When he'd left Douglasville he'd thought it was his son's forgiveness. No more. He had given up hope of that.

Grumpy stopped the van, got out and stretched. The wind dropped and he heard the sound of a stream gurgling near a small tree-covered hill. He locked the van and walked fifty yards or so. He stopped, pushed up his Greek fisherman's cap, untied the madras bandanna from his neck, and wiped his forehead.

The late afternoon sun blazed with intensity. Before him sat a most strange contraption: combination truck and shack, loose-joined as if created by a mad industrial sculptor. Could this be what he'd been seeking... or was it only a mirage?

The faint strain of what could have been a guitar or lute accompanied a low, raspy singing voice of indistinct gender. He walked up to what he thought was the door and knocked. The music continued so he tapped again. The song stopped. Footsteps padded in his direction. Someone pulled a curtain to the side of the crescent moon window above the door.

Grumpy waved. The curtain flopped straight. He waited a few moments, tapped a third time. A guttural voice said something in a language Grumpy didn't understand.

"Can you help me?" he asked.

Another gargle, including a phrase with the words American something-or-other seeped through the still-shut door.

"Yes, I'm an American."

The door opened a crack.

"Vhat you vant?"

Grumpy remembered Sarah's tales of her dealings with Gypsies. "I would like to speak with the madame."

"About?"

"I have questions. I hope she has answers."

The door closed again. Footsteps moved toward the front of the vehicle, a soft conversation filtered out, then silence. As he reached to knock again, the door swung open.

A short, stocky man with a bushy mustache and long black hair motioned Grumpy inside.

"Thank you." He climbed up the short ladder.

The interior of the caravan could have been designed by a Hollywood art director. Wood-fronted shelves filled with mysterious jars and a jumble of odd-sized containers lined the walls. The furniture was small, covered with beautifully woven fabrics. Grumpy blinked back tears and took several breaths, his nostrils burning from the intense mixture of incense, garlic and other herbs in the air.

"You have questions for Madame Tucheskyah?"

"I am really looking for a teacher."

"Teach you vhat?" The man's dark, suspicious eyes measured Grumpy, who was glad he had decided not to change out of his denim traveling clothes. Any hint of wealth might have been a problem.

"To read the crystal ball."

The man shook his head. "This she does not teach. It is only for knowing."

Grumpy nodded. "Then I would like Madame Tucheskyah's help in opening my knowing."

The suspicion intensified. "You speak too vell for an American."

"My mother had the knowing."

"Why did she not teach you?"

"Young men are fools. By the time I shed my foolish coat, she had passed over."

"Why you want to read the crystal ball? So you can entertain your friends, maybe join circus?" A smile crept across the stocky man's face.

"No." Grumpy laughed.

"Maybe you want to invest your money in American stock market, become rich."

"I have been rich, it brought me no pleasure and little worthwhile knowledge."

"We are poor, that brings no pleasure either." The man waved his tired arm, a gesture of futility. "What makes you think Madame Tucheskyah will teach you?"

"I'm not sure." Grumpy reached into his pocket, pulled out a pendant: an upside down silver heart overlaid with a golden crescent moon. "But she may agree, once she sees this."

The man's left eyebrow raised, he looked again at Grumpy, this time with a warm sadness. "Your mother give you this?"

"Yes."

"Vhat did she tell you when she give to you?"

"Every heart has its own moon—"

"And every moon, its own heart." came from the front of the vehicle.

Startled, Grumpy turned to see a middle-aged woman sitting in the curtained passage. Gnarled tight, her crippled hands were nubbed batons at rest in her lap. Her hair shot red and silver flames from both sides of her head, precariously balanced on a thin, swan-like neck. But it was her molten eyes that were truly afire.

Grumpy caught his breath.

The woman's full, dark red lips slowly formed a magnificent smile. "Valka, we will need a bottle of wine and some bread and cheese. Today we celebrate."

The short man frowned. "Celebrate what?"

"The return to our family of a lost brother." She engulfed Grumpy with another smile. "I believe he has searched for us a long, long time."

❦

Doug sneezed several times. He stood up and excused himself from the dinner table.

"I'm tired," he said, avoiding Nanny's gentle reach.

"Are you coming down with a cold, Doug?"

He shook his head and left the dining room and climbed the stairs with leaden feet. Unlike his classmates, Doug had never been glad to see Friday come, preferring the noisy halls and classrooms to the quiet of home on the weekends. So what if he didn't really have any friends, he still enjoyed being around the kids. Now it didn't matter if he ever went back to school.

He punched the bannister. It was his own fault. He'd known not to answer that note. Would he ever learn? The moment the last bell rang, he'd thrown on his coat and gloves and hurried around to the gymnasium door. Although wary about the note, his curiosity had forced him to check it out.

Rounding the corner, he skidded on the icy sidewalk and nearly collided with a large snow-woman. Arms outstretched, she wore only a babushka and a huge brassiere, from which hung a sign: "Nanny loves you, Dougie." A small pyramid of snowballs was stacked at her feet.

It really was funny. He would have just laughed if the first snowball hadn't hit him square on the back of the head, right on his birthmark. The second knocked the sign face-down in the wet snow. Others came whizzing by, so he shielded himself behind the snow-nanny. He let four or five more streak past before he reached down and sent one of his own toward his attackers—all of whom had desperado-like scarves covering their faces.

"Quit hiding behind your nanny," shouted one of the boys.

"Yeah, come on, pussy. Fight like a man."

One desperado stood up and Doug let fly, reaching down quickly to launch another. The first missed its mark, but not the window behind. A scream followed the sound of breaking glass, when the second missile hit the boy smack in the face. He went down as if shot.

The other boys ran away. Doug stood, frozen. A teacher's face appeared in the window. Damn. Mrs. Stipple. She shouted at Doug, then saw the injured boy on the ground. Doug knew he should stay to help his victim; however, he ran toward the front of the school where Fiona would be waiting.

Once home, he waited nervously for the telephone to ring while he did his homework, his stomach knotted from an unsuccessful attempt to digest dinner. He wouldn't answer any of Nanny's questions about the day, about why he was so out of breath when he jumped into the car.

Doug heard the phone ring, just as he got in bed. He pulled the covers over his head and waited. Five minutes later, Nanny came in.

"Doug?"

"Yes."

"Why are you hiding under the covers?"

He peeked out and squinted. "The light kinda hurt my eyes."

She reached over and felt his forehead. "Well, you may be coming down with something. You sleep, and we'll see how you feel in the morning."

"Okay."

"Just think, tomorrow you'll be ten years old."

He tried to smile. It came out more like a wince. She kissed her fingertips and touched his forehead.

"Nice dreams."

She turned out the light and Doug twisted and turned, trying to find comfort. None came. His nerves felt rattled. He pulled the pillow over his head to block out the buzzing that suddenly invaded his being.

A moment later he found himself in a corner of a dark cave, huddled under sheepskin blankets, waking from a deep sleep on a rough pallet of straw. Outside, dawn was just breaking.

The sound of the first cock's crow made Ogmios stir. The graying, clan bard and seer opened his eyes and sat up, to look beside him at his beloved Fionnaghal and over at their three small children, all peacefully asleep under their woolen fleeces. Fionnaghal moaned and snuggled deeper into her warm, lambskin cover.

"I must go check the stones," Ogmios whispered, not to wake the children. He got up, put on his sheepskin coat and pulled his woolen head-covering well down, over the large, ugly birthmark that covered much of the back of his head.

"Take care, dearest Og," whispered Fionnaghal, her dark, soulful eyes peering out just above the cover. "The path may be dangerous from ice."

"Have no fear. I have the feet of a goat," said Ogmios, lifting his foot.

"More than the feet of one," she said, exposing her body to the chill morning and his warm eyes.

On any other day, Og would have jumped into the bedding to prove her right, but this was not the time. He tiptoed to the mouth of the cave, then stopped to look over at the rest of the clan, still sleeping quietly.

May the Gods protect you all, he thought, as he began the tortuous climb up the steep, narrow pathway. At the top of the cliff, Og paused to look in the sky where the stars—the tears of the night—were winking out, one by one.

Down below, as the dense, whitish haar lifted slowly from the surface of the sea, Og could see the work of a magic paintbrush: A few little reed coracles, used by the clan fishermen, appeared first in the foreground; then, in order, the sandy brown, kelp-spotted shore of the loch, the green slopes leading to the blue, misty hills and glens, and finally, the outlines of the mountains behind. All was still, motionless and soundless, as if the painter-god had slowly unveiled the beauty of the scene for Og's eyes alone.

The smooth surface of the sea-loch erupted with hissing mackerel, shattering the serene silence. A screeching, hungry osprey swooped, then dove and splashed into the surface of the water, now shimmering in the bright, reflected rays of the rising, red sun. Mother Earth had come alive again.

Og sighed and took a deep breath of the fresh, clear air. He loved the faint smell of the sea, the kelp and fish.

A black spot, two thousand feet up in the brightening cobalt sky, swooped down silently. Suddenly it become a huge sea eagle, a gray, smearing streak, plummeting for its prey: The osprey screamed, taking violent evasive action. After the impact, a little cloud of feathers marked where the angry, wounded osprey had dropped its wriggling breakfast. Og watched the sea eagle snatch the hapless mackerel in mid air and, spreading its enormous wings, fly triumphantly away.

Og peered up the glen, saw the clan's sacred circle of stones that stood silhouetted against the sky, atop the distant hill. The wind shifted, intensified, bringing an icy breeze from the west. He tightened the fleece around his waist, resecured a second fleece over his shoulders.

The gods had positioned this little land between the sea and the loch as if to diminish the fury of stiff westerly breezes before they gathered force and whipped on to the east. Og gave thanks to the God of Warmth for his clothing.

He continued up the narrow, winding path to the bottom of the lush glen, where some of the clan's cattle grazed on the relatively flat land between the hills, rumps to the wind. The call of a corncrake clack-clacked through the crisp air. Og did not search for the source, knowing this bird turns its head as it calls, making it almost impossible to locate. Some of the more superstitious clansmen attributed the grating, elusive sound to the rasping moan of some lost spirit. But Og knew better.

He crossed the field and climbed a stone dike, which divided the verdant terrain and kept the sheep and goats away from the pasture that had been allotted to the cattle. Og raised his eyes to look at the horizon, about a mile away. The standing stones were outlined clearly against the brightening sky. As he forded the burn which wound its way through the valley, eventually spurting out and down from a crevasse in the cliff face to the sea, Ogmios stooped to drink.

Before cupping his hand for water he checked the location of the cattle. Smiling, he remembered the advice his father had given him so many years before: "Always drink upstream from the herd."

He shook the icy water from his leather-clad feet in a mock goat dance, then continued climbing, certain that things would go well.

At the circle, Og walked to the headstone, bent down to pick up the slate and the sharp flint with which he made his daily marks. He counted six vertical scratches before noticing a small mouse peeking from its hole at the base of a huge stone.

"It's been six days since the winter solstice should have passed," Og explained to his companion. "The sun needs to show herself soon, or the clan will call for a new seer. And I will once again have to fish to feed my family."

The mouse twitched its nose and whiskers.

"For days, Mother Sun has hidden behind the thick clouds. They were so low, I had to use the sun-stone to find my way from the ledge to the circle and back again."

The sun-stone consisted of a rare, calcite-spar from the land of ice—a special crystal that polarized sunlight by changing from pale yellow to blue when held vertically and turned perpendicular to the sun. It always proved invaluable when visibility was zero.

"My father taught me how to use it," Og said to the mouse. "He also taught me the secrets of the stones as his father taught him.

"So many secrets." He rubbed his hand along the sharp, square edge of the nearest stone, remembering the questions he had asked his father. Where did they come from? How were the huge stones quarried, brought here, and raised? "I would like to understand that mysterious procedure. It would be most useful to the clan," he mused.

There was a ballad about the stones, but not even a hint of their origin. In the clan, Og was not only the seer, but also the bard; so it was natural that an appropriate couplet came to mind as he prepared to do his job. He sang:

"... And thus our guardian stones
   were caused to float in air—
   Like in the sea, as doth a boat..."

A hundred men couldn't move one of the stones. It did not matter what magic the ancestral clan had used to build the guardian ring. Now that it was here, there was no need to build another.

Og entered the circle. He sat on a small, round stone about sixteen inches high, positioned precisely at the center. Facing the tallest stone, due south from the seat, he looked left, at the narrow gap between the next two stones to the east.

"I hope the sun has stopped its journey southward and has started to return," he said, as an important verse came to his mind:

"If the seer seeth that the sun doth dance,
 or stop its regular, loving motions,
 Take to the hills and caves near the top,
 All safe from the flooding oceans.
 Thus to save maternity;
 This through all eternity."

Og shielded his eyes and squinted, carefully examining the position of the sun as it rose from the sea. He had to move his head to see the edge of the shining, red disk.

"At last!" he cried. It was as he had hoped.

"The life source of the clan has passed the winter solstice—the bottom of its annual journey—and returns." He grinned at the mouse. "All goes well. There will be another summer."

Relaxed now, Og smiled. The accumulated tension of the uncertainty of the last six days drained swiftly from his body. The seer had seen. Now, he knew.

"The planting will begin in seven days less than three months." He made the seventh vertical scratch on the slate with the flint. "Only eighty-six more until the seeds go into the ground."

Relieved that the days were getting longer, Og sighed, got up and went to the edge of the upper cliff. He stopped to look at and listen to the dark green waves, foaming and thundering against the rocks far below.

Fionnaghal stood on the ledge, arms outstretched, singing to the curious seals. A huge, friendly, inquisitive bull approached, a benign expression on his face. She waved to him. Og could almost hear her clear, melodious voice, seemingly in tune with all living things.

He saw their three children watching her from the safety of a grassy knoll on the wide, irregular ledge that separated the upper cliff from the lower one.

To the right, Chief Oengus stood alone at the dark mouth of the cave.

He looked up at Og, who returned his gaze. Not a word was spoken. Not a sound was heard, except for the sea, the howling wind and the screams of the terns, gannets and gulls out in the sea-loch, diving for their breakfast. Og made no gesture or sign to the

Chief. Not a muscle twitched in either face and, even though both had the eyes of eagles, they were too far apart to see each other's craggy features. Both knew the importance of the moment. Og sent his thoughts to his chief.

Oengus turned and called the clan from the black cave. They assembled immediately and Og watched the chief raise his hand for silence.

"Friends," he intoned, "It appears that the Gods again look upon us with favor. The stones say the Mother sun will soon provide the warmth and light we need to sprout our seed, thus to ensure our survival and that of our livestock. In three months you can begin the planting. But today, we prepare for our annual feast of celebration."

Doug felt a light shake on his shoulder. He opened his eyes. His nanny smiled and whispered, "Happy birthday, Dougie."

He yawned and stretched, then he saw the package she held behind her.

"Is that for me?"

"Maybe after a kiss."

He jumped up, threw his arms around her neck and planted his lips on her cheek, one hand groping for the package. She gave it to him.

He tore the wrapping from the present, opened the box. Twenty-four hand-painted lead soldiers in full Scots Guards battledress complete with kilts, stared at him. The bagpiper's cheeks were puffed out. The other soldiers stared ahead in stoic readiness.

"Oh thanks, Nanny. They're super. Can I play with them now?"

"Just until lunch. Your father is supposed to be here for cake and candles. He's going out tonight."

Doug dressed quickly, wolfed down his breakfast, then hurried toward the glassed-in porch, carrying the soldiers and a small shopping bag he'd lifted from the kitchen.

He glanced behind him, then opened the door quietly so Nanny wouldn't know he was going outside without his coat. A gusty wind blew small, dry snowflakes around him as he ran to the rockgarden by the winterized, Olympic-sized swimming pool.

He was back inside in seconds.

"Ten-shun," he said, kneeling down to position the row of soldiers.

What a wonderful birthday. He would spend the morning building a castle for them to defend, using water from a pail to wet the sand. He reached into the bag, pulled out the slender stones he had just selected. He arranged them in a circle, the design that had somehow formed in his mind.

When Nanny came to call him for lunch, she stared open-mouthed at his creation.

"Doug." she said, kneeling at the edge of the box. "Where'd you get those wee stanes?"

Doug stood and brushed himself off.

"My clothes are still clean."

"Stanes—Stones... there." She pointed to them. "What made you arrange them like that?"

"Dunno." He knelt next to her. "They just seem to belong that way."

"We used to call them standing-stone circles in Scotland. There's a famous one in England— Stonehenge."

"Stonehenge? I don't think—" Doug frowned. "—What were they used for?"

"Who knows? Some think they were ancient astronomical observatories. Others say they were used for human sacrifices, or other pagan rites."

"Gosh, I just thought it looked cool."

"Well, all right, Doug, it doesn't matter." Nanny said, smiling. "Now come have your lunch."

"Is Dad here?"

"Not yet." She put her arm around him and led him into the breakfast room. "Come on, laddie."

They ate in silence. Doug took small bites and chewed each of them forever, occasionally glancing at the clock. When his plate was nearly empty, Nanny reached across and tapped his hand.

"How 'bout a game of cards?"

"Sure." He brightened up. "What shall we play?"

"Poker," she said, noting the gleam in his eye. "But this time, I'm going to teach you about wild cards."

"Wild cards?"

"You'll see. Now drink up quickly."

Doug finished his milk in three quick gulps, then practically dragged her to the card table in the library.

Doug caught on to what wild cards were and how they were used so quickly that Nanny joked that he must have been a Mississippi riverboat gambler in a former life.

"I don't know, Nanny," Doug said. "Could be. Our teacher read a story in school about paddle wheelers with tall, black stacks. She made it so real I could almost smell the smoke and hear the old steam whistles."

"Then you just roll up your sleeves, young man. We'll have no fancy gambler tricks in this game."

"Who gets to pick what's wild?"

"I'll pick first." She turned the deck over. "Let's see. How about One-eyed Jacks...no... Split bearded Kings.

Doug came at her in a flash. "What are those?"

"Well," she said, "One-eyed Jacks have only one eye: Their heads are in profile, so you can't see the other eye. On most decks they're the Jacks of Hearts and Spades."

She took one out of the deck and held it up.

"And the kings?"

She removed all four kings from the deck.

"If you look closely, Doug," she said, "you can't tell if the King of Diamonds has a split beard. See how he faces to the left, with his beard curling up to his chin?"

"Yes, Nanny, said Doug, "He looks sad."

"Well, I don't know if he's sad or not, but look at the King of Hearts. Do you see how his beard is split in the middle? It even curls up towards his cheeks"

"He looks like a big sissy." Doug said.

"Don't know about that." She pulled out another. "But here's the King of Spades. See his beard?"

"Yes, Nanny, It's split like the others, but he looks like he's waiting for the answer to a question."

"Interesting," Fiona said, then pulled out the last king. "Now, here's the last king: The King of Clubs. See how his curly black beard splits—"

Doug recoiled. "He's mean. I don't like him."

"Doug," Fiona said, "These are only playing cards—"

He buried the card in the deck "He's nasty."

"Why do you say that, Laddie?"

"It just popped into my head."

"All right. Never mind," she said, shuffling the cards again.

"Please don't make the King of Clubs wild. I hate him."

"Mustn't say 'hate,' Doug," she cautioned, counting out equal stacks of wooden matches for the betting. "You can 'dislike him intensely.' But never hate."

"Sorry, Nanny." Doug scowled at the king when his dark face appeared on the bottom of the deck during the shuffle, then, whispered under his breath, "But I still hate him."

Doug peeked at the front door several times while she dealt out the cards. He bit his lip, then smiled.

"How about we play until one of us runs out of matches, then we'll have your cake?" She smiled. "You're father will just miss out."

He nodded, pushed five match sticks to the center of the table. She'd given him three queens—and not a king to be found.

The application lay on his desk like a beautiful woman's hand. If Avisson reached across to grasp it, it was possible that the hand would be withdrawn in disgust and he would be a laughing stock.

Margaret, Dr. Ramis' secretary, must have put it there. To taunt him, maybe? No. She didn't seem to understand the subtle complexities of the Foundation's work, but was still the most faithful employee. Her unflagging optimism and willingness to try, where other secretaries (and even a few junior administrators) gave up, made her a favorite of upper management, but the object of scorn for everyone else.

Anyway, it was only an application for a temporary residency at the Edgar Cayce Institute in Virginia. As the Assistant Director of the Douglas Foundation for Psychic Research, Avisson might receive extra consideration. Still, he wasn't good at hoping for things.

His failed marriage had proved that.

He picked up the application. One page. Typical of the Cayce Center to be so direct. Who are you? What have you done? Why do you want to do this? He knew he couldn't bullshit his way into a residency. Not like some members of the Douglas Foundation staff, i.e. Dr. Ramis. He shook his head, chiding himself at the thought. The man had his strengths, his skills. He took care of the politicking and fund-raising, leaving Avisson to oversee the actual research.

Six months. One hundred and eighty days of solitude and study, in the thick woods surrounding the Cayce Institute. A cottage like Thoreau's, clear night skies that had opened the minds of Aristotle, Socrates, and Plato; the peace and quiet that writers such as Emerson had employed, to plumb the secrets of existence in the quest to expose man to his universal nature.

Avisson sighed, reached for a pear. Who was it said "When Nature has work to be done, she creates a genius to do it?" He was sure he'd read it at the University, though it had seemed to echo in his head since childhood.

He walked to the window, opened his arms to the winter night sky.

"Bring on your genius, Mother Nature," he called out. "I'll do the rest."

He cocked his head, listening. Nothing. He shrugged, took a bite of the pear and curled his lip. These South American pears were either raised in bad soil or the refrigerated trip north had removed their zing.

Andrea had laughed at his habits throughout their six-year marriage. He never could explain his preference for cold showers, even in the middle of the worst winters. She claimed he got up so early every morning only to escape her company; that he preferred the sullen trees to her morning breath. Near the end, he did not disagree.

He took another bite of the pear. Maybe things would have been different if he'd just once taken her offer of an apple. They never even opened the bottle of vintage Cabernet that one of his clients had given him as a wedding present. It had never seemed appropriate to both of them at the same time. Another minor, but typical source of conflict.

Alas, that was their problem. They were as different as apples and... pears. Both were now better off: he wound up with the bottle of Cabernet and she got custody of the alimony checks.

He stared at the application. "Why do you want to do this?"

If he didn't want the residency so badly, he might just tell them the truth. It was a crazy notion. But someday, if he ever found the time, he would write it up. Even give Andrea the credit she deserved for unwittingly giving him the initial idea.

"Stop looking at me with that patronizing expression," she'd yelled at him one night, a few weeks before she made him move out.

"But you're acting like a typical Capricorn," he said, immediately realizing his mistake.

"Ugh!" She tore at her hair. "Just once, I wish you'd look at me like a woman, instead of some stupid sign of the Zodiac."

"I'm sorry if I understand you," he said.

She grabbed him by the shirt. "I just hope I come back as something different next time, maybe a Leo, or a Scorpio—Yeah, a Scorpio. Man, I hope I do run into you again, give your 'let's-balance-the-scales' Libra-ass, a run for your money."

His laughter was not meant to insult her, but it did. He tried to explain how much he was intrigued by her idea, but she was past listening.

Three weeks later, the moon was in Mars and his Libra-ass was out in the street.

He studied the random notes he'd made on his pad concerning possible Zodiacal Influences on the Soul's Progression. The central theme was very simple: If the time and date of birth determined the planetary influences on one's present life, might not the time and date of death be part of a formula that determined the influences on the next existence?

Too crazy for the Cayce people. Such a radical idea might put him out of the running.

He lifted the page and began a second series of more conventional ideas, to fill out the application. Recapitulating client experiences, actual case histories, was not so radical an approach and might put him in the running. If he played it right, he might just get lucky. And if he didn't get time off soon, he'd probably strangle that Mrs. Clark and all the rest of his New Age clientele, with their dream catchers and prosperity candles.

After much thought, he finally finished his notes. He sighed, paper-clipped the application to his pad, and dropped it on Margaret's desk on his way out. He could trust her to type in the information and get it in the mail on time.

There just had to be a good way to preserve local pears to see him through the winter. He'd stop at the library in the morning, after his cold shower and his walk.

Peter put down the stack of drawings and reached for his coffee. He pushed Felicity's image out of his mind and slid the papers into a file marked "P.D. MacBrayne IV."

"How does Doug react when he sees these?"

The teacher shrugged. "Never says a word."

"But he did stand up for himself during the snowball fight, right?"

"Broke a window and gave one of the kids a black eye before running for the car."

Peter nodded. "That's some progress, I suppose."

"Mr. Douglas-MacBrayne, are you sure this course of action is right for the boy? He seems so eager to please."

"Don't be fooled, he's manipulative in his own way. That's why it's so important to me that his teachers keep the pressure on, not let him get away with anything."

"I'm sorry, but public schools just don't have that kind of control over the staff or the students. We're not a military academy."

"And you wonder why people are so disenchanted with the public school system?" Peter saw the teacher's jaw jut. "Think about it a moment. Someday, Doug will run Douglas Industries—the very life blood of this town. Being 'eager to please' isn't going to make him a great leader."

"He's only nine years old—"

"Ten. Today's his birthday."

"Then I suppose you'll want to get home."

Peter shook his head, glowered. "Look, I don't expect you to agree with my methods, but this is the only way he's ever going get toughened up."

The teacher stared at him.

"Thank you for keeping me abreast of the situation. I'll make sure your continued cooperation is noted, during the budget discussions by the School Board next summer."

He dismissed the teacher with a short nod, reached for his coffee mug. His fingers thrummed on the table. He didn't need a piano to play this tune.

The world of Janina and Valka—brother and sister—was without borders even in 1982. They knew the back roads that skirted the towns never failed to bring them customers. As an apprentice, Grumpy sat to one side, watching Valka spread the cards for all Janina's readings. After two years of silent observation, Grumpy had begun to see that although the details differed, everyone's basic question seemed always the same: "How can I avoid the pain of living?"

Gentle with the simple folk, Janina was short with skeptics. She had no desire to prove her visions correct, nor to convert mocking disbelievers.

Weather permitting, the three would sit outside around a small table, eating the meals Valka always prepared. Whenever Janina's swan neck tilted, her head swaying from the day's efforts, Valka would carry her into the back room for a nap, while Grumpy washed the dishes.

Often, alone in the quiet of the forest, images floated around him, faces from his past leered from the trees, voices murmured in the breeze. How far he was from Douglasville—no family, no familiar structures around him. His emotions swirled unchecked, unchanneled.

The first time he had felt such disorientation, such disconnection from his real life, an unexpected nausea rose from his belly and he leaned against a tree to steady himself.

"Here," Valka said, offering an open bottle of wine. "This will help you find your stomach."

"Thanks." Grumpy took a long swig. "I don't know what came over me."

"There are many ways to be drunk." Valka laughed, took the bottle and drank. He wiped his lips on his sleeve. "Every day in America you see same people, same land, buildings and roads. Your eyes and ears are accustomed only to what they know."

Grumpy nodded, took the bottle.

"Out here, living this Gypsy life, everything is new, every day. You look for old patterns. Listen for words from old friends." Valka tapped his head. "Confusing, Yes?"

"Very much so."

"Good. You cannot learn until you are confused." Valka pointed to a small farm, through a gap in the trees. "The dirt in field must be tilled—confused—before seed put in to grow new crop."

"Then I must be getting ready to learn a lot, because my head is spinning."

Valka slapped him on the back. "Janina, she is good farmer. You will be happy with what grows in your head."

Each night after her nap, Janina went over the more memorable readings of the day. But no matter how hard he listened, Grumpy couldn't quite decipher the revolving kaleidoscope of the cards: faces, sticks, swords, and cups that arranged themselves in the secret combinations of past and future.

One evening, they camped outside the town of Vilnius. He stared at the cards, empty of any new wisdom, leaned back in disgust. Janina reached over with a gnarled fist and stroked his beard, now grown long and shaggy.

"You try too hard."

"If I can't master the cards, how will I ever be able to read the crystal ball?"

"Why is that so important? Maybe you will not like what you see."

For a moment he considered just giving up. There were so many things she refused to talk about—especially those he felt he needed to know. She had told him only that her mother sent her to America to be educated, brought her home after college. But whenever he asked about the relationship between Sarah and her mother, she either steered him away from the subject, or ended the conversation.

"Maybe I should start calling you Madame Tucheskyah again."

They sat in silence, Janina staring at her crystal ball, Grumpy staring at her.

He looked into those molten eyes, revisiting all the wondrous places he had been before finding her. The ancient Aztec temples, the Mayan calendars he rubbed his fingers across, coming away only with today's dust, the secret Inca caves. The Buddhist temples of Japan, the sapient Confucian logic, written on parchment that had survived thousands of years; the holy mud of the Ganges River. Throughout, he remained ignorant of, insensitive to all but physical sensations.

"It is important that you find out for yourself," she finally said.

But why? She would have a better chance of deciphering the meaning of the muddled images that swam inside his head.

"You need to see the world through your mother's eyes," she said, repeating a statement she had made over and over again.

"Why?"

"The answer to why is always because." She smiled. "Empty your mind of everything except the because."

He slowed his breathing, using the Buddhist technique he had learned at the Ashram near Calcutta. Images fought for his attention, but he released them. A moment of calm enveloped him. It lasted only a moment as another onslaught of busy thoughts attacked. He let them pass through him. Next came colors: orange sunsets, the underwater aquamarine off the coast of Bali, jade green forests, the deadly onyx laughter of Pacific monsoons. All passed.

After several minutes, he reached into his vest pocket, pulled out a photograph he had received that afternoon in a package from Fiona. It had come via his agent in Paris. He handed it to Janina. Her eyes flared as she raised it between two twisted fingers.

"And who is this?"

"My grandson, Doug."

"Your mother wants you to see him through her eyes."

Janina rested her chin on folded hands. Grumpy had learned to wait whenever she assumed this pose: part pyramid, part sphinx. Finally she broke the silence.

"How much did Sarah tell you about my mother?"

"Only that when I found the other pendant I would find the answer." Grumpy shrugged. "But I don't even know what to ask."

"Do you understand the symbolism of the heart and moon?"

He shook his head.

"Then that is where we will start."

"And the rest?"

"That is up to our mothers." She held up the picture of Doug again. "I warn you though, it may take several more years. Is it worth it to you?"

Grumpy took the picture, smiled. "I've been away his entire life, traveled thousands of miles. I can't quit now."

"Why did you leave him?"

"I didn't leave him. I went before he was born."

She nodded. "You left when your wife died?"

He nodded.

"And your son—this boy's father—he blamed you for her death."

"Yes."

She looked down and caressed the pendant that hung around her neck. When she raised her eyes again, there was a new fire, a different dancing light.

"All that happens has happened before and will happen again. This is the basis of all knowing. Where mankind's relationship to the universe of stars is concerned, every moon has a heart and every heart a moon. When one sets, the other rises. This is the basis of all being."

Grumpy swallowed hard, wrestled with the images swimming in his mind. "And you see all this in the cards?"

"The cards mean nothing to a true reader. They are puppets for an audience that does not understand the real theater of the spirit."

"And the crystal ball?"

"A window to the human heart."

Grumpy frowned. "I don't understand. It seems that the theater of the spirit would be harder to see than the human heart."

Janina's voice went low and deep, as if coming from her stomach. "The learning is difficult because when you use the crystal ball, you are not seeing the human heart with your own eyes."

"Whose then?"

"When you look through the ball—" she took a slow deep breath, "—you look through the eyes of God."

She let her head dangle, kept her butt in the crook of the sofa and her legs curled over the back, as if she were waiting to be gutted by some cosmic hunter.

"Go on, Mrs. Clark." Avisson swiveled his chair, ignoring her display, a tactic he'd grown accustomed to for the past several months. "Tell me how you think the ginseng affects your dreams."

"Well, it's as if God himself is entering me. You know?"

"No, I don't. Tell me about it."

"It's these new candles I'm using, I'm sure of it. They're hand-rolled beeswax, and the ends are shaped like—you know, a little fireman's helmet thingee?"

"Shaped like a penis?"

"That's it."

He heard her shift position. Two years of working with her had taught him not to turn around to see the next display. He had come to know her moods as well as her antics.

"I kneel in front of the bedtable, take one of the licorice ginseng lozenges and suck on it while I light the candle."

Another change in position. His mind made pictures to the sound of her dress. He pushed the images aside.

"Where's Larry during all this?"

"Downstairs in his study. He's working on the Scorpio Slasher murder case. You know, the one where the killer claimed whenever the moon was in Mercury he was compelled to rape and strangle a stripper." She giggled. "I told Larry he should have the guy plead temporary astrology."

In spite of himself, Avisson smiled. "What was Larry's response?"

"He didn't get it." She sighed. "But then, I haven't had the dream since he took the case, either. Thank heavens I have my new sleep ritual."

"Do you feel anything out of the ordinary before you go to sleep?"

"A kind of tingling." Her voice went all smokey. "That's when I know I'm going to have a good night."

Avisson closed his eyes as she spoke. The dream starts out the same every time: She's walking in the woods and sees a young man sitting on the lowest branch of a huge oak tree, swinging his legs. She begins to dance in front of him, taking off a different article of clothing with each spin. The boy ages as the pile of clothing grows larger. Finally, she is naked and he is middle-aged. He jumps from the limb and grabs her by the hair, throwing her down on the pile—which has now become a feather bed. She spreads her legs and he climbs on top, putting his hands around her neck supposedly to keep his balance, his feet still on the ground. He doesn't lay on her, just hovers above. But his penis is long, and every time he juts into her, she can feel it almost to her throat. She climaxes just before she passes out from a lack of breath.

"How do you know that is God?"

"Well, at the very end, I look up into his face, and he's become a very old man, a grandfather type. Know what I mean?"

Avisson grunted, rested his head against the chair. He didn't have the heart to tell her that the dream was more psychological than divine—Freud could make a comeback based on it. Still, it was breakthrough stuff for anyone interested in the truth about themselves.

He pictured her son, obviously the boy she wanted turned into a man to pleasure her. Then the grandfather—a painfully simple childhood metaphor for a woman as sexually extravagant as she.

Shit. He was hoping to shift her away from dream therapy, but with this...

The door opened, Dr. Ramis stuck his head in. "Sorry to interrupt."

Avisson spun around, relieved that Mrs. Clark was now sitting primly on the sofa.

"Is something the matter?"

Ramis grinned, handed Avisson a long envelope. "Margaret said you'd want to see this, immediately."

Avisson pulled the letter from the slit, read it with widening eyes.

"Dear Dr. Avisson. The Cayce Institute for Psychic Studies is pleased to inform you that your application for residency has been accepted. Your proposed thesis: Zodiacal Influences on the Soul's Evolution, much interested our Board. Please contact this office at your earliest convenience."

He looked up, stunned. Margaret had typed the wrong notes, submitted them to the Cayce people and he'd still been awarded the residency. Ramis clapped him on the back, having read the letter over Avisson's shoulder.

"Quite a feather in your cap—for all of us, I suppose." He glanced at Mrs. Clark. "Of course, we'll all pitch in to take over your caseload."

He stuck out his hand to the woman. "Armen Ramis, Director of the Foundation."

"Cleo Clark. Pleased to meet you, Dr. Ramis."

"Call me Armen."

"Do you work with clients also, Armen?" Mrs. Clark cast an evil glance toward Avisson.

"Why, yes I do, Mrs. Clark."

She sat back in the sofa, arms in a mock crucifix. "Please. Call me Cleo."

Avisson took his nose out of the letter, looked at the two of them. He wasn't psychic, but he didn't need a crystal ball to see what was going to happen in this particular future. He would warn Ramis later. Right now, he would go home and celebrate—on the way, he would buy half a dozen pears.

And—there was a bottle of Cabernet that had waited too long to be opened.

❦

When winter storms slowed their journeys south, the gypsies would travel to the nearest town where relatives lived. Janina could not tolerate the cold. In the second year of Grumpy's apprenticeship, they stayed with Cousin Adina who had a small cafe and bookstore at the edge of Budapest. Janina gave readings in the back. To pass the time, Grumpy dusted shelves and helped make the steaming, dark brew that cut the cold for shivering customers.

Then Adina caught the flu. Grumpy and Valka managed the shop until she recovered. The harsh, guttural language never quite rested easily on Grumpy's American tongue, but he learned to communicate with his hands and eyes. Several mature women made attempts to woo him, but he resisted.

"Vhy do you not make these women happy?" Valka asked. "The nights are cold enough, no?"

"It doesn't seem right," Grumpy said, putting the finishing touches on a cappuccino.

Valka shook his head. "You are vaiting for true love?"

.This made Grumpy laugh. After a moment he grew serious, watching the steam from his drink rise through his fingers. "I'm ashamed to say I've never really known love, true or otherwise."

Valka clinked his cup against Grumpy's. "Do not fear, my friend. You may not know love, but it knows you."

Two customers entered. Valka rose in welcome. Grumpy sat with his back to them. He could not stem the tears that rolled from his eyes and disappeared into his beard. He heard Janina call his name, wiped his tears and went to the back room.

She was sitting across from a young woman.

"Would you lay out the cards for me?"

Grumpy joined them at the table and began to shuffle slowly. He tried looking at the woman as Valka did when performing the same function. At first she avoided his gaze, then raised her eyes to look right into his. He blushed, fumbled the cards.

"Sorry."

The woman looked at Janina who translated, adding more words than Grumpy thought necessary. The woman smiled.

He put the stack down for her to cut into three separate piles. He picked them up and turned the cards face-up, one-by-one: two children with cups dancing around a woman, the three of swords intersecting in the heart, the devil sitting on his throne, the lovers card—upside down.

Janina spoke in Hungarian. Grumpy heard only the sounds. His head began to swim with images. He saw a man shouting. Behind the young woman stood a shadowy young man in a baker's apron. Suddenly Grumpy understood: the shouting man was her father; the shadow-man, her lover.

Hands trembling, Grumpy turned over several more cards which seemed innocent enough, but the images in his mind grew clearer: the father spoke to the daughter as one would to a wife. Then the tower. Disaster. The death card. Change. The chariot. Travel.

She was pregnant. Had come to Janina to find out which man was the father.

Janina and the woman were staring at him.

"Tell me what you see," Janina said.

He told her. The swan neck bobbed agreement. Janina translated, the woman's face contorted. Confirmation.

"What do the cards say she should she do?."

The kaleidoscope turned. The information shined in his head like sunlight through a stained glass window. The tower card showed two people falling from the top of the spire. One, falling feet first, was surrounded by a dark cloud, the other seemed more to have jumped and was surrounded by splashes of energy.

"Though every option seems disastrous, if she does not act, it will be much worse."

Janina translated. "Go on."

"The death card means she must kill her father's domination of her. She must make his hold over her die."

"Good. What else?"

"She must travel, go away with her young baker."

Janina's eyebrows lifted in appreciation. She nodded and spoke to the woman.

Grumpy turned over the last card, the rainbow—a happy ending.

The woman's expression was determined, but fearful. She reached across and took Janina's withered hand, then bowed to Grumpy and left.

After several silent moments, Janina cleared her throat. "Now tell me the rest of what you saw."

"The child is her father's." Grumpy took a deep breath. "She will leave with her lover, but she will die within a year or two."

"If that is so," Janina said. "Why the rainbow?"

"Her lover will take good care of the child. The little girl will grow up to be happy and loved—properly."

"And you saw this in the cards?"

He shook his head.

"Then how did you know it?"

"I think—I sensed it, that's all." He frowned. "Shouldn't we have told her she was going to die?"

Janina smiled sadly. "She already knows."

Peter leafed through the last few pages of the preliminary annual report, then threw it on the desk.

"Are these figures accurate?"

Dan Downey, the comptroller, shifted uncomfortably in his chair, took out his handkerchief, wiped his thick lenses, then mopped his brow and pointed nose. "You were in such a hurry, Peter, some of the numbers are ballpark, but can't be far off. At worst they're within five percent."

Peter walked to the window, looked out over the buildings that comprised Douglas Industries.

"It's not going to be enough—"

"What do you mean? We're in the black, probably the second most profitable manufacturer in the entire shoe and leather-goods industry."

"True. And who's the most profitable?"

Downey shrugged. "Eterna-Sole, I'd guess."

"Good guess."

Peter ran his hand over the thick logbook, begun by his grandmother, continued by his father and now him. It told the story of a company that had produced shoes and leathergoods for more than seventy years. A company founded by his crystal ball-reading grandmother, then, after her death, run down by his happy-go-lucky father.

Recently recorded was how Peter had established tight fiscal controls for the first time in the company's history. He had brought in conservative managers who developed new processes that required retooling, resulting in increased productivity and higher profits from reduced labor costs.

"Just being in the black isn't going to be good enough." Peter sat behind his desk. "We're headed for a takeover fight."

"With whom?"

"Think for a moment, Dan. What's the easiest way for a company our size to leapfrog into the big leagues?"

"Buy up other companies."

"That's exactly what I think Eterna-Sole wants to do, and we're on their list."

Oh, come on, Peter." Downy laughed. "Have you been reading your grandmother's crystal ball?"

Peter's hand slowly fisted. His bowtie bobbed twice, then stopped. He cleared his throat, tossed a file marked "Confidential" on the desk.

"Read it."

Downey scanned the pages, looked up. "Where'd you get this?"

"Grandma had her methods, I've got mine."

"So they are going to try to take us over. What's our next move?" Downey put the folder on the desk.

"It's a longshot, but the answer just might be in here." Peter patted the corporate history. "The first World War was responsible for the company's fastest growth: Army boots, belts, saddles. The leather industry boomed and the company blossomed.

"The Great Depression of 1931 hit the company hard, but Sarah dug into her savings and bought up a local tannery, which reduced our manufacturing costs, and gave us a small, but measurable advantage, at least until 1938."

"What happened then?" Downey asked.

"That was the year plastics first came into commercial production. Sarah wanted to buy machinery to get in on the ground floor. Most of the Board didn't see any relationship with the leather goods industry, but Sarah did."

"A pretty standard business morality tale," Downey said. "Not unlike the head of a large manufacturer of steam locomotives, who publicly announced these new-fangled diesel locomotives would never run on the main lines and would only be fit for switching and yard work."

Peter nodded. "Or when the inventors of Fiberglass offered an exclusive license to one of the biggest producers of insulation in the country. One of its top officials turned them down, saying it would never replace magnesia insulation, or especially asbestos."

"Asbestos. Yeah. I see we had the same text in business school," Downey said. "But how does this apply to this takeover bid?"

"At that time, Sarah persuaded half the Board to make the investment; then cast the deciding vote herself. Today, there are more varieties of plastics on the market than you can shake a stick at. But the one we're concerned with in this situation is Polyvinyl Chloride."

"PVC?" Downey frowned. "We're already one of the largest producers of flexible PVC in the world. It wouldn't be cost effective to expand in that area. We wouldn't get the return..."

"Dan, think. Right now we fabricate a lot of soft PVC into inexpensive belts, ladies' purses, men's wallets, all sorts of things, but the competition is stiff and there's little profit."

"And we make more money on our leather goods, for higher priced, similar items, especially shoes." Downey looked at his watch. "Where are you going with this?"

"Leather shoes have a couple of advantages—the fact that they breathe and have a 'hand' or feel, that people prefer. But PVC costs a lot less. Not only the material, but the labor. Take shoes, for example: To make them from leather, you need a good quality hide and an operator skilled in selective die-cutting, to get the maximum number of high-quality parts from each skin. The trim, or scrap, can be sold for only a pittance.

"On the other hand, little skill is needed to die-cut PVC. And the waste can easily be recycled: You simply throw it in the hopper, melt it down and roll it out again. The problem is, PVC doesn't breathe or have the rich, soft hand, or feel of leather."

"Can't we just change the formulation?"

"We can add plasticizers, but the shoes wear out faster. We've tried hundreds of formulations."

"People don't expect cheap shoes to last," Downey said. "If you'll pardon the pun."

"No," said Peter, ignoring it. "But here's the point. If we can beat Eterna to an artificial, PVC-based leather that will breathe and that people will like wearing, we'll not only head off the takeover but start playing with the really big boys, as well."

"Where are we, research-wise?"

"We've tried everything, including micro-spiking, but that makes the PVC too porous and the holes are objectionably visible. We have a chemical team, working hard, rearranging molecular structure, but everything they've come up with has missed the mark, too."

"Why don't we just give up?"

"You just want to rollover and let Eterna-Sole win?" Peter lurched to his feet. "Right now, the main financial difference between the two companies is that we have to support Sarah's goddamned Douglas Foundation for Psychic Research and the Douglasville Orphanage. If we can get out from under them, we can pump that money into research. That may just give us the edge."

"The Foundation is chartered. We're stuck with it."

"Yeah, unless the directors vote to shut it down. In which case the charter is null and void."

"Never happen. They're sitting on a golden goose."

Peter smiled. "Ever been bitten by a goose? Hurts like hell."

"You've got something up your sleeve?"

"Let's put it this way. Many directors of non-profit organizations don't realize they're financially responsible if that organization is sued. Faced with such a situation, how do you think the directors would react?"

"Is somebody going to sue them?"

"This is just a hypothetical discussion."

"Come on, Peter. I know you better than that."

Peter slid another file across to Downey, who read, occasionally shaking his head.

"Jesus, this reads like a bad TV movie."

"All true, though." Peter grinned. "And extremely useful."

"Has the husband seen this?"

Peter shook his head. "Not yet."

"Could be nasty, if he did."

"That's right, especially given that he's well known as an expert litigator. And Douglas Industries, given our relationship to the Center, is vulnerable also. Deep pockets, and all."

"Will this be enough to cut our ties?"

"Not on its own. But it's a good start." Peter stood. "Now, to the question at hand. If the relationship between Douglas Industries and the Center is dissolved, can we fight this takeover?"

Downey sat still, stared straight at Peter for nearly a full minute. "Possibly. But we'll still have the Orphanage. It's political suicide if you knock that out."

"I've got a big sleeve. The Orphanage will be taken care of at the same time. Now, just tell me what's possible."

"Depends."

"On what?" The wings of Peter's bowtie began flapping.

"Peter, I'm basically an accountant—"

"One who makes fifty thousand a year as comptroller of this company."

"But still an accountant."

Peter rolled his eyes. "The point, Dan."

"The point, Peter, is that accountants deal with numbers. I don't know all the numbers yet."

"They're right there, in the report."

"I don't mean those numbers." He sat on the edge of his chair, mopped his brow. "Before I agree to do anything...I need to know *my* numbers."

Peter's bowtie landed. "Then it is possible?"

Dan nodded. "In the universe of numbers, everything is possible."

❦

Heaven. He had gone on sabbatical and arrived in heaven. He had no idea the state of Virginia was so beautiful. The second night, Abe (he had discarded the Dr. Avisson in the spirit of a true sabbatical) sat on the small, screened-in-porch at the front of his cottage. The cicadas began a concert that moved in perfect synchronization from one stand of trees to the next. For an eternal moment, it sounded as if the stars themselves were singing to him, each constellation in the zodiac taking its turn.

He closed his eyes, tried to visualize the faint waves that arrived from space every moment of every life... arrived with what? Instructions? Did the astrological aspects: birth, moon rising—the powerful indicators of potential, coded not unlike the DNA helix—give the structure of possibility, of meaning, to seemingly quixotic qualities?

A streak of faint white flared in the dark sky, then evaporated. Abe suddenly saw the immense possibility of his thesis and, at the same moment, the probability that he might never prove it.

If reincarnation were true and individual souls were indeed affected by karma, it made sense that most probably those souls came back within the different grapefruit sections of Leo, Virgo, Sagittarius, etc., because each sign brought with it certain good qualities and failings appropriate to the development, or evolution, of a soul. One time, a meticulous, regal Leo; the next, a dark, reckless Scorpio. A stubborn Taurus, for example, might be followed by a duplicitous Gemini; the pluses and minuses inherent in each sign, providing the karmic game plan for successive incarnations.

He opened his eyes, looked again at the legion of stars. In a book he read, some guru wrote that the soul's long journey to enlightenment was akin to an eagle flying over a mountain, a silk scarf in its beak. Each time the eagle passed, the scarf would barely touch the peak, scraping off a few molecules, an infinitesimal bit of granite.

"The soul becomes enlightened, only after the eagle's scarf has flattened the mountain," the guru wrote.

Abe thought he understood it then, but now, listening to the ventriloquist cicadas give voice to the stars, he felt the long, arduous path to enlightenment, opening deep within him.

He would not be able to prove that the soul returned based on a system of zodiacal balances. But someday, someone might arrive who remembered and could access his or her past lives and might also remember enough about those lives to pinpoint through inference, (or perhaps old, old records), the approximate birth dates, death dates and the corresponding astrological signs for each.

"When Nature has work to be done, she creates a genius to do it."

He suddenly missed the Foundation, realized he had been foolish to grow resentful there. If and when nature sent her genius, the Foundation would be crucial to the research.

The cicadas increased their singing. Abe joyously tossed his head and laughed. What a marvelous, perfect universe.

At first, Grumpy thought it was a branch banging against his camper, but a voice followed and he shook himself awake.

"Grumpy." It was Valka.

He wrapped himself in a blanket and opened the door, flapped his arms, shivering in the cold, windy night.

"What is it?"

"Come. Janina needs to speak with you."

Grumpy dressed quickly, followed him to the caravan. Janina sat in dim candlelight.

"You must prepare to leave." She looked up at him. "Right away."

"Why?"

"I can't tell you. But you must leave now."

"Now? It's not even light yet."

"Yes. You must leave now."

"But we haven't finished. I don't know enough to—"

"Your grandson is in danger."

"Doug? What danger?"

"It has begun. He knows and the evil knows too."

"What evil?"

She wrapped her arms around her chest, her head went backwards, the silver-streaked, red hair flowing. For the first time since he'd met her, he saw fear in her flaming eyes.

"You must go home. That is your place now."

"But what do I do? How do I help him?"

"You must help him without his knowing. He must not know you have returned."

"How the hell do I do that?"

She smiled. "You have grown your disguise over the years we have traveled together. The rest you learned in Adina's shop."

"Adina? What—?"

"You came to us a businessman. As a businessman you shall return."

He nodded. He could see it also. "Okay, but how do I fight this evil?"

"You remember the lesson of the pendant?"

"Yes."

"Repeat it to me."

"Every heart has its moon and every moon has it's heart. But—"

"There is one thing more. Every moon has its dark side, as does every heart." She looked up into the night sky. "There are great spirits around the boy, of both darkness and light. Your son holds the key that opens the doorway to the future and protects the present and the past."

"Peter? How does he..."

"Your son holds the key. That is all I can say."

"Hmm... May I please use your surname, Petrovitch, as my own?"

"Of course."

"You have a suggestion for my forename?"

Janina thought a minute, looked at Valka, who was deep in thought. Suddenly, a huge grin spread across his face.

"Why not call yourself 'Vorchalkin?'" he suggested.

Janina's eyes glinted. She smiled. "That's just marvelous."

"What's marvelous?" asked Grumpy, "What does 'Vorchalkin" mean?"

Still smiling broadly, Janina looked him straight in the eye. "It's from the old Russian, 'Vorchat' meaning to grumble, or growl. In this form, it refers humorously to someone who's always out of sorts. In a word... 'Grumpy'."

She snuffed out the candle and was swallowed by the darkness. Grumpy shook hands with Valka, climbed into the front seat of his van and started the engine. As he pulled away from the site he knew in his heart Janina was right...except he would call himself "Valka." Otherwise, some smart-ass might guess his identity, if he happened to know old Russion.

His gypsy days were finished. It was time to go home.

Chapter Four

June 1982

Peter opened the newspaper, quickly found and scanned the article written in expansive prose about the upcoming hospital fund raiser—a costumed Medieval Fete. He scowled. The article made no mention of the bash being in honor of his fiftieth birthday, as promised by Cathy Downey when she cajoled him into having it on the estate. He reached for the telephone.

"Downey? Peter."

"Yes, Peter. Did you change your mind about taking my cousin to the Fete?"

Downey had tried to entice him into attending the Fete with some female cousin, visiting from New York.

"Dan, I told you before, I'm a little old for a blind date and, I sure as hell am not wearing a costume."

"Come on, Peter. You haven't had a serious date in ten years. Em's a great girl. Wait 'till you see her costume. I promise you, no queen ever looked this sexy."

"That's not what this call is about. I'm not sure having the Fete on my estate is such a good idea."

"You're kidding. Right?"

"No. I'm really uncomfortable about having a crowd of strangers here."

"Peter, there's no time to arrange another site."

"What about the County Fairgrounds?"

"All torn up with new construction."

"Damn." Peter clicked his coffee cup with a spoon.

"If you back out now, my wife's going to kill both of us. A great number of people have spent a hell of a lot of time putting this together."

"I realize that, but I'm worried about security. That's my home, you know."

"Peter..." Downey exhaled loudly. "I've spent the last seven months covering our respective corporate asses—at your request. If you scuttle now, we may attract scrutiny we don't need."

"By canceling a fund-raiser for a very good reason?"

"What reason? Your paranoia? Holding the Fete at your estate is great PR. Makes you seem more accessible."

"Hey, come on, Dan. I'm plenty accessible."

"Sure, in your usual stand-offish way."

"What's your point?"

"Manipulating paperwork is one thing, but stepping out personally and showing yourself as the man who leads the company—and the town—will help us considerably, when it comes time to announce moving the psychiatric clinic to the orphanage. We're not out of the woods on this thing, yet."

Peter sighed. "So I'm stuck with this?"

"Hell, why not just think of it as a huge birthday party in your honor?

"Isn't that what it is?"

"Peter."

"Joke, Dan."

"Ha, Ha. Look, the staff will take care of everything. Just relax and turn fifty."

"Thanks for reminding me." He looked out the window, saw the first workers already erecting the main tent. "All those people, they're already trashing the place."

"We'll have a special clean-up crew out here, immediately after it's over. There won't be a scrap of paper on the ground, I promise."

"It's not paper I'm worried about. It's the porta-potties."

Downey's laughter was cut short as Peter hung up and spun away from the window.

Damn this fund raiser. There was no way to tell Downey the deeper reason he wanted to cancel. It was bitter irony that Douglas Industries provided so much money to support the hospital, but when his mother and his wife needed treatment, the doctors hadn't been able to keep either one alive.

How different his life might have been if both or even one, had survived. Maybe he wouldn't feel so...so alone.

Peter was glad his father was still traveling in God-knows-what country. He'd seen the postcards from all those strange places, the odd rambling messages scratched on the back. There was no way Peter would let his soft-headed father ruin Doug with his harebrained philosophies. Especially now that Doug was exhibiting the worst elements of both his great-grandmother and his grandfather. Why was Doug so wimpy? The crying had stopped but the boy still crumbled at the least bit of criticism. Peter would have to instill some backbone in the boy if he were going to survive as an adult. Even bringing Fiona over had been a mistake. She was supposed to be an accomplished Scottish nanny, but Doug had her wrapped around his finger.

And now the two of them had become a team against Peter, instead of being grateful for what he had given them. Doug had surely inherited his intelligence from the MacBrayne side of the family, and Fiona was probably better paid than any nanny in America. He gritted his teeth.

It wasn't fair. He shook his head. Doug's arrival took Felicity away from him, then Fiona stole Doug away. The boy even seemed to like a grandfather he'd never met, more than his own father. The king of the castle is supposed to receive tribute from others, not the other way around. The time had come to show everyone who was really in charge.

Peter slapped his hand on the table, confirming his decision. The cook stuck her head into the dining room.

"Did you want something, sir?"

"No, sorry."

She disappeared hurriedly into the kitchen, Peter grabbed the telephone and dialed quickly. "Dan? Peter. I changed my mind about your cousin. Is she still available?"

"Available? Hell, I brought her here just to meet you."

"Great," Peter said. Right, first a thief, now a pimp. "I'll pick her up tomorrow night, at seven."

"We can bring her."

"No, I have something special in mind."

❦

Doug stepped away from the large canvas and wiped the perspiration from his forehead with the inside of his elbow, then peered at the picture he was copying. Not bad really. The castle was a little fuzzy, but the clouds looked real enough. From a distance. He took another step backwards and bumped into something.

He turned. "Sorry."

"No problem." Sally was painting a garden. Some of her flowers looked more like psychedelic mushrooms. "These look stupid."

Doug shook his head. "They're just not finished yet."

She chewed on her bottom lip, her eyes scrunched.

"Maybe if you made the petals bigger..."

"Maybe I should let Jimmy finish it." She pointed off to the left.

Jimmy looked as if he had more paint on his shirt than the large canvas backdrop, but there was no denying his painting was the best. A manor house stood deep in the background, behind an intricate green maze of hedge.

"Well, ours aren't so bad. Anyway, they're just going to be used as scenery at the Fete." Doug leaned down to put more water in one of the jars of tempera.

"What're you wearing tomorrow night?" Sally put a new petal on one of her flowers. It now looked like a hot-air balloon.

"Nanny got me this really cool Peter Pan outfit."

"Did Peter Pan live in the Middle Ages?"

Doug shrugged. "I don't care about that. You'll understand when you drive past the shrubbery at the gates."

"You can tell me."

"No. It'll spoil it for you."

She approached him, holding the paintbrush like a lance. "Tell me now... Or else."

Doug grinned, assumed what he thought to be an appropriate fencing stance with his paint brush.

"En garde."

Sally giggled, parried several times, then thrust toward Doug's chest. He spun out of the way, tripped over a jar of paint and went reeling toward Jimmy. Jimmy moved out of the way like a toreador and Doug fell right through the maze onto Jimmy's canvas.

Doug tried to pull himself up quickly, but Miss Stipple arrived in an instant. She stood looking at Doug, her arms folded over her chest, eyes blazing.

"You just won't quit clowning around, will you?"

"It was an accident."

"It was thoughtlessness, as usual."

Jimmy let out a short sob. Miss Stipple went over to put her arm around his shoulders.

"Don't you worry, Jimmy. Why don't you see what you can do with Doug's panel?"

"But Miss Stipple—" Doug tried to climb out of the broken canvas. Another part tore.

"Mr. MacBrayne, you are going to be too busy repairing this panel to worry about yours"

"Yes, ma'am."

"And just because this is day camp, don't think your father won't hear about it."

The teacher guided the forlorn Jimmy to Doug's panel while Doug tried to extricate himself without doing more damage. He looked up, hoping Sally might come to help him, but she had joined the other in comforting Jimmy, by discussing what he might do to improve Doug's painting.

He was almost free of the panel when he noticed Jimmy staring at him. When the other boy was sure the teacher and Sally couldn't see, he slowly curled all his fingers but the middle one. That he stabbed in the air toward Doug.

Doug made a face and flipped him back.

"There's no need for obscenities, Mr. MacBrayne."

God, the woman had eyes in the back of her head. "Miss Stipple, it wasn't meant for you."

"Oh, for whom? For Jimmy, because you ruined his painting? Or for Sally? What did she do?"

"It wasn't..." Doug stopped. This was already lost. To continue would only make things worse.

"You go to the counselor's office. I'll be there in a moment."

Doug trudged off. As he passed Chas Miner, one of Jimmy's friends, he felt a few drops of water. Doug wiped his neck. Yellow paint.

"Cut it out, Chas."

"Stick it, Dougie."

"Come on, Chas." Doug assumed a boxing stance.

Chas stood with his gangly arms straight down on either side.

"What's the matter, Chas? You chicken?"

Doug circled Chas, flicking pretend punches, when he was unexpectedly pulled backwards by his collar.

"You can't even follow simple instructions, can you Mr. MacBrayne?" Miss Stipple. "Well then, I'll just have to take you there myself. And call your house."

"No one's home. Nanny said she would be out shopping today."

"Dear me," Miss Stipple said, continuing to pull Doug along. "Then I suppose we'll just have to call your father."

"No! You don't have to call Dad."

"Well, someone has to collect you."

"Oh please, Miss Stipple. I'll sit quietly until Nanny's finished shopping. Please don't call my father."

"You should have thought about that before you destroyed Jimmy's painting." She turned him to face her. "You, with all your advantages, picking on a boy like Jimmy. You should be ashamed."

At that moment Doug understood. She hated him for the same reason Jimmy did. Could it be so simple as having a rich father? He looked into her face as she sat him down outside the counselors' office. The now-familiar vibrations began, the moment she walked inside. He could barely feel his shoulders quiver or his head slump.

The porch disappeared and he felt the blistering heat of the sun. There was no wind, not a cloud to be seen. The hot sand burned his feet as he staggered toward a small grove of trees that surrounded a pond. An oasis in the desert. His lips were cracked and broken. All he could think of was the water that waited for him and a chance to remove his armor.

Grateful for the shade, he lurched toward the edge of the pond, where he gulped without stopping.

"Do not drink so fast. Your insides will explode."

He looked at the woman who stood before him.

"What?" He reached for his sword. "Who are you?"

"Please." She backed away. "I meant not to frighten you."

"Who are you?" He scrambled to his feet, dizzy but on guard.

"I am Gemilla, of the family Kasheen."

"An infidel?"

She frowned, not knowing the term. "And you? Why do you speak our words?"

"My name is James Davidson, I learned your tongue from an infidel captured during the last Crusade."

"What is this infidel?"

"A lost soul, a barbarian who has not yet been introduced to God."

"We follow Allah."

"There is no salvation unless one accepts the teachings of Christ. Those who do not believe in our Holy Father are doomed to an eternity in Hell." He swayed, barely able to stand. "What are you doing out here all alone? Are you not afraid?"

"This is my family's land." She looked around. "My brothers will soon arrive. They will bring their sheep so they may drink."

He withdrew his sword, looked around. He barely had the strength to hold it.

"You must rest." She took a step toward him. "We will not hurt you."

His instinct told him not to trust her, but his legs buckled and he began losing consciousness. The treetops spun and he felt her arms around him, cradling his head. He looked into her eyes: one gray, one black.

"Here, drink some, slowly." She put the cup to his lips.

"Domina Christo..." he whispered.

❦

Looking like the victim of a hold-up, Fiona giggled and squirmed as the seamstress pulled the measuring tape from under her upraised arms.

"Sorry, forgot I was ticklish."

The seamstress nodded, her mouth tight from years of holding pins, then marked the size on her pad. She went for Fiona's hips—another ticklish moment. Fiona wiggled and blushed.

"Guess I'm not used to this sort of thing."

"No problem," the seamstress said, rolling her eyes. "That's the last of it anyway."

"Normally I buy my clothes off the rack," Fiona said, then realized the other woman would have figured that out by herself.

"Miss McLean, it'll take me a quite few minutes to check our inventory of Medieval costumes for one your size. You can wait here, or step next door and have a cup of coffee. I'll come get you when I'm ready."

"Next door?"

"A new cafe-bookstore just opened." The seamstress leaned over, whispered. "Personally, I give them six months. Imagine, thinking that people would want to drink coffee while they look for books."

Fiona's first inclination was to wait in the costume shop, but found the woman so disagreeable that she would have waited at the dry cleaners to get away from her. She grabbed her purse.

Outside, she considered finding a bench to enjoy the balmy day. She could use a few minutes to herself. Things had been so hectic around the estate since Peter told the staff that the annual Hospital fund-raiser would be held there—on his birthday. He had been so puffed up, so full of himself as usual, that he didn't even see that Mrs. Downey, the chairperson, had finagled him into letting them use the estate for free. The committee could care less that it was Peter's fiftieth birthday. They just knew the attendance would be high because people would want to take a peek inside the grounds of the Douglas-MacBrayne estate.

Not that the idea of a Medieval Fete wouldn't be fun. And Doug was so excited. Many of the children from his class would participate and he was looking forward to having them there for the first time.

Fiona glanced at the sign above the entrance. The Crystal Cafe and Bookstore looked harmless enough. Maybe she would have a cuppa and find a new mystery author. She pushed through the door and found herself in an entirely different world than she had expected. The place looked more like a Gypsy tea room than a strip-mall bookstore. The room was dim except directly above the bookshelves, which were illuminated by small track-lights on the ceiling. An ornate, wooden coffee bar graced one corner. Behind it a young woman was concocting some kind of steamy brew. Across the room was a small counter, where sat a mysterious-looking man with a long, salt-and-pepper beard. He looked up when she entered.

"Welcome to the Crystal," he said. "Liquid or literature?"

"Beg pardon?" Fiona asked.

"Coffee or books? What's your pleasure today?"

She smiled. "Maybe both. What do you recommend?"

He studied her intently, pointed to a chair by one of the tables. Fiona sat. He whispered to the girl behind the bar, then went to the shelves where he selected a book from a lower shelf.

The girl brought a cup of tea and placed it in front of Fiona. The man took the seat across from her, put the book next to the tea. She read the title: *Masterpieces of Murder*, by Agatha Christie.

"My goodness, Mr.—"

"Vorchalkin Petrovich." He reached across and shook hands. "But everyone calls me Valka."

"Fiona McLean. But how could you know…?"

He grinned. "Lucky guess about the book, maybe. But with your accent, I figured I couldn't miss with the tea."

"Well, I…For a moment, I wondered if you were going to read my palm, next."

His smile seemed almost wide as his beard was long. "I could do that, Miss McLean. But I'm really better at reading the Tarot."

The seamstress stuck her head inside. "All set, Miss McLean. Come pick out your costume."

"I'll be there in a few minutes." She turned to Mr. Petrovich. "Sorry, maybe you can read my cards some other time."

"How about tomorrow night at the Fete?"

"You'll be there?"

"Wouldn't miss it for the world." He tugged at his beard. "I rented a booth as soon as I heard about it."

Something was terribly wrong. Avisson examined the artwork on the walls of the recently redecorated reception area. Too high-tech for his taste. Colorful lines and circles, intersected by stripes, rings and irregular blotches of different hues, gave the impression of a corporate Rorschach. He saw his reflection in a polished glass surface. A mountain man's craggy, old-fashioned face, dotted with warts peeking through a partial beard, stared back at him. Perhaps he should have shaved before returning to work.

Freud had a beard, why couldn't the Assistant Director?

Still, from the tone of the new decor, maybe he should have just stayed at his cottage in the thick woods surrounding the Cayce Institute. He had been reluctant to leave Virginia, thought he would be glad to be home.

But this wasn't the home he had left. Driving in, he'd noticed the sign in front of the complex had been redone. They had finished the Douglas Foundation, leaving off the founder's first name. No space remained for the second part: for Psychic Research. A passerby would think it nothing more than an ordinary psychiatric clinic. Maybe this was the situation his college faculty advisor had foreseen, when he insisted Avisson major in Psychology and only minor in Parapsychology.

He quieted the paranoid thoughts racing through his mind. Margaret would tell him what was going on. He pushed open the double doors marked "Administration."

A white-smocked, blonde receptionist looked up and smiled. A black, white-lettered sign said, "Dorothy Slimson."

"May I help you?" she asked

"Uh... where's Margaret?"

"Margaret? Oh, yeah. She transferred."

"Then I need to speak Dr. Ramis."

"Can't."

"Why not?"

"He's not here."

"When will he be back?"

"Oh, not for a long..." she pursed her lips, "Early retirement."

Avisson scratched his head. Hawthorne wrote Rip Van Winkle, Woody Allen filmed Sleeper, and now after a six-month sabbatical, *he* had returned to discover someone had sent his resume into the Twilight Zone.

"Miss Slimson, is anyone running the place?"

"That would be Dr. Kautsch." The receptionist had the telephone in her hand. "Would you like an appointment?"

"No."

Now she was confused, too. "Then how can I help you?"

"I'm Dr. Avisson. I think I'm the Assistant Director here."

"Oh, Dr. Avisson." She straightened in her chair. "Dr. Kautsch should be finished with his meeting in a few moments. They're finalizing plans for the Fete."

"I can come back. He's not expecting—"

"It's costume. All the staff is expected to attend." The telephone buzzed and her attention shifted, before he could ask more questions. All business.

He didn't need a dream interpreter, to help him with this one. It was a veritable nightmare. Eight years working hard to bring science to parapsychology and vice versa, now seemingly down the drain. Avisson already missed the laid-back atmosphere at the Cayce Institute. The excitement in everyone's eyes over their groundbreaking research into what seemed to be the very mystery of human existence. So much more important than treating the mind as a computer, which required only rudimentary, perhaps chemical adjustments, to return a person to functionality of a sort. At the Cayce Institute, what the AMA practitioners considered mental health was thought of as only scratching the surface.

He shook his head. Science versus Metaphysics—the same old Civil War. He felt like a Confederate soldier who'd awakened smack in the middle of a Union encampment.

"Dr. Avisson?"

He looked up to see a hand extended in his direction. He stood and shook it, looking into the dark-haired man's face. White smock, of course. And thick glasses above a salt-and-pepper goatee and a broad, insincere grin.

"Sorry to keep you waiting, Avisson. Conference call about the Fete."

"Fete?"

"Costumes, booths, music, food. Great fund-raising project that will help augment next year's budget.'

"Any increase has to be good news." Avisson smiled, stopped when he saw the grim look on his new boss's face.

"By the way, you'd better get a costume. Everyone's expected to attend. It's tomorrow night."

Kautsch led the way into his office, motioned for Avisson to sit, then picked up a blue file marked Personnel. "Lots of changes in the making, Avisson. You've returned just in time to be part of them."

"I'm looking forward to sharing my research from the Cayce Institute."

Kautsch seemed to be studying Avisson's face. What was he looking for? "Anybody ever tell you how much you look like Abraham Lincoln?"

Avisson had heard it so often, he just nodded. "You said there were changes in the making."

"Uh, yes."

"Will that impact the research in psychic studies?"

"Psychic studies." Kautsch's eyebrows narrowed. "Perhaps you should understand something right off the bat. It's true that the institute was started by Sarah Douglas to investigate the paranormal, but I was hired with the understanding that my first priority is to shift the focus."

"I don't understand. The institute was started specifically to study psychic phenomena."

"Eighty percent of our funding comes from Douglas Industries. When the company was run by Mrs. Douglas, her main outside interest was just that—studying psychic phenomena. Now that Peter Douglas-MacBrayne, her grandson, is running the show, the board feels the Foundation must accommodate his interests."

Avisson squirmed in his chair. "And what would those be?"

"I haven't met him yet, but the board is expecting to move in the direction of pure psychiatry." Kautsch smiled. "Anything but the paranormal."

So he hadn't been paranoid. Everything was different. He sat in shock, as Kautsch outlined the circumstances that brought the change to the foundation: Dr. Ramis' gross indiscretion with a female patient, the husband's threatened law suit, the huge, potential exposure for Douglas Industries.

Avisson nodded. He'd had a bad feeling about that Clark woman, about Ramis' handling of the case. She was too pretty, her dreams too erotic. Avisson had been glad his boss had taken over when he went on sabbatical. Kautsch was saying something.

"I'm sorry," Avisson looked up at him.

"I was saying that the Board settled out of court, apparently thanks to Peter Douglas-MacBrayne, himself."

Kautsch went on to explain the Board's decision to rewrite the organization's statement of purpose. All the preliminary steps to sever the relationship with Douglas Industries—which would in the end lead to complete self-sufficiency for the Foundation—had been taken.

"And they hired you to 'make some changes.'"

"Within six to twelve months, this organization will be completely self-supporting—no longer dependent on outside sources of income."

Avisson sighed. "You've seen my background. If the focus has shifted, what the hell am I doing here?"

"That's a good question. To be perfectly frank, I initially wanted to give you your ah...professional freedom." Kautsch went behind his desk, sat in his chair and crossed his legs. "But one of the directors insisted we keep you on."

Avisson shook his head. "Then what exactly will I do?"

"You're a trained therapist. Why don't we start there?" He tossed a thin folder on the desk. "In fact, here's your first case."

"The background?"

"English teacher at a local public school. Suffers from depression and acute alcoholism."

Kautsch's voice was neutral, almost too much so. Although Avisson had just met him, he was already quite sure there was a sinister agenda submerged behind his new boss's seeming indifference. He glanced through the file, spoke without looking up.

"Any particular reason you want me on this case?"

Kautsch lips curled into a partial smile, straightened again. He couldn't seem to take his eyes off Avisson's face. "It really is uncanny how much you look like Lincoln."

Avisson shrugged. "I take after my mother."

❦

Doug's eyelids fluttered and opened. Miss Stipple stood in front of him, a cup of water in her hand.

"Here, drink some. You must have fallen asleep."

He sat straight, thanked her and took the cup.

"Your father will be here any minute."

"Was he angry?"

"He didn't sound happy."

Doug finished the water in the cup and leaned against the porch railing. He couldn't stop staring at Miss Stipple.

"Is something the matter, Mr. MacBrayne?"

"I was just wondering," Doug said. "Do you wear contact lenses?"

"No, why?"

"Your eyes, they're two different colors."

She nodded.

"What causes it?"

"I have no idea."

She turned away, as if uncomfortable with the subject.

"Miss Stipple?"

"Yes?"

"I didn't mean to ruin Jimmy's painting. It was an accident."

"You always seem to have accidents where Jimmy's concerned. If you would pay more attention to what you're doing, these things wouldn't happen."

"Is that why you don't like me?"

Her neck jerked, as if she had been slapped. "I don't dislike you, Mr. MacBrayne. I simply can't tolerate careless or impertinent behavior."

Doug saw his father's Bentley pull into the front parking lot. Startled, he stood up.

"My father's here."

Miss Stipple rose next to him. "You go ahead. He already knows what happened."

Doug took several steps toward the door, stopped and turned. "Miss Stipple, I'm sorry for messing up."

Her face tightened. "In the future then, think about what you're doing."

"I will. I'll try. But I just wanted you to know that I'm sorry…for everything."

Her mouth tightened—she looked as if she might cry. Doug turned and ran to the steps where his father met him.

"When I have to leave the office because you misbehave, there need to be some changes."

"I know, Dad. I'm sorry."

"Sorry isn't enough. You're grounded."

Doug wasn't sure what that meant. His father almost never let him go anywhere without him or Nanny, anyway.

"Grounded?"

"Confined to your room. House arrest."

"But Dad…what about the Fete?"

"What about it?"

"Nanny got me this cool Peter Pan costume."

No response.

"Some of the kids from school will be there…" He could see that tack would not change his father's mind. "Besides, it's your birthday party and I wanted to—"

A sharp look from his father shut him up. His father drove in silence for five minutes, bowtie dancing an angry samba.

At the edge of town, his father suddenly turned the wheel and made a right turn.

"Aren't we going home?"

"We have to make a stop first." The Bentley turned again. "Do you really want to go to the Fete?"

"I'd like to, Sir."

"Then you will go... on one condition."

"Okay." Doug sat back in his seat, relieved.

"Don't you want to know the condition?"

"Sure. What is it?"

"You can go, but you must wear the costume I get for you."

"But Nanny already has one for me."

"Do you want to go to the Fete?"

"Yes." Doug gulped. "What costume—?"

"You'll see, tomorrow night."

Jimmy climbed off the bus and gazed around. This place was even bigger than the zoo, but smelled better. He followed Miss Stipple and the other volunteers as if in a daze, captivated by the shrubbery, shaped as Peter Pan characters. The group passed through the shadow of the immense house on their way to the fairgrounds.

"Look," Sally called out. "They have their own church."

"Chapel," Miss Stipple corrected.

"Must be awful sinners to need their own chapel," Jimmy whispered to Chas Miner.

"I wonder if they have their own priest, too." Chas whispered back.

"Probably. They own everything else in this damn town."

"Hey, careful." Chas looked around. "My father works for them. He says that if it wasn't for Douglas Industries, there wouldn't even be a town."

"Yeah, well if it wasn't for them, my mother—"

"Now pay attention, children." Miss Stipple clapped her hands, took a clipboard from under her arm. "You have each been assigned to work in different areas. Check this list and find your booth."

Jimmy and Chas wandered through the fairgrounds, slipping in and out of the small tents, laughing at the men wearing tights and codpieces, whistling under their breath at the women wearing low-cut dresses and prop-up brassieres.

"Musta been fun to live back then," Chas said, eyeing a particularly buxom woman.

"Bet it wasn't anything like this." Jimmy watched, mesmerized by a juggler who had six oranges flying in the air.

"How do you know it wasn't?"

"I don't." Jimmy spotted Miss Stipple heading their way and ducked under a canvas flap. He listened as the art teacher berated Chas for not being at his post, grinned at the scuffling sound of his friend being dragged off, probably by his ear.

"Hello, young fella."

Jimmy turned. An old man with a long beard, sat behind a card table, adjusting the turban wound around his head.

"What are you supposed to be?"

The old man grinned. "A gypsy fortune teller. And you?"

Jimmy shrugged. "A kid in a stupid costume."

This brought a laugh. The old man extended his hand. "Valka Petrovich."

When Jimmy didn't shake, the old man's arm fell to his side. "I take it you're not enthralled with the idea of working the Fete,"

"Didn't have much choice."

"Where are you supposed to work?"

"Some stupid food booth, handing out turkey legs to assholes."

He nodded. "Sounds sufficiently stupid. Would you like to help me?"

"Doing what?"

"I need an assistant."

"Doing what?"

"What do you like to do?"

"Draw. I like to draw."

"You any good?"

Jimmy took a pad of paper and pencil from the table and made a quick sketch of the gypsy. When he looked at it, the old man whistled.

"You sure as hell would be wasted, handing out turkey legs to assholes." He looked up. "What do you say? Want to be my assistant—you can sketch the suckers... ahem, the customers. I'll charge 'em an extra five bucks. You get half if you want it."

"But I don't have my stuff."

"We'll get it."

"Miss Stipple won't go for that."

"This Miss Stipple gives us any trouble..." A funny glint entered the old man's expression." ...and I'll give her the evil eye."

"You can do that?"

"Yeah, I can." His voice was conspiratorial. "But I have a hunch you can do it, too."

Jimmy smiled for the first time.

"Okay." The old man rose from the chair. "Now, do you have any supplies at home, or must we buy some?"

"I got 'em."

"Okay. Where do you live?"

"You know where the orphanage is?"

Jimmy waited for the sadness to enter the man's expression, the look adults always got, when they realized they were talking to an orphan. This Petrovich guy never batted an eye.

"Okay, then. First we find this Stipple woman, then we get your stuff." He motioned Jimmy to lead the way.

After ten minutes of searching the midway, they found her in a frenzy, a pencil precariously stuck into her beehive hairdo.

"There you are. Jimmy, I should send you home right now. What's the idea skipping out on—"

"Madame." The old man stopped her. "This young man will be my assistant for the rest of the day. His skills are much too valuable to be wasted on crass culinary pursuits."

"And who might you be?"

"Valka Petrovich." He bowed. "Fortune teller extraordinaire."

"But you're not on the list."

"Please, Miss Stipple. Mr. Petrovich is going to let me draw his su...his customers."

"That's right, and the extra proceeds will go to the hospital."

Miss Stipple frowned. "I don't know..."

"Tell you what. I'll do some extra drawings for class. Please, Miss Stipple?"

The teacher squinted at the old man. He spread his hands and smiled.

"It's for charity." He sidled closer. "And I'll even give you a free reading."

She recoiled, as if confronted by a cobra.

"Please, Miss Stipple?"

Finally she relented. "Okay. But don't expect extra credit for this, Mister Lyden."

"Great." Jimmy started toward the parking lot. "Come on, Mr. Petrovich.

But the old man just stood and stared, eyes wide.

"Are you coming? We have to get my stuff."

"Yeah, sure," he said. "I'm right behind you, Mr. ...Lyden."

Once upon a time, there was a girl named...Doug put his pencil down. Was it Rapunzel who was trapped in the tower, or Snow White? He couldn't remember...

Outside, he could hear the final hammer blows as the last tent pegs were driven in the ground. He had seen the students climb off the bus and gather around Miss Stipple. She stood like a maypole, waiting for streamers. He knew he should be down helping but feared going against his father's orders. House arrest. That's what Dad called it.

He put his chin on the window sill, watching the banners being erected. Some of the workers were already in costume. Off in the distance, he heard what sounded like hoofbeats. Strange, there were no horses nearby.

The pounding increased. He closed his eyes.

❧

Pride welled in James Davidson's chest as he sat in the saddle, armor gleaming in the sun, lance held vertically at his side.

The king and queen acknowledged him and he tilted his lance in return. The crowd roared approval.

"Death to the infidels!" shouted a woman from the front row. "Feed them to the wolves!"

James searched the column ahead for Akmed, the Christian infidel. How did this Arab feel about hearing his people slandered? For months, the two of them had sat in the Arab's hovel, going over the words, the magic keys to understanding this strange nomadic people. The man seemed to be as fervently Christian as any bishop, but James was never quite sure of his sincerity. Prayer in front of one's captors was one thing, true belief, another.

The king handed a proclamation to the crier to enunciate the goals of the forthcoming crusade: Land, Treasure and Souls...slaughtered, sent to hell. Those who refused to believe, would die. The number of victims would be proved by severing the right ear. A heavenly tithe.

James turned at what he thought was Margaret's voice. Must have been mistaken. Her refinement would not allow her to shout loud enough to be heard over this din.

There were many reasons to go on such a perilous journey, but even more to return victorious. Marriage and an estate awaited him—the only real hope of property for a second-born son.

At the end of the parade, he would signify to the crowd that he fought in her name, on her behalf. She would keep his colors until he returned.

He pulled the crested scarf higher on his neck to keep the sun off the red clump at the back of his head. Experienced crusaders told tales of heat that could cook a man's hands and feet, winds that drove the sand like tiny arrows into an uncovered face, nights where the cold actually froze men while they slept.

Across the fairgrounds, Damien Arbuthnot knelt before Bishop Rawlings. The crowd quieted as Rawlings raised a large, jeweled cross in one hand and a chalice filled with sacramental wine in the other.

"Domina Christo, Sanctus..."

A bee flew into James's visor. He wheeled his horse about, his right hand searching for the angry buzzer. The reins slipped from his left and the horse bolted toward the stands, just as the stinger pierced the bridge of James' nose. Blinded, he fought to stay on the panicked mount. The crowd's laughter turned into a roar of fear. He felt the awful collision with the stands, flew into emptiness and was seemingly lifted by the screams that filled the air.

He landed away from the kicking horse, his fall cushioned by spectators. He lay gasping, fighting to open his breastplate.

"Ye gods, man!" A deep voice boomed above him. The pandemonium stilled, except for one shrill wail.

James struggled to sit up. The dead bee dropped out of the helmet he lifted from his head. His forehead burned, tears blurred his vision. But he could see well enough. Ten feet away a woman cradled a small child in her arms. She shook the rag doll, as if brute force might reanimate it. No response.

James' groom and several others captured his horse which now limped on three legs, the fourth bent at an impossible angle. One of the grooms plunged a sword between the creature's ribs. The ground shook as it went down in a heap.

His fingers searched for the stinger without success. He soon realized he was looking for proof to show the mother that it had been an accident. He closed his eyes, buried his face in his hands.

She needed no proof.

One of the Bishop's assistants attempted to comfort her with Latinate whispers, over the child's still form.

A shadow loomed over him. Arbuthnot stood, blocking the sun.

"You understand the meaning, do you not?"

"Meaning, Sire?" James squinted at the corona that surrounded the Duke's head.

"You have cast an evil aura over our crusade. We are doomed, unless you are willing to make a sacrifice."

"Sacrifice?"

"You must eschew your intended's heraldry."

Arbuthnot reached down, pulled James to his feet with a mighty arm, then turned to the mother.

"Fifty extra infidels, to replace your child."

She looked at the Duke with glazed eyes. James staggered toward her, went to one knee and bowed. He tore Margaret's scarf from his neck and handed it to the woman. She took it in trembling hands, her face tight.

"The name. I must know the child's name."

"W-w-willum."

James stood and faced the crowd, raised his sword to the king.

"Your highness, from this day forth, I forsake love and property. I fight for you and our Holy Church in the name of the child, Willum."

The king raised his scepter in acceptance.

James trudged through the crowd of peasants which parted to make way for him. He never looked back at Margaret. His eyes were too filled with tears, his heart with shame.

❦

·The vibrations slowed. With two fingers, Doug wiped a small line of spittle from his chin. When his eyes focused, he looked out the window at the people below. He felt closer to those he saw in his dreams—day or night.

Rapunzel had it good, he thought. At least she could let her hair down.

A tap at the door. Nanny entered carrying a long box.

"Here's your costume, Doug."

She put the box on the bed and both stood looking at it.

"I guess I should open it."

Nanny bit her lip, raised her eyebrows. "What do you think it could be?"

"A jailbird suit?" Doug forced a giggle.

"Well, let's untie the string and find out." She loosened the knot. "Go ahead, lift the top."

Doug did. He stared inside. His worst suspicions were confirmed, as was his greatest fear.

His father must truly hate him.

Birthmark

Grumpy heard the laughter outside his tent and asked Jimmy to check it out. The boy returned a moment later.

"You have to see this."

"What?"

"Just come look."

Right in the middle of the Middle Ages stood Abraham Lincoln, surrounded by medieval waifs and bosomy women. The look on the man's face would have matched the dead president's, had he found himself in a similar time-warp.

"Are ye here to free the serfs, Mr. Lincoln?" Grumpy called out.

Avisson blushed, nodded. "Apparently."

"Come sit a spell, it's safe in here."

Lincoln pushed through the jeering crowd and bent over to enter the gypsy tent. He tipped his tall, black stove-pipe hat.

"Abraham Avisson. Thanks for the rescue."

Grumpy extended his hand. "Valka Petrovich and my esteemed assistant, James Lyden."

"Sirs." The president shook Grumpy's hand, reached for Jimmy, who simply shrugged. "But the woman where I got the hat had been so admiring, said I fit the part perfectly."

"That you do, Mr. President," Grumpy said. "Right costume, wrong century."

"Well, Lincoln was ahead of his time, wouldn't you say?"

"No." Grumpy shook his head. "I think he came along just when he was needed."

"What about people who believe they were born at the wrong time—that they should have come earlier or later?" Avisson placed the hat in his lap.

Jimmy got his pencil and began sketching.

"I think everything happens as it's supposed to," Grumpy said. "People usually misinterpret much of what happens."

Avisson smiled. "Good gypsy answer."

"That's an easy one. Nothing gypsy about it." Grumpy let his hand hover just above the crystal ball. "But then, you already knew that, didn't you—in your work investigating the paranormal?"

That got both Avisson's and Jimmy's attention.

"What's paranor...?" Jimmy asked.

"Paranormal investigation is the scientific study of phenomena that can't be explained by physical science," Avisson said.

Jimmy put his pencil down.

Grumpy smiled. "Things that go bump in the night. Ghosts, spooks, psychics, reading peoples' minds, seeing the future. That cover it, Doc?"

"Crude, incomplete, but accurate."

"A common gypsy failing." Grumpy spread his hands. "Care to see what else the ball has to say?"

"What's the rate?"

"Five for the reading and five for a sketch by my assistant." Grumpy grinned. "I assume you can write it off?"

"Not these days, my friend." Avisson handed over a ten dollar bill, pointed to the crystal ball. "But you probably saw that already."

"There's a difference between knowing and seeing," Grumpy said, pocketing the money as he studied the globe in front of him.

After several moments, he reached without looking for the Tarot deck and gave it several casual shuffles. He frowned. Rolled his eyes. Snorted. Began dealing out the cards. He studied the layout, returned to the ball.

"Why, damn those..." Grumpy said, pushing himself away from the table.

"What's the matter?" Avisson revolved the brim of his hat with his fingers.

"The last part's not about you." Grumpy returned the tenner. "This one's on the house."

"What about the drawing?" Jimmy tore it off his pad.

"I'll pay for it." Grumpy handed the boy a bill. "Why don't you take a break, Jimmy? Grab a bite and have a look around."

Jimmy was about to resist, then noticed he'd been given a twenty.

"I'll be back soon."

"Take your time," Grumpy said.

He waited until the boy was gone.

"Avisson, things look a little screwed up where you work."

"That's an understatement."

Grumpy nodded. "They're going to get a lot worse before they get better."

"I kind of figured that."

"Well, hang in there." Grumpy swept the tarot cards into a single pile. "Just remember, there's no such thing as slow dancing with the devil."

"Meaning?"

"Stay on your toes." He stood and walked Abraham Lincoln to the tent flap. "And come have coffee some time at the Crystal Cafe and Bookstore."

"That's you, huh?"

Avisson put the stove pipe on and stepped outside. Grumpy watched him go, smiled. Only a true metaphysician would wear street clothes to a costume party.

❦

"Come on out, Doug. Let me see."
"No."
"Why not?"
"Because I look stupid."
"We'll all look stupid. It's a costume party."
"Not this stupid."
"Open the door, Doug."
"No, you'll laugh."
"I won't."
"Promise?"
"Yes."

The door opened and Doug clomped out. Fiona smiled, but it was difficult to hold the laughter. The silk outfit was a patchwork of bright colors, arranged in no particular order. His feet looked like two silk sausages with green balls tied on the big toes. But the hat was the coup de grace. Also silk, it looked as if someone had dropped a giant, multicolored starfish atop his head. Each arm ended with a ball similar to those at the ends of his sausage feet.

The dam burst. She laughed as seldom before, but managed to catch Doug's sleeve as he started to retreat into his room.

"Hold on…"
"You promised!"

Gasping to catch her breath, she held him at arms length, tears of laughter streaming down her face.

"Oh, Doug. It's.. it's…"
"Awful."
"No. It's the best. People are going to love you."
"They're going to laugh at me." He lowered his head.
"That's right, they will." She pulled his chin up. "And that's what will make them love you."
"They laugh at me at school. I know they don't love me."

Fiona fought the sudden rush of protective anger rising within her. What she thought was only a splinter of pain in the boy's eye, inflicted by an insensitive father, actually went much deeper: He was getting it at school, as well.

"Doug, people can't make fun of you unless you let them."

"Oh? How am I supposed to stop them?"

"Not stop them, join them—have fun with them."

"How?"

"Start with tonight. Do you know what the court jester's job was, in ancient times?"

"To make a fool of himself?"

"Not really. The jester made fun of himself and everybody else. Because the jester looked so funny, he got away with it. People knew it was his job to make fun of things—like the government—especially whoever was in charge."

"Kind of like a clown at the circus?"

"Right, only smarter. The jester says things ordinary people wish they could say but don't have the humor—or the guts."

Beneath the silk starfish, Doug's serious expression almost made Fiona laugh again. She held back. Any more convincing and the idea would be too much hers. After another moment's reflection, his jaw jutted, determined. He strode into his room, over to a bookcase, found the book and opened it.

"Nanny, how many serfs does it take to change a light bulb?"

"I don't know, how many?"

He rolled his eyes. "None. They didn't have electricity in the Middle Ages."

She laughed, hiccuped, her eyes teared. She pulled the handkerchief from her sleeve and dabbed her eyes.

"Oh, come on, Nanny. It wasn't that funny."

"Yes it was, Doug."

She wanted to crush him with a huge, loving hug, but stopped herself.

"You study up, while I finish getting dressed."

She hesitated a moment at the door, watching the starfish boy completely absorbed in his book, the arms of the hat waving in the air as he scanned the pages. Up to now, she had been pleased with who he was, but at this moment she had a glimpse of who he might become.

And no mother had ever been so proud.

❦

Peter had spent almost two hours in his private office bathroom trying to assemble the outfit he had rented from the Douglasville Costume Shoppe. Dizzy from the strong smell of spirits that filled the room, he couldn't get the elegant, black beard to stay in place. The instructions showed how to part it at the chin, each half curling away from the other, up towards the ears. He tried to comb it in this fashion, before attaching it to his face—each time without success. In frustration, he decided to stick it on first, then comb it, as if it were real.

After several applications of spirit gum and almost a can of hair spray, he stopped fussing. This was as good as it would get. After a long, critical look, he turned from the exhausted bathroom mirror, went into the main part of the office and quickly finished dressing. Standing in front of the big, full-length mirror that hid his private bar, he finally put the silver crown on top of his thick, black wig.

"Not too bad, for an amateur," Peter said aloud.

He threw the long, black cloak over his shoulders, strode across the room to the door. With a final, approving glance in the tall mirror, he swept out the door, climbed into the rear of the limousine he had rented for the evening and told the driver where to pick up his date.

A woman with long, straight black hair and pancake-white complexion met him at the door. Her lips, painted a deep red, matched the blood-colored rose pinned to the bodice of her black, silk gown.

"Pleased to meet you, Mr. MacBrayne—or should I call you 'Your Highness?'"

"Call me Peter," he said with a royal smile. "And I must say, you make a fitting escort."

"I will, once you help me with this."

Peter took the gold crown and placed it on her head.

"There, you've just graduated from Princess."

The chauffeur held the door for the royal couple. Once inside, she moved closer.

"Cousin Dan tells me you haven't been with a woman for nearly ten years." She ran her finger down his fake ermine lapel. "Is that true?"

"There are many things about me that your cousin Dan doesn't know."

"I thought he was your second-in-command?"

"Your cousin is basically an accountant—the chancellor, if you will, of my kingdom."

"You didn't answer my question."

"The chancellor is more or less equivalent to a knight."

"Yes?"

"Well, knights know only what kings want them to know."

She smiled, snuggled closer. "I know something about that heraldry stuff, too."

"What's that?"

"The difference between a princess and a queen..." Her hand caressed the black beard. "...is, that for a queen, once a knight is not enough."

❦

Jimmy stood on a chair so he could see. He worked his tongue around the edge where the ice cream met the cone, to keep the melting chocolate from dribbling on his hand. He scanned the crowd, trying to capture as many images as he could. Sometimes the pictures melded together. Instead of one panel depicting a dog-trainer and another a juggler, he saw a man juggling poodles.

He returned to reality when the emcee announced a change in the evening program: A court jester that went by the name of "MacBrayne the Insane."

Sure enough, there was Doug, hogging the spotlight as usual.

Jimmy spit out a blob of chocolate as the crowd applauded raucously. Of course they would suck up to him. Didn't everybody?

"Do you know why they called it Mid...evil times?" came over the loudspeakers. "Because it was only half bad."

Groans, laughter. Applause. Gimme a break. Jimmy was about to jump from the chair after two or three more topical but corny jokes, when a trumpet blared off to the left.

Every face turned to look at the entourage heading for the stage. Pipers piped and dancers gamboled, in front of a covered caisson carried on the shoulders of six half-naked giants—linemen from the varsity football team.

Doug looked at a piece of paper handed him by the emcee. "Ladies and gentleman," he cried into the microphone, "it gives me great pleasure to introduce tonight's guest of honor, the man who helped to make this all possible. He's celebrating his fiftieth birthday, and Douglas Industries is celebrating its seventy-fifth."

Jimmy's stomach tightened, he closed his eyes.

"Ladies and gentlemen, serfs and serfettes, please put your hands together for the King of Douglasville, Peter Douglas-MacBrayne, the Third, and his lovely Queen 'Em."

The caisson door swung open and for a split second, it appeared to Jimmy as if a living face-card had escaped the deck and come to life: in front of the crowd stood the Queen of Spades. They roared their approval.

Jimmy put his hands over his ears. He didn't want to hear the next applause.

Fiona saw the question on Doug's face and moved closer to his side.

"You're doing really well, Dougie."

"Thanks," he said, not taking his eyes off the Queen. "Who is she, Nanny?"

Doug barely got the words out when Fiona saw him stiffen. She followed his eyes and saw Peter emerge from the caisson, looking for all the world like the King of Clubs, a mighty scepter in his hand.

Suddenly, Doug's screams and cries for help shot through the PA system. Fiona tried to hold him but he squirmed and wriggled in a mad panic to escape.

Peter immediately changed from a beaming, beneficent ruler to a confused and angry despot. He strode up to Fiona who could barely keep Doug from flying off the stage

"For God's sake, what's the matter with him?" Peter tried to push his cape out of the way with the hand that held the scepter. Doug screamed again and leaped from the stage. The crowd broke his fall, then he was away.

Peter snatched the microphone from the ground. "Please calm down. It's all part of the show."

The crowd murmured, a few sarcastic laughs showed they really didn't buy that.

Fiona stood on tiptoe trying to find Doug. She was shaken roughly by an infuriated Peter.

"What the hell is the matter with that boy?"

"I haven't the slightest idea what's come over him, sir," said Fiona. "But you carry on. I'll find him and quieten him down, soon enough."

Doug pushed his way through the crowd, bouncing off of as many fete-goers as he missed. Sweaty and panting, he finally made it past the last tent and found an empty path.

He staggered dizzy and sick, toward the family chapel, which loomed out of the dimness. It seemed to be covered with layers of sin, pain and absolution—almost as thick as its sturdy stone walls. When he walked past the far end, Doug suddenly felt the familiar chill coming on. He shuddered and looked around. Nothing. He wrapped his arms around his torso to warm himself. His eyes grew heavy. He sat down, leaned against the stone steps leading to the chapel entrance. He tried to open his eyes but everything was foggy. Not sure if awake or asleep, he felt himself get up and push the door. Anything to get away from his father, who now seemed more an enemy than ever.

Voices. They were looking for him. He staggered inside, surprised to see candles glowing on the altar. In the flickering yellow light he thought he saw the figure of a tall, broad-shouldered man, kneeling on a hassock in front of the altar. Eyes closed, the man's hands were folded around a silver crucifix, in prayer.

Doug rubbed his eyes, all thoughts of his father's terrifying costume gone.

The priest must have sensed Doug's presence. He looked up as if startled, then floated through a pair of dark red curtains at the rear of the chapel.

Still queasy, Doug walked to the altar and leaned against it. The vibrations had never been this strong. He fought to keep his eyes open, but the room spun around him, the candles blurring with the stained glass windows—a constantly revolving kaleidoscope.

He found himself floating, body-less. Felt like a cloud with eyes, looking down on an angry crowd outside a large manor house. The people carried torches and kept shouting something that sounded like "Away with the Cheviot!"

The view was dizzying but persistent. He watched a ram slaughtered in the middle of the crowd, then thrown onto the steps of the manor. A woman with a large, bloody bandage atop her head and a fiery torch in her hand ran forward to taunt a man standing on the vestibule steps, a long musket in his hands.

He raised the gun as if to fire. The crowd fell back.

"You don't scare me none, you English-sucking bastard," she cried.

The gun remained aimed directly at her. She did a little dance, screaming out other vile names and waved her fire like a magic, orange wand.

❦

Jimmy tiptoed to the window and peered in to see Doug leaning against the altar, an almost lifesize crucifix towering above him. Could he be asleep? Jimmy spotted the jester hat lying on the steps, snatched it up. A plan formed in his mind. He slipped around to the front. The crowd's applause and phoney laughter burned in his ears. He pushed the chapel door open and stealthily crept inside.

The candlelight cast spooky shadows. He nearly bolted when a mouse skittered across his feet. He took a deep breath, frog-walked up the aisle nearest the far wall. He remembered Sally's comment about the MacBraynes having their own church.

He thought of his mother, the dim memory of her face hovering above him. All he had left was pictures of her. Old, cold photographs.

A rage of anger coursed through him, but he held it in check. Getting Doug in trouble at school was nothing compared to what Jimmy could do to him here. Especially after having seen how frightened the boy was of his father.

He clutched the jester hat and clambered atop the altar. Christ in a jester's hat, that would be a good one. Checking Doug once more, Jimmy started to heave himself up.

One of the candelabras toppled toward the red curtains that hung from wall.

Startled, he ran to the front door, then remembered Doug. He looked over his shoulder. The blood drained from his face. The altar was ablaze. Shit, he'd done it now. When he opened the door, he released a scalding wind which almost blew him off his feet.

He dropped the jester hat on the steps and ran for cover in the shrubbery.

❦

Grumpy stood outside his tent. He had seen it all: Peter's argument with the Queen of Spades, ending when she ran away in a huff; Abe Lincoln Avisson introducing Peter to an unknown, goateed man, costumed as a medieval healer—half barber, half butcher—who had his arm around a buxom blonde, in a low-cut, peasant outfit. Then, he spotted Fiona, obviously searching for Doug. There'd be no reading for her tonight.

Grumpy slipped into his tent to pack his things. He stiffened. Had someone yelled "Fire!"? Then came the chorus, screaming. He shuddered—Janina had been right about his coming home.

❦

Fiona's stomach did a pancake-flip when she saw flames shoot from the chapel roof. She raised her skirt and ran toward it. Her breath came in short gasps. Doug was in there, an obvious place to hide from his father.

Several men and women were standing around the entrance when she arrived.

"Let me through," she said. "I think someone's in there."

One of the men grabbed her.

"Don't go in," he said.

She flailed at him with her fists. "Doug's in there. I just know it."

"We already looked inside," another man said. "There's nobody there."

"Are you sure?"

"Just flames now."

She sagged, sat hard on the ground, then saw the jester hat at the foot of the steps.

"Oh, my God," she said, scrabbling on her hands and knees to pick it up. She looked up at the blazing chapel. "Doug!"

Chapter Five

Doug's eyes fluttered. He sniffed. His clothes smelled of smoke but the air was thick, moldy. Groggy, he tried to sit up, but his head spun. He coughed. Hard to breathe.

To his left a tiny candle flickered, its yellow light cast shadows against blackened stone. The room, or whatever it was, was small. He was propped against a long, rectangular marble box.

The back of his neck tingled. Afraid, he forced his eyes to explore the area. He was sure he wasn't alone.

"H-hello?"

The air seemed to move in the darkness beyond the candlelight.

"Is anybody here?" He tried to rise. His lungs ached, his hands felt miles from his arms, legs rubbery.

"Am I dead?"

This time a deep chuckle came from the darkness.

He twisted around. "Who's there?"

"Do not be afraid." A man's voice, half echo, half breeze.

"W-why not?"

"I will not hurt you."

As Doug's eyes adjusted to the darkness, he read the letters engraved on the side of the long, marble box: Sarah Douglas.

He gulped. "Am I dead or something?"

"Why would you say that?"

He didn't have an answer. "Could you come out where I can see you? I'm kinda scared."

The figure of the priest Doug had seen in the chapel moved into the light. This time, despite the dimness, Doug could see every feature of the man's handsome face, the neatly trimmed bushy eyebrows, the shock of thick, reddish hair and the white rim of the clerical collar, barely exposed above a long, flowing black cassock.

"Hello, Doug," The figure said.

"How do you know my name?"

"I am... or rather, one might say, I was Father Hector, the Parish Priest here, a very long time ago, my boy." There was a touch of sadness in his deep voice.

"Where are we?"

The man's hand caressed the marble box. "In your great-grandmother's mausoleum."

Doug scurried away, stopped at the edge of the candle's power. "My great-grandmother's in there?"

The priest smiled. "Her earthly remains are."

"Why are you here, now? If you used to be the parish priest..."

"I never really left."

"Well then, how come I've never seen you before?"

The priest put his thumb and finger on his chin, pondering the question. "I think it has something to do with vibrations. But I am not a man of science. Ut multa paucis verba, alea jacta est."

"What does that mean?"

"It means, in brief, 'An irrevocable decision has been made,' my boy. In any event, it doesn't much matter."

Doug frowned. "How did I get here?"

"You fell asleep in the chapel. When the fire started—"

"Fire?"

The man nodded. "Yes, your family mausoleum was the only place I could think to bring you so you'd be safe."

"You carried me?"

"Something like that." Father Hector shrugged. "I couldn't let you just burn."

The final images of his dream came to Doug. The woman threw her torch at the manor house. At least he thought she did. Hard to remember. He looked up. The priest was staring at him.

"How is it...I mean...why are you here?"

"I've been waiting for you."

"Me?"

"Yes, I'm here to teach you about your other lifetimes."

"Lifetimes? I thought they were only dreams."

The tall man smiled. "One way or another, everything is a dream."

"Are you a dream?"

This brought a laugh. "Sometimes even I, think that." There was a sad note in his voice. "All I remember is riding back to the manse, after an...er, interview with the Bishop. I fell from my horse and was severely trampled. Then I woke up here."

"Trampled? Shouldn't you get to a hospital."

Hector brushed away the idea. "I'm in no pain now. It was a long, long time ago."

"When was it?"

"Seems just like yesterday." He gazed around the crypt. "The year was 1885, I believe."

Doug worked the abacus in his head. "That means... your physical body... died 95 years ago?"

"I have reluctantly concluded... and am quite certain it did."

"Are you a...ghost?"

The priest smiled. "The church doesn't exactly subscribe to that particular nomenclature."

"Then what are you? An angel?"

Now the priest laughed. "Not hardly, lad."

"Then what do I call you?"

"Why don't you just call me Hector?"

Jimmy stood shivering in the night cold, watching the firemen finish putting out the flames. The walls of the chapel remained, but the roof had fallen in. Yellow-suited men walked around with fire extinguishers, spraying bursts of chemical fog at hot spots.

A hand landed on his shoulder. Jimmy jumped.

"Hold on, boy. It's just me." Petrovich smiled at him. "Scary stuff, fires."

Jimmy nodded.

The old man pointed to the woman who sat weeping, clutching the jester hat.

"His nanny looks pretty upset."

More silent agreement from Jimmy. He thought back to the snow-nanny he and Chas had built during the winter term, felt his cheeks begin to burn, despite the chill.

"H-have they found his—him yet?"

Petrovich shook his head. "I don't think he was in the chapel."

Startled, Jimmy looked up. The old man grinned.

"Gypsy intuition."

Relief flooded over Jimmy. There was no real reason to believe the old man. He just wanted to—badly. A sob broke through the surface and he felt himself being pulled to the man's chest, where he cried quietly into the beaded tunic.

"Scary stuff. I know. You go ahead and cry." He stroked the boy's head. "You're safe, now."

Peter stood staring at the burned-out shell of the chapel. He felt everyone's eyes on him. They'd been looking at him since Doug careered screaming from the stage. He knew what they were thinking. It was his fault that his only child was crazy, went running off and set fire to the chapel. That stupid cousin of Downey's had come right out and said it. He'd sent her packing in a hurry.

His insides clenched. If Doug really had been inside the chapel, there was no way he could have...

"How are you doing?" It was Kautsch, the new Director of the Foundation and his buxom assistant, called Slim something. Downey had introduced them earlier, well before the unanticipated fireworks. "Are you okay?"

Peter would have shrugged, but his shoulders were too heavy. The Fire Chief approached, face smudged with soot and sweat.

"We've searched the wreckage, sir. There's no trace of him."

"Then where is he?"

"Well, sir..." The man took a deep breath, "sometimes, if a kid accidentally starts something like this, he panics and runs off. There's enough people here to search the grounds. Why don't you have someone check the house?"

Peter nodded, set his jaw and walked over to where Fiona sat. "We're going to organize a search of the estate. Why don't you check the house."

She looked up. "The house?"

"Yes, the house."

"Wasn't he in the..." She pointed to the chapel.

"Apparently not."

"Thank God." Tears started again.

"Get hold of yourself, Fiona. We still don't know where he is."

She nodded, stood shakily and started toward the house, still clutching the jester's hat.

Peter went past the Fire Chief, who was organizing his men and some volunteers from the crowd. He went up to Dr. Kautsch and his blonde assistant, who were among them.

"I appreciate your helping out this way. It means a lot to me."

Kautsch smiled. "Just happened to be in the neighborhood."

The Chief barked orders. The searchers dispersed. Peter joined Kautsch and "Slim," as the doctor called her. As they walked along, Peter found himself babbling about the difficulties of raising a boy without a mother. Kautsch seemed sympathetic.

"Has Doug ever done anything like this before?"

"Not really," Peter said. "Some minor problems at school. Kid stuff. You know."

Kautsch nodded. "I do. In my experience, especially with children of single parents, this kind of 'acting out' builds slowly over a period of time. There's almost no way for parents to detect it early."

"I guess that's what therapists are for." Peter squinted as he searched the nearest clump of trees with his flashlight. "Do you have any experience working with kids?"

"Only fifteen years." Kautsch laughed lightly. "Some of my patients will be continuing with me at the Foundation."

"Fifteen years..." Peter sighed. "God, am I glad you showed up."

"So, you've been watching over our family all this time?" Doug sat on the marble box, swinging his legs alongside great-grandma Sarah's remains.

"I have. Of course, I've looked after the chapel and the graveyard, as well."

"Then could you be called our Guardian Angel?"

"Guardian maybe, my dear boy. But Angel? Most definitely not!"

"Why not?"

"I... I committed a mortal sin."

Doug's eyes opened wide. A mortal sin. He'd heard about them in Sunday school, but never met anyone—much less a priest—who ever admitted to such an act.

"But all you had to do was go to confession. That would have made it all right, wouldn't it?"

"Of course. And I was on my way to confess to the Bishop." His shoulders slumped. "That's when I was trampled!"

"But if you were on your way to confess, surely God would take that into consideration. After all, you meant to confess."

"Ah, good point. But I'm not sure that only intending to, counts."

Doug nodded as if he understood.

"I am afraid my sin was so abominable, so revolting...even had I properly confessed, I would still go to Hell...Timeo terra incognita. I fear the unknown, my dear boy."

"But what could a priest do that was so bad?"

Hector's face contorted, Doug felt the pain from where he sat. Hector spoke without seeing him.

"She had a halo of blonde, wavy hair which cascaded over her shoulders and gave her the appearance of an angel from Heaven. The first time she came to early morning Mass, she knelt, placed her white, slender hands together, and closed her eyes in prayer for about ten seconds. She sat by the aisle at the end of the fifth pew. When she first looked at me, I nearly stumbled off the pulpit. Her eyes were hazel. They spoke to me, as if saying 'I want you, Father.'"

"I don't understand. What did she mean?"

Hector acted as if he hadn't heard.

"At first I looked away." Hector swabbed a snow white handkerchief across his forehead. "It was all I could do to deliver a coherent sermon. I found myself hesitating each time I glanced her way. Those eyes..."

"What did you do?"

"Nothing. For twelve years I had been the priest here. Never before, had anything like this happened to me." He glanced up at Doug. "I'd never been tempted."

"Tempted to do what?"

Again, Hector ignored the question.

"For the next four weeks, this woman attended early Sunday Mass and, on each successive week she moved one pew closer. After Mass, I always shook hands with every member of the congregation. Each week she held my hand longer and longer. Oh, the look in her eyes..."

"Couldn't you just tell her to stop?"

Hector chuckled. "Perhaps, but the truth is I liked it. It felt like a sin, but more like a game. Figured she was just tempting me, and if I told her to stop or sent her away, then I'd have failed in my mission as a priest."

"So it was like a battle of wills?"

"Exactly." Hector gazed at Doug. "And I was sure I could win, help redirect her on the path of righteousness."

"That doesn't sound too bad to me."

"It wasn't. In fact, I think I was winning, until she showed up at a special midnight Mass and asked me to light a candle for her son. Said the baby was deathly ill. In fact, things were so bad, she shouldn't have come, but the baby might require last rites. I followed her home. I waited in the parlor while she went into the other room to check on him." He wiped his brow again.

"Was he okay?"

"There was no child. When I opened the bedroom door, there she lay, completely naked..."

Doug's experience with female nakedness came from old medical books tucked away in the attic, in his grandmother's dusty steamer trunks. His mind filled with drawings of women, with red lines marking arteries and organs.

"What did you do then?"

Hector wrung his hands, turned away as he whispered, "Everything."

Whatever "everything" meant, Doug sensed it was something priests weren't supposed to do. Hector glanced over his shoulder, gave Doug a wan smile.

"The next week she left the village without a word to anyone. I was so overwhelmed with guilt, so ashamed of my weakness, I found it almost impossible to conduct services for days. I started drinking, a little bit to get me through the services, a little bit after the services; a little more before I went to bed to dull my dreams. I didn't realize until later that I was pretty drunk most of the time."

"Did anyone else notice?"

"Everyone." Hector rubbed his mouth. "Until finally someone told me they'd called the Bishop—he was on his way. I became so petrified I rode away from the chapel so as not to confront him."

Doug nodded. How many times had he found excuses to stay in his room, when his father was in a bad mood?

"Then I realized I had a tremendous opportunity. All I had to do was confess to the Bishop, take my punishment, then all my inner torment would cease."

"So you rode back here?"

The priest nodded. "I felt so free. It was simple: I would confess and all my sins would be washed away, just as I had been telling my parishioners for those twelve years. I dismounted when I reached the grounds of the chapel and led my horse around back to tie up." Hector shuddered, his voice soft and mysterious. "Once I went inside the rectory and saw what was going on... I knew I was lost."

"But why? Wasn't the Bishop there to hear your confession?" Doug concentrated, trying to picture the Bishop. "Or wouldn't he listen to you?"

"Oh, I'm sure he would have," Hector said. "But I didn't want him to."

"But why not?"

Of all the sad smiles that had passed Hector's face during the telling of the tale, this last was filled with the most pain. He struggled to keep his dignity. Hector reached out as if to put his hand on Doug's shoulder, then pulled it away.

"Well... when I went inside and heard the Bishop speaking softly in the rectory, I thought he might be praying. He wasn't praying, and he wasn't alone. I ran out, jumped on my horse and we started away as fast as we could go. Unfortunately, the horse tripped, I was thrown to the ground and the horse rolled over me." He grimaced, started to buckle, then righted himself.

"That's when you died?"

Hector nodded.

"What of the Bishop?"

"I vaguely remember him giving me last rites."

"But isn't that like confession? I mean, doesn't he ask God to forgive all your earthly sins?"

"That's true, lad."

"Then why are you still here?"

Hector stared through the little stained glass window, high on the wall of the vault. The scene depicted a hand reaching down from heaven toward several people reaching up.

"Dear boy, for your sake I hope you won't encounter this for years, but there is a tunnel, an entrance that leads to the afterlife. All I know is that it is there waiting for me. Beyond it lies judgment for all my sins."

"And you're afraid to go into it? Even if the Bishop did give you the last rites?"

"Yes." Doug started to speak. Hector stopped him. "I am afraid... because I think the Bishop was in no position to forgive anybody's sins."

"But as Bishop, isn't he one of the highest priests in the church?"

Hector nodded.

"Then you should be okay."

"As you go through life, my son, you'll come to learn that some men of high religious position are not necessarily men of true spirituality, or virtue."

Doug frowned. "But if he's the Bishop—"

"I won't go through the tunnel until I'm sure that I've been forgiven. That Bishop wasn't the right person to confess to."

"Why not?"

Hector thought for a moment.

"Well, if you cheated on a test and saw someone else cheating on the same test—from whom would you ask forgiveness, the teacher or the other student you saw cheating?"

"The teacher, I guess."

"When I find that teacher, that's when I'll be able to confess." Hector smiled. "And that's when I'll go through the tunnel."

Doug watched Hector kneel, cross himself. He wanted to ask more questions, especially about the tunnel, but heard a voice calling him from outside the vault. He jumped down and walked over to the door.

The sun was just rising over the treetops. Men walking like zombies were combing the area. He looked around for Hector.

He was gone.

"Doug? Doug MacBrayne, where are you?" The shouts echoed through the early mist.

The vibrations stopped, just as Doug was mulling over Hector's problem, trying to figure out just what test the Bishop had been cheating on. He was suddenly so tired, he could barely push open the heavy vault door. "Over here," he squeaked, then collapsed against the jamb.

❦

Two firemen arrived before Peter did. He elbowed them out of the way and knelt beside his son.

"Doug. Doug."

The boy's eyes opened, mere slits. "Daddy?"

"What happened?"

"Fell asleep. Woke up in there." He pointed to the mausoleum.

"How did you get there?"

Doug shrugged, drowsy. "I guess he carried me."

"He?"

"The priest... the man in the chapel."

"What man?"

The Fire Chief tugged on Peter's sleeve. "Mr. MacBrayne, let us check him over, first." He asked for an oxygen kit. "From the smell of his clothes, at the very least he's suffering from smoke inhalation."

Peter patted Doug's shoulder and stepped out of the way. He looked at the smoldering chapel, measured the distance to the graveyard. He caught Dr. Kautsch doing the same thing, drew him aside.

"You heard what Doug said?" Peter whispered.

Kautsch nodded.

"What do you think?"

"Well, unless he really caught an arsonist in the act, which I doubt, I'd say he's invented the perfect alibi. Even better than Richard Kimball's 'one-armed man' in The Fugitive."

"Alibi?"

"Doug knows he's the only one, other than the firemen, whose clothes smell of smoke, five hours after the fire's out. That looks bad. So, he wants us to believe that the man who started the fire is really a nice guy, underneath, who takes a big chance carrying the only witness to the crime to safety."

Eyes hard, Peter looked at Doug.

"There is one problem with that scenario, Mr. MacBrayne."

"What's that, Kautsch?"

"In the end, Kimball turned out to be innocent."

Peter nodded. "That's television for you."

❦

Fiona returned to the dining room after making sure Doug was asleep. She poured herself a cup of tea. Peter sat at the table, dark circles under his eyes. He acknowledged her greeting with a short nod. He motioned the cook to bring him coffee, cleared his throat.

"Probably should send some coffee out to the firemen."

Fiona nodded. "Where'd they find Doug?"

"He was right in the family vault. Went there to hide after setting the chapel on fire."

"He told you this?"

"Something like that."

She shook her head. She'd take Doug's word over Peter's, even during a lying contest.

Peter took out a business card and pushed it across the table to Fiona. She looked at it. Dr. Leon D. Kautsch. Child Psychiatrist.

"You want Doug in therapy?"

"I do."

"But why?"

He studied his cup for several moments. "If you don't know, perhaps I made a mistake in hiring you."

A sharp red anger surged through Fiona, but she held her tongue, recognizing the implications of the statement.

"No disrespect intended, sir. I—I was only wondering if it's because of last night—"

"To tell you the truth, I understand all about last night. Doug overreacted, but I suppose his response was understandable, given the situation."

"Y-you understand?"

"I do."

"Then why a therapist? Doug was just caught off-guard by your costume."

Peter stared at her, shook his head. "It wasn't the costume."

"No?"

"Think, Fiona. Last night was the first time Doug has seen me with a woman." His voice was confident. "Perfectly natural for him to be so upset. And I'm sure we'll discover that the chapel fire was only another accident. You know how clumsy he is."

Astonished, Fiona stared at Peter. "How clumsy Doug is?"

Peter seemed almost happy. "He said something about falling asleep in the chapel and some man carrying him out during the fire, but Dr. Kautsch agrees that this is probably just a defensive lie."

"And so you think Doug needs a therapist?"

"Well, you have to admit, between his problems in school, his lack of friends, now this display in front of the whole town..."

Fiona bit her lip. He was one slap away from knowing the real reason why his son might need therapy.

"Dr. Kautsch says—"

"You've already talked this over with him?"

"Yes, last night during the search. He has an amazing sensitivity, saw right away how Doug would be jealous of Em, how normal it would be for Doug to go to the chapel. All that insight, and he hadn't even met Doug yet." Peter grinned, looking into his cup as he stirred it. "Can you imagine how much he will be able to do with Doug, once they meet?"

A shudder passed through Fiona when she heard, "...once they meet." She would have resisted, if he hadn't started the conversation with the implied threat. The last thing in the world she wanted was some strange shrink to get inside of Doug's precious head and start rooting around. Especially a psychiatrist Peter liked.

"What...I mean, don't you think you should check his qualifications? At least get a recommendation?"

Peter waved his hand. "Hell, I know a good man when I see one."

Fiona held her tongue. "When are we supposed to meet with the good doctor Freud?"

"Kautsch. Monday afternoon. Two o'clock."

"All right, if we must, but I'll take him."

"And Fiona, but..."

"Yes?"

"No coaching."

The cook walked through the dining room, pushing a cart loaded with a coffee urn for the firemen and the clean-up crew. Fiona rose, placed her napkin on the table, pushed it nearer the plate so Peter wouldn't notice the tight knot she had tied into it.

❦

Grumpy sat in the rear of the Crystal Cafe, hidden from the customers by an ornate screen. Sundays tended to be quiet and Kim, the barista behind the coffee bar, loved being in charge.

His hands roved over his clear crystal ball. He knew better than to try to will the answers to the surface, but wasn't sure he had the patience to wait this time.

Off in a far corner of his mind he could hear Janina chuckling. He sent her a mental "ha, ha" and refocussed on the ball.

A conglomeration of images flowed and swirled within the crystal: Peter in his King of Clubs costume, Abraham Lincoln Avisson, a jester-clad Doug, serf Jimmy, and fair maiden Fiona. Others hovered indistinctly at the periphery: Downey, whom Grumpy had hired years before as a mouse-eared, young accountant; Kautsch, the supposed mind-healer; his buxom, blonde companion; the spinster Stipple.

Next he checked the auras: Peter's estate: brown and stagnant; Douglas Industries: pulsing blue; a gray, monochromatic rainbow had one end in the Foundation headquarters, the other in the Orphanage; the entire town of Douglasville: dim, light-absorbing, instead of shining.

Grumpy looked deeper. There were superficial causes—the effects of a deeper, spiritual malaise. He let the images go abstract, flowing together into lines and swirls of color. When the mass hit its peak revolving speed, Grumpy pulled a mental sword from its scabbard and drove the blade deep into the center of the crystal.

The swirling mass opened He caught a brief picture of a man in black and white, his head bleeding some kind of fire.

Then the crystal cleared. That was all he would see for now. He walked to the counter, leaned on his elbow. Why had he waited so long to try to figure this stuff out?

The noise started as muted singing, then became a chant. Grumpy peered through the front window. People carrying signs. He walked to the door, shook his head. He had wondered how long it would take them to find him.

Christians Against Witchcraft.

Grumpy smiled, called the leader over, a heavyset woman wearing a white dress.

"Would your group like some coffee or tea?"

Her eyes sharpened. "We're here to inform the public, not socialize."

Grumpy shrugged. "It's a free country."

"For the moment," the woman said, turning on her porky heel.

Birthmark

As soon as she walked into the waiting room, Fiona recognized the woman behind the reception desk as the "Slim", Kautsch had introduced to Peter at the Fete. Her name tag said Dorothy Slimson, and although the voluptuous blonde typed with effortless speed, it was also quite apparent that her skills might transcend the secretarial.

Doug headed for the pile of magazines and books on a circular table in the middle of the room, while Fiona walked to the desk.

"You must be Miss McLean," Miss Slimson said, then pointed. "And that must be Doug."

"Peter Douglas MacBrayne IV, for the record."

Slimson jotted it down. "If you'll just fill out this form, the doctor will be with you in a few moments. He's almost finished with another client."

Fiona sat next to Doug and completed the form, while he discarded one magazine after another. She smiled. He was looking for one with more words than pictures. He gave up. Fiona patted his arm, followed his eyes as he smiled at a young woman who sat near the door, filing her nails. In her late twenties, she wore a bright yellow skirt that came to just above her knees. Her pleasant overall appearance contrasted sharply with the permanent sneer, seemingly etched on her prim, prissy face. She glared at Doug. He shrugged.

"What's that?" Doug leaned over Fiona's arm for a better look.

"Just a form for the doctor."

"About me?"

"Yes."

"What do they want to know?"

"Childhood diseases, current conditions. Kind of like a weather report, only it's about you."

Doug found a book and leafed through it.

Fiona had almost finished when the doctor's door burst open. A small, eight-year-old, brown and yellow carbon copy of the waiting mother erupted into the room. Mother got up, quick as a cat, grabbed the squirming little menace by the hand. Seeing Doug, the brat wrenched from her mother's iron grip, ran over to him and slapped the book out of his hands. Making an ugly face, she spat at him.

The nurse stood. "It'll be about ten minutes, Miss McLean." Then she disappeared into the doctor's office, carrying the form Fiona had filled out.

"Godammit, Belle," said mother, "you stop that this minute." To no one in particular she added, "after all this time you'd think we might be getting somewhere... Belle, come here!"

The tiger cub circled the table, just beyond her mother's reach. Nostrils flaring, Belle snarled. Fiona pictured two small horns sprouting from her forehead.

Doug quietly retrieved his book. He sat down and watched them race around the table, an amused expression on his face.

The next time the little fiend shot past, Doug stuck out his foot and tripped her. Quick as a cat, the angry mother leaped, lifted her kicking, screaming cub off the floor. Belle bit her mother hard on the upper arm, breaking the skin.

"Dammit," the mother yelled and slapped Belle square in the mouth. The girl put her finger to her lip and noticed a fleck of blood. As she began to wail, the mother whirled, focusing on Doug.

"You're lucky this is a thick carpet, you little punk." She stroked her daughter's hair. "You might have broken my baby's neck."

Before Fiona could speak, the mother lugged her cub out into the hall, slamming the door. Two pictures shifted on the wall. Fiona got up, straightened them and returned to Doug.

"I wonder how long the doctor's been working with her," Doug said.

"Not long enough—"

"Or too long."

They both giggled and Fiona reached for a magazine. Her worries about the doctor subsided. Between herself and Dougie, they could handle anybody.

Ten minutes later, Miss Slimson came to say the doctor wanted to see Fiona first... alone.

A warm, rosy glow—that had not been there before—radiated from the nurse's face. Looking closer, Fiona noticed faint wrinkles in her previously immaculate uniform. A few stray hairs had escaped from what had been a tight bun.

Fiona turned to Doug, "You'll be all right, dear? I shouldn't be very long."

"Of course, Nanny. Don't worry about me."

As she followed the nurse to the doctor's door she noticed the woman unconsciously rubbing her right buttock.

Dr. Leon D. Kautsch sat in his overstuffed, black leather chair, smoothing wrinkles from his white coat, wiping traces of lipstick from his mouth with a tissue. With a deft, practiced motion, he opened his desk drawer, took out a bottle of pills and popped one, pausing in mid-swallow to welcome Fiona.

"G-good afternoon, Miss McLean. Please sit down." He adjusted his thick, bottle-bottom spectacles and stroked his neatly-trimmed, salt and pepper goatee. "I'm running a bit late, so let's get right down to business."

Fiona offered a respectable thank you and sat in one of two dark brown chairs, opposite the Doctor's heavy desk. A red couch stood by the wall to her left, near the desk and the doctor's chair. She sniffed something vaguely familiar in the air. On the couch, a blanket and a small pillow were in disarray.

The doctor noticed Fiona's glance at the sofa and blushed. His slippery smile made Fiona uncomfortable.

"Mr. MacBrayne gave me some background on young Peter—"

"Doug."

"Oh, yes. Doug." He glanced again at the information sheet. "You obviously spend more time with the boy. What would you say are the challenges—psychologically speaking—he's up against."

"Psychologically speaking," Fiona said, raising an eyebrow. "I don't think Doug is challenged in the least. He is one of the smartest and most well-adjusted children I have encountered in almost forty years as a nanny."

"Yes, of course. Mr. MacBrayne told me you might not want to speak openly about young Peter's...Doug's problems."

Fiona resisted the urge to snap the condescension off his face by twisting the end of his nose. She knotted her fingers around her purse.

Fiona said, "His primary problems, as I see them are that he has the vocabulary of a college graduate and an understanding of what's important in life that far transcends his age."

Again, Kautsch nodded. "His intellectual abilities are not in question here, Miss McLean. The entire town witnessed the boy's traumatic reaction to seeing his father with another woman. It's quite apparent to me that the boy has some issues, problems with his father, including a fear of abandonment. After all, he did lose his mother at birth. It's quite obvious—"

"Excuse me, Dr. Kautsch."

"—that a boy of his age would resent—"

"Dr. Kautsch."

He glanced up. "Yes?"

"Do you want to talk about theories or Doug?"

Again, that slippery smile. "Maybe we should start with you?"

"Me?"

"Yes. I admire your protectiveness of the boy. Mr. MacBrayne told me how you moved right in, took the boy under your wing...perhaps even felt that you could replace his mother." He spread his hands. "It's only natural that a certain co-dependence would occur."

"Co-dependence? What's that?"

"You must not watch TV talk shows."

"I don't."

"Well, co-dependence involves a relationship between two people that is based on their weaknesses, rather than their strengths. Doug is the proverbial motherless child..." Kautsch's gaze intensified. "And you are the proverbial childless nanny."

Fiona leaned over the desk, cutting the distance between then by half.

"I am not the subject here, Doctor."

"But you are part of the scenario. That makes you part of the problem."

"Since you put it that way, Doctor, let's talk about you." She moved closer still.

"That's hardly—"

"No, doctor. You are now part of the scenario, that makes you part of the problem."

"Miss McLean, I don't think—"

"Oh, but I do think, doctor. And I'm an eccentric old Scots woman, which gives me the right to say what's on my mind. And I'll tell you what I think."

Kautsch tried to smile, failed.

"I think, doctor, that you recognized an opportunity regarding Mr. MacBrayne and his son. Everyone knows his wife died during childbirth and that he is raising his son alone. When you saw Doug go flying off the stage away from his father, I think you saw a way in and took it."

Kautsch's face went scarlet. "Miss McLean."

"Hell, call me Fiona, Leon. Let's get cut all this crap, as you Americans say. Yes, I'm protective of Doug. His father is at the office ten to twelve hours a day. He does his best, but his best is only part of what Doug needs."

"That's a pretty strong statement, Fiona."

"Well, I have strong feelings when it comes to Doug. It's true I love the boy. Anyone who spends more than a few days with him loves him, too. And in this case, I believe his father may have done him a gross disservice by enlisting a psychiatrist, based on having shared only a few observations during a charity fete."

"I have fifteen years in practice, to justify my worth to my clients, Fiona."

"I'm sure you do, Leon. But before you get to look inside Doug's head, we'll have to get a few things straight."

He started to rise. "I think, Miss McLean, that—"

"What's the matter, doctor? What happened to Fiona? You get to question other people without answering to your own methods? I think that's unreasonable."

"Unreasonable? I'll have you know—"

"Have me know anything you want. But you must prove yourself to me, before I'll let you get close to inside Doug's head."

"I believe a call to Mr. MacBrayne is in order."

"That's fine. And right after that, let's call the State Licensing Board. Let me ask them if it's professional for a psychologist to be screwing his secretary between clients."

"How dare you!"

"Trust me, Leon, I dare almost anything where Doug's wellbeing is concerned. Hell, if that little Belle is any example of your fifteen years of practice, you've got a long way to go before you get it right. You'll have to show me better than I've seen already, or you'll never get near Doug."

Kautsch stared at her for almost a minute and a half. She sat upright in her chair, looking him straight in the eye. He finally cleared his throat.

"That little girl you met in the waiting room was sexually molested by her grandfather from age two until last year. She didn't speak for nearly a year, at one point. The mother is a society whore, who spreads her legs for any man who drives a Jaguar or other comparable vehicle." His eyes never wavered from Fiona's face. "Miss Slimson is my lover. She's thirty-two years old and the most accomplished assistant I have ever employed. She works six days a week and still finds time to care for her ten year old son. It's true that we occasionally make love between patients—with some of the horror tales I hear in this room, I should drink a fifth of whiskey a day. But I don't."

"Dr. Kautsch—"

"Please. Let me finish." He turned and waved his hand toward a wall, filled with diplomas. "I have spent a decade and a half studying about and then trying to undo the damage close relatives do to children." He swung around to face her. "I am not a perfect man, but I am the best goddamned child psychiatrist for three hundred miles."

"I understand, it's just that—"

"Doug is special to you." He nodded. "And I am a flawed, imperfect human being. But when it comes to children, understanding their problems, seeing the truth of their situation, helping them find their way out of the maze their parents have created for them—I'm the best I've ever met."

Fiona stared at him long and hard. Finally, she stood, extended her hand across the desk. Kautsch hesitated, then took it.

"Dr. Kautsch, I'm Fiona McLean, it nice to meet you, at last." She sat down. "After all, I've heard so much about you."

Kautsch replied with a real smile, followed by genuine laughter. Fiona joined in.

"Fiona, I would appreciate it if you would never repeat anything I just told you."

"If you'll do the same for me."

He shook his head. "I wouldn't have the nerve."

"Would you like to meet Doug now?"

"You raised him, right?"

"That's right."

"How much trouble am I going to have with him?"

"Lots, doctor. I'm a pussycat, compared to him."

Kautsch started to reach for the intercom.

"No fair calling in reinforcements."

Kautsch winked, asked Miss Slimson to send Doug in.

"Oh, and doctor?"

"'Yes?"

"Whatever you do, don't let him talk you into playing Scrabble."

Peter donned a white hardhat and followed the Fire Chief into the burnt shell of the chapel. Three workers from the salvage company were hoisting the charred crucifix. Peter shuddered. The figure on the cross looked like an Egyptian soldier immolated by an Israeli missile, during the Seven-Day War.

"All the evidence points to the fire starting right behind the altar. Curtains there, right?"

Peter nodded.

"Well, near as we can figure, looks like one of these candelabras got knocked over." He shook his head. "All this old wood. Hell, just match-sticks, waiting for a spark. Lucky it didn't go up years ago."

"No sign of anyone...else?"

"Anyone else?" The Chief paused in his note-making.

"My son, Doug, said he saw someone, a man, maybe a priest."

The Chief smiled. "Hell, sir. If I was nine years old and got caught in a church fire, I'd see a lot more than a priest, I can tell you."

Peter's smile was wan. "Do you need me for anything?"

"Want to look over the official report before I turn it in?"

"Do I need to?"

"Well, sir...you've been very kind to the Fire Department over the years. There may be something you don't want your insurance agent to know about... regarding the fire, candles, etc."

"Very considerate, but just file it as you wrote it."

"Thank you, sir."

Peter limped gingerly through the wreckage. He waited until he was halfway to the house before letting the smile play across his face. The chapel, gone. The clinic, next.

"Pretty soon you won't have anyplace left, Grandma Sarah," he said under his breath.

He made a bee-line for his car. The hell with insurance and fund-raisers. He deserved a round of golf.

He punched in the number of the pro shop as he drove past Captain Hook and the croc. "Peter MacBrayne here. I need a tee-time as soon as possible."

"Fine sir," the voice said. "Unfortunately, your regular caddie is at the dentist."

"Doesn't matter. Anybody'll do."

"Well, I hate to say this, but all we have is a new boy. If you could wait an hour or so—"

"No, that's fine. I'll be glad to show him the ropes." Peter grinned, hadn't felt this happy for a long time. "And tell Sandy I want my Old Tom Morris putter out of the display-case in the pro shop."

A gasp. "You're going to play with that?"

"Why not?"

"It's worth a fortune. Aren't you worried—"

"A great golf club is like a beautiful woman: neither are any good behind glass."

"Yes, sir. I'll have it waiting for you."

Peter whistled as he drove. If this was any indication of what it felt like to be fifty, he couldn't wait for the rest of the decade.

🌿

Doug watched Kautsch jot a few notes, then look up.

"Well, young man, you've had quite a time."

"Yes, sir."

"Do you have any questions about what we're going to do here?"

"You're going to ask me questions, and depending on how I answer, you decide if I'm crazy."

Kautsch began to object, then realized he was being baited. "Miss McLean warned me about you."

"Nanny wouldn't say anything bad about me."

Kautsch nodded. "It wasn't bad. It was good stuff. Most kids aren't as smart as you. How do you feel about that?"

Doug shrugged. "Not much I can do about it."

"So, you don't mind being smarter?"

Doug saw where Kautsch was headed. "Everybody's smart in their own way. Nanny says there's book-smart and life-smart—and all kinds of smart in between."

"Your nanny's pretty smart, herself, isn't she?"

"Sure."

"And she loves you a lot."

Doug nodded.

"Maybe more than your father does?"

"No." He thought about it, closed one eye, watching Kautsch with the other. "Different."

"Different in what way?"

Doug smiled. He could see how this was going to go. Kautsch smiled too, put his pen down.

"See how it works?"

"Kinda like peeling an onion." Doug jabbed his finger into his chest. "Except I'm the onion."

"That's right, but every time you peel off another layer, you get to see more of yourself. Get to know more about yourself."

"And so do you."

Kautsch tapped his pad with his pen. "Does that bother you…my getting to know more about you?"

Another shrug. "I don't know you."

"Well, I'm doing this because your father asked me to," Kautsch said. "Your father wouldn't do anything to hurt you, would he?"

Doug was stopped. The answer required the right words. "Not on purpose."

Kautsch smiled. "And Nanny? Would she do anything to hurt you?"

"Never." It blurted out.

"So, she does love you better."

Doug shook his head. "She knows me better, spends more time with me. Dad has the company to run."

Kautsch smiled in appreciation. "A very exact answer. Good. I like exact answers." He leaned forward, his tone shifted. "So, why don't you tell me exactly what happened the night of the Fete?"

"Everything?"

"As you remember it."

Doug looked Kautsch straight in the eye. "This is the real test, isn't it?"

"Test?"

"All that stuff before, about Nanny and Dad, that was just a quiz... but this is the test."

Doug was about to tell him everything: seeing Father Hector, falling asleep against the altar, waking up in the mausoleum, but the vibrations started. Softly at first, then building, but for some reason not reaching the usual intensity.

"I was scared, see. Dad's costume, it didn't look like him. Anyhow, I ran and hid in the chapel. And I don't know, when I leaned against the altar, I might have bumped one of the candelabras accidentally, you know?"

Kautsch nodded, scribbling away.

"So I ran away. I'd screwed up real bad. Heck, this was Grandma Sarah's chapel."

"Is that why you went to the mausoleum?" Doug looked at Kautsch. The doctor raised his eyebrows. "To apologize to your Great-grandmother for burning down her chapel?"

Doug grinned. "Gosh, you are good."

Kautsch nodded. "That's why I get the big bucks."

They both laughed, slapped their knees. This wasn't going to be so bad. Heck, a piece of cake.

"Okay, Doug. Now that we know you're smart and I'm good, let's figure out how we can make your life at home a little easier." Kautsch leaned forward in his chair, his hands laced atop his head. "This week, try to find out what your dad wants more than anything else in the world. Then you think of something you want more than anything else in the world—and we'll see if we can find a way to accommodate both of you."

"You mean, I can ask for anything I want?"

"Within reason, yes."

"And you think Dad'll let me have it?"

"Maybe. But that's something we'll talk about at next week's session. It's called 'give-and-take.'"

No matter what color the paint, orphanages still exude a sense of loss, of incompleteness. Grumpy sat on a faded, salmon-colored sofa while the receptionist called the Matron.

Sarah had been both wrong and right to fund the place. Right, because lost children need a place to be found, or at least to find themselves. And wrong, because a building alone can never be a home. And, as long as the building existed, some people who might have taken a child into their own home, wouldn't.

He got up as the matron approached. A bowling ball with arms and legs, she rolled more than walked.

"How can I help you, Mr. Petrovich?"

"I met one of your children, and was impressed with the lad. Thought I'd see if I could help."

"All donations to the orphanage are tax-deductible."

"I was thinking more of personal and direct help."

"Such as?"

"You tell me."

Her eyes x-rayed Grumpy. Nothing even remotely resembling a smile crossed her face.

"We don't encourage personal relationships with people outside the orphanage."

"I would think it would help the children feel part of the community."

"You would think…" She folded her arms. "But the truth is that orphans are like puppies. People like to bring them home for Christmas, then take them back to the Pound after Easter."

Grumpy winced. "Has that ever happened to Jimmy Lyden?"

"So that's who you met?" She sputtered. "Incorrigible boy. Nothing but trouble."

"He was a great help to me at the Fete. I think he's very talented."

The x-rays increased in Roentgens. "Where are you from, Mr. Petrovich?"

"I've just finished ten years traveling around the world. Been in Douglasville a few months. I own a bookstore here."

"And you thought I'd just turn over one of our children to you because you asked? Because you have a bookstore, and maybe a little house, and now you'd like a kid to play with, too? Does that complete the picture?" She put her face right next to Grumpy's. "Where's Mrs. Petrovich?"

Grumpy held his composure, smiled sadly. "She's dead."

The Matron blinked, stepped away. "Oh."

"And I don't expect you to turn Jimmy over to me." He pulled out a Crystal Cafe business card. "I'd like to help. Pure and simple.

It's obvious he's got tremendous talent. I'd like to make sure that talent has the opportunity to blossom."

She held the card as if peering through the twin microscopes of her eyeglasses, searching for contagious protozoa.

"I hardly think Sarah Douglas intended us to shelter young minds, only to expose them to the likes of you and your establishment."

Grumpy nodded, pulled out a small pad of paper. "Could you tell me your name, please?"

"Stella Groebnick. Why?"

"Mr. Peter Douglas-MacBrayne, Junior, is the principle investor in my store. He is currently on a purchasing tour in Europe, to identify new inventory for our Autumn season." Grumpy snapped the pad shut. "I'm sure he'd like to know that the people running the orphanage his mother started—the one he has supported all these years—hold his spiritual views in total disrespect."

"I had no idea..." the bowling ball deflated.

"Ms. Groebnick, I am not your enemy. Nor am I a pervert interested in a young boy." He pulled out his handkerchief and cleaned his glasses. "It would seem that the world has already hurt Jimmy enough."

She nodded, a tinge of red returned to her cheeks. She realized there was no real threat to her position.

"You really like working with the children, don't you?"

Her eyes softened as if he had divulged a secret no one else knew. Grumpy smiled.

"It's hard, having to discipline children who don't understand that what you're asking of them is no different than what their parents would have, isn't it?"

Behind her misty eyes, Grumpy saw the broken dreams of a slender little girl, who matured plain and round. A romantic heart surrounded by steel ribs. It hurt him to see it.

"I will help you with all of the children, Miss Groebnick," he said in the soft voice of a lover, "if you will help me with Jimmy."

He reached across and took her hand, not in a shake, but more as a friend.

"Is Jimmy here?"

"No... he just started a new job."

"Good for him. Where?"

She glanced at the clock on the wall behind Grumpy. "Oh, gosh. I have to pick him up in an hour, but the other children—"

"Where is he working? I'd be glad to pick him up."

"Are you sure?"

"Positive."

"Do you know where the Country Club is?"

"I know it quite well."

"That's where you'll find him. He's learning how to become a caddie."

❦

Thwack!

Jimmy craned his neck to follow the flight of the ball. A pigeon flew into his line of sight and his eyes automatically tracked the bird.

"Did you see where it went?"

"Think so," Jimmy said, "though a pigeon blocked my view at the last second."

"Don't worry, it faded to the right."

Jimmy heard the unspoken, 'I was watching, even if you weren't' that lurked beneath the man's false empathy. Jesus Christ, of all the golfers that could have showed up for Jimmy's first day. Why does the MacBrayne family have to stick another snotty nose into his business?

And the old man was as big a know-it-all as his kid:

First hole: "The bag isn't so heavy if you hold it like this."

Third hole: "Please don't make noise while I'm getting ready to hit."

Seventh: "When we're on the green, don't walk between the ball and the cup; your footprints might interfere with the roll of the ball."

Ninth: "Don't pick a ball up to identify it, even in the deep rough. Let your player do it."

Eleventh: "Stand still and be quiet, when I'm addressing the ball."

Sixteen: "Keep up, caddie. You're always supposed to get to the ball before your player."

The weight of MacBrayne's huge bag of clubs was beginning to take its toll. Jimmy walked faster, trying desperately to close a gap of about twenty-five yards. He took it all in sullen silence. The guy was just a jerk, wouldn't let up. Of course, watching the father in action explained a lot about Doug. Between having a funny-talking nanny and this bowtied Bozo for role-models, the kid would never grow up to be anything.

For the first time in his memory, Jimmy was glad he lived at the orphanage. Old Matron "Grab-your-knickers" left him alone most of the time, and the other kids fought their own battles. Any time the other "inmates" tried messing with him, he just whipped out his pen and publicly humiliated them. He'd lost a few fist fights, but never a draw...

They finally arrived at the eighteenth.

"Now this eighteenth hole is the toughest par on the course," MacBrayne said, teeing up his ball. "I've never come close to a birdie here. For some reason, I usually struggle just to make a bogey."

Jimmy went through the mental file card he had drawn when the caddie-master had explained: A bogey was an evil gangster laughing at the missed shot, tossing one ball in the air; double-bogey—two balls; a triple—three. Par on a hole was Mama Bear stirring her soup pot, with the proper number of balls—white potatoes—floating on top. She had a cartoon balloon over her head, "Par is printed on the scorecard." Jimmy had been told that very few members would score better than par on any given hole, but he had drawn his mental cards, just in case: A birdie was a blue heron, sitting on her nest, with one under her. An eagle landing with a club in each claw, signified two under par. An eagle with two heads: a double eagle—three under. Finally, a hole-in-one was a pure white playing card, with golden letters "ACE" at the center.

Thwack.

There is something universally awe-inspiring about a perfect drive: The ball arrows into the sky, a long, white blur that falls and rolls forward in the middle of the velvet green fairway.

Jimmy followed its flight, no pigeons this time. Peter watched, driver in hand, his mouth open.

"Gawd, that felt good."

"Looked good, too." Jimmy held out his hand for the club. MacBrayne stared at him, still dazed.

"I've finally got my chance to get a birdie on this hole." He let Jimmy take the driver. "It's like breaking a wild horse, once you tame a hole, it's yours forever."

As they walked down the middle, Jimmy felt himself willing another good shot. There was something cool about being part of MacBrayne's defeating this final hole. In his head, Jimmy could see the way he would paint it. The fairway and trees far below; MacBrayne driving; a second MacBrayne hitting off the fairway; The last MacBrayne on the green, finally using that wacky old putter, he said he bought in Scotland; and in the foreground, the blue heron fluttering her applause.

"Five wood," MacBrayne said, reaching out his hand. Jimmy gave it to him. "And not a sound."

Jimmy swallowed his lips, crossed his fingers. Made sure every part of him was still. He'd never seen an adult so scared, so excited.

MacBrayne squared his feet to the ball, turned and looked at the pin. A lake protected the green on two sides. A kidney-shaped sand trap guarded the front. The clubhouse looked down on the green and up the fairway, toward the tee, behind them. He looked at the ball. The pin. Jimmy rolled his eyes. Just do it, he urged silently.

The club came away from the ball, then up, glinted in the sun, then became a blur.

Whoosh. Thwack.

Both pairs of eyes lifted, followed, dropped. MacBrayne turned to Jimmy.

"Holy cow."

Jimmy pointed. The ball stopped ten feet from the pin. MacBrayne nodded, exchanged the five wood for the ancient putter, which he caressed as they marched to the green.

"This club was handmade and used by Old Tom Morris, a famous Scottish pro and club-maker. He won the British Open with it, several times, I think. Don't even ask what it's worth."

Jimmy shrugged. What the hell was the British Open?

They climbed the hill to the green. MacBrayne pointed to the flag.

"You tend the pin. I'll need it in the cup to help me line up, but be sure to pull it out as soon as I hit the ball."

"Why can't I do it now and hold the pin to one side?"

MacBrayne shook his head. "I told you I need it in. When the ball is a yard or two on its way, pull it out."

"Okay."

MacBrayne leaned over, measured the putt, took several practice swipes. His arms moved backward, gently forward.

They watched the ball as it rolled precisely on line, heading for the hole. Jimmy tugged the pin. It was stuck. He pulled harder but still no give. Finally he gave a mighty heave with both hands, but succeeded only in lifting the metal cup an inch above the ground, out of the hole.

The ball hit the side of the cylinder, smack in the middle and bounced away.

MacBrayne's Adam's-Apple bowtie danced furiously. Eyes wider than egg yolks, he walked over, snatched the flag-stick from Jimmy, twisted it free and repeatedly jabbed and jammed the cup, until it was back in place.

"Hold this, goddamn it."

Jimmy took the flag-stick, held it the way he had wanted to in the first place. Apoplectic, MacBrayne walked to his ball, gave it a cursory glance, tapped it at the hole.

It missed.

"A bogey." He said, stunned. "I have the best drive and approach shot in my life and score a bogey." He looked at his putter, then at Jimmy. "And you, because you couldn't get the pin out of the cup—" He raised the club. "—you just sabotaged the most important shot of my golfing life."

Sensing what was coming, Jimmy dropped to the ground, using the over-sized bag as a shield. He heard the whoosh and felt the breeze from the putter as it whirled past where his head had been a split-second before, then sailed on into the lake.

❦

Same clothes. Same office. Same person—even with a beard. But Avisson felt as if he'd been strait-jacketed, no longer investigating the paranormal. He was now supposed to correct the abnormal. He leafed through the file. Not a lot here, except of course Kautsch's handwritten note, paper-clipped to the folder: "Straight counseling. No weird stuff."

Avisson punched the intercom button. "Margaret, when Mr. Sharpe arrives, please send him right in."

"He's here now."

Avisson smiled. Rescuing Margaret from the secretarial pool had been a small triumph, but a victory, nonetheless.

The door opened and Clint Sharpe entered. As soon as he saw the shade of his new client's skin, Avisson began chuckling, fought to keep from outright laughter.

"Something funny?"

"No." Avisson couldn't quite stop. "It has to do with our new director. I was pretty sure he was a jerk. Now I know it."

Another chuckle escaped and Sharpe wheeled as if to leave. Avisson came around his desk, reached to take the man's arm, thought better of it.

"Please. I'm sorry. Let me explain."

Sharpe turned. "Why?"

"Maybe you'll find it funny, too."

He thought about it. "And if I don't?"

"Then you can work with somebody else."

Sharpe nodded, folded his arms.

"Thank you." Avisson pointed to his own face. "Who do I look like to you?"

Sharpe rolled his eyes. "A shrink with a beard."

"Any historical figure?"

"Kind of...what's the point?"

Avisson smiled. "When the new director gave me this assignment, he said I was perfect for you. Now I know why."

"Jesus, he is an idiot." Sharpe seemed to trying hard not to smile, but the irony snagged him. He reached out his hand. "Mr. Lincoln, Clint Sharpe."

"How do you do, Mr. Sharpe... Abraham Avisson." He shook his hand, asked Sharpe to take a seat. "Now that we've established that I work for an idiot, why don't you tell me why you drink, even during school hours?"

Sharpe shook his head. "God, that's smooth. No foreplay, no kissing up. Just 'Wham, bam, Freud's your man.'"

Avisson kept his expression neutral. "Does it have anything to do with being the only black instructor at your school?"

"Definitely not."

Avisson smiled. "Then why?"

Sharpe dropped his head, spoke through his knees to his shoes. "God, I thought I'd be ready for this."

"Take your time. There's no hurry."

"No, you don't understand." Sharpe's eyes closed. "I know exactly why I drink. I just can't tell you yet."

"Why not?"

Sharpe's face was full of silent pleading. "Because I don't know you well enough."

"For what?"

The answer was a whisper.

"I'm sorry, I didn't hear."

"Because I don't know you well enough to cry in front of you."

※

Grumpy took it all in from the clubhouse terrace. There was Peter, sure enough, and Jimmy, wrapped in a towel, watching the greenskeepers drain the lake.

Grumpy shook his head. The grinning clerk in the pro shop hadn't been kidding, after all.

The sight of Peter and Jimmy together was a small shock. Of course, he hadn't seen his son in ten years except costumed as the

King of Clubs at the Fete. Time had thickened Peter's slender body into a bulky, middle-age frame. The typical CEO.

Would Peter recognize his father? Grumpy doubted it. Not so much the beard, but his own body and spirit had changed radically over the decade. A dissolute corporate executive, Grumpy had long lived off the fat of his father and mother's efforts. Rotund, bleary-eyed, a consumer of everything within reach.

His adventurous travel had taken all that out of him. He now weighed one-hundred-sixty pounds, about fifty pounds less than when he left Douglasville.

Grumpy's disguise was time and the beard, plus the fact that he was indeed a different man than the one who had left. He walked down to where they stood by the edge of the lake, without removing his sunglasses.

"Problems, eh?" Grumpy affected some of Valka's accent. "What you lose, solid-gold ball?"

"No, a valuable club." Peter snapped his fingers at Jimmy. "You ready to go back in?"

Jimmy looked at Grumpy, who winked.

"Sorry, I am here to collect boy. He need to go home."

"But what about my club?"

"The lake will be drained soon. You'll find it, yourself."

Peter glared, Grumpy smiled. "Come boy."

Jimmy ran to his side. Grumpy put his arm around his shoulder. "Did you get paid? What about tip?"

Jimmy shook his head. Grumpy looked at Peter.

"He gets his money from the caddie-master."

"But don't you want to give boy tip for diving after valuable club?"

"What? After he made me lose it?" Peter turned, started to limp away.

"The boy lost club?" Grumpy turned to Jimmy. "How you lose man's club?"

"I ducked when he chucked it at me."

"Hey, mister," Grumpy shouted. "You threw club at this boy?"

Peter ignored him.

"I'm talking to you. Who do you think you are?"

Peter stopped as if hit in the head. He turned, face purple, stalked toward Grumpy.

"I am President of this golf club, and my name is Peter Douglas-MacBrayne, the third, if you must know."

Grumpy snorted. "You behave like this? Your father and grandfather must be ashamed you carry their name."

With that, Grumpy and Jimmy walked away, Peter's invectives sailing past them. Jimmy tried to speak several times, but stopped.

"What's on your mind, Jimmy?"

"I hope I didn't cause you any trouble."

"What trouble could you cause me?"

"Well, he's the most powerful man in town. He could screw up your business."

Grumpy laughed. "He can't screw up my business and he's not the most powerful man in town."

"He's got the most money."

"Maybe," Grumpy said. "But I'm the only Gypsy in town."

"You're not scared of him?"

"Not in the least."

"Then neither am I."

"Good boy." Grumpy opened the car door. "Sorry I messed up your tip."

"That's okay, I don't think I would have made a very good caddie anyhow."

"Well, what would you think about working in a bookstore?"

"Don't know."

"Well, think about it. The job is yours if you want it."

"Do I have to read them? The books?"

"No, just stack them and help Kim with the coffee bar."

"That could be fun."

Grumpy ruffled the boy's hair. "With you around, it will be great fun."

Jimmy pulled his comb from his pocket, made a face as if to say, Please, don't do that.

Dr. Kautsch led Doug to the door.

"Miss Slimson, please make another appointment for Doug." He nodded to Fiona. "Is four o'clock next Monday okay?"

"That'll be fine, Doctor."

"Good." He shook Doug's hand. "It's a pleasure meeting you, Doug. We'll start in earnest next week. Monday, Wednesday and Fridays."

"Thank you, Dr. Kautsch."

After Fiona and Doug left, he turned to his assistant.

"Any more appointments, this afternoon?" asked Kautsch.

"No. That's the last for the day."

"Good. Lock the front door."

"Leon, I don't have time for another go. I've got to pick up Kit in twenty minutes."

"It isn't what you think, Slim. This is going to be a tricky case. I've got to talk to the father tomorrow."

"About what? The boy seems all right to me."

"My guess is he is. That's the problem."

Slim stood with a hand on her hip, waiting. "Okay, what's on your sneaky little mind."

"Well, the richest man in town comes to us, seeking help for a son who really doesn't need it." Kautsch took two steps, raised his finger in the air. "Now, if we tell him that there's nothing wrong with his son—"

"Which there isn't."

"As far as we can tell. But consider the family history. Granny Douglas was a crackpot. Used a crystal ball to predict the stock market, where she did very well. Then took some of the money to set up her foundation to do paranormal research."

"Sixteen minutes." She held up her wrist to show her watch. "I can't be late."

"Listen, once we finish converting the Center from spooks to wackos..." He smiled. "Our patron, Mr. Douglas-MacBrayne, won't need us anymore. Probably cut all ties with us."

"Ten minutes."

"Unless the kid—"

"Unless the kid has problems—though he doesn't—and we help cure him... over a very long period of time."

"See how smart you are?"

"What about Miss McLean? She could be trouble."

"Hell, she's big trouble. But we reached an understanding."

"Oh, and what was that?"

"As long as I appear to be sincere and don't threaten her relationship with the boy—"

"But I thought MacBrayne said he wanted to—"

"He does," Kautsch took her by the shoulders, "but that's where you and I come in."

"How so?"

"The more he learns he can trust us, confide in us—"

Slim smiled. "The sooner MacBrayne will send Nanny packing."

Chapter Six

Why was Aunt Agatha kissing him? He tried to push her away, but couldn't find her in the darkness. He wanted to pull the covers over himself, but there weren't any. He was not in bed.

Phineas woke fully, lifted himself to a sitting position. A sharp pain pierced the back of his head. He rubbed his birthmark, pulled his fingers away. Blood.

The puppy that had been licking him jumped into his lap. He stroked the dog, looked around dully. Had he passed out? Hit his head? To his left, the bitch moaned. Ah, he'd returned the pup, turned to see the split-bearded man. The villain must have hit him with whatever he'd been hiding behind him.

Phineas reached into his pocket for his rag, realized the rest of the truth. He'd been robbed. Damn, should have given the money to Mrs. Grimsby when he had the chance. Now it was gone. Tomorrow he'd be in the street. He stroked the puppy's head.

The puppy licked his bloody hand. Phineas was pathetic enough for begging but people wouldn't put money in a bloody palm. Even begging had its protocol. So he looked around for something to clean it, found a crumpled up piece of paper. He opened it, spit into his hand. As he started to wipe, he saw the words:

> MALE SCRIVENER
> To Assist Blind Poet.
> Respond in person to:
> J. Milton, Artillery Walk,
> Burnside Fields

Phineas' heart pounded. J. Milton, blind poet? It could only be the great man himself. He looked down at the puppy. If he hadn't tripped...even the blow to his head...could something good come out of such an awful event?

As Phineas turned to limp out of the alley, he heard a small yip and turned to see the puppy right on his heels.

"No, pup. You have to stay here with your mum." He bent to scoot the dog over. "Tell you what. If I get the job, I'll come back for you."

He stood shakily, leaned against the wall to rearrange his clothing. Who would believe that such a disheveled beggar was a Cambridge graduate. Thank heaven Milton was blind.

Phineas stumbled up the steps to Milton's door and knocked. It was opened by a tall, black Nubian with a brilliant smile, which vanished when he noticed Phineas' condition. Without a word, the manservant took him by the arm, ushered him into the pantry, then dipped a cloth into a bowl of water and gently wiped the blood from the back of his head. Smiling, he handed Phineas another cloth to clean his hands and face.

"Thank you, my kind friend," Phineas said. "Will you please take me to Mr. Milton?"

"You business with Master?"

Phineas reached into his pocket, pulled out the crinkled announcement.

"I'm here to apply as Mr. Milton's scrivener."

"Terrible sorry, sir." The Nubian frowned. "Job filled."

All that had been holding Phineas together was the hope of securing this position. He slumped. The servant quickly poured a goblet of wine and put it before him. Phineas drank slowly. All was lost. No job, no money, no room.

"He didn't hit me hard enough." Phineas muttered.

"Pardon, sir?"

"The man who clubbed me. If he'd hit me harder, I might be dead. I am anyway."

"No, sir—"

"Grutto! Grutto." A voice called from another room.

The servant nodded, motioned Phineas to stay and hurried out. He returned several minutes later with a smile.

"You luck today, sah."

"Luck?" Phineas sat up. "What do you mean?"

"Man he hire no show up. Now look for new man." A huge hand clapped Phineas on the shoulder. "You want talk him?"

"Yes. God, yes."

"Good. He in study." He pointed through the door. "Dis way."

Phineas started out, stopped. "Your name is Grutto?"

"Yah, sir."

"Phineas Davies." He reached out and shook the Nubian's hand. "May I ask you a question?"

Grutto nodded.

"Why did you help me? If Mr. Milton had already finished interviewing applicants..."

Grutto smiled. "In my country, sah, when man hurt, we help."

Phineas shook his head. "And they call England civilized."

The study was nearly as dark as the alley had been. For a moment Phineas was afraid to enter. A gray shaft of light filtered through a gap in the heavy purple curtains hung in front of the window, on the far side of the room. There was the man himself, sitting between two busts. Phineas recognized Cromwell; the other appeared to be Aristotle. To Milton's right was a small table with a stack of paper, a quill pen and an ink pot. A coal fire glowed red in an ancient, wide-hooded Tudor fireplace.

As Phineas entered the room, he gazed at the books that lined the walls. Over Milton's left shoulder hung a small, gilt oval frame with three miniature portraits—vignettes—of three young, solemn-faced girls staring stiffly straight ahead. Daughters?

Phineas approached fearfully, spine tingling as he encountered the enormous energy emanating from Milton's presence. Hunched in his heavy chair, the writer's sightless eyes stared straight ahead. His aquiline, hooked nose contrasted with the rest of his nearly feminine features. Thick bags of puffy flesh hung below the eyes, joining the shadows in the room to give the impression that the man's vision was lost deep within two endless caves.

"Pray, who is there?" Milton called out.

"Phineas Davies, sire." Phineas gulped. "I have come to see...if you will hire me...I need a job, desperately...."

"You may need a job, but what makes you think I need you?"

"I found your announcement."

"And you're just now applying for the position? It was filled a week ago."

"Grutto told me..."

"Grutto? How do you know my servant's name?"

"I asked him, sire. He told me." Fear and pain caused Phineas to take several deep breaths. "He...he also said you needed someone because...the last one..."

"Why are you out of breath? A young man your age?"

"I found your notice crumpled up in an alley and ran the entire way."

"Come closer, then."

Phineas hobbled over.

"Is there something wrong with you? Why do you walk so haltingly?"

"I was born with a twisted spine."

Milton ran slender fingers through his graying, shoulder-length auburn hair. Now he seemed to be struggling to speak.

"Understand, Mr.—"

"Davies."

"Mr. Davies. I, as well as anybody, am aware of the prejudice against one's infirmities." His finger brushed his eyes, returned to his lap. "But I have a terrible intolerance for tardiness. I wouldn't want even to interview you, unless I could be certain you would be on the job promptly every day."

"Oh, sire." Phineas gulped. "You have been my idol since long before I graduated from Cambridge. I—"

"Cambridge?" Milton's face relaxed. "I, too, attended Cambridge. But your accent is too mellifluous to be from London."

"I hail from the village of Cmfwp, near Ludlow Castle..."

"My God, man. That was where they staged my masque, 'Comus.'"

"I know. I saw it."

"But that was thirty years ago, nearly to the day. How old are you, Mr. Davies?"

"I was only six at the time. But I remember it well. My Aunt Agatha took me."

"Impossible." Milton shifted in his chair. "My 'Comus' was played in honor of the Earl of Bridgewater during his inauguration as Lord President of Wales. Only the family, friends and the estate staff were in attendance."

Phineas nodded, then remembered Milton couldn't see his gesture.

"True, sire. But my Aunt Agatha's brother was head gardener. He arranged to sneak us in. From that very day, you became my idol." He lowered his voice. "And I decided to become a writer."

"Have you become one?"

It was an awful question, with an even worse answer. Phineas was glad the poet was blind so he wouldn't be able to see the shabby clothes, the straggly hair—the failure, who sat before him.

"Do you consider yourself a writer, young man?"

"Mister Milton, there is no man alive who loves words as much as myself." Phineas wrung his hands, wishing he could flee his idol's presence, rather than make the galling admission. "But, as a youth, when I developed that ambition, I didn't realize that becoming a writer involved so much more than the simple and joyous love of words."

Milton nodded. "There is nothing more difficult than telling a hard truth about oneself."

The poet shifted in the chair and slowly but unerringly put his right foot on a tattered, velvet-covered hassock.

"My gout bothers me once in a while, my boy. I have a second unfortunate affliction, myself...And have you read my 'Comus' since you saw it as a child?"

"Several times."

"Good. And would you agree then that the central theme involves chastity?" Milton pointed a slim finger in Phineas' direction. A sly, crooked smiled crept across his face as he waited for the answer.

Another misery. Phineas shook his head. "Forgive me, but I think not."

Alert, Milton's foot jolted, then relaxed on the hassock. "Well, then, what exactly do you think the theme was?"

"I...to me...the theme concerns individual freedom."

The crafty smile slowly resolved into a congenial grin. "Go on."

"Well, I learned from 'Comus' that there are consequences, especially personal responsibilities, which necessarily accompany free choice. I learned that the illusory temptations of vice, often appear insidiously more attractive, than if one were to remain virtuous."

"Ah, virtue!" Milton clapped his delicate hands together. "The ultimate goal of every government. Wouldn't you agree?"

Phineas grinned, saw the trap yawn open. "But you, yourself, wrote that self-discipline could never be imposed by the State. How can an individual ever hope to cultivate his own virtues if the government constantly imposes them on him? It is a common thread throughout much of your work."

"So it is, my boy." Milton leaned forward. "But you worry me."

Phineas looked up quickly. "I do?"

"Yes. I can see that if I hire you as my scrivener, I shall always have to be on the alert with your hovering over my ideas so closely."

"I mean no disrespect." Phineas cast about, desperately trying to find the words to save the situation. He had not anticipated that his admiration of Milton's work would endanger his chances at working with the man.

"Sire, most intelligent people in Britain consider you a great poet. I agree. But, if you will forgive me, I think of you as an even greater political writer."

"You do, Mr. Davies?" Milton's smile broadened, nearly cut his fragile features in half. "And just how did you arrive at this astonishing conclusion?"

"It started with some of the principles in 'Comus,' but really came home to roost in your 'Areopagitica.'"

"You read that, too?"

"Aye, and I can't think of any more apt statement to Parliament than when you said, 'The State shall be my governors, but not my critics.'"

Milton nodded. "Some misunderstood the meaning."

Phineas laughed. "I have no doubt of that. But you also wrote something that I think applies to your concerns about hiring me as your scrivener."

"I did?"

"Yes. Later in the same piece, you wrote: 'Where there is much desire to learn, there of necessity will be much arguing, much writing, and many opinions: for opinion in good men is but knowledge in the making.'"

The poet was quiet. Phineas sat on the edge of his seat, unable to read the decision forming in the other man's mind. Finally, Milton shifted in his chair and spoke.

"Mr. Davies...I firmly believe good poetry serves to tame the wild beast in mankind...And I have had plenty of opportunities to witness man's inhumanity to man, especially in recent years." He paused, sat more erect. "Accordingly, several years ago, I decided to begin an epic poem—the one I have been preparing to write, for my entire life."

Phineas, in the presence of a god preparing to outline his plans for a new Eden, remained quiet, unwilling to interrupt.

"I have decided to return my attention from the subject of national freedom, to individual freedom; to try to explain the ways of God to mankind. I have now given this interview careful thought. When the previous scrivener did not arrive today, I must admit I was in a foul humor, because I want nothing to interrupt this work." He smiled. "For a moment I was afraid I was going to be forced to have one of my children accomplish the transcription."

"Wouldn't that have been easier for you?"

"Bah, if I had sired a son, perhaps. But I have been cursed with daughters only—three of them—each as useless as the next, when it comes to the world of ideas." He grinned, leaned in Phineas' direction. "However, between my having had only daughters and the fact that my previous scrivener couldn't wake on time, Providence appears to be on both our sides in this endeavor."

"Sire?"

"I would like to ask you if you would be interested in helping me complete my epic?"

"There is nothing I would like more."

Milton held up his hand. "Your qualifications are excellent, but there is one thing that remains to be seen."

"What is that?"

"Relax, my boy. We need only to check your handwriting." He pointed to the table. "I will dictate. You will transcribe. My wife will check the quality of your penmanship."

Relieved, but afraid his nerves might ruin his script, Phineas went to the table, sat down and carefully dipped the pen into the ink.

"Ready when you are, Sire."

"Let me think..." Milton paused, cleared his throat and began. "Better to reign in hell than serve in Heaven..." He waited as Phineas wrote. "Are you finished?"

"Yes."

"Elizabeth! Will you come here, please?"

"Coming." A woman entered, nodded to Phineas and put her hand on Milton's shoulder. "What can I do for you, dear?"

"I want you to examine this young man's penmanship. Is it adequately legible?"

Milton's wife examined Phineas' work. "It is both legible and well-turned. Far better than the last."

"Thank you, Mrs. Milton." Phineas looked up gratefully.

She frowned, disappeared as quickly as she had arrived.

"Now, my lad," Milton said. "I would like to employ you on a trial basis. When can you—"

"Immediately, sire, if you wish."

Milton laughed. "Tomorrow will be soon enough. Could you be here by eight o'clock?

"Yes, without fail. And thank you. Words cannot express my gratitude."

"Good work will be sufficient—and promptness."

Phineas rose to leave.

"Mr. Davies, would you do me the favor of obtaining several quills, some ink and paper. I have a dread fear of stopping work for lack of preparedness."

"I would be happy to, but..."

"Yes?"

"It's embarrassing, but I was robbed on the way here..."

"My God! What on earth...?"

"A brute of a man, with a split beard, clubbed me from behind in an alley. He took my purse."

"We live in such ugly times, Mr. Davies." Milton shook his head, opened a small box, on the table next to him. "I'm sorry about your misfortune."

"On the contrary, sire. It was good fortune. When I awoke, I found your small poster, right beside me. I never would have seen it had he not attacked me."

"Here, young man, take this crown as your stipend for a week in advance."

When Phineas reached for the coin, Milton took his hand. "Perhaps we shall indeed make something good out of our misfortunes—you with your twisted spine and I with my useless eyes."

"Have you a title for your work, sire?"

"I do indeed." The sly smile returned. "It's to be called, 'Paradise Lost.'"

Phineas clutched the small packages—one of sausage, cheese and bread, the other filled with the writing materials. As he hurried across the uneven cobblestones, he could not help but smile at everyone he encountered. He saved part of his grin for Mrs. Grimsby. Although he couldn't blame her mistrust, he would enjoy handing her the rent and disabusing her of the notion that he was a beggar.

The week's pay in advance was more than he'd earned in months.

Filled with the image of his success, Phineas almost missed the pitiful whimpering in the alley he'd just passed. He lurched to a halt, spun and looked inside. Heard the sound again.

The dark danger of the alley shimmered in his mind. The back of his head throbbed as he remembered the vicious attack. He fingered the remaining coins in his pocket. Should he risk another bang on the noggin for a promise to a tiny pup?

Then he thought of the paper, found crumpled beside him when the licking pup returned him to consciousness. A mournful yelp curled from the alley. He would keep his promise.

He took a hesitant step into the bricked gloom, waited for his eyes to adjust to the light. The alley appeared empty, but it had seemed so, before. Five steps further and he located the source of the sound. Cautiously, he knelt beside the bitch. She was no longer breathing.

"Here, pup. Where be ye?"

A snuffle came from behind the corpse, then a small head showed itself. Phineas tucked his packages under one arm and lifted the pup by the scruff of its neck.

"Here you are. We'll do all right, the two of us." He settled the dog into one of his wide pockets. "After all, I owe you a great deal."

As Phineas started out of the alley, he heard scuffling from the far end. He hurried into the light of the street where he stopped, leaned puffing against a doorway, three shops down.

"I don't know what we've just escaped from, pup, but we'll not go in there, to see." He stroked the brown and tan head. "What say we hie home to celebrate?"

The pup snuggled deeper into his pocket, looked up at him from within.

"What's the matter, pup?" He thought for a moment, then smiled. "I suppose we should give you a name, eh?"

He looked at the sign on the shop where he had leaned, "Alasdair." It seemed a fancy name for such a small bundle of fur, but it fit.

"And I'll call you Alley, for that's where you were found."

❦

Doug awoke with a grin. Very possibly that was the best dream yet. He touched his cheek, could still feel the place where the puppy had licked him. Cool. He'd give anything to have a puppy now, but doubted Dad would let him, especially after the latest scuffle with Jimmy Lyden.

It would have been okay if Jimmy had drawn another cartoon about Doug. He was used to it. But when Doug saw the panel titled "McBrain Drains the Lake," featuring his father wearing his famous bowtie, with a golf club up his ass and a ball on top of his head, he had to take action.

One quick punch to the eye, a trip to the counselor's office and this time, Nanny to the rescue.

At their second session, Dr. Kautsch called Jimmy's cartoon "passive-aggressive," and launched into a spiel about kids not realizing the consequences of their actions.

"That boy wouldn't have drawn the cartoon if he knew he was going to get punched," Kautsch said. "On the other hand, sometimes there are good consequences that can't be seen either."

One of the things kids don't know about the world is what he called "give and take."

"Kids are used to taking things. They want apples from the refrigerator, they take them. Now, the fact that mom can't make an apple pie because they ate the apples never occurs to them." Kautsch almost always swiveled in his chair when he thought he'd made a clever point. "So, Doug. When you want an apple, if you say, 'Can I have this apple if I go to the store to get another?' more than likely your father will agree."

But there's a big difference between apples and puppies. Unless...

Doug kicked the covers off and slid out of bed to see if Dad's car was still in the drive. It was. Perfect. He washed his face, rinsed out his mouth, then dressed quickly and ran downstairs.

"Good morning, Dad." Doug said, slipping into his chair. "Oh, good morning, Nanny."

She half-smiled. "Are you ready for breakfast?"

"Yes, please." Doug's eyes shone as he watched his father, waiting for him to turn the next page of the newspaper. At the first movement of the wrist, Doug launched his question.

"Dad, do you ever dream about golf?"

The page stopped half-turned. He lowered the paper and looked at Doug. "Golf?"

"Yeah, or like work. Do you have dreams about stuff you're going to do the next day, or things you may want?"

His father thought a moment. "I can't really say one way or the other. I guess when I wake up, all that stuff goes away. Why do you ask?"

"Well, I had this dream last night... that I had a puppy. It was so real, it felt like it licked me just before I woke up."

"Dream-puppies are a lot less trouble than real ones," his father said, rustling the paper as if to resume reading.

"Oh, I know, Dad." Doug took a sip of juice. Orange courage. "And I'd really like to have a puppy, but I'd like to make a deal with you."

The paper was now flat on the table. "A deal?"

Doug nodded, avoided looking at Nanny. This had to be just between him and Dad.

"Yeah. I was thinking. Sure, I'd like a puppy..."

"You said that."

"Oh, yeah. But the question is, what do you get out of me having a puppy? I mean, I don't even know if you like dogs. Do you?"

His father scratched his chin. "I guess so."

"Did you have one when you were growing up."

This brought a faint smile. "Yeah, I did. At least, she was a family dog. A beagle."

"What was her name?"

"Billie."

"Billie the beagle?" Doug grinned. "What happened to her?"

His father's face clouded. "We never knew. Some kind of animal must have gotten her in the woods. She just didn't come home one day. We never found her."

"Gosh," Doug said. "Did you ever have another one?"

"No."

Doug lost his courage for a moment. His father actually still seemed sad about losing his dog.

"You said something about a deal?" His father smiled. "So, what do I get out of you having a puppy?"

Excited, Doug jumped up. "You mean I can?"

"Let's hear the deal first."

"You get a caddie."

"A caddie?"

"Yeah. If you let me get a puppy, I'll be your caddie."

His father looked at Nanny. She shrugged. News to her, too.

"How often?"

Now Doug looked at Nanny. She smiled.

"Once a week should be sufficient—fair enough?"

Doug and his father both nodded.

"For how long? As long as you have the dog?" This was said with a grin.

"How about..." Doug thought for a moment. "What's the hardest hole, the one you have the most trouble with?"

"Eighteen."

Doug nodded. "Okay. Until the day I shoot... what do you call it... par?"

"It's a par four."

"What do they call it when someone does better than par?"

"A birdie is one under. An eagle is two."

"Okay, on the day I birdie number eighteen, I don't have to be your caddie anymore."

His father laughed. "The day you birdie eighteen, is the day I become your caddie."

"Then it's a deal?" Doug reached out his hand.

"Deal."

They shook. Nanny looked as if she had something in her eye. She excused herself and left the table. Doug attacked his eggs with vigor. He couldn't wait to tell Dr. Kautsch how well the 'give and take' idea worked.

❦

Slim led Downey into the office. Kautsch couldn't help notice the man's surreptitious glance at her behind. Just what was the etiquette regarding one man ogling another's secretary?

"Dr. Kautsch. A pleasure to meet you."

"And you, Mr. Downey." Kautsch sat in his chair. "Is there any reason why Mr. Douglas-MacBrayne isn't joining us?"

"This is only preliminary. The Foundation's conversion to the orphanage facility can move either quickly or slowly—as we deem necessary." Downey stopped speaking when Slim arrived with coffee. Waited until she left. "We want you in on the planning, for obvious reasons."

"In other words, I'm covering your asses."

Downey shrugged. "Not much to cover, really. Nobody's going to argue with having the facility help children, instead of researching weirdos. We only want to be free of the fiscal responsibility."

"I'm going to need some guarantees."

"Such as?"

"I've put my career on the line to come here. Psychiatric careers are no different from corporate: as long as you continue to climb, you succeed. If you stumble at any step along the way—you're marked as suspect for years. Doesn't even have to be your fault."

Downey stood up, walked over to the wall displaying Kautsch's diplomas and awards.

"You may not believe it to look at me, but I was a helicopter pilot in Vietnam. We'd go in, drop our grunts in the middle of nowhere, wait for them to engage the Gooks. When one side or the other ran out of bullets, we'd fly in and scoop up who and what was left." Downey laughed to himself. "Only a little more dangerous than commuting in L.A."

"Interesting analogy."

"Yeah, well sometimes new crew members would show up. All gung-ho, but still wanting to survive. It was something you could see in their eyes, except nobody wanted to look that closely." Downey sat on the edge of Kautsch's desk, still talking toward the diplomas. "So this Captain Carruthers arrives. Fancy pedigree, top scores, instructor for awhile, the whole schmear. The first time we go troop-scooping in a hot zone, Carruthers starts to pull out. Self-protection, see. He didn't want to lose his aircraft, 'cause the Army spent x-millions on the damn thing, and it would be a mark against his record if he lost a ship."

"Let me guess. His own troops shot him out of the sky. Or they killed him in his sleep."

"Romantic. Probably should have killed the bastard." Downey picked up his empty cup, put it down. "As other choppers went down, pilots killed, wounded, and all that, Carruthers kept getting promoted. Finally, he ran the outfit. Stayed in Nam five years, never lost a chopper. He was decorated at the end."

"The point of this little morality tale?"

"The accountants ran the Vietnam war and almost every skirmish ever since."

"That's why you became an accountant?"

"I was one before I got drafted." He grinned. "Most people don't know how crazy most accountants are. If they did, they probably wouldn't hire us." He leaned on the desk with both hands. "Some day, I'm going to buy a helicopter franchise from the now-retired General Carruthers, but I need real money to do that—and digging Douglas Industries out of the hole and making them a successful, mega-corporation is my ticket."

"Admirable ambition. But I still don't see how General Carruthers applies to my situation here."

"Simple. I don't want you to be a hero, or to do anything stupid. I want you to protect your own self-interest every step of the way. This facility can do some good and still be self-supporting. We'll give you the tools, you do the work—and you'll be compensated according to your personal success."

Kautsch had filled half a page with doodles and sketches. One showed a dollar-sign lying on a sofa, a dialogue balloon above it. Obviously the doctor saying, "How long have you felt like the root of all evil?"

"Dr. Kautsch?"

"He looked up. "Sorry, I was thinking," he said.

"Which time-schedule do you feel more comfortable with: six or twelve months?"

"Let's see." Kautsch made a few more scribbles on the page. "Six months means we put the orphans out right in the middle of the Christmas season. Does that fit with your community image?"

"Jesus—"

"Didn't think so." Kautsch doodled a helicopter chasing stick children, bullets puffing at their feet. "On the other hand, if we make the change at the end of the school year, only a few will notice if some of the kids don't return, after summer vacation."

"I see how it can work." Downey leaned over, to look at what Kautsch had drawn.

"There's another option." Kautsch covered the pad with his arm. "One that will create less dislocation for the children and ensure the first year or so of the Children's Clinic."

"That being?"

"Those orphans that can't be farmed out, will be kept as the first patients of the clinic." Kautsch smiled. "After all, being an orphan is traumatic. They are really wards of the state, so let the state pay us to take care of them."

"But they're just orphans, not mentally disturbed."

Kautsch came around the desk, clapped Downey on the shoulder and guided him toward the door. "Trust me. After a couple of sessions, I can find mental disturbance in anyone."

Avisson skidded around the corner, barely missing Dr. Kautsch, walking another man to the front exit. He nodded to them, then pounded up the hallway. He burst through his office door, nearly colliding with Clint Sharpe.

"Mr. Sharpe, so sorry I'm late. I forgot we changed your appointment to this morning."

"No problem, I just got here a minute ago."

"Did Margaret offer you coffee or something?"

"I'm fine, thanks."

Avisson led the way into the office. Sharpe sat, folded his hands on his knees. He got up a moment later and walked to the bookshelf.

"What's this?" He held up a small jar containing what looked like gold foil.

"It's called an apport," Avisson said, "sent by a psychiatrist in Florida. That came out of the face of one of his female client's during a session."

"Came out of her face?"

"Yes. The woman he calls Miss Katie, has apported everything from semi-precious stones to flowers and that 'gold' foil."

"Why? How?" Sharpe put the jar down.

"Don't know. That's why he's studying her."

"That's weird."

"Yes." Avisson smiled, finished preparing for the session. "There are many things we don't understand about the human mind, human experience—without even going into the reason why."

"Man, you sure have a habit of hitting the target, right in the center."

"Excuse me?"

Sharpe seemed to be gathering strength, breathing deeply, his eyes closed. When he spoke, his voice came from way down in his solar plexus.

"I drink because I don't know why..."

"That's what we're here to find out. Once we find out why you drink—"

"No." The black man shook his head. "I drink because I don't know why..." Each word came out of his mouth slowly, a piece of flesh torn from his tongue. "...God. Killed. My. Little. Girl."

They sat silent for several minutes. Sharpe's hands shook but nothing else moved. Avisson got up, took the specimen jar from the bookshelf, held it up.

"Thank you," he said. "You've just helped me see how this stuff comes out of that woman's body."

"I have?"

Avisson put his hand on Sharpe's shoulder. "There are emotions so pure, so elemental...so difficult to express, that when they are finally expressed, it doesn't have to be with words...the feelings themselves are like pure gold."

Sharpe's eyes, which had remained clear, suddenly filled with tears.

"I was doing okay. Why'd you have to say that?" He pulled out his handkerchief and dabbed at his eyes. "Damn."

"How about we have some coffee and you tell me about your daughter?" Avisson hit the intercom.

᪆

Doug tried hard to concentrate on the assignment, but he couldn't shake the idea that tomorrow he might have a puppy. Augie Trumbo used a wheelchair because of a congenital back problem. He got to bring his dog, Honey, to class with him: a yellow Labrador Retriever. Honey impassively watched the antics of the students, nonchalantly accepted the many pats on the head as she accompanied her master between classes.

Doug suddenly realized that Miss Stipple was standing behind him, watching him stare at the large sheet of paper on the easel.

"Daydreaming again, Mr. MacBrayne?"

"Sorry." He smiled. She scowled. "I'm getting a new puppy. I guess I can't stop thinking about it."

She nodded. "That is a big event. But do you want to hurt those girls' feelings?"

She directed Doug's eyes to the stage, where Sally and her three best friends were modeling for the rest of the class. The four had become inseparable over the past school year. They called themselves "The Moles." There was even a rumor that they had tried smoking and threatened to beat up one of the less popular girls if she told on them.

Jimmy had designed a Mole logo for their jackets, where the M served as the face, with the L-nose between the O- and E-eyes. A lazy S underneath contributed a funny kind of smile.

Doug tried sketching the four girls as they sat on the small stage at the front of the room. He came close to the way their arms and legs were casually splayed, but was afraid to do their faces.

Sally caught him staring at her and stared back. At first, there was a flash of that old smile, the one she gave him the first day of school, but now she looked angry, somehow resentful.

When Doug returned to the sketch pad, the vibrations hit him hard, stronger than ever.

Tukla could feel, even smell a storm hiding beyond the tall monument of ice the gods had left behind, before his grandfather's grandfather had gone out into the snow for the last time.

Tukla urged his dogs forward. There was perhaps one hour of stingy light left. One of the treacheries of spring—that the sun should tease the eyes. He cursed himself for waiting those extra minutes by his ice hole for the seal that kept stealing fish off his hook.

How foolish to stand so long with spear poised. Stupid creature, if it had come up for air just once, Tukla would be bringing home enough dinner for a week, plus a new covering for the baby soon to arrive. Instead he and Nikami would face another night of clinging hungrily together.

"Kontuk!" He shouted into the wind. "Kontuk!"

At the sound of his name, the lead dog surged forward. Tukla shouted again but the wind drove moist breath into his face. His cheeks burned with shame at the thought of facing Nikami's hungry eyes, again with empty hands.

If her father hadn't forbade their marriage, they would not have been forced to run away, to be together. The man was too old, his sack dried to powder. He had forgotten about love between a man and a woman.

So what if Tukla was better at carving tusks than fishing? The old man even had an answer for that.

"Tukla, you will only be good at carving the ivory other men bring to the village."

And the others had laughed. Even Tibuk, his best friend, joined in the taunting. "The only spear you know how to throw is the one between your legs, Tukla."

Nikami alone loved him. Only Nikami saw his inner beauty, in spite of the ugly birthmark that looked a little like an elephant-seal snout growing on the back of his head. Besides, any other woman would mock him for coming home empty-handed. But Nikami would open her arms to him, pulling him beneath the coverlet, chipping a hole in the ice of her hunger to let him fish within her.

Tukla sent his whip toward Kontuk. The dog yelped, almost realizing he would have to wait another day as well. He blamed his father's death first, then his mother. A man should live long enough to teach his son how to hunt and not leave him to his mother's simple-headed encouragement.

"Every man knows how to fish," she would tell him at night. "Very few can turn ivory into magic."

His own hunger churned. Tukla held onto the sled as he felt his stomach trying to devour his own small store of fat. How many days since they'd eaten? Three? Four? Each day left a deeper hollow in his beloved Nikami's cheeks. If he had speared that seal, they would have had meat and blubber to warm the igloo, instead of trying to share each other's diminishing heat through the night.

And the baby. Another joke of the gods, sent to prove Tukla's unworthiness.

The dogs slowed their pace. Tukla raised his whip.

"Kontuk!"

The dogs stopped in their tracks. Kontuk growled, ruff straight in the air. For a moment Tukla could see nothing ahead of them, but a moment later he was reaching into the sled for his spear.

Seven, no eight large wolves came raging over a snow drift to his left. Tukla hurried to release the dogs so they could defend themselves.

"Ha-yee!" he cried as the wolves closed the gap.

Birthmark

Kontuk braced himself as the snarling, lead wolf launched at him. Tukla had barely released the last dog before the fight was on. He waded toward the wolves, slashing his spear at every exposed flank. Their bared teeth reminded him of Tibuk and Nikami's father—everyone who had ever laughed at him. His fury peaked, as he threw himself into the dog and wolf melee.

After an eternity which might only have been ten minutes, the battle was over. The three remaining wolves limped off. Tukla examined his eight friends where they lay panting by the sled. Two were mortally wounded. Tukla petted them gently before finishing them quickly, ending their pain.

He slit open one of the wolves, sliced off sections of meat, gave each dog a small piece to renew its strength. Kontuk waited at the front of the sled. Tukla gave him the largest piece of meat before harnessing him.

While the dogs chewed on their enemy, Tukla piled the carcasses onto the sled. He buried his two friends so the scavengers wouldn't find them until Spring; then called his team to their feet. They rose slowly, stiff from the cold and the battle. They sniffed at the wolf carcasses, uneasy about turning their backs on them.

Tukla pushed as hard as the dogs pulled, while they slowly made their way home. Tonight, he and Nikami would eat all the meat they could swallow. Tomorrow, he would remove the hides. The day after, they would return to the village—a man and a mother-to-be.

The wolves had fought their hunger together. He and Nikami would rejoin their own pack.

His boyish pride had put them all in danger. Now that he had seen the frenzied fury of the hunger-maddened wolves, the angry face of his woman's father and the mocking smiles of the others would no longer intimidate him. They were right about him: he was a boy pretending to be a man. But the boy had entered the fight with the wolves and emerged a man. He would hold them all spellbound for at least a week with the tale of this mighty battle.

Yet even as these proud thoughts raced in his head, a sober, mature reflection filled his mind: he would say nothing of his adventure. Let them wonder how the two of them had survived the harsh winter. Maybe in a year or two, if he found the right walrus tusk, he would carve a toy in the shape of a wolf for his child.

Miss Stipple clapped her hands to signal clean-up time. Doug shook his head and started putting away his pencils without looking at what he'd drawn.

"Is that what we look like to you?" It was Sally.

"Oh." He inspected his drawing. Four wolves in the snow.

"Are they dead or sleeping?" She asked.

"What do you think?"

"I think they're dead." She turned and walked away.

"Sign your drawings and leave them on my desk," Miss Stipple pronounced from the front of the room.

❧

Kim shouted up that she needed to get some groceries and supplies before opening. Grumpy waved where he sat on the balcony just above the Crystal Cafe sign. He tossed a large envelope on the table and sighed. He'd gone over the report three or four times. He shook his head, he had been stupid to hope...

Brief, unambiguous, the information was damning.

"Subject: Molly Lyden. Born 1931. Died 1973. Never married. Last known employer, Douglas Industries. Terminated November, 1968. No reason given. One child, James Ulysses Lyden. Born October 30, 1969. Father unknown. Subject died of complications after mastectomy. Detailed medical reports in Health and Welfare file. Child permanently assigned to Douglasville Orphanage upon mother's death at her request."

The picture came clear: after Peter discovered Grumpy and Molly's affair, he'd fired her.

Lost job. Lost benefits. Lost hope.

Their romance had not been storybook. Grumpy was trapped in a loveless marriage, one that not even drinking himself into a daily stupor could make bearable. The consummate career secretary, proud of her abilities, Molly loved her job, her freedom.

And they nearly loved each other.

Expert at crossword and anacrostic puzzles, Molly's teasing invitations always involved little notes that hinted at her whereabouts:

"Don't go out during the Arab fast day, Hamlet," translated to read, "Ramada(n) Inn, Room 2B."

"Crosby's top song from best film, Gettysburg begins," meant, "Holiday Inn, room eighty-seven."

Molly snubbed him the morning after he couldn't decipher "Saturday Night Fever Star, Henry Cabot makes boxcars." She had spent the night alone, in room twelve at the Travel (Travolta) Lodge. After that, whenever confronted with her obscure clues, Grumpy didn't dare have his first afternoon drink until he had the answer.

Coward that he had been, Grumpy hadn't stayed to face Peter's anger, hadn't protected an innocent woman. No, he'd left home with his American Express card and a snoot full of remorse and booze. While he was sucking tequila in Latin America, Molly was discovering what it meant to be blackballed in a town like Douglasville. While he was sailing the Pacific to the Orient, she was on welfare, trying to cope alone, pregnant. And finally, when he was climbing tall mountains in Nepal, looking for the meaning of life, she was clinging to hers, while incompetent welfare doctors cut into her body in a fruitless, fatal search for rampaging cancer cells.

Grumpy did the math again. The last time he and Molly were together was in October, 1968. Jimmy was born on October 30, 1969, twelve months later.

Did the fact that the dates proved Grumpy could not be Jimmy's father reduce his sense of obligation?.

A tap at the door below and Grumpy noticed the time. Five minutes after ten. He was late opening. Kim would be upset. He hurried down with the keys and opened the door.

Fiona McLean was waiting on the sidewalk.

"I hope I didn't disturb you..."

"Retail never sleeps." He held the door for her. "Please come in, Miss McLean."

"My charge is at day camp this morning, so I thought I'd take the opportunity to steal away for a cup of tea." Her nervous smile didn't fool Grumpy.

"Missed you at the Fete the other night." He led her to the same table of her first visit. "I meant what I said about giving you a reading."

"That's not really why I'm here."

Grumpy smiled, put his hand over his heart. "Why, Miss McLean, are you here because you find me irresistible?"

"Mr. Petrovich!" Her cheeks blazed.

"That's not it?"

She shook her head. "What I'd really love...is a nice hot cuppa and a quiet place to do some serious thinking."

"Hot tea and a zipped lip. Coming right up." He bowed.

Fiona thanked Mr. Petrovich for her tea and dropped in a sugar cube, idly stirring with the spoon until she could no longer feel the little lump. She looked into the small bowl. Who decided how much sugar went into a cube? Was it the same as a teaspoon? In that case, who determined the size of a teaspoon? Someone had invented or established a measure for nearly every aspect of life: a sugar cube, a cup of margarine, a pint of ale, a gallon of milk, an acre of land...

She shook her head and sipped her tea. So what if Peter and Doug did have a good morning? It had been quite touching to see the two of them talking almost like father and son. So why was she upset? Jealous?

"Can I get you some more hot water?" Petrovich held up a metal pitcher.

"No thanks," Fiona shook her head, "I'm in enough hot water as it is."

"You? This I do not believe." The man sat across from her. "Who would be so foolish as to make trouble for you?"

"Me."

"Ah, that makes sense." He nodded gravely. "What kind of trouble?"

"I think I've become co-dependent."

He stared at her for a moment, then laughed. Fiona blinked, thought about what she said, blushed and began chuckling herself.

"Oh, my goodness. What a silly thing to say." She reached for her tea, changed her mind. "You must think I'm an idiot."

He shook his head. "No, not at all. It's just the last thing in the world I expected you to say. Caught me off-guard. The idea of you being weak, co-dependent..."

He grabbed a cup of his own and filled it from Fiona's pot, raised it in a toast. "Here's to one of the healthiest individuals who's ever entered this store."

"Please, don't make fun of me." Her eyes dropped to the table, a piper's inhale away from crying.

"Oh, my dear Miss McLean." He came around to her side of the table, rested his hand on her shoulder. "I would never make fun of you."

"I just realized that I do love Doug too much—that's the boy I take care of. He's the dearest thing in the world to me. Today, he and his father had a real breakfast together, acted like father and son for the first time in years—and I'm ashamed to say I was jealous."

"What's the matter with being jealous?" He filled her cup.

She frowned.

"I'm sorry," he said, noticing, "did I do something wrong?"

"Well, my cup was only half-empty."

"Now it is all full."

"Thank you, but I had just the right amount of sugar—one cube per cup... You filled it, and I can't break a sugar cube in half... so the taste is..."

"Not to your liking." He took the cup, emptied it in the sink, and refilled it. "There. Thanks for the lesson."

She nodded. "You're welcome."

He put his elbows on the table and leaned his chin on his laced fingers. Looked at her. She smiled, fidgeted, looked around the store, then finally returned his gaze "Why are you staring at me?" she asked.

His eyebrows raised. "I'm just trying to imagine what idiot taught you jealousy was bad."

"Everybody knows that."

He shook his head. "I don't. So, unless I'm from another planet—"

"You mean you aren't?"

For a moment Fiona was afraid he wasn't going to laugh, but he did.

"Some people say jealousy is a sign of insecurity, but I think it is more a sensitivity that should be listened to," He said. "How long have you been this boy Doug's nanny?"

"Since the day he was born."

"And the mother?"

"Died in childbirth."

"That makes you the mother."

She shook her head. "Just the nanny."

"What other person has spent as much time with him? Who knows him better? Who else would throw herself in front of a car to save him?"

She smiled weakly. "No one, I guess."

"That's right. Now, you say this morning the father treated the boy like his son for the first time in years...it's my guess that the father's been kind of stupid where it came to the boy. Am I right?"

"He's been busy."

"And hurt. He thinks the boy's birth cost him his wife. He's not too lovable, so another wife who really loves him isn't going to happen.. He thinks this boy took away his only love."

"Probably."

"And he's taken it out on the boy all these years. So, when he suddenly starts acting like a father, you don't trust him. He hasn't exactly earned your trust over the years, has he?"

"Not in the least."

"That tells me you have every reason to be jealous. The father hasn't done anything to earn the boy's love—but he gets it all the same. Is that fair?"

"In truth? No."

"It isn't fair, and you hope that the boy will someday see the whole truth. But that may never happen."

"That's kind of dreary."

"Sorry." He smiled. "It would be dreary if we were here only to do things and be around for each other. I happen to think there's a lot more than that, to this being alive business." His hands went out in a *"who-me?"* gesture. "I don't know what's behind it all or why, but I believe there's a universal purpose."

"Is this Gypsy folk wisdom, or something?"

Petrovich laughed, then grew serious. "I know the story very well. I lost my son to his mother, an angry, selfish and spiteful woman."

"You divorced her?"

"She died."

"So, how do you and your son get along now?"

"We don't. We haven't talked for years."

"But, you're so nice. So kind and wise. How could your son not see that?"

"He's still wearing the lenses his mother gave him to look at me with." He leaned over, took a sugar cube and popped it in his mouth. "What kind of lens do you want your Doug to use to look at the world with?"

"His own, one of his own choosing."

Petrovich nodded. "Has the jealousy helped?"

She smiled. She could feel it across her face, like a sun coming over a mountain—a warm understanding. She slid her cup over.

"Is there enough for a refill, Mr. Petrovich?"

"I believe so, Miss McLean." He took her cup. "If not, we can always make more. Around here, there's plenty of hot water for everyone."

❦

Avisson turned off the tape, grabbed a pear and devoured it. He could no longer stand listening to the man pouring out his pain, nor could he open his mind again to the image of this brilliant, agonized fountain of guilt, remorse, self-hatred, bitterness.

When the ordinary activities of the world break a man's heart, he may weep for days, weeks or months. When a poet is an accidental accomplice to breaking his own heart, there is no refuge, no end to the tears, no salvation.

The words are too available. The understanding too clear. The verdict intones, moment after moment, in one's own voice: Guilty. Guilty. Guilty.

"She was the perfect combination of brown sugar and sunlight," Sharpe had said. "From the moment she pushed her little head out from that place where my wife, Mandy created and nurtured her.

"She was so sweet, we just had to call her Candy."

Clint poured himself more coffee, added nothing to it, and sat down. He described the little garden in the yard, where he and Candy planted a few packets of seed.

"She was fascinated when the plants grew and blossomed. 'Oh. Look, Kakoo,' she called, 'see the pretty flower.'"

"Kakoo?"

"Her name for me." He sipped, put his cup down and crossed one leg over the other. The first sign of comfort since they began talking. "It was an orange marigold. She carried it around all afternoon, even through dinner. That night, as we were reading her favorite book, *Through the Looking Glass*, she insisted we press the flower between the pages so it would be there always.

"Quite good foresight," Avisson said. "Considering—"

"But that's probably the worst part, Dr. Avisson." Sharpe became agitated. "It's all gone. Anything of importance, almost everything that she touched and cared about—is gone."

"Somebody take them?"

Sharpe shook his head. "She was such a little squirrel. It became a big joke between Mandy and me. We couldn't let her know we really liked something she made or found, because she'd hide it somewhere, and we couldn't find anything she ever hid.

"In second grade, she got an 'A' for a sketch of a little angel, with three doves hovering nearby. I liked it so much, I got a cheap frame and put it on my desk in the corner of the living room."

"Gone?" Avisson had his pen in his mouth.

"Evaporated." He motioned with his hands. "Then there was this beat-up doll, a Raggedy Ann snuggle-pillow she got for her first Christmas. Slept with it every night from then on. In the morning, she'd make her bed and slip Raggedy Ann under the pillow. Said the doll needed her sleep during the day because she kept watch over Candy at night."

He stopped for a moment. Avisson looked away as Sharpe's eyes moved toward the ceiling.

"After the funeral, when Mandy finally screwed up enough courage to pack away Candy's bedclothes, she noticed it wasn't under the pillow. We tore the house apart. Gave up."

"Clint?"

"Yes, Dr. Avisson?"

"You've told me about before and after. Can you tell me what happened on that very day?"

Caught, Sharpe's eyes widened in panic. The energy in his voice went dull, fearful, as he remembered.

"She'd had this bad cold. You know kids, they can be really sick but still have all the energy in the world? Well, it was Saturday, I was grading papers and Mandy was off to the mall. Normally Candy would go with her mom, but..."

"But she had that cold."

"That's right." He took a deep breath. "Anyway, I was working on the porch and she was bouncing her ball off the garage door, doing a play-by-play. She was a great mimic. She would listen to something on television or in a movie, and we'd hear it for a week. So she'd bounce the ball, it would go way high in the air and she would shout, 'Back, back, back, way back... gone!' and stuff like that. Catch the ball and then throw it with all her might against the door and shout, 'Yer owt!'"

"Quite the ballplayer."

"She would have made Jackie Robinson look like a piker. First black woman to play in the major leagues, if she ever got the chance."

"What happened then?"

"I was in the middle of a letter I was writing to William F. Buckley, Jr., you know, the world-famous conservative?" Avisson nodded. "She walks up to me, like Arnold Schwartzenegger in Terminator and she says, 'I'll be back.' I looked up at her, because there was a most unusual tone in her voice. So, I said, 'What, honey bun?' and she repeats, 'I'll be back,' then runs off to the driveway again with her ball."

"And?"

"She didn't...come back, like she promised."

"A car?"

Sharpe nodded. "I heard the bang of the ball on the garage door. She yelled, 'Oh, pooh.' Then a screech of tires..."

He could go no further.

Avisson sat silent for several minutes. Sharpe never moved.

"How long before the drinking started?"

"On the way home from the cemetery."

"Why drinking?"

Sharpe looked up. "Is that a serious question?"

"Very much so. Some people become promiscuous, others resort to violence, still others lose themselves in their work..."

"Dr. Avisson, I am an educated black man, not an easy position in this society. All through university, people asked me what sport I played—all the other blacks were bouncing basketballs and throwing their bodies around on the gridiron. No one believed I was there to hone my intellect. The library was near enough to the football stadium for me to hear the cheers, but I was blessed with tremendous powers of concentration. When I focus on what I'm studying, nothing intrudes." He clenched his hands. "Not even the sound of my little girl running down the driveway, out into the street."

Avisson waited for the toxic radiation of the last comment to subside. He glanced at Sharpe's curriculum vitae.

"Says here you were a Ph.D. candidate and selected to attend the Iowa Writers Workshop for Poetry. Pretty prestigious stuff, perfect launch to a promising academic career."

"Maybe, for someone who's sober long enough to do the work."

"That's our next task, I guess." Avisson smiled. "That is, if you want to continue."

"Sure, unless you think it's too late."

"Too late?"

"Well, I don't think I'll be invited to the Writer's Workshop again. I vaguely remember that my last letter to them was less than poetic and more than a little incoherent."

Avisson walked to the front of his desk, leaned against it. "Hell, many of the great poets had a drinking problem. Some consider addictions in artists a sign of greatness."

"Maybe so, but my career in academia is pretty much washed up without a doctoral degree."

"That's true. But I've known Ph.D.'s that took ten years. You have plenty of time."

Sharpe shook his head. "The committee was pretty upset with me the last time they met. A couple of them even stalked out of the room."

"Why?"

"I made a pretty strong case that FDR was to the American Constitution what Satan was to the Garden of Eden."

"What was the title of your thesis?" Avisson hid his grin.

"Modern Conservative Politics in the works of John Milton."

"Provocative. Would they give you another chance?"

"Maybe. But I'm not ready."

"When will you be?"
"When I stop siding with Satan."

❦

Doug bounced against the headrest. Nanny looked over with a frown.

"Sorry, Nanny," he said. "I didn't think it would be this hard to find a puppy."

"Well, it is a pretty important decision. I'm glad you're being selective."

Selective? All the puppies were cute. They'd stopped at every place Doug had found in the Yellow Pages: The Puppy Palace, Pups Are Us, Puppy Kingdom. Then there were the kennels. Doug had been kissed on the nose by baby beagles, Labradors, German Shepherds, Rottweilers, Wolfhounds, Scotties (Nanny's choice), Great Danes, Irish Setters, Dachshunds, and a few he didn't recognize.

But not the right one. He could tell by looking in their eyes.

Nanny reached over to pat his arm. "Don't get discouraged, there are puppies to spare. You'll find yours."

Doug nodded, disbelieving. As they drove past a small fruit stand, out of the corner of his eye he saw a handmade sign: Buskie Pups.

"Please stop, Nanny."

"What?"

He pointed to the sign. She pulled the car to the side of the road, then eased into the parking lot. Doug was out in a shot. He ran to the woman at the cash register.

"You have puppies here?"

She nodded. "You want one?"

"Can I see 'em?"

Another nod, followed by a tilt of the head. A young girl of five or six walked over, took Doug by the hand and led him around the corner of the building.

"Why do you call them Buskies?" Doug asked.

"Their momma is a Beagle and the papa was a Husky." She giggled. "My mommy made it up."

Doug heard them before he saw them: a female and her four pups, in a run-down fenced area with a small lean-to for shelter. Three of the pups had ganged up on the fourth, who stood its ground in the corner, playfully growling and warning the others off. The three conspirators shared their mother's black and tan markings. The fourth was silver, with subtle tones of black and tan beneath.

"We call that one Alaska, 'cause he looks like his daddy, blue eyes and all."

At the sound of his name, or maybe just the girl's voice, Alaska looked over. One glance confirmed what Doug had felt as soon as he'd seen the sign.

This was his dog.

He knelt and clapped once. "Come here, Allie."

"Alaska," the little girl complained. "He won't answer to—"

But the puppy did answer. He bounded straight into Doug's hands, outstretched over the low fence. Doug lifted and held the puppy against his chest. Alaska licked Doug's face as if it were chocolate-covered.

"You just gonna take him?"

"Sure, why not?"

The little girl shrugged.

Nanny walked up, saw the pup and smiled.

"Looks like that's your dog."

Alaska panted happily as Doug carried him to the car. Doug petted him and smiled all the way home, whispering in his ear.

"I knew I'd find you if I waited. I just knew it, Allie."

Chapter Seven

"Who would like to help me demonstrate the next dance?" Mrs. Thornbush pointed at Doug with a pudgy, red-tipped finger. "Mr. MacBrayne?"

He gulped, shuffled forward, past the jeering grins of the Mole-girls.

"I'm not a very good dancer," Doug said.

"Nonsense," Mrs. Thornbush said. "Everybody can dance, once they're properly taught."

She took each of his hands, assumed a waltz position, nodded for the music to start. Augie bounced the phonograph needle on the record, causing the music to start six or seven bars in. Mrs. Thornbush dragged Doug with her, in a vain attempt to join the music. Then she stopped, counted by nodding her head, and pulled Doug along again in a whirling cloud of flowery dress and overpowering perfume. Dizzy, he could hardly feel his feet touch the ground. Mrs. Thornbush was almost carrying him.

"I-I-I—" Doug tried to escape her grasp, but her head had hot-air-ballooned into the cloudy music. He was her tether to the dance and she floated around him, her hard-soled shoes tapping against the linoleum. Doug tried to keep his feet moving, but out of her way.

The music hit a crescendo. Mrs. Thornbush spun Doug away, only to lose his sweaty palm and send him flying into a clump of laughing students. They caught him and shoved him out into the circle, where Mrs. Thornbush stood, shaking her head.

"Mr. MacBrayne. If you can't cooperate, or at least pay attention when I'm teaching you very simple steps, how can you ever hope to pass this class?"

He didn't answer.

She folded her arms across her chest and glared at him. "You won't be a boy forever. Someday you're going to be a man, and men should know how to dance."

He nodded, sat down. He had struggled with dance class all semester and would have given up, if they'd let him. They wouldn't. So he suffered whenever the music started.

The irony was that everything else in his life was nearly perfect. It was as if the addition of Allie to the family had smoothed over everything that had been wrong before. Doug and his father actually laughed and joked. There were still the occasional blow-ups at the golf course, but Doug knew it had more to do with the golf than with his caddying—which while imperfect, was improving. In a strange way, Doug would rather have his father yelling at him than at any of the other caddies.

At home, Doug no longer sat at his Rapunzel window, longing for a friend. All he had to do was whistle or call, and the ever-growing bundle of silver-gray fur would come bounding to be hugged and scratched.

When he finally told Nanny about his problem with dance class, she sat on the edge of his bed.

"Did I ever tell you about Dancie Reid?"

"Who's that?"

"Well, he taught the weekly dancing classes I attended as a teenager in Newtyle," she said.

Doug laughed, visualizing Nanny as a bobbysoxer. She gave him one of those hush-or-there'll-be-no-story looks. So he pulled the bed covers over his abacus, up to his chin.

"Ah, Dancie Reid," Nanny began, "was a thin, wiry man, of medium height. He had neatly trimmed, salt and pepper hair, and always wore a navy suit to his classes and most times, a conservative tie and a white shirt.

"He was a great fiddler, a superb dancer. You should have seen him, pedaling his bicycle over the lonely, Scottish country roads, between the hills, through the glens, rain or shine. Dark coattails fluttering behind him in the wind, black violin-case strapped securely on his back. Despite the long bicycle ride, he always smelled so good. It was about ten miles from his home to our schoolhouse; so I never could understand why, after that long ride, his cologne, or whatever it was, hadn't worn off before he got there."

"Did you have a crush on him?" Doug asked, a sparkle in his eye. Nanny tapped his hand.

"We girls all did in the beginning, but because he was a strict taskmaster, everyone dreaded making a mistake. He seemed never to miss anything; when you made a misstep, he was there like lightning, by your side. Then you'd smell the lotion, hear the fiddling stop and you'd feel the rap of his slender bow on the top of your head.

"Not only was it humiliating, it hurt. He couldn't abide mistakes. I was a good dancer, but whenever we changed steps, I would be confused for awhile—then I'd get one of those raps. It got so bad I thought about quitting the class... but of course I didn't dare. Everybody learns to dance in Scotland."

"What did you do?"

"Well, every week, a wise, old woman used to bring her granddaughter. She saw me getting whacked, so she pulled me aside after one particularly bad evening. It felt like I had knots all over my head." Nanny rubbed the top of her head and grinned. "I think I still have one or two bumps to show for it."

"Come on, Nanny. Did he hit you that hard?"

"Never you mind..."

Doug rolled his eyes. "Nanny."

"Well, this old woman, she comes up to me and says, 'Your trouble seems to start whenever the solo dances begin, where the steps are more complicated.' I agreed, but what to do? 'Darlin', she says, 'you're doing a different dance in your head than with your feet. Learn the dance in your head first, then your feet will follow, with practice."

"Did it work?"

"It did, I'm glad to say, for my head's sake."

"What was your favorite dance?"

"The 'Cumberland Reel,' was everyone's favorite. Different colored ribbons hung from the light-fixture in the middle of the room. Each of us took a ribbon, and backed away from the centre to form a circle.

"As the music began, we danced in and out, twisting and turning, weaving the beautifully-colored streamers into sort of a braided rope of ribbons.

"Then, when Dancie played the signal on his fiddle, we reversed the procedure, our direction of movement, unweaving as we went, until each of us held his own ribbon in front, free from all the others. Then we were back in our circle, exactly where we started.

"Finally, we'd dance several steps to our right, then to our left. The streaming ribbons gave the effect of a moving Maypole.

"We had really great fun: not only was it our favorite dance (we all knew it the best,) but it was always the last one of the evening."

"I wish our dancing was more fun." Doug chewed his lip.

"It will be, once you get the dances straight in your head."

"How long will that take?"

"Well, once you realize that dancing is not really about the steps."

"Tell that to Mrs. Thornbush."

"Do you think she is a good dancer?"

"She knows the steps…"

"Sure, but does that make her a good dancer? Did you enjoy dancing with her?"

"No."

"Why?"

"I guess because I didn't know the steps, and she seemed to be dancing without me."

"Remember that. Really, good dancers always know where their partners are."

"So, how do I become a good dancer?"

"Everywhere you look, Doug, you'll see people dancing. You can't always hear the music, but it's there. If you watch people closely enough, you can see how they move, why they do certain things, how they relate to each other…it's just like dancing. When you really start seeing them, then you'll hear the music that nobody else hears."

"And I'll be able to dance well in class?"

"In class, you start by learning the steps."

"That means listening to Mrs. Thornbush?"

"Of course." She grinned.

"Nanny. You just snookered me, didn't you?"

"Not any more than usual." She kissed him on the forehead. "No more talking. Good night."

That night, the world of dance and people came together in Doug's head. From then on, every time he saw a group of people, he would notice how close or far they were from each other. How two people would unconsciously shift when joined by another.

A line at the grocery-store became a slow conga. Kids in class swayed away slightly when the teacher approached. A group of boys slowed their pace when approaching a group of girls. Unless, that is, the girls wore the Mole insignia, in which case, the boys avoided them entirely—all the boys except Jimmy, who seemed to enjoy a special status with this gang of Amazons, which was what Chas Miner called the girls—behind their backs.

The music stopped.

"Who's next?" Thornbush pounced on a boy trying to hide behind a book and pointed at Augie, who sat by the scratchy record player, for another tune. Doug closed his eyes and pictured her feet, then his own. He could feel the pattern of the steps synchronize with the music. When the music stopped, she asked for another volunteer. Doug raised his hand.

"Another go, Mr. MacBrayne?"

"Yes, please, Mrs. Thornbush."

This time, he kept the pattern in his head, let it flow down to his legs. The music stopped. No bones broken.

"Much better, Mr. MacBrayne. Much Better."

Phew. Doug returned to his seat, gazed out the window at the greening fields of Spring in Douglasville. Another of Nanny's lessons had saved the day.

The final bell rang and the classroom exploded, students flying for the door. Doug dropped one of his textbooks and bent down to get it.

"You going to the Crystal?" Sally whispered to the Mole standing next to her.

"Yeah, but my mom's ragging me about it. Says it's not a place for 'nice' girls."

"Exactly!" Sally high-fived the other girl. They started out, then Sally saw Doug as he stood. "You shouldn't eavesdrop."

"I wasn't. I dropped a book."

"Yeah, I'm sure."

Doug wondered how to say it? "Look, Sal. I did hear what you said, but not on purpose. I don't even know what the Crystal is."

"God, don't they ever let you out of the castle?"

"Castle?"

"You are unbelievable." She rolled her eyes, strode away. Then stopped at the door. "For God's sake, Doug, you won't ever find out who you really are if you don't break loose occasionally, get out of that prison they've got you in."

"I know who I am."

"Right. You know who your nanny thinks you are, who your father thinks you are...anybody else have a clue?"

"My dog, Allie."

She threw up her hands. "I give up. They win." Started out the door. "Nice almost getting to know you."

Doug stood there, stunned. He gathered his books and saw Mrs. Thornbush vigorously erasing the word "Waltz" from the blackboard. When Doug reached the doorway, she cleared her throat.

"Young women can be difficult to understand, Mr. MacBrayne." Her smile was confectionery. "Don't let the fact that she seems angry fool you into thinking she doesn't like you."

"Why should liking me make her angry?"

"My husband, Rupert, and I were together for thirty years..." Her eyes misted. "We loved each other very much, but sometimes fought like cats and dogs. It's just part of the mystery." She smiled, suddenly a coquette, thirty years younger. "You'll understand, once you know how to dance."

Doug nodded and left. Maybe poor Mrs. Thornbush was a better dancer than he thought.

Grumpy bid Fiona good day and returned to his post behind the counter, to prepare for the change of shift. Between three and four every afternoon, the clientele of the cafe underwent a radical transformation. The mothers of grade-school age children left in station wagons to collect their darlings and were replaced by students dressed in every imaginable costume and unimaginable hair-style.

Grumpy watched the migration from behind the counter. Occasionally, the timing would become skewed: a stray, maternal wildebeest would be passed by one of the young, leather-jacketed jackals or hard-eyed, budding lionesses. But sparks never flew. Peace at the watering-hole was maintained simply by Grumpy's benign gaze. Universally loved by his customers, none would think of letting him down inside the store.

Jimmy arrived, sans entourage. Grumpy raised an eyebrow.

"Where are the girls?"

The boy glanced behind him, shrugged. Then grabbed a cloth from the sink and began cleaning tables. Grumpy smiled. Old "Grab-your-knickers" sure had been wrong about Jimmy: Incorrigible had turned out to be "encourageable." And Grumpy had kept his promise to the boy, never asking him to read any of the books. But it didn't stop Jimmy from leafing through the pages, looking at the art work from literally every age of man, devouring the imagery, burning it into his artistic consciousness.

And the boy listened, closer than he let on. Once, he hovered nearby, while Grumpy and Abraham Lincoln Avisson, (his name in the store) discussed the doctor's research into the astrological influences in reincarnation.

"But if I can't prove it, Petrovich," Avisson said, leaning forward in his chair, "what good is all this work?"

"So what's the big deal about proof?" Grumpy saw Jimmy smirking behind Avisson. The boy had listened in on so many conversations, he knew when the old man was baiting someone, waiting to spring something important. Grumpy winked.

"How can we ever bring science to metaphysics if we can't provide proof?" Avisson asked.

"Turn it around, my friend." Grumpy smiled. "We should be bringing metaphysics to science. Science is younger, it should be subservient to the older discipline. Metaphysics has something science will never have."

"What's that?"

"Belief."

"That's what scientific proof brings."

Grumpy shook his head. "True belief is knowing the rightness of something without proof. Science is actually in the business of disbelief."

Avisson sighed. "Okay, but how do I make my thesis believable?"

"Do you believe that astrology and reincarnation are linked?"

"I believe they may very well be. That's what I'm trying to prove."

"How many books have you read on the two subjects?"

"Maybe fifty or more, of each."

"Done any past-life regressions?"

"Sure. I've interviewed a number of people who remember past lives. All circumstantial evidence, though. Nothing earthshaking."

"What more do you need?"

Avisson thought for several moments. Nodded. "It would be ideal, I think, to have twelve people, who not only remember being born under each astrological sign, but who also remember having died under each of the twelve signs—including birth and death dates and location of each, so I can check the astrological patterns, if any."

"That's a pretty tall order."

"Hell." Abe shook his head. "If it was easy, someone would already have done it."

"Okay. Why not start with one person?"

"Do you have anyone in mind?"

"No, but I have a hunch one is on the way."

"Who?"

"I don't know, Abe. That's up to the Universe."

"What do I do in the meantime, just wait? Put my all my research on hold?"

"So, what's your hurry? Why'd you do the research in the first place? Who are these invisible judges who have made you afraid to take a chance, by waiting for the right person or people to come along and help you unlock this secret? It's going to take a quantum leap to uncover any truth behind this." Grumpy walked to the coffee bar for a refill. "Don't be such a chickenshit."

"Look, I'd be glad to play the Universe's game, but with all the changes at the Foundation, my life is a little confused at the moment."

Grumpy saw Jimmy leaning with his chin on the broom, absolutely entranced. He winked at him. "Confusion is good."

"Gee, thanks," Avisson sputtered.

"Really. You don't begin to learn until you're confused. When you plow a field, aren't you confusing the dirt, which makes it easier for the seed to grow? Did you ever learn anything from a state of knowing?"

"I give up." Avisson grinned, embarrassed. "Man, am I glad you weren't around when I was at university."

Grumpy laughed.

Avisson stood, dropped a five-dollar bill on the table. "See you, Gypsy."

After he left, Jimmy walked up, smiling, showing his unusually well-kept teeth. "Do me a favor, okay?"

"What's that?"

"When you have something to teach me, just tell me you're doing it."

Grumpy looked into the piercing eyes. He put his hand on the boy's shoulder, nodded.

"Hey, Jimmy. How about some service?" The Moles had arrived.

Grumpy watched the girls' eyes, filled with the satisfaction of ordering their anti-hero around, and noted how he accepted such treatment within the confines of the store—but only from the girls. Anyone else would be quickly put in his place by "the green gaze"— Jimmy's version of the evil eye.

The front door banged open. An idiot shoe salesman walked in. He had come from the bowling-alley with a bimbo on his arm and begun to order Jimmy around to impress her. Jimmy just stood, staring at the man.

"What'sa matter, kid? Got shit in your ears? Two cappuccinos. Chop, chop." He smiled at his girl, who looked at him as if he were Gene Kelly.

Stare. Silence.

"I thought they trained 'em better at the Looney Bin? Come on, kid, make those cappies to go." He squeezed the girl's waist. "We're on the move."

The gaze was full green. No movement.

One of the Moles sitting at a far table shook her head, said to another girl in a sing-song voice, "He doesn't know the magic word."

The Gene Kelly impersonator turned. "What? You mean I gotta say 'please' and 'thank you' to get served around here?"

The Mole shook her head. "The magic word is asshole. Stop acting like one and he'll serve you."

The man blushed, started to get angry, grabbed the pin-girl by the arm and stalked out.

The Mole-girl high-fived her friends, then looked sheepishly over at Grumpy. "Sorry, Mr. Petrovich."

Grumpy nodded. "Normally, I would suggest using the Old English term, 'Arse-hole,' but I believe under the circumstances, the asshole in question wouldn't have understood." He motioned to Jimmy. "Give that young lady a hot chocolate, on me."

The scene had inspired another drawing for the BOOK. This one bore an uncanny resemblance to the shoe salesman, snapping his fingers and ordering "Two cappies, to go," surrounded by a thick red circle with a diagonal line through it. Beneath it the words: "No Arse-Holes."

The BOOK was a large, three-ring binder filled with plastic page-protectors. When people wrote poems, sent letters—good and bad—or photos and drawings, they all went in to the book. Grumpy couldn't remember who started it, it was just there, one day.

A man in an expensive suit walked in, saw Jimmy sweeping, asked him a question. Jimmy pointed to Grumpy and the man went to the counter.

"You the owner?"

"Nice suit. Am I being sued by somebody?"

"No." The man stuck out his hand. "Larry Clark."

Grumpy shook hands. "Am I being sued?"

"I am a lawyer," Clark said, "but this isn't about you or your store."

"How can I help you?"

"I need information on astrology."

"We've got a whole section on it."

Clark shook his head. "I don't have time for books. My client goes before the Grand Jury next week. I don't need to become an expert, I need to find one."

"What's the charge?"

"Murder."

"Ah, so you're representing the Scorpio Slasher."

"An unfortunate moniker, but yes."

"Is your client innocent?"

"There are extenuating circumstances."

"An abused childhood? I don't think the courts will go for that these days."

Clark smiled. "No. I think I can prove my client is only dangerous during certain periods... based on his astrological chart."

"What kind of defense is that, for a litigator of your reputation."

"The only one I've got."

"And you expect to win?"

Clark shrugged. "Ever hear of the Twinkie defense? That guy got off and his case was even flimsier."

"I guess I was out of the country. Who'd your client kill?"

"Eleven victims over the past fifteen years."

"What happens if you don't get this guy off?"

"He'll probably get the electric chair." Clark frowned. "Actually, my client said he wouldn't mind dying, if he knew he would come back as any astrological sign other than a Scorpio."

"I can't help you with that..." Grumpy pulled out his business card and wrote down a phone number."

"Who's this?"

"Dr. Abraham Avisson. Tell him I referred you."

Clark shook Grumpy's hand and left. Grumpy gazed around his store. People coming, going. Scientists, metaphysicians, lawyers...who could have ever guessed that retail would be so exciting?

❦

Doug stared at the passing scenery all the way home, ignoring Allie, who kept sticking his head out the rear window, nose to the wind. Sally's taunt echoed so loudly in Doug's mind, he didn't hear Nanny's question.

"Sorry, I didn't hear you."

"How was school?"

"Okay." He slumped in his seat, put one foot on the dashboard. Nanny cleared her throat and he dropped his foot to the floor. "Nanny, have you ever heard of something called 'The Crystal?'"

"It's a bookstore-cafe kind of place."

"What kind of people go there?"

"Oh, all kinds, I suppose." She turned and smiled. "I've only been a couple of times."

"Any kids?"

"Not when I was there, but I usually go during school hours."

"Could we go after school, sometime?" He reached over and pulled Allie's nose from the window.

"Sure. I think you'd like Mr. Petrovich."

Doug swung around. "Who's that?"

"The owner. He's very nice."

He peered closely. "Is he a friend of yours?"

She laughed. "I suppose so, though I don't know him well enough to call him a friend."

Doug continued staring at her.

"Really, I hardly know the man."

His eyes narrowed. He noticed a slight blush creeping up her neck as she pretended to concentrate on the road ahead. Finally, he clapped his hands and laughed. "Allie, Nanny's got a boyfriend!" He broke into a fit of giggles and Allie jumped onto the front seat to see what the commotion was about. Doug ducked to avoid the licks. "Cool."

"Douglas MacBrayne, that'll be enough of that." Nanny was beet-red. "Allie, you get in back."

Boy and dog wrestled all the way home. Nanny parked the car and sent them out to play, as soon as Doug changed his clothes. He grabbed his small set of golf clubs and headed for the temporary driving-range his father had built alongside the burned out chapel. Peter had had it surrounded with a chain-link fence while he decided whether or not to rebuild it.

Doug practiced smacking whiffle balls and Allie raced like mad to retrieve them. Whenever Doug hit one really high in the air, Allie would run, jump and catch it in his mouth. He would prance back proudly, but never give Doug the ball the first time he asked. Sometimes, they would engage in a game of catch-me-if-you-can, although Allie would only be caught when he was ready.

After one such go-around, Doug faked several swings just to get Allie going. He laughed and Allie came back, arctic blue eyes focused hungrily on the ball.

"You'll never catch this one." Doug waggled his hips, took a mighty swing and hit the ball with all his might.

The ball sailed high, just as a wind-shift hooked it toward the graveyard. Allie raced after it, watching the ball's trajectory as he ran. He stopped about five yards from the low, cemetery wall.

"Get the ball, Allie. Go on."

Allie turned, but didn't budge. The fur on his neck stood straight up.

"What's the matter, boy?" Doug ran to his side, tried to pat his hair down. "You afraid of ghosts?"

A low rumble came from Allie's throat.

"Chicken." Doug hopped the wall. "Never thought I'd see the day you'd be afraid of anything."

As soon as he bent over to pick up the ball, the vibrations started. Dizzy, he spun around and thought for a moment he might hit his head on a gravestone. A hand shot out from nowhere, steadied him. He looked up into a face silhouetted by fading sunlight.

"Hello, Master Douglas."

"Hector?" Doug blinked. "I wasn't sure if you were real or a dream."

"Thank you for remembering me, in either case." The priest bowed his head. "I've been looking forward to talking with you again."

"You have?"

Hector nodded, pointed to the fenced-in chapel. "Look what they've done."

"Dad doesn't know what he wants to do yet." Doug scratched just below his birthmark. "Though Nanny doesn't think he's going to rebuild it."

Hector nodded. "He doesn't understand why your Great Grandmother kept it up. If he did, he wouldn't hesitate to rebuild it."

"You know?"

"Aye, lad." Hector looked to heaven. "Karma and the passage of time have inextricably bound me to your family."

"What did Sarah do?"

"It didn't start with Sarah. Actually, you have to go way back to Scotland in the 1840s, to a little parcel of land on Loch Fyne near Dundarave Castle. The Laird had seeded half the female tenants on his estate, at least the comely ones, but distrusted his wife because she suddenly had a son, after four successive daughters."

Hector laughed, slapped his thigh.

"The old goat believed the malicious, but false rumors that she had sought the connubial assistance of one of the grooms to provide a male heir, who would carry on the MacBrayne name."

"Hey, that's my name!" Doug sat upright. Hector nodded, then continued.

"Unfortunately, the Laird snubbed his son, a strange, broody young man, born mostly deaf, with only half a left ear. The lad did however, have an uncanny eye, could sketch and color any living creature. Unfortunately, he was almost useless for anything else.

"Useless, that is, until he discovered the granddaughter of the retired gamekeeper, one Kirsty Campbell, whom he wooed in the strangest way. He left drawings of her on the front porch every morning. Kirsty was so afraid her grandfather would see the pictures and go after the young man, she took to rising every day at dawn, to remove the art from the porch.

"Soon enough, Kirsty was summoned to the castle to work in the kitchen for an upcoming festival. It was only a matter of time and circumstance before the young Laird would have his way. He told her of the coming Cheviot..."

"What's that?" Doug leaned against a headstone.

"Sheep. He said his father planned to convert the estate into a sheep-farm and would evict most of the tenants. But, if she would submit to him, she and her grandfather could stay on. The boy did love her, you see. When she became pregnant, the gentle fool even asked his father to let him marry her."

"He wouldn't, right?" Doug asked.

Hector shook his head, a deep sadness entered his voice. "This poor simpleton knew only how to draw, that he loved Kirsty—and she was going to have his child. So he went to the Rector, thinking the Church might intercede."

"Couldn't the Church force the father to let them marry?"

Another shake of the priest's head. "If the Laird let one bastard in, he'd have to take responsibility for all the others."

"What's a bastard?"

"An illegitimate child. Born out of wedlock."

"Oh, yeah."

"Well, the Church was politically and financially indebted to the Laird, so the young man's request was denied. They found the poor lad two days later, dead of a gunshot wound."

"What happened?"

Hector seemed to go into a trance, a timelessness went into his eyes as he spoke, as if reading from the sands of time.

"The Factor of the Dundarave Castle Estate arrived the next day and tethered his sleek, black stallion to a branch of the stout Rowan tree that stood swaying, just outside the gray, stone cottage. The wild, blustery wind tore at the thatched roof, ripping at the beige reeds, having white-capped its way across the waters of Loch Fyne, a sea-loch in the west-central Highlands of Scotland.

"The palefaced factor clamped his cap to his head, gathered his cloak around his shoulders and approached the stone cottage. From his modest shelter in the lee of a gray boulder, an aging, brown-and-white hound raised his tired head and snarled, exposing toothless gums. Undaunted, the factor knocked on the wooden door. Young, pretty Kirsty Campbell answered, her pink cheeks made brighter by the cold and her curly brown hair captured by a scarf she wore when cleaning.

"Ach. Mr. Dalgleish. Will you come in out o' the cold, and have a cuppie? I've just put the pot on the stove."

"No thank ye, Miss Campbell, I've no time for that, today. I've come only to fetch your grandfather."

"He's gone for a short walk," Kirsty said, "but he should return for his tea, in an hour or so. Would you like to wait?"

He looked at her with eyes colder than the wind outside. "There's trouble here, Miss Campbell. I give you fair warning to be ready to vacate this house and leave the estate by the end of next week. The Laird will countenance no arguments."

The color drained from Kirsty's cheeks. "But my family's been on the estate for generations. What have we done wrong? Why do we have to leave. Where are we to go?" Kirsty paused. A light came into her bright blue eyes. "Is it because o' the bairn?" she asked, patting her stomach, "I'm only a few months along, Mr. Dalgleish. No one need ever know about the young Laird and…"

"The young Laird is dead."

The information struck Kirsty like a slap from a heavy hand. "How did he die?"

"Shot."

Tears welled in Kirsty's eyes. She twisted the ring on her finger. A gift from the young man, it had belonged to his grandmother. She spoke in a whisper.

"I suppose you'll be needing grandfather to help hunt for the killer."

"I know who the killer is, I'm just waiting for him to return."

"Return? From where?"

"From that short walk."

Hector waited until Doug's eyes widened with understanding.

"The old gamekeeper didn't really kill the young Laird, did he?" Doug said.

"Probably not." Hector nodded. "But the Laird blamed Kirsty's grandfather, anyway."

"Why?"

"Because, in the eyes of the Church, if the young Laird was thought to have committed suicide, he couldn't be buried in the church cemetery. Sacrificing Kirsty's grandfather was not so important to the Laird, as keeping the official family record clean."

"Was her grandfather put in jail?"

"No. He was hanged."

"And Kirsty?"

"She married a crofter, one Kenneth MacBrayne."

"A crofter? Was he related to the Laird?"

"Yes and no." Hector leaned over, a ghostly conspirator. "Some said Kenneth was the spitting image of the senior Laird himself."

"Another b-bastard?"

"As I said, there were a great many of them around." Hector smiled. "When she was a pretty young scullery-maid in the castle kitchen, Kenneth's mother had been forced to submit to the amorous advances of the senior Laird. After Kenneth's birth, she took the MacBrayne family name as her own, not an uncommon custom, in those days.

"So, when her son, the illegitimate Kenneth MacBrayne, married Kirsty, he gave the MacBrayne family name to the expectant mother."

"Did Kirsty have the baby?"

"Yes, eventually. A boy."

"Wow! Was that my great-grandfather, Hamish?"

"No, Hamish came later," the priest said. "I suppose it would have been your great, great-uncle."

"What was his name?"

"They named him for the young Laird, his real father." The priest's eyes became prankish. "Let's just say his name rhymed with rector."

※

Peter adjusted the goggles. He felt foolish. Nothing looked particularly dangerous in the laboratory. No Frankenstein appliances or bubbling vats. But maybe that was why they had still not discovered the secret to a marketable artificial leather.

A young lab-technician fumbled a beaker as Peter and Downey passed. Carter, the whale-shaped Director of Research, blew out an exasperated spume.

"Mr. Knapp, this is not the Nobel committee, just the men who sign your paycheck."

"Yes, sir."

"A Berkeley zealot. Hopes to help us develop artificial leather...to save the seals, or whatever." Carter did not bother lowering his voice as he steered Peter and Downey toward a bank of microscopes. "Purist."

He said the last as if he were saying "Leper." Peter glanced over his shoulder. The young man noticed he was being watched. He blushed.

"How long has he been out of school?"

"Three, four years." Carter adjusted one of the microscopes.

"Do you really want someone that inexperienced? This is top priority."

Carter slipped a slide into the carrier and focused. "The best research is going on at universities, especially the big names. They've got government money, for state-of-the-art equipment and information-sharing by computer. Obviously, our industry isn't willing to do that. He's a steal."

He rolled his chair to the next microscope and focused it. "Look in there. What you have is a cross-section of leather cells. Compare that with what you see here."

Peter looked at the first, Downey at the second. Then they traded places.

"They look nearly identical," Peter said. "Does that mean we're close?"

Carter's elephantine head tilted, waggled negatively. He tossed a sample of brown material that looked like leather. "Feel this."

Peter did, handed it to Downey.

"Feels like rubber," Downey said.

"Told you," came from across the room. Knapp looked like an old open-cockpit pilot, with his goggles on his forehead. "What you're holding there, gentlemen, used to be leather."

"But it feels like rubber," Downey said.

Knapp moved close. "What you're experiencing is spiritual and cellular dissonance." He seemed so proud of himself, Peter was reluctant to let him know that he had no idea what the young man was talking about. "We took leather and mashed it up, broke it down and reconstituted it. Made the same kind of paste we use to mold our flexible PVC."

"I thought our goal was to turn plastic into leather, not the other way around." Downey scratched his head.

"The point here, has to do with texture." Knapp pulled the skin on his arm. "All leather is basically just skin. Human skin has a spiritual connection with animal skin, because the two perform the same function. Leather has a cellular harmonic, that we just can't reproduce with plastic—yet."

Peter rose from the counter where he sat. "So, is this a convoluted way of saying the project is a failure?"

"Not at all. The research to date has shown us lots of ways how not to make artificial leather." Knapp's tone was inspired. Carter cleared his throat in a not-so-subtle warning, but the younger man wouldn't be stopped. "Consider what oil is—just vegetation, forests, even dinosaurs that were crushed millions of years ago. They have gone from an animate to an organic state, put in the evolutionary blender, so to speak. Trying to make leather out of plastic is like trying to make a dinosaur out of oil. That's where the spiritual and cellular dissonance comes in. Even cotton, plant that it is, has more life to it than dead oil. And over the centuries, we've grown accustomed to the feel of cotton against our skin. It's the same with leather."

"But not plastic." Downey said.

"Hasn't been around long enough." Knapp was rolling, evangelical. "That's what's so important about recognizing the spiritual part of it. We can line the molecules up precisely, but the experience of the material has to match that of leather—the feel of it, its 'hand' and the fact that it 'breathes'. When it does, people will wear it."

Peter turned to Carter. "Do you know what the hell he's talking about?"

"Of course." Carter nodded. "That's why we hired him."

"I still don't get it." Downey rubbed the reconstituted leather, looked at Carter. "How is all this Voo-Doo going to help us patent this product?"

"Everyone in the industry is trying to develop artificial leather. Between the skyrocketing cost of raising cattle and the growing animal-rights movement, the company that first finds the answer will control the industry for five, maybe ten years." Carter shifted his bulk. "What Knapp says might sound crazy, but he's not the only one saying it. We're all searching for a process, he's looking for the answer. If we find it first, it may be because of him."

Peter and Downey left the laboratory and walked slowly across the quadrangle to the administrative offices. Before going inside, Downey stopped Peter.

"You know what we have to do."

"Pump more money into research as soon as we get rid of the Foundation and the Orphanage," Peter said, "

"Yeah, but we should get Carter out of there as soon as possible."

"Why Carter? He's heading up the project."

Downey shook his head. "Because, he's shot his wad and is following this kid the whole way. We've done the basic research, it's the genius-spark that's missing. Carter was right about it being Knapp."

"You're not worried that he's too young?"

Downey smiled. "What happens if we need to raise more money? Who can we front? A fat pig like Carter, who looks like he eats investors for breakfast? Or a young, personable scientist, who's perfectly positioned between the Sierra Club and Albert Schweitzer?"

Peter stared at him. "And they think I'm ruthless."

"Gotta think straight if you're gonna think big."

"Who are you quoting now, Dan?" Peter asked. "J.P. Morgan?"

"It was either Einstein or Mae West. I don't remember which."

❦

Avisson had just finished reviewing his notes of his last session with Clint Sharpe when Margaret buzzed him.

"There's a Mr. Clark here to see you."

"I don't have him on my calendar. Are you sure there hasn't been some mistake?"

"He was recommended by a Mr. Petrovich."

"Oh. Send him in."

Avisson came around to the front of his desk. Clark, a tall, well-dressed man, entered and reached out to him.

"Larry Clark. Thanks for seeing me on such short notice, Doctor."

"Larry, as in Larry and Cleo Clark?"

"Why, yes."

"Clark, as in the threatened lawsuit that cost Dr. Ramis his job?"

"Yes. Does it bother you that someone should be made to account for unprofessional behavior?"

"I suppose not. But why are you here?"

"Petrovich recommended you to me, regarding the possibility of your testifying in an upcoming case."

"As a therapist?"

"As an astrologer." He pulled out a sheaf of papers, tossed several on the desk. "As you can see from the planetary alignment in this poor soul's chart, he was destined to kill. A Scorpio with Pluto in the eighth house. Tragic combination."

"I believe your wife suggested he plead temporary astrology. Is that your tactic now?"

Clark laughed. "No, but temporary insanity based on demonstrable, astrological pressures."

"Who's going to prove them for you?"

"You are, Dr. Avisson. According to Mr. Petrovich, you're the only one who can."

Avisson spun his chair, turned away. He needed to consider this carefully. A year ago, he would have thrown himself passionately into the case. This was one of the reasons the Foundation had been started.

Kautsch's note hovered in his mind. "No weird stuff."

On the other hand, Petrovich had thrown Avisson a challenge. He spun his chair to face Clark again.

"No guarantees. The judge might throw both our asses out of the courtroom for even suggesting this."

"True," Clark said, speaking through the temple he'd made with his fingers. "But win or lose, my client needs your help, Dr. Avisson."

"I can only testify to the believed astrological influences. I won't bend things in his favor just to save his life."

"You don't understand." Clark waited a moment, found the right words. "If my client loses, he wants the court to put him to death."

Avisson stood, paced around the desk, pulling at his beard. "You say that Petrovich recommended me to you?"

"The guy at the Crystal Cafe. Yeah." Clark looked up. "Will you take the case?"

"I'll start the research, but you need to know that I won't take one side or the other." He wrote down several items. "And I'll need to see the prisoner at the jail with his answers to these questions."

"What's all this for?"

"To see if we can take him back into some of his past lives."

☙

Doug was stunned. Was he actually talking with a dead relative? "Why didn't you tell me all this last time?"

"I didn't want to shock you too much, what with the fire, and me being... well, you know, don't you?"

"I guess so," Doug said. "But isn't it better to meet a gho...a spirit you're related to, than a total stranger?"

"Maybe." Hector spread his hands. "But you're the first live person I've ever really talked to. I don't know the protocol."

Doug sat thinking for several minutes. "So, I'm truly related to the Laird of Dundarave, through Kenneth MacBrayne, right?"

"Yes, though there's no proof."

"And the Laird kicked Kirsty off the land, then she and Kenneth came over. That's how all this started?"

"Half of it. The other part of the story began near Loch Leven, at Burleigh Castle."

"Another Laird?"

Hector winced slightly. "Afraid so."

Doug rolled his eyes. "More bastards?"

"Just one. Your great-great-grandfather, Douglas. Peter the first, I suppose."

"Where was this?"

"He ran away to Gray-Yards, near Loch Tyne, up north by Inverness." Hector chuckled. "But this time, Morag Douglas, Peter's wife, who came from a Highland family of spitfires, called Monroe—gave them what-for.

" 'Our family has been farming the Laird's lands as far back as anyone can remember,' Morag told the Gray-Yards Factor, when he came to roust them off the property.

" 'Mrs. Douglas,' he said, 'the fact the land has been farmed has nothing to do with it. The decision has been made. The whole lot of you are to go. If we must, we'll get the police. Or,' he added ominously, 'we'll even get soldiers, if necessary. It's the law.'

" 'What sort of law is it that let's the Laird throw us off land we have farmed for him since the beginning of time? And farmed very well, too, I might add.'

" 'It is not your land. It belongs to the Laird, Mrs. Douglas. You and your neighbors are all tenant-farmers and therefore his employees. It is my unpleasant duty to tell you that you are all getting the sack, but I'm happy to say the Laird is prepared to make a financial settlement.'

" 'But what are we to do? Where will we go?'

" 'The Laird will pay for your transport to Glasgow and for your fares aboard one of the sailing-ships to Canada. To those who go without a fuss, he will even give a little extra. Your cooperation will help you get a good start in the New World.'

"Morag frowned and looked the factor straight in the eye.

" 'Is this the truth?' she asked, 'Rumors have been rife in the land that the 'Clearance' of a family from the Highlands is not normally accompanied by any financial consideration, whatsoever.'

" 'I tell you the truth, Mrs. Douglas. On my honor.'

" 'Well, on your honor...why have these Clearances come to us?'

" 'The reason is as it has been everywhere else: sheep.'

" 'Sheep?' Morag said. 'We are being evicted to make room for sheep? Has it come to animals over people?'

" 'Blunt, but true.' the Factor said, reddening slightly. 'But it really derives from the economics of the situation: Because of the bad weather, the short growing season and the poor quality of the tired land, you tenant-farmers are barely able to scratch out a living and—you remember the potato blight a few years ago?'

" 'Ach! How could I forget?' Morag replied. The hardships of the terrible famine they all endured flashed into her mind.

" 'Well, the Laird hasn't forgotten, either. There have been no payments in either cash or crops for two years. The Laird's patience has run out.'

" 'But sheep...'

" 'Even as poor as it is, the land will provide well enough for the Cheviot, Mrs. Douglas. Furthermore, they are easy to tend and shear. Whereas people need constant feeding, clothing, schooling and taking care of, in general.'

" 'And I suppose there's good money to be made from the selling of the wool?'

" 'That's correct.'

" 'So what it boils down to is the Laird thinks he has lost money in farming, and he can make money from sheep?'

" 'He knows it. Now, if you'll be so good as to tell your husband. As I said, the Laird will be generous with all of you.'

"The generosity came in the form of notices that were posted, listing the names of those to be out of their homes in a week. The crofters were enraged. No one complied. Two days later, the Factor brought the police into the village while the men were out in the fields. And, without warning, they forcibly evicted the women, the old men and the children. They tossed all the furniture into the street and set fire to every roof in the village.

"Some of the women resisted by throwing stones and whatever. The police response was brutal, vicious. Furious, almost insane with outrage, Morag tore a leg from her flimsy kitchen table and went for the Factor. A huge policeman clubbed her head. She fell unconscious onto her pile of pitiful furniture.

"That evening, after the police left, their terrible but 'lawful' duty done, Morag Douglas, large with child and wearing a bloody bandage on her head, led an angry mob to the manor house. The people carried burning torches and shouted, 'Away with the Cheviot!'

"Three men carried a ram into the middle of the crowd, slaughtered it and threw it onto the steps of the manor. Morag taunted the Factor who stood on the vestibule steps, a long musket in his hands.

"He raised the gun as if to fire. The crowd fell back.

" 'You don't scare me none, you English-sucking bastard,' Morag cried.

"The gun remained aimed directly at her. She did a little dance, screaming more obscenities and waved her fire like a magic, orange wand. Then she let it fly, straight for the manor house. The rest of the crowd followed suit, filling the sky with flaming torches.

"The Factor discharged the musket, knocking the bandage and a piece of scalp from Morag's head. She dropped like a stone. At first the crowd thought she was dead, but she staggered to her feet a few moments later, and calmly replaced both scalp and bandage.

"When the police arrived, they arrested Morag and the other leaders, but the blazing manor was beyond saving. Later that night, a number of men, led by Peter Douglas, freed the jailed crofters and the pregnant Morag.

"Most of them quietly left for Glasgow on foot, with all the meager possessions they could carry.

" 'Maybe I should have stayed in jail,' Morag said one evening, shivering against the November cold in a hay-filled barn. 'At least we might have then been transported to Australia as convicts. The winters there aren't nearly so severe as what they say of Nova Scotia.'

" 'Yer no criminal,' Peter said through clenched teeth. 'And that's the last I ever want to hear mention of what happened at Gray-Yards.'

"Fiery as Morag was, she would rather face the Factor's musket again than Peter's anger. She smiled, patted his hand, before falling into a deep sleep."

Doug had a question, but wasn't quite sure how to frame it.

Hector grinned.

"You wonder how I know all this if I wasn't born yet?"

"I guess."

"The two families' first years in Nova Scotia were bitter and hard. Between the cold and lack of money, the only entertainment was the telling of stories; so the stories of the Clearances were told to us children over and over again."

"Okay, but where did they meet the MacBraynes?"

"Three weeks after Kirsty's grandfather was hung, in early December, the MacBraynes and those neighbors who did not decide to move to the Lowlands or south to England, stood huddled on the wharf, near the Glasgow City Centre. Two small rowboats ferried the passengers out into the misty harbor, where the black-hulled, wooden barque stood at anchor, its four masts waiting for the white sails to be unfurled.

"Kenneth MacBrayne stood tall, his dark beard in contrast with his pale face. One arm was placed tenderly around Kirsty's shoulders. A few herring gulls squawked around the icy harbor, landing every so often on bits of flotsam in the murky water. The smooth, weathered stones of the wharf reeked with the strong smell of fish.

Kenneth wondered if they had made the best decision. Some of their less-adventurous neighbors had gone south to England, but had not been heard from. He gathered his cloak to protect him from the chill.

Soon enough, it was their turn to be rowed to the ship. Hand-in-hand they walked down the stone wharf on the north bank of the River Clyde. Evicted from what they considered their own Eden, they had their own paradise within, the heritage of the clans in their blood. They faced the uncertain future proudly, but fearfully.

The impassive, ruddy-faced seaman watched as they cautiously climbed into the small boat and took their seats. His competent, gnarled hands moved the oars effortlessly through the still water until they arrived alongside the formidable ship. Kenneth looked up where the bowsprit joined the bow and saw the name of the vessel, painted in white letters on the grimy, black hull. He pointed it out.

"Look, Kirsty. There's the name of our ship, 'The Land of Hope' and underneath, it says, 'Mackie and Thomson, Glasgow.' Her name seems quite appropriate for our going to Canada, don't you think?"

"I certainly hope so." said Kirsty, with a wan smile. "But I wonder if they change the name for the return?"

"Why would they do that?" asked Kenneth,

"It probably returns here, to get more poor souls like us, don't you think?" she replied. "My guess is they'd only need to make a small change. Wouldn't "Land of Dim Hope" be appropriate for the return voyage to Scotland?"

"Don't be bitter, Lass."

"I am. And a bit sad, too. But I'm mostly scared, Kenneth, scared by what we left behind and of what lies ahead. I've heard that some call these vessels 'coffin ships.'"

A rope ladder hung from the gunnel almost down to the still surface of the water. A stocky man, with a gray beard and an officer's cap looked down on them, disinterestedly.

On the main deck, they looked around. There were people everywhere. Kenneth showed a seaman their tickets, asked about the compartments. The man just laughed and pointed below deck. Kenneth threaded his way through the throng of Scots on deck and found the steps leading down to the hold. As he descended into the darkness, he was overcome by an odor so strong, so virulent, he almost retched.

It was obvious that the interior of the ship had been used for countless voyages identical to the one on which they were about to embark and that it had not been cleaned or disinfected between trips.

His eyes adjusted to the darkness below deck: The entire area was lined with nothing but flat boards, joined to make wooden shelves about four feet wide. He counted five levels high and saw the boards were supported by brackets nailed to the inside of the hull. Not a bed nor a bunk anywhere in sight. He made a quick calculation and, gasping from the foul air, returned to the deck.

The crew hoisted the two rowboats on board. Kenneth heard the rattle of chains lifting the heavy anchor from the muddy harbor bottom. Other crew members were aloft, unfurling the sails, which turned out to be roughly patched, stained and gray, rather than the pure white his imagination had expected. He found the Captain and grabbed him by the arm.

"I have changed my mind! We don't want to go to Canada."

"Well now, ain't that too bad?" The Captain sneered. "My ship is full and we're under sail. You're too late, mister."

Kenneth elbowed through the crowd of buzzing passengers and found Kirsty standing by the rail. They looked back at the city of Glasgow as it receded in the frigid mist.

Suddenly, a familiar, wailing drone skirled across the still waters. A hush came over the crowd on deck. A lone, kilted bagpiper stood at the end of the wharf, pipes to his mouth.

As he played "Auld Lang Syne," Kenneth and Kirsty MacBrayne, tears streaming down their cheeks, noticed a tall man and his young wife standing nearby. The girl had a large, bloodstained bandage on top of her head and held her protruding stomach.

"My name is Douglas, Peter Douglas. And this is my wife, Morag." said the man, extending his hand. "We have been cleared from Gray-Yards, up Inverness way. Some say it should be called Grave-Yards."

Kenneth introduced himself and Kirsty, said they came from the MacBrayne Estate, by Loch Fyne.

"A dirty business, these Clearances," said Peter Douglas.

"Aye," said Kenneth. "But there's one thing they've not kept in mind by replacing men with sheep."

"And what would that be, Mr. MacBrayne?" Morag spoke for the first time.

"If there's ever a war, the sheep won't take up arms to defend our country," Kenneth said. "These profitable Cheviot ensure Scotland will never again be free."

Glasgow had long since disappeared. The wind picked up and there was a chop on the surface of the dark green sea.

"Then we'll find our freedom elsewhere," Kirsty moved closer to Kenneth.

In the next few days an occasional wizened sailor would look in on the dank, foul hold at the bottom of the gangway and wonder if this group of Scots would try to clean it up, as had all the others.

No matter what the weather, during the early days out of Glasgow, the seas were always calmer than when they reached the wild Atlantic, west of Ireland. Well before that time, the women covered their noses with their kerchiefs, scrounged some pails, brushes and soap and did their best to remove the accumulated filth.

On average, they slept three to a shelf: most often man, wife and child. The MacBraynes and Douglasses, given that both women were pregnant, often shared one shelf. The men took turns walking the deck, while the others slept. The wind shifted and the ship came about to a chorus of creaks and groans from the beams and planks in the hold, accompanied by the sound of the rising wind, which shrieked like a wounded banshee in the rigging. Waves began braking over the bow.

Now out in the vicious, rolling swells of the North Atlantic, the deposits of urine, vomit and worse, would accumulate faster than they could be cleaned up. Before they had embarked on their journey, all the evictees were told they could bring only clothing and food with them. So they sold what they could of their pitiful possessions, in what was obviously a buyer's market. After a few weeks at sea, little food remained, so they were forced to buy from the Captain's ample stores, at outrageous prices.

It soon became apparent the Douglasses had no spare cash whatsoever. They had even sold some of their clothing to pay for passage, and had nothing left for food.

Kenneth and Kirsty, on the other hand, even after four weeks at sea, had spent only a fraction of what they had fetched by selling the ring given to Kirsty by the young Laird. Kenneth discussed the situation with Peter Douglas: They would share and share alike until, God willing, they arrived in Canada. They would then, somehow, start a shoe-repair business. Peter Douglas would teach Kenneth MacBrayne the trade, in exchange for his financial help.

Six weeks out of Glasgow, the big storm hit. Having gathered force since before midnight, by the middle of the next afternoon, the wind was of hurricane strength. The ship, almost invisible in the pelting, stinging sleet, tried to maintain its heading, to no avail.

Enormous swells tossed the five hundred and eighty ton, square-rigged barque as if it were a log shooting rapids in some icy mountain stream. Wind-whipped, white-frothed breakers combed the deck of the hapless vessel, their dark green teeth gnashing at the railings. The passengers were impossibly huddled below. Most were either seasick or sick with fear. The stench was almost unbearable.

The Captain had long since ordered all sail taken in. Everyone prayed the storm would blow itself out. No one noticed it was Christmas Eve.

Morag went into premature labor, while Kirsty tried to hold her to the shelf they shared. The men fought to bring water and some clean rags to the shelf, but after a long night of trying to calm her, at daybreak, the battle was lost.

The roiling seas, as if understanding the nature of the moment, subsided for the impromptu service. The child was wrapped in spare cloth and returned to God.

Kirsty held and rocked Morag, whose pain had made them closer sisters than any blood."

Doug was quiet as Hector finished the tale of the voyage, the landing in Halifax, the bitter winters, during which the two families shared everything, even Hector's ultimate birth and early childhood.

"Should I not have told you this story?" Hector asked.

"No, I'm glad to know." Doug took a deep breath. "I'm just sorry Morag's baby had to die."

Hector nodded. "Every story of life involves death. I believe that's what makes living so heroic—men and women continue to struggle, knowing all the while that death awaits them."

"Death and that tunnel you're afraid to go through?" Doug smiled.

"Everything has its reason, Master Doug," Hector said. "Even my cowardice."

❦

As he walked along the corridors of the orphanage, Peter couldn't help feeling even more certainty in the transition that loomed. Sure, each of the forty bedrooms seemed homey enough. But the children may as well have been at a private school. They still ate their meals communally—and camp is for the summer, not all year round.

The architect and the state standards inspector each carried clipboards and spoke in hushed, conspiratorial tones. Dr. Kautsch acted like a prospective real-estate buyer, unconsciously tapping the walls and checking the swing of doors and eyeing the symmetry of wall and ceiling junctures. When he realized Peter had caught him at it, he grinned.

"My mother used to get dizzy if she walked into a room and the walls and ceilings were crooked. She made me go in first, to check for her."

Peter smiled. Why were all psychiatrists so batty?

Miss Groebnick rolled along with them, hustling off to get whatever information or papers were required, only to rejoin the group with a breathless display of efficiency. Peter could see the questions in her eyes, but was loathe to answer any yet. Everything was too preliminary, and any premature disclosure of the plans could quash the entire deal.

What with Downey initiating the negotiations with the investment bankers the following week, any delays from this point on would leave the door wide open for Eterna-Sole.

"What are your plans for the orphans' relocation?" the state inspector asked.

Peter and Kautsch looked at Miss Groebnick. Her face blanched. Peter spoke quickly.

"Should any of the remodeling require relocation of the children, their temporary accommodations will exceed existing standards."

Miss Groebnick gulped. Kautsch hurried to add, "And if construction occurs in the summer months, the Foundation will be happy to pay to send the children to summer camp." He turned to the round woman. "They would like that, wouldn't they?"

She nodded, still pale.

The tour finished, Groebnick was called to answer the telephone. Peter and Kautsch walked the inspector and the architect out to their cars and made arrangements to meet in another week. When they drove away, Peter grabbed Kautsch by the sleeve.

"I thought you talked to both of them about keeping quiet."

"I did." Kautsch carefully took Peter's hand from his arm. "The man's a bureaucrat. You can't make them do anything."

"Yeah, well, where is the money coming from to send them to camp?"

Kautsch shrugged. "Downey's working on that one."

After Grumpy waved goodnight to Jimmy and put the car in gear, he saw Miss Groebnick hurry down the steps toward him. He lowered the passenger window. She leaned in, breathless.

"Thank you, Mr. Petrovich. I just wanted to let you know that Jimmy won't be able to work at the store tomorrow night."

"Oh, is everything all right?"

"Just some State-testing. They come in periodically. It took me five years to get them to do it after school so the children wouldn't miss their lessons."

"Thank you for letting me know, Miss Groebnick." The woman lingered in the rolled-down window. "Is there anything else?"

"Well, I really shouldn't say—except—how often do you speak with your principal shareholder? Didn't you say it was Peter Douglas-MacBrayne, Junior?"

"Yes. We communicate quite regularly. Why do you ask?"

She leaned in. "Can you keep something confidential?"

"I believe so."

"If you speak with Mr. MacBrayne in Europe, would you ask him to come home as soon as possible?"

"Why, is something the matter?"

She nodded, on the verge of sobbing. "They want me to find a camp that will accommodate all the children this summer...for some remodeling...they said."

"Who's they?"

"Mr. Downey and that Dr. Kautsch."

"I would think letting the kids go to camp would be a nice thing, don't you?"

She shook her head.

"Why not?"

"We had extensive remodeling two years ago. We don't need it now."

"I see."

She pinched his sleeve gingerly. "Please, don't let them take my children away."

Chapter Eight

At first, Fiona didn't realize the noise she heard at the back door was Allie scratching. She opened it after he barked sharply, twice.

"Why, what's got into you, Allie?" She pointed. "Go find Doug and tell him supper's almost ready."

Allie barked again, turned a quick circle, then looked at Fiona with canine impatience. He took three steps, stopped to see if Fiona was following.

"If this is some kind of trick you and Dougie have cooked up…" She removed her apron and followed him.

Allie would run a bit, stop and wait for Fiona to catch up, then continue. Peter had just stepped out of the Bentley when they crossed the driveway. He called to her.

"So now he's got you walking the dog, Fiona?"

"No, sir," Fiona called back. "Allie seems a might upset about something. Thought I'd better check."

"Where's Doug?"

"Don't know," she said.

Peter handed the driver his briefcase and joined Fiona as Allie led to the graveyard by the chapel. Allie stopped, barked again, fur raised on his neck.

"What is it, boy?" Fiona said.

Snarling, Allie took one bound and leaped over the low wall. Fiona spotted Doug, lying at the base of a headstone.

"Oh, my God."

"I'll get him," Peter said, and vaulted over.

Fiona, trembling, watched Peter scoop up the boy and carry him out. Allie stayed close, whining.

"Is he hurt?" Fiona asked?

"Either passed out or asleep." Peter knelt, keeping Doug's head upright. "Are you okay, Doug?"

The eyes fluttered. The mouth began to chew the air. "What...?" He opened his eyes and looked up.

"Are you okay, Doug?" Fiona was right by his father's side.

"Guess I fell asleep." He rubbed his face.

Fiona felt his forehead. "My God, lad. You're cold as ice."

"I'm sorry."

"What happened?" His father sounded angry.

Doug looked around, saw Allie and smiled. "I was hitting whiffle balls. One went over the wall and..."

"And what?" Peter asked.

"It was him!" Doug's eyes searched the graveyard. "The guy who pulled me from the fire."

"What? Who?"

"Father Hector. He's part of our family..."

"Dougie, hold on now." Fiona looked worriedly at Peter. "It must have been a dream."

"No, not twice. It couldn't be." Doug looked at his father. "He's been here since the early 1800s."

"What are you talking about? He would be well over a hundred years old." Peter frowned.

"No. He died. A horse trampled him. But he's afraid to go to the tunnel."

"Tunnel?"

"Where you go when you die."

"That's it." Peter threw up his hands and walked toward the mansion. "I've heard enough."

"But, Dad—Sir?"

"Enough." He whirled and pointed to Fiona. "And you. I want you to call Dr. Kautsch and make another appointment for Doug to see him immediately. If not tonight, then tomorrow morning, first thing."

"But—"

"No buts. Do it."

Peter stormed inside. Fiona wrapped her arm around Doug and they followed.

"Sorry if I got you in trouble, Nanny."

"No trouble, lad." She kissed the top of his head. "No trouble, whatsoever."

Clint hadn't meant it to happen. He'd promised Mandy he would never drink at school again, but packing his things took more courage than he had at the moment. He looked around, dully.

Maybe he would be better off. The snot-nosed kids at the school pissed him off, pure and simple. They were supposed to be preparing for college but not one of them could write a single paragraph without a grammatical error. A few weren't even sure what a paragraph was. And that didn't take into consideration the sheer paucity of ideas or concepts in their vacuous renderings.

Imagine, boycotting his classes because he refused to grade tests on a curve. Couldn't they see he was doing it for their own, long-term good? So what, if some of the lazy ones hoped their grades would be "automatically" improved if the best students goofed off once in a while, thus moving the curve to the left?

Why should average students get honor grades if the A-students stay home with the flu? That's what grading on the curve can do: It can't be logical. It's only a mechanical devil. And there's to be a "debate." A debate? Huh.

"Please think of grades in economic terms—as if a grade were money." Clint had said to the debating team: two surly members of the Student Council, two men and a woman from the Board of Education—plus Dr. Johnson, the wimpish Principal who had set up the charade of a debate when it became clear that, on his own, he would be unable to make Clint grade on that damned curve. For his part, Clint had been foolish enough to welcome the debate, thinking he would be dealing with open-mindedness.

"For the purposes of this discussion—" Clint smiled at the opposition; then at the audience, where sat every student from his classes. Perhaps they thought he hadn't prepared his position carefully. "—and for the sake of this discussion, let's agree that grades are the equivalent of real-world dollars, where the better your performance, the more money you get."

He moved to the blackboard. "Let's say that an "A" is worth $90; a "B" is $80; a "C" $70, and so forth.

"Now, the traditional system of measuring achievement has been used with great success for generations of students who have been accepted, or rejected by colleges, based on a uniform standard of accomplishment.

"On the other hand, grading on a curve assaults the standard, by diluting and/or obfuscating it. If, for example, the highest grade on a given test is 70, the curve will cause the top ten percent of the class to get an "A," period." Clint grabbed a piece of chalk and wrote "Voila!" on the blackboard, "Those who should have gotten only $70 will get $90 for their poor result. The standard has thus been relaxed, assaulted: Inferior work has been overly rewarded. And...your chances of getting into the college of your choice...have been unalterably reduced."

The opposition stared, stony-faced. Some of the kids applauded. Clint recognized every one as an A student.

"This process of decay has pervaded our entire educational system. We are graduating too many ill-prepared students, sending them out into the real world, where most will remain badly educated until the day they die...and may never realize it was their tenured teachers, grading on a curve, who betrayed them."

Clint looked the opposition straight in the eye. "Now, before you vote, please consider this question: "Can you ever properly tell the difference between Right and Wrong, by a show of hands?" He then turned to face the audience, mostly his own students. "No matter how it turns out, I promise I will never betray you, never...even if it costs me my job."

He opened the top drawer of his desk and looked inside. Shit, no breath mints. That weasel, Johnson, was probably on his way here already, would walk in sniffing the air like some airport drug-dog.

Screw him. They'd already done their worst.

Clint slipped the pint from the bottom drawer into his briefcase. Evidence gone. Ha.

He looked at his notice of suspension and probation: "Inebriated during class." The report was as mediocre as were most of the students. No poetry, no energy. Drunkenness was a spiritual undertaking, almost by medical definition. He didn't just get loaded, plastered or smashed. Why couldn't they have said his intoxication was Bacchanalian; that he wasn't simply a lush or a sot, but a dipsomaniac? It would be easier to accept the judgment of his moronic educational peers if they could only rise above their linguistic disabilities.

He picked up the current issue of National Review, put it in the box with his books and personal effects. Clint's love of words could be blamed on William F. Buckley, Jr. Either on him, or Mr. James Davis—maybe both.

The two men couldn't have been further apart in the real world, but they were twin pillars in Clint's personal ideology. Bill Buckley was a well known conservative, whereas Jim Davis owned a small junkyard, just off Ashland Avenue and 47th Street on Chicago's south side, near where Clint was raised. But Clint might have never found Buckley if it hadn't been for Davis.

Years before, Clint and four or five other boys earned extra money after school by helping separate waste paper at the junkyard: newsprint in one pile, corrugated and cardboard in another, slick magazines in a third. When things got slow, the other boys would grab magazines with pictures in them, dream about someday owning the things they saw.

Young Clint soon tired of looking at the picture magazines. A waste of time. One afternoon, Mr. Davis saw him slip a copy of National Review under his shirt.

"Where you going with that, boy?"

"School." Clint hung his head. "I... there's lots of words I don't know in here."

"Gonna ask your teacher?"

"No. I can find 'em myself." He puffed himself up to his full height. "Going to the library. Got a big dictionary there."

Mr. Davis played with his goatee, nodded, grinned his one-gold-tooth smile.

"Make you a deal, boy. You take that magazine." He held up a gnarled finger. "When you think you know what all the words mean, bring it back. Then I'll pick out some tough ones. I'll give you ten cents for every one you get right."

"Okay!"

"But you gotta pay me ten cents for each one you don't."

Clint thought a moment, stuck out his hand. "Mr. Davis, you got a deal."

Clint pushed himself from his chair when he heard Johnson at the door. He had his briefcase in one hand, the box in the other, just as the principal entered.

"Thanks for opening the door. I wasn't sure how I was going to do that."

"I'm sorry about this, Mr. Sharpe." Johnson stared through weasel lenses. "Of course, your medical benefits will continue through your ah... probation and counseling."

Clint smirked. "If only it were as easy for a person to be open-minded about his philosophy of education as it is to make him stop drinking, eh?"

Johnson blinked twice. I'm sorry. I don't see the connection."

Clint nodded. "That's why you're the principal and I've been suspended."

He walked past the man without saying goodbye.

❦

Avisson stopped to stare at the figure on the bed behind the isolation cell door: Pudgy, baby-faced with a serene expression. If the man had not already admitted to the police that he was the Scorpio Slasher, Avisson would never have believed it.

Avisson tapped on the bars. The man looked up, smiled nervously.

"May I come in?"

He nodded. The guard released the lock.

"They told you I was coming, right?"

Nod.

"My name is Dr. Avisson, Mr. Sabey. I am—"

"I asked for an astrologer." The voice carried more hurt than anger.

Avisson smiled. "I'm both astrologer and therapist. I'm not sure what we'll be able to prove to the jury, but I'm willing to try if you are…"

"I killed them women, and I'll kill even more if I ever get out. It's my unavoidable destiny."

Avisson stared at him. "Who taught you that?"

"What?" Sabey looked at his fingernails.

"Who taught you that killing these women was your unavoidable destiny."

"It's all in my horoscope, my birth chart." He shrugged. "I'm a Scorpio with Pluto in my eighth house, and then Venus trined by Mars…nasty, nasty stuff."

"Bullshit." Avisson closed his briefcase, started to rise. "Someone's been feeding you a clever defense." He looked Sabey in the eye. "If I'm going to help you, I want the truth…not Larry Clark's manipulated 'realities.'"

Sabey stared for several moments, measuring. Nodded, very slightly. His eyes shifted, a tone of mockery came into his voice. He was no longer a disinterested prisoner.

"Yeah, I wanted to kill those bitches, those frigging cows." He moved forward on the bed, spoke evenly. "That knife was connected right to my penis, know what I mean? Every time it went into them, they came—red, see. But I could feel it, deep inside me. And I always knew which one was next. Waited for exactly the right moment each time, didn't I? Always exactly the right bitch. Sent 'em back, I did. Orders from the Universe, Dr. Avisson. I was following my orders from the Universe… and I followed 'em exactly."

Avisson sat down. Sabey grinned.

"Truth ain't very pretty, is it?" He waved his hand, stood up, defiant. "None of them believed it was me in the beginning. Cops, prosecutors, grand jury, hell, Larry Clark—asshole that he is—was the only one who knew, right from the beginning."

"So, what do you want from me?"

For a moment, Avisson thought Sabey was going to grab him by the neck, but the man simply brushed a bug or something off Avisson's shoulder. The gesture was light, unconscious.

"I want to know..." His head seemed to hurt him, or the thought he was trying to get out was a mental gallstone, okay when nestled inside, but painful to pass. "...when would be the best time for me to die."

"But that's impossible to predict."

"No it ain't." Sabey shook his head emphatically. "Look, I don't care what you have to do...send me back into ten or twelve past lives...I gotta know that I don't have to live like this again. Shit, dying don't mean nothing..." He held up his hands. "I've squeezed life through these hands like it was orange juice for breakfast. My insides were hungry for that feeling. Eleven times, I was grabbed by something that made me kill those women. I don't ever want nothing to control me like that again. Get it?"

Avisson nodded.

"Good." Sabey lay down on his bunk. "You gonna hypnotize me or something?"

Avisson found his voice. It cracked. "Have you ever been hypnotized before, Mr. Sabey?"

The man turned his head slightly. The baby face had taken on a whole new demeanor. "What do you think it was like when the Universe ordered me to kill those women?"

❧

Doug sat cross-legged on the sofa. Dr. Kautsch shifted slightly in his winged chair to the right, cleared his throat.

"Did you tell your father everything you just told me?"

Doug shook his head. "He didn't want to hear about it. He just walked away."

Kautsch nodded. "How do you feel...about his 'walking away?'"

"Well," Doug plucked at his pants cuff, "I suppose if it hadn't happened to me, I might not believe it either."

"Very astute, but how do you feel about not being believed?"

"Feel?"

"Does it make you angry?"

Doug shrugged. "Not much I can do about it, can I?"

Frustrated, Kautsch rubbed his hands down his face. "Let me ask you this: Does your nanny believe you?"

"I think so. Yes."

"Does it make you mad that your father doesn't believe you, when your nanny does?"

Doug grinned. "I'm not mad, and it doesn't make me angry."

Kautsch nodded, even smiled a little. "I give." He leafed through his notes. "You said you felt a vibration after you went over the wall. Have you ever felt anything like that before."

Now it was Doug's turn to study Kautsch. He stared at the doctor, not sure what he was looking for.

Kautsch squirmed. "Have you ever felt anything li—"

"I heard you." Doug's sharp tone surprised even himself. "Sorry, I was thinking."

"Thinking if you ever felt it, or thinking how to answer?"

"What might happen if you don't believe me."

Kautsch exhaled loudly. "Doug, it doesn't really matter whether I believe you, or anybody else does, for that matter. We each have our own reality. Feeling free to express that reality, becomes the basis for all your future interactions." Kautsch put his pen down. "Do you understand what I'm telling you?"

"I think so." Doug frowned. "But whenever I try to tell Dad about things I think or feel, he doesn't want to hear about them."

"Does his disbelief make them any less real to you?"

"Not a bit."

"Then tell me about some of them."

Doug took a deep breath and launched into a detailed description of the vibrations, the odd dream-like state that overtakes him—how he then wakes up in strangely familiar places, that seem like other worlds, where the diverse casts of characters include a clan of hunter-gatherers, monks, crusaders, a London scribe (with a dog named Allie), an island seer in a stone circle and even a wolf-killing Eskimo.

Finally, Doug described his two encounters with Father Hector. He talked at length. Kautsch remained quiet, making notes, checking the tape recorder. Doug folded his arms when he was finished. "Well, what do you think?"

"Think or believe?"

"Do you believe I experienced these things?"

"I do."

"Are they real?"

Kautsch shrugged. "I'm a therapist, not a philosopher. I believe these things are real to you. What you choose to do with this reality determines what we do next."

"Do you think I choose these things? That I'm making them happen?"

"Not in the least." Kautsch put his pad down. "Finding the cause of these dreams or episodes will take a very long time. But I assure you, it's worth doing."

"So, this is not something spiritual, it's all in my mind?"

Kautsch smiled, leaned across and patted Doug's knee. "Remember, Doug. I'm a psychotherapist. As far as I'm concerned, everything is psychological."

Doug smiled thinly at Kautsch. The doctor's tone was amiable, but the look on his face was that of a ravenous cat that had just swallowed a canary...whole.

The vibrations started, felt like approaching thunder. Doug excused himself to go to the bathroom.

"Why don't we pick it up from there, next time?" Kautsch said. "I think we made some real breakthroughs today."

Doug nodded, left quickly. Later, in the waiting room, he took Nanny's hand and started out the door.

As soon as he touched her, the vibrations stopped.

❦

Peter leaned forward in his chair. God, Downey was good. The rapt attention of the other directors had been broken only by their frequent applause.

Downey stood at the end of the long, mahogany Boardroom table. Using flow charts, two computer screens, and a slide presentation, he had outlined a radical vision of Douglas Industries' future in just under thirty minutes.

In a breathless, dizzying display of fiscal strategy, Downey described a scenario he called "Dominoes of Decision." The momentum of every decision naturally and logically carried each part of the new business-strategy forward to the next domino.

"We must become masters of the obvious," he said at one point, "and it's obvious that the current corporate structure—which was appropriate in the 30s and 40s—is now holding us back. By converting to a Delaware Corporation, we will realize significant tax relief, and can raise the large investment necessary to bring Ultraleather to the marketplace."

On cue, his secretary pushed a key on the computer keyboard and a row of upright dominoes began to fall.

"But—" he snapped the pointer against the nearest flow-chart, stopping the falling dominoes. "—by creating two classes of stock—voting and non-voting—we will encourage a large influx of investment cash, without requiring our top decision-makers to waste valuable time by answering to a horde of inexperienced, speculating investors."

A new row of green dominoes, a dollar sign on each, began to cascade. He touched the computer screen. The cascading stopped abruptly.

"Raising cash isn't our only reason to offer non-voting stock to the public." He walked around the table, put his hand on Jim Knapp's shoulder. "That's why we have Mr. James Knapp, who will explain the progress we've made over the past several months in the development of Ultra-Leather."

Knapp, caught off-guard, looked around wildly for an escape route. Downey laughed.

"Don't worry Jim, we'll let you go to your lab in just a few minutes." He leaned over, whispered, then stood up. "Don't go into the science, just give them the gist of what you're up to."

Knapp stood, cleared his throat. "As you may soon discover, I wasn't prepared to made a presentation..."

Several directors chuckled.

"However, we have made significant strides in the race to develop artificial leather." He grinned, seemed in control. "Our laboratory samples are superior to anything now known in the industry...

"At the outset of our development program, there were only two significant obstacles: The hand, or feel of the material and its ability to breathe like leather. We've solved the hand/feel problem and are quite literally on the verge of achieving adequate breatheability, under manufacturing conditions.

"To this end, months ago, we initiated what we call the 'Porosity Program.' Our results to date have been spectacular."

Better prepared than he had let on, Knapp reached under his seat, took out a box labeled TOP SECRET, and opened it. "Here you are ladies, gentlemen, please take a piece and feel it."

Oohs and ahs followed the box as it went round the table. "What you have is a piece of the very first, laboratory-made Ultraleather, which passes our stringent requirements for breatheability."

"Marvelous," Gerald Walsh said, the only surviving non-family Director, who had known Sarah Douglas. "Congratulations. I have a question."

"Yes, sir?"

"I know you have been working on this for months, but exactly how has it been accomplished?"

"I'll make it as short and non-technical as I can. You all know we have tried spiking the PVC, to make holes in it."

Every Director, except Peter, nodded.

"Then we tried micro-spiking, which was less objectionably visible, but didn't pass the spec. Finally, one of our men had a brain storm…"

Downey nodded, interrupted. "The man's name is Jim Knapp."

Knapp blushed, continued. "Well, okay, I did think it might be interesting if we got a hold of some microbes that liked to eat PVC."

"What?" came the chorus. Every Director except Peter sat on the edge of his seat.

"Believe it or not, there are microbes that will eat almost anything, except perhaps the precious metals. We found a couple of strains known to eat petrochemicals and sure enough, one of them likes PVC. So, to make it short, we put about a zillion of them in our lab mix, rolled it flat, and waited."

"And they ate holes in it?" Walsh asked, astonished. He held his sample close to his old, watery eyes. "Well, I can't see them."

"Right. But they're there. The porosity test results prove it. We went from micro-spiking to microbe-eating, and there it is, in your hands. And if you feel it carefully, you will find the hand soft, pliant—even better than real leather."

Stunned silence broke into thunderous applause.

Walsh cleared his throat. "How soon will it be ready for the marketplace?"

"It will take time and money, sir. Money for more research and lots more to get into volume production: Incubating vats, piping, special manufacturing equipment, and so on. Everybody knows how hard it is to bring a sample from the laboratory into full-scale production—to get the bugs out, so to speak."

Nervous laughter rang round the table. Knapp blushed.

"It will also take time and obviously…the more money, the less time."

"How soon will we be able to get it onto the market?" Walsh demanded.

Before Knapp could launch into a long explanation, Downey intercepted him.

"Ever the marketing genius, eh, Mr. Walsh?" He patted the white-haired man's shoulder. "The point is, our industrial informants tell us we are currently leading in the race to develop this new product. And once we secure the patent—" He pointed to the charts again. "—the figures will move even higher, the market value of our stock will go through the roof. Increased dividends will of course follow."

"Can't eat research," Walsh said gruffly.

"That's true." Downey signaled his secretary, who pushed the computer execute key. Suddenly, the computer screens exploded with images of huge dollar-dominoes moving at breakneck speed, the clicking sound filled the room like a plague of locusts. The camera never zoomed in far enough to show the entire pattern, just the tiles descending diagonally, in sequence.

The show paused abruptly. The room became silent, then filled with applause when the directors saw the final image:

One huge dollar sign, alongside the gold "D" and "I" of Douglas Industries, was spectacularly outlined in sapphire blue.

After the ovation Downy handed out copies of the proposal. "Ladies and gentlemen, you will vote at our next meeting in two weeks. Meanwhile, please study the numbers carefully. We will expect your input, but after that meeting, as soon as we have your approval, we must act quickly to forestall any takeover attempts during the transition."

He stood next to Peter, who extended his hand. A flash went off. Peter couldn't stop smiling. History was about to be made—in his favor.

Doug was glad Fiona didn't press him about his session with Dr. Kautsch. His insides felt jumpy enough without having to go through another explanation. The part of him that had hoped the pictures of the past were just dreams had been shattered. Perhaps he should never have told another soul. The "dreams" were too real, too much a part of himself to be anything less than...than what?

Absorbed in his interior cross-examination, for a moment he didn't notice where they were, when Fiona parked the car. He glanced around the shopping center. They'd never been here before.

"What's this?"

"Thought you might like a treat."

His smile was grim. He was not sure he could eat anything, even a treat. "I'm not—"

"Come on, you'll like it."

He stepped out of the car and looked around. Then he saw the sign. His whole insides seemed to relax and a sweet calm replaced the tension with which he'd been wrestling. He blinked away a little water that came from his eyes as Nanny put her arm around his shoulders. She really was the smartest person on earth, especially when it came to knowing him.

As they entered the cafe, Doug's excitement turned to caution. Jimmy stood behind the coffee counter, running a machine that looked part-locomotive and part-cow, with spigots spouting steam. Arranged at several of the tables were the Moles. Sally sat in a corner pouring through a large book. Two high school students lounged by the window. Doug had had precious little previous contact with older kids. They seemed like young gods to him.

Doug steeled himself for the reaction he usually received at school, then felt a mild protectiveness toward Nanny, especially when he remembered the snow effigy—but there was no reaction. Two of the Moles noticed him first, but their eyes returned to whatever they were working on. Doug smiled. Indifference was better than scorn.

"Why don't we sit here?" Fiona said. "This is my table."

"You have your own table?"

"My regular table, I should have said." She handed him the menu. "Why don't you figure out what you want?"

Doug read the folded-in-half cardboard: Latte, Espresso, Cappuccino, Italian ices—

"Would you like something to drink?"

Doug looked up, past the menu. Jimmy stood by their table, an order pad in his hand, pen poised. Neutral.

"I'm not sure what everything is." Doug blushed.

Jimmy nodded. "Try an Italian ice. We got cherry, passion fruit, mango, blackberry and pina colada."

Doug was tempted to look at Nanny for help, but not in front of Jimmy. "Could I have a mango?"

Jimmy nodded, took Nanny's order for hot tea and walked away.

"Can I look around, Nanny?"

"Of course."

Doug wandered the aisles, letting his eyes drift over the stacks: Philosophy, Jungian Psychology, Religion and Myth, Native American, Astrology, Tarot. He encountered two Moles. Talia and Susan stood in front of a section entitled 'Wicca.'

"What's that?" he asked.

"Witchcraft." Talia said. She wore a short black skirt over a longer, gray dress on which the Mole insignia had been reproduced five or six times using some kind of white ink or paint.

"Why don't they call it Witchcraft?"

"Because some people who don't like that name would give Mr. Petrovich problems."

"They already picket the place on Sundays," Susan said.

"Who? Why?" Doug asked.

"Christian Fundamentalists." Talia shrugged. "I don't know why."

Doug continued his inspection of the shelves. The placement of small artifacts from around the world seemed helter-skelter, but he sensed that the owner, this Petrovich, had reasons for everything he did. Doug rubbed the belly of a large, wooden Buddha.

"That's supposed to bring good luck."

Doug whirled and found himself looking at a slender man with a long, gray beard.

"You must be Fiona's friend," he said, sticking out his hand. Doug shook it.

"Douglas MacBrayne, sir."

"Petrovich, Valka Petrovich. I'm happy to meet you, at last."

The man's eyes backed up his statement. Never had Doug seen such deep interest and what looked like affection. No wonder the store was popular, if he looked at everyone that way.

"Do you approve of my little establishment?"

Doug nodded. "I've never seen any place like this before."

"That's probably because it all came out of my head." Petrovich grinned. "Funny head, funny store."

Doug smiled. "And nice people."

This seemed to catch Petrovich in an odd way. He cleared his throat. "Yes...ahem, well...why don't you continue looking around, then join Fiona and me when you're finished?"

"Thank you," Doug said. He listened to Petrovich's footsteps, then casually turned to see the man put his hand on Nanny's shoulder in greeting. She looked up and smiled at him. Doug's eyes narrowed. He'd been right. Nanny did have a boyfriend!

Jimmy delivered the Italian ice and hot tea, then spun on his heel and stormed behind the counter. He had hoped to keep his feelings hidden, but seeing Mr. Petrovich make a special trip to the rear of the store to shake MacBrayne's hand had infuriated him.

He banged two mugs in the soapy water. Banged them again during the rinse. Petrovich glanced at him, returned to his conversation with the nanny.

Sally walked over. "Are you okay, Jimmy?"

Jimmy shrugged.

"What's the matter?"

"I didn't think Petrovich would fall for it...that's all."

"Fall for what?"

Jimmy nodded toward Doug. "Well, he was sucking up to MacBrayne, wasn't he?"

She laughed, barely hanging on to the stool.

"What's so funny?"

Sally put her elbows on the bar, folded her hands together. "It's not Doug he's sucking up to. Don't you know anything?"

"Huh?"

She turned, leaned on her elbows and whispered out of the side of her mouth. "It's the nanny he's after. Look at him, he's practically drooling in his beard over her."

"Get off it," Jimmy whispered back.

She raised an eyebrow. "Women know these things."

"Maybe women do, but girls don't."

She stuck out her tongue.

"Ooh, that's really adult."

One bounce took her off the stool. She grabbed the Italian ice from the table and strode to where Doug sat, leafing through a book on ghosts. Jimmy's eyes burned an angry tattoo into her back, but she never turned around.

"Your ice is melting." Sally handed Doug his drink.

"Thanks. I forgot about it."

"Whatcha readin'?"

"Book on ghosts. It's pretty good."

She tipped the cover, checked the title. "You believe in them?"

"Do you?"

Sally frowned. "Am I going to have trouble with you, too? It's not polite to answer a question with a question."

"Sorry." He slurped his icy drink through the straw. "I do believe in them, yes."

"Ever seen one?"

He nodded.

Her eyes grew large. "You're kidding, right?"

Doug shook his head. "I talked to one, twice."

"Get outta here!"

"Shh. It's a secret. I don't want anyone to know."

"Not even Nanny?" Sally grinned.

"No, not even her. Not all of it, anyway."

"Well..."

"What?" He looked around.

"Are you going to tell me, or not?"

Doug thought a moment, his head bobbed slightly. "Okay, I'll tell you, but you have to tell me a secret about you, too."

Sally shook her head.

"Why not?" Doug leaned forward, whispered. "Why should I tell you my secret when you won't tell me one?"

She bit her lip, looked around the store. "Because your secrets can't possibly hurt as much as mine."

Doug stared at her, unable to connect the look on her face with the implication of the statement. She put her hands on her hips, impatient for his answer.

"Okay, I'll tell you. But not here."

"Where?"

"In our family graveyard. That's where he lives—the ghost."

Now it was her turn to think. She nodded slowly. "When?"

"After school, next week."

She shook her head.

"Why not?"

"It's got to be dark." She moved closer, whispered. "Midnight, tonight."

❦

Avisson rewound the tape, relaxed in his chair and rubbed his eyes. He wished he could rub the words and sounds from his ears, also. Sabey was truly deranged, a pure psychotic. If the jury ever heard any of this, there would be no way they would put him in jail. The scientist in Avisson should have been intrigued by such a subject. The killer's human side had been completely repressed. Sabey thought about killing all the time. He breathed death. That he had thus far killed only eleven times, was due to his utter willpower, a perverse self-discipline that had nothing to do with his victim, and everything to do with Sabey's warped sense of destiny.

Larry Clark hadn't invented the horoscopic defense. Sabey was obsessed by his own astrology. Convinced he was special, he looked at killing as his birthright. Death was a tool. Sabey viewed himself as a universal scalpel, honed and glistening, to be used precisely— as only he saw fit.

Avisson punched the 'play' button.

"People don't judge tornadoes, forest fires or hurricanes," Sabey said, pacing his cell. "They are afraid of them, run from them, protect themselves as best they can... but they understand they are facing nature."

"Thoughtless nature?" Avisson asked.

Sabey turned, his eyes blue lasers. "Thoughtless, but not unknowing. We are all phenomena of a scheme so vast..." He smiled at Avisson, a door closed behind his eyes. He licked his lips, seemed to transform from mammal to reptile.

Avisson shuddered.

Sabey's smile became a sneer. "Are you sure you're up to this?"

"This?"

"Getting me off."

"I didn't realize that was my job." Avisson held the other man's gaze. "I thought you wanted to determine the right time to die."

The reptile transformed into a mammal. Sabey fell on the bed, curled into a fetal ball. When he was as tight as he could make himself, he spoke in a child's voice—a small bully. "You'd better go now, before the universe realizes how close you are to me... you never know what the next set of orders might be."

Avisson rose from the chair, punched the stop button on the tape recorder. Somewhere deep inside him, he heard a different boy's voice asking if what his brother had was catching, like a cold.

"No, dear. It's all in his mind."

Avisson reached for his coat, slipped it around his shoulders and headed out the door. He needed to walk while it was still light. He didn't trust the dark at the moment. Perhaps it had something to do with the echo of Sabey's laughter in his ears, or perhaps it was the deep memory of the little boy's question. The voice had sounded like Avisson's, but he didn't have a brother.

At least not one he remembered.

❦

"Thanks for the ride, Mr. Petrovich." Jimmy slammed the door, started up the orphanage steps.

"Jimmy!" came from the car.

The boy turned. Petrovich rolled down the window.

"I'm sorry," Jimmy said, "I didn't mean to slam the door."

"Don't worry about that." Petrovich seemed to search for the words. "Look, Jimmy, some funny stuff might come up in the next few weeks—"

"What kind of stuff?"

"Not sure. But listen. Just hang in there, have faith, you know?"

Jimmy didn't, but he nodded anyway.

"Sometimes, things aren't what they seem to be." Petrovich closed his eyes, reopened them. "But no matter what happens, or how bad things may get, I will always be around to help you...to take care of you...one way or another."

"What's the matter, Mr. Petrovich?" Jimmy blanched. "You're not dying or anything, are you?"

"No, nothing like that. You just roll with the punches and you'll be okay. You hear?"

"Yes, sir."

"See you tomorrow, after school."

The window closed. Jimmy climbed the steps slowly. He heard the tires crunch gravel as the old Chevy headed toward the exit, but he could still feel Petrovich's eyes on him. He really did like the old guy, though he didn't understand him half the time.

Voices and footsteps echoed down the hall as Jimmy entered through the big doors. He stopped halfway in, glanced over at the parking lot, saw the expensive cars. So, the bigwigs were here, obviously in the conference room, next to old "Grab-Your-Knickers" office. He checked to make sure no one was looking, then slipped into the mop room. He hid his knapsack behind the stacked cartons of soap and toilet paper, climbed the step-ladder that leaned against the far wall. He lifted a large, water-stained fiberglass ceiling tile and pushed his head into the darkness above. Feeling around, he found his flashlight off to the left, clicked it on.

The passageway always reminded him of Star Trek: If the Enterprise really existed, he was sure the ship's plumbing had to have a system of crawl spaces like those that ran throughout the orphanage. He took off his shoes and made his way on hands and knees toward the conference room. He arrived at the vent and peeked through just in time to hear Grab-Your-Knickers say, "That's not what I meant."

"What did you mean?" came a rough voice from an invisible source. "You don't think orphans ought to go to summer camp like normal kids?"

"No. Of course they should. It's just that we remodeled the entire facility several years ago, it seems like a lot of money for—"

"The money spent on the physical plant is none of your business. Your job is to keep operating costs within your budget."

"But a whole summer away? The children—"

"Ms. Groebnick." This second voice was calmer, more measured, but just as insistent. "What we need from you is recommendations on summer camps. Did you get the information or not?"

"I did."

"Well..."

"Comparing costs and activities, the best one that will take the boys—all twelve of them—for the entire summer is Camp Shambala." Jimmy heard the sound of shuffling papers. "And it's new, only an hour-and-a-half away. The eight girls can attend another camp, just outside of town called—"

"Thank you, Ms. Groebnick," said the rough voice. "Please send my office a memo outlining the costs, including transportation."

"Do you want to see the brochures?"

"Not necessary. If you think it's what we need, that's good enough."

"Thank you, Mr. Downey."

"That'll be all, Miss Groebnick."

She didn't move.

"Is there anything else?"

"I—I was wondering." She wrung her hands. "Should I be looking for another job?"

The one named Downey looked at the other man who spoke as he came into view. He had a salt and pepper goatee and thick-lensed glasses.

"There will be some changes, Miss Groebnick, but you have a position here as long as you want it."

"Thank you, Dr. Kautsch." Her voice quavered. "I like the children a lot. Don't know what I'd do—"

"You have nothing to worry about."

"I just mean—"

"You have nothing to worry about."

"Thank you, Doctor." She scurried from the room, obviously relieved.

Jimmy sat up straight, suddenly ashamed of all the fun he had made of Miss Groebnick. It never dawned on him that she actually liked the orphans.

"Leon, what did you have to do to get Shambala to take the kids for the entire summer?"

"Money for additional staff. Miss Slimson will cover nursing duty four days a week. I think I found a good nurse from the hospital whom we can depend on to cover the other three days."

"Why not use Groebnick, as long as we're paying her anyway...?"

The goateed one shook his head. "We need her here, working for us."

"You sure you're want her around after the changeover?" The rough voice asked.

Jimmy returned to the vent.

"Timing is everything, Downey. She just wants to keep her job. She doesn't care about those kids anymore than we do."

"I'm not so sure. She seemed pretty sincere."

"Greed makes people do all sorts of things."

"You mean, like turning an orphanage into a loony-bin?"

The goateed doctor laughed. "Wait until those spoiled little shits get back from camp and see a ten-foot fence around their precious little country-club."

"They're going to freak out, Leon."

"Exactly, my dear Downey. Orphans into delinquents...Voila: State funding."

Jimmy closed his eyes, concentrating on not screaming through the vent at the two assholes. This must have been what Petrovich was talking about—changes coming. And he expected Jimmy to stay loose? Roll with the punches?

"Did you talk to MacBrayne about his kid, yet?" Kautsch asked.

"No, we've been tied up with the stock transfer."

"Don't let it go too long, I need that kid at the camp for at least a month."

"I'll do what I can, but Peter's pretty protective of him. He's terrified he'll be kidnapped, or something."

"Yeah, well if he's serious about getting rid of the Nanny, the kid is going to camp." He handed Downey Miss Groebnick's brochures. "Stop and talk to him on your way home."

"I still don't see what—"

"Look!" Kautsch exploded, "No one can complain about us sending the orphans off to camp if MacBrayne sends his own kid, right?"

"Yeah, but—"

"No buts. You get him on board—and right away—or we're looking at another year before we change over. Can you afford to support the Orphanage and the Foundation for another year?"

"No, and I wish you'd quit asking me that."

"Just don't forget that we must have control of the kid to control his old man."

"Jesus, Kautsch, don't you ever worry that there might be a Hell?"

"Oh, there's a Hell all right," he laughed, "But I'm betting that Freud is the devil."

"And if you're wrong?"

"Then we're both screwed."

The two men left the room. Jimmy breathed aloud for the first time in what seemed like an hour. He'd never felt so angry, so helpless. How the heck was he supposed to hang loose, with this kind of stuff going on?

❦

Avisson looked across the street to see if the lights were still on in the Crystal Cafe. About to step off the curb, he felt more than heard the car behind him. He jumped to his left as the bumper clipped his heel. He rolled over twice, then collided with a prickly shrub. He looked over his shoulder to see who had tried to kill him. A battered blue Ford, driverless, as far as he could tell.

He rolled gingerly away from the shrub, feeling it cling to his clothing. The passenger door of the blue Ford had burst open, the driver sprawled across the seat.

"Oops."

"Oops?" Avisson limped toward the car. "You almost kill me and all you can say is—"

The driver lifted his head from the seat. His eyes were unfocused, blood-shot red. "Doc?"

Avisson sighed, shook his head. "Clint, what the hell...?"

"Probation. Th'fuckers. Goddamn curve killed me."

"Nearly killed me, too." Avisson leaned down. "Can you sit up? We've got to park this car properly, then see if we can get some coffee in you."

Upright, Sharpe slumped quickly, but Avisson got the door closed and hurried around to the driver's side. He reversed off the curb and parked just as he spotted Petrovich's Chevy pull in front of the Cafe.

"Are you open?" Avisson yelled through the window.

Petrovich peered, recognized the voice, waved him over.

In a bad comic routine, Avisson got Sharpe out of the car, steadied him long enough to lock it; then half-carried him across the street to the cafe. Petrovich wore a smile, but his eyes expressed concern.

"Celebrating?"

"One of my clients. Tried to run me down." Avisson pushed one of Clint's hands toward Petrovich. "Clint Sharpe, meet Valka Petrovich."

"Oops," Clint said, then staggered. "Fucking curve."

Petrovich looked at Avisson, eyebrows raised. Avisson shrugged. "Code?"

"For what?"

Another shrug. "For fucking curve?"

Petrovich laughed.

Avisson grew serious. "I don't think we'll find out what's wrong until he's sober."

"Bring him in. I'll fix him an old Gypsy remedy."

"What's that?"

"Double espresso and a slice of lemon."

"That's a Gypsy remedy?"

Another grin. "It's about the only thing I know how to make."

The telephone rang and Petrovich answered. Avisson carefully sat Sharpe in a chair, leaning his elbows on the table to keep him steady.

"What happened, Clint?"

Sharpe pulled an envelope from his pocket, handed it over. Avisson opened it.

"That's great work," Petrovich said to the phone. "Yes, Camp Shambala. Right. I'll see what I can do. Call me the minute you learn anything new."

Petrovich hung up the phone and walked to the coffee counter.

Having read Clint's letter, Avisson put it down. "Petrovich, you need any help here at the store?"

"You looking for a job?"

"Not yet, but I know someone with a Masters degree in English who needs something until the Fall semester."

"Our friend there?" Petrovich asked.

"Oops," Sharpe said, falling through the pyramid Avisson had constructed from his arms, head and hands.

"Yes." Avisson reached over to prop him up.

Petrovich shook his head. "A bookstore would be too confining for a man who spends the whole school year inside a classroom."

"You have another idea?"

Petrovich nodded. "Yeah, it just came to me." He carried over the cup of espresso, waved it several times under Sharpe's nose. "I think what we have here is a born Camp Counselor."

"What?" Avisson shook his head.

"He's experienced with kids..."

"Yeah, so what?"

"His complexion is perfect."

"What's that got—"

"Won't sunburn much."

"Are you sure about that?" Petrovich shrugged and Avisson sighed. "Okay, what else?"

Pause. "Well...I need someone."

"Someone or anyone?"

"Someone who can be trusted."

"Oh, a drunk teacher on probation. Great recommendation. I can see camps all up and down the coast clamoring to have him."

"Someone I can trust."

"What makes you think—"

"He's your client, that means he trusts you. You trust me. I trust him."

"Hell of a lot of assumptions right there." Avisson put his hands to his head, groaned. "Make me one of those damned expressos, Gypsy. Now, I feel drunk."

"Oops," Clint said with a happy smile.

❧

After Nanny said goodnight, Doug closed his eyes and tried not to think about going to the cemetery with Sally. The very idea made his heart go choppy.

Besides, he had three hours to go. He would have been able to sit up talking to Allie, if he hadn't told Nanny the dog might have fleas. She insisted his 'buddy' stay down in the laundry room until a flea bath could be arranged. There would have been no way to climb down the rope fire ladder with Allie in the room. He would have awakened the entire household.

Doug had thought about setting his alarm, but knew that either Nanny or his father would hear it. That meant staying awake. He tried to find the calm he'd felt when he had entered the bookstore. The place was so peaceful, happy. Reminded him of a watering hole he'd seen on some nature TV program, where all the animals made peace and drank together before resuming their roles as predator and prey, out in the savanna.

As he drifted, he pictured the smile of the owner, Petrovich, and how much Nanny seemed to like the man. He thought he should feel jealous, but the man seemed too genuinely nice to dislike in any way. Nanny's got a boyfriend. He smiled, then let his mind wander the bookshelves. So many books, ideas, lives.

A slow, deep thrum began to work through him, coming from deep within. At first he thought it was the vibrations again, but this was different. It seemed to come from the other side of a tall wall that separated him from what felt like an ancient place.

He thought of meeting Sally, tried not to close his eyes but his nostrils filled with the smell of... honey. Then it started.

Stotl reset the crystals, inserted the shred taken from a ceremonial coconut-carving that had been retrieved from the island he was studying. The hologram displayed images of seven native dancers, feet and arms flying to a silent beat. He adjusted the shred and the focus tightened on the dancers' feet. He glanced again at the longitude and latitude where the coconut had been found, then replaced the shred with a slab of honeycomb from the same general geographic area. He shifted the crystals to slow down the holographic image of the dance the bees did, when they returned from the nearby meadow.

He checked his calculations again. Closer. Both dances indicated a similar, root pattern. The honeycomb and coconut had been collected within five miles of each other. The common mathematical denominator worked at the local level, but would not extrapolate to the intersection of longitude and latitude, as he suspected.

What was he not seeing?

He turned and spun the crystal globe on the table, watching the light refract through it, gleaming from a point at the center of the—.

"Of course!" Stotl shouted, leaping from his stool. "True longitude and latitude take their positions as projected from the center point, not from the external overlay."

"What are you jabbering about?" Bentov, the map master stood, arms folded.

"But I've proved it," Stotl said.

"Proved what?"

"My theory linking aboriginal and bee dances. From a navigational standpoint, it means that we can isolate..."

Bentov held up his hand. "Proved? I thought you were a serious scientist?"

"I can express mathematically that..."

"Too late." Bentov waved him off. "Write up a summary and submit it to the Geophysics Council for consideration—that is, if it does relate to mapping."

"Very much so. Using this formula, our mappers will be able to move exactly to—"

"Enough." Bentov moved toward his own cubicle. "Submit it to the GPC. They will determine its usefulness."

Stotl turned his back and grinned. Bentov was just being his cantankerous self. He must have known Stotl was onto something. Otherwise, he would have asked to see it and then decide if the Council should have a look. This way, he had already given his tacit approval.

"Stotl?" Bentov leaned from the doorway. "Of course, I have to see your formula first."

Stotl nodded, but the grin didn't fade. If Bentov had been reading his thoughts, then he also knew it worked.

Somewhere, Stotl thought he heard laughter. Couldn't be Bentov, who hadn't laughed from the moment Stotl first met him. He glanced around the otherwise empty room. A chill ran up his spine.

Doug awoke. The smell of honey evaporated. He tried to look over the wall that had seemingly lowered for the dream, but it was back in place. What kind of name was Stotl? He thought about asking Dr. Kautsch, but Doug hadn't liked that funny smile the doctor wore at the end of the last session. Gave him the same uneasy feeling as the laughter at the end of the dream.

He glanced at the clock. Ten minutes after nine. He fell against his pillow. He'd never make it to midnight.

Clint turned off the lights and engine, rolled into his driveway and sat for a moment. He could see Mandy's silhouette in the front window. She would be furious, which meant absolute silence. Being the wife of a sporadic alcoholic is worse than one who is drunk all the time. She never knew what to expect. Hell, for that matter, neither did he, casting about blindly half the time, never knowing what would set him off. If only he could see further than one or two minutes in front of his face, his life might be different.

This was just another part of the punishment, of that he was certain. Otherwise why would he be born with such strong, irrational feelings about responsible freedom? Why was he afforded an education, then not allowed to use it? Why give him a daughter, the light of his life, then extinguish that light?

"You coming in?" Mandy. He hadn't noticed her at the car window.

"Yeah. Sorry."

"For what?"

He looked at her as he hadn't for a long, long time. "Everything, Mandy. I'm sorry for everything."

She nodded. "Me, too."

"There are some things I have to tell you."

"Come inside."

He shook his head. "No, we'll go in after, okay?"

"Sure."

"I got suspended, put on probation this afternoon." She already knew. "Then I got drunk, almost ran over my therapist."

"I thought you liked him?"

"I do. I was drunk." He ran a hand through his short, curly hair. "He took me to a cafe, made me drink something called a Red-Eye."

"More booze? Nice cure."

He shook his head. "Double espresso in a cup of regular coffee."

"You'll be up all night."

He smiled. "Yeah, with any luck."

She eyed him suspiciously. "You seem pretty happy for a man who just lost his job."

"Suspended. But I have another one."

"Doing what?"

"Camp counselor."

"I thought you didn't like kids."

"Don't. Hate 'em." He reached out and took her hand. "But I love you and this is a way to keep some money coming in and maybe change some of my attitudes."

"Where is this camp and how long will you be gone?"

"About ninety minutes away."

"Just how long will you be gone?"

"All summer."

"And what am I supposed to do while you're gone?"

"Decide if you want to stay with me…" She flared. He held up his hand. "… and if you think it would be a good idea to try and make another baby."

Her left eye fluttered, upper lip quivered, and for a moment, Clint thought she might faint. He jumped out of the car and held her.

"Mandy?"

She folded against him, her face buried in his shirt.

"Are you okay?"

At first he thought the moisture seeping into his shirt was her tears, but then he felt the soft pressure of her teeth on his breast.

"What do you…? Ow!" He tried to look at her, but she giggled and burrowed in, deeper. "Hey, girl. What are you up to?"

"You think you can just go away for the summer and not leave me something to remember you by?" She bit at his chest again. He jumped away. She laughed, grabbed him by the shirt. "I already know that I want to stay with you, and that I want to make another baby with you."

"You do?"

"Get your double-espresso butt up those stairs." She slapped him on the behind. "'cause we're gonna start making that new baby tonight, you hear?"

"I hear you, honey."

"Don't you honey me."

He winced.

She gave him another swat.

"Ow! What was that for?"

"That was for getting suspended." Another smack.

"What was that for?"

"For getting drunk."

She came at him again and he ducked, but she didn't swing. Instead she stood on tiptoe and gave him a kiss.

"What was that for?"

"That was for loving me enough to ask a stupid question like 'Do I want to stay with you?'" She bit his lip.

"Ow! Darlin'."

"Believe me now?"

"Yes."

"Good, don't forget it."

"Don't think I will, ever."

He followed her up the stairs.

Peter adjusted the light on his study desk and leafed through the packet one more time. Even someone as carefree and inattentive as his father would be able to see what switching to a Delaware corporation would mean to his stock. Non-voting stock could be rendered nearly worthless by a hostile board of directors. With any luck, the packet wouldn't catch up to him within the two week time limit. So the question was, where the hell was the old man?

Peter shuddered. This should be giving him more pleasure than he felt at the moment. Not that he owed the old bastard anything. He rubbed his leg, closed his eyes.

"Some day you'll understand," his father said after a ten-year-old Peter came limping home from school, tears streaming down his face, because of his schoolmates' taunts and cruelties.

"But Father, I don't understand. If we're rich like everyone says, why can't we get my foot fixed?"

"Money doesn't fix everything," the father soothed. "Everything you learn about having a foot like this will make you stronger in the future."

Young Peter turned to his Grandmother Sarah, who simply nodded. He would have accepted it, if he hadn't sought his mother's confirmation. She turned away, angrily, he thought. It was not until Peter was older that he realized the look on her face had been one of disgust and hatred. Disgust by the thought that her husband and mother-in-law would lie to him, and hatred for having tried to make her an accomplice.

Thus, the day after he graduated from high school, she had surprised him with tickets to Europe for the two of them. The itinerary was extensive: nine countries in twelve weeks.

Once they were airborne to London, she handed him a stack of postcards.

"What are these for?"

"I want you to start filling them in and addressing them now. After we get to Heidelberg, I don't think you'll feel much like it."

Peter flipped through the cards, one depicting scenes of each city on the itinerary.

"But why can't I do this, as we go along?" He looked at the blank cards. "I'll have more interesting things to say then."

She smiled and patted his hand. "As soon as we arrive in London, we catch a connecting flight to Frankfurt, then a train to Heidelberg. You have an appointment tomorrow afternoon with Herr Doktor Klug von Messerwerfen."

"Who's he?"

"The world's finest reconstructive surgeon." She put her hand on his leg, squeezed.

It took a moment to sink in. He looked at the stack of postcards, nodded, sat upright in his seat. "Dad and Grandma Sarah don't know, do they?"

"No."

"How are you going to pay for it?"

"It's all taken care of."

"They'll be angry."

She shrugged. "I've been angrier for a long, long time."

She picked up her pen and began writing the first postcard from her own stack. He watched her hand for several moments before realizing what he wasn't seeing: her wedding ring. His eyes went up to her wrist: nothing; up to her neck and ears: nothing. Nothing.

He smiled. Everything came into focus. For years he'd heard her harangue his father, complaining about his cheap Christmas gifts, birthday presents. If she couldn't have his love, at least he could make some symbolic gesture...say, in diamonds. How she had mocked him, cajoled him. Peter heard a good part of it, had pitied his mother her dismay.

Now, she had traded her material self-respect for this plan to rebuild his foot.

He leaned over and kissed her on the cheek, then picked up his own pen and began writing.

Peter sighed. Herr Doktor von Messerwerfen had said the boy's foot was the most hideous example of Kyllosis he'd ever encountered. He suspected some teratogen, (such as thalidomide, developed years later) might have been involved, but no trace was found. X-rays confirmed that where most people have five toes, Peter had only a single bone, or mono-dactyl. Hence, the Kyllosis, or clubfoot, was most aptly named in Peter's case.

"The doctors in the United States claimed it was inoperable," his mother said, while Peter sat on the examination table, his club foot swinging. "Is that true?"

Messerwerfen nodded. "Ja, before five, six years ago, no hope. Now..."

"Yes?"

He held up his hands, fingers spread like Chinese fans. "My mother, she wanted me to be sculptor. Jah. My father, he say 'Doktor!'" Messerwerfen grinned. "I love them both very much." He gently took Peter's misshapen foot in his hands, looked at the boy. "I will sculpt you a new foot, ja?"

Peter gulped. "Ja."

"Zer gut."

The pain between the five separate surgical procedures was excruciating, but Peter's mother stayed by his side throughout, reading to him from books and tourist brochures about the various places they were supposed to have gone, had they followed the itinerary.

She never turned away when he wept, just dried his tears and continued reading.

"How can you stand it, mother, watching me like this?"

"I love you," she said, simply. "When you love someone, you stay close, no matter what."

One week before their scheduled return, his mother called home to say Peter had fallen and broken his ankle. The doctors in Heidelberg seemed very competent. They had cast the leg and provided appropriate crutches. Peter should have no trouble making the return trip. He might need some help getting around Yale the first semester and there would be physical therapy after the cast came off.

When she finished, Peter stared at his mother. "You don't believe he'll actually fall for it, do you?"

"I don't care whether he does or doesn't." A mischievous light came into her face. "But the longer they don't know, the more foolish they'll feel once they do."

"Oh, Mother, what about hotel bills, train fares...photographs?"

She pulled a camera from her bag, snapped his picture.

"You left the lens cap on, Mother."

She snapped again.

"But, Mother, you're shooting blanks—" He stopped. She had him. He looked at her bare fingers. "And your jewelry, how will you explain that?"

"Stolen while I was bathing, probably two or three days from now."

"And when the cast comes off, and I can walk without a limp?"

"Do you remember where we stopped, just a week before you broke your ankle?"

He rolled his eyes. "There've been so many places—"

"France. Remember Lourdes?"

He nodded. "Where pilgrims go to be healed."

"My boy can walk!" She lifted her eyes to heaven. "It's a Miracle."

Peter could tell that Grandma Sarah knew right away, but didn't let on. His father never said anything directly to Peter, once it became clear how he had been snookered, though Peter overheard the man arguing with his mother later that night.

"You have no idea what you've taken away from him," his father said, heatedly.

"Yes I do," his mother spat back. "I've taken away the shame he feels, the ignominy of being a cripple, the pain of walking differently from others."

"If he felt any shame or ignominy, you taught it to him, not I." There was a pause. His father seemed to be gathering strength or courage. "Did it ever dawn on you that he may have been born that way for a reason, to learn something? You just may have interrupted his karma."

"Oh, get away from me with all that reincarnation mumbo-jumbo. All I know now is that I've made my son happy and you wouldn't. That's what really bothers you, isn't it?"

After a long, deadly silence, Peter heard his mother say, "What are you doing?"

Alarmed, he put his hand on the door knob, but did not turn it.

"Writing you a check."

"You think you can buy your way into my son's heart?" She laughed. "You forget your own lesson: Money can't fix everything."

It was the last thing of importance he ever heard pass between the two of them.

Peter frowned, sighed and placed the packet for his father in the envelope. He sealed it for the next day's mail. Then he read Downey's memo, glanced at the attached brochure. Shook his head. No way was he going to let Doug out of his sight for the whole summer. A week, maybe. Three months, never.

❦

An owl hooted outside. Doug sat upright. He glanced at the clock. Darn. Five minutes past midnight. He hurried to the window, lifted it and looked out into the darkness.

"Hoo. Hoo."

"I'll be right down," he whispered loudly through cupped hands.

"Hurry up," came from the black void.

Doug fed the rope ladder out the window and let it down until he felt it hit the ground. He secured it, leaned out, grew dizzy, put his leg over the sill. His tennis shoe bounced off the wall, sounded like a gunshot.

"Shhh!" came from below.

"I know," Doug loud-whispered back.

He made his way down the ladder, which was designed for emergencies, not stealth. After what seemed ten or fifteen minutes, his feet touched ground. He looked up to his window. Shook his head. Going up would be worse, much worse.

A hand shot out of the darkness and grabbed him.

"You fell asleep, didn't you?"

"Duh. How'd you guess?"

"Which way to the cemetery?"

"Come on."

She took his hand and Doug led her to the chapel. She started to say something as they passed the kitchen wing of the house but he hushed her, waited until they were nearly at the chapel.

"Sorry, but Allie might have woken up if he heard you."

"Your dog?"

"Yeah."

She gazed at the chapel, then back at the dark mansion. "Do you like living there?"

He shrugged. "I guess."

"Doesn't it get lonely?"

When he didn't answer, she squeezed his hand. The feeling shot up his arm like a shock—the kind that gets a heart going after it has stopped.

They came to the low cemetery wall. Doug hesitated.

"What's the matter?"

"Waiting."

"For what?"

"The vibrations." He thought about the episode he'd had just before falling asleep. "Oh, shit."

"What's the matter now?"

"I'm not sure he'll show up."

"Why not?"

He explained about the vibrations, how they usually arrived whenever anything like this happened.

"I'm not sure I'm good for more than one-a-day, that's all," he said.

"For God's sake, Doug, we're talking ghosts here, not vitamins."

"I'm just saying, I don't know if he'll show up, that's all."

She harumphed, then said sexily. "You just wanted to get me out here in the dark, didn't you?"

Doug's heart began to race again. An animal skittered between the headstones and Sally grabbed his arm. They both laughed, but she didn't let go.

He helped her over the low wall and they walked toward the mausoleum.

"How'd you get here?" Doug asked.

"Hitch-hiked."

"You're kidding, right?"

"Yeah. I rode my bike."

"You aren't scared being out this late?"

She shook her head. "There's scarier things at home."

He wanted to ask "Like what?" but they were at the mausoleum door.

"What's in here?"

"My Grandma Sarah and a bunch of other relatives."

"Cool. And this guy..."

"Father Hector."

"Yeah, Hector. He lives in here with them?"

"I don't think 'lives' is the right term."

"Hangs. Floats. Haunts." She went to open the door. A padlock secured it. "Dammit."

"If he's around, that padlock won't make any difference."

"But I was hoping to meet your grandmother." She pulled on the door. "Come help me, Doug."

She turned when he reached for the door and kissed him, locking her arms around his neck. Caught off guard, Doug instinctively drew away, but she held tight.

As the kiss continued, Doug's heart resumed its wild pounding and he suddenly felt the onset of the vibrations. The two feelings mixed together, braiding within him the strong, emotional staccato of sex with the smooth, slippery sensation that took him out of his body. Just as the divergent feelings threatened to tear him in half, he spotted Father Hector out of the corner of his eye.

"There," he mumbled through the kiss; then extracted himself from her grip. "He's over there."

Her breath was coming in deep gulps, she turned and gasped, "Where?"

"I saw him right over there." He pointed.

She turned to face him. "You mean, there really is a ghost?"

"Of course. Why do you think we're here?"

She smiled. "Midnight kissing's more fun than ghost-busting."

"Come on." He took her by the hand and started after the apparition. "I want you to meet him."

She dug in her heels. "Can't we just stay here, finish what we started?"

Doug stared at her. "I don't believe it. You're afraid, aren't you?"

"Am not."

"Are too."

"All right, have it your way." She snorted, grabbed his hand. "Let's go find Brother Nectar."

"Father Hector."

"Hector, Schmector. Let's just go find the son-of-a-bitch."

Fiona wasn't sure if her indigestion had awakened her, or was it Allie's whining in the laundry room? She turned on the light and glanced at the clock. Nearly one in the morning. Maybe an old Agatha Christie would put her to sleep. Downstairs, she fixed herself a Pepto Bismol and opened the laundry room door. Allie bolted through the kitchen and up the stairs.

"Ach, you scamp, get back down here before you wake up the whole house."

Allie had nosed Doug's door open by the time Fiona got there.

"Darn ya, Allie" she whispered, tiptoeing in. "If you wake him up, I'll…"

But Allie was already across the darkened room, illuminated only by the hall light. He had his paws on the sill, his nose sniffing out the open window. He whined, then wheeled and headed out the door and down the stairs.

Confused, it took Fiona another moment to realize that Doug was not in bed but had climbed down the ladder to the ground. Allie's frantic scratching at the front door echoed up the stairwell.

Fiona pulled her robe tighter and scuttled downstairs.

"Douglas MacBrayne," she muttered, "when I get my hands on you, laddie…"

She grabbed a flashlight from the kitchen counter and whisper-called Allie to the back door. "Now, we've got to be quiet, you hear?"

Allie wanted out, was gone like a shot the moment Fiona opened the door. She hurried after him, using words under her breath she hadn't said for thirty years. It didn't surprise her to find Allie growling at the cemetery wall.

She heard giggling off to her left and snapped the flashlight in that direction. Allie launched over the wall. Two faces ducked behind a gravestone. One of them was Doug. Fiona called his name. Then she heard tussling.

"Get off me, Allie." It was Doug. "You traitor."

"Douglas MacBrayne, you come out here where I can see you, right now." Fiona shone the light toward the sound.

Doug stood up. "I'm right here, Nanny."

"Tell your friend to stand up, also."

"What friend?"

"That one." Fiona flashed the light on a pair of legs sticking out from behind a nearby stone. "Don't mess with me, lad. Not at one o'clock in the morning."

Doug leaned over and restrained Allie, who was licking the accomplice's face. Then he helped the person up and the two walked toward her.

"It's just me and Sally, Nanny."

Fiona grunted. She knew her from the cafe. The leader of the Moles, according to Petrovich—who had also told Fiona his interpretation of the club name.

"Care to tell me what you two are doing out here in the middle of the night?"

"Looking for Father Hector."

Fiona shook her head. "Couldn't you have done that after school?"

"But, Nanny, this is after—"

"Don't be smart, lad. There's still trouble waiting for you here."

"It's all my fault, Mrs—Miss—"

"Miss McLean. And it's both your fault." Fiona flashed the light on Sally's face. "How'd you get here?"

"Bike."

"Well, come into the house, so I can call your parents to pick you up."

"Please, Miss McLean. I can make it home okay, I swear."

"Child, if anything happened to you, I'd never forgive—" Fiona saw the look of terror on the girl's face. "Okay, how far is it? I'll drive you."

"But Dad'll wake up." Doug tugged at her arm.

"I'd be home before you even got your keys, Miss McLean."

Fiona shook her head. "Where's your bike?"

"Over in the bushes by the side of the house."

"All right, you skedaddle, but I expect to see you tomorrow at the Crystal so I'll know you're okay."

Sally reached up, gave Fiona a warm hug, then ran off to her bike. Allie started after her, but Doug whistled him back. They stood outside until the crunch of Sally's bicycle tires faded, then they went inside.

"Your dog has fleas, huh?" Fiona whispered to Doug, pointing to Allie. "Never again. Understand?"

"Yes, Nanny."

"And, Doug."

"Yes?"

"Be sure to wipe that lipstick off your mouth before you hop in bed."

He blushed, wiped his mouth with his sleeve, walked upstairs, Allie in tow—still chiding his faithful companion for his disloyalty.

Nanny giggled, reached for her antacid, realized her indigestion was gone. She touched her cheek where the girl had kissed her and shuddered thinking of what Petrovich had told her.

The look of terror on the girl's face confirmed the worst. What an ugly world, when young girls feel safer on the streets at night than in their own homes.

Fiona trudged to bed. She wouldn't need a mystery to put her to sleep, tonight.

❦

Peter stood in his darkened bedroom window, portable telephone in his hand. He'd almost dialed 911 for the police, but when he realized it was Doug in the cemetery—this time with a friend—he held off.

Something was surely going on out there and he was quite certain neither Doug nor Fiona would tell him anything about it.

Maybe Peter's father had been right that sometimes parents had to take extraordinary measures to ensure a son's development.

Peter dialed the telephone, listened to the recording. His secretary's voice said to wait for the beep.

"Grace, this is Mr. MacBrayne. I want you to make arrangements for my son to attend Camp Shambala for the full summer. Dan Downey has the dates.

"And then make airline and train reservations for Miss Fiona McLean to Dundee, Scotland, leaving the same day as Doug." A sly smile played across his face. "Just to confirm, Grace. Make that a one-way ticket to Scotland."

Peter clicked off the telephone, gazed out the window at the dark night. "We'll just see how you like that, Miss Fiona McLean."

Chapter Nine

The drive to Camp Shambala had taken an hour longer than Doug had been told. The sign said "Road Construction," but meant they were blasting a new, two-lane highway out of a rocky hill—at that point too near the old road for safety. Not only was the noise deafening, but Doug's frustration became almost unbearable when he figured that ten minutes remained of the journey.

At last they pulled into the overgrown driveway and parked in the unweeded lot. Doug jumped out, thanked and said goodbye to the driver and began dragging his suitcase behind him, Allie straining ahead at his leash.

Who ever heard of keeping a dog on a leash out in the country? Besides, this Camp Shambala looked more like Camp Shambles. He couldn't remember what he'd pictured when Dad told him about the forthcoming "summer adventure," as he put it, but so far, everything smelled musty and looked dilapidated and shabby.

"It's on a big lake, surrounded by summer homes and a few other camps." Dad had said. "I used to go there when I was a kid. Grandma Sarah had a summer place on the shore."

"Wow, you mean we still have land there?"

"She gave it to her maid when the woman retired. Sarah was funny that way." Dad shook his head. "But look, I just know you'll have a good time. Some of your friends from school will be there,"

Who could that mean? Doug sighed. Dad just didn't understand that Nanny was his only friend. He blotted out the image of her climbing into the airport limousine. She had wanted to visit the camp, to make sure it passed her standards, but Dad had vetoed that, saying it would just embarrass Doug. Now Doug wished she'd been allowed to come. She had looked so forlorn as her fingers touched the window, a brief goodbye.

Just the way he felt at this minute.

Allie veered off the path toward a tree and Doug tugged him back, up on his hind legs.

"Don't go getting all wacky on me, Allie," Doug said. "At least not before we find our bunkhouse and I can unload this stuff."

Allie gave in reluctantly, then tugged again. Doug fell to one knee. Something passed over his head, disappeared in the brush on the other side.

"Hey!" Doug shouted, trying to see what it was. "What the heck was that?"

Another whatever whizzed over his head.

"Hey!" Doug covered his head with his arms, looked out from underneath. "Go get 'em," he whispered, releasing Allie.

Allie tore into the underbrush, snarling. There was a shriek, a commotion in the leaves, and a figure burst from cover.

"Yeow!" Chas Miner tried to shake Allie from his gym shoe, but the dog hung tight. "Hey, get this mutt off me."

"Tell me why you're shooting arrows at me, first."

"Way over your head. I shoot at everybody. It's my job. I'm Camp Indian this week."

"That's a little dangerous, isn't it?"

Chas shrugged. "No. I'm such a bad shot, and besides, I use rubber tips."

"What if you shot someone in the eye?"

"Then a billion nagging mothers will have been right." He threw up his hands. "Jesus, MacBrayne, you've only been here five minutes and you already sound like my mother. Lighten up, you're at camp. We're supposed to act like hooligans. Get it all out of our systems by Fall."

"They told you that?"

Miner rolled his eyes. "Let me guess, this is your first time at camp, right?"

Doug nodded.

"Damn, another tenderfoot." Chas breathed out a stream of frustration. "Come on, which bunkhouse did you draw?"

"Artillery Walk." Doug held up the sheet of paper. "Why does that sound familiar to me?"

Chas looked at it, began to laugh. "I dunno, but you got screwed, dude. Jesus, it's Uncle Milty's place."

"Who's that?"

"You'll find out." He pointed to a path that led up the hill to the left. "Just follow that trail."

Allie lunged again at Chas, mistaking his paroxysms of laughter for danger. Doug tugged the leash sharply and started up the path.

Fifty yards up the hill he saw it, a large log cabin that resembled the two others he'd seen on the way, except this one had a rickety, rustic picket fence surrounding it and campers working in front.

One of them spotted Doug. "Look, guys, fresh meat. Better call Massah Sharpe."

The cry went out and the front door opened just as Doug reached the rickety gate. A tall black man, wearing white shorts, shirt, and hat stood at the door, fanning himself.

"Well, well, what have we here?"

"Doug MacBrayne, sir. They told me I was assigned to this bunkhouse."

"Fine, fine. Plenty to do here, as you can see." He turned and waved his fan at the boys. "Back to work, my summer slaves. You don't want to miss the afternoon swim."

The seven other boys stopped their gawking and threw themselves into hoeing and raking the front yard. They seemed to be raising more dust than doing anything productive, but the black man gazed at them with benevolent eyes.

"Come along, Mr. MacBrayne. We'll get you a bunk and then fix you up with a rake or a hoe." He noticed Allie. "And leave that creature tied to the gate. Caninae Prohibitus."

"What do you mean, dogs are forbidden? My father paid extra, so Allie could come to camp with me."

Some of the benevolence left the man's eyes, but a new glint replaced it.

"You've studied Latin, Mr. MacBrayne?"

Doug shook his head. "No, but I understand the roots of some words."

"Really? Well, I'll tell you what. I'm a fair man, aren't I lads?"

"Yes, Master Sharpe," came the obligatory reply.

"Very good." He turned to Doug. "You like words? Well, we'll have a competition, play a little word game. If I win, the dog sleeps outside."

"And if I win, Allie sleeps inside, right?" Doug grinned.

"Something like that." Master Sharpe took off his hat, wiped his brow with a handkerchief. "Have you ever played Scrabble, Mr. MacBrayne?"

Doug frowned, scratched his head. "A few times, but not lately; so you may have to explain the rules."

"No problem there, I'm good with rules. Am I not, boys?"

"Oh yes, Mr. Sharpe," they called in a chorus.

Doug smiled. His father may have been right after all. Camp just might turn out to be more fun than he expected.

Avisson stood before the grease-pen board behind his desk. Down the left hand margin he had written the eight identities he had thus far encountered during the hypnosis sessions with Sabey. Across the top were columns designated: Birth Sign; Believed Era; Personal Qualities; Significant Remembered Events and Actions; and Approximate Date and Time of Death.

None of the columnar data was conclusive, especially the estimates for birth and death dates, but Sabey had remarkable clarity for such details, particularly when deeply hypnotized, as he had been the past few sessions. If playacting, he should get an Academy Award, or whatever they give for Best Performance by a Multiple Schizophrenic.

There was a tap at the door, which opened. Dr. Kautsch stuck his head in.

"Bother you for a moment, Avisson?"

"Sure." Avisson beckoned to his boss.

Kautsch stood next to him, studied the board. "Sabey?"

Avisson nodded.

"Wacked, right?"

"Completely."

"What's this Birth Sign?"

Avisson coughed. "Ah, past life astrology. It's Sabey's contention that he had no choice but to kill those women, according to his birth date, and the fact that he's a Scorpio with Mars rising—"

"I thought I told you we didn't want any of that New Age crap anymore?"

"You did, but this is part of the patient's makeup. Hell, it's his lawyer's line of defense. Want me to ignore it so they'll take him to another facility?"

Kautsch shook his head. "No, but—"

"Besides, we may have hit on a new way to expand, exponentially, the cost of treatment we provide to patients."

Kautsch's eyes narrowed. "You're messing with me, right?"

"No." Avisson ran his hand down the line of Sabey's personalities. "Whether or not we psychiatrists like it, people are asking us more and more about the possibility of having lived before. If the trend continues, soon half of America will believe in reincarnation—that we have lived before."

"So what?"

"If they also believe that those past lives influence their present life, then we may have to start treating past life symptoms, to heal present psychoses." He raised his arms. "Voila! Each individual might represent six or seven different past life patient opportunities. The accountants will love it."

Kautsch stared at him. "You are messing with me."

"Only a little bit." Avisson smiled. "But the part that really makes you angry is the part that you think—deep down—may be true. You just don't want to admit it."

Kautsch's goateed face split, showing yellowish-white teeth. "Perhaps, if you like thumbnail analyses. Which I don't."

"No, I suppose not."

The two men stood, looked at the board. After half a minute, Avisson cleared his throat. "You wanted to see me."

"Oh, yes. It actually does have to do with Sabey." Kautsch pulled a folder from under his arm. "Just what are the odds of a jury finding him mentally competent?"

"If this were California, I'd say ninety-nine point five percent. Here in New Jersey: sixty-forty."

"Do you think Sabey's worth studying, from a research standpoint?"

"He's unique, which both adds to and diminishes his value as a subject. Why?"

"We may both wind up winning from this—accidentally, of course."

"How so?"

"Not sure, yet. Just stay with him, and keep me updated. As soon as I know something tangible, I'll tell you."

Kautsch left. Avisson sat behind his desk, put his feet up and closed his eyes. Cleo Clark begat Larry Clark, who begat the savage, Sabey. Dr. Armen Ramis begets Dr. Kautsch, who begets what?

Something monstrous, no doubt. Kautsch and Sabey had the same look in their eyes: the amoral predator, and no astrological sign covered that.

❦

Grumpy looked at the list, shook his head. No way he could finish everything in time. He glanced at Kim, who was showing the new girl how to make a cappuccino. The phone rang. He nodded for Kim to answer.

"It's for you, Mr. Petrovich."

"Take a message."

"I tried. He says it's important. A guy named Jacques something from Paris—"

"Okay." He put the phone to his ear, continued jotting notes. "Allo, Jacques. J'écoute."

He half-listened while his agent described the special delivery envelope from Douglas Industries. Should he open it? What should he do?

"Same as always, Jacques: assign the proxy to Gerald Walsh." He rested the handset on his shoulder, while completing his checklist. "I'm sure it's all very important. But I'm juggling about twenty things here, at the moment. Just assign the proxy. Yes. Bien, bien. Oui. Merci. À bientot."

"Who was that?" Kim asked. "He sounded terribly sexy."

"The president of France. He wanted to know if they should attack Germany or England."

Kim stuck out her tongue.

Grumpy laughed, looked around the store. "You sure you'll be able to handle things?"

Kim rolled her eyes. He took it as a yes.

"Right. Then I'm off." He checked his watch against the store clock. Twenty minute window. "If everything goes according to plan, you'll see me in a week. If not, I'll be back tomorrow."

Kim put her hands together and looked at the ceiling.

"Ha, ha," Grumpy pushed the door open and stopped. His car had a flat tire. He turned and pointed at Kim. "Stop praying. Look what you've done already."

Fiona sat heavily into the airport seat opposite her gate, wriggled several times to try to get comfortable. No use. God, this was a mistake. She knew it from the moment she saw the ticket next to her plate at the dining room table. She knew it the moment she saw the glint in Peter's eye, his false bravado and insincere expression of gratitude.

"Lord knows you deserve a vacation," he said. "Lord knows I'd love to get rid of you, forever," she read into his thoughts.

She was pretty sure that it hadn't been his idea. Peter never plotted, especially with such cunning. No, someone else's hand was behind this caper. She could sense it, smell it.

And the rat she smelled must be Kautsch. Though she had no real evidence, this cheese had a psychological aroma to it. It was too innocent on the surface. Peter, with all his faults, could be relied on for blatant, autocratic moves. This was slippery, oily and slick.

She shouldn't be leaving the country. That much she knew. Putting thousands of miles between her and Doug was a tragic mistake. But what else could she do? If she stayed behind on some pretense, it would prove to Peter that she was—a blush filled her cheeks—co-dependent.

Okay, she couldn't argue with the fact that it would be nice to visit Dundee, see Kate and Sandy, and that old witch, Maggie.

Fiona sighed, settled into the chair. How she used to love summers in Scotland. The air, so filled with the blue salt of the sea and the green sugar of the glens. Not like New Jersey, where the summer air collapsed in the lungs from the heat and humidity, and one scurried from one artificially-cooled, commercial cavern to another.

And, oh God, to see a landscape not plastered with billboards promoting underarm deodorants, or leering camels with cigarettes jutting from their dromedary lips, liquor ads where women bent over, half the heinie showing, as if their butts alone could induce a hangover.

Could it be that Peter had been right? Even if mistakenly so? This vacation might turn out to be a well-needed holiday—a joyous one at that.

A new smile filled her face. Heartened, excited, Fiona looked around at her fellow travelers.

"Will Miss Fiona McLean please pick up a courtesy phone?" Came across the public address system.

Fiona looked around. The message repeated. She hurried to a uniformed worker who pointed to a row of white telephones. She picked one up, gingerly.

"This is Fiona McLean."

"Miss McLean, a Mr. Petrovich called and asked that you meet him in the VIP lounge immediately. If he's not there yet, please wait for him."

She found the lounge, waited in line for several minutes to speak to the receptionist. She explained her mission. The girl pointed to her left.

"Mr. Petrovich, here's your party, I believe."

BIRTHMARK

Fiona looked up to see a short, stocky man with a bushy mustache and long, black hair moving toward her. She turned back to the desk.

"I'm sorry, there must be some mistake. I'm supposed to meet Mr. Valka Petrovich."

"I am Valka Petrovich," the man said with a thick accent. "Who are you?"

Again to the receptionist. "I'm sorry, I don't know this man. I—"

Then she saw her, the middle-aged woman sitting in a wheelchair. Her crippled hands, gnarled tight, were at rest in her lap, her hair shot red and silver flames from both sides of her head—precariously balanced on a thin, swan-like neck.

Fiona caught her breath.

The woman smiled. "Valka, do not frighten Miss McLean."

The short man frowned. "Frighten?"

"How do you know my—?" Fiona looked past them, saw a familiar face, reddened by exertion.

"Fiona!" the other Valka Petrovich called, "I'm so glad we caught you in time."

Bewildered, Fiona leaned against the counter. She looked at one Valka Petrovich, then the other. Shook her head. "You aren't brothers, like that boxer who named all his sons 'George,' are you?"

Her own Petrovich smiled, sadly, it seemed, pointed to the dark-mustachioed man. "Fiona McLean, please meet the real Valka Petrovich, and his sister, Janina. They've just arrived from Bucharest."

Fiona nodded to each of them, not willing to give in to her feelings for the wheelchair-bound Janina just yet. "If he's the real one, who are you?"

The man squirmed like a schoolboy caught in his first lie. The eyebrows raised, a wince formed, the shoulders twisted.

"For God's sake, man, are you Hitler's long lost nephew, or what?"

Her friend stuck out his hand. She took it, gingerly. "Miss McLean, we haven't been properly introduced. And that's my fault." He took a deep breath. "My name is Peter Douglas-MacBrayne, Junior. Doug's grandfather, also known as Grumpy."

Fiona blinked, gulped. She automatically pumped his hand once and released it. "Please to meet you, at last, Mr. Peter Douglas-MacBrayne, Jr." She turned to the Petrovichs. "And pleasant making your acquaintance, even if briefly." She drew herself up. "And now, if you'll excuse me, I have a plane to catch to Scotland."

She walked toward her gate, half-hoping he'd follow, half-praying he wouldn't. She'd never slugged anyone before, at least not at the same time she was crying.

❦

Doug chewed his lip, arranged and rearranged the letters before him, but no other word rose to the surface. He sighed, played what he had. It wasn't enough to dent Mr. Sharpe's lead.

"Pity we're almost out of letters," the man said, "I've enjoyed the competition."

Doug marked the score for his move, then glanced around the room at the faces of the other campers.

The dining hall had filled, magically. Somehow everyone in camp had heard about the great English Master, Goliath/Mr. Sharpe, being challenged by the diminutive David/Doug. It was a strange feeling having everyone root for him. And here he was, letting them down. Obviously, playing against Nanny had not prepared him for the real world of Scrabble. Hell, he was getting trounced. His eyes met Jimmy's from the rear of the hall. Jimmy flipped him the bird. Doug shrugged.

"Don't try to lull me into thinking you're not paying attention, Mr. MacBrayne." Sharpe arranged his tiles on the wooden holder. "It's obvious you've played more than you let on, but probably not someone as good as I am."

"It does look like you've got me, sir. In fact—" Suddenly interrupted by the now almost-familiar chill, Doug also heard a strange laugh. He looked around to see if anyone else had heard, but all eyes were glued on Mr. Sharpe, who was concentrating, hard.

"Aha!" he cried, placing all seven of his tiles vertically down the left side of the board, using the "O" in oracle, already in place. "I love a grand finish."

Chas Miner read the word out loud. "Hey, that's not how you spell exercise." He elbowed Doug, who glanced up from his tile holder. "Don't let him cheat you."

Doug's smile was glum. "It's pronounced almost the same as 'exercise,' but 'exorcise' means to get rid of a ghost."

"Ooooo!" came the chorus from the other kids.

"Exorcise." Sharpe grinned. "As in 'now you don't have a ghost of a chance,' MacBrayne; so get ready to make that shelter for your dog to sleep in tonight—outside."

Doug groaned as he counted out the points: "That's 18 for the word, times three is fifty-four for the triple-word score, plus the

50-point bonus, for using all seven tiles. "That puts you ahead by 221 points, Mr. Sharpe."

"Well, don't be too disappointed. I've beaten the pants off of plenty of Ph.D. candidates." He grinned, reached for the bag of wooden tiles. "You've got nothing to be ashamed of —"

"Wait, I haven't drawn yet." Doug looked at the E and Q on his rack, withdrew the remaining five tiles and put them on the wooden tray. Someone snickered behind him: Doug had inadvertently spelled out U ARSE. Laughter rippled through the crowd, as the joke spread.

"What's so funny?" Sharpe asked, rubbing his chin.

"Just a silly mistake," Doug said, suddenly missing Nanny, who disapproved of his using risque words, "You may be smart for your age," she'd say, "but you can still mind your manners."

He shuffled his letters, thankful for the U, which he put to the right of the Q. He then took the R and E and put them at the left of his tile rack. Fully aware that he needed a huge play, to have any hope of even coming close, he studied the board carefully.

"That's all the tiles. It's your last chance." Sharpe said, shaking the empty bag, "So take your best shot. But I'm afraid there's no hope for you, lad."

A quick chill struck Doug. He shuddered, looked up quickly to see if Sharpe noticed. He hadn't. When Doug's thoughts returned to his letters, a word suddenly appeared in his mind.

"I've got one!" he cried, then placed the tiles in order, along the bottom of the board, spelling "R-E-S-Q-U-A-R-E-D." He put the first R on the open, red triple word-score at the bottom of exorcise, creating the noun "exorciser."

Sharpe frowned, grabbed the dictionary, while Doug counted the points.

"Let's see, the Q is on a double-letter score, so that's 20, plus 8, equals a word-score of 28; times three for the first triple-word score, makes 84; times three again, for the other triple-word score. That comes to 252, plus the 50 for using all my letters. That makes 302, and, finally, three times the exorciser word-count adds 54,"

Stunned, Sharpe recounted twice, then once more.

"Good God, that's 356 points." Sharpe put down his pen, thinking it just might be a Guinness world record for a single play. All he could manage to say, was "You've won, MacBrayne."

Bedlam broke out in the hall. Boys pounded Doug on the back, even as he stood and extended his hand to Mr. Sharpe, who accepted it, bowed; then walked out, very stiffly, carrying both the Scrabble box and what remained of his dignity.

In the midst of the congratulations, Doug felt a slight pinch on his arm. Jimmy stood next to him.

"Meet me outside, in ten minutes," he whispered. "And don't let anyone see you."

Doug pointed to Allie, who was himself surrounded by admiring fans.

"Chas'll take care of him for you."

Jimmy disappeared. Doug waded through the boys and gave Allie a hug. He looked up at all the smiling faces. He'd felt Nanny's absence so terribly, just a few moments before, but now—now he felt something different, something brand new. He caught his breath and nuzzled Allie's neck.

They weren't alone anymore.

🍎

Fiona looked up from her book. The screen said her flight would be delayed two hours. This did not surprise Fiona. Not that she thought Peter Douglas-MacBrayne, Junior, had the power it took to delay her departure, but rather that the moment seemed to dictate that she would not be able to make such a clean getaway.

That Petrovich woman, she seemed to have the power to ground a plane, wheelchair notwithstanding.

Fiona thought about Maggie. Did each country's mystics exhibit different personalities? Scottish Maggie was so improper, a wild-haired hag. On the other hand, this Janina seemed to come from the land of vampires and werewolves. No doubt a true Gypsy, she appeared very civilized and proper.

Just seeing the woman had wrenched Fiona's insides. The last time she'd felt something like that with an adult was when she first met Felicity Douglas MacBrayne. Obviously, Doug had tugged at her insides from the very beginning, and now that she knew that her Petrovich was also a MacBrayne, that explained his effect on her.

But was it good to have all these connections? With no close family in Scotland, Kate and Sandy had been the only Scots she was really connected to, but that was more proximity than real connection. Even the occasional letters between her and Kate had a certain chatty reserve, whereas everything connected to the Douglas-MacBrayne family, except Doug, seemed to hit Fiona below the belt, for better or for worse.

So now, why this ambush at the airport? What do two Gypsies from Bucharest and a Scottish nanny on her way home, for the first time in thirteen years, have in common?

Fiona tried concentrating on her book again, without success. She sighed, put the book in her bag, began to look around the room. She stopped when she spotted Janina Petrovich no more than ten feet away, sitting quietly in her wheelchair, her eyes staring down into her own lap.

Oh, no. Fiona was not going to fall for this little trick. Neither Petrovich nor Douglas MacBrayne Jr., could make her give in by sending Janina to fetch her. Fiona took out her book, started reading again, found herself looking up every few minutes to see if Janina had changed position. She hadn't.

She wasn't going to talk to the woman. Didn't even know her. But every time she glanced over, she noticed another detail. The woman's silver earrings, dangling splendor; the way the artificial light pooled in the translucent area below her eyes; the way the baton-hands quivered, despite the woman's appearance of perfect stillness; the impression of fire, given off by Janina's hair, hair that just had to be hot to the touch.

Certain that an hour had passed, Fiona checked her Timex. Ten minutes. At this rate, she would soon have Janina's every feature memorized and catalogued.

And Fiona would be raving out of her Scottish mind.

The man sitting at the end of the row nearest Janina got up, stretched, then walked away. Janina's eyes never left her lap.

Spouting frustration, Fiona gathered her things and moved over, to sit next to her.

"Thank you, Fiona," Janina said softly.

"For what?" Fiona asked, a bit testily.

"For making the first move. I'm not very good at asking for help."

Fiona had been ready to do battle, but this caught her completely off guard.

"What does Petrovi-Mr. MacBrayne want you to do?"

"It's not about him. He thinks this is all his idea, but it's really mine." Janina raised her eyes for the first time. Fiona felt herself falling into them. Janina continued in a soft, matter-of-fact voice. "Grumpy thinks he brought me here to trick me into seeing a specialist. He and Valka think they are so clever, two foxes."

Her smile cut Fiona's resolve in half. One of the nubbed hands reached over and rested on Fiona's wrist. The hand looked so alien, she hadn't expected it to be warm to the touch.

"Like all men," Janina said, continuing in her soft voice, "they only know what they think. That is why I need your help."

"Can I say 'maybe?' Until I hear your proposal?"

Janina nodded. "It is a very simple one. It is time to find and train my replacement."

"Replacement, as what?"

Janina grinned. "That is not so easy to explain."

Fiona held Janina's hand. "But maybe Grumpy and Valka are right. Maybe you do need a specialist. Maybe you will recover your strength and be able to do whatever it is you do."

"Ah, but I have never in my life been stronger." Another grin. She leaned over slightly, spoke in an even lower whisper. "Do you think it is easy to delay a trans-Atlantic flight?"

Fiona's eyes narrowed, trying to see if Janina was kidding. The woman's eyes burned, deep coals. She was not.

"Fiona, I'm dying. I need to find my replacement."

A door slammed in Fiona's heart. She caught her breath, felt claustrophobic. No way. No way was she going to replace another dying woman. She'd done it once and look what it got her.

The nubbed hand stroked Fiona's arm.

"You are not to be my replacement. But in the process of finding one, we may be able to help save some other girls from themselves—" Janina's smile took on even more mystery—" and you might just find your heart's desire, as well."

Fiona was not strong enough for these people, with their comings and goings, their being born and dying. She was a simple Scottish lass, trying to lead an ordinary life. Where did all these Gypsies come from?

"We are like your 'Little People,'" Janina said, as if reading Fiona's mind. "We don't 'exist' at all, until you really need us."

Fiona sighed, collected her things, and walked beside Janina as they made their way out of the terminal.

"You use a crystal ball, too?" Fiona asked.

"Yes."

"Will I be able to see Doug in it?"

"Maybe," Janina said. "But where we're going, it may be easier to use a telescope."

🙶

Flushed with victory, excited by the prospect of new friendships, Doug was feeling particularly amiable, even toward Jimmy Lyden. He did have a quick flash of regret at having left Allie in Chas's care, especially after the "Camp Indian's" attack earlier in the afternoon. If this were an ambush, Doug wouldn't have Allie to warn him.

No Allie. No Nanny. He was truly on his own. The thought caused more wonder than concern. After all, he'd defeated Mr. Sharpe, even when it looked so impossible, near the end. Nanny would be so proud of him. Dad would probably scowl, remind him that Mr. Sharpe held Doug's fate in his hand for the rest of the summer and, having defeated him might not be such a good idea.

But Doug hadn't really been thinking about winning. Heck, it would have been all over if Sharpe hadn't said—what was it? "No hope for you, lad."

That set off all kinds of alarms in Doug. Something that refused to let him lose—at least not this time.

"Hey, MacBrayne-less. Over here."

Just once Doug would like to nail Lyden when he wasn't all ready for him. Oh, to have the upper hand, just once. He cantered to the clump of trees where Jimmy leaned. At first Doug thought he was smoking, but it was just a long weed stuck between his front teeth.

"I heard about you taking out Uncle Milty, that was pretty cute."

Doug shrugged. "Just got lucky at the end."

"Maybe, but you gotta start being more careful."

"Careful?" Doug stared at him. "Why?"

"We don't know how Uncle Milty fits in—"

"Why do you call him 'Uncle Milty'?"

"You'll find that out at bedtime." Jimmy waved the idea away. "Look, the important thing is to be careful what you do with any adult, and if anything strange happens, let me know, so I can figure out how it fits in."

"What strange stuff? And why should I report to you?"

Jimmy clenched and unclenched his fists slowly, closed his eyes for a moment. "Look, I don't like you, you don't like me, but—"

"Wait a minute." Doug shook his head. "I know you don't like me, but don't tell me what I feel. I may not like the things you do to me, but I never said I didn't like you."

"Yeah, yeah, whatever." Jimmy spit the weed from his mouth. "The point is, something bad is going on, and we know it's going to screw up the orphanage, maybe the school, and possibly the whole town. And your dad's involved, too."

"You're crazy."

"No, I'm not." A funny glint entered Jimmy's eyes. "Chas told me this is the first time you've ever been to a summer camp, is that true?"

"Yeah, but what does that prove?"

"Nothing. But where's your Nanny right now?"
"Going to Scotland, for a vacation."
"How many vacations has she taken before this?"
"None."
"Gee, sure sounds like your father wanted her out of the way."
"You're really crazy."
"Oh, yeah? Ever hear of a guy named Dr. Kautsch?"
This stopped Doug. He nodded. "I know him. So what?"
"Guess who runs this camp?"
"Some guy named Merriwether—I read the brochure."
"And you believe everything you read, right?"
Doug sighed. "Why would they lie?"
Jimmy frowned, thought for a moment. "If I prove to you they're lying, will you keep your mouth shut and your eyes open?"
"I guess."
"Hold out your hand."
Doug did. Jimmy pulled something from his hip pocket, jabbed Doug's palm. Doug cried out, grabbed his hand and watched the first drops of blood seep through his fingers.
"It ain't too bad, but I'd go see Nurse Slimson, if I were you. The Infirmary's up the hill from the Arts and Crafts Building." Jimmy winked. "That's where they have the most accidents."
Jimmy skipped down the path before Doug could say anything. Nurse Slimson. He knew her. If she was there, maybe Jimmy was telling the truth. He gazed at the red oozing from his throbbing hand. The vibrations began and Doug felt the trees around him evaporate, only to be replaced by a different forest.

᭝

Ashna noticed the berry patch and licked his lips. When he returned, he would bring berries to Huva. Maybe that would lift her spirits. For the past few suns she had been listless, afraid. Water sprang to her eyes when he asked if she were ill.
He was almost to the secret cave when he heard a crashing sound in the bushes to his right. At first he thought to investigate, but if it was a bear or other large creature, he might be injured or even killed.
Besides, he had little time to make new drawings, better ones. The last hunt had only produced half the usual results, though Ashna had drawn more animals than normal.
Now Tehuti spoke of moving camp, because of their diminishing number.

Off to the right, Ashna finally spotted the source of noise. His brother Hamar's head could be seen through the branches below, halfway to the stream where they all washed and drank. Ashna raged from the mouth of the cave, falling and sliding down the hill after him. He called to his brother, hurried along on his crippled legs as fast as he could move. Hamar continued toward the stream. Ashna cried out again.

Hamar stopped, stood waiting for Ashna with his hands behind him.

Ashna did the open hand of greeting. Hamar grunted, did not signal back. Ashna showed his open hand again. No response.

"It is forbidden," Ashna snarled.

Hamar shrugged, did not look at him.

"It is forbidden," Ashna said again.

Hamar looked up, then past Ashna, his eyes filled with fear. Ashna turned. There stood Tehuti.

Tehuti raised his hand. Ashna did the same, then looked at Hamar, whose hand was also raised—and covered with blue, red, and yellow pigments from the cave.

"Show me the painting-cave," Tehuti commanded.

Hamar shook his head.

Tehuti pulled an arrow from his sheath, fitted it into his bow. "Show me the cave."

Ashna moved between the two men. "My brother—"

"Move out of the way, deformed one," Tehuti said, "or you will die, too."

"Ashna—" came from behind him. But before he could turn to his brother's voice, something whistled past his ear. He raised his hand to Tehuti.

"Do not—" Ashna stopped as he heard gagging, choking sounds behind him. He turned to see Hamar topple to the ground, one of Tehuti's jagged arrows lodged in his throat. Ashna knelt beside his brother.

"Huva—hide Huva." Hamar gasped, as the life left his body.

Ashna stood and slowly began hobbling to collect the rocks he would need to cover the body. It was the only way he could contain the useless rage that boiled within him.

"No," Tehuti shouted. "Clan leave now. No time."

Ashna emptied his eyes of his anger, looked at Tehuti dully, stooped and picked up several more rocks. Tehuti slipped the notch of another arrow into the bowstring, pulled back. Ashna continued the burial of his brother. Tehuti would not shoot him. He could strike down Hamar, for having the pigment on his hands—proof of doing the forbidden—but not Ashna, who exhibited no such evidence.

Tehuti leaped upon the four-leg. "We leave now, deformed one."

Ashna nodded, continued piling the rocks on his brother's body, while Tehuti rode away. Every now and then, Ashna would glance at the stream. In his fury to discover his brother's guilt, he had stopped him, mere footsteps from washing the evidence from his hands in the stream.

That fury had cost his brother his life.

"Hide Huva," Hamar had said.

Ashna heard wailing down below. He dropped the last of the rocks on his brother's grave and hurried down the hill. He burst onto the first plateau only to see Tehuti pull Huva onto the four-leg with him. Still far above, Ashna looked away, but the wind blew the distasteful sound straight into his mouth.

He would never catch up with them. Even if he did, was he not helpless against Tehuti?

Ashna hurried back to the cave, entered without looking to see if anyone was near, then clambered toward the rear. The moment he lit his small lamp he understood Hamar's warning—and why his brother had painted.

There was the four-leg, grazing while Tehuti was doing man-woman with—Ashna put the lamp closer to the wall, fell gasping to the ground.

All he could see of the woman was her face, looking away from Tehuti—but the pain in her dark, soulful eyes was evident, as was her identity.

Somehow, Ashna would have to find them, bring her back. Tehuti must not be allowed to keep her. Ashna rose, carefully washed his fingers in the small bowl of water, then armed them with the only ammunition he possessed: his pigments.

❦

Doug blinked, looked at the woman in the doorway of the small infirmary. He didn't recognize her, but she seemed vaguely familiar. If forcing Doug to the nurse's cabin was Jimmy's way of proving a conspiracy—

"Yes?" The nurse smiled. "Is something the matter?"

"I cut my hand." Doug lifted it to show her.

"My goodness, so you have." She took him by the wrist. "Come inside, we'll get you fixed up in a jiffy."

BIRTHMARK

"Where's Nurse Slimson?"

"She had to stay home. Her son is sick. I'm filling in today."

Doug pondered this, while she washed his hand thoroughly in the sink, then had him sit on the examination table in the middle of the room.

"What'd you cut yourself with?" She asked, reaching for a bottle of hydrogen peroxide."

"A can lid, by the mess hall." He read her name tag. "Miss Peabody."

"We'd better check your record, see if you've had a tetanus shot." She frowned. "What's your name?"

He told her. She looked it up. "Well, Doug. We're going to have to give you a shot, just to be on the safe side."

Doug's eyes opened wide. "But the lid was really clean. It had just been washed for recycling."

She looked at him sideways from the refrigerator from which she had just removed a clear bottle. "Funny, when you first walked in, I thought you were a brave young man. I can't imagine how I could have been so wrong."

Doug rolled his eyes. He was stuck, in more ways than one. He rolled up his sleeve. "Go ahead."

"That's better." She smiled. "But I have one more piece of bad news: Down with the trousers."

He groaned, rolled over on the table and slipped his pants down. "Yes, Miss Peabody."

"You can call me Prudence," she said, extracting the needle and wiping the skin with an alcohol swab. "I figure anybody who lets me stick a needle in their gluteus maximus when I first meet them, can call me by my first name. What do you say, Doug?"

"Okay, Prudence" Doug said, pulling up his pants. "As long as I don't have to get a shot every time I see you."

"That's kind of up to you, wouldn't you say?"

Doug nodded, thanked Prudence and left, vowing silently to smash Jimmy the next time their paths crossed.

When Jimmy saw that the alternate nurse was on duty, instead of the expected Miss Slimson, he realized that MacBrayne might not believe in the conspiracy, let alone help. Cutting MacBrayne had been a stupid mistake on Jimmy's part, but maybe having the naive punk still against him might actually be safer. That is, unless he'd told the nurse that Jimmy had cut him.

Things were such a muddle in his head. If only Jimmy could talk to Petrovich.

He cleared his throat, spit into the underbrush. All this nature was clogging his breathing. Probably allergies. He could feel it coming, first the sore throat, then the earache, and finally headaches so bad he wanted to scream. When the latter came upon him, his eyes would go all out of focus and he would see the world as if through a thick, wavy lens.

He hated the thought that it might come over him here at camp. Bad enough at the orphanage, but at least there, they left him pretty much alone, and the only ones at camp who knew this happened to him were the other orphans, not the KWIPS (Kids With Parents) from school.

He looked up at the sun through the forest canopy. The afternoon swim would be starting soon, but he had already made it clear to the camp staff that he followed his own schedule. That fool, Merriwether, had tried to have a "sit down" with him, but Jimmy had hit him right off with his patented "You think you can punish me any more than life already has?" speech, then assured the man that although admittedly eccentric, he wouldn't do anything dangerous or illegal.

At least, not so they'd know about it.

Off to his right, a small stream gurgled. Jimmy pushed through the thick undergrowth to get a sip of water. Allergies or no, he did like it here in the woods. Everywhere he looked he saw another drawing or painting. Didn't matter whether he painted them or not, the scenes existed as soon as he saw them, framed in his mind. Some he instinctively knew he couldn't paint. His hands didn't know enough—yet.

Images of things were easy to depict. But he wanted to paint the ideas of things: a bird's song; the perfume of pine needles, crushed between fingertips; the panic of a squirrel at the whoosh of an owl, winging through the night forest; the way the trees and ground shake for a moment after every blast of the road construction. Best of all: what the heart feels like, after searching the cloudy night for the moon and seeing it appear suddenly on the other side of the sky—these feelings were the other side of the pain that made it worthwhile.

Jimmy's ear throbbed and the ache began to corkscrew into his head. He knelt beside the stream and cupped his hand to drink. Just as he was about to lap it with his tongue, he smelled something rotten. No, just plain nasty. He sniffed his hand, looked into the water. There were little gray strands running through it, catching on rocks and collecting in pools. He wiped his hands on the mossy bank, stood and began walking upstream, to get above the source of contamination.

The undergrowth along the bank was so thick, he had to jump from rock to rock the last fifty yards. The visible part of the stream emerged from the base of a tall, craggy hill. He pushed through the last few green sentries and finally came to an opening in the hill. The cave entrance, supported by a frame of old, sagging timbers, was blocked by a series of crossed, weathered planks and a large, flaking sign, that instructed intruders to "Keep Out."

Jimmy smiled in spite of his approaching headache. How was he supposed to resist such an invitation?

At the start of their limousine ride, Fiona had been glad she'd made Valka/Grumpy switch places with her, so she would not have to sit looking directly at him. But that meant either look out the window or into Janina's serene face. The woman's serenity was an odd counterpoint to Fiona seething insides. She couldn't shake her anger, even after Valka/Grumpy outlined his plan. It still galled her.

"A Nanny Camp? Are you crazy?" She had spun in her seat. "What would you have done if I had continued to Scotland?"

"Found an emergency replacement," Grumpy said, "or canceled due to illness."

"But these girls are all signed up, right? And under what pretense?"

Grumpy's shoulders shifted. "No pretense. We intend to teach them parenting skills, baby-sitting skills, if you will. They're at an age when they're going to begin caring for children. The more they know about what's ahead of them, the better they'll do."

"How many?"

"Seven of them."

"That means seven families made plans." Her finger punctured the air in front of Grumpy's nose. "And if you just canceled, they would all be hung out to dry."

"I would have compensated them."

She shook her head. "You don't get it. Just because you have all the money in the world, doesn't mean your little charades might not hurt people. You're thinking is almost as warped as your son's."

"Possibly," he started slowly, "but my intention is very dif—"

"Intention?" She sputtered. "The best intentions are automatically distorted when you lie or deceive along the way."

"But some people can't deal with the truth."

She glowered at him. Was this the man she admired, liked, so much? How could changing his name have made him so stupid? "What you mean to say is, it's harder to get your way when you have to tell the truth at every step."

His eyes went to the real Valka and to Janina for help. Valka shrugged. Janina smiled. Neither spoke.

"I guess I really screwed up," Grumpy said, taking a deep breath and letting it out slowly. "I'm sorry."

"Yes, well—" Fiona still had some steam in her. "—next time use your heart instead of your money, you might get what you want a lot faster."

That ended the conversation, except for Janina, whose smile broke into small chuckles, which she tried to stifle, but eventually gave way to. The other three stared at her. After half a minute of low laughter, she smiled.

"I'm sorry. It just struck me as funny. Grumpy travels all over the world looking for Gypsy answers, then spends several years with Valka and me—when the entire time, there was a Scottish Gypsy, right here at home."

The tension broken, Valka suggested a glass of wine to celebrate their arrival, then pulled a bottle from his rucksack, while Grumpy pushed the button that opened the bar.

"Where are we going, anyway?" Fiona asked.

Grumpy told her.

"But that's near where Doug—"

He nodded. Smiled.

Her eyes narrowed. "And let me guess—these seven girls include the Moles, right?"

"That's right."

Fiona accepted her wineglass from Valka, clinked against the others', then did a double-take as Grumpy said, "To Camp McLean."

"To Camp McLean," she repeated. Her gaze met Janina's over the brims of their glasses as the two women drank.

When she took her lips from the glass, Fiona understood: the plan, the camp, the Moles' participation—it all confirmed the source of Janina's power, and the ingredient necessary for her replacement: pain, and lots of it.

Fiona had seen such pain in another's eyes, and recently. She shuddered, thinking that someone so young had already paid such a high price and was still so afraid.

Afraid to go home.

Birthmark

❦

Doug lay on his bunk. Whether it was the fresh air, the great pick-up softball game that took most of the afternoon, or the overly heavy dinner of meat and potatoes, he was exhausted, and happily so.

Everything was so funny here. The three bunkhouses each housed eight boys—twenty-four in all. And the counselors. Bernie Klinger, who looked more like a mad composer than a camper, was in charge of the Hole-In-The-Wall bunkhouse, where Jimmy and Chas were asleep. That suited Doug fine. He liked his cabin-mates. Particularly Augie Leopardi and Johnny Manfred. Augie lived at the orphanage. He had the dark features of an Italian (he had told Doug his name meant Leopard in his father's native tongue and Doug hadn't let on how obvious it was). Johnny was a shy boy with glasses, a year younger than Doug, but who seemed to look up to Doug as if he were an older brother. Apparently Johnny had five sisters. He was the youngest in the family and seemed lost without the girls, who pampered him.

The other bunkhouse was run by a college student, Nigel Wilson, who kept after everyone, to pick up litter, not to use too much water. He wore a t-shirt that read, "Screw the Timber Industry, Just Save the Spotted Owl."

Then there was Tex and Bonnie James, and their three-year old son, Jesse. Tex ran the craft shop and Bonnie cooked. Tex looked half Indian and Bonnie had the lightest complexion Doug had ever seen. Her hair looked like pale blonde silk. She wasn't exactly pretty, but she obviously adored Tex and Jesse, and her looks improved whenever she looked at either of the men in her life.

He decided that Greg Sturgis, in charge of the waterfront, was really part fish. Another college student, Greg had obviously spent his high school years as a lifeguard. His face was absolutely fierce when he told the boys the rules they would obey in the water and on the beach. They were supposed to go canoeing in a couple of days. Doug was sure the rules would be even stricter, then.

He reached over the side of the bed to stroke Allie, who probably would have been purring were he a cat. Allie had been declared Camp Mascot. Never had he received such petting, nor so much surreptitious food at dinner. There seemed to be more food hitting the floor, than the throats of the campers.

Doug grinned. Keeping secret the cause of his cut hand had inadvertently raised his status: Miss Prudence Peabody was a camp favorite, and to be administered to by this pretty, red-headed angel of mercy (and object of universal boyhood lust) was another notch in Doug's belt.

He giggled to himself, when he realized he was one happy camper.

Even so, he had groaned with the others when "Massah Sharpe" announced it was bedtime: that he would read them to sleep from his favorite, Paradise Lost.

"You'll be asleep in two minutes," whispered the boy in the next bunk. "It's worse than Sunday School."

"For your information, Mr. MacBrayne—" Sharpe trimmed the wick on the hurricane lamp, which at once filled the cabin with a soft, golden glow— "Paradise Lost is an epic poem about the Garden of Eden, written in the 1600's by John Milton, who was—"

"I know, blind." Doug stifled a yawn. He felt Sharpe staring at him. "I'm sorry, Mister Sharpe. Did I say something wrong?"

Sharpe shook his head. "You know about Milton?"

"I guess so."

"You guess so. Is it similar to your having told me this afternoon that you hadn't played much Scrabble?"

"No." Doug blushed. "I don't know why I remembered or knew that Milton was blind."

"Well, shall I read, or are you going to surprise us by reciting the poem from memory?"

"How long is it?"

"About two hundred pages."

"Guess you'd better read it, huh?" The boys laughed, and Sharpe looked as if he were going to react badly. Doug sat up. "That was a joke, Mr. Sharpe. I'd really like to hear you read it."

He began. There was another soft chorus of groans from around the room, but Doug was rapt. Sharpe's expertly-modulated voice became Heaven and Hell, angel and devil, Adam and Eve. Milton's words—so incomprehensible to the other boys—roared through Doug like a furious fire. He knew this from deep inside himself. He knew it the way he'd known Allie. And when the vibrations started, he went without resistance.

❦

At the end of the first week of work, going over the already-completed pages of the manuscript, Phineas found himself immersed, nearly drowning, within the thick beauty and sharp description of Milton's picture of the battle between Satan and God, the battle for dominance in Heaven.

He paused from his reading and glanced over at Milton who was gazing, sightless into his own dark distance.

"Sire?"

The poet turned toward the scrivener.

"Yes."

"I've been thinking about Satan."

Milton chuckled. "Not surprising. Where have your thoughts taken you?"

"When you wrote in 'Aeropagitica,' that 'The State shall be my governors, but not my critics,' it now seems, in Paradise Lost, that you have Satan acting on the reverse principle, in part, during the battle for Heaven: that he was willing to take the criticism of the Almighty so long as he was not ruled by Him."

"There is some merit in that, but is there a profound point?"

"Oh no. My question goes more to the concept of free will and the nature of God's purpose in allowing Satan both to wage a losing battle and then to be exiled."

"God's purpose?"

"Surely, if God is all powerful, he could have prevented the uprising. Even you hint at the possibility of God's purpose when you had Satan say to one of his underlings, 'To do aught good never will be our task, But ever to do ill our sole delight, As being the contrary to his high will Whom we resist. If then his Providence Out of our evil seek to bring forth good, Our labor must be to pervert that end, And out of good still to find means of evil; Which oft-times may succeed, so as perhaps Shall grieve him, if I fail not, and disturb, His inmost counsels from their destin'd aim.'"

"Where do you see purpose in that statement?"

"Well, just as God created the light out of darkness, it seems to me that Satan's stubbornness has that same purity—or lack of it. So Satan is fulfilling God's purpose for him, and in doing so, has set up the likelihood of free will for us on earth."

Milton shook his head. "I'm sorry, Phineas. I am not following your reasoning."

"Well, sire, you have written that Satan is 'One who brings A mind not to be chang'd by place or Time. The mind is in its own place, and in itself Can make a Heav'n of Hell, a Hell of Heav'n. What matter where, if I be still the same, And what I should be, all but less than he Whom Thunder hath made greater? Here at least We shall be free; th'Almighty hath not built here for his envy, will not drive us hence: Here we may reign secure, and in my choice to reign is worth ambition though in Hell: Better to reign in Hell, than serve in Heav'n.'"

Again, Milton chuckled. "Those last words were the very first of the poem you heard."

"Yes, and they have stayed with me."

"But what of free will?"

"As you can see, the idea is still forming. But I have this picture of Heaven as one place, then God created earth which is at one remove. Now, Satan described Hell as a place 'furtherest' from God's reach—which would imply that Earth is somewhere in the middle, pulled between the two. That is where your idea—that the mind is its own place, which can create a Heaven out of Hell or Hell out of Heaven—is so profound." Phineas smiled broadly. "I can think of no better illustration of free will."

"Yes, the point is complicated, but nonetheless correct. Are you suggesting I make changes to what I've written thus far, perhaps to clarify?"

"No, sire. But since you are next planning to write about the Garden of Eden, I thought you might keep that point in mind regarding Adam and Eve's adventure."

"You see a correlation?"

"Just as Satan followed his nature, waged war, and chose to rule the kingdom of hell rather than serve in Heaven, Adam and Eve chose to rule Earth, to escape God's 'criticism' though not his governance—in leaving Eden and moving away from God's presence."

"But surely they were tricked by the serpent, Satan's messenger?"

"Ah, but here's the rub. We know of Satan's pain in being confined to hell—though his pride masks it. We also know of Adam and Eve's fear and shame at leaving—though they left all the same. But nowhere, is there any mention of God's regret."

"How is man to ever know of God's feelings?"

"We cannot. Rightly spoken. But just as self-discipline can never be imposed by the State—could God be any less wise? How can man ever hope to cultivate his own virtues if God constantly imposes them on him?"

Milton raised his finger into the air as if to rebut, then paused, seemed to grasp both Phineas' meaning and the use of the poet's own ideas in supporting it. He lowered his hand, stroked his chin, broke into a chortle, then full laughter.

"I knew I should be wary of you, scrivener. The idea is provocative—even if it is mine, twisted to your own purpose." He wiped his brow with a handkerchief. "I'm not sure how I will use this piece of mental chicanery, but we shall find a way, shan't we?"

"God willing."

"Yes, God willing." He turned to face Phineas, deep in thought. "Would you do me a favor, Phineas?"

"Certainly, sire."

"I would like you to read me something you've written."

"But—"

"Tut, tut. Don't be modest. I think it's only fair, since you have all this knowledge of me through my words. Shouldn't I at least have some insight into your own self, by hearing the process of your thinking."

"Please understand that I'm not resisting your request out of modesty or subterfuge." Phineas took a deep breath. "The simple truth is that I haven't written anything."

"Not even a poem?"

"Nay, sire."

"But don't you have anything you want to tell the world, Phineas?"

"Perhaps. But I have not the slightest idea where to begin."

"That's all right, my boy." A wry smile crossed Milton's pale face, "I will make it an assignment, as if you were in school and I were your teacher."

"Do you truly think I could write poetry for one of the greatest epic poets who ever lived?"

"Thank you, but please don't look at it that way. Just pretend you are the pupil and I'm the instructor."

"When would you like to see this assignment?"

"Oh, no hurry. Whenever you like." Milton stretched his gouty leg, stifled a yawn. "I believe we should end early today. Will you ask Grutto to come in, on your way out?"

Phineas got up, turned away, then noticed Mary, Milton's youngest daughter, standing by the door. He started to speak, but she put her finger to her lips before tiptoeing quietly through the door opposite the kitchen.

"Is something the matter, Phineas?"

"My foot must have fallen asleep while we were talking." Phineas said. "I'll fetch Grutto now."

As he limped into the kitchen, Phineas wondered how long Mary had stood there. So absorbed was he in the conversation, he'd not even noticed her. Was the girl so interested in her father's work that she would risk being caught eavesdropping?

He shrugged off the question, then told Grutto of Milton's request.

"You wait, Phineas." The Nubian said, then quickly went into the study.

Phineas sat on the edge of a small table, pondering the last conversation with the poet. He felt he had been unable to express clearly the image he had, of the similarity between Satan being driven from heaven and the fate of Adam and Eve. Was it really part of God's plan, or simply souls gone awry? Why would someone choose to leave Eden? Leave Heaven? What could be so important?

A quiet cough behind him caused Phineas to turn and see Mary standing in the doorway.

"Thank you for not giving me away to father."

Phineas nodded. "There didn't seem to be any reason to."

"Well, thank you all the same." She twisted a long auburn curl. "He believes girls can't understand what he writes, but I do."

"Have you read his writings?"

"Yes, whenever I can steal a look."

"And?"

She blushed. "Well, beneath all those fancy words, he shows a pretty clear picture of things."

Phineas smiled. "You speak rightly."

He started to say, 'For a girl,' but held off.

"Mr. Davies?"

"You can call me Phineas, Mistress Milton."

"If you will call me Mary."

"M—M—Mary. Can I help you with something?"

She bit her lower lip. "It's hard for me to keep up with his work when I can only read bits and pieces. If you were to—"

"Have you ever asked him if you could read it? I'm sure he would be pleased to know that one of his daughters—"

"But he wouldn't. He believes I am just as stupid as he thinks my sisters are."

"Surely—"

A crash sounded in the study, followed by the poet's curses.

"Grutto, you idiot! What have you broken now?"

"The vase, master. I sorry."

"Well clean it up, confound you, man."

Phineas looked at Mary, who was blushing. The red in her cheeks set off her blue eyes. She brushed a glistening, auburn strand from her face. Phineas caught his breath.

"He's so mean to him, and Grutto never speaks up, just quietly accepts father's harsh words."

"I like Grutto very much, but I can understand your father's impatience with his clumsiness."

"Oh, but you're wrong." Mary dropped her eyes. "I'm sorry, I didn't mean to speak like that, especially to you, Phineas."

Phineas felt a slight pull within his chest and his own cheeks coloring. Dangerous thoughts hovered, thoughts sure to get him fired and to incur her mockery.

"You see, it's father who is clumsy, but he won't admit it to anyone. So he blames Grutto, just because he thinks he is a savage." She shook her head. "Do you think that's fair?"

Phineas stared at her. "Y—your father is a great man—"

"A great writer, yes. But a great man would follow his own teachings."

Another mild commotion in the study brought Mary closer to Phineas. He leaned away.

"Listen, would you explain the new sections of the poem to me, Phineas?"

"Yes, I would, but there is rarely time, once your father and I finish each day. How could I explain—?"

"Every Sunday afternoon, Grutto accompanies me to the park. We could meet there."

He tried to picture her casually strolling amidst the plague-ravaged street-people, especially those who inhabited the park.

"I don't think—"

"Oh, please?"

Her face was inches from his, her breath a peppermint sigh. Phineas nearly groaned.

"Wh-what time?"

"Just after two."

"But won't Grutto—"

Mary smiled. "Why do you think he asked you to stay?"

Doug awoke, looked around and realized everyone was asleep. A shaft of moonlight came through one of the screened windows. It was a clear line of light. He smiled at the dream, reached over and rubbed Allie's head.

His father had been right, and he should know how grateful Doug was. He would send him a postcard tomorrow.

Peter could not settle. He wandered from room to room, not sure if he were trying to escape the loneliness, or find something to soothe the ache. This was what he wanted, wasn't it? A whole summer alone, a way to become a bachelor again, instead of just a single parent.

He sat on Doug's bed for five minutes. Every year since Felicity had gone, it had become harder for Peter to believe Doug was his son. The boy is so unlike me, he thought—but not unlike some in my family. Another mystery.

He went into the hall, stopped and peeked inside Fiona's room. He'd never been in there. He pushed the door open, flipped on the light. The silence made it seem more museum than bedroom. What few things she'd left behind were more decorative than useful.

A faint smell of lavender water reminded Peter of the very scent Fiona had used when he first met her at St. Andrews, those long years ago. He looked out the window and wondered what she had thought when she had first seen the extensive view of the flower and vegetable gardens, part of the vast front lawn and the driveway winding out to the country road, Peter Pan and his mates at the entrance.

Peter smirked at the moth-eaten Agatha Christie novels and the well-worn Bible on the little bookshelf above her bedside table. He opened the bathroom door to find a threadbare tartan robe, hanging forlornly from the single hook. He smiled, shook his head. Fiona had made such a big deal out of telling him that those members of the Clan MacLean who left the island of Mull traditionally dropped the 'a' in Mac, to become McLeans. So persnickety.

When he passed by the highly-polished dressing table, his eye caught a small, wooden box. Locked. Peter stopped, looked sheepishly over his shoulder, pulled his penknife from his pocket and pried it open. Inside was a small diary. He grabbed it, wondered why she hadn't taken it with her.

He ripped it open and began reading. Only two pages had any writing on them. Dated yesterday and the day before. The final entry said, "I shall miss the laddie, but I leave, happy that he and his father have been getting along so very much better of late."

"So, she took Volume One with her," Peter said aloud, "I'll bet there's a whole lot of rotten meat in that one." He closed the diary, returned it to the box and clumsily pressed the jimmied lock into place. Any old busybody could have done that, he thought.

On his way out, he saw it, hanging from the wall behind the entry door: a corkboard, literally smothered with memorabilia. Each brass thumbtack, every brightly-colored pushpin secured a handmade card, a message from Doug, countless notes and dated drawings—each a piece of the whole history of Doug's affectionate adoration. No—love for his Nanny.

Suddenly sick and angry, Peter closed his eyes, as if to shut out his utter humiliation; then staggered from the room. Had to leave the house. Too quiet. Too empty.

Too full.

Chapter Ten

"Good morning, ladies," Fiona began, then rested her hands on the makeshift lectern and leveled her gaze at the girls splayed across the sofa, the settee and the chairs, in the large living room. They reminded her of a post-modernist painting, limbs seemingly disconnected from their bodies, bent into odd shapes. Behind the "neo-nannies," as she had overheard Sally describe the group before breakfast, stood Grumpy and Valka. Janina sat off to the side by the door, her hands at rest in her lap, her eyes scorching the girls with an eager intensity that even Fiona found arresting.

The girls waited, listlessly, bored by the silence.

"I said, 'Good morning, ladies.'" Fiona's voice rose slightly with the color in her cheeks.

Sally's hand fluttered in the air.

Fiona nodded. "Yes, Sally."

"We don't know what to call you, ma'am." When Fiona looked confused, Sally continued. "Are you a camp counselor, our teacher, or the—nanny-master?"

Giggles spread across the room. Grumpy started to smirk, but cut it short when Fiona shot him a quick frown.

"My name is Fiona McLean," she said, allowing the McLean to resonate. "It is true that this is a camp, though a somewhat different camp than you may be accustomed to attending. I am not a teacher. I know how to do what I do—for I am a nanny." She paused. "As for the 'master' part, that we shall have to discover together, wouldn't you say?"

Shrugs. One girl, Darla, a petulant brown-haired snipe, blew a large pink bubble. It exploded. She high-fived a green-haired girl next to her, and all the girls laughed.

Fiona's temperature increased visibly. It was apparent she was about to lose the struggle to maintain her composure, when a raspy sound came from near the door.

The sound was repeated.

The laughter trailed off as one-by-one, the girls and eventually everyone in the room, looked at Janina. Wearing a funny smile, she motioned for Valka and he walked to her side. She said something in another language. He looked at her quizzically, then reached over to flip the light switch up: on. She motioned again and he flipped it down: off.

She giggled, spoke in her reedy voice. "Switch up, light on. Switch down, light off."

No one spoke. The moment seemed so simple, so idiotic, there was nothing to say.

She spoke again to Valka in the raspy tongue. He pulled a knife from his pocket and undid the switch cover. He carefully turned the switch upside down and reattached it to the wall. Then he flipped it down and the light came on.

"Thank you, Valka." Janina turned to the group. "Switch down, light on."

"So, what's it mean?" Sally asked. "Are we here to study electronics?"

"Yes, in a way you are right, Sally." Janina's smile glowed, her hand rotated in front of her chest. "All of our emotions and feelings are electric. We have switches for all of them within us. One for respect. One for love. Even one for sex."

"I like that switch," whispered Darla, then blushed when she realized that everyone heard.

"I like that switch, too." Janina grinned. "Sometimes our switches get turned upside down, just as Valka did here. When that happens inside your heart, you can't love who you really love, you can't respect those who respect you.

"And the worst part is that the person who turned the switch around, who hurt you, will have control of your feelings until you decide to reverse the switch, the way it belongs inside you."

She waited. The color drained from Darla's face. Several others wore shocked expressions. Sally's demeanor never changed.

"Miss McLean has a great power within her. She has knowledge and a great capacity for love and understanding. If you give her your attention, she will give you what she knows and that knowledge will make you stronger and better than you ever imagined."

Janina coughed and fell silent. Several girls jolted in her direction, but she held up a baton hand. "I am fine, thank you." Then motioned for Fiona to continue.

Fiona nodded appreciatively to Janina, then smiled at the girls. "I am a nanny. I have had the privilege of taking care of other people's children. Perhaps some of you will follow in my footsteps. Others may be lucky enough to have children of your own, who will need your best care and attention."

A round-faced black girl, Carrie, raised her hand. "Miss Fiona, if we gonna learn how to take care of children, where they at?"

Fiona nodded. "In order to learn how to take care of someone else, you have to start by knowing how to take care of yourselves."

Sally sat upright on the sofa. "You mean, we're not just going to be baby-sitting all summer?"

"Nothing of the sort." Fiona glared at Grumpy who shrugged. She walked around to the front of the podium. "This is your summer vacation. To be sure, there will be things to learn, but mostly it's going to be fun."

"Your fun or our fun?" came from one of the girls.

Fiona grinned. "Probably a little bit of both, and never enough of either, I'm sure."

❦

Doug floated through the morning activities. He passed through a shy phase while washing up before breakfast with ten other boys at communal sinks. Then there was a mad rush down the trail to the dining room, Doug shouting gleefully with the others, completely losing himself in the throng. His giddiness at being surrounded by so many people began to subside during the craft hour as he focused on selecting a project.

Some of the boys were working with leather, scarring the smooth surfaces with prefabricated designs. Others trimmed and notched slender branches, using leather strips or twine to attach sharpened stones to make arrows, and rocks to make tomahawks. Every project harkened to early, Native American life, but all seemed too simple or uninspired to Doug.

Jimmy, Chas, and several other boys from the Hole-in-the-Wall gang, were huddled together in the far corner of the craft room. Whenever they noticed Doug looking their way, they closed ranks and blocked his view. He shrugged and wandered through the rest of the craft area. Ceramics, carving, sewing (pouches), carpentry (mostly birdhouses), and finally—puppet-making.

Doug's eyes lit up, while he watched several boys fashion crude papier-mâché heads to float atop cloth bodies.

"May I?" He asked Tex.

"Sure, son. Know what you want to make?"

"I think so." Doug grinned, dug his hands deep into the bucket of papier-mâché. He knew exactly what he was going to make.

❦

Fiona had just flopped into her overstuffed chair and put her feet up on the small ottoman in her room, when she heard a small knock. The girls were supposed to be with Gertrude Schmidt, the heavyset cooking instructor that Grumpy had found—who knew where. She started to struggle out of the chair, decided against it.

"Who is it?"

"Me, Grumpy."

"Go away."

There was a long silence. Then another tap.

"Please, Fiona, I have a surprise for you."

Muttering, she was barely able to extract her aching bones from the chair and limp to the door.

"This better be good," she growled as she opened the door. "I feel like I have a hundred Leprechauns pulling at my ankles every time I try to move."

Grumpy smiled. "Think you can make it out to the deck?"

She shook her head, but followed him anyway.

The deck was a kind of widow's walk on the second floor. The girls' bedrooms were all on the first floor. The second was reserved for adults. The arrangement had seemed like a good idea, though climbing up the stairs after each session, was tiring. Fiona never realized how easy she had it minding just Doug. Keeping track of seven girls, even though they had become willing enough to cooperate, was more taxing than she ever imagined.

Grumpy opened the double doors leading to the deck, and allowed Fiona to go out first.

"Ta da!" He cried, pointing to a large telescope on a tripod.

"So we're going to look at the stars—" Fiona's eyes were exhausted slits. "—in the middle of the afternoon?"

"We're going to look at one star in particular. Come see."

She sighed, shuffled over.

"Just look through that eyepiece. It's already aimed and focused."

She bent over, put her eye to the telescope and saw blue. The telescope was focused on water.

"Very nice." She started away.

"Keep looking."

Again she bent, put her eye to the contraption. This time, a head popped out of the water. She was looking at Doug. She smiled. He submerged again. Another head popped up. A different boy. Doug again emerged. He and the other boy began pushing water in each other's faces. Then the boy threw himself on Doug and pushed him under the water.

"My God," Fiona gasped, "he's drowning Dougie!"

"Keep watching." Grumpy laughed.

She looked again. Dougie popped out of the water like a cork, laughing, a mock fierceness on his face, as he returned the favor to the other boy and sent him down into the drink. She watched, fascinated at being able to observe him so closely from such a distance. Grumpy showed her how to zoom out, to widen the viewing angle to take in the entire scene. A small group of boys were splashing in the water around a large, raft-like structure thirty feet from the dock. At the wider angle, Doug was indistinguishable from the others. She wondered aloud at this, that her eyes could fool her.

"He's a regular boy," Grumpy said. "Does that strike you as odd?"

"No, I guess I just never expected him to be so—"

"So normal?"

"Yes."

Grumpy laughed. Fiona blushed.

A whistle blew across the lake and the boys reluctantly left the water. Fiona followed Doug's progress onto the beach, arm-over-shoulder with the same boy he had battled in the water. She stayed at the telescope, until he was swallowed up by obstructing trees.

"Does he know I'm here?" she asked, straightening up.

Grumpy shook his head. "Do you want him to know?"

"No, I guess not." She sat in a deck chair. "It's just so strange. It was hard enough letting him go to school, you know. Being around him twenty-four hours a day—I know it's selfish—but I hated giving him up for those six or seven hours a day. He's such a delight."

"I can see that."

"You can?" She looked at Grumpy for a long moment. "Then I don't understand how you could have been gone so long."

"No, I don't suppose you could," he took a deep breath. "Sometimes I wonder how it happened, myself."

"Sorry, I don't buy that." Fiona snorted. "That's just not good enough. You had to know what your son is like, what effect having a man like Peter for a father would have on the boy."

Grumpy seemed startled at her ferocity, and though he looked as if he might flee, he didn't. He sat in the chair opposite Fiona, hands clasped together.

"What I am going to say is not an excuse. I won't pretend to say that what I did was right. I made mistakes with Peter, as I'm sure Peter has made with Doug." He peered across the lake, squinted as if looking far beyond what he could see with his eyes. "When my wife died, I realized that I had been wrong for most of my life, that I made bad decisions involving the people who were given to me, either by family, by choice or by accident. I'd like to say that great wealth cripples those who have it, but I cannot. My mother was one of the most capable people I ever met, poor or rich."

"I would liked to have met her," Fiona said.

"Ah, she would have loved you, Fiona." Grumpy smiled at her. "She would have approved of you."

"Did she approve of your wife, Peter's mother?"

Grumpy was thoughtful. "Sarah never really disapproved of anyone. She seemed to see the world in much larger terms than we ordinary mortals tend to." He chuckled. "But my wife never really approved of Sarah, you see. I didn't really understand that, until it was too late."

"Too late?"

His head bobbed. "Yes, I guess it was about the time Peter was five years old. He was born with a club foot—"

"He was?" She remembered his limp, which seemed to mirror his emotions. "So, you had it fixed when he was five?"

"No. That was my first mistake, I guess. " His eyes went out across the lake. "I listened to Sarah, who felt that Peter's foot was a karmic brand, a kind of "scar" from a former life and that if we did anything about it, we would be hurting his soul's progress."

"Karmic brand? What on earth is that?"

"Sounds kind of silly, now, doesn't it?" Grumpy winced. "Some people, particularly in the East, believe that we live a great number of lives, that we are reincarnated time and time again, learning lessons each lifetime, that we carry forward into the next, until we achieve perfection. When we do something particularly bad, we may bring a reminder of that deed with us, this time."

"I've heard a bit about that. Don't really believe it, though."

Another nod. "Reasonable. Not necessarily an easy thing to believe. Lots of people use it to excuse bad behavior. Takes a lot of thinking about. I didn't really start thinking about it until I'd been away for several years. Once I started, I knew I couldn't return until I understood how it fit into my life and the lives of those I cared about."

"So, you understand this now? This reincarnation stuff?"

"I think so, some of it." Grumpy pulled out his pipe. "Mind if I smoke?"

She shook her head. "Go ahead."

He filled his pipe, tamped it down, then lit it. "Funny—"

"What's funny?"

"When I was Valka Petrovich, it was much easier to talk about things like this. Now that I'm Peter Douglas-MacBrayne, Jr., again, it feels odd."

"Maybe it's not as true for Peter the Second as it is for Valka the second."

He peered at her, understood the reference to Janina's brother, then laughed. "You are a pip, Miss Fiona McLean, a real pip."

She inclined her head, then lifted it. "Now, Peter the Second, I would very much like to hear the whole story."

"Which one? The story of my trip? The story of my marriage?"

She looked at her watch. Dinner with the girls would be getting started in forty-five minutes. "Why don't you start wherever you want."

"Not a lot of time."

"Oh, I don't know." Fiona settled in her chair. "It seems we have all summer."

❦

The afternoon sports period was a complete disaster for the boys of Artillery Walk. Doug and his bunkmates first lost at volleyball to the Walden Ponders, then at softball to Jimmy's group—all of whom seemed to have an extra spark, a kind of extra-competitive spirit that Doug and his cohorts couldn't quite match. They weren't better, at least not as far as Doug could tell. But they wanted to win more than the Artillery Walk boys.

Doug pondered this during the free period that followed sports. He had seen Jimmy, Chas, and a boy named Bobby take off for the woods and at first thought to follow them to see what they were up to. He might have, if his teammates hadn't been so discouraged.

"What'll we do now?" Doug asked, trying to smile. "Anybody got any ideas?"

"I think we should make a whole bunch of white flags tomorrow, during craft period," said Augie Leopardi, lying flat on his back in the grass. "Then we can surrender before we even start playing any game in the afternoon."

Some of the other boys chimed in, describing other ways of forestalling further humiliation. They could make dresses, or pretend they were priests and that losing was part of their vows. There were other, similarly distressing ideas designed to protect their egos. Doug drowsed as he listened, barely noticed the vibrations until he was swept away.

Ashna staggered down to the empty encampment. Everything and everyone was gone. He sat in front of the fire circle he had shared with Huva and his brother. Tehuti would drive the tribe hard, moving as fast as he could make them. Even if Ashna walked day and night, he might never catch them. How would he eat, how would he protect himself from the creatures that stalked lone ones such as he was, now?

And if he caught them, what would he do? Swallow an arrow as his brother had? What good could he do for Huva—dead? What good could he do anyhow, so far away?

He closed his eyes, lay down in the dirt. Perhaps the vultures would come to end his questions.

Pictures drifted in and through his head. He saw Tehuti, Huva, Hamar, the tribe. Tehuti was the strongest, could do anything he liked, really. But his rules all seemed aimed against Ashna. All his mockery was reserved for the crippled one. He could easily have killed Ashna when he killed Hamar. No one would have challenged him.

But he didn't.

Deep inside Ashna's head, he suddenly knew that Tehuti was aware that Ashna continued to make the drawings to help the hunt, even though he had forbade it.

But he had killed Hamar for having paint on his hands.

Ashna sat up with a start.

Could it be? Was it possible that Tehuti was afraid of Ashna? But what could Ashna do to defend himself from Tehuti? Tehuti was stronger, laughably so. Tehuti had the four-leg. Tehuti could send an arrow almost two hundred arm-lengths, to kill a deer. Ashna could barely pull the bow.

All Ashna knew how to do was make pictures. The pictures were good. They brought the animals close, so the hunters could kill and the tribe could eat.

Ashna shook his head. If the pictures could bring the game close to the encampment, why couldn't pictures bring the tribe back? If his pictures had that magic, then he could draw Tehuti staying clear of Huva. He could make Tehuti blind. He could wither his arm. He could make Tehuti dead on the ground and have the spirits of his ancestors come collect him.

Ashna laughed, stood, did a hobbling dance around the cold fire.

He did not need to fight Tehuti, he simply needed to paint him and let the magic do the rest.

He half-knelt in the dirt, put his finger into the ashes. He applied war lines to his cheeks, a gray lightning bolt down his forehead, and a circle on his chin. Then he splashed ashes on his shoulders, on his chest and all down both legs—the good and the bad.

Almost completely covered, he stood, raised his fist in the air and let out a raspy whoop.

"You come face me, Tehuti," he cried. "And you bring my Huva to me, unhurt—or by the sky that sings above us, I will draw such terrible pictures from my anger, that you will not be able to hide from me, even for a hundred lifetimes."

Doug awoke with a start. Johnny Marks was shaking him.

"Come on, Doug. We'll be late for dinner."

"Oh, sure. Thanks." Doug rose and stretched, then walked with Johnny toward the dining room. Halfway there, Doug spied a truck unloading a large box behind the laundry room.

Doug stopped him. "Say, Johnny. What are you working on in crafts?"

"Just a stupid pig carving board for my mom. Why?"

"Want to help me with something that will be a whole lot more fun?"

"Sure, what?"

"You'll see, tomorrow. But you can't tell anyone. It's got to be a surprise. Okay?"

"Sure." Johnny grinned. "Can we go eat now?"

"In a minute." He dragged Johnny with him to the laundry room.

The two boys watched as a new washing machine was removed from its large, rectangular cardboard box.

"Can I have that, mister?" Doug asked.

"What you want it for?"

"Arts and Crafts."

The man shrugged. "Sure, saves me taking it back on the truck."

"Great," Doug said, then motioned Johnny to help him carry it behind the building.

"We gonna make a fort?" Johnny asked.

"Better than a fort." Doug said. "When we're finished with this, everyone'll wish they bunked at Artillery Walk."

Avisson sat quietly, while lawyer Clark read Sabey's psycho-astrological chart. Every once in a while, a paragraph or line would cause the lawyer's eyebrows to raise. Once he even looked over, but Abe ignored him, until the barrister had completed the brief. Finally, he put the file down, took off his glasses and rubbed his eyes.

"Is this shit true?"

Avisson shrugged. "As far as I can tell. All the sessions were tape-recorded. Either Sabey's the most brilliant actor to come along since Richard Burton, or he was really under." Avisson rolled some tension from his neck. "I've hypnotized probably two hundred subjects, I'm pretty good at knowing when someone is faking it."

Clark nodded. "Think a jury will buy this?"

A shrug. "Who can tell? I suppose if you pack the panel with prospective jurors who have called the psychic hotline at one time or another, you may have a chance, at least for mental incapacitation."

"You think we should go for crazy?"

"No." Avisson shook his head. "But I think the pattern shows that Sabey only kills under certain astrological conditions. He's a psychopath, all right. Perfectly amoral when he's under the influence, so to speak. No remorse. He's not exactly a sympathetic character."

"He's a bloody killer, pure and simple." Clark tried to relax in his chair, his hands clasped behind his neck. "On the other hand, we could get a fair amount of press out of this."

"Is that good?"

"For me, it's great. Win or lose, or even if I get somewhat of a reduction from First Degree Murder—my business should double at least."

"What about Sabey?"

Clark leaned forward. "You want him out on the streets?"

"Hell no," This, Avisson knew for sure. "On the other hand, the influences seem pretty regular. I'd hate to have the state stick a needle in his arm, before we had a real chance to study him for several years. They had that guy Dahmer in jail when he belonged in a facility where he could have been studied."

"Dahmer, the cannibal? You don't think he got what he deserved?"

Avisson's face screwed with thought. "He killed and got away with it for years. Regardless of what he did to his victims after they were dead, he was a killer. For that, I suppose he deserved to die. But think about this: What if Dahmer had been part of that Mormon group that tried to cross the Rockies—wasn't it in the late eighteen-hundreds? They wound up eating the dead in order to survive. Or, what if he had been a missionary to one of the cannibal tribes? Perhaps he had been eaten alive in a former life and that awful imagery had been brought deep in his head, from before his birth, this time? If we had been able to study him, without constraint, who knows what we might have learned?"

Clark sputtered. "Look, I like winning cases—or at least lessening the charge on my clients—that's a kind of victory. But I'm still an officer of the court." He leaned forward. "Believe it or not, I still believe in jurisprudence. But if we have to start revising our laws to allow for this karma stuff—Why, hell, man, we could be trying traffic tickets for years, just sorting out the potential past life influences."

"Tough problem, isn't it?" Avisson smiled. "I'm not saying that every case has its root in a prior life experience. But what is our justice system anyway, except an imperfect reflection of God's justice? Most rules for society are based on spiritual laws.

"If a crime committed this go-around, has its root in an injustice from the distant past that requires some kind of balancing, or karmic retribution, in order for the involved souls to advance spiritually—then who are we to call it a crime, even though, under our 'system' we find it illegal?"

"That is a real can of worms."

"True," Avisson pulled at a wart on his face. "But consider this: 'When nature wants something to happen, she creates a genius to do it.'"

"Who said that?"

"Don't remember, but it seems apt here. Even though Sabey is a criminal genius, in a way, if we want to start tracing culpability through several lifetimes, can you imagine a better start? I mean, my God, the man has recounted six past lives."

"No judge is going to go for this."

"You're probably right. But we have to start thinking about it, sometime."

"Okay." Clark was all the way into it now. "Let's say there's some other past life influence—karma or whatever—beyond the six you have documented here. And let's say that someone you know and care about deeply, in this lifetime, was involved in a terrible crime from ten lifetimes before and Sabey is just waiting to whack this person?"

"Yeah, I get it. So we get him off and three or four years from now, Sabey takes this person I care about out.."

"Well, how do you feel about it?"

Avisson was quiet for nearly a minute. "Mr. Clark, do you believe in God?"

Now it was Clark's turn to think. "Yes, I believe I do."

"What if you got a drunk driver off on a technicality in the law and six months from now, that drunk driver kills your wife. How would you feel?"

"A little sad," Clark said, "I do like Cleo, although she can be a major pain in the ass. But to tell the truth, I wouldn't blame myself. If God, or whoever, wanted my wife up in heaven, then who am I to keep them apart?" He shook his head. "Lord knows I've never been able to keep her from anyone else, who wanted her."

Avisson blushed. Clark shook his head.

"Not you, too?"

"No." Avisson breathed a sigh of relief that he was able to tell the truth.

"But she offered, right?"

A quick nod and a deeper blush.

"That's okay, Avisson." Clark smiled. "I've always approached Cleo like my clients—innocent until proven guilty. And quite frankly, I never ask my clients if they did it or not, because just knowing could get in the way of defending them."

"Very philosophical of you."

The lawyer shook his head. "Very practical. I like Cleo—a hell of a lot more than I like most of my clients, I might add. She's actually a pretty good wife. People love her at cocktail parties. I get a hell of a lot of business done at those parties."

Avisson looked closely at Clark's eyes as he spoke. There was undoubtedly more, under the words, unstated. He realized that the man actually did love his wife for who she was. He really didn't care what she did out of his sight. Now, more than ever, he was glad he had never taken Cleo, the temptress, up on her countless offers.

Larry Clark, successful, cynical lawyer, loved his wife. Somehow the knowledge made Avisson happy. Another thought entered his mind, more insidious, more discomforting. Larry Clark had not initiated the firing of Abe's former boss. The threatened lawsuit ran counter to what Clark had just expressed about his relationship with his wife. That meant that someone, probably at Douglas Industries, had finessed the information into the resignation and had something more in mind, beyond just getting rid of the Foundation.

"What's the matter, Avisson? You look like someone just kicked you in the stomach."

"Oh, uh, I just remembered I was late for an appointment."

"Must be awfully important. You look pretty shook up."

Abe shook his head. "It is and it isn't. Not now anyway."

"Well, what else do you need before our appearance before the Grand Jury?"

"A couple more sessions with Sabey, just to finalize the report and to check out any other past life things that might make him dangerous to anyone out in the public."

"You think you can find that out?"

Abe shrugged. "Maybe not, but it's worth a look. I would hate to keep that needle from Sabey's arm if it meant that someone who has done a pretty good job this time, or someone important, might be in danger."

"I'll get the paperwork for you to see him—how many more times?"

"As many as you can arrange."

"Then it's done."

Clark stood, extended his hand across the desk. "Shall we make a little legal history then, Doctor?"

Avisson took his hand. "Why not?."

˜

After one week of solid work, Doug was happy with what he had accomplished in the craft room. But that was nothing compared to the change at the sports center. Even Johnny, who had been so ready to surrender after the first day of games, had a brightness in his eyes as he assisted Doug in the workshop and then followed him out to do battle in the sun. And it didn't matter that the losses on the field continued.

Doug had called his teammates around him, at the beginning of the week.

"Listen," he said, low enough so that Jimmy's teacher couldn't hear him, "I have a plan that will drive those guys crazy."

"You mean since we can't beat them?"

Doug shrugged. "We don't know that, but you're probably right. Listen, most of the fun in winning is watching the other guys slink off the field in defeat, or have them argue with each other and get mad." Doug took a deep breath. "If we just pretend we're happy to be out on the field, and enjoy playing the game—and if someone makes a good play, regardless of the team, we applaud and look happy."

"Gee, you want us to be good sports. Wow, that's quite a plan!" Gene Wheeler was a good hit, absolutely no-field, ball player.

"Well," Doug said, "it's not being good sports, if we do it knowing we're going to drive them crazy. Good sports would mean we really meant it—and you don't have to mean it. It's reverse psychology."

"My mom uses that on me all the time," Augie said.

"Does it work?" Wheeler asked.

"Yeah, I guess it does."

"Well, hell," Wheeler punched his glove.

"What have we got to lose?" Doug asked.

No one had an answer. Doug put on a phony grin, they all followed suit, and went out on the field.

It took a few days of Doug and Johnny leading the good-natured laughter, but it eventually infected the entire team. The others weren't quite sure why losing had become so much fun, but they joined in Doug's loud enjoyment of the other team's superior play. They applauded great catches, looked with awe at long fly balls that soared over their fielders' heads. In volleyball, they whistled at spikes that sent them sprawling in the dirt.

They had all watched their leader, Doug, sucker Massah Sharpe into losing at Scrabble when it was important, and they sensed that some similar turnabout was in the offing, when it came to their competitors on the field. Ironically, they played looser, made better catches, and hit the ball better themselves. Not enough to win, but the margins were closer, and not so humiliating.

Every afternoon during the free period, Doug and Johnny would hie themselves off to the workshop. Even as he entered the shop, Doug always noted that Jimmy and his cohorts headed off into the woods at the same time.

When Johnny got hit in the head with a line drive, it was Doug who accompanied him to the infirmary. He looked forward to seeing Prudence again, but this time he met Miss Slimson. He smiled, when he saw her.

"Hello, Miss Slimson," he said, brightly.

"Why, Mr. Doug, how are you enjoying camp?"

"Very well, thank you."

"What have we here?" She put her arm around Johnny's shoulder. "Hit your head, did you?"

She led Johnny to the far end of the infirmary and looked into his eyes to check for concussion. "Nothing too serious. Does it hurt a lot?"

Johnny shook his head.

"Well, it looks like you're going to have a fine goose egg on your forehead for a few days, but it doesn't look like anything's broken."

She prepared a bag of ice and showed him how to hold it to keep the swelling down.

"Doug," she said, "I see in Miss Peabody's report that you cut your hand the very first day. How did that happen?"

So much had transpired since then, Doug had almost forgotten about the incident with Jimmy.

"Aw, just cut myself on a can lid." He stuck out his hand. "Nearly all better, far as I can tell."

She looked at his hand, took some ointment and spread it across the palm. "There, that should finish the job. Anything else bothering you?"

He looked at her, dropped his shoulders. "Not really. I'm having a great time."

"That's wonderful. Any more incidents?"

"Incidents?"

"You know, like you told Dr. Kautsch about. He asked me to sort of look after you."

"Oh." Doug hesitated, did he really want to go into it with Johnny there? "No, in fact, I sleep really good here."

"Must be the fresh air."

"Yes, that's it. The fresh air."

"Thanks, Miss Slimson." He hurried toward the door with Johnny.

"You're welcome, Doug. Come see me sometime, it gets a little quiet here."

"Sure. Though the counselors keep us kind of busy."

"I'm sure they do." She gave him a big smile.

When they were outside the door, Johnny looked at him with even more respect than before. Doug laughed.

"What are you looking at?"

"I think she likes you," he said, incredulous.

"Naw, I just knew her back home."

Johnny shook his head. "No, I see my Ma look at the postman exactly the same way."

"Your mom likes the postman? What about your dad?"

"He lives in Cincinnati. They're divorced."

Doug put his arm around Johnny's shoulder. "That must be tough for you."

"Not too bad," Johnny said. "He's a lot nicer to me there than he ever was at home."

As they walked down the path, Doug thought again that maybe he had it pretty good with Nanny and his dad. Sally was scared stiff about her home, and Jimmy had nobody at all. No, Doug was one lucky camper. Lucky indeed.

❦

Sally wiped a splash of flour from her nose. She grinned at Talia, whose white cheeks gave her the look of a mime. All the girls were up to their elbows in bread dough, while Fiona walked around the long table, commenting on the consistency of each girl's loaf, encouraging here, adding flour or water there, aiding in the folding-in process, that would make the wet glop into bread, after the baking.

Just as the loaves were finished and inspected by Gertrude, then put into pans for baking, Janina rolled into the room and laughed.

"You all look like Indians," the gypsy woman said, "with angelic markings."

Sally blushed, then widened her eyes when Janina called her name.

"Yes, ma'am?"

Janina looked to Gertrude. "May I borrow Sally for a little while, this afternoon?"

Some silent piece of information passed between the two women before Gertrude nodded.

"I wish to go down by the lake, Sally. And I'd like your help in navigating the path."

"Sure," Sally said, avoiding the questioning gaze of the other girls.

"Thank you."

They traveled the newly-poured concrete path toward the lake, listening only to the soft whir of Janina's electric wheelchair. Her hair moved backwards in the light breeze, and her pale skin glowed in the sunlight.

Sally walked on the grass next to the walkway, shutting out the sounds of laughter that echoed from the kitchen, where the girls clanged pots and utensils in the cleaning-up process.

Janina stopped at the wooden dock and sighed.

"I did so love swimming, as a young girl like yourself."

Sally raised her eyebrows, didn't speak.

Janina giggled. "My favorite was what you Americans call 'skinny dipping.' With the boys, of course."

"You—?"

"Swam, kissed, swam—nothing sweeter than a kiss under water—with the right boy, of course."

"Of course." Sally was glad Janina was looking at the water, couldn't see her blush.

"Does it surprise you, that I did those things?"

Sally shook her head. "No. I just didn't know—when—"

Janina grinned. "Oh, I was a normal girl—even until I was thirty-five or so."

Sally could hear the question in her mind, but couldn't make her mouth form the words.

"Then this—condition struck." The woman turned with a brilliant smile. "Came as a complete surprise to me, I can tell you."

"I'll bet."

"I was a dancer. Gypsy-dancing is very popular in Europe. We used to travel around to all the great cities. We played in theaters, opera houses, dance halls. Didn't matter where, we just danced."

Sally frowned. "I don't understand."

"What dear?"

"Well, the girls say that you can read the future: tarot, stuff like that."

Janina shrugged. "What don't you understand?"

"I guess—well, how does a dancer learn how to do that stuff?"

"Ah." Janina moved her chair to look directly at Sally. "It is actually easier for someone like a dancer, though it is not something learned, but uncovered within the self."

This completely confused Sally. Janina reached out and touched her hand.

"When I was little, I could do many strange things with my mind. I could move marbles, just a little, but enough to notice. If I was playing cards with someone, I knew what cards they were holding, and I couldn't help myself from cheating."

"Wow, really? Could you read people's minds?"

Janina nodded. "I suppose so, in a way. But, let me ask you: Do you think it is a good thing to know what people are thinking?"

"Sure, that would be cool."

"Yes, I can see why you would think that. But consider this. What if they were thinking bad thoughts, or were seeing that you were lying or doing something bad, that you didn't want them to know. Do you think this knowledge would be a good thing?"

Sally's mouth twisted into a knot. "But—"

"Knowing what another person is thinking is a terrible responsibility. And there are people who would do bad things to someone who had this gift."

Sally looked at Janina's hands. "Did people do this to you?"

Janina didn't seem to hear her, carried on talking. "When my mother saw that I was special, she forbade me to use the gift. She was afraid that someone from the government would find out, and take me away from her. So she taught me to hide."

Did you?"

"Yes. We all did, actually. During World War II, I was a very little girl, but things were very bad for gypsies in Europe. So, in some ways, I was hiding ever since I was little, anyway."

"And after the war?"

"After the war, the communists controlled our region, so it was more important than ever to hide. That's why I became a dancer, and then a drunk."

"A drunk?"

"I believe in America they now call them alcoholics. I felt and saw so many things I knew I shouldn't—or that others didn't—I drank wine and vodka to kill the feeling, blot out the images."

Sally peered at the woman through thin slits. This didn't seem like a confession. Janina stopped, laughed a little, waved one of her baton hands.

"But I did not mean to bring you down here to speak of the past. It is your future that interests me."

"My future?" Sally snorted.

"Yes, dear. I believe you have a wonderful time ahead, just waiting for you around this corner."

Sally remained quiet. They moved along in silence for several moments, then she glanced over at the house. Fiona and Grumpy were on the second-floor deck, looking across the lake through a telescope. She tried to figure out what they were watching, but it seemed to be just another camp.

Despite her early misgivings, Sally had to admit that she was having fun. She didn't mind all the cooking and work in the kitchen nearly as much as she thought she would. The Nanny Master, Fiona, seemed strict, but underneath her teacher's veneer, the woman obviously liked the girls. And Janina. Sally shivered. She felt that she really loved this woman, without understanding why. She was the most unusual person she had ever met, and the most honest.

There was something strange going on, she decided. This whole Nanny camp was not what she thought it would be. There was plenty of time for swimming and playing games in the yard. Also, a big screen TV had been installed in the living room, where the girls watched movies on the nights when Janina or Fiona were too tired to tell them stories—though Sally really believed their tiredness was feigned, to keep the girls from getting overly used to hearing their tales.

Janina's were the best. She talked of soldiers, of the funny theaters she played in. Whenever she launched into one of her anecdotes, everyone forgot that she was crippled. When she talked of dancing, it was as if they could see her gliding right in front of them.

And then there was Mr. Petrovich, who claimed to be a long lost relative of Janina and her brother, Valka. How was it that cousins should have the same name?. She wasn't sure she liked the nickname he had picked for himself: Grumpy. But that was what everyone called him, now.

No, something was going on, but she wasn't sure whether it was all good or a little bad, or maybe some of both. Didn't matter. She was out of the house for the summer and had begun to feel really free, for the first time, ever.

She looked at the back of Janina's head. How could someone in a wheelchair be so cheerful all the time? She had to be in pain, just look at her gnarled hands and twisted feet. But she always wore a smile and seemed genuinely happy to see the girls even when nothing special was going on.

She suddenly realized that she didn't want this summer to end, not ever. She could stay here forever. She rested her hand on Janina's shoulder and was rewarded with a squeeze from the woman's baton fingers.

In a flash, she saw a young Janina sitting in a dank room, a single bulb burning in a light above her head. Janina's fully formed, ungnarled hands were strapped to a chair. Several men in bad suits were shouting at her. She kept her eyes straight ahead. Then a man walked toward her, some kind of prod in his hand. The prod had a long cord that led to the wall.

"You like to dance, don't you, pretty one?"

Janina stared straight ahead.

"One touch from this, and you will limp till they carry you to the grave."

Still no response.

"Two touches, and you will ride on wheels." He rubbed the prod along her fingers.

"Look at these beautiful hands. You could do commercials for American television, perhaps their famous soap, or jewelry. Yes. These hands were definitely made to be photographed wearing jewelry."

He leaned close to her ear, whispered. "You help us, we help you. It is simple. No?"

The young Janina never wavered. Never closed her eyes, just looked straight ahead.

Angrily, the man switched the prod on, then jammed it into Janina's leg, just above the knee.

Sally cried out, crumpled to the ground. Janina shifted as best she could in her chair. She reached out to the girl.

"Are you all right?"

Stunned for a moment, Sally nodded, lifted her self upright.

"Why couldn't you just tell me what happened to you?"

Janina sighed. "It was the only way to find out."

"Find out what?"

"If you were who I thought you were."

"And who is that?"

Janina's hand patted Sally again. At first, Sally flinched, afraid that the images would return, but they didn't. Only warmth.

"We shall talk of this, during our time together. Okay?"

"Okay."

As they traveled the walk, Janina kept her hand on Sally's. The hand was so warm. So broken, and yet so warm. Sally felt tears on her cheek, but she kept pushing the wheelchair forward.

Janina had been right. It was not fun to read another's thoughts.

That night "Massah Sharpe"—as all the boys now called him, Doug included—opened Paradise Lost to begin reading. With Johnny's help, Doug solemnly pulled a large, cardboard box from the other side of his bunk, and walked over to the counselor's chair. Without a word, he put the box down, opened it, and pulled out a plastic bag. He placed the box on its side and put a small stool inside.

Sharpe looked at him, stupefied. "Mr. MacBrayne."

"Yes, Massah Sharpe?"

"Would you care to explain?"

"It will all be evident in a moment, Massah Sharpe."

"Then may I begin reading?"

"In a second."

The other boys hid their giggling behind hands across their mouths They watched Sharpe's internal fury building, as if Doug had lit a fuse on a Fourth of July skyrocket. They all cringed, anticipating its explosion.

When Doug climbed inside the box, pulled the flaps in behind him, Sharpe sizzled.

"Mr. MacBrayne!"

"Yes, Massah Sharpe?"

"I appreciate the performance art aspect of this little display of disobedience, but I command you to come out at once."

"Just another moment, sir."

If Doug's voice had carried any hint of mockery, Sharpe might have sealed up the box and had it shipped to Timbuktu. But the young man's deferential tone never wavered.

"Okay," came from inside the box. "You can start reading now."

"And you intend to listen from inside the box?"

"Something like that."

"And I have your permission to begin now?"

"Yes, please."

Now all the boys were interested. Sharpe looked around the cabin. Normally, when he started reading, they lapsed into a kind of faint, or coma. Often falling asleep when he was only a page or two into it.

He opened the book, cleared his throat. Began reading. With the first word out of his mouth, beyond his view, the opposite end of the box opened, and the boys began laughing. He stopped reading, stood to see what they were laughing at. But when he tried to see around the other end, the doors snapped shut.

"Mr. MacBrayne."

"Yes, Massah Sharpe."

"This is very disruptive. I order you to show me what you are doing."

"No, sir."

"No?"

"It's for the boys. It's not for you. You already know the story."

"Please, Mr. Sharpe," Augie beseeched, "couldn't we just keep going?"

"We'll be good. We'll pay real good attention," Johnny chimed in, "we promise."

Sharpe looked at them, searching for signs of deceit. None on any face. He shook his head.

"Okay. Into your beds." he leaned down to the flap end of the box. "Mr. MacBrayne."

"Yes, sir?"

"You win again."

"It isn't about winning, sir." There was a pause. "I am trying to help you. You'll see."

"Hmpf," came from Sharpe.

He went to his chair, opened the book, cleared his throat. The flaps opened again. The boys keened forward.

"And the devil said—"

That night, the boys heard every word. As soon as he was finished with his planned section, he closed the book. The boys looked up.

"That's all? Can't we do another section?"

He shook his head in wonder. "No, if I did that, we'd run out before camp is over."

The flaps on Doug's box closed, there was a shuffling inside, then the back opened and he peeked out.

"If we finished Paradise Lost, maybe we could do another book, after that?"

Sharpe gazed at him. Nodded. He opened the book, Doug closed the back flap and the same shuffling sound was heard. Then the front flap opened and Sharpe continued reading.

At the front of the box, the flaps opened to reveal a small curtain that hid Doug from the boys. Two puppets, one devil and one angel, were acting out the words Sharpe spoke. When appropriate, Doug switched the puppets around. He had the Devil, several different angels and a figure with long, flowing white hair. Doug had been less sure about that one than the others, but the boys recognized God as soon as they saw Him and they liked Him best of all.

Massah Sharpe only read one other section, then turned off the lights and told the boys goodnight. Doug lay under his blanket, grinning from ear-to-ear. He was too excited to sleep. The boys had been so happy, so involved with the show. He'd never felt anything so wonderful in his life. The sounds of sleep gradually filtered through the bunkhouse, and Doug's eyes began to droop. He was almost asleep when he heard a footstep off to his right. He turned his head and saw a large, dark figure—Mr. Sharpe—tiptoeing to the box. Sharpe lifted the rear panel softly, pulled Doug's bag of puppets from inside, and opened it. There was a long sigh. Then the bag was returned to its place.

Doug let his hand slip off the bed, to rest on Allie's head, then closed his eyes.

Clint returned to his own bunk and sat slowly, making sure the springs didn't squeak. He couldn't quite understand the confusion he felt toward Doug. During his years of teaching—a reluctant profession—he had looked upon children as small enemies. There was a natural wall between him and them that went beyond the age difference and the fact that he taught in mostly white schools. He simply didn't have patience with their lack of knowledge, unreasonable on his part, he understood that, but he couldn't help the way he felt.

Now, after the second worst moment in his life, getting fired from his teaching job—this boy shows up in his bunkhouse, and single-handedly turns his reading of Paradise Lost into great fun. Clint chuckled. He had known the boys would hate listening to the old-English tale. He really was only reading it for his own enjoyment, and to exact a small revenge on the humiliation of being forced into this counselor job. Tonight, the boys had clamored for more.

Doug had even been right in keeping it from him. That made it more exciting for them, an illicit adventure. He chuckled again, as he slipped under the sheet. Maybe when they finished with Paradise Lost, he would begin War and Peace. That would teach them! He sighed, felt the pull of sleep at his eyes.

"Goodnight, Kakoo," he whispered to the ceiling. "I hope you got to see the show tonight. It was a pretty good one."

As with every night since she died, his little girl remained silent. And also, as with every night since that dreadful day, his eyes welled with tears, just before he fell asleep.

But for the first time since that day, he felt almost happy to be alive.

*

"Thought you might be out here, Fiona." Grumpy walked across the second floor deck toward where she sat, near the telescope. "Any activity across the lake tonight?"

"The trees block everything but the beach." She smiled. "But I was actually just looking at the stars."

Grumpy looked upward. The moonless sky made the stars twinkle brighter than usual. The two of them stood quietly watching for nearly three minutes. Grumpy knew he was eventually going to have to tell her the last part of his story, about Jimmy's mother and his tragic betrayal of a woman he almost loved. It was the difficulty in telling her this last part, that had finally shown him how much he had come to care for Fiona. How much he valued her opinion of him.

He suddenly felt very old, very tired. The sigh that came out of him was surprisingly loud. Her chuckle confirmed that she had heard it for what it was.

"Why don't you just tell me?" Her voice was kinder than he dared expect.

"I guess"—a deep breath— "because it is the one moment in my life about which I felt feel truly ashamed."

"Shame's not the worst feeling in the world, you know."

"It isn't?"

She shook her head, barely silhouetted by the light from her room. "No. I would say the inability to feel shame would be far worse."

"Ah, true enough."

And so he told her, including the part about Jimmy, and how much he wished the boy had been his son, though the arithmetic of his birth date was against it. She remained silent throughout, even a minute or so after he fell quiet himself.

"That's quite a story," she said finally.

"Yes, I suppose it is."

"I'm glad you told me. I would have hated to hear it from anyone else."

All he could do was nod. His heart was all seized up and he was afraid to even breathe.

"Does Jimmy know?"

"No. At least I don't believe he does."

"You know you're going to have to tell him someday."

This brought another sigh. "I know."

He desperately wanted to ask her—what? If it mattered? If she thought she might still be able to care about him? Did she even care about him now? At least in that way? Before he could open his mouth and make a fool of himself, she spoke, low and even.

"Did you know that I almost didn't get to be Doug's nanny?"

"No, I didn't."

"I shared a house with a younger woman, who Peter preferred over me." She smiled, painfully. "I knew Felicity wanted me, I could see it in her eyes, but Peter chose Kate instead. I was crushed. It had seemed so right to me, but I was willing to accept my fate."

"Then how—?"

Fiona chuckled, told him about Maggie, the winning football ticket. How glad she'd been to come to America. How much it hurt when Felicity died.

"Do you know that your son has only been on one date since she died? And even then, he ended it quickly when there was a chance that Doug might have been hurt in that fire."

"What are you getting at, Fiona?"

"Peter, for all his faults and fears—and without even realizing it—has made Doug the center of his life. He may be the worst father imaginable, but there is no mistaking that he spends more energy than anyone I ever met caring for his son. Those two need each other in ways they may never see, never realize."

"Yes, I can see that."

"You may regret not being a better father to Peter, but you will regret it even more if you fail Jimmy."

Grumpy started to speak, but Fiona held up her hand.

"Hear me out." She turned, her feet on the ground, to face him. "But not out of debt to his mother—out of joy for the boy. For the sheer pleasure of being part of his life. You have been given a second chance, but you'll have to put your shame away to take advantage of it."

Grumpy nodded. "I've come to realize that ever since he came to work with me at the store."

"Good."

"And I think I've thought of a way to make it all more complete." He smiled. Thought about going down on one knee, then realized his hands were shaking. He laughed when he noticed, and clasped them together. "That is, if you're willing."

She noted the funny look on his face, saw his distress, and frowned. "Uh oh," she said softly. "Oh, no you don't, Peter Douglas-MacBrayne, Junior."

"What?"

"I have a feeling I know what you were about to say, and I'm going to ask you not to. Please don't even think about it."

He blushed, looked up at the stars. "I suppose you're right."

Several minutes passed in silence.

"Are you still going to Douglasville next week?"

"Yes," Grumpy said brightly, happy to change the subject. "Can I get you anything?"

"A couple new mysteries would be nice. As much as those girls tire me out, I still find a few chapters before bed helps me get to sleep."

"Done."

"Thank you."

"No, thank you, Fiona." His heart tightened again. "Thank you very much."

❦

Peter couldn't stop staring. Warm sensations still tingled throughout his body and he knew he still wore a silly grin, but couldn't seem to wipe it off his face. God, it had been what, thirteen, nearly fourteen years? A cloud of perfume hovered above the bed. He reached out, but all he touched was air. An illusion. Was this real?

He let his hand hover just above her breast. Was she asleep? She said she needed to get home, but another minute wouldn't hurt. The house had been so empty since Doug left for camp and Fiona went to Scotland. He had been so much more empty, for so long. He had forgotten what it was like, the wonderful drowsy, excited, warm and succulent sensation of sharing his bed with someone.

Felicity's image entered his mind and he gently pushed it away. It wasn't fair that he should still love her so much when she had been gone so long. But now, his eyes devoured the beautiful figure of the woman who lay beside him. What luck, meeting her in the street that way. A drink. Just to talk. She had so much insight, besides being so beautiful. No—better than beautiful. Desirable. It had been so many years since he felt this.

She stirred. He pulled his hand away. One eye opened. That smile. Such a clever mouth.

"Sorry, I must have dozed off."

"Just for a moment." Peter caressed her hair. "I knew I should wake you, but you looked so beautiful, so peaceful."

She stretched. "What time is it."

"Just a few minutes past midnight."

She sat up, didn't cover herself. He liked that.

"I've got to get going. My baby-sitter is going to kill me."

He pursed his lips, couldn't prevent the pout.

"Now, dear, don't be that way. If I had known—"

He laughed. "If I had known, I would have done something, I'm sure."

Now she laughed, reached for him, drew him close. "You did plenty." Her eyes narrowed. "I can't believe that you haven't been with anyone for thirteen years."

He smiled. "You inspired me."

"Then it's mutual."

She rose, started to dress. She was one of those rare women who was just as beautiful clothed as naked.

He put his feet over his side of the bed. "I'll drive you home."

"That's okay. I have my car, remember?"

"Oh, yeah." He slipped on his pajama bottoms. "Do you have time for a nightcap?"

She shook her head. "Don't like to drink and drive."

He nodded.

She pulled her cotton sweater over her head, shook her hair. It fell into place. She truly was amazing.

"When can I see you again?"

She paused, one stocking halfway up her leg. "The rest of the week is kind of busy. Maybe over the weekend."

"God, so long?"

She walked over, patted his cheek. "After thirteen years, you've become a greedy, greedy boy."

He grinned. "It's only going to get worse, you know."

She looked at him, sighed. "Yes, I suppose it will."

"Will you mind, my wanting you so much?"

"I won't, but—"

"Ah, the mysterious boyfriend."

"Yes." She grew serious. "I didn't expect anything like this ever to happen. I'm not exactly in the habit of sleeping with men on the first date."

He laughed. "And it wasn't even an official date."

"I'll need some time, to sort things out. Can you be patient with me?"

Now Peter grew serious. "I've waited these many years to meet you, to feel these things again. Yes, I can be patient."

"Good." She leaned over, kissed him. Held his lower lip in her teeth and growled, "And I promise you'll be rewarded for your patience."

For a moment, he actually thought he might faint. Just the taste of her, the smell, the look.

She started out.

"When can I call you?" He asked "Tomorrow during the day?"

She stopped, turned in the doorway, shook her head. "I'm at the camp again tomorrow." She smiled. "Shall I say hi to Doug for you?"

Now it was Peter's turn to shake his head. "No, I don't think that would be such a good idea—yet."

"I guess not. Good night, Peter."

"Good night, Dorothy."

Her eyes grew bright. "Please call me Slim."

Chapter Eleven

Downey smirked when he first spotted Kautsch, who definitely looked more turtle than psychologist, in his white hard hat, as he gingerly picked his way through the construction zone around the orphanage.

"Hardly looks like the same place, does it?" Downey said when Kautsch reached his side.

"Amazing." He frowned. "Things are so torn up, though. Will it be finished by mid-August?"

"They'll have the chain link and the landscaping finished for sure. May have some of the inside left to do, but we'll shuttle the kids around from one wing to the other if we have to."

Kautsch nodded. "How's the isolation-ward coming along?"

"The state inspector was here this morning. He said if we continue following the plans, we should achieve the rating you said we would need."

"Good."

Downey shifted his feet. "Still don't understand why that unit was so important. It's nearly a quarter of the budget."

"Long-term, Downey," Kautsch took out a cigar, bit off the end and lit it. "We can only make so much money off sick kids. We might be able to do a little bit better with alkies and druggies, but the funding for those is still dependent on insurance and grants."

"Makes sense, but I still don't understand the heavy security."

"The best funding of all," Kautsch sent a plume of smoke that was quickly dispersed by the breeze, "is housing the criminally insane. The prison system gets more money than any other sector, no questions asked."

"We have any of those in Douglasville?"

Kautsch smiled. "Not at the moment, but we will—"

"If you have anything to do with it, right?" Downey stared at him.

Kautsch turned. "What's the matter with that?"

Downey shook his head. "Just never ever met a shrink who sounded so much like a lawyer, that's all."

"Why thank you, Mr. Downey. I take that as a compliment." Kautsch grinned. "That is how you meant it, isn't it?"

"Of course," Downey said.

"Good," Kautsch gazed at the crew working on the isolation ward. He turned for a moment at the sound of a car in the drive, then squinted into the sun. "We've got a long way to go to pull this little scam off, Downey, and it's important that partners are nice to each other. Every step of the way."

❦

Grumpy put the car in gear and pulled away from the curb in front of the orphanage. Valka sat quietly, next to him, waiting. After they had driven several blocks, Grumpy pulled the car to the side of the road, stopped. He rested his head on the steering wheel.

"You feel okay, Grumpy?"

Grumpy shook his head. "I feel sick."

"Your stomach?"

"No, my heart."

"Oh, God," Valka reached over, hurriedly started to undo Grumpy's collar, "I drive you to hospital."

Grumpy shook his head. "Not a heart attack. My heart hurts for what they are doing at and to the orphanage."

"Ah." Valka sat up straight. "These are bad men, no?"

"Yes."

"Can you stop them?"

"I don't know." He suddenly remembered what he had told Fiona, his feeling of having failed his son by not fixing his foot sooner—his cowardice, after his wife died. But deeper, from another place within him, he heard Sarah murmuring. "Don't make things happen, you have to let things happen. Sometimes the universe needs bad things to happen to the people we love, to make them better.'"

He shook his head. "Valka, we're going to need Janina to help figure this one out."

"Maybe." Valka looked out the passenger window.

"Maybe? Did I hear you right?"

Valka nodded, still did not turn to face Grumpy.

"Valka, what do you mean?"

When the man did turn to face him, Grumpy saw a pain new to his experience. Valka, the steadying influence for the past several years, the man who cooked, cleaned, drove the funny wagon, cared for his sister better than any nurse, looked frightened, grieving, mortally wounded in the eye.

"Fifteen years ago, my sister, they let her go. Let her come home."

"Who?"

"The communists. They kept her to study her powers."

"She never said any—"

"She cannot speak of it. She went to a place inside herself where they could not find her, where she would not have to feel what they did to her."

Grumpy lowered his eyes.

"One day, they just let her go. I picked her up." Valka shook his head. "When they took her, she was a beautiful girl. When she smiled, men fainted. When she danced, they came to life. That was our Janina."

Grumpy tried to picture Janina dancing, laughing like a regular woman. He could see that only in her eyes, not her body.

"The sister I picked up, was much worse than how you know her now. We hugged. I carried her to the wagon. Drove her to see our mother. After the first tears, they did not speak for days. But my mother, she held Janina's hand."

"Was there nothing for them to say to each other?"

"Not in words. My mother, she was giving Janina the knowledge, the knowing. For two months, they held hands through most of the day. We saw no clients. We made no money. It did not matter. People came to us from the villages, as we traveled. They gave us food, coin. The people knew."

"Knew what?"

"That my mother was leaving."

"Leaving—" Grumpy saw it now. He understood. He remembered his own mother's long weeks of coma. Every day, he would go hold her hand, drunk as he was, more out of instinct than anything. What had she given him? Why had it taken so long to surface within him? He turned to Valka. "I don't want Janina to die."

The rough man's eyes were red. Water struggled at the surface, dropped in a slow procession down his cheek.

"Neither do I, brother. But she will be angry if I tell her so. She will say I have no faith."

"Yes, I can hear her saying just that."

"But I have faith." Valka became animated. His arms waved in the car. "It is just that I love her. She is my only sister. I do not want to be so strong that I do not miss her. Do you understand?"

Grumpy reached across and took Valka's dark, callused hand in his own. "I understand, Valka. I do."

"You must promise me you will not tell her I cried. If she finds out, she will do something terrible."

"No, she wouldn't. What could she do that was so terrible?"

Valka's misery was now mixed with a look of deep fear. "If she knows I have cried, she may cry herself. I could not stand the thought of those tears."

"I shall not tell her, Valka. I promise."

"When she was a little girl," Valka's eyes looked straight ahead, at nothing. "If she was in a field, she was like one of the flowers. If a flock of birds were above us, she became one of them. When the sky was blue, so were her eyes." He sighed. "When the communists held her, people would say to me, 'Valka, do not grieve so for your sister. Get a wife so you can forget her, until she returns.' But how does one forget a sister like Janina. Tell me, how does one forget her?"

"We don't forget her." Grumpy leaned his head against the top of the seat. "Nor shall we—ever."

❦

Doug was now joined in the craft shop by all his bunkmates. They were making a new set of puppets for the next book. The whole camp was buzzing about the Walkers, as they were now called. What had been derision over Sharpe's reading *Paradise Lost*, now became a kind of envy. Even Jimmy's small clot of conspirators couldn't help occasionally glancing over, to check the puppeteers' progress.

Once it had become obvious that Sharpe knew about the puppets—which only took a few days—the washing-machine box was replaced by a makeshift stage. The boys took turns handling the puppets, so Doug could sit on his bed and watch with the others. Where the boys in the other bunkhouses groaned about bedtime, the Walkers hurried up the hill, eager for the pre-bed festivities.

Sharpe read with new enthusiasm. Sometimes they would read twenty or more pages before stopping—and that was only reluctantly accepted.

When it came time to choose a new book, Massah Sharpe actually let his slaves decide. With six weeks of camp left, the boys selected five books, and broke up into teams to make the puppets for each.

The regular camp activities continued perforce. The Walkers had been having so much fun losing at baseball, soccer and volleyball, that the Walden Ponders joined in the fun, until they almost stopped keeping score when they played each other. The Hole-In-the-Wallers never lost. Jimmy pushed them, despite the grins of the opponents, walking off in disgust when the losers would shout 'Great game!'

At the campfires, held in the center of the camp compound every other night, Bernie, the Hole-in-the-Wall counselor, played his guitar, while Tex James strummed his ukulele and sang old Native American songs, cowboy songs, and songs by someone named Cole Porter.

Merriwether, the camp director, seemed confused by all the happiness that had arrived so unexpectedly. His wife, MerryLou, and Bonnie James surprised the boys with a duet.

Doug grew tan and muscular. He laughed throughout the day, and Allie bounced around, next to him. One night, Sharpe complained of a sore throat, so Doug read from the book. He stopped once, when he noticed Allie snuggled up to the Massah's leg and the black man reached down to pat the dog's head.

That night, the vibrations came just as Doug closed his eyes.

🌱

The manuscript pages accumulated into the separate books of Milton's new opus. Phineas dutifully transcribed the poet's words, celebrating the end of each week by meeting Mary and Grutto in the park. At first, Grutto stood off to one side watching the passers-by, while Allie gamboled at his feet, but eventually he joined their conversations. Phineas used the opportunity to teach him to read and Mary continued the secret reading lessons at home.

One blustery Sunday, as November prepared to spill into December, Phineas made his way to the park, picking his way through the streets carefully. Everywhere he looked there were more signs of the plague, people passing each other gingerly, averting their eyes and covering their mouths. One woman seemed to be shadowing his footsteps. Every time he turned around to look at her, she crossed herself. Finally, she moved into a doorway and disappeared.

He arrived in the park to find Mary and Grutto involved in a quiet but intense, argument.

"Dear ones," Phineas said, hobbling quickly toward them. "I cannot believe my eyes. Such great friends should never argue."

Mary rushed toward Phineas and put her arms around his neck, sobbing. He looked up at Grutto for an explanation, but saw only pain in the Nubian eyes.

"What calamity has befallen you?" He took Mary by the shoulders and held her in front of him. "Is your father ill?"

She shook her head.

Phineas glanced again at Grutto. "Tell me what is the matter?"

"The mastah want leave London."

"Leave, but why?"

"The sickness."

Phineas nodded. "But he is only trying to protect us. Surely that cannot be bad."

Mary looked up wildly. "Grutto, show him."

The Nubian pulled an envelope from his coat pocket and handed it to Phineas. The letter was addressed to Milton's agent in Buckinghamshire. The instructions were simple. The man was to find a competent scrivener to assist Milton in the completion of his latest work.

Phineas slowly refolded the letter, put it into the envelope, and returned it to Grutto. He then went to sit on a bench, his own eyes filling with tears. Mary sat beside him and took his hand.

"I have an idea, dearest Phineas."

"No, mistress," Grutto said. "You cause trouble for Phineas."

"Trouble?" Phineas looked up.

"I know father admires your work. He so rarely compliments anyone, but he always speaks highly of you."

"But the letter?"

She nodded. "He does not always think about other people's needs. But there may be a way, if you're willing."

"What? I would do anything."

Mary took Phineas' other hand, cradled both within her own. "If you were to ask father for my hand in marriage—"

Phineas started, pulling his hands from hers. "Your hand—"

"Yes."

He stared at her.

"What a wondrous thought." He shook his head. "But why would you want to sacrifice yourself, your happiness, for the likes of me? I know you love learning about his poem as we go along, but this—"

She smiled. "Do you really believe that I am so interested in the poem?"

Truly stricken, he turned to Grutto, who shrugged. He turned back to Mary. "I am sorry, but I cannot believe that a beautiful woman such as yourself would find my ugliness so—"

She put her finger to his lips. "Hush, Phineas. You are a fine man with sharp intelligence—rare qualities in London today." She lowered her head. "However, if you find me unappealing—"

"No," he said, taking her hand. "Darling Mary, you are the most beautiful woman I have ever seen. My hesitation comes from my knowledge of myself."

"Then, if you find me sufficient, and I find you more so, there should be no hesitation."

"What if he says no? After all, you are the daughter of a great man, and I am just a lowly scrivener."

"You are the best assistant he has ever hired. You know his attitude about women. We are not nearly so important to him as his work."

"Except we are working on the very last pages already. He doesn't need me anymore, anyway."

"Do you believe this is the last thing he will write? Look at it this way, if we marry, he's not just getting a son-in-law, he's also getting a permanent scrivener."

"But what if he fires me for asking?"

She held up the envelope with the letter to the agent. Phineas nodded.

Grutto stepped forward. "Miss Mary, we must go now."

She stood, took Phineas' hand, her eyes charged with a fearless gleam. "Promise me you will ask father, and quickly."

Phineas followed their progress as they left the park. He felt rooted to the rough seat, frozen with fear and amazement. He could hardly imagine no longer being witness to the poet's creation. On the other hand, the possibility of sharing his life with Mary was a miraculous consideration. But how even to broach the subject with Milton?

He put his head in his hands. A low, long moan escaped his lips. Several people walking past skirted him warily.

❧

Over at Camp MacLean, a similar harmony had settled over the girls. Fiona was never so proud as in the mornings. She knew she had finally gotten through to the girls when they started making their beds without a fuss before coming down to breakfast. That had been a major hurdle. Here Janina had come to her rescue, explaining to the girls that the best dreams come when one takes the time to make the bed after sleeping in it.

"Our dreams wait for us all day. They watch us, listen to our hearts, preparing the story they will tell us when we close our eyes. If you don't make your bed, the dream from the night before gets stuck in the rumpled sheets and blankets. When you make your bed after sleep, that is a signal that you want another, better dream, the next night because you are showing respect to those who bring your dreams."

That got half the girls making their beds. Then Grumpy told them about Native American dream catchers: small hoops of wood with feathers and rocks laced within, by woven string. They all went out into the woods to get the materials they needed to make their own.

"Make them for each other," he told them. "It's better as a gift than when you make one for yourself."

Two days later, he surprised them with a bag filled with a colorful assortment of feathers, small bones from different animals, and gems. These were incorporated into their creations and exchanged. Every bed was made from the day the dream catchers were hung on the wall above their heads.

In the mornings after breakfast, the girls sat around with Janina and told her of their dreams.

"I was growing these carrots, you know, in the backyard," Talia said one morning. "But every time I would pull one up, you know, by the green part, there was never anything there."

"Weird," Darla said.

"Yeah, I thought so, too." Talia turned to Janina. "I haven't eaten carrots for a week, so I don't get it."

"You don't get why you dreamed of carrots?"

She shook her head.

Janina smiled. "We all have two minds—actually several minds, or sections of the brain that come together, to help create the mind. Inside these sections, is everything you've ever seen, thought, tasted, known in your whole life."

"You mean like a video recorder?"

Janina laughed. "Exactly. Sight and sound, but also touch, taste, and the most powerful of all—smell."

The girls wrinkled their noses. "Eee-eu!"

"What does that have to do with carrots?"

"Well," Janina tapped her chin, thinking. "When you think of carrots, whose picture comes into your mind?"

"Bugs Bunny." Talia said, and received an elbow in the side.

"Not from a cartoon, silly," Susan whispered.

"No, it could be from a cartoon," Janina pointed to the television across the room. "Remember, your mind is capturing everything you see and hear. So television is a very powerful part of your memories. Does this Bugs fellow eat carrots?" Janina giggled. "Of course, he is a rabbit, silly of me. But is there anyone from your family who you associate with carrots?"

Talia chewed her lip. "I guess my father. He has this garden out in the back yard. He's always out there after work, weeding and stuff."

Janina nodded. "And your father, do you do a lot of things with him. Does he take you to movies or to the ice cream parlor?"

"Naw," Talia shook her head. "He's always too busy. My mom said we might go on a family vacation this year, but then they heard about this camp." She shrugged.

"I'm sorry," Janina said softly.

"No, I really like it here, I really do." Talia hugged a cushion to her chest.

"But you'd rather have gone on a trip with your mom and dad?" Janina rolled closer to her, stroked her hair. "It's okay. I think I would have rather gone with my parents, too."

"Yeah."

"Well, then, your father has this garden, where he plants vegetables. He puts in the seeds, waters them, lets them grow, and takes them out of the ground to be eaten, used for food. Right?"

"Yes?"

"In your heart, you plant the seeds of love for your father and your mother. You do what they say, try to act in a way that will make them happy, you love them with all your heart. But when it comes time to pull the carrot, to harvest your love and effort, there is no carrot. They do not see all you do with regard to them. You have worked so hard, but get no food from the love you give them."

"That's what my dream is about?" Talia asked.

"Maybe. That is what I see in what you told me. It is not too good to interpret every dream, or try to give everything a meaning you can understand. Your deep heart and your mind have their own code, a way of speaking to each other. It is not always so important to break the code." Janina swiveled her chair slightly, so she could see all the girls. "This is the importance of dreams, the importance of always telling yourself the truth about your feelings—even if you can't always tell others. Your dreams help you see what you are feeling at the very bottom of yourself. That is where all emotions start."

"What I don't understand," Susan said, "is where all these emotions and dreams come from?"

"Good question," Janina beamed in the girl's direction. "Because no one really knows."

"Then why even talk about it?" Sally fumed.

"What do you mean, Sally?" Janina asked.

Frustration was etched across Sally's face. She took several deep breaths. "Oh, I don't know what I mean."

"That's okay, philosophers and scientists, priests and metaphysicians have been asking themselves the same questions for centuries. You don't have to know what it means—except what it means to you."

"But what if you're wrong? I mean, whatever we do, everyone tells us were wrong." Sally's knees were bobbing like pistons. "If we think something different from our parents or teachers, they tell us we're wrong. Every time I fell down when I was little, I would go crying to my mother and tell her it hurt, and she would always tell me that it didn't hurt and to stop crying."

"And it did hurt, right?" Janina asked.

"Hell, yes."

Janina sighed, folded her hands in her lap. She suddenly looked very tired.

"My dear girls," she started, "I won't pretend that the world doesn't have its problems. Your parents and teachers were taught how to act by people who didn't really know how to act themselves. All I can tell you is that most people really do the best they can, but when you learn something different or better in the future, that's what you have to do for yourself and for your children, if and when you ever have any."

"Then that means the future is all up to us." Sally seemed dejected.

"Don't be sad, dear—or any of you." Her eyes scanned the faces of the girls. "This being alive is a miracle, even at its worst. I can't prove it to you, because everyone has to find it out for themselves."

"But it's so hard, Janina," this from Susan.

"Yes," Janina agreed, "but things change, almost always for the better, if you let them. It happened for me."

"Really?" came from several of the girls at once.

Janina tapped her wheelchair. "When I was your age, I was just as headstrong, and in some ways, just as angry. I was bound and determined that nobody was ever going to push me around." She waited for a moment, her eyes bright. "But now, everyone pushes me around." She giggled. "Otherwise I would never get anywhere."

The girls giggled with her, except for Sally.

"Are you saying that your life is better in a wheelchair?"

"Yes, I believe it is." She spoke quickly before the disbelief set too firmly in their faces. "I see the world from an entirely different perspective than I would if I were walking. When you can walk, stand on your tiptoes, you see what you are accustomed to seeing at that height. But I see people's hands, I watch the way they walk. I see their eyes from underneath them instead of straight on."

"So you know more?"

"No, I see a different side of them. One of the reasons people are so uncomfortable around people with disabilities is they sense that the person sees them the way no one else does." Her smile grew expansive. "My darlings, I've had my time dancing, and laughing, and running through the fields. Now I get to roll around, and there is always someone with me. When I could walk, I was often alone. Now, I am never alone. That is a good thing, I think."

Each of the girls took in this information differently. Janina waited a moment, then finished.

"Who knows, if I weren't in a wheelchair, I might never have wound up here, and I wouldn't have missed meeting all of you for anything in the world."

As usual when Janina spoke, it was obvious she meant what she said.

Jimmy sat in the bow of the canoe and Chas in the stern. The other five canoes had surged ahead.

"Come on, Jim. They're beating us."

"This isn't a race. Hasn't Doug taught you anything about the sin of competition."

Jimmy smiled. He could just see Chas' confused expression, but didn't turn around to look at him.

"What are you up to now?" Chas asked.

"Me?" Jimmy chuckled. "What makes you think I'm up to something?"

"Because I know you better than anyone."

Jimmy nodded. Fair enough. "Okay, I wanted the others to get ahead."

"Why?"

"Look over to your left, at the bank there."

Chas turned and looked in that direction. "Looks like a big house. What of it?"

"Look at the second floor, the deck there."

Chas peered. Suddenly a glint, as if from a mirror, sparkled. "What's that?"

"Don't know. I've seen it a few times. My hunch is someone's watching us."

"Who?"

"Gee, I don't know, Chas. That's what I thought we'd find out."

"Hm."

Jimmy continued to guide the canoe out of the line the others were following. Gradually, they drifted toward the big house. Back at the camp beach, they could hear Fisher's ever-present bullhorn calling them.

"Canoe four, you're drifting too far east."

Jimmy lifted his oar out of the water and waggled it as Fisher had taught them. When he put the oar in again, he paddled in the direction of the house.

"Number four!"

When they were forty yards or so from the bank, Jimmy stood, turned around to wave to Fisher. Chas looked startled.

"Hey, Jim, what the—"

Jimmy splashed into the water. He tried to climb in, but only managed to capsize the boat, sending Chas into the drink as well.

"Wha!" Chas cried, then went under. He bobbed to the surface, his life jacket slick with water. "You jerk, what do we do now?"

"Swim for shore."

Chas narrowed his brow, spit water from his mouth, and started stroking toward the bank. Jimmy swam effortlessly, next to him. They could barely hear the sputtering bullhorn from their own camp.

"What do we do when we get there?" Chas gasped.

"They bundle us up in a blanket and give us hot cocoa, what else?"

Chas nodded.

It took them fifteen minutes to reach the shore. When they staggered onto the beach, a short, dark man met them.

"Your boat sink," he said.

"Yes, sir." Jimmy sat on a rock to catch his breath.

"You at camp across there?"

"Yes, sir," Chas said, flopping next to Jimmy.

"Then I help you get back."

"Do you have something to drink?" Jimmy asked, innocently.

Valka smiled. "You swim through lake filled with water, and still thirsty?"

"Yes, sir." Chas said.

"No one here now, I am caretaker. I get boat." He turned and headed for the dock, a few yards away.

"Well, that really worked, Sherlock." Chas shook his head, water flying from his hair.

"Oh, I don't know." Jimmy motioned with his head toward the house.

There were people inside all right—girls, in the kitchen area. And on the second story deck, a telescope was aimed right at Camp Shambala.

They didn't have time to discuss it. The dark man waved them to climb into the boat. Jimmy pushed Chas ahead of him, sneaking several glances at the house as they went. They climbed in, made for the spot where their boat overturned. The man helped them right it, then tied it to his boat, and motored across to Camp Shambala.

Fisher thanked the man profusely, but the dark man waved him off.

"It was nothing. The boys, they needed help." Then he motored away.

Jimmy and Chas watched him leave, then turned to face the music from Fisher.

"What were you boys doing out there?"

"Well," Jimmy started, "we hit a kind of current or something. Anyway, the boat just kept drifting. I guess I'm not as good a rower as Chas, so I thought we would change places. When I stood up, I lost my balance and went into the lake. I guess I need to work on climbing into an overturned boat, next."

Fisher eyed him closely. "Yes, I guess you do. We'll start on that tomorrow."

He stalked off, and Jimmy leaned close to Chas.

"We're going back across the lake."

"Are you crazy? It took him all of five minutes to catch us this time. Fisher won't let us near the canoes if we try it again."

"Not during the day, stupid," Jimmy said, looking at the big house. "We'll do it after everyone goes to sleep."

"But there's a chain that goes across the canoes, and he padlocks them at night."

"Yeah, what's your point."

"You got a hacksaw?"

"Don't need one." Jimmy smiled, pulled a small key out of the pocket in his swimming trunks. "Ta da!"

"Where'd you get that?"

"It's the spare. Merriwether had it in his office."

"When'd you get it?"

"Remember last week when I volunteered to help on the cleaning crew."

"Yeah, I wondered about that."

"So, now you don't have to wonder anymore."

Chas stared at Jimmy.

"What's the matter now?" Jimmy asked.

"Just wondering which prison I'm going to have to visit you at when we're older."

"Ha!" Jimmy slapped him on the back and they headed toward the mess hall. "Never happen, pal. Nobody's ever gonna lock me up."

Fiona found Grumpy in the study. He was sitting back to the window, looking at a sheaf of papers. She thought to announce herself, but stood and watched for several moments. He had been so quiet since his return from Douglasville. At first she thought it had been a reaction to her turning down his implied—well, what she'd thought might be a proposal of marriage. She blushed at the very thought and cleared her throat.

"Yes?" He turned. "Oh, hi, Fiona."

"Good afternoon, Grumpy. What are you reading?"

"Ah, just some business papers."

"Good business?"

"No, but nothing too worrisome." His smile was wan, pinched.

"What's going on?"

"Thought you might want to know, we had a pair of visitors."

"Oh, who?"

"Jimmy and another boy. Their canoe capsized and they swam to shore."

"Jimmy?" Grumpy sat up. "Is he okay?"

Fiona chuckled. "I was watching them through the telescope. From what I saw, looks as if Jimmy did it on purpose to try to see what was going on here."

Grumpy nodded. "That sounds like him. And you can bet he'll be back. But I didn't hear any commotion."

"Valka met them at the bank, took them away in the motor boat."

"At your request, I imagine."

"Yes," Fiona grinned, "the last thing I want is to have my girls mixing with boys from back home."

"Your girls." A new light entered Grumpy's eyes. "I like that."

"Well, they are." Fiona blushed. "But more Janina's, in another way, I guess."

"You've done very well." Grumpy's voice was soft, affectionate. "Better than you thought, right?"

She nodded.

"But not better than I thought. I knew you would do very well with them. You have the stuff."

"Is that Valka the Second or Peter the Second talking?"

"Both." He grinned. "And a lot of Grumpy the only."

"Well, I came here for another reason."

"Oh?"

"Yes." She twisted her handkerchief in her hands. "I—uh, have been doing some thinking. A lot, actually. I gave you quite a bit of trouble that day at the airport. I just wanted you to know that I appreciate how things have turned out."

"Thank you, Fiona, but you were right, that day. I've thought quite a bit about it, myself. You were absolutely right to dress me down the way you did. I was dead wrong. We could have done this without all the subterfuge."

"Maybe. But we won't know, will we?"

"No, but it was a good lesson for the future."

"Good, but that brings up another thing I've been thinking about what you started to ask me the other night that I asked you not even to think about, remember?"

"I don't think I'll ever forget. What about it?"

"Well, I wanted you to know that I do like you immensely. You're probably the only man since my husband, who I've found interesting in any way." She put her hand to her mouth. "Oh, dear, did that sound as terrible to you as it did to me?"

Grumpy laughed. "Not at all. I know exactly what you are saying."

"You see," she sighed, "I made a vow, to myself more than anyone else, that if I ever had a baby to raise from, well, from a baby, I would put all my energies into its life. I would dedicate myself to raising it, even if it meant I never fell in love again."

"And you made that vow regarding Doug, right?"

"Yes. And I believe it was the right thing to do."

"So do I."

"You do?"

"Yes, dear." He put the folder of papers on the table next to his chair. "I realized after I brought up the subject, how inappropriate it was for me even to think that. Again, you were right. I love Doug, too.

That first time you brought him into the bookstore, I could see that he had become quite a wonderful young man, and it was all due to you."

"No, it wasn't. You may not realize it, but you helped a great deal."

"How?"

"Your gifts. If you only knew how much he looked forward to any word from you. And Peter, bless his blind heart, he just doesn't know the boy. Every time you sent something to Doug, no matter how small, it was always exactly what he wanted. You have an uncanny knack where that boy is concerned." She went on to tell him of the fight over the abacus, Peter's reaction, the trip to the orphanage, Doug's funny dream.

Grumpy was nodding by the time she finished. "Amazing, but I have a feeling I may have boxed myself in a bit."

"How's that?"

"Well, he knows me as Valka Petrovich. How is he going to react when he discovers I'm really Grumpy?"

"Hm." Fiona slipped her hanky into her dress pocket. "One good thing, Doug is far more forgiving than I am. Once he understands the reasons behind it, he'll be okay."

"I hope so."

"No, it will be okay. That's what I was trying to say the other day about spending so much time with him. He really is the most extraordinary person I have ever met, my prejudices notwithstanding." She started for the door, stopped. "And I can honestly say I've only met one other person who even comes close to him, in my view."

"Who's that?"

Her smile was that of a young girl's. "You'll have to figure out that for yourself."

"Not even a hint?"

Now she became a schoolteacher, chastising a student who missed an answer purposely. "Not even a hint."

Grumpy's heart was warm as he reluctantly turned his attention back to the papers he'd received from Jacques, in Paris. Once again he'd been so concerned about what he was doing, he'd not heeded his business manager's warning.

But it was all clear to him now. Whatever Peter had up his sleeve, Grumpy would not be able to exercise his voting-stock to fight him. In fact, with the corporate change that had been instituted, Grumpy didn't really have a vote any more. Peter must have brought in someone really sharp. He never could have thought of this ingenious screw-job, on his own.

Grumpy's stock had been reclassified as Non-Voting B certificates. Still holding value and subject to dividends, but no longer active regarding the day-to-day operations of the new Delaware corporation. On the surface, this would not have been a bad thing, but if the company ever experienced a downturn, there would be nothing the B-stockholders could do to fight the Board. In fact, if the stock plummeted, Grumpy could be completely wiped out.

There was a major shift going on: The changes Avisson described at the Institute, coupled with the new construction at the orphanage, was pretty clear: The Douglas Corporation would no longer be officially connected with either facility. It all had to be the doings of the man with the goatee and the ill-fitting hard hat who oversaw the construction at the orphanage. Grumpy had seen nothing but a dark cloud around that man.

He rose slowly. He had been avoiding Janina, because of what Valka had told him about her condition. She was so intuitive, she would read his eyes in a minute. Perhaps if they talked about these other things, the potential events, he could hide his fear for her.

Maybe he would call Abe later in the evening. He missed that Lincoln look-alike. There weren't too many men that Grumpy trusted and liked upon first meeting, but Abe was one of the special ones. Actually, Valka was, as well.

Maybe things weren't so bad. For the first time in his life he had two male friends with whom he would be close until he died. And even Fiona had opened the door again, albeit just a sliver. Still, with two good friends and a potential partner like Fiona? Hell! Nothing could stop him.

That is, of course, except himself.

That night, Jimmy and Chas sneaked out of their bunkhouse, tiptoed down to the beach, silently undid the chain, and paddled slowly out into the lake. The almost full moon made heading toward the lights of the house that much easier.

"When we get close," Jimmy whispered, "we'll turn to the left and land beyond the lights. That way, it won't be so easy for that Mafia guy to catch us again."

"Mafia?" Chas gulped. "Jesus, Jim, do you think they have guns and stuff?"

"Gee, I don't know, Chas. What do you think?"

Chas missed Jimmy's sarcasm.

"I want to go home. I don't want to get gunned down."

"Try not to wet your pants in the boat, okay?" Jimmy chuckled, "I was only kidding, Chas."

Chas grunted.

They finished the trip in silence, landing just south of the private dock.

"What do we do now?" Chas helped Jimmy tie the boat to a tree limb.

"We go see who's up there."

"Oh, God."

"Okay, chicken shit, you wait here, then."

"But it's dark."

Jimmy sighed. "What do you want to do, stay with the boat, or come with me?"

Chas thought a moment. "I'll stay with the boat. If I hear anything, I'll get her ready to shove off."

"Fine."

Jimmy slipped along the water's edge, keeping low to the bushes. The lights glowed on the second floor. Another light shone at the rear, on the ground floor. He tiptoed to the window and peeked inside.

A young girl with her back to the window was sitting across from a crippled woman in a wheelchair. He wasn't sure if they were talking or just holding hands. The young woman nodded, then turned her head to one side.

Jimmy gasped. It was Sally. He ducked down, hoped the woman in the chair hadn't caught sight of him.

What the hell was Sally doing here? And who was that fiery-looking woman?

He lifted himself up, to peek again. Sally stood, getting ready to push the woman out of the kitchen. The dark man met them at the kitchen door and took over from Sally. Jimmy ran to the next window. The man and the woman went one way, Sally the other. He followed her progress by the lighted then darkened windows. One light stayed on, at a frosted window. He listened, heard water running. Must be a bathroom.

He tapped at the window, heard the water shut off. He tapped again. The window opened slightly.

"Who's there?"

"Shh. Is that you, Sally? It's me, Jimmy."

"Jimmy!" she exclaimed.

"Sh. Not so loud. Jesus."

"What are you doing here?"

"I'm at Camp Shambala, across the lake. What the hell are you doing here?"

"Nanny Camp."

"Nanny? As in, Lame-brain MacBrayne's nanny?"

"Yes."

"Who's that woman in the wheelchair?"

"Janina. She's a gypsy."

"Ah." As if that explained it. "Who's the Mafia guy?"

"Mafia? You mean Valka?"

"Not Mr. Petrovich. The dark short guy."

"Valka Petrovich. He's Grumpy's long lost something or other. He's Janina's brother."

Jimmy tried to understand, couldn't. "Sally, do they have you on drugs or something. Nothing you've said makes any sense."

"Neither do you, standing outside in the dark in the middle of the night."

"Yeah, yeah. Who else is here?"

"The Moles, a couple of other girls. Fiona and Grumpy. Mrs. Schmidt, who teaches us cooking."

"So, this is a Nanny Camp. Are they making you baby-sit kids or something?"

"No."

"No." Defeated again, Jimmy tried to think. "Is Mr. Petrovich—my Mr. Petrovich—is he here?"

"Yes, that's Grumpy."

"Ah." His head swirled with all this new information, none of which made any sense.

"I have to get to bed. Before Fiona finds out."

"Wait."

"What?"

"Can you sneak out and meet me sometime?"

"I don't think so."

"Why not?"

Silence.

"Why not?" He repeated.

"Because I don't think I want to. Fiona and Janina trust us." She started to close the window. "I have to go. See you at home, in a few weeks."

"Sal—"

The window shut tight, locked. Then came the sound of footsteps from the other side of the house. A flashlight beam. Jimmy ran away from the beam as quietly as he could. As he tiptoed under the second story deck, he thought he heard Mr. Petrovich's voice say, "I told you he'd be back."

Jimmy wasn't sure if it was pride or something else in that voice. All he knew was, he had to get out of there quick before the dark guy caught him. He ran down to the bank. No boat.

"Chas!" He whisper-shouted. "Where the fuck are you?"

"Out here," came from the black water.

More footsteps decided Jimmy's next move. He ran out to the end of the dock and jumped in feet first, to keep his hair dry. As he started swimming toward where he thought Chas and the boat were, something from behind hit him on the shoulder. Was it a bullet?

He looked up and saw an orange life jacket floating by his right arm. He slipped into it and swam on, to the canoe.

When he reached Chas, he expertly flipped into the seat and sat dripping for a moment to catch his breath.

"How'd it go?"

"Very interesting."

"What? Come on, tell me."

"Weird stuff. Hard to describe."

"Mafia? Did they have guns?"

"No, you putz."

"Putz? Why am I a putz, now?"

"For making me swim all the way out here." He put his paddle in the water and they headed toward camp.

Petrovich, or now Grumpy, had told him to hang in there, that some strange things might be happening. So far he'd been right. But why hadn't the man who seemed to like him so much told him he'd be right across the lake? And what was he doing with MacBrayne-less's nanny?

Sally used to love to sneak out. She'd never needed an excuse—just to get out was good enough for her. So, the nanny had won over Sally and the Moles. Had she turned old Petrovich against him as well?

His anger grew as they approached Shambala. MacBrayne had pretty much pulled the wool over everyone's eyes here at camp, as well. Shit, the twerp had taken the fun out of baseball, soccer, volleyball. All anyone ever talked about was the puppet shows at Artillery Walk before bed. Big deal.

Maybe it was time to take MacBrain-less down a notch. He'd wait for the right moment, then kaboom! No more happy camper.

He was chuckling softly by the time they landed, pulled the canoe up on the beach and replaced the chain.

"Phew," Chas said as they started up the path to their bunkhouse. "That's a relief."

"There really wasn't anything to be scared about. It wasn't a Mafia hangout, just a big house."

"No, I was worried you were mad at me or something."

"Nah," Jimmy put his arm around Chas's shoulder. "I was just thinking."

"Oh, about what?" Chas was nervous.

"About the cave. I think I've figured out exactly how we can use it."

Chas waited. "You're not going to tell me, are you?"

"Not yet."

"Because you don't want to scare me, right?"

"Yeah, that's it."

"Shit. Now I'm really worried."

Sally couldn't get to sleep. Jimmy's bizarre arrival at the bathroom window spooked her. It was a reminder that there were only a couple weeks left of camp, and she would have to return home—to Douglasville, her father, school. The idea of leaving Camp McLean and Janina weighed her down. Fiona had implied that they would have the camp again next year. That would give her something to look forward to, help pass the time.

If anyone had told her she would enjoy sitting with a crippled woman and holding her hand for an hour or so every night before bed, she would have laughed in their face. Now, the thought of returning home, sleeping in her own bed, wondering when her father was going to get drunk and —

She looked up at the dream catcher. Janina had given her a small heart-shaped stone to attach to it. She glanced out the window at the moon, which would be full in three days. Valka said they would have a moon dance, an old gypsy tradition. That might be fun. He made it sound all mysterious and wonderful. What was it Janina had said that day, that being alive was a miracle? Maybe that was something that happened to people when they got old and realized they had lived longer than they had time left. Maybe that made life more miraculous.

That's exactly how she felt about the time remaining at Camp McLean. The camp season was more than half over and the sadness of that felt like a kind of death. She would have to try to explain it to Jimmy when she saw him next. She smiled as she thought of how he had tapped for her attention, standing outside the bathroom window like Romeo and Mr. Clean all rolled into one.

She wondered if she would wind up marrying Jimmy. No, probably somebody else. She thought about that night she kissed Doug in his family's graveyard. Doug would probably grow up to be a really nice man. There would be no way to choose between the two of them. They each had their good points and bad. Jimmy was too crazy. He was surely destined to be some kind of famous artist, probably living in New York. Doug would take over control of the family business and be a New Jersey suburbanite. Neither option sounded quite right.

No, she would be like Janina: unmarried, mysterious.

Sleep overtook her quickly, but she awoke an hour later, perspiring. Her dream had started with fire and ended with a kind of prison cell. Bars on the windows, but she was on the outside looking in. She could not see who was in the cell. She reached up and touched the heart with her fingertip.

The fear from the dream faded. This time she slept peacefully.

※

The day started out strangely. Doug ate breakfast with his bunkmates, but Jimmy kept smiling at him. Friendly. His nemesis even helped Augie with the design of a puppet, during the craft hour. At lunch, the new Jimmy continued his funny mood. But the clincher came during the volleyball game. Jimmy's team seemed to have caught the sportsmanship bug. The competitiveness was gone. Compliments abounded. Doug knew he shouldn't have felt uneasy, but when it came to Jimmy, he just didn't trust him.

But maybe he was being unfair.

During the free hour, he took a quick dip to get rid of the sweat from the afternoon's play and spotted Nurse Prudence standing alone at the far end of the beach. He grabbed his towel and ran up to her.

"How are you?" he said, dripping wet.

"Doug! How's your hand?"

"Perfect, thanks to you." He held up his palm to prove it.

"I've got a surprise for you."

"What's that?"

She had a funny, crooked smile. "We've met before."

An odd, dizzy feeling swept through Doug. He tried to think of all his funny dreams, the waking ones, to see if he could remember seeing her. Nothing.

"Oh, yeah. When I cut my hand."

She shook her head, the smile broadened. "Nope, before that."

"Well, you did seem kind of familiar, but I—I don't remember."

"I know you don't." She tousled his wet hair. "I didn't, myself, until a few days after meeting you here."

"Wow." he shook his head. "I'm pretty good at remembering people. I'm sure I would have remembered you. How old was I?"

"Let's see." Her fingers pulled at her chin. "You would have been about, I guess, a whole minute old."

"A minute?" Then it dawned on him. "You were there when I was born? Really?"

She nodded. "I weighed you, and gave you the APGAR test. That's what nurses do to make sure all of a baby's parts work—fingers, toes, eyes, hearing, etc. I put your name-band around your wrist. I remember because there were so many letters."

"Gee." A cloud passed through Doug's eyes. "Did you—did you know my mom?"

"No." Prudence suddenly remembered the other part of the moment. "Oh, dear. I'm sorry, Doug. I didn't think."

He shrugged. "That's okay, I just thought—"

"No, that was stupid of me." Her face was red.

He smiled at her. "It's okay, really. I know she was okay. Where she went I mean."

The vibrations hit harder than ever before. Doug's eyes rolled up into his head and he collapsed on the sand.

Embarrassed as she had been, Prudence spun into action. She knelt and checked his pulse. It was low, steady, but very low. She checked his tongue to make sure he hadn't swallowed it; then started calling for help. Greg Fisher, the lifeguard, came running and carried the limp boy to the infirmary.

When Clint Sharpe showed up a few minutes later, Doug's eyes had begun to flutter. He opened them and focused on the worried faces of Sharpe, Fisher, and Prudence. Merriwether came running in, just as he sat up on the bed.

"How do you feel, Doug?" Prudence asked.

"Good." He blinked several times. "Good, really."

"It was my fault, I completely forgot about your mother."

Merriwether elbowed past Sharpe. "What's going on?"

"Doug fainted on the beach."

"Fainted? Did you call the doctor?"

Prudence looked at him. "I checked his vital signs. Thy were OK." She looked at Doug. "Has this ever happened to you before?"

He nodded slowly. "A couple of times. When I remember certain things."

Merriwether snorted. "What kind of things?"

325

Doug stared at him. "Stuff from before."

"Before?" Merriwether frowned.

"It's my fault," Prudence said, taking his pulse. "I should never have mentioned that I was there when he was born."

Merriwether was more confused. "What's the matter with that?"

"His mother died during his birth."

"That was very stupid of you, Miss Peabody. I'm going to talk to your supervisor about this. I think we may have to reconsider your position here."

"No!" Doug swung his legs over the side of the bed. "It's not her fault. The vibrations started when I remembered taking my mother to the other side. It's always like that. It wasn't a bad thing at all."

Merriwether whispered to Prudence. "Call the doctor. I want—"

"Dr. Kautsch knows. He's my thera—uh, doctor."

"Doug, you're obviously delirious. We'll call the doctor to check you over and —"

"It's true," Doug maintained. "I saw everything."

"How can a baby see those things, much less remember them?" Merriwether asked.

"I was not a baby. I hadn't gone into my body, yet, because I was aware that the embryo might not survive its birth. But when they decided to perform a Cesarean section, I decided to do it.

"On the way, I met my mother and took her to the light. I knew it would comfort her. I came back and entered my body, only after I knew she was safely there." He smiled. "It was very nice for her, Prudence. It wasn't a bad thing at all. It never is. People just think it is, because they aren't sure about what happens. They fear the unknown."

"And you know, I suppose."

"Yes, I do. And I can prove it."

That silenced Merriwether, but only for a moment. "And just how do you propose to do that?"

"Tell him, Prudence."

"Tell him what, Doug?" Prudence could hardly find her voice.

"Tell them about that funny doctor who yelled at you."

"You know about that?"

He nodded. "Do you remember why he yelled at you?"

"Of course." She seemed reluctant to say more.

"Go ahead, it's okay."

"Yes, Miss Peabody, we're all dying to hear why this funny doctor yelled at you."

"Wait," Doug hurried over to the table, took a piece of paper and wrote something on it. Then turned and smiled. "Just in case you don't believe that I know what happened."

He handed the paper to a bug-eyed Clint Sharpe, who held it like a dead snake.

"Well, I made the APGAR tests on Doug: reflexes, length, weight. All that. But I put down something like eight pounds one ounce. And Dr. Fussinbacke—"

"That was his name?" Doug asked. "That figures."

Prudence smiled. "Quite appropriate."

"What did Dr. Fussy-whatever say?" Merriwether tapped his foot.

"He weighed Doug, himself, and found he then weighed eight pounds and just over two ounces."

"So, you made a mistake."

"No, I didn't. That scale was extremely accurate."

"But that doesn't prove anything."

"Ahem." Sharpe cleared his throat. "Look at this." He handed the paper to Merriwether. "Go ahead, read it."

"After my soul re-entered my body, I weighed slightly over an ounce more than when Nurse Peabody weighed me."

"That's preposterous!" Merriwether stalked toward the door. "I don't know what kind of game you all are playing—" he pointed at Prudence— "but I want Dr. Kautsch called immediately."

"I'll do that right away, sir."

"See that you do." He slammed the door behind him.

"Phew," Prudence said. "He's really angry."

Doug lowered his head. "Sorry I got you in trouble, Prudence—again."

"He doesn't matter." She hugged him. "I'm just glad you're better. You scared the hell out of me."

A soft sob came from the other side of the room. Both Doug and Prudence looked over at Clint, who looked stricken, tears running down his cheeks.

"Mr. Sharpe?"

He shook his head, gathered his heart, looked at Doug. "Is it true? When someone dies, do they go to this light thing you mentioned?"

"Yes, sir."

"And your mother, she didn't hurt anymore?"

Doug shook his head. "Not a bit. On the way to the light, she told me how glad she was to be rid of her old, diseased clothing. Actually, she felt wonderfully well."

"She did? Hmm. So, this light—it's a good place?"

"Yes. I've been there many times, and past it, to the other side. There, they always know me as 'Alzar.' It's a better place than you can possibly imagine.

"That's good." Sharpe tried to smile, couldn't manage. "Excuse me, I need to be alone for awhile."

Doug and Prudence watched him leave in silence. They went to the window and followed his progress down to the beach. His hands were in his pocket, his gait a slow shuffle. When he was out of sight, Prudence pulled Doug close, her arm around his shoulder.

※

Jimmy watched Doug across the mess hall. He'd heard about the fainting spell on the beach, and all the howdy-do at the infirmary. Not so much what happened, but Merriwether was pretty pissed-off. He asked Tex about it after softball, and the man said he overheard Merriwether calling some doctor named Kautsch. The Walkers' counselor, Mr. Sharpe, was nowhere to be seen.

Jimmy leaned over to whisper to Chas. "I think we should do it tomorrow night."

"Uh oh." Chas had a mouthful of food.

"Listen," Jimmy whispered harshly. "Our boy's fancy doctor is coming tomorrow. I don't know what went on, but it must have been serious to have his precious shrink show up. And look, no Massah Sharpe."

"So, what are you planning to do?"

"Take him across the lake."

"What?"

"Yeah, but I need you to do two things."

Chas held out his wrists. "Yes, officer, I'll go quietly."

Jimmy punched him on the arm. "It won't be anything like that. All you have to do is trip him in the mess hall tomorrow and I'll make sure he spills his food on me."

"Gee, that'll teach him, all right."

"Just do it."

"Okay. What's the other thing?"

"I want you to watch his dog. Just until I get back; then we let the dog loose when I get back."

"But Allie's liable to wake up the whole camp." Chas scratched his head. "Wait—when you get back? You're going to leave him there?"

"That's right."

"Ooh, that's really mean. They might kick him out of camp."

"Exactly."

Chas mulled this over, shook his head. "Won't work."

"Why not?"

"Doug'll never go, he's such a wimp."

Jimmy grinned. "Oh, he'll go all right, especially when I tell him who's over there?"

"Who?"

"His precious nanny, that's who."

"Jeez, why didn't you tell me last night?"

"I wanted to finish the plan. Besides, you might have spilled the beans."

Chas looked hurt. "No, I wouldn't have."

"Okay, then, I was wrong. I'm sorry." He pushed his dessert over to Chas. "And to prove it, you can have my cake."

Chas glanced at the cake, then at Jimmy. "Why do you hate him so much?"

"Don't know, really. I just do, I guess."

"Gosh, that's a great answer."

"It's the truth."

※

That night, Clint stood before the boys.

"I have two requests tonight. First, I'd like you all to start calling me Clint. That's my first name." He smiled. "And second, I wonder if it would be okay if I worked the puppets while someone else read."

There was a moment's silence. Johnny Marks, who was behind the stage, looked at Doug, who nodded. The boy walked over and handed the puppets to their leader.

"Here." Then he laughed, ran over to his bunk and jumped on it.

Clint put a puppet on each hand. "Now, who's going to read?"

The boys looked at Doug, he nodded to Augie, who did a "who-me?" then walked to Clint's chair and picked up the book.

"Once upon a time," he started, glanced up to see all the boys encouraging him with their eyes. He grinned. "Once upon a time, there was a great teacher, a one hell of a bunkhouse counselor." He looked over at Clint, who wore a confused look. "Everybody in the camp called him Massah Sharpe, but the people who liked him best, his friends—called him Clint."

The boys all applauded and laughed. Clint stood and took a bow. "Now, hurry up and read from the book, before Merriwether comes up the hill and makes us turn off the lights."

※

Avisson sat in his living room, staring at the dreaded bottle of Cabernet, on the table next to his chair. There were only a few swallows left. He wouldn't even need a glass to finish off the last remains of his failed marriage. He could just tilt the bottle to his lips and drink.

But it wasn't his marriage he was mourning, nor the awful changes at the Foundation.

Maybe it was the loss of his professional innocence, now gone, shattered quicker than a teenager's virginity during her first all-nighter at the beach.

No, not even that. This was worse.

And it happened so quickly, so innocently. Sabey was deep under, talking a kind of distracted gibberish. Suddenly, the man was involved in a heated conversation with himself. Or two selves. But they were selves of such alien dimension, that Avisson nearly brought him out of it to stop what they were saying.

"He's done enough," a meek voice said. "He can rest now."

"He was sent to kill twelve. And twelve he shall do." This voice was harsh, brutal, ugly.

"The Influences call for choice. You know the—"

"Choice!" Roared the ugly one. "He belongs to me. He is my instrument. He must exact the revenge, or the other three will mean nothing."

"But you're reading the energies wrong. He has suffered enough. He will carry this with him through the next ten times. That is too much to ask."

"Nothing has been asked. It has been decreed!"

"You weren't there. You didn't see the whole story. There is much beyond your anger, that applies here."

"Enough!" Cried the harsh one. "I was there. What I know, I know. You will not interfere any longer."

Then Sabey gave a strangled gasp, gripped his throat, and fell so silent, Avisson was afraid to touch him. When he finally got up and went to check, one eye opened.

"Do not touch me." The cold voice remained.

Avisson withdrew his hand. The blood emptied from his face. After several minutes, Sabey slowly awoke. He yawned, stretched. Looked over at Avisson, who'd returned to his chair.

"Any luck, Doc?" The look on his face indicated he knew something of what had transpired.

"Maybe."

"Don't maybe me, Doc. You know as well as I do—there's one more to do, isn't there?"

Avisson shook his head. "You have a choice, Mr. Sabey. You've had a choice in this, all along."

"No I don't, Doc. I haven't had any choices, ever."

"Well, I'm going to do my best to protect you from yourself, then. I can do that much."

That funny, ugly smile covered Sabey's face. "You really believe that, don't you, Doc?"

"Yes, I do."

"I guess we'll just have to see, won't we?"

"Yes, Mr. Sabey, I guess we will."

Avisson reached for the bottle, quickly downed the last few swallows. The wine hit the back of his throat with the impact of a bug against the windshield. He gagged, slammed the bottle down on the table. Goodbye, marriage. Goodbye, innocence.

Hello, pure evil.

Then he clicked on the television and did something he hadn't, for as long as he could remember.

He watched a bad situation comedy.

The drive to Camp Shambala had left Kautsch out of sorts. He hated the out-of-doors, felt much more comfortable within the confines of an office, a hospital, any place but where bugs could bite and the sun could burn him.

"Give me the city, anytime," he muttered.

"What?" Slim shifted in the passenger seat.

He downshifted going around a curve. "Nothing."

They drove on for several more miles.

"Has Doug said anything about missing Miss McLean?"

She shook her head.

"How about his father?"

Another no, though a bit of color crawled up her neck.

"That's a good sign, I suppose."

She nodded, lost in her own thoughts. He glanced at her in the rearview mirror, reached across. She gave him her hand, but it was without life. The fingers just rested within his grasp.

"Slim."

"Yes?"

"Are you okay?"

"Yeah, just, Oh, I don't know." She pulled her hand away, folded it under her armpit.

"You want to talk?"

She shook her head.

His eyes burned the road ahead. They drove in silence until the turn-off to the camp. She showed him where to park and pointed to the infirmary.

"Why don't you get a cup of coffee from the mess hall and I'll fetch Doug."

"Mess hall," he sighed. "With a name like that I'll bet they don't have cappuccino."

"This is a camp for kids, remember?"

He searched her eyes, but she turned and walked away.

Ten minutes later, after retrieving a cup of hot brown liquid from someone appropriately named "Tex," he made his way up to the infirmary. Doug came running down the path toward him.

"Dr. Kautsch!" he cried.

For a moment, he thought the boy was going to hug him. He wiped the dark mood from his face and smiled.

"Well, hello, Doug. How are you?"

"Absolutely great!"

Even before they made it inside, Doug was recounting all the small miracles of life at camp. A litany of small victories and exciting moments that came so quickly, Kautsch gave up trying to write any of them down. He waited until Slim left them alone, and tried to slow Doug's beaming narrative.

"That's wonderful, Doug. Sounds like coming to camp has turned out to be a good thing." He smiled. "I vaguely remember your being rather anxious about leaving Miss McLean and your father."

Doug blushed. "Seems kinds of silly now, doesn't it?"

"Not at all," Kautsch tapped his pen on the pad. "Perfectly natural. Anytime we face an unknown, there's always fear. Fear makes us more alert, helps us to survive. Which you seem to have done admirably."

"Well, the people here are wonderfully nice." He started to launch into the cast of characters, but Kautsch again slowed him down.

"Why don't we focus on what happened on the beach yesterday? That appears to have been somewhat traumatic—fainting and everything. Know what I mean?"

Doug nodded, but his smile never wavered. "I know that it would probably seem that way to anyone else, but it really was pretty wonderful."

"Wonderful? Fainting is wonderful?"

Doug shrugged it off. "That part was a little different, but it didn't hurt. I mean, I didn't hit my head or anything. It's just that the vibrations came on kinda sudden, faster than usual."

"These vibrations, were they different than the other times you experienced this phenomenon?"

"No, just faster. When Prudence asked me —"

"Prudence. That would be Nurse Peabody?"

"Yes." Doug grinned. "She said I could call her Prudence after she gave me a shot in the—uh, gluteus maximus."

Kautsch chuckled. "Yes, I suppose that would provide a certain familiarity. "Why did she give you a shot?"

"I cut myself—" Doug cleared his throat "—on a piece of tin, the first day here."

Without looking up, Kautsch made a note on his pad: For the first time, Doug had lied, and about the cut. A less experienced therapist might have stopped and called him on the lie, but Kautsch knew better. There would be a more propitious time to trip the boy up, bring out the truth in a different context—when he didn't have his guard up about the incident.

"Is your hand better?"

"Oh, yes. All healed up." Doug held up his palm to show him.

Kautsch nodded. "And your butt?"

Doug laughed. "Even better."

"Good. Now let's go back to yesterday. Why do you think the vibrations were so strongly triggered? Thinking about your mother's death? Your birth?"

Doug thought for a moment. "No, I think it was remembering the light. It was so strong, so beautiful."

"The light?"

"Where I took my mother after she died."

"You took her?"

"Yes, I guess you would say my soul led her soul. At least that's the way it felt, or how I remembered it."

"Have you ever remembered it before yesterday?"

"No."

Kautsch took a deep breath. Wrote several sentences.

"Something wrong, Dr. Kautsch?"

He looked up. "No, Doug. This is an important moment for you. Everybody has certain questions, feelings about their birth. That's one of the reasons we celebrate birthdays. To mark the day every year, to remind us of where we came from, how we got here."

Doug listened carefully as Kautsch continued.

"When someone's mother dies bringing him into the world, it can haunt him—even without his realizing it. One of the ways to deal with the feelings of guilt about it, is to make up a story that helps him get past it and carry on with life."

"Y—you think I made this up?"

"No, not really, Doug. Remember, when these other incidents have come over you, they were always at moments of extreme emotional pressure. You've been faced with tough situations. In this instance, you've been cut off from your nanny and your father. You appear to have dealt with that very well, at least on the surface, but it stays underneath, lurking, looking for an opportunity to rise up. When Miss Peabody mentioned that she was there when you were born, the hidden feelings of guilt could have mixed in with that subliminal fear of being apart from your support system, and boom, you fainted."

"I can see that," Doug said thoughtfully, "but it doesn't feel that way."

"Well, good." Kautsch saw doubt on Doug's face. "No, I mean it. That release of these two hidden emotional bombs, could mean that you have released both, powerfully, and their influence might be lessened as you go along."

When Doug remained silent, Kautsch pushed forward on another front.

"Have you had any other incidents, of the vibrations, I mean?"

"Yes." Doug appeared cautious.

"When was that?"

"The first night here. Our bunkhouse counselor, Clint was reading to us from Paradise Lost."

Kautsch's eyebrows raised. "Doesn't exactly sound like proper reading for a bunch of campers."

"Not so bad." One of Doug's shoulders raised, lowered. "But as soon as he started reading, I started to remember a—"

"Remember? Or vibrate?"

"They're kinda both."

"Okay, go on."

"Well, I was this writer, or poet. Long time ago, I think. Anyway, the man who wrote it was John Milton. I knew he was blind. And I think I was helping him, you know?"

"Helping?"

"Yes, as his scribe."

Kautsch rubbed his forehead. He felt the anger rising from the drive to camp, his frustration with Slim's emotional distance cutting into his professional reserve. This rich kid, coddled and protected at every turn, needed to be brought down to earth.

"Quite frankly, Doug, I have to tell you what I think about that, for your own good."

"Sir?"

"It's time we talked about the difference between fantasy and truth, because if you don't learn it, and learn it soon, you're going to be in real psychological trouble."

"Dr. Kautsch, I—"

"You're too smart, Doug, to keep kidding yourself this way. It just isn't healthy."

"But—"

"No, let me speak for a moment." Kautsch let the pad fall into his lap. "You arrive in camp, feeling insecure and you conspire somehow to cut your hand, so you can go to the nurse's station, get some sympathy, perhaps from a woman nurse. A nanny is called a 'nursemaid' in some quarters."

"I didn't—"

Kautsch waved him off. "You get the sympathy that you so desperately need, the attention—"

"I didn't conspire to cut my hand—"

"No?"

"No. It was an accident."

"Oh, come on, Doug. You don't really expect me to believe—"

"I didn't do it!"

Doug rose from the chair. He was about to say, "Jimmy cut me with a knife because I didn't believe him," but stopped. Jimmy's warning came to his mind: "Ever hear of a guy named Dr. Kautsch? Who do you think runs this camp?" He stared at the man across from him.

"Doug?"

He shook his head to clear his thoughts. He could feel the vibrations starting, deep, deep within him. But he pushed them away. It took all his will to do so, but eventually he felt them recede.

"It was Allie," he said softly. "He had this tin can with the lid half off. When I tried to take it away from him, the lid cut my hand."

"Why didn't you just say that?"

"I was afraid that—" Doug bit his lip. "—that my dad would take him away from me."

Kautsch spoke softly. "Doug, I'm sorry that I was so rough on you. I knew you were lying when you first said that. I'm afraid it offended me. I knew there was a good reason, but I'm human too." He smiled. "That's not easy for me to admit."

Doug just nodded.

"I told you once before, that I see everything in psychological terms. These visions—vibrations—that you experience, I believe they all have a psychological basis. You are a very smart young man and that is to your credit. But your intelligence often masks deep hurts, powerful emotional conflicts that get translated in very strange ways. This is nothing to be ashamed of. When you saw your father with that woman at the fete, it was a natural response for you to run away, to retaliate by accidentally starting the fire at the chapel. When you get here, you seek comfort with the nurse. When you are faced with a new group of boys and a counselor who reads from Paradise Lost, you respond by imagining that you helped write it—so it raises your importance in their eyes. When you meet someone who was there when your mother died, you see yourself as guiding your mother to Heaven. None of these are bad things, Doug. But someday you're going to have to face up to the fact that they are the creations of a very fertile mind that is protecting itself from the pains and fears of ordinary life. The sooner you realize that, the sooner you can use this amazing intellect of yours in a more constructive and appropriate fashion."

Doug felt like stone. He heard what Kautsch had just said, but his mind was going over all the things he had told the man. If this had come up a week earlier, he might have agreed with the doctor, or even allowed a certain amount of doubt about his feelings. That is, if he hadn't known absolutely within his heart that the light existed.

In this stunning moment, he realized that Jimmy had been right. It wouldn't be an easy admission, but he would tell him so, first chance he got.

"Thank you, Dr. Kautsch." Doug stood up. "I need to think a bit. Do you mind?"

Kautsch shook his head agreeably. "I understand completely."

"Thanks."

"I'll be here overnight, Doug. If you want to talk again before I leave in the morning, just come knock on the door."

Doug mumbled he would do just that, then headed out.

He spotted Jimmy on the volleyball court and called him over. Jimmy came over.

"Hey, Doug. What's up?"

"You were right."

"About what?"

"About this camp. About Dr. Kautsch. All of it."

Jimmy took this in. "You ready to help?"

Doug said yes.

"Good." Jimmy looked around. "Meet me here during the free period, I have something to show you."

"What?"

"You'll see."

"Okay."

"And Doug—"

"Yeah?"

"Don't wear yourself out today."

"Why not?"

"Because tonight we're taking a canoe ride."

"Where to?"

"To see a friend of yours."

"Who?"

Jimmy smiled. "You'll see."

Chapter Twelve

Doug followed Jimmy through the woods, relieved to be away from camp and Dr. Kautsch, who watched everything he did and everywhere he went. His teammates had wondered at Doug's irritability, but hadn't said anything about it. Doug could not tell them how embarrassed he was by the man's presence. Even when some made jokes about the guy with the sun block all over his face, swatting clumsily at mosquitoes, Doug was in no humor to laugh with them.

Miss Slimson seemed in a bad mood also. Several times he saw Kautsch speaking to her, but she would only shrug. Kautsch's face turned red and he returned his attention to Doug.

He and Jimmy met behind the mess hall during the free hour. Chas and Augie volunteered to watch Allie, who strained at the leash to go with his master. The first time they tried to walk away, Doug had to return to Allie and order him to stop whining. They decided then and there that Allie would stay in the Walden Pond bunkhouse with one of the orphans. That way he wouldn't wake anyone up when Doug and Jimmy sneaked out of their respective beds into the night.

"So, what's the big secret out here?" Doug asked when they were out of earshot of the camp.

"We found a cave."

"Yeah? That's pretty cool."

Jimmy nodded. "Well, it may come in handy sometime. Since you've joined us, I thought you should know about it too."

Doug didn't quite understand, but he didn't say so.

"See," Jimmy continued. "If we ever need a hideout, or a place to just cool our jets, we've always got this cave."

Five minutes later, Jimmy was pushing brush away from the side of a hill. He stopped, pointed down to the lake. "See that old dock down there?"

"Yeah."

"If you ever get lost, just keep going around the lake until you see that dock, then just come straight up here."

"Gotcha."

Jimmy cleared the last few branches away from the side of the hill. Then the opening and the old warning sign came into view.

Doug whistled. "That's cool."

Jimmy grinned. "Wait till you see the inside."

He grabbed a flashlight from a sack by the front of the cave and motioned Doug to follow him. As they walked inside, Doug whistled again.

In one corner was a stack of canned goods, obviously stolen from the mess hall. There was a small table, a few chairs, and an old rug in the middle of the space that created sort of a living room.

"This is what you guys have been sneaking off to do everyday?" Doug asked.

"Yep. Pretty cool, huh?"

A sleeping bag was rolled up in one corner, and there were various other supplies.

"I don't get it," Doug said. "Why would you need these things at camp? I mean, things aren't so terrible there, are they?"

"No, in fact, they're pretty cool, as camps go." He reached up and lit a candle stuck in the rock face. "But if things ever go really wacky at home, we can always come here and hide out, while we figure out what to do."

"Hm." Doug wandered around, touching here and there, wiped the dust off on his pants. "You really think you'll need it?"

"Who knows?" Jimmy flopped down into one of the chairs. "But I'd rather have it than not. What did Kautsch say that made you change your mind?"

Doug snorted. "He's just a jerk. He doesn't believe anything I tell him. I figured out today that he's just been pretending to listen to me. He twists stuff around, just to make me look bad. If I felt he was right, I wouldn't mind. But he seems awful creepy to me now."

"Well, consider this your safe place, too."

"Thanks." Doug sat across from him. "So, who are we going across the lake to see. This friend of mine?"

Jimmy's face beamed. "Where did you say your Nanny went this summer?"

"To Scotland."

Jimmy waggled his finger. "No she didn't."

Doug sat up. "Nanny's across the lake?"

"Yep."

"Wow." He shook his head. "What's she doing there?"

"From what I saw, she's been watching you through a telescope all summer."

Doug laughed. "Leave it to Nanny."

"What time do you guys get to sleep?"

"Probably ten tonight, because of the campfire."

"Okay, ten-thirty, you meet me at the dock."

"What about Allie?"

"Chas'll be there to take care of him."

"Cool." He grew serious. "Jimmy?"

"Yeah?"

"Thank you."

"You're welcome." Jimmy gave him a thumb's up. "Just remember, if you get lost, just follow the lake until you get to that old dock."

Doug gave him a thumb's up back.

❦

Grumpy sat across from Janina. He had thought of a hundred different ways to begin the conversation, but now that she was sitting right there, he couldn't find the words.

"Why don't you just say it, Grumpy?" Janina's eyes were bright.

"Say what?"

"That you know about what is going to happen to me. That you are worried. That you don't know what to do next." She smiled. "Do you think I didn't feel terror when I knew my mother was leaving us?"

He sighed. "No, I'm sure you did."

"I will tell you, dear friend. You have given me a great gift. With Sally, with these girls. Meeting Fiona. You have made the last moments of my life quite beautiful. I hope you understand that."

He felt tears, fought them. "I know what you have given to them. How different their lives—all of our lives will be because of you."

"You are so funny." She laughed, a tinkling. "You are so convinced that you are not worth knowing, that you will not accept good when you hear it."

"This conversation is not about me."

"You are so serious!" This produced another laugh. "If you do not become more happy, I will not tell you about the heart-moon that we both carry."

Now he smiled, but wanly. "I don't think I want to hear it if your telling me means what I think it does."

"Stick your hand out, where I can reach it."

He did. She slapped his hand.

"There, now you have been punished. Do you feel better?"

He rolled his eyes. "Please, don't make fun of me. Do you understand how much this hurts?"

Her tone softened, but grew more serious. "Yes, I do. But I also know how valuable the pain is. I know where it will lead you, and it is a good thing. I will not take it away from you."

"But there is so much more to do, to get ready for. So many things are happening. We need you to stay."

"No you don't. Besides, I could not change this if I wanted to. This is the time. The future belongs to you, as much as it belongs to them." She pointed in the direction of the girls' rooms. "Now, are you going to hear about the heart-moon, or shall I have Valka write it down so you can read it."

"Tell me." His voice was filled with defeat. Her eyes sharpened. He sat up. "Please tell me. I'll be good, I promise."

"You told your mother that, but you didn't keep your word." She smirked. "You think I don't know you, after all this time together?"

"All right. I'll be as good as I can be."

"That's better." She reached for her cup of tea, hooked it with a gnarled hand and sipped. "The heart-moon amulet signifies the combination of blood and spirit. It has great power, but only to those who are descended from one family. However, simply having the heart-moon does not mean that one can use the power. Your mother and my mother were given the amulets by their mothers. My mother gave mine to me. Yours to you."

"What does the amulet do?"

"The amulet does nothing. It is a legacy from the beginning of our family, many lifetimes before."

"So, you and I are really related?"

"Not in the blood, but in the spirit."

"I don't think I understand."

She nodded. Thought for a moment. "You know that souls live many lifetimes here on earth. Each follows a path. But each soul is part of a family of souls. Souls of the same family, when they encounter each other, often recognize each other, without knowing exactly why. They just feel a kinship, a closeness. On the other hand, there are occasional encounters with a person whom you immediately feel is an enemy. This is not rational in human terms, but very much so in spiritual terms."

"You mean, like light and dark?"

She shook her head. "That is too facile a description. It is more karmic in nature than that. I do not have all the answers, but when the world was created—you remember the story of Cain and Abel, from the Bible?"

"Yes."

"That is the best way I can describe these two kinds of souls. One creates, one kills. One is full of love, the other full of hate. They are drawn to each other when they find each other in a lifetime. This is not conscious. Neither one knows consciously how to find the other. That is a magnetism that is beyond my knowing. But when it happens, there is a battle. Each time the creative soul wins, there is less evil in the world, for a time."

"And when the killing soul succeeds?"

"Then there is more evil." Janina's demeanor saddened.

"What of the heart-moon? How does that enter into this?"

"The evil soul obeys the moon and fears the heart, which is the only protection against the killing one."

"So, if and when I encounter this soul, I will be protected?"

She shook her head. "It is not for you. It is to be passed on to someone else."

"To Peter? I don't believe he would accept it, much less believe in it."

"No. It will be passed on to your blood. You will know when the time arrives."

"When I die?"

"Perhaps. But you will know when the time arrives."

He understood.

"And your heart-moon. Who will you pass yours on to?"

She smiled. "I already have."

Grumpy's eyes widened. "If you have passed it on, then you do not need to die."

"Give me your hand."

He hesitated. "I don't need you to slap me again."

"Give me your hand."

Reluctantly, he reached out to her. She cupped his hand with her gnarled fingers, moved it to her lips and kissed him. Then she caressed her cheek with his hand, kissed it again and released it. He looked at her.

"It is that soon?"

"When the girls leave here, I go also."

"And what if I lock the doors and refused to let anyone go?"

"Then the state will come, call you a dirty old man, and you will go to jail for kidnapping."

He smiled, his eyes smarting.

"But you must promise to do something for me, after I am gone."

"Yes?"

"You promise?"

"I promise."

"When I am gone, you must find Valka a good woman to marry. He has given up his life to care for me. He has done too good a job. He must replace me in his heart with a woman who will teach him of the world instead of the sky."

Grumpy thought about Valka's confession in the car. His tears. "He will not do it. He loves you too much."

"He will do it if his brother Grumpy tells him to."

"I'll try."

"And Grumpy, my beloved friend. There is one other thing I must tell you, and you must hear it without denial."

"What is that, Janina?"

"Your mother, Sarah. She is very proud of you."

He had promised himself that he would not cry in front of her, but it was a promise he could not keep. She pushed the electric button and rolled past him. Her hand brushed his face, then she was gone from the room.

At dinner, Kautsch sat at a table surrounded by young campers. They were respectful at first, but the novelty quickly wore off and they soon fell into their normal banter. Throughout the meal, he watched Doug, who wore his baseball camp backwards, as was the fashion. The boy showed none of the effects of their conversation earlier in the day. He seemed bright and happy.

Slim, on the other hand, alternated between glowering at Kautsch and smiling at Doug. In the years that she had worked for him, with the exception of dark moods just before her period, she had been emotionally consistent toward him. He could not understand why she was shunning him. The appointment book at the clinic had been full, and they hadn't had sex all week. He couldn't quite write off his feelings as simple horniness, though. She was definitely within herself, in another place, as far as he was concerned. He didn't like it one bit.

At the head of Doug's table sat a black man wearing spectacles. He seemed quite jovial with the boys and they obviously revered him. Kautsch mentally went down the list of the employees, but couldn't remember anyone named Clint.

The one called Tex walked in halfway through dinner, called out, "Sharpe, you have a telephone call." The black man rose to answer it.

Kautsch mulled this through. Clint Sharpe. Where had he heard that name? Then it hit him. Clint Sharpe was the alcoholic school teacher he'd assigned to Avisson. It was a joke, assigning the Lincoln look-alike to the black man. But how did he wind up here?

He made a mental note to ask Merriwether, then glanced at Slim. Again, she was looking at Doug affectionately. If he didn't know her better, he'd think they were lovers. He looked at Doug. The boy had filled out, just a few extra pounds, but he definitely was going to look like his father, except for his blond hair—.

Kautsch dropped his fork. Several boys stared at him, continued their banter. He reached under the table to retrieve it, came up red-faced. Not from the exertion. He didn't know what might have happened between Doug's father and Slim, but he was now convinced that something had.

He caught her eye, silently mouthed the words, "After dinner," and jerked his thumb in the direction of the infirmary.

She nodded.

Then several things seemed to happen at once. Doug tripped and spilled his tray of food on another boy. There was a tense moment as it appeared there would be a scuffle. But the boy just helped Doug to his feet, cleaned himself off and order was restored. However, in the confusion, one of the other boys had cut himself accidentally. Everyone gathered around while Slim put a napkin on the cut and led him up to the infirmary to clean the wound and bandage it.

Kautsch paced out front, angry at the delay in confronting her. Then, when the boy came out, Doug and several other boys met him. Doug made a big show of letting the boy have Allie for the night to help him get better. The boy beamed, accepted Allie's leash as if he had just won an Academy Award.

The delay meant he wouldn't be able to talk to her until after the campfire. Kautsch muttered something about Neanderthal rituals, but followed everyone down to the clearing.

He watched dolefully as Slim joined in the singing of the dreadful songs. Then came a veritable amateur night of twangy guitar and not-so-bad violin. But Kautsch was on the verge of exploding.

He desperately wanted to walk over and turn Doug's baseball cap around. Perhaps that would hide more of the face that looked so much like his father's.

But he didn't. He joined in the final chorus of "Kum-baya, my Lord, Kumbaya," then made polite noises as the boys drifted away to their beds.

BIRTHMARK

Slim walked silently, fiercely, ahead of him toward the infirmary. When they arrived, she pointed to the chair.

"Just wait awhile. Let everyone get settled down. You look like you're going to yell and I want you to cool down before we talk. No sense having the whole camp in on this."

He sat. He twiddled his thumbs. He knew she was right. He hated the thought that anyone else might become aware of his anger. He was a professional. He had gone through twelve years of school and six years of intensive therapy in preparation for his work.

But none of that had prepared him for the feelings that surged through him at the moment.

Cool down? Right.

Luckily the night was a scorcher. No breeze. Just heavy humidity that stuck to the boys' skin as they slipped beneath the sheets. Everyone commented on how much they were going to miss having Allie in the bunkhouse, but Doug reminded them that the dog would comfort the wounded boy from Walden Pond and they quieted.

"What if a bear comes in the night? Who's going to warn us?"

"Hell, you forget how smart Allie is." Doug laughed. "If a bear ever came in here, he'd be the first one out the window."

They all laughed and settled down to sleep.

In twenty minutes, Clint started snoring and Doug slipped out of bed, grabbed his clothes and tiptoed out the door.

He stayed close to the buildings on his way to the dock, but stopped for a moment near the infirmary. Dr. Kautsch and Nurse Slimson were talking. The psychiatrist didn't sound very happy. Doug would have continued on his way if he hadn't heard Kautsch say, "Of all people, why did you have to pick Peter MacBrayne?"

"What?" she replied.

"Hell, bad enough you have to cheat on me, but with Doug's father? Right when we're so close to—?"

"I didn't plan to sleep with the man, it just happened."

"It just happened," mocked Kautsch.

Doug sidled up to the window, making sure to stay out of its light.

"So you think you're going to replace the Nanny that easily, Slim? You think that fucking his father is going to make Doug think you're his mother?"

"Don't be crass. It isn't like that at all."

The meaning of the conversation sunk in quickly. Doug pushed his hat off his head and stepped on a box to see inside. Miss Slimson and his father? Replace Nanny? Was that why his father sent him to camp? So he and Miss Slimson could—"

The wooden box cracked and Doug jumped off. The voices inside stopped. He ran for the dock, staying in the shadows. He knelt behind a tree stump and watched as Kautsch opened the door of the infirmary, looked around. When he went back inside, Doug scurried the rest of the way.

Jimmy was waiting for him off to the left, the rope holding the canoe in his hand.

"Geez, what took you so long?"

Doug tried to catch his breath. "Clint took longer than usual to go to sleep."

"Well, hop in."

Doug did. Jimmy pushed them off the beach and they started out toward the light across the lake. As they paddled, Doug replayed the conversation he'd just heard in his mind. He wished he could confide in Jimmy, but despite their budding friendship, he just didn't feel like he could fully trust him yet.

At least Nanny was close. Just a few minutes away. She would help him understand all this. He glanced at Jimmy in the moonlight.

"How did you find out Nanny was there?"

Jimmy chuckled. "I'd seen someone watching us from the balcony the past week or so. So I pretended to fall overboard yesterday and went ashore there."

"Really? So Nanny knows we're coming?"

"No. Some gypsy brought us back in a motorboat."

"Nanny and a gypsy?" Doug was stupefied. "I don't get it."

"Neither do I." He paddled a bit to the left to get on course. "I told you, something weird was going on in town."

Doug nodded thoughtfully.

"Keep quiet," Jimmy said and they pulled closer. "When we get there, I'll drop you off and stay thirty or forty feet to the right of the dock. Over there." He pointed and Doug nodded.

"When you come back, just whistle—but real soft. I'll whistle back."

"Okay," Doug whispered.

~

There was a soft knock on Grumpy's bedroom door. He closed the book he had been reading, walked over and opened it.

"Come, quietly. It is Janina," Valka said. "We need to take her to the hospital."

"Damn, okay." He hurried to grab his keys off the bureau. "Did you tell Fiona?"

"Yes, she has gone to awaken Mrs. Schmidt. We don't want to bother the girls until morning."

Grumpy nodded. "Are you okay, Valka?"

Valka shook his head. "No."

"Where is Janina now?"

"I have put her in the car. Hurry."

Grumpy tucked in his shirt, followed him quickly past Mrs. Schmidt, who was wearing a robe over her nightshirt. They walked to the car. Fiona was in the rear seat, holding Janina's head in her lap. Grumpy got behind the wheel.

Valka stood beside the car.

"Come on," Grumpy said.

Valka shook his head.

"I cannot watch her die."

Fiona rolled down her window, "You and I are family now."

Valka nodded, leaned inside to kiss Janina's forehead. "Go in peace, my sister," he whispered. Tears rolled down his cheek.

Grumpy threw the car into drive and sped away. Valka straightened, looked up to the sky. Walked slowly into the house.

Doug had nearly made it to the house when he saw the two men approach a car in the driveway. The light in the car flashed for a moment when one of the men climbed inside. He saw Nanny already there.

He started to call her, but was afraid. He crept closer, hiding behind a hedge. Nanny rolled down her window, spoke to the man beside the car.

"You and I are family now."

The man nodded. Then leaned into the car and hugged her.

Doug stopped in his tracks.

The car sped away, the man looked up to the sky, then went into the house. Doug saw his face in the porch light. He was swarthy.

His mind whirled. He couldn't make sense out of anything that he had heard that night. His father and Miss Slimson. Now Nanny and this gypsy fellow?

And where was Nanny going so late at night?

He turned and went slowly down to the beach, turned right and walked thirty or forty feet. Whistled.

No answer.

He whistled again.

Nothing but silence.

Jimmy had done it to him again. When was he going to learn not to trust that bastard? He looked across the lake. The camp seemed miles away. A fierce rage rose in his chest. It was all so obvious now. His father had wanted him out of the way, so he could pursue Miss Slimson without Doug around. He couldn't believe Nanny would betray him. But he'd heard it with his own ears. She and the gypsy were family now. That could only mean one thing.

Everybody had somebody else now—except him. He had to think this through. What had Kautsch said to him that afternoon? He needed to learn the difference between reality and fantasy.

He had taken his mother to the light, hadn't he? Yes, he knew that.

As he trudged along the water's edge, a bright flare, perhaps a falling star, shot across the sky. He felt the vibrations start, but he didn't care anymore. The last thing he remembered was the old dock Jimmy had pointed out. It wasn't so far away. And the cave was just up from it. If he could only get there, he'd have a place to sit and think.

Ogmios again sat on his stool in the middle of the circle of stones. There was a stranger in the sky last night, he thought: a dreug—a traveler—a comet. Could it be an ill omen? He wondered, then dismissed it from his mind and watched the sun rise from the sea between the two stones directly to his left. He made his daily mark on the tablet.

Returning to the stones that evening at sunset, Og watched the sun sink behind the hills, between the two stones directly to his right—straight across the circle from the morning's sunrise. Taking his flint, he drew a diagonal line across the mark he had made that morning. This "X" marked the time of the Vernal Equinox.

As he returned to the top of the cliff, Og had a strong, intuitive sensation of being watched. There was an unfamiliar scent of trouble in the air, so strong that it momentarily blinded him and deadened his sense of feeling. The swiftly approaching nightfall held its breath. Og bent down to pick a small sprig of white heather for luck.

There can not be anything to that scent, Og thought, I must be mistaken. The rest of my Clan is on the ledge, or in the cave, preparing the evening meal. But the comet, his intuition and his nose had been right.

As he forded the burn, two strangers attacked. They had what seemed to be horns growing from their heads. The fight was short and swift. Og's brute strength enabled him to strangle one of his assailants. But the other escaped, running across the peat hags, toward the hills in the north.

After the battle, Og returned to the top of the cliff. He saw Oengus in the dim twilight below. Their minds exchanged thoughts.

The Chief called the clan outside. "Our seer hath seen again. And even now the days equal the nights in length. Sleep well, my friends, tomorrow will indeed be busy, for it is then, we will begin the spring planting."

Oengus said nothing to the clan of what Og had telepathed about his encounter with the strangers. He wanted to get the details first.

At daybreak the next morning, Oengus accompanied Og to the edge of the burn where the stranger's body lay.

"Horned-headed men, you said, Og?" said the surprised chief, "Why, he wears only a helmet, adorned with the horns of a bull."

"So I see, my Chief Oengus, but the light was dim last evening and I was taken by surprise."

"What do you think we should do?"

"Nothing comes to me. With his yellow hair and beard, the man is not of our kind. I can not think why they would want to attack me."

"Nor can I, unless they had been spying and thought you had discovered them. Do you think we should post a guard at the top of the upper cliff? Perhaps there are more of them."

"Yes. I think it would be wise and prudent to do so."

A few days later, Og awakened one morning, greatly disturbed. Fionnaghal noticed his distress.

"My dearest Og," she began, her dark, soulful eyes searching his creased, craggy face, "What troubles you? Please tell me."

"I did not sleep well. Last night, I dreamed of a fleet of long, narrow boats which came from the sea, and up Loch Tuath. Their coarse sails had strange markings on them. Rounded discs were attached outside the hulls, alongside each oarsman. Then the scene shifted. I saw a horde of long-haired, yellow-bearded men scaling our lower cliff. Each man wore a helmet on his head. Horns protruded above the temples."

"Oh!" cried out Fionnaghal, "A dream in color has always been prophetic! What will you do?"

"Chief Oengus will decide."

Og rose and found the Chief already awake, a grim expression on his face. They traded an ancient verse without speaking:
"Beware the longboats so swift and thin,
Fair-haired warriors ensconced within.
Rough sails and strong oars do thus propel
Satan's angels from the depths of Hell."

Og and the Chief went to the mouth of the cave, crossed the wide ledge, and looked out over the sea, under the low, heavy overcast sky. Tiny specs on the horizon grew larger and drew ominously closer as they watched.

"They have come," thought Og.

"Yes," thought back the Chief, "Five boats means one hundred warriors, and we are but forty, not counting the women and the children."

"It is the women and the children they want. There is still time to hide them."

"No, Og. It is already late. We must prepare for the attack. Sound the alarm."

Og got his horn, climbed quickly to the top of the cliff and blew three short blasts. Every clan member stopped what he was doing and scrambled onto the ledge. They piled stones and boulders at the edge of the cliff, high above the shore of the loch. They carried red hot coals from the cave and started little fires about every ten paces along the rim of the ledge. Precious logs and heavy branches were piled nearby. The women herded the children into the cave. Standing behind the piles of rocks, the men of the clan waited, watching in silence as the boats drew closer.

There had been invasions from over the seas in the past. Many ballads about them had been passed down through the generations. The songs had taught them how to fight.

The clan prepared well for the attack, but not well enough. The warriors approaching by sea were only decoys.

The escaped spy had told his chief the exact location of the clan cave, giving an accurate count of the men they would have to fight, the animals that would be theirs for the taking. He described the young clan women in glowing terms. A master strategist, the king of the invaders planned the attack cunningly and carefully. He was in no hurry. He split his force and landed most of his men in the cove on the north shore of the island. He left a token force to guard the boats and rafts they had brought to carry the prisoners and animals.

The land army waited until Og's horn warning cleared the pastures atop the upper cliff. Then, unseen by the hapless defenders on the ledge, the invaders quietly positioned themselves on the high ground, above the clan cave. Og and Oengus had not considered the possibility of an attack from above and behind.

The outcome was quickly evident. Oengus, wishing to avoid senseless slaughter, put his weapon down and raised empty hands high above his head, in abject surrender. A great moan rose from the clan, and the fighting stopped.

The Chief motioned to Og, who knew what he had to do. In front of the downcast defenders, he raised to his greatest height and addressed his brothers.

"Weep and wail not, my friends. You have lived good lives and, the Gods willing, your souls will live beyond the death that these strangers have brought us. Our Chief has prevented the worst part of a terrible slaughter: Our women and children will survive; so all is not lost."

Og turned to the chief, sorrow written on his craggy, wrinkled face. Good bye, my Chief, he thought, Woe that neither the second sight nor the stones, provided a warning of this catastrophe.

Good bye, Og, my good friend, thought back the Chief, You have long served us well. Fret not. Then, turning to his people, he spoke.

"Fear not, my friends. They will take good care of our women and children. And mind you—our seed in some, and the blood of our children, will ensure that the essence of the clan will survive. Be brave, my men, as you prepare for the death that surely comes upon us—now."

With heavy heart, Og went into the cave to say goodbye to Fionnaghal and their children. Suddenly, his heart became much heavier: He smelled an acrid odor wafting from the massive stone urn among the fire stones. Og looked at the bare stalks of hemlock lying in disarray on the ground. He saw the more potent roots and fruit were missing.

"What have you done, Fionnaghal?" he called, a tremor in his voice, "Surely you haven't—"

"Og, my dearest. I've saved the last for you," she offered a stone cup, half full of the deadly drink.

Og shook his head and watched the lethal poison take its paralytic toll of the children, the baby first to go.

"But why?" was all he could say.

"Because," stammered Fionnaghal, "I will not allow my children to be taken into slavery—or worse! And without them, my life has no meaning."

He stood, open-mouthed, witnessing a crime worse than being taken as slaves. A mother killing her own offspring.

"My darling Og," gasped Fionnaghal, as the poison began to take effect, "For me, there is no future."

That said, the paralysis overcame her. She collapsed onto the straw by the children, her dark soul-less eyes rolling up, to stare at the cave's bleak ceiling. Her spirit departed.

Og stood a minute, said a sad, silent prayer and bade goodbye to his family. Then, heaving a deep sigh, he walked to the mouth of the cave, just in time to see the chief of the invaders, a huge, bloody cudgel in his hands, heading for Oengus. The rest of the victors had formed a circle around the two chieftains and began to chant in unison, faster and faster.

"Konge Knekke, Sire! Kill! Konge Knekke, Sire! Kill! Konge Knekke, Sire! Kill! Sire! Kill! Sire! Kill!"

There was no doubt that this dark warrior was the leader. He stood out above his blond compatriots, from the tips of his fine boots to the top of his raven, curly locks. Not a horned helmet, but a small, jeweled band circled his head. Compared to his men, his clothes looked almost tailored, and his face carried a dark, arrogant, superior sneer. But the most unusual feature was his black beard. Neatly combed and trimmed, it fairly glistened in the light. Most astonishing of all, it was parted in two, just below the chin—each part curled up and away from the other, toward his ears.

The invading King raised his mace. The club descended with full force, striking Oengus behind his right ear, crushing his skull and killing him instantly. The cruel King then stepped over Oengus' lifeless body and delivered the blow that broke the spine of what little resistance might have remained in the defenders' minds. Gloating, he put his hands on his hips and laughed.

Upon a signal from Konge Knekke, the victorious invaders separated the victims into two groups. The young women and the children were moved to one side. The rest: all the men, the old women over twenty-five, and the infirm, were lined up and beheaded on the spot. The victors rolled the bodies over the edge of the cliff into the sea and carried the severed heads into the deepest recess of the cave, where they were covered with soon to be blood-soaked sand.

The storm descended on Mull in a fury. Lightning flashed, stabbing the land. Thunder reverberated, echoing back and forth between the dimming, hazy hills. A glorious rainbow appeared in the north: a half-circle of gorgeous color.

The Clan of Crackaig had fallen. The secret of their stone circle would die with them.

Og was the last. He could hide in the cave, but he had no reason to live. His family, dead. The clan males, annihilated. The survivors, bound for slavery.

Og stepped into the light. He called to the leader, this ugly Konge Knekke. "Come, you bastard. Bring your cudgel so I may join my family and my friends."

The ugly, split-bearded man could not understand Og's words, but he heard the challenge. He roared, ran toward Og with the club upraised, brought it down on Og as fast as lightning. Og felt the thunder of the blow throughout his entire being.

He laughed at the man and an instant later, died.

The vibrations slowed, stopped. Doug looked at the old dock. He knew he could probably reach Camp Shambala in another hour or so. But he needed to be alone and the cave was much closer. There he could think, then sleep. Jimmy had been right about the hideout.

Doug pushed through the bushes and found the cave. Ogmios had died by leaving the cave. Doug had found a reason to go inside one.

Kautsch awoke suddenly at the sound of men calling "Doug!" throughout the campground. He staggered out, met Slim at the infirmary door.

"What's going on?" she asked.

"Don't know." He grabbed the black man by the arm as he was hurrying past. "What's going on?"

"Doug MacBrayne is missing."

"What?"

"He wasn't in his bed this morning and no one has seen him since last night."

"Shit," Kautsch said.

"What's that?" Clint Sharpe said, pointing just below the window of the infirmary. He walked over, picked up a baseball cap. "This is Doug's." He turned to Slim. "Did you see him last night?"

She exchanged a glances with Kautsch. "N—no. I heard a sound outside the window, but that was just before I went to sleep. I thought it was only an animal."

Sharpe glared at Kautsch. "You're his therapist, right?"

"Yes, I am." Kautsch tried to look dignified in his robe.

"Was Doug upset by anything you talked about yesterday?"

Kautsch reddened. He did not appreciate being interrogated in such a stern manner by a mere camp counselor. But he held back from what he wanted to say and just shook his head.

"No, in fact he was better than I anticipated."

"Shit," the black man said. He waved to Merriwether, who hurried out of his bungalow. His wife, MerryLou, held the screen door open. "Over here," he cried, "We've got to organize a search."

When they were out of earshot, Kautsch sidled up to Slim. "Still think you did the right thing by fucking the boy's father?"

"Don't try to blame this on me, Leon. You're the one he overheard last night."

"Oh, don't worry," Kautsch said, re-tying the sash on his robe. "I know exactly how I'm going to deal with this." He started away, stopped, turned. "Get dressed. We've got to help find this poor, psychologically-distressed boy before the bears eat him."

"Fuck you, Leon," Slim said, then hurried inside the infirmary and slammed the door.

☙

Sally awoke with a start. In her mind, the dream lingered. In it, Janina had come to her, kissed her on the cheek, told her she loved her and would always be with her. Then—and this was the part she couldn't wait to share when they discussed their dreams—the crippled woman, now whole, walked out the door and was engulfed in the bright light of the hallway. Just before she vanished, she did a pirouette, arms raised high above her head.

Sally took the heart moon from her dream catcher, put it around her neck, then threw off her covers and walked into the hallway, dim in the morning light.

Valka was sitting at the dining room table. his eyes red with tears, shoulders slumped.

"Valka?"

He looked up.

"What's the matter?"

"She is —" he could not finish.

Sally knew. In her bones, in her heart, in her mind. She waited for tears, waited for a terrible piercing of her heart, but none came. She nodded, walked over and put her arm around his shoulders.

"I love you and I will always be with you."

His eyes opened wide, startled. "You—you saw her, too?"

"Yes, Valka." Sally caressed his hair, kissed his forehead. "I saw her go into the light. She is safe now. She is in no more pain."

He nodded, but the water still flowed down his cheeks.

"And Valka—" her smile burned through his fog, "Where she is, she is dancing. Her legs are strong and I saw her dance, right into the light."

"This you saw?"

"Yes, Valka."

He noticed the heart-moon around her neck. A small smile worked its way across his trembling lips. He reached for it, kissed it.

A car stopped on the gravel drive. Two doors opened, closed. A moment later, Grumpy and Fiona walked in, together. They saw Valka and Sally.

"My sister dances in heaven, doesn't she?"

Fiona nodded, her eyes red.

Valka stood, hugged her. "Do not be sad, my new sister." He pointed to Sally. "She saw Janina dance in the light. That is good enough for me."

Obviously exhausted, Grumpy took Fiona's hand. Valka led them to the dining room table.

"You eat. Then sleep a little. Tomorrow night is the full moon. We will dance with my sister then. Now, you rest."

When Doug heard the sound of the searchers off in the distance, he quickly went outside the cave and hid the entrance with as many branches and bushes as he could find, then wriggled inside and waited for them to pass.

He wrapped the sleeping bag around his shoulders and sat, Indian-style. He felt the vibrations coming on, but resisted. He didn't want to be disturbed by anything. The pain from the night before had diminished and he realized that for the first time in his life, he was completely alone. It was not a bad feeling.

Not that he wasn't angry or confused. He just wanted to think without interruptions. The faces of all those he knew in his life swirled around him. Some with love, some with something much less than love. As he let his mind drift, he could feel the pull of what others wanted for him, from him. Everyone else seemed to want something. He couldn't discern what each was after, but the sensation of their pull on him was profound.

Then the pattern began to form: Every time he saw or experienced something good, he got in trouble. The first time the vibrations came, with Grumpy's Christmas abacus, his father got angry and they had their boxing bout. When he discovered Father Hector out in the chapel, his father grew angry again. Now that he remembered taking his mother to the light, Dr. Kautsch turned on him.

Why would such miraculous visions be met with anger and rejection?

He glanced around the cave. In one corner was one of Jimmy's drawings. Not a drawing really, but an embellished version of the Mole insignia, executed in his funny hieroglyphic code. Despite Doug's anger at the orphan, he had to admit that Jimmy always managed to get him, one way or the other. He couldn't really deny that.

He stared at the drawing. Jimmy hadn't wanted Doug to tell anyone that he really knew how to write. He had conned everyone into believing it, from the start. No one ever messed with Jimmy. Whatever Doug's nemesis was doing with his artwork, he was able to keep it to himself because no one could decipher it.

Doug smiled. Unwittingly Jimmy had given him the answer. All Doug had to do was not to let anyone know what was going on when he had one of the vibration "attacks." The trouble never came from the attacks, but from his *telling* about them.

For a moment he considered doing a victory dance but he could still hear voices nearby. It wasn't the time to show himself. There was still the problem of Nanny and her new family, whatever that meant. No. If he emerged from his cave, they would discover him and he might never find out what was going on across the lake. He would hang tight until darkness fell, then sneak over to the big house. Who knew when he would have this much freedom again? Might as well savor the delicious feeling, while it lasted.

❦

Supper at Camp Shambala was a desultory affair. Only Jimmy ate with unusual gusto. He studiously avoided Chas' searching glances, shaking his head whenever his friend managed to catch his eye. The rumor spread throughout the campers that the State Police had brought a special water unit to troll the lake, looking for the missing camper's body because an overturned canoe had been found late in the afternoon.

Sharpe looked pale. The psychiatrist's face remained red and he chewed his nails incessantly. Merriwether paced outside his front door.

Several rescue vehicles arrived followed by a large, fancy car that had kicked up dust all the way to the mess hall. The counselors met outside, having left instructions for the boys to finish dinner.

Peter MacBrayne's voice rattled through the woods from the moment his feet hit the dirt. Jimmy smirked as the man tore into Merriwether, then Kautsch—everyone within range of his anger.

"You and you great fucking ideas," he shouted at Kautsch. "I told you I wanted to get rid of the Nanny, not my son."

"This is not the time or place—" Kautsch began.

"Don't give me any of your shit. I want my son found, and quick."

At that point, Nurse Slimson pulled Peter aside, whispered to him.

"Doug overheard what?"

Then the police took over. Two men in wet suits headed for the dock. The knot of adults followed. The boys all raced to the screened windows to have a better look. Chas grabbed Jimmy's arm, pulled him aside.

"What the hell did you do with Doug?" he whispered.

"Nothing. We went across the lake; then I left him there. You know where he is, as well as I do."

"The cave?"

"Probably."

"What about the canoe?"

Jimmy smiled. "Nice touch, eh?"

Chas sat heavily on a bench. "Man, you're going to get us killed, you know that?"

"Naw," Jimmy sat on table in front of him. "This is Papa MacBrayne's show."

"Yeah, for a little while, until they figure it out."

"Figure what out?"

"Easy." Chas snorted. "They're so dumb. All they have to do is let Allie go. He'll lead them right to him."

"Shit." Jimmy scratched his head. "You're right."

Chas brightened. "You know, we would look like real heroes if we suggested it."

Jimmy nodded. "Yeah, we would. Only one thing."

"What's that?"

Jimmy stood, walked over to an empty window. Chas followed him.

"What, Jimmy?"

"We could do that, sure." He turned and faced Chas directly. "But who wants to look like heroes to this bunch of assholes?"

"So what do we do?"

"Easy." Jimmy grabbed a handful of potato chips. "We wait until they figure it out all by themselves."

Sadness is a cruel tool. In one person, it is an awl that etches lines of pain into the soft clay of the face. In another, grief breaks through the subtle dams that have checked unwanted emotion from spilling into view.

Stunned as he was by the night's events, Grumpy could not help but be amazed by the effect of Janina's death on the small group that made up the Nanny camp. Whereas he had expected Valka to be disconsolate, the brother hurried from Mole to Mole, from Fiona to Mrs. Schmidt, offering encouragement and assurances. Fiona, whom Grumpy had expected to be stoic, wept unabashedly. The Moles themselves—tough, street-wise creatures as advertised— were, with the exception of Sally, traumatized. Their eyes were red and the nectar of pain flowed down their young, apple-cheeks as if their very flesh had been wounded.

Sally sat by the window, occasionally glancing over at the group, but her eyes gazed mostly at the rising moon, which lit the night with only mildly less brilliance than the sun that had just slipped below a crown of thick pines.

His own reaction surprised him. When his mother died, Grumpy got drunk, blind drunk. He wept into his martini, called it "drowning the olive." His wife's death had produced the same desire for drink, but at the time, he was ashamed that he could not cry. Now, he had no desire for booze. His eyes remained clear, while he watched the others grieve. Nor did he feel the need to comfort anyone. The grief was probably good as it became part of their experience. It was necessary and in a strange way, fulfilling. Perhaps it might have been different for him, he realized, except for Janina's kiss on his hand. He could still feel her lips, and the gentle brush of her love for him still resonated against his fingers.

There seemed to no comfort for any of them, until the wail of Valka's accordion began to fill the room with a powerful tone of musical mourning that matched their feelings, lifting their eyes to his figure in the doorway.

"Come," he said, with a tilt of his head, "we must sing her to heaven, while the moon is bright."

They trooped outside to the bare circle by the dock where Valka had spent the afternoon stacking wood. Valka never stopped playing, but asked Grumpy to light the pyre with a gasoline-soaked torch. As the flames rose toward the moon, Valka's playing rose in a frenzy, encouraging the others to dance for Janina,; to give their legs to her, to pound the ground and remind the earth that their sister and friend had been on the earth, had gone from the earth and was now sailing to the moon on Valka's musical space craft. Louder and faster they danced, shouting and singing wordlessly, but replete with spiritual meaning.

Grumpy wove in and out among them, linking arms when arms appeared, softly touching faces when they arrived in the firelight. At times, the music disappeared within the loud crackling of the fire. At other moments, the heat from the flames unnaturally cooled the sweat that ran down his face like tears. Ordinary sensations dissolved into ethereal images. At the height of the dance he reached out and she was there, a red flame that took his hand and moved past him. He braided his way through the other dancers and met her again and again. She was laughing, her eyes bright with the music and the fire.

And they all saw her and took her hand in turn. And they all laughed with her. This dance of death that had brought her back to life had an enlivening effect upon the dancers, each of whom experienced it in his own way.

Doug knelt at the edge of the dock, watching the strange ritual. His eyes, dark and hurt, followed Nanny. How could she betray him this way? He barely heard the music. There were the Moles, Petrovich from the cafe. Doug's legs ached from the bramble tears of his journey through the dark woods. His head ached from lack of food. All spun angrily before his eyes. What right did they have to be so happy when he hurt so?

Then he heard a familiar barking behind him. He turned to see a flurry of flashlights. There was no place to run or hide. He could either approach the dancers or turn to face his pursuers. Vibrations buzzed toward him from several directions. He launched himself toward the pyre. He had to tell her, before they caught him. She had to know how much this hurt.

Just as he was about to reach her, something caught between his legs. There was a loud yelp and he looked down to see Allie, his leash tangled at Doug's ankles. Flashlights emerged from the woods. A shout. Father? His body pitched forward. A familiar pair of arms grabbed him. More cries. A shouting confusion. He looked up into her eyes.

"Doug?" she cried, hugging him to her.

"Nanny," he whispered.

Then, he was yanked away, looked up to see his father's dark scowl.

"Dad?"

"What the hell is going on here?" Peter MacBrayne thundered.

The two groups converged. Policemen, Camp Shambala counselors, the Moles, the swarthy man, others, all swirled together.

"I should have known," his father shouted. "Every time he pulls a stunt like this, you're involved."

Nanny reached for him.

"It wasn't her, Peter," Petrovich said. "Doug just showed up out of nowhere."

"Who are you?" Then a dark silence. "You—Father!"

"Grumpy!" Nanny cried.

Doug stared. Petrovich. He looked into his father's face and saw sheer hatred. He turned to look at Petrovich.

"You're my Grumpy?"

The man nodded. A shard of ice stabbed Doug's heart. He shrugged off his father's grasp, walked up to the bearded man.

"You're my grandfather?"

"Doug, I'm sorry. I couldn't say anything be—"

Doug spun on his heel, started away from the group. He bumped into Jimmy, who was also staring at Grumpy. Then, Doug turned to Nanny.

"You knew?"

"Not—"

"You knew!"

He wanted to faint. Wanted the vibrations to come and carry him away. But nothing happened. There was no escape. He walked to his father, took his hand.

"I want to go home, Dad."

Startled by the request, his father drew him aside. "You've got some explaining to do, young man."

Doug shook his head. "I don't understand anything, Dad. I really don't."

Horrified, Fiona stood stock still. The flames flickered behind her, but she felt nothing. She watched Peter and Doug walk several paces away, stop. Peter turned.

"You're fired, Miss McLean!"

"But, you promised—on your wife's—"

"Don't even mention my wife, you—you—" His throat bulged ominously, almost dislodging his flapping bowtie; then, he pointed to Grumpy. "And you. If I even catch you near my son, after this, I'll—I'll—"

Then he turned, guided Doug away.

Grumpy's arms hung at his side. Fiona's pain rooted her to the spot. She could not go to comfort Doug. The Shambala group headed away, except for Jimmy. Grumpy looked at him, took a step forward. Jimmy stepped back, shook his head.

"Liar," he said, then hurried after the rest.

A black cloud covered the moon.

Chapter Thirteen

The snow was gone but the wind still carried the last frigid perfume of winter. Peter noticed the slight rouge in Doug's chilly cheeks as the boy teed up his ball.

"I'm going to out-drive you, Dad."

"Don't worry about hitting it far, Doug," Peter replied, "Just concentrate on your swing."

Doug grinned, nodded and bit his lower lip while he addressed the ball. A smooth, powerful swing. Swoosh-thwack! The ball flew straight down the middle, landed just short of Peter's and rolled a few yards past it..

Peter's eyes bulged. He gulped. Tried to suppress his protesting ego. "Good shot." was the best he could manage.

Doug looked carefully at his father, wondered if the pattern of "anger following good" would surface. For only a moment, he wished he'd sliced the ball into the woods.

But Peter managed a wry smile, as they walked down the fairway. "I don't know whether that was luck, or skill, Doug. It doesn't really matter. This is our first outing this season; so let's enjoy it." Inside, Peter thought that perhaps Doug had inherited some of his competitiveness, after all.

He observed Doug out of the corner of his eye as they walked in silence toward their second shots. A year ago, he would have never guessed father and son would be golfing together, on the first day of Spring. For once, his bowtie rested, calm as a clam.

Funny how ordinary life has a way of dulling the sharp edges of the past. After enough time has passed, the gleam diminishes from the brightest memories, leaving at best a dull luster. On the other hand, dark and frightening experiences, viewed over a long stretch of ordinary months, hold less power over the observer and bring less fear with each passing stretch of regular time.

BIRTHMARK

For this insight, Peter had to thank Dr. Kautsch and the sessions at the doctor's new office at the orphanage. Although Doug seemed somewhat less vivacious than before, he was also almost normal. Gone were the smart-aleck retorts, the constant challenges to Peter's authority. Gone also, thankfully, were the strange fainting-spells that had created such distance between father and son.

Indeed, it finally had come to roost that the Scottish nanny must have been the cause of all the trouble, for, from the day eight months earlier, when Peter had fired Miss McLean, Doug had been a model, if somewhat muted, son and student.

Not that Doug was completely out of the woods yet. Kautsch had made that abundantly clear. Fourteen and a half years of tutelage from the Nanny had etched deep patterns that might take years of therapy to undo. For that, Peter steadfastly took full responsibility. In his grief over losing his dear Felicity, he had allowed the Scot far too much leeway over his son's upbringing and well-being and, even though it had apparently been caught in the nick of time, the years they now faced undoing the damage would be something they would share, accomplish together.

Peter had even gone so far as to curtail his relationship with Miss Slimson. It grieved him greatly to do so, but he considered it part of his fatherly duty not to endanger Doug's mental well-being by continuing the romance. Kautsch had helped here, also. Even offered to fire the woman if Peter felt it would be too uncomfortable either for Doug or himself to meet her in his office.

After a frank discussion, Doug had impressed Peter with the suggestion that their situation should not impact a single mother, raising a child.

Peter had not been impressed with his father's and Miss McLean's shallow attempts to maintain contact with the boy, even after Peter threatened a court-imposed restraining order should they persist. Well, they had a surprise coming to them.

He smiled when he saw Doug's second shot fly straight at the green, but it fell short, to the right of the sand trap, leaving an easy pitch at the pin.

"You keep that up and you'll be Junior Club Champion in August."

"I'd rather just play with you." Doug blushed. "If that's okay, Dad."

A gust of wind watered Peter's eyes as he took the seven iron from his bag. He wiped his eyes with his sleeve and lined up the shot. He wished the feeling would last forever: this alien, transcendent sense of well-being and love that surrounded him. He looked up, down, concentrated.

At the top of his back-swing, the beeper in his back pocket hummed. Peter flinched, and watched with dismay as the ball snapped to the left and rolled soundlessly into a huge bunker.

"Damn it," he muttered.

He jammed the club into his bag and checked the beeper.

"Who is it, Dad?" Doug asked as they trudged toward the green.

"Jim Knapp, from our research department." He pulled his cell phone from his bag and dialed. "Knapp, Peter here. What's up?"

He listened while Knapp complained that he hadn't been consulted about an article on UltraLeather, in an industry trade magazine.

"Jim, look, you stay there. I'll see you in a couple of hours. I know all about that article, I authorized it." He rolled his eyes at Doug with a wry grin. "Yes, I did. We have to start the ball rolling on this, to raise the investment capital to produce it, remember?"

He mouthed to Doug that he would be finished in moment.

"Jim, you don't understand. In order to build the equipment to test larger batches, we first have to raise the money. Chickens and eggs, Jim. Chickens and eggs." He laughed. "No, Jim, I don't suppose chickens go out on a limb to lay their eggs, but we do. Look, I'll be there as soon as I can. You hang tight."

He replaced the phone in his bag.

"If it's important, Dad, we can—"

"No, let's finish our round. Though it does mean I won't be home until late, tonight. Will you mind eating with Mrs. Fitch?"

"No. I'll just hit some balls until dinner. Then I have my homework, anyway."

"Good boy." Peter ruffled his hair. "One thing you have to learn if you're ever going to take over Douglas Industries, son. There's business and then there's golf. You can do a lot for your business during a round of golf, but you can't do anything about your golf game at the office."

Grumpy placed the phone gently in its cradle, slumped in his desk chair and sighed. Fiona looked up from the coffee bar.

"What's the matter?"

He rubbed his eyes, looked up. "That was my lawyer. He says I have no recourse with regard to my stock."

"So Peter wins?"

He nodded. "Lock, stock and corporation."

She walked over, put her hand on his shoulder. "I'm sorry."

He patted her hand. "I guess I'll have to put off that round-the-world trip, for another year or so."

"Didn't you already take that trip?"

Now he smiled. "One of the best things I ever did. And the worst."

She grabbed a dishtowel, waved it threateningly. "You can stop that talk right now. Just because things look gloomy, doesn't mean they won't straighten out later. You have no idea how important those gifts you sent to Doug were to him."

"It's not just that." He rubbed his throat. "Everything seems so—so lost, right now. Neither of us can talk to Doug—you have to admit that's my fault."

"No I don't."

"Yes it is. And Jimmy. He trusted me, maybe the only person he ever trusted, and I let him down with another one of my self-protecting lies."

"What would you have done differently?"

"If I'd known what—"

"But that's the point. How could you have known? How could anyone have predicted all this?" She leaned closer, forced him to look into her eyes. "Do you know why fortune tellers can't see their own future?"

"No, why?"

"For the same reason you can't change the past. If you could, you probably wouldn't do any better than you did the first time."

"I don't think I like that answer."

"Good." Fiona turned and headed toward the coffee bar. "That means it's probably true."

He evil-eyed her back.

"And get that silly look off your face," she said without looking. "It's nearly time for the Etiquette Hour."

Grumpy swiveled in his chair. "Is that this afternoon?"

"Yes, why?"

"Abe's coming by."

"Metaphysical chess?"

"Ha, ha."

"Well, you boys can play in the back room. I'll call you if we get busy."

Grumpy stared at her. A warm sensation of well-being washed over him. For the moment, the confusion of the past year fell away. He was filled with gratitude that Fiona was here with him. He realized he was happier here in the store with her than he had ever been at any time in his life.

"What are you staring at?" Her arms were folded in front of her.

"Uh, sorry, just thinking."
She peered closer and he blushed.
"Thinking?"
"You know me, metaphysics—"
"Yes, I do know you."
He grinned. Now she blushed. The door chimed as it opened. They both turned to see a man in a very bad suit.
"May I help you?" Grumpy stood.
"Yes, does a Fiona McLean work here?"
"Yes, that's me." Fiona smiled. "What can I do for you?"
The man reached into his jacket and pulled out his wallet and identification. "U.S. Department of Immigration and Naturalization Service. I need to ask you some questions."

Jimmy stepped from the school bus and followed the other students through the open gate. He nodded at the guard who was busy checking names. A moment after he was past the guardhouse, the gate slid closed. Jimmy's shoulder's hunched as the metal clanged.
"Lyden!" the guard called after him.
"Yeah, what?"
"Kautsch wants to see you in his office."
"Tell him I have to finish my homework." Of course, Jimmy's homework was a series of nude drawings, the latest in a series he called Perfect Women.
"You tell him," the guard said. "He said he wanted to see you as soon as you got off the bus."
Jimmy kicked a stone in the driveway and slowed his step. Every second he had to spend with the bearded, leering psychiatrist seemed like an eternity. He couldn't understand how MacBrayne could stand spending an hour at a time with the man, three days a week—at the orphanage, no less. Having MacBrayne come to Jimmy's home, albeit an institution, seemed a violation of his boundaries, which Kautsch was always talking about.
Shit, leave it to MacBrayne to come out of last summer, smelling like a rose. Sucking up to his old man had really done the trick, apparently. He was free as a bird, while Jimmy and the other orphans had returned to discover their home had been turned into a prison. Oh, the buildings had the same look, but between the double-wired fence, the guardhouse at the gate, and the new construction, that looked more like pillboxes than residences—the casual elegance of the Douglasville Orphanage was definitely gone, forever.

He dragged himself up the stairs and walked through the administration wing toward Kautsch's office. At least he would get to see Nurse Slimson. She was worth the trip. The boys at the home all had theories about her and Kautsch, but Jimmy had scoped the two of them out with his painter's eye and came up with nothing. As far as he could see, she chilled right out when the Doc was near her.

"Hello, James," Miss Slimson said as he entered. "Dr. Kautsch is waiting for you."

"Hi, Miss Slimson." He stopped at her desk. "What does he want?"

She shook her head. "Not a clue."

Jimmy nodded, tapped on the inner door.

"Come in."

He peeked in. Kautsch waved him to a chair. Jimmy sat. Kautsch shuffled through some papers on his desk for a whole minute; then reached behind him and pulled out, of all things, Jimmy's portfolio.

"Want to tell me about these?"

"Just drawings." Jimmy shrugged.

"Rather explicit, if you ask me."

Who asked you? thought Jimmy, remaining silent.

"Especially for a boy your age. Care to tell me who your models are?"

"Nobody. They come out of my head."

"Out of your head—" Kautsch smiled. "I won't deny they're very good. But I'm afraid we have a problem."

Jimmy clenched his teeth. Kautsch looked at him.

"You have to understand that we are responsible for all aspects of your development. And when we detect potential psychological, uh, situations, we have to take precautionary measures."

Jimmy rolled his eyes. "More tests."

Kautsch nodded. "Yes."

Jimmy stood, extended his hand. "Are you gonna keep my drawings?"

"Yes." Kautsch shook his head. "They will have to stay in your files."

Jimmy's eyes narrowed. He turned, walked out the door, gave Nurse Slimson a quick salute and went into the hall. A plan was forming in his head. He had been stupid to leave those drawings in his room. Warden Kautsch had his sneaks go through the rooms regularly. Old Grab-Your-Knickers probably scammed them. Well, it was time to begin fighting back.

Outside in the fading daylight, he glanced at the new buildings. They were nearly completed, and they certainly were not designed for orphans. Whatever he came up with, it better be good and he better figure it out quickly. The way Kautsch operated, Jimmy was sure one of those new rooms was waiting for him. He just knew it.

❦

Kautsch watched the door close and chuckled. He leafed through the boy's portfolio again, selected his favorite pose of a naked young girl with one foot on each of two uneven parallel bars. He rolled it up and secured it with a rubber band. Suitable for framing, he thought, and for inclusion in his private collection.

This Jimmy would make the perfect client. Art by mental patients was selling like hotcakes. Maybe bring it out as a coffee table book.

He reached behind him and extracted a file marked "Triggers." The orphans had proved more normal and malleable than he had first anticipated. There was still time, though, as the construction was off schedule. He lifted James Lyden's page from the file and made a notation: "Take away art materials." His finger drifted down the list of Triggers. Each indicated its own anti-therapeutic device: For a molested foster child, pushing the envelope on getting her to discuss her father would be a sufficient trigger. Another had a phobia about spiders. Time for a visit to a pet store next week. Claustrophobia meant getting locked in, accidentally of course. Low self-esteem would get an orphan a series of tasks that couldn't be accomplished and a dressing down for failure. The beauty of attacking these weaknesses was the ease with which they could eventually be healed and sent out, assuring a constant flow of successes until some really sick kids could be found.

The phone jangled. He pushed the speaker-phone.

"Yes?"

"Larry Clark on one."

"Thank you, Miss Slimson."

He removed the phone from its cradle and leaned forward. "Hello, Larry."

"Dr. Kautsch. We go to trial next week. Just wanted to make sure you had everything ready, at your end."

Kautsch opened another file. "Got everything right here. Psychological evaluation, facility update, recommendations—the lot."

"Has Avisson been briefed?"

Leon rubbed his nose. "Uh, well, he's handling the psychological profile. I'll be testifying as to our recommendations."

"Doesn't that split the effect? I mean, the jury's going to have to absorb two testimonies that way. Juries tend to dislike psychiatrists, in the first place."

"Larry, I've testified hundreds of times." He jotted a quick note to himself. "In this kind of situation, juries tend to hate spending money on a psychological criminal. So, Abe testifies to the man's mental capacity; then I come in from the administrative standpoint and show them they will save money, if they find him incapable and let us house him."

There was a short pause. Clark continued, "But the question of disposition, normally comes after the verdict. I don't see how I can work it into the trial portion."

"You figure that one out, Larry. You're the lawyer. You want to win this, right? Well, your job becomes easier if the jury knows what's going to happen to this lunatic. Most communities live in fear that a hometown criminal will be caught out-of-state, brought back into their community and eventually released there. This way, they'll know exactly where Sabey is, all the time."

"I still don't know—"

"Come on, Lar—show them the economic benefits. Let's say it costs a hundred thousand dollars a year to keep him penned up. Every politician thinks that every tax dollar spent in a community, gets multiplied at least six times as it flows through the cash registers around town." Leon grabbed a cigar and lit it. "Keeping this money in Douglasville may be the only positive thing Sabey has accomplished in his life. Hell, he's better than a new road project."

"Of course, all of this is dependent on me getting a loony verdict instead of murder one."

"I don't see any trouble with that."

"You don't?"

"Of course not. This is Douglasville and justice here, like everywhere, starts with politics—"

"Yes?"

"And politics here, like politics everywhere—"

"Yes?"

"Starts and ends with money."

There was a long pause, a loud exhalation of breath.

"Still there, Larry?"

"Yes. I was just thinking, you would have made an incredible lawyer."

"I take that as a compliment, Larry."

"Oh, it is, don't worry."

"Larry?"

"Yes, Leon?"

"Did you take care of that other little matter we discussed?"

"Yes. Anonymous tip, just as you suggested."

"Good."

"Leon, does this have anything to do with our case?"

"Larry. Everything has something to do with everything."

"Can I quote you?"

"Go ahead." Kautsch laughed. "It's a free country."

"How's Abe doing?" Fiona asked.

Grumpy cracked open the office door, to peek into the store. He smiled. Abe had been flustered when first asked to take over the Etiquette Hour, but once Grumpy told him the news about Fiona and the fact that the Etiquette Hour was so-named to keep parents from wondering about the metaphysical content of the discussion, he had launched into presenting astrology to the girls with relish.

"He's doing fine," Grumpy said and returned to his chair across from Fiona. "Looks like it's the most fun he's had in years."

"He's not talking over their heads, is he?"

This brought another smile. "These girls knew Janina. No one will ever talk over their heads as long as they live."

For a moment, Grumpy thought he might have made a mistake by mentioning their departed friend, but Fiona's wince lasted only a moment.

"Do you think Peter turned me in to Immigration?"

"I would say that's as good a guess as any."

She nodded, sipped at her tea. "I really don't know what I would do if I returned to Scotland, except to try to land another Nanny job."

"You could, but you'd increase your misery tenfold."

"But nannying has been my life—"

He shook his head. "You've been a mother for the past fourteen and a half years. Doesn't matter how old the child you might care for, everything it does would remind you of Doug at that age. You'd cry yourself to sleep every night."

She started to retort, stopped.

He looked closely at her. "I thought you said the crying stopped."

"It did—" she played with her spoon— "sort of."

Big sigh. He reached across and took her hand. For once she didn't resist. His tongue blocked the siphon of his speech, all the words clogged in his throat. It was the perfect moment to ask her. She would have had to say yes, to stay near Doug. She would have done anything to accomplish that, even marry an old wreck like him. But the words wouldn't come. He looked into her eyes. She was ready to be asked. It was just that simple. Yes, would be the only answer. But he couldn't say the words. His eyebrows knitted. Was he afraid? No. Did he not love her? Of course he loved her. She had taught him love.

Then what was it?

"It's okay, Grumpy. I'll figure something out."

Why wouldn't his tongue work? "F—Fiona. I—"

"Sorry to intrude." Abe stuck his head inside the room. "But the girls wanted to tell Fiona goodbye. Make sure she's feeling better."

"I'm coming." Fiona extracted her hand from Grumpy's and rose. She stopped at the door, turned to face him. "It really is okay."

She straightened her dress and pasted a bright smile on her face. The girls sat expectantly, hands in their laps.

"Did you enjoy speaking with Dr. Avisson?"

They all nodded.

"Fiona?" Susan raised her hand.

"Yes, dear?"

"I don't get it."

"What don't you get?"

"Well, it seems like everything we've been learning—from last summer to this afternoon—all this stuff about life, and the stars, and astrology...oh, I don't know."

"Keep going, Susan." Fiona leaned against a tabletop. "You were doing fine."

"I just don't understand why we can't learn about these things in school. They seem a whole lot more important than who crossed the Delaware River to attack the Rednecks."

"That's Red Coats, dear." Fiona lifted her hand to still the giggling that broke out. "Where I come from, the Red Coats are considered quite close to rednecks; so I don't think you were far off."

"Suzie's right, Fiona." This from Sally. "We've learned more about life—about how to live our lives and be happy—from you, than all the years we went to school put together."

"Why, my goodness, girls. I don't know what to—" Fiona's hand fluttered to her chest. She caught her breath. A large tear trickled down her cheek.

The stricken girls rose at once and surrounded her.

"Are you okay, Fiona?" They asked in a jumble, clumsily caressing her arms and hands.

She pulled them close to her, awash in their funny perfumes, sensing the occasional pinch of a buckle here, a spiked earring there. They were the oddest young ladies she had ever met, but she loved them much more than she had realized, even a moment ago. She glanced over and spied Grumpy and Abe watching from the office door. She smiled, released the girls.

"Okay, ladies. I want to say a few things, and I want you to listen and not say a word."

Theirs was one unified and solemn gaze.

"Good." Fiona took a deep breath. "First, I want you to know that I have been happier teaching you than anything I have ever done before. And that you, too, have taught me a great deal."

Sally started to speak, but caught herself.

"I'm going to tell you a hard truth. I was in that office for the past hour or so, feeling terribly sorry for myself, because the immigration people want to make me go back to Scotland." There was a audible, negative murmur, but Fiona silenced it with a wave of her hand. "They may win, these immigration people, but that doesn't mean I'm going down without a fight."

"But what can you do?" Darla couldn't stop herself.

"Do you all remember what Janina taught us, about the most powerful weapon on earth?"

The mere mention of their departed goddess heightened the moment for all. Sally raised her hand. "She said it was love, Fiona. But are you gonna love the Immigration people?"

"Well, not exactly. But I can say something that I should have said months ago, but was too proud and stubborn to admit, to myself or to him." She turned to face Grumpy. "I love you, Peter Douglas-MacBrayne, Junior, and I think you should marry me."

꙳

Grumpy stared open-mouthed at Fiona. Then he looked at Abe, who smiled.

"Methinks you would do well to say yes," Abe whispered in his ear. "Or these young lionesses might just tear you limb-from-limb."

Grumpy's mind flashed to the time, only minutes before, when he had been unable to make her the same proposal. Why couldn't he speak then? What had he been waiting for? What had held him back? Across the room, behind the girls and Fiona, a soft glow emanated from the table where he did his readings. The glow from Janina's crystal ball increased, until he realized that it was the omen, the answer he had been waiting for.

Fiona followed his gaze, as did all the others in the room. The glow brightened, casting shards of fiery reflections around the room. Who was he to argue with Janina and another of her miracles?

"Yes, Fiona McLean," Grumpy said softly. "It would be my honor to have you as my wife."

The brilliant sunset was just about gone, but Doug persisted. The feel of the club in his hands was smooth. The whiffle balls fairly flew into the darkening sky. Allie ran like a greyhound after them.

Doug knew there was homework to finish but the mindless swinging, losing his thoughts in the motion, letting his body just flow, was too seductive to leave just yet.

Everything seemed so far away. The moment of absolute solitude in the cave the previous summer had taught him a valuable lesson. Until that moment, Doug had belonged to everybody, anybody else but himself.

Something had snapped in the madness of that moment around the campfire. All the anger and hurt he had been feeling went down some invisible drain within him. Oh, there were still moments when he thought he could hear Nanny's footsteps outside his door. But he knew it was his imagination. Even the revelation that Petrovich was his grandfather didn't matter anymore. Sally tried to explain some crazy tale of a woman in a wheelchair and a legacy, but he couldn't follow any of what she said. Might as well have been Swahili. He saw her as a stranger now, not as the girl who had kissed him in the family graveyard. A big part of him had remained inside that cave, lying dormant in the sleeping bag cocoon. A caterpillar, waiting to grow wings.

Allie dropped a ball behind him and Doug glanced at the hulk of the old chapel. No, not all of him was in that cave. He would love to have a few more kisses with Sally, speaking Swahili or Burundi, but that could wait. Then he had to grin. The first time he told his dad he was going to hit some whiffle balls, the look on his face was priceless. Doug saw him watching from the kitchen window, and noted the relief on his face when Doug hit the balls away from the chapel.

All that craziness was gone. He didn't believe Dr. Kautsch's psychobabble about stress and trauma-induced hallucination. When backed against the wall, Doug had told him about the vibrations in the cave, Ogmios and Fionnaghal, how she poisoned their children. There was nothing in Kautsch's entire experience to explain away that one. He had just nodded, with that "I see" look of his and made some notes. Father Hector, the Chinese monk, all had seemed more real than that. Finally, Doug stopped fighting Kautsch. He didn't fight anyone anymore. Not even Jimmy. Something happened to Jimmy that same night. But where Doug found a place of quiet within himself, Jimmy seemed to be growing tighter and tighter, every day.

❦

Clint marked his place, put the book down and stretched when he heard Mandy's footsteps in the living room below. He glanced at his notes, nodded. A good day's work. The summer camp had jarred something loose within him and he had taken up his Ph.D. thesis again, with renewed vigor and insight.

"Clint?"

"Be right down, honey."

"That's okay, I'll come up."

He smiled as he listened to her inevitable routine. First she hung her coat in the closet, then went into the kitchen. A woman's habit, he supposed. Next came a quick face-rinse in the downstairs bathroom. Cleaning off the germs and smells of the hospital. Then a turn in the living room, not to check on Clint's housecleaning, but more to see the nest. All subconscious.

Now her footfalls on the steps. A brief pause beside Candy's picture. Not so subconscious. Today, she lingered. It usually meant he would hear about some child who was ill, who had been admitted to the hospital. Couldn't begrudge her that.

This time she stayed. He walked to the hallway, looked down at her. She was staring at Candy's photo, whispering softly.

"Honey?"

Tears streamed down her face. His heart lurched and he quickly moved to her side, a jolt of terror stopping his breath.

"Mandy?" He put his arm around her waist, pulled her to him. She molded herself against him, sobbing. "Sweetheart."

But she couldn't speak properly, only cry. As she poured her pain into him, Clint could not help but realize how weak and ineffectual he was. How he had depended on her for the past few years and how this torrent felt so endangering to his heart. But he remained quiet against his racing thoughts. Phalanxes of questions rose and receded. He stayed still, held her as tightly as he could.

They stood glued to each other for minutes. Finally, the sobbing slowed, she wiped her wet cheeks against his shoulder, then finally looked up into his face. The tears threatened again, but she held them back, swallowing hard.

"What is it, sweetheart?"

"I was going to tell you first, but thought—" she glanced at the picture again. "I guess I didn't realize that I would feel guilty."

"Guilty?"

"Funny." She nodded, sniffled. "Didn't even know it was in there, you know?"

He didn't know, but nodded anyway. Couldn't speak for fear of what she would tell him.

"Tonight, driving home. There was the most amazing sunset. Like the sky was on fire." She brushed a stray thread from his shirt. "And I thought it would be okay, you know? Then, coming up the steps, when I stopped and looked into Candy's eyes, I knew it would be okay. But this guilt rose up out of nowhere. Well, not nowhere, I suppose. From inside me. How could this be happening, after—"

"Mandy." Clint could not contain himself any longer. He took her hand, gingerly he thought, but she winced, so he loosened his grasp. "Honey, you're scaring me. What happened? What's inside you?"

She smiled, gazing at their daughter's picture. "Sorry, dear, one of those girl things, I imagine. Caught me off-guard that she would have known already, that's all."

"What!" Clint cried. "What does she know? What do you know? What's the matter, honey? We'll get through it. You'll see. We can get through anything—together—really."

She caressed his cheek, her eyes as full of love, as if he had just spoken the most wonderful poem ever written.

"I love you, Clint."

Misery struck. Now he knew she was dying. His eyes closed, he felt his balance start to give way. Vertigo. He groaned.

"Honey?" Mandy pinched his wrist. "Hang on there, Clint."

"Oh, God, Mandy."

"It's not bad, I swear. Clint. Come back, honey. Don't go away."

His eyes fluttered. He thought for a moment he would vomit. Then she was kissing him, covering his cheeks and mouth, his eyes, with soft kisses. Her lips were warm. He swallowed, took a deep breath.

"Clint," Mandy said, directing his eyes to Candy's picture. "What was it she wanted more than anything in the world. Do you remember?"

He wouldn't have remembered his name, if she hadn't spoken it at the moment. He shook his head.

"She wanted a little baby sister, remember?"

Somewhere off in the dim past, he remembered her having sung a little song, practicing for when she had a little sister to take care of. He nodded.

"Well—"

"Well, what?"

"That's what I'm trying to tell you." She straightened his shoulders, held him away from her for inspection. "You're going to be a father again."

"You're—you're not going to die?"

"Of course not, whatever made you think that?"

It didn't matter. Not a bit. He gathered her close again, covered her face with kisses. He could hear tinkling laughter off in the distance. The distinct smell of brown sugar wafted around him. And a little voice, whispering a name. He strained to hear it. Finally was able to repeat it.

"What?"

"Her name."

"What name?"

"She just told me her little sister's name."

"Who—wha—" Mandy shook her head. "We don't even know if it's a girl yet."

"It is." Clint smiled. "Canditu. That's what she wants us call her. Canditu."

Chapter Fourteen

A marriage late in life is normally a quiet song, often without words, hummed in the silent corners of two well-traveled hearts. But when the hearts belong to two such as Grumpy and Fiona, two who have touched the lives of so many others, the song becomes an anthem to the secret hopes and unspoken dreams of many.

Fiona watched with amazement as the Moles took on the roles of bridesmaids, molding the traditional wedding-accessories to their own, eccentric visions. She laughed as one-after-the-other arrived with pictures of potential wedding gowns, clipped from magazines. Fiona had neither the figure nor inclination to sport either a leather dress as one suggested, a backless plasticine affair, or a lesbian, hemp tuxedo, offered by a magazine with the unlikely title of Grunge Q. She drew the line at the mere mention of a tattoo and announced there would definitely be no discussion regarding the piercing of any part of her body.

Undaunted, cheerfulness unwavering, they came at her with suggestion after suggestion, regarding everything from cake to punch to the shower. The honeymoon was another verboten subject, though the hard-bitten cynics' eyes never failed to glaze over at the slightest hint of post-nuptial antics.

Not that the men were any better. The combined news of the imminent marriage and the Sharpe's forthcoming bundle of joy had turned Clint, Grumpy and Abe into giggling schoolboys. They would huddle in the corner, laughing and playing chess, whispering together, until a customer approached, which made them paste on serious expressions.

Immigration would not bend on the matter of Fiona's leaving the country. She could indeed marry Grumpy, but would have to leave the country and return again. The couple decided to honeymoon in Dundee, thus satisfying U.S. Government regulations and allowing Grumpy to see where Fiona had lived. A message was sent to Valka, but his last known address was a post office box, in the former Yugoslavia.

All seemed harmonious and blissful, except for three question marks on the guest list. The first was Jimmy Lyden. Grumpy called the orphanage and left word for Jimmy to please call him. He received a call from Dr. Leon Kautsch, who suggested they meet before the message was passed along. Grumpy agreed.

The second and third were Peter MacBrayne III and IV, respectively. Once again, the task was Grumpy's. He sent a short note to Peter at the office, asking to meet, but hadn't heard, with only a week to go before the wedding.

❦

America had grown accustomed to serial killers, but the trial of the Scorpio Slasher put Douglasville on the map. Larry Clark's unusual defense brought media coverage from as far away as Japan in the East, to Helsinki in the West. The ordinary citizens of Douglasville were suddenly thrust into the spotlight, forced to become experts, at least of their own opinions. Whereas Abe Avisson maintained a relatively low profile, Leon Kautsch became a veritable beacon of Astro-psychological information.

"The Age of Aquarius of the sixties brought us to an age filled with new considerations, new opportunities, new challenges," he told one battery of microphone-wielding reporters. "There is hardly an American who doesn't check his or her horoscope at least once a week and I would venture to say that the vast majority check theirs every morning. Even Nancy Reagan, the First Lady, has a personal astrologer."

"Do you use tarot cards in your evaluations of clients?" One Italian reporter asked.

"Let me make one thing clear," Kautsch smiled, "The Douglas Foundation is a psychologically-based treatment-center. We study the workings of the human mind, in response to the world. It's not our job to say that astrology is true or real, but rather to study the effects of such beliefs on the activities of the people we treat. In other words, astrology is not one of our tools for observation or treatment, but we do recognize that people are influenced by their beliefs, regarding their astrological situation. When those beliefs lead to aberrant behavior, such as in the case of Mr. Sabey, the defendant, then we must take those into consideration."

Abe watched the performance with mild disbelief. All these months he had been skirting around the issue with his Director, never imagining that Kautsch was absorbing what Abe was saying, much less being able to fashion it into such a coherent statement.

He expressed his wonder during a break at the Crystal Cafe. Grumpy laughed. "What did you expect? Kautsch is a chameleon. One moment he's blue to hide in the sky, the next red, invisible against the flames. All I know is that our business is up sixty percent."

Abe sighed. "But it's become a circus, all these people rushing to appear intelligent about a subject they knew nothing about two weeks ago."

"Abe, you have to look at the larger picture."

Avisson lifted his cup before sipping. "Tell me, Socrates, of this larger picture."

"Methinks I should check my coffee for hemlock." Grumpy grinned. "It doesn't matter what brings people to consider new ideas, so long as they do. Sure, these neophytes don't know a thing about astrology, but they are suddenly seeing it in a totally different light. You know yourself how people suddenly relax when they find an answer to a problem in their life that they haven't been able to conquer on their own. Look at Alcoholics Anonymous. I know what it's like to be a drunk, the hopelessness of it."

"You went to AA?"

Grumpy nodded. "For a little while. It wasn't for me, but I saw people who had no hope of ever changing their lives, suddenly grasping a handhold. They found a moment of rest from being out-of-control and used that moment to change their behavior—eventually their lives. The same can happen here. If people see that their astrological chart has certain ingredients that have tripped them up in the past, they can at least stop blaming themselves for the moment, understand that they were born with certain liabilities, relax, and then find a way to go on."

"Believe me, I understand that part."

"Do you? Abe, the thing that AA, astrology, past lives, all have in common, is the sudden understanding that the person is not alone—they are part of something, a process or scheme larger than themselves. Call it God or the Universe, or Gaia—whatever—but they are not alone. And most important of all, there are reasons for their presence here on earth. Doesn't matter if they don't completely understand the reason; grasping that moment of being connected to it all is the first ray of hope." Grumpy leaned closer across the table. "It's because they suddenly understand that the God, or wisdom that created everything, created them as well, and they are part of everything, too."

"And our boy Sabey? What hope does he have?"

"Hitler taught us that charisma is not enough for political leadership. Great evil is a terrible thing. But from what I can see, great good always rises up against that evil. The Holocaust has been a moral signpost for decades, just as slavery reminds us that individuals have to make up their own minds about other human beings. Governments cannot do it for us."

"I ask again, and Mr. Sabey?"

Grumpy sighed. "As far as I can see, he's done his terrible deeds. All we can do now is protect the public from him."

They sat in silence for several minutes. Abe's face was contorted. Lincoln could never have looked so sad.

"What's wrong, Abe?"

"I'm an astrologer, not a psychic, but I have a bad feeling about my patient."

"Meaning."

"Just a feeling, and a sense of confused responsibility." Abe looked up at the ceiling. "You see, I don't believe in the death penalty, not at all."

"I would have been surprised if you told me anything different."

"Yes. Well, here's the problem. From my work with him, I think he's right—"

"That the Universe has been instructing him to kill?"

Abe shook his head. "Not in the least. The ingredients are there: the rising signs, several trines, conjunctions—all the potential that he made choices about. No, I think he's right, about dying at a certain time to make sure he comes back with different feelings, a different life-potential."

"Really?"

"It amazed me. I charted what I could of his past lives. There is a direct path to this lifetime, almost a bee-line—if you will—to the kind of person he has become. It's very subtle in other respects and I have no idea what kind of karma is involved, but there is definitely a thread."

"Have you told him this? Or Kautsch? Or Clark?"

Another shake of the head. "Not on your life. Remember, I don't believe in the death penalty. If I tell him the date I have figured out, he will change his plea from insanity and beg to be killed on that date. The judge and jury would probably have to go along with him—after all, if they buy his defense, they would have to buy this."

"What about client-doctor privilege? Doesn't he have the right to know?"

"I don't think the Hippocratic oath takes in astrology, Grumpy." Abe wiggled his cup, his lips pursed. "But the problem is worse than just telling him."

"Yeah?"

"Yeah. You see, according to the chart, he is in a tight, astrological spiral. Meaning he would probably come back with many of the same—ah, liabilities."

"Meaning?"

"Meaning, if he doesn't die within a certain window of opportunity, this time, he'll repeat the cycle, time and time again, until he does hit it."

"Jesus Christ. So if he doesn't get the death penalty, and lives out his life—"

"The next window of opportunity for his astrological situation, if I've figured it properly, comes again in one hundred and seventy-eight years."

"What are you going to do with this?"

"Nothing." Abe looked Grumpy straight in the eye. "I told you, I don't believe in the death penalty. But right now I'm going out, to buy some fresh pears."

❧

Doug pulled his French book from his locker, stuffed his gym bag into the empty space. The hallway was nearly empty and he cursed the knot in his shoelaces for making him late. That would mean a difficult discussion with Mademoiselle Torchiere in French, explaining why he had missed the second bell.

He turned to go and nearly bumped into Sally.

"Sorry, Sally. I didn't see you there."

"I know. I've only been here for two minutes."

"Oh, I guess I was—excuse me, I'm late."

"I need to talk to you, Doug."

"Sure." He glanced around. "Uh, when?"

"Can you meet me tonight, in the graveyard again?" A teasing smile played at her lips.

He shook his head. "Sorry, I don't really go there anymore."

"Poor—what's his name again, Nestor?"

"Hector," he said, then wished he hadn't.

"Poor Father Hector must be lonely."

"Not my problem."

Now the smile became a pout. Her hand snaked up to his neck, teased his hair near the small birthmark. "I promise it will be worth your while."

He could hear the clock ticking. Every second just expanded the time he would have to stand in front of the class with Miss Torchiere.

"Sally, Allie got us in trouble last time, and there's no way he'll stay quietly behind in my room. Things are different now that— They're just different now."

"Then where, when? You tell me, Doug. It's important."

He sighed. "Look, there's a small grove of trees on the other side of the house. I used to play there when I was little. You can't miss it. Looks like a picnic area."

"Midnight?"

"No way. It has to be right after school or not at all."

"Okay, I'll meet you there."

"Fine."

He started to go, but her hand pulled him toward her. She planted a kiss on his lips. His eyes widened. She smiled.

"I told you I would make it worth your while."

Her laughter followed him down the hall.

❦

Peter's Adam's apple bobbed nervously, while he fingered the letter. He wasn't sure whether to laugh out loud, or scream with anger. How dare his father do this? The sheer effrontery of the man, thinking somehow that Peter gave one whit for this mockery of a wedding. What did his father think, that Peter might start calling Miss McLean "mother" now? That he in any way approved of this ceremony, an obvious immigration scam, to allow her to stay in the country? God, the woman was incorrigible. First Doug, now his father. There were apparently no limits to her manipulative powers.

He punched the buttons on his phone and waited through several rings.

"Dr. Kautsch's office."

Ah, he'd forgotten how sweet she sounded.

"Dr. Kautsch's office. May I help you?"

"Hi, Dorothy, this is Peter." She caught her breath. He smiled, ruefully. "Can I speak with Leon?"

"Sure, I'll get him on the line."

"Thanks." A dull ache rose from his groin. He made a note to ask Leon for an inside number so he didn't have to go through this every time he wanted to talk to the man.

"Peter. Leon here. How can I help you?"

"A situation has come up, regarding my father and Fiona. I thought I'd alert you and ask your advice."

"Go on."

"Well, it seems they're getting married. At the end of the week."

"My hunch is you're sitting there, holding an invitation."

"More or less. My father wants to meet me, discuss having Doug and me attend."

"Ah, thought so." There was a shuffling of papers. "What do you want to do?"

"I sure as hell don't want to go, but I don't know how Doug would take hearing about it, secondhand."

"Hmmm. You're right."

"And I don't want to make the decision for him. I mean, I wouldn't mind just saying no. This is exactly the kind of situation that triggered his stuff 'from before.'"

"Precisely."

"So, what do you suggest?"

"Doug's been doing wonderfully and it's a shame that this has come up. On the other hand, it might be a good test of his new sense of balance. I agree you should leave the decision to him, just be sure you let him know that you're behind him, either way."

"Ah."

"What's the matter, Peter?"

"Well, if he wants to go, I would feel obligated to accompany him, to make sure things stay on an even keel."

"And?"

"Well, I have to tell you I hate the idea of going. I really do hate it."

"Does it bother you that your father is getting remarried?"

"No, not exactly. Well, yes, I guess so."

"It's not an easy thing, Peter. No matter how grown-up we get, our parents are our parents. When one or the other chooses a new partner, it brings up tough feelings. Perfectly natural."

"Perfectly natural."

"Peter, can I ask you a question?"

"Shoot."

"Have you ever seen your father in a relationship with another woman?"

"Not exactly."

"How exactly?"

"Well, just before my mother died, he had been having an affair with one of the secretaries at the office. A real sordid deal. It killed my mother when she found out."

Kautsch whistled through the phone. "That's tough, Peter. No wonder this hurts."

"It doesn't hurt, really. Just that Doug—"

"Peter."

"Yes?"

"I've grown very fond of you and Doug. He's my patient, but I've come to consider you my friend. Can I be blunt?"

Peter paused. "So long as I don't have to come and lie on your sofa, be as blunt as you like."

Kautsch chuckled. "That's what I like to hear. Sarcasm in the midst of pain. This won't hurt. At least not a great deal. But I promise you'll feel better when it's over."

"I can hear the dentist drill already."

More laughter. "Wonderful, Peter. Now, I want you to tell me exactly what happened between your father, your mother, and this affair."

With a groan, Peter launched into the story of Grumpy and Molly Lyden, his mother's shame and broken heart. Peter's vow that he would never have anything to do with his father again.

"Whatever happened to this Molly—uh—"

"Lyden. Not sure. I fired her, of course. Grumpy took off for Europe and left the whole mess for me to clean up. I believe she died, cancer or something."

"Would there still be a file on her there?"

"I believe so. Why?"

"Well, even though Doug has been doing well, I'm sure there is still residual hero worship and natural ties to Miss McLean. If I can show him the truth about his grandfather; then he may not want to go to the wedding and we can weather this thing, with the least amount of upset."

"I'll have my secretary find what we have and send it over."

"Great. Oh, Peter."

"Yes?"

"How do you feel?"

"Better, actually."

"Told you so."

Now Peter laughed. "That's why you're the doctor, right?"

"Absolutely."

"And why you get the big bucks. What do I owe you for this session?"

"Shall we say—the usual?"

"Okay, I'll get a tee time. Thursday okay for you?"

"Great. And the winner buys lunch."

"I guess that's fair."

"It sure as hell is, Peter, since you always win."

Peter rang off and buzzed his secretary. "Eileen, could you get a tee time for me and Dr. Kautsch on Thursday? And find the number of my father's place, the Sistine Cafe, or something like that, would you?"

"Right away, sir."

Peter relaxed. What did he ever do before Dr. Leon Kautsch arrived in his life?

Sally was waiting for Doug in the grove. He walked slowly toward her, cautiously measuring the feelings rebounding inside his chest. Maybe meeting her here would be a mistake, bringing her to this place of so many childhood memories. The birthday when Nanny had given him the toy soldiers, her remark about the "wee stanes," all the times they sat here, looking at the shapes, the figures in the clouds—her wonderful stories.

Allie shot toward Sally, bounding with his usual happiness. Doug clamped tight on his emotions and wore a tight smile in answer to hers. She appeared, as ever, calm and assured. What did girls know so early, that boys didn't?

"Hi, Doug," she said, patting Allie with strokes that went the length of his back.

"Sally."

"It's nicer here during daylight."

"Yeah, guess so."

She looked at him closely. He blushed.

"A lot has happened over the past year, Doug."

He nodded, tossed a stick for Allie to chase. He watched Allie run. Looking directly at Sally was too dangerous. She was still too beautiful and he felt as if he looked at her too much he might start to cry.

"What's the matter?" She reached for him, he moved away.

"Nothing."

"Come on. Where are you? Ever since last summer, you've been so distant. You don't talk to anyone, you don't laugh anymore. Are things that bad?"

He smiled, ruefully. Was quiet so bad? "Things are actually pretty good," he said softly.

"I'm glad to hear it." She tore a new blade of grass, chewed it. "I've got a favor to ask you."

He waited.

"A big favor." She searched his face. "But before I ask you, there's something I would like to know."

"Okay."

"Is there something wrong with me? Do you— I don't know. What did I do wrong?"

The question caught him off guard. His head wobbled. "Nobody did anything wrong. Especially not you."

"Then what is it? It's like no one can touch you. You're in school, you do your assignments, answer questions in class, but you might as well be a ghost."

He tried to keep the fear out of his eyes, turned away. He felt her hand on his shoulder. She pulled him around and embraced him. She smelled like vanilla.

"It's okay, Doug." Her voice was a mere whisper, her breath smelled of peppermint. "You do what you need to for your life."

He stayed in her arms for the longest time, feeling her against him. He was less aware of the particulars of her body than of the sensations, frozen winter streams gurgling to life, as if his very blood had been blocked and now renewed its travel. An aurora borealis burst inside his head. Not distinct images, but dancing reflections of red and blue, purple and green. Funny rainbows, not arched and striated but cubed, colors inside of colors moving, spreading in simultaneous dimensions.

His breath returned to his lungs with a rush. He pulled away from her slightly, looked into her eyes. She was Sally, but different from the one who had kissed him last year.

He caressed her cheek, his eyes full of wonder. When was the last time someone had hugged him?

Now it was her turn to grow shy. They had encountered a place within each other that was similar, unexplored, intimate beyond their years.

"What is your favor?" He wasn't sure if he had spoken or just sent her the message with his mind.

She blushed, lowered her eyes.

"Please, ask me."

She took his hands, pulled him to a log. She straddled it, facing him, kept his fingers laced within hers.

"Now it seems silly. Not right, you know?"

"More reason to tell me," he said.

Her laugh was light. "Oh God, Doug. You'll laugh at me."

"I doubt it."

She took a deep breath, closed her eyes. Then opened them, leaned forward. "I was going to ask you if you would be my date for a certain upcoming party. It's this Saturday."

"That doesn't sound so terrible."

"Ah, but you haven't heard all of it." Another chuckle. "Because, if you had resisted at all, I was going to offer myself—all of myself—to you, to make sure you'd come with me."

"All of—"

She nodded, her eyes bright and shiny. "All of me."

Doug gulped. He knew in his head what she was talking about, but his body was having a completely unfounded reaction.

"This party, why is it so important to you?"

"Two of my best friends are getting married."

"A wedding? You want me to go with you to a wedding? What's so important?—I mean so—I don't know, scary about that?"

"Well, we haven't exactly talked for a long time. I wasn't sure how you felt about things."

"Things?"

"Between us. Between you and—"

Danger signals raised the hair on the nape of his neck. He extricated his hands from Sally's and stood over her.

"This isn't about my going with you, is it?"

She shook her head.

Allie, alerted to Doug's emotional shift, moved next to him.

"Who's getting married, Sally. Who are these best friends of yours?"

She chewed her lip, stood slowly. "I'm sorry, Doug. I was wrong to come, even to think—"

"Who's getting married?"

She started away, he caught up to her. "Tell me."

"You'll find out soon enough, Doug."

"That's not fair, Sally."

Her eyes were clouded. Her whole body had an attitude of defeat.

"Doug, when are you going to get it? Life isn't fair. It just isn't ever fair."

Doug watched her trudge away. Allie was caught between chasing after her and standing next to his master. He whined, licked Doug's hand.

The smell of vanilla disappeared in the light breeze and there wasn't the slightest hint of a rainbow. The vibrations started. At first he panicked, fighting against the loss of control. Then he gave in.

Phineas looked into his small looking-glass, while he washed his face. The ninth of December, in the year of our Lord, 1666. Today should have been a celebration marking both the end of writing Paradise Lost, and Milton's birthday. Instead, he felt as if everything good in his life were ready to topple over a precarious cliff and he would fall with it, screaming into the abyss. Phineas shivered as he splashed icy-cold water on his face.

When he reached for the cloth to dry himself, his hand bumped against his gift for the poet. He dried his face, then picked up the small, mahogany figure of a man on horseback, delicately filigreed with silver. The rider, who appeared almost part of the horse, had a leather quiver of tiny, silver arrows slung across his back. The horse stood on its hind legs as the archer drew his miniature, silver bow—an arrow pointed straight ahead past the horse's neck.

🙿

Phineas had bartered the silversmith down from two crowns to three shillings, and whereas the blind poet would not see the beautiful craftsmanship, he would be able to feel its magnificence. More importantly, Mrs. Milton might come to understand that although Phineas might be poor, he was a man of sufficient sensibilities to marry her daughter.

He blushed at the thought that this humble gift might sway the great man in Phineas' favor, but the vision of Mary's fearless eyes gave him courage where he had none of his own.

He dressed carefully, wrapped the carved figure in soft paper, then reached for a folded sheet of parchment. This was the other weapon in the battle to protect his life—the poem Milton had asked him, months earlier, to write—far more precious and dangerous than the tiny archer's arrows.

Thus armed, he left his room and bumped into his landlady.

"Mr. Davies?"

"Good morrow, Mrs. Grimsby."

"When you didn't leave for work this morning, I was worried that you might be under the weather."

"Thank you for your concern, but I'm fine." He smiled at the narrowing in her eyes, a hawk looking for some small mouse of information—looking carefully at his skin, for hints of the plague. "We're celebrating Mr. Milton's birthday today."

"Ah, and how is your famous employer?"

"He's fine, as well, Mrs. Grimsby."

He hurried past her, then slowed once he reached the street. How uncanny of her to come snooping on the very day that his peace and her rent were threatened by the Miltons' impending departure. He'd often heard her boasting to the neighbors about her prize lodger. How would she react, should he be discharged? Phineas clucked and shuffled up the street.

Still early for Milton's late-afternoon birthday party, Phineas walked slowly through the streets and alleys of London, barely noticing the wet, feathery flakes that floated to the ground around him. The resultant nimbus around the occasional street lamp gave areas of the city an ethereal look. Phineas knocked on Milton's door.

Grutto opened, nodded, led him to the study. Mrs. Milton stood at her husband's side, daughters in the background shadows. Mary gave him a searching look, he smiled at everyone. Despite the perennial fire in the hearth, Milton sat huddled against the cold, the customary, coarse coat hiding his short, silverhilt sword.

"Phineas is here, dear," said Mrs. Milton, "It looks as if he has brought something."

"I have, Mrs. Milton. A birthday present for your husband." He walked over and handed him the mounted archer. "Let me give it to you before any other guests arrive. A most happy birthday to you, sire. And may you have many more."

"But I thought this party was to be in celebration of the completion of our little effort," exclaimed Milton, with a touch of sarcasm. "A little polishing of the last pages is all that remains."

He took the present, felt it carefully, sensitively. Phineas could feel Mary's questioning eyes pouring into the back of his head, did not turn around.

"Why, it feels like a man on horseback—rather an archer." cried Milton. "Is this—yes—a taut bow. I can tell the workmanship is excellent, my boy. It must have cost far too much. It is most kind. Thank you, so very much."

"You are welcome, sire, but have you grasped its symbolic significance?" replied Phineas.

"As you know, my boy, literary symbolism is not unfamiliar to me, but I really do not know what you are talking about. Please explain."

"Sire, you have spent your entire adult life, symbolically charging through the unillumined, intellectual alleys of London; brandishing your sharp, arrow-like pen; shooting your brilliant, enlightened words straighter, truer and further than most men can see—in your unending promotion of the cause of freedom."

"Well, that is quite a metaphor, Phineas. Though I think you have overstated—"

"Nay, Sire. Let me continue: Symbolically, as the archer-horseman, you wish men to bridle authority, not to be bridled by it. You have written logically that censorship stultifies creativity; that in order to improve the productivity of the people, the best thing any government can do, is to get out of their way—"

"That last bit was primarily your thought, Phineas," Milton said, surprising Phineas with the rare compliment.

"Shall we compromise, by saying we explored the idea together? After all, you did the actual dictation."

"Be that as it may, my boy, I would like to take this opportunity to thank you for your contribution to my most important work, to date."

Phineas blushed. "Sire, that is not—"

"Tut, tut. Normally I do not approve of taking spirits, except for the occasional glass of wine at dinnertime. But today is an exception. Grutto! Grutto! Oh, where is that stupid Nubian, when he is needed?"

Grutto stepped just inside the room. "Yes, sah?"

"Bring in the wine, now."

"Yes, sah."

"Sire?" Phineas said quickly. "If you will permit me, I would like to offer the second part of my gift."

"Surely, Phineas. This archer is sufficient."

"You asked me months ago, to write a poem. I have done so and would like to read it to you now."

Milton leaned forward in anticipation. "Ah, wonderful. Please do read it."

"If you will excuse me," Mrs. Milton started toward the kitchen door. "I'll just check on Grutto's progress."

"No, please, Mrs. Milton." Phineas held up his hand. "I would like you to hear this as well, if you don't mind."

She stopped. "Well, certainly."

Phineas pulled the folded parchment from his pocket, looked at Mary briefly, then cleared his throat.

"I beg your forgiveness firsthand, sire, for the audacity of having written this, but you and your lovely family have given me the courage to do so."

"Please, Phineas. Do not be afraid of our criticism. We have been fortunate to count you as our friend." The poet shifted his gouty leg on the settee. "Now, please continue."

Afraid to look at anyone, Phineas began to read:

"There is this garden called the human heart.
A blissful place, where all emotions start.
This bower for the soul, wherein grows belief,
Where pain of life can find loving relief.

This garden is once the place that Adam claimed
To find his mate of flesh, his Eve so named—
A poor and naked wretch whom God soon promised life;
Then offered knowledgeable fruit and a comely wife.

The same as me, who poor and broken, landed at your door.
You, divine poet with your own Eve, gave me work and more
To etch your illumined thoughts into paper with ink,
To be the first to hear the magic of all you think.

But now, like Adam in the warm embrace of this bower
Do I beseech your favor at the apex of this per'lous hour.
For like that original pair who sought to wed for life,
I ask permission to make your daughter Mary, my wife"

Milton, who had been smiling and nodding, stopped. His eyebrows knotted, when the meaning of the words came clear. Phineas glanced at Mrs. Milton, now pale, also watching her husband.

No one spoke. After several moments, Milton pointed in the general direction of his wife.

"Margaret, please take Mary upstairs. I will call for you later. Everyone else will leave Phineas and me alone."

Mrs. Milton took Mary by the arm and led her out of the room. The other two sisters hurried into the kitchen. Once both of the doors were closed, Milton sighed.

"My dear, dear friend, I'm afraid you've put me in an intolerable position."

Phineas started to speak. Milton stopped him with a brief wave.

"Would you care to tell me how you and Mary reached such friendly accord?"

Phineas told the poet of Mary's desire to understand "Paradise Lost," of teaching Grutto to read.

"Mrs. Milton and I have decided to go to Buckinghamshire, Phineas. To escape the Black Death—the plague." He paused. "I was going to tell you today, but you apparently already know. True?"

"Yes, sire. Mary told me."

Milton sighed. "Did she also tell you I was planning to ask you to move there, as well?"

Astonished, Phineas looked at him. "But, sire—she showed me an announcement, looking for a new scrivener."

Milton nodded. "I had that posted to appease Mrs. Milton. She was against my inviting you. She is jealous of the time we spend together, our—rapport."

"Then I may accompany you, sire?"

"Just yesterday, I had convinced my wife of the efficacy of retaining you. Unfortunately, your proposal of marriage to my daughter has made you even more of a threat."

"But you, sire. How do you feel about my marrying your daughter?"

"Were it up to me alone, I would approve." He smiled sadly. "After all, having a scrivener in the family would be quite convenient."

"Then could you not speak with your wife?"

"I'm afraid not. She suffers from a terrible jealousy—even of my children from previous marriages. She would make my life a veritable hell."

"What if I—"

"Retracted your proposal? Are you that fickle, man?"

"No, sire."

"Then I'm afraid there's no hope for you, lad." Milton attempted to smile. For the last time, Phineas watched the familiar, slender forefinger point at him. "Phineas, you have no idea how much I will miss our conversations. You made significant contributions to my work, particularly with respect to certain political philosophy."

"I did think you were being overly influenced by Cromwell, sire."

"Perhaps, perhaps. You have saved some money?"

"Yes, sire, thank you. And with God's help I will soon find something else to do. Meanwhile, I have my dog, Allie."

"Then I wish you luck, Phineas Davies." Milton extended a fragile hand.

After fervently, but gently, shaking the great man's hand, Phineas went to the dark hall, eyes streaming with tears. He found Grutto in the kitchen.

"Good bye, Grutto, my friend," he said, embracing him.

"You go?"

"Yes, I go. I will miss you."

"Thank you for teach me read English my friend."

"You are welcome, Grutto. I wish you luck. Take care of the mistress and master—and the daughters."

"Yes, no see you again?"

"It's not likely, Grutto. Goodbye."

"Goodbye, Pinyus friend!"

The black man clasped Phineas' hand, squeezing it gently. He brushed away a tear with the other. Turning, Phineas walked slowly out the front door to the cobblestone street. He stopped and gazed up at Mary's window. He thought he saw her for a moment, but the curtain fluttered and the image disappeared.

"Come, Allie," he called.

She got up, yawned and stretched. He reached down to pet her.

"Let us go home."

Doug awoke to Allie's worried and insistent growl. He reached over and patted him on the head.

"I'm okay, boy."

Doug sat up and Allie tried to crawl into his lap. There was no fighting him. He put his cheek against Allie's nuzzling affection. He preferred Allie's kisses to the bigger question: would he tell Dr. Kautsch about this new dream or not? He glanced past the house to the burned chapel. No answer.

Peter stared at the newspaper, glanced at Dan Downey over the top of it. "Front page of the Wall Street Journal? We're actually on the front page?"

Downey grinned. "Payoff time, Peter. Welcome to the big leagues."

His eyes raced down the article. The accolades jumped out at him: New process. Artificial leather. Major breakthrough. Environmental groups name Douglas Industries "Green stock" of the future.

"How high is the stock now?"

"We jumped twenty points this morning alone, Peter. Nearly a thirty percent increase in value." Downey lit a cigarette. "We've been fielding calls from banks across the country. Hell, even a few internationals: Japanese and Dutch and Indonesian. You know them, first in, last out."

"Good, Dan. Very good." Peter walked to the window. "What are our options?"

"Well, that depends on what you want to do. We can split the stock and expand our fiscal base that way, or work with a bank, with stock as collateral."

"What's the difference?"

"If we split, we take on thousands of new partners. But we dilute your holdings and voting power. If you decide to use your stock as collateral for a major research-funding loan, we only have one partner —no matter which bank we choose. Then, when the process goes into production, you maintain control of both the decisions and the profits." He smiled. "Of course, you could just sell out now and spend the rest of your life in Tahiti."

"Yeah, I would do that, if I were my father." He looked at Downey's confused grimace. "Sorry, another issue entirely. Speaking of which, though. What happens to his non-voting stock?"

"The increase is only on the active, voting stock. His shares became another class entirely, when we moved the corporation to Delaware."

"And if he wanted to sell out now, based on this news story?"

"No one would touch it. Why invest in non-voting stock when you can get the premium stuff?"

"Just checking. I need to keep him under control."

The intercom buzzed.

"Mr. MacBrayne, Mr. MacBrayne is here for his appointment."

"Thank you, Eileen. Give me a minute, then send him in." He turned to Downey. "Speak of the devil."

"You want me to stay?"

"No. Thanks, Dan. This is not business. Nor pleasure, for that matter."

Dan left and Peter arranged himself behind his desk. His bowtie throbbed momentarily, but a quick look at the Journal calmed it. He pushed the intercom.

"Send him in, Eileen."

Peter snorted lightly when the door opened and his father entered. What had he been worried about? When he had glimpsed the man during the craziness last summer, he had been shocked. Now he saw that the beard only partially obscured his face. Yes, he had lost weight and no longer had the alcoholic haze in his eyes that Peter had grown up seeing, but he was the same dissolute character behind the soft glow of health.

"Thank you for seeing me, Peter," his father said, standing before the desk. "You look well."

"I am well." No pleasantries came to mind. "How can I help you?"

"I—uh, wanted to invite you personally, to my wedding. You and Doug."

"Ah, yes. To Fiona McLean." He kept the bitterness out of his voice. "And what purpose would our attending serve? Mine? Doug's? Or yours?"

"I would hope all three."

Peter chuckled. "Very political answer."

"I suppose it is." His father nodded, steadied his gaze. "Peter, may I tell you something, something I should have said years ago?"

"I suppose so."

"When I left, and started traveling, wandering, I learned some things I wish I'd known when you were young."

"How to read tarot cards? What would that have helped?"

A shrug. "No. I learned that I had been wrong, wrong-headed for years and years. That I made terrible mistakes, ones I couldn't undo no matter what I said or did now. I would like to apologize for those mistakes."

"Very generous of you." Peter stood, his knuckles on the desk pad. "And I suppose I'm supposed to say, 'That's okay, Pop. All is forgiven.' Is that what you expect?"

"No."

"Good." Peter pulled at his cuff. "Because all is not forgiven. Never will be. Your deceit killed my mother. Your deceit recently sent my son into a tailspin that he is just now recovering from. I can't see that you've learned anything."

"Peter—"

"No!" Peter thundered. "I can't change the past. You killed my mother, broke her heart. How dare you even consider marrying again and expect me to join in happily? Especially to that Scottish woman. You were gone, you weren't here to see Doug's fits, the traumas he endured. Your marrying Miss McLean is the worst possible thing you could do to him."

"Miss McLean is—"

"A conniving spinster—as far as I can see—who poured her hidden lunacies into my innocent son." Peter limped around the desk. "If you wanted us to be part of this charade, why didn't you come before you asked her to marry you? Why weren't we part of the decision?"

"Would your response have been any different?"

"Not in the least." Peter wiped a fleck of spittle from his lip. He closed in. "And you, what makes you think you will do any better with her than with mother—or Molly Lyden?"

The name hit his father with the intended effect—a slap. Peter gathered his control, spoke slowly and with menace.

"Your selfishness and inconsiderateness killed my mother. Your cowardice killed Molly Lyden. What defect is going to finish off Miss McLean?"

"I cannot argue with your view of the past, Peter." His father cleared his throat. "As to the present and the future, all I can say is that I have learned more about my faults than I ever realized and I work very hard to overcome them, or at least not to inflict them on others."

"Oh, really?" Peter lifted a sheet of paper from a folder. "Was this Janina Tucheskyah one of your lovers? Seems being near you did her a lot of good, wouldn't you say?"

He could see the color rise in his father's face. His jaw tightened, then just as quickly relaxed.

"Peter, I guess I underestimated how much you hate me. I hope that someday you can find it within yourself to forgive." Peter started to speak, the father held up his hand. "Not for my sake, in the least. But for your own peace of mind."

"I'm touched." Peter said bitterly. "As for your wedding, I doubt that I will be attending. But Doug will get to decide for himself if he wishes to do so. I hope he decides against it, because I feel that nothing good will come of this. For his sake, I hope I'm wrong."

His father inclined his head, turned and walked out of the room.

Peter waited until the door was closed then limped to his chair, bowtie aflutter. His leg throbbed and his stomach was in a knot. He glanced at the Wall Street Journal, but there was no comfort there. His hand shook as he reached for the telephone.

"Let me talk to Leon."

❦

Grumpy's hands were shaking so violently that he could hardly turn the key in the ignition. He pulled out of the parking lot with exaggerated slowness, trying to keep his mind on driving and away from the conversation with his son. The man had surely inherited his mother's traits.

Before he could let that thought travel to its natural destination, he stopped it. No, Peter was just interpreting facts the way he saw them, unforgiving, but blindingly accurate. What had Janina told Grumpy, "We are all agents of the universe. When someone tells us something about ourselves we don't wish to hear, the universe is always speaking to us through them."

Well, Grumpy got the message loud and clear. But how to interpret it? He picked an imaginary daisy and began plucking petals in his mind. "We marry, we don't. We marry, we don't," he mumbled as he drove to the orphanage. By the time he pulled up at the guardhouse, he had just plucked clean the largest daisy in existence with no clear answer.

The place looked even more foreboding than it had during the summer when he and Valka visited. Abe had said Kautsch was a real operator, but only now was Grumpy beginning to see the scale of the man's ambition. This would not be an orphanage much longer. And when the transition came about, perhaps Jimmy could—that Grumpy and Fiona—

He cut off the thought and made his way to the Director's office. No sense counting chickens until you build the coop.

A very attractive nurse met him at the door. She had the kind of smile that made a man wish he were twenty years younger. Maybe Thirty.

"Dr. Kautsch is expecting you, Mr. MacBrayne."

Freud's soulmate reached across the desk and shook Grumpy's hand.

"How can I help you, Mr. MacBrayne?"

"Well, Dr. Kautsch, as you may know, Jimmy Lyden worked in my store last year. He was a very good employee, by the way."

"I'm glad to hear that."

"Yes, well. As you probably also know, there was a bit of a mix-up last summer."

"I was there, Mr. MacBrayne. I witnessed your Bacchanalian ritual around the bonfire. Very—"

"Gypsy?"

"Original, at any rate."

"Yes. Well, certain information came to Jimmy before I had a chance to explain things. That information has badly damaged our relationship."

"Children take a long time to get over being lied to, Mr. MacBrayne, particularly by those whom they have deemed trustworthy." Leon pulled a cigar out of the humidor and lit it. "But it's compounded when the child in question is an orphan with negative feelings about trust to begin with."

"I am aware of the problem, Doctor, and I would like to help, if I could."

"You think that some kind of rapprochement with Jimmy would help him, is that what you're saying?"

"I would like to try to repair the relationship, and I think that might help him, yes."

"Well, normally I would agree with you, Mr. MacBrayne. But quite honestly, I have to tell you that I doubt it. We are charged with maintaining the wellbeing of the children here. We recognize they have been abused by life, cast adrift and left alone through any number of circumstances." He opened a file. "If I were speaking with any other man than you, I believe my attitude might be different, but in this case, I believe your presence in his life is entirely detrimental."

"May I ask in what way?"

"Of course. Let's see. You had an affair with his mother. Cut her free when it was convenient for you. She became pregnant, was fired, lost her health benefits. Gave birth to Jimmy. Died when he was an infant."

Grumpy sighed. The hand of Peter. "All true."

"Yes, well, to compound the problem, you strike up a friendship with the boy, under an assumed name, obviously to protect yourself for some unknown purpose. You gain the boy's trust, then lose it when your real identity is revealed." Kautsch looked over his glasses at Grumpy. "We try to teach these children to trust their instincts, Mr. MacBrayne. That becomes incredibly difficult when the people in their lives undercut that trust by lying and portraying themselves falsely. Bad enough when it's family—we can't control what families do to children. But we can control when strangers, who have no vested interest other than their own specious feelings of guilt or some other subtext, ask to become part of these children's lives."

"I won't deny the mistakes I have made, Dr. Kautsch. But that is in the past—"

"I'm glad, Mr. MacBrayne, that you have some remorse. I, as much as anyone, recognize that people can change. Otherwise, my job would be hopeless. But let's face the facts. You have a history of duplicitous behavior motivated by pure self interest. Were you a younger man, with a number of years of proven change under your belt, I might be more interested in your situation, but habits of a lifetime are difficult to reverse. Even now it seems to me that you are only interested in reestablishing your relationship with Jimmy and have him attend your wedding to prove somehow to Miss McLean that you are a worthy man."

He closed the file and stood.

"That is not sufficient reason in my book, to permit you to have access to Jimmy."

"There's nothing I can say or do to change your mind?"

"You don't really know the boy, do you?" Kautsch inhaled deeply on the cigar. "He hates the entire MacBrayne family. He reasonably blames you for killing his mother. He is constantly tormented by your grandson at school. Now, you have lied to him about your true identity. What's next? Maybe spill some punch on him at the wedding?"

"That's really uncalled for, Dr. Kautsch."

"Oh is it?" Kautsch came around the desk. "I have spent quite enough time trying to repair the damage done by you and your fiancee to these two boys. I prefer to use my energies in a more profitable manner. Your wishes are the very least of my concerns."

Grumpy stood and looked at the man for some time. He was trying to see him through Janina's eyes. But all he saw was darkness.

"You're wrong, Dr. Kautsch. Time will prove it so."

"Then time shall be my judge, Mr. MacBrayne. If that's what you are calling yourself, this week. Now, I have work to do."

"I'll bet you do, Dr. Kautsch. I'll just bet you do."

Grumpy turned and strode out of the room. He felt dirty having the man know about his past, about Molly. Yes, he had been a fool, and selfish. Abe had been right when he said Kautsch was a smooth operator. He knew all the right things to say and the right moment to say them. But Abe was wrong when it came to thinking that Sabey was pure evil. Sabey was evil all right, but Kautsch, hidden behind his guise of healing, was the purest evil Grumpy had ever encountered.

And regardless of what Jimmy thought of Grumpy, there was no way he was going to let Kautsch win.

His father seemed preoccupied during dinner, so Doug remained quiet. After fifteen minutes, he looked up to see his father watching him. Doug smiled.

"You're awfully quiet tonight, Doug."

"Sorry. You appeared to be thinking. I didn't want to interrupt."

"Ah, I was. How was school today?"

"The same." Doug shrugged. "How was work?"

"Real good. Our stock shot through the roof today. Was up more than 37 points at closing."

"Wow."

His father must have realized Doug didn't entirely understand. "Some of our stockholders made a million dollars today."

Doug's eyes widened. "In one day?"

"Yup."

"Wow."

There was a quiet moment. Doug cleared his throat. "Dad?"

"Yes, son?"

"Can I ask you a question about girls?"

The eyebrows raised, two bobs of the bowtie. "Sure."

"Nothing like—you know."

"Good. I'm not exactly the world's expert."

Doug blushed. "If a girl asks you to a party, and even though she likes you, there seems to be another reason she wants you there, what would you do?"

"What was the other reason?"

"I don't know. Just a hunch, you know?"

"Hmm. Doug you like her?"

"Very much."

"And she likes you?"

"Yeah, though not boyfriend and girlfriend, you know? Though maybe. Gosh, I don't know."

His father laughed. "And you never will know, that is. Women are funny creatures, Doug. They get mad at you if you figure them out, but they cry if they think you don't understand them."

"Gee. What are we supposed to do?"

"Well, you could always become a priest."

The infectious banter nearly made Doug say, "Like you?" but he stopped himself.

"Dad?"

"Yes?"

"Can I ask you a personal question. Serious?"

"Sure, Doug. What is it?"

"Well, I know that Dr. Kautsch thinks that seeing you at the Faire that time and hearing about you and Miss Slimson upset me. But I think I was just caught off guard, you know. When I think about it now, I kind of like the idea of your having somebody."

"That wasn't a question."

"Guess not. Sorry, I didn't mean to stick my nose in your business."

"No, Doug. I was just kidding." His father unbuttoned the top of his shirt. "To tell you the truth, I don't know if I ever will get married again. I mean, if it was going to happen, it might have before now."

Doug nodded. "I guess. I like Miss Slimson, you know. If you ever decide—"

His father laughed. "If I do, you'll be the first to know, how's that?"

"Fair enough." Doug grinned, took a bite of meat. "Would you mind if I went to that party with Sally?"

"Saturday? No, in fact I'll drive you if you want."

"That's okay, it's in town. I'll get a ride from Mrs. Fitch."

"Well, let me know." He patted his pocket, as if he just remembered something. "Oh, I got an announcement you might be interested in. An invitation really. I'm not going and since you're busy now on Saturday, I guess it doesn't matter."

"Invitation?"

"Yes. Your grandfather and Miss McLean are getting married."

Stunned, Doug stared at his father. "Nan—Grum—"

Peter's head bobbed up and down. "I think they're getting married for convenience. You know, so she can stay in the country. You have to be a citizen, or marry one to stay."

To cover his reaction, Doug took a mouthful of food. He now knew immediately what party Sally had been referring to.

"How do you feel about that, Doug?"

A shrug of the shoulders. "I guess it's their business."

"That's what I thought." His father put the invitation away. "I suppose it's only right that we buy them a gift, even if we don't attend."

Doug thought this over. "I think if we just send our best wishes, that would be enough."

"You think so?" His father smiled, insincerely. "Then, I'll have my secretary do a telegram. What do you think about that?"

"Okay." He swallowed hard. The food hit the bottom of his stomach and settled there.

Somehow, he knew no telegram would go out.

❦

Jimmy lay on his bunk, his hands twined behind his neck. The light fixture in the ceiling was lit, but no images formed. Normally, he could put someone like Kautsch out of his mind and let the pictures come, take him away with them, with their formation and becoming. But all he saw was a large, round blackness, swirling above him, a disk that swallowed the light, folded any images into it's oppressive funnel.

He wasn't surprised that the nanny and Mr. Petrovich-cum MacBrayne were getting married. He saw it in their eyes the first time she came into the cafe, even though Sally thought he didn't. Painters see things, even things they don't want to know. The colors and shapes that reveal the world are sometimes not about beauty or art; they can bring truth with them—wanted or not.

How happily Kautsch sneered out the information about the invitation to the wedding, smacking his hungry, dog-lips over the bones of truth he had uncovered about the old man's relationship with Jimmy's mother.

"How does this make you feel?" He had asked. "Betrayed? Violated?"

Jimmy remained calm. As angry as he felt about Grumpy's actions, there was no way he was going to give the psychiatrist any piece of himself. The man was enjoying his meal of all this enough, without adding Jimmy's feelings for dessert.

"I feel sorry for him," Jimmy said bluntly.

"Sorry?"

"Sure," Jimmy snorted. "Imagine, a man that old needing a nanny."

How the mind-wolf laughed. Jimmy laughed with him. He understood the man's need to be seen as an emotional conspirator. Jimmy knew the game. He had drawn and painted enough pictures that his subject thought portrayed beauty but which really showed a hidden piece of ugliness that wouldn't be recognized until later.

Jimmy understood Kautsch much better than the man understood the boy.

"See this." Kautsch pointed to a locked cabinet behind his desk. "These drugs help people. Sodium pentothal, for example, helps people tell the truth when their conscious mind won't let them. Sometimes they remember things they thought they'd forgotten. Lying is like a drug for some people. They use it to forget the reality of their lives, to disarm the shame they feel over their actions.

"What people like the older MacBrayne don't understand is that the very intimacy they think they're protecting with the lie is being destroyed by the very same act, right within them." He walked around to the front of the desk. "Then they wonder why people don't trust them. They make everyone else the scapegoat for their own fears. Do you understand, Jimmy?"

"Yeah, I get it."

"Good." He took another puff on the cigar. "But I happen to believe that people get to make their own choices. I suppose I could forbid you from going to the wedding, but I don't think that would be fair. So, tell me, do you want to go to the wedding? You've been invited."

Jimmy borrowed the sneer. "Only if I could be sure of catching the bouquet."

Another bout of wheezing laughter. Kautsch sent him from the office with a clap on the back and the smell of cigars clinging to his clothes. Jimmy stopped at the janitor's closet to make sure the construction hadn't sealed off his run of the facility.

The last thing he wanted in the world was to celebrate such a stupid idea as this wedding. But Jimmy knew he would be there and he was sure MacBrayne would be there, one way or another. All Jimmy had to figure out was what gift to bring. Suddenly a smile crossed his face. MacBrayne would be at the orphanage Friday for his session with the good doctor.

Jimmy clapped his hands and sat on the edge of the bed. What better gift for a bunch of liars than their very own scapegoat?

Chapter Fifteen

The air duct was filled with dust. Jimmy had to pinch his nose to keep from sneezing. There were no workers around on Saturdays, but it also meant people weren't following any schedule and he didn't want to get caught by accident.

Luckily, Kautsch had taken the office next to the conference room. That made negotiating the pipe shafts easier. Jimmy had listened in on enough meetings to make this trip blindfolded.

·He reached the vent behind Kautsch's desk. Now came the tricky part. He lifted the metal grate and put it beside him. There was just enough room to slip through, but he had to be sure he could climb back up. The credenza was just high enough for him to catch a foothold and still reach the opening in the wall.

It had been so easy Friday afternoon. He had mustered up some tears and rushed into the office. Slimson was sympathetic, but Jimmy insisted on seeing the doctor.

"He's with someone, Jimmy," she said. "Just sit down and relax. He'll be out in half an hour."

"Please, Miss Slimson," Jimmy sobbed. "I just figured out something and if I don't talk to him right in the middle of it, I'm afraid I won't understand it later."

Reluctantly, she buzzed the inner office. Kautsch was sharp with her but consented to come speak with Jimmy.

Jimmy refused to begin until Slimson left, another nice touch he thought. Then launched into his "breakthrough."

"You see, Dr. Kautsch, I had this flash, like why I draw instead of write. You see, it seems to me that everyone has lied to me—except you, of course. And they use words to lie, to hide what they're really doing, who they are. So, I don't trust words."

"I see, Jimmy. Very good."

"But they can't hide what they look like when they lie. They can't hide their faces, their bodies. They can't hide where they live.

Nature doesn't lie, Doctor. Nature is the truth. So when I draw things, people, the things I see—that's my way of shoving the truth at them. Telling them I really see who they are, what they're doing."

Kautsch's eyebrows lifted. Jimmy smiled through his tears. "If you hadn't talked to me the other day about liars and what happens to liars, I don't think I would have understood this."

The doctor's wise nod almost made Jimmy laugh, but he covered it by wiping his eyes with his sleeve.

"The question now, Jimmy, is what are you going to do with this insight?"

"Gee, I don't know."

Kautsch smiled, actually tousled Jimmy's hair. "Don't worry about it. Seeing it, is enough for now. Think about it over the weekend and we'll talk next week. What do you say?"

"Okay."

"I've got to get back inside. Are you all right?"

"I am now, thank you." Jimmy looked grateful. "I know you have work to do, I'm sorry I disturbed you."

"No, Jim. This is my job and you're very important to me. I'm glad you told me this. I think it's very important."

"Thanks."

As soon as Kautsch returned to his office, Jimmy combed his hair in the office lavatory. Why did he hate it so, when anyone messed with it, especially Kautsch? He glanced at his fingernails, grinned at the mirror, felt better and left.

Back in the office, Jimmy was tempted to see if Kautsch had written anything about the interruption, but he didn't want to take the time. He pulled the pick set from his pocket and headed for the medicine cabinet.

Footsteps sounded in the hallway and Jimmy looked around frantically for a place to hide. The small sofa catty-corner to the wall made a perfect niche. He dove behind it, checking quickly to see how apparent the hole in the wall was from the desk. Then ducked as the door opened.

The smell of cigar smoke filled the room. Kautsch. Jimmy heard the creak of his chair, the phone being lifted and dialed. There was a short wait.

"Peter, this is Leon Kautsch. I'm not entirely sure about this, but I thought I should let you know. That party Doug was going to with the girl, Sally? Well, I believe she's taking him to the wedding. I'm not sure he knows, but I'm worried there might be another episode if that's what it turns out to be. I'll look for you at the golf course. If you get this message and you're somewhere else, contact my service. They'll beep me."

Next came the sound of the filing cabinet being opened. A riffling of papers, then closed again.

"Shit," Kautsch muttered.

The chair creaked again, footsteps to the door. A pause, then the door opened and was closed again.

Jimmy waited five minutes, then flew at the medicine cabinet. Normally, he would have left no evidence of his opening and closing it. But he broke the lock, took what he wanted and closed it tightly, but unlocked.

He looked at the file cabinet. Made a mental note to return some time, to see exactly what Kautsch had in there. That could wait. He still had to break into the high school and then there was a party to liven up.

Doug waved goodbye to Mrs. Fitch and rang the doorbell. He heard a feminine voice call from upstairs and a moment later the door opened. A man in suit pants and a tee shirt looked at Doug through bleary eyes.

"Don't want any," he mumbled and closed the door.

Doug pulled out the slip of paper Sally had given him, checked the address. He thought about ringing the bell again, but decided against it. If that was Sally's voice he heard, she'd be down.

A moment later the door opened and a breathless Sally pulled him inside.

"Sorry about that. Dad forgot you were coming."

She looked wonderful. Her dress was made of a soft material that floated around her, more a cloud than clothing. Her blonde hair fell to her shoulders and glistened.

"Doug! Your mouth is hanging open."

"Sorry." He awoke from the dream and grinned. "You look absolutely—"

"Come on in," she cut him off. "Dad and mom want to meet you."

She led him into the living room where the man who had closed the door on him sat across from his wife. Mrs. Witzel wiped her hands on the apron she wore over her housedress and reached out to shake hands with Doug.

"Nice to meet you, Doug. Sally has told us all about you."

Sally rolled her eyes. "Dad, this is Doug MacBrayne."

Birthmark

A sharp glint pierced the bleary focus of Mr. Witzel's glance as he reached out a desultory hand in Doug's direction.

"Nice to meet you Mr. Witzel, Mrs. Witzel," Doug said.

"What time will you be home?" Mr. Witzel murmured.

"Probably ten or eleven," Sally said, wrapping a light silk shawl around her shoulders. "I don't think the reception will go past then."

"Make it ten."

"Daddy—" Sally protested.

"Ten or not at all."

She sighed, took Doug's hand and started for the door.

"Have a good time, kids," Mrs. Witzel called out.

Doug and Sally stood on the porch for a moment. They could hear voices being raised inside.

"Let's go, Doug."

They walked hand-in-hand for the first block. Sally's step lightened as the distance between them and the house increased. Doug was trying to figure how such a beautiful daughter could have been produced by the pair he had just met. Sally caught him looking sideways at her and squeezed his hand.

"Stop peeking at me. You're going to make me blush."

"Sorry, it's just that you look so—so—"

She laughed gaily. "Garish? Horrific? Plague-ridden?"

"Beautiful. And grown up. It's scary."

"Why do you think my dad was so weird? He hates the idea that I'm going to be dating boys soon." Her voice imitated the valley girls of television sitcoms. "Like I haven't been already, gawd."

"You've been on a date?"

She looked at him as if he had just asked her if she spoke English.

"Plenty of them." She put her arm through his and pulled tight against him, tilted her head and whispered, "I've even smoked cigarettes and drank a beer. Actually, a bunch of beers."

"Did you like it?"

It must not have been the question she was expecting because she didn't have a reply at hand. She thought for a moment. "I guess it's not everything it's cracked up to be, but I felt really cool, and that was the important part."

"Well, you're cool enough without those things, if you ask me."

She smiled, kissed him on the cheek. "The perfect Doug answer. God, you're going to break hearts."

"I hope not."

She patted his hand. "It's going to happen anyway and I hope you remember me—that I was the one who predicted it."

"I don't think I'll ever forget you, Sally."

This silenced her. They walked another block and entered the downtown area. For a moment Doug thought he saw his dad's Bentley and flinched.

"What's the matter?"

"Nothing."

She looked around. "Ah, Papa doesn't know you're going to the wedding, does he?"

"No. He's really mad at my grandfather about something. I guess they don't get along. I just figured it would be better to tell him I was going to a party with you."

"Well, that's the truth. Your code of honor is still intact."

Doug stopped.

"What's the matter?"

"Why do you do that all the time?"

"What?"

"Make fun of me."

"Sorry, I didn't mean to hurt your feelings."

"I don't know if my feelings are hurt, but I don't get it. I mean, why even invite me to go with you if you think I'm so stupid."

"What's the matter with having a code of honor? Kind of like knights and chivalry and all that."

"But you make it sound—I don't know—like a mockery."

She laughed a little. "There, that's a Doug statement if I ever heard one. Mockery. I don't know anybody else who uses words the way you do." She turned to face him. "You're the smartest person I ever met. Sure, you act funny, but not a bad funny, just different. There's nothing wrong with being unique."

"There's a difference between unique and eunuch."

This took a moment to sink in, then she laughed out loud. "Oh, God, that's priceless."

"Well, Sal, I really don't understand. Like, why was it so important for me to come to this with you? You have the Moles. All your friends from the cafe. Why me?"

"I like you. That's why."

He shook his head. "Not enough. Come on, I'm not going another step until you tell me. What was it you said, that you were going to give me 'everything' if I came with you? It must be pretty important."

"Okay." She sighed, chewed her lip. "I'll tell you, but only if you promise me something."

"What's that?"

"That you'll still come with me and we'll have a great time and dance and laugh. That's what I really want. I really want to celebrate today, and I thought being with you would help in that."

He looked in her eyes. Was she kidding? "Okay, I promise to be a regular prince charming."

"Double promise?"

"Triple, quadruple, quintuple promise."

She took a deep breath. "Okay. I wanted you to come with me because I thought—No, I *knew* it would make Fiona extra happy if you were at her wedding."

It was so obvious, Doug was surprised he hadn't realized it earlier. He felt a sudden pang. Part wounded ego that Sally didn't want him for her own reasons and another part for the feeling of having been selfish and frightened.

"Let me get this right. You were willing to sleep with me to get me to come to this wedding?"

"Well, yeah, I guess I would have."

"To make Nanny happy."

"Yeah."

He shook his head. Would wonders never cease. Now it was his turn to laugh.

"What's so funny?"

"I was just thinking, all those years that everyone made fun of her, of my having a nanny, and here you, the leader of the pack, would give up the ultimate—well, to make Nanny happy."

Sally did not share in the humor. "And what's the matter with that?"

"Nothing, just seems funny."

"It's not funny. Fiona is a great woman. Maybe the second greatest woman I ever met. I happen to love her very much and I'm amazed that you could hurt her the way you have, over the past eight months."

"Me!"

"You. Did you know that she cries herself to sleep every night? She misses you so much, and you—you just hide in that great big mansion, not once thinking about how she's feeling."

"You don't know anything about it, about how I feel. What I'm up against." Doug's face grew red from anger and embarrassment. "You're free. You get to go out on dates, smoke cigarettes and drink beer. My father watches me like a hawk. I have a fucking psychiatrist checking everything I feel, three times a week. How do you think that feels?"

Doug trembled with rage. Sally's eyes were wide. She reached out to take his hand, but he shook her off.

"Doug?" Again her hand stretched out. "Please. For me."

The moment his hand was within hers the anger drained from him. His breathing was ragged.

"We're just kids, Doug. Our life doesn't belong to us yet, not all of it. Her voice was soft and low, painful. "Do you remember that first day at school?"

"Yes," he said hoarsely.

"I thought you were the most beautiful thing I had ever seen. I still do. I think I'll always think that, no matter what happens, or where we go in our lives."

"You must not look in the mirror much," he whispered.

"What?"

He glanced at her, shy, his eyes still warm. "You're the beautiful one."

He could see a smart answer rise up, then subside within her. "Still want me to go to the wedding with you?"

"If I can go with you, Doug. I would like that very much."

"And we'll sing and dance and laugh and have the best time ever?"

She shook his hand. "The best time ever."

Grumpy peeked out through the office door and smiled. The cafe had been turned into a beautiful if somewhat eccentric standby wedding chapel. The sun shone brightly through the large front windows, which meant the ceremony itself would take place in the back garden.

Heavy footsteps above meant that the Moles, with their fashionable heavy boots, were helping Fiona with her last minute preparations. He grinned as he remembered the argument of the afternoon before, when the girls tried to convince Fiona that combat boots were the only way to march into matrimony.

Mandy and Clint Sharpe spotted him and walked over.

"Grumpy, I have to tell you that the cafe looks prettier than a Las Vegas drive-through wedding chapel," Clint said,

"Clint!" Mandy elbowed him. "Not everybody has to know where we got married, or how."

Grumpy laughed, accepted Mandy's kiss on the cheek and her best wishes for the day.

Clint gave him a thumbs-up, then escorted Mandy to the outdoor seating. Grumpy craned his neck, finally spotted Abe rushing through the door, his best man tails flapping in his wake.

"Sorry, Grump," he said, panting. "Got called to court because it looked like the jury was going to bring in a verdict this afternoon."

"Did they?"

Abe shook his head. "False alarm. I just hope they don't beep me during the ceremony."

"What does Clark think?"

"Well, they paged Kautsch just before I left. Not sure exactly what that means, but Larry seemed to think it was a good sign."

"Well, I'm glad you made it. Somehow it wouldn't have seemed appropriate without you."

"Well, I've been practicing my 'emancipation proclamation' toast for the reception." He tapped a round, satin disk—a stovepipe hat folded down onto itself. "Couldn't resist—after all, I was wearing it when we first met."

More clumping upstairs sent both men's eyes upward. "Abe, could you ask Fiona if I can talk to her for a moment before the ceremony?"

"What? And risk bad luck—"

"I have gypsies on my side," Grumpy said, pushing Abe toward the front entrance.

A moment later Abe motioned to Grumpy.

The Moles, sans Sally, lined the stairway as Grumpy climbed the steps to the apartment above the cafe. Talia snapped his picture. He made the appropriate "Don't break your camera" comment, then tapped at the door. The Moles wore appropriate bad-luck frowns, but he just smiled, collected himself and entered.

Fiona sat in the living room, beautiful in a light green dress. Grumpy's eyes brightened in appreciation.

"You look lovely, Fiona."

She blushed. "Thank you."

He walked to her side, knelt and took her hand. "There's something I need to say to you before we're in front of everybody."

Her glance sharpened, but she held her tongue when she saw his eyes.

"Earlier this week, I went to both Peter and Dr. Kautsch. I was hoping that Doug and Jimmy would somehow find their way here for the wedding."

She nodded, moisture glistening in her eyes. "I thought you might."

"You did?" He pursed his lips. "Yes, well, as you can imagine, neither conversation was very cordial."

"Raked you over the coals?"

"Yes. And I want to apologize for messing things up. If I had done things differently, we might have all—"

She put her fingers to his lips. "Peter Douglas-MacBrayne Junior, if you had done things differently, we might not be getting married. We both know this trouble is not your doing." She caressed his cheek. "The very fact that you went into the lion's den to try to make me happy—two lion's dens, for that matter—makes up for their missing the ceremony."

"Well, I just wanted you to know that I regret my mistakes, and I intend—"

"Hush, dear." She pointed to the doorway. "Those girls, those funny, silly, loving girls, are the proof that what we are doing is a good thing. Doug and Jimmy will be okay. I feel it very deeply. But those girls have a chance in life they never would have had without you. So you and your tuxedo get downstairs and wait for me. I'll be there in a few minutes."

He leaned close to kiss her, she smiled, turned away. "Please, I'm engaged."

"Not for long, dear. Not for long."

❦

Fiona sat with her hands folded in her lap after Grumpy left. She savored this moment of being alone, seemed like the first in weeks. She looked up to the ceiling.

"My dear friend up there, I've been careful in my life not to ask you for too much. But now, you see, I'm about to marry a very fine man." She put her hand to her chest. "I was married once before to a good man and you took him quickly. Only you know the reasons and I have no argument with you over that."

She sighed, look at the mirror over the mantle. Looked away.

"You see, this time feels like something very important. This man you've given me has wonderful qualities that have just come to the surface for him." She hesitated. "I'm not asking you to give me years and years with him; that's between you and him. But I am asking that you help me help him, properly. I'm a stubborn Scots woman and he's a gentle American. I know these traits are going to come into conflict and I just hope that you'll help me know how to be a good wife to him."

She rose, straightened her dress. "And one other thing. If you could help me not faint during the ceremony, I'd appreciate that, too."

A tap at the door ended her prayer.

"Come in."

Sally peeked inside. "You alone?"

"Yes, what is it, Sally? I'm just about to come downstairs."

"I've brought you your present. Thought you might like to see it before the ceremony."

"Sally," Fiona said, not masking her frustration. "Couldn't it wait?"

"No."

She disappeared. The door opened again. Doug took a step inside.

"Doug—" Fiona took a step toward him.

"Hello, Nanny."

"You've come—but—"

He smiled, on the verge of tears.

"Don't you cry, Dougie, or I'll ruin my makeup."

His smile wavered. "I wanted to wish you a happy wedding."

She took another step toward him, afraid he might leave before she got a chance to hug him.

"Are you okay, Doug?"

He shrugged. "I'm okay now."

She reached out her hands and took his. "Me too, Doug. Now."

Then he was in her arms.

"I'm sorry I couldn't talk to you, Nanny. I'm so sorry."

"Shh, Dougie. It's all okay now."

"Sally told me how it's been for you. If I had known I would have—"

"Hush, darling." She kissed his cheek. "I just missed you, that's all."

The music started downstairs and Fiona held him at arms length. "Can you stay for the reception?"

"You bet, Nanny."

Her eyebrows raised. He grinned.

"Dad thinks I'm at a party with Sally. We're safe."

"Just like Romeo and Juliet, eh?"

"I'm glad you're marrying Grumpy." He squeezed her hand. "Kinda keeps everything in the family."

"That it does, Dougie, darling. That is does."

He pulled away from her. "I'll be downstairs, okay?"

"Okay. Tell them I'll be right doon—in me waddin' goon."

He grinned, left.

She looked up at the ceiling and mouthed, "Thank you." Then went out on the landing where her funny daughters waited to take her to her new husband.

Jimmy glanced at his reflection in the window of the cafe. Replaced a few strands of wayward hair and wiped the dust from his clothing. One quick check-over and he pushed through the swinging glass door. Someone was speaking outside. Jimmy spotted the punch bowl, frowned. It was empty. He slipped into the empty kitchen and opened the refrigerator. On the top shelf sat a gallon container of fruit punch concentrate. He carefully unscrewed the top, took the little bottle from his pocket and emptied it into the punch. He replaced the top, shook the container, then closed the refrigerator.

The music started outside. He walked quickly to the kitchen door, peeked out and marched through. The guests were applauding. He wasn't sure he could escape, unseen, out the front door, so he walked to the counter where he used to work. He was just behind it when Grumpy and Fiona walked into the cafe, holding hands.

They stopped when they saw him. Grumpy smiled.

"Jimmy! You made it."

"Can I get you an espresso, Mr. Petrovich." Jimmy grinned, his white teeth gleaming. "Or are you drinking tea now?"

Grumpy looked at Fiona, as if for permission, which was granted, headed toward Jimmy, hand outstretched.

"I'm so glad to see you."

"Me too, sir."

The other guests were now trickling into the cafe.

"Jimmy, we're going to be gone for a couple of weeks. But will you come visit me here, after we get back? There's so much I want to tell you."

"Yes. I would like that," Jimmy said. "Now you two go have fun. I'd feel more comfortable if I could stay behind the counter during the reception. Like the good old days."

"Anything you want, Jimmy. Anything you want."

Jimmy smiled. Clint and Abe walked in, both greeted him happily. For a moment, Jimmy thought he might have made a mistake. He considered spilling the contaminated punch. He had taken one step toward the kitchen, but then saw Doug walking arm-in-arm and laughing with Sally.

He scurried behind the counter, fingering the empty bottle in his pocket. MacBrayne would no doubt take off his jacket sometime during the party. Then the game would be over and Jimmy could head home.

BIRTHMARK

Maybe it was the elation over the skyrocketing price of Douglas Industries stock, or perhaps it was the anger he had released at his father, but whatever the cause, Peter was shooting his best round of golf ever. He was one under, through seventeen.

His drive on the eighteenth was long and straight. Halfway to his second shot, he heard his name called in the distance. He turned to see Leon Kautsch hurrying toward him.

"Peter! Peter, wait."

Peter leaned on his club, gazed up at the heavens. "You're never going to let me break par, are you?"

Before the heavens could answer, Kautsch came puffing up to him.

"Peter, I'm glad I found you."

"What's the matter, Leon?"

"It's Doug."

Peter dropped his club. "What about him?"

"He's gone to the wedding. I'm really worried that he may have some kind of relapse."

"To the wedding? I thought he was going to a party."

"Yes. But he failed to mention that the girl is one of Miss McLean's bridesmaids."

"Goddamn it!" Peter shouted, kicking the club.

"Sorry, but I thought you should know."

"Come on, Leon. I'm going to—"

"Don't be hasty, Peter. Why don't we just go there and collect Doug. With a minimum of fuss. We don't want to make too big a thing of this, at least not in front of everybody. It might set him back. Moreover, if you appear only disappointed, but reasonable, we just might salvage things."

"Yeah, well—"

Peter reached down, grabbed his club. He was so angry, he could hardly see well enough to follow Kautsch to the parking lot.

He would be reasonable all right, right up to the moment he got Doug home.

Doug slipped out his jacket and sat next to Sally. He smiled at Fiona, whose eyebrows raised appreciatively. He blushed. Sally surreptitiously gripped his hand.

"Normally, we would be toasting with champagne," Abe said, balancing the stovepipe hat on his head as he raised his cup. "But because Grumpy is too cheap to get a liquor license, we'll have to settle for punch. Is everyone's glass filled?"

Doug glanced around, momentarily blinded by Talia's constant picture-snapping. Kim stuck out her tongue for the camera, while she wheeled the punch bowl around on a small cart.

All glasses filled, the assembled guests raised them as one. Abe smiled.

"Four score and about a thousand years ago, Grumpy MacBrayne came into this world." He waited for the laughter to subside. "And no more than twenty-nine years ago—" he nodded toward Fiona, who blushed and nodded in turn "—our lovely Fiona also came into the world. We have come to honor their union."

"Hurray for Fiona!" came from the Moles.

"Before I continue, I would like to read a special message that just arrived." Abe raised his hand, unfolded a telegram. "My dear brother Grumpy and my sister Fiona. I am sorry I cannot attend your wedding for I am too far away. But I want you to look at the moon tonight. In its smiling face you will see a hint of the joy this news has brought to my heart. Signed, Valka Petrovich Tucheskyah."

Grumpy nodded, then gave Fiona a light kiss. She blushed, but the smile never left her face.

"Love has no age, knows no time," Abe continued. "But as we put our lips to our cups, Grumpy and Fiona, we want you to know that we are drinking to your happiness and your joy. May the years be gentle with your hearts and long with your affections."

"To Grumpy and Fiona," came from the crowd. All downed their drinks. Kim hurried around refilling glasses.

Abe smiled as Grumpy winked at Jimmy, who was drinking from a can of coke. The groom stood.

"Please refill your glasses everyone," he said. "I think we're all thirsty enough for another toast."

There was a brief wait while Kim made the rounds with the punch. Then Grumpy faced Fiona.

"To my bride, I am eternally grateful." He turned and faced the crowd. "To my friends, our friends, I would like to say how your presence here warms my heart. Your sharing this day with us makes it even more sacred, more joyous." All rose and drank. Next he waved his cup at Clint and Mandy. "To the Sharpes—who have their own reasons to celebrate—I wish you nothing but happiness and a minimum of morning-sickness."

There was more laughter. Clint stood and bowed. Mandy blushed. Sally squeezed Doug's hand. He squeezed back.

Everyone drank again.

"I'm never going to get married," one of the Moles cried and dropped her cup. "God, I hate my grandfather."

Several people suddenly began speaking incoherently. Grumpy looked stunned, placed his hand on the table to steady himself. Doug started to rise, lost his balance.

A confused bedlam broke out. Doug's eyes swam. He heard the voices, felt a powerful wave of nausea overcome him. He thought at first the vibrations were coming on, but this disorientation was coming from within him, his whole body seemed disconnected from the room.

Sally dropped his hand. "Don't, please don't," she cried out.

Out of the corner of his eye, Doug saw Jimmy walking toward him. People were crying loudly. Jimmy ran to the telephone. Just before he lost consciousness, Doug saw Nanny, holding Grumpy in her arms, sobbing. Then he heard his father's voice calling from the door. Off in the distance, there may have been sirens.

The lamp sputtered. Phineas felt more than saw the flickering shadows on the wall, above the pile of straw that served as his bed. The lamp's oil was nearly gone. A sigh began from deep within him, never made it to his swollen lips. He raised his right hand. Even in the failing light, the spots on his skin seemed much darker than the last time he looked.

How long had he lain here? An hour, a day, a week? He could no longer tell. Mrs. Grimsby had long since stopped pounding on his door. That silence, her acquiescence, could only mean her death. Had her father in heaven stopped laughing, now that she had joined him?

Phineas tried to chuckle. Couldn't. A short cough brought up more blood. He wiped feebly at his chin, felt the wetness on his shirt. He arched his neck, dropped his head, as the stench of his illness caught at his nostrils.

A quick, shuddering chill forced him under the pile of rags that served as his bedding. A whitish shadow gleamed against the wall. The angel of death? Had she no manners? How could she stand the rotting perfume that must greet her dire task?

His eyes closed, not enough strength to keep them open. He was startled by a scratching sound across the room. A rat scampered the length of the floor. What was the etiquette here? Would it wait for him to stop moving completely? Was he like the rubbish-collector who came at the end of the angel's banquet to remove the evidence?

The scratching stopped. Phineas forced his eyes open. The rat sat up, nostrils and whiskers twitching.

"Shoo!" Phineas whispered, sitting up half way.

Not long now, the rat seemed to signal with the wipe of a paw across its face.

Who would remain to count the dead at the end of this plague? Gingerly, Phineas moved his hand to his leg as an itch broke through the wet delirium. Would the fleas leave anything for the rats? The effort made him collapse. Straw sticks ripped at the fresh, festering wound which lay squarely upon his birthmark. A bed-sore there? he wondered.

No, it seemed somehow connected to food. When had he last gone out? The fog in his brain became laced with scarlet fissures of wavering memories: He would leave the city. Use the last of his savings to escape the plague. One last trip to the market for some provisions. Trudging along the cobblestone to the marketplace, past the shadowy lane near the High street. Small cries. A boy, wearing the clothes of gentry. Crying, lost. What was he doing without his parents?

"Hey, leave off, you two," Phineas had called to the shadowy figures that had knocked the boy down, were pilfering his purse.

The boy looked up. Those dark, soulful eyes. Strangely familiar.

The short thug looked up. "Bugger off, mate."

But those soulful eyes pulled Phineas into the lane. "Don't hurt the boy. Take his purse, but don't hurt—"

The large one turned. That awful, diabolical black beard, split at the chin. The boy grabbed for his purse. The club caught him like a calf. A killing blow. The dark eyes sparked, evaporated—soul-less.

Phineas wanted to run. Couldn't. Those eyes. He knew them. The club went into the air again. Phineas turned. The force of the blow drove him against the brick wall.

His mind cleared. Aunt Agatha had called his birthmark lucky. Lucky for that club—made a good target.

The back of his head now mush, Phineas could still feel the thugs rifling his pockets, taking the last of his money.

Three crowns stolen, a cracked one given.

The corners of his parched lips turned up into a sickly grin, then fell.

Who would bury him now that death was so close? Would his friend, as promised and paid, take his poor remains to that tiny graveyard with the three headstones that marked the trinity of Davies? Mother, never known. Father, rarely seen. At least Aunt Agatha had stuck around, seen him through Cambridge—before her meeting with the angels.

He'd had such a simple plan for his death. A prescribed epitaph:

> Here lies Phineas Davies, Poet, Scrivener.
> 1628-1666
> I have never ceased to wonder
> Since on this poor plane I have been
> Why people mean not what they say
> And seldom say what they mean.

Another bloody cough shattered the granite image. Too complicated now. What with corpses being burned instead of buried. The ghoulish sick, who warmed their hands on the fire. Was that to be his legacy to the world? Would the writer who never emerged, be fuel for a dying hag's last mote of warmth?

An acrid plume of smoke slowly filtered under the door. Could they have built a pyre so close to the building that—he coughed. Where was Allie? His faithful dog would warn him of any real danger.

He groaned. His ragamuffin companion had met the same club in the alley. Who would mourn the loss of these two strays, mongrel and scrivener?

The faint flame from the lamp's spirits and the essence of Phineas' physical being simultaneously flickered, sputtered, went dark.

Tears stole the last bit of living moisture from his eyes. Milton had been right. Paradise was lost.

❦

Doug's eyes fluttered open. He blinked twice, turned his head. Nurse Slimson sat beside the bed, writing on a clipboard. He moaned. She looked over.

"Doug?"

"Hi." He was groggy, his mouth crawled with spiders, which had taken all the moisture away. He tried to move his arm, but it was tied to the bed. A tube with liquid, dripped into his arm, ran up to a bottle hanging from a metal sleeve.

"Where am I?"

"In the hospital. You're pretty sick."

"Sick?" He tried to sit up, couldn't. "Oooh. My head."

Nurse Slimson pushed a button by the bed. She reached over and felt his forehead. "Dr. Kautsch will be here in a second."

"Dr. Kautsch? What's going on?"

"Don't talk just now. We have to wait for the doctor."

"But—"

The door opened, Kautsch entered. His face was grim.

"Doug."

"Dr. Kautsch. What happened?"

"That's what we like to ask you."

"I don't know. I was at—" he searched his memory. "—at Nanny's wedding. Then—I don't remember."

The door opened again and a man wearing a shiny black suit entered. Doug looked at him.

"Hello."

"Doug," the man said, then turned to Kautsch. "Has he said anything?"

"Not yet. He only remembers the wedding and getting sick." Dr. Kautsch sighed. "Doug, this is Detective Nielson. He needs to ask you some questions."

"Okay." Doug's head spun slightly. He opened his eyes again. "Detective—"

"Doug, we need to know how much sodium Pentathol you put into the punch, the day of the wedding. There are some very sick people. And anything you can tell us will help." He coughed. "And of course, if you help us, things will go easier for you."

"Sodium what?"

"Pentathol, the drug you took from Dr. Kautsch's office on Friday afternoon."

"I didn't—" he tried to sat up, the restraints stopped him. "I don't know anything about that."

"Doug," Dr. Kautsch said firmly. "We found an empty container in your jacket pocket that had traces of the drug. Then we found the prescription bottles in your locker. Did you put it all in the punch, or just some of it?"

"I didn't—" Tears welled in his eyes. "I don't know anything about it. I swear."

Nielsen's voice was hard. "Doug, there's no use lying. We found the evidence in your pocket and in your locker at school. Do you know Mrs. Sharpe?"

"Clint's wife? Yes, not well, though. Why?"

"Because she's pregnant, Doug. Your little stunt might just kill her baby."

"Pregnant?" He vaguely remembered part of the toast, just before he passed out. She was sitting next to Clint, smiling. "I don't know anything about any bottles or prescriptions."

"Doug—" the detective raised his voice. Dr. Kautsch grabbed his arm.

"We'll let you think about things for awhile, Doug. But don't take a lot of time. We need your cooperation, otherwise you could be facing a murder charge."

"But I didn't—"

Kautsch put his fingers to his lips. "You just think, Doug. And think very hard. What happens to you over the next few years depends on your willingness to cooperate with the police."

"But I—"

"Just think."

Kautsch started to guide Nielson out, turned and sent a warning glance to Nurse Slimson. She nodded, lowered her head.

Doug closed his eyes. Sally's voice sang in his head. "The best time ever, Doug. The best time ever."

Peter rushed toward Dr. Kautsch as soon as he closed the door to Doug's room.

"How is he?"

"A bit groggy."

"Did he say anything?"

Kautsch glanced at Nielson.

"Mr. MacBrayne, you have to understand that we have an official investigation in process here."

"But he's my son."

"I understand, Mr. MacBrayne." Nielson tapped his pencil against his notebook. "But your son is facing assault charges. Poisoning twenty-seven people, and possibly killing a fetus—this is not a matter of simple delinquency."

Kautsch cleared his throat. "Detective, I'm sure Mr. MacBrayne understands the seriousness of the charges."

"All I want to know is what he said."

Nielson glared at Peter. "Your son says he didn't do anything. Given the evidence against him, I would suggest you get him a good lawyer. Now, I have to interview more of the victims. If you'll excuse me."

Nielson stalked away. Peter's shoulders slumped.

"This is all my fault. I shouldn't have let him know how angry I was at his grandfather."

"There's no way this could have been predicted, Peter." Kautsch put his arm around him. "We're lucky that Doug has been in therapy and that I have a complete psychological profile on him. I promise you he won't go to jail. We have the new facility all set up. It's not going to be like home, but at least he'll have people he knows caring for him. We'll get him through this. You'll see."

"Thank you, Leon." Tears flowed down Peter's cheeks.

Clint pulled his hospital robe tighter around him and took Mandy's hand again. She responded to the pressure of his grip but without strength. The door opened.

"Mr. Sharpe?" The detective again.

"Yes?"

"Can we talk for a minute?"

"Do we have to?"

"It would help." The man took two steps inside the room.

"Okay, go ahead."

"Well, I've been talking with the doctor. He mentioned that Doug has had these hallucinations, or dreams about having been a—scribbler—"

"Scrivener?"

"That's it. A scrivener for some guy named Milton?"

Clint almost choked, recovered. "He was a poet in the 1600s. Wrote 'Paradise Lost.' "

The detective made a note. "Was that made into a movie?"

"Not that I know of," Clint said, holding his sarcasm. "It was an epic poem."

"Yeah. Well, here's my question. The Doctor says Doug was in your cabin. You were his counselor last summer?"

"That's right."

"And you read to the boys from this 'Paradise Lost?' "

"That's right." Clint looked at the detective. "What does this have to do with anything?"

"We're trying to establish motive, Mr. Sharpe. We're dealing with a very sick young man—" he held up his hand to stop Clint from speaking, "—who has a vivid imagination at best, and destructive hallucinations at worst. If he somehow associated you with this Milton fellow and if this scrivener character from the hallucination had some beef with Milton, then that helps explain why he poisoned the punch."

Clint shook his head. "Sorry, Detective, but I don't buy it. I spent all summer with the boy. I still don't believe he could have done that—hallucinations or not."

"If I hadn't read the psychological report of the boy's therapy over the past year or two, I might agree. But there are too many weird associations between his hallucinations and the people at the wedding." The detective folded his notepad. "Mr. Sharpe. Ever hear of John Wayne Gacy? The Chicago serial killer who was a clown for children's birthday parties. Or Jeffrey Dahmer, the cannibal from Milwaukee? No one believed what they did, either. At least in this case, we have a chance at stopping a greater tragedy further down the road."

Clint returned his attention to Mandy. What greater tragedy could there be than losing this second baby in his wife's womb? He didn't trust himself to talk to the detective any further.

"I hope everything turns out okay for you, Mr. and Mrs. Sharpe."

Clint nodded. Mandy squeezed his hand again. He leaned over and kissed her fingers.

Grumpy and Fiona sat in the Emergency Room waiting area, holding hands. Peter burst through the swinging doors, limping noticeably, bow tie fluttering furiously. He stopped when he saw them, Grumpy rose, unconsciously shielding Fiona from his son's malevolent gaze.

Peter pointed, started to speak, his face red.

Fiona rose, but Grumpy held her.

"He must have seen Doug."

"Don't say anything now. It'll only make things worse."

Peter looked around wildly, as if for another exit. There was only one way to leave. He stalked past them, muttering.

A nurse approached.

"We've tested your blood. The doctor thinks you'll be okay to go home tonight. But if there are any more symptoms, come back immediately."

"And the others?" Grumpy asked.

"Well." The nurse looked around. "Only one really serious case. Everyone else will go home tonight or in the morning."

"And Mrs. Sharpe?" Fiona whispered.

The nurse shook her head. "I can't tell you anything."

"Thank you." Grumpy took Fiona's arm as the nurse walked away. "We'll wait a couple of minutes, then go home, okay?"

"Shouldn't we stay? I mean, I don't know what to do."

He nodded. "Neither do I, dear. Neither do I."

Abe tied his hospital gown and shuffled out of his bathroom. He was surprised to see Leon Kautsch standing by the window looking out at the stars. His boss turned, smiled.

"How are you feeling, Dr. Avisson?"

"I've had hangovers that were worse."

Kautsch nodded, pointed to the night sky. "Funny things, stars. By the time the light gets to us, it is millions of years old. To some it's just light, to others, the light tells tales of alien beings, advanced civilizations whose abilities are beyond our comprehension."

"You sure you didn't drink any of that punch?"

Kautsch chuckled. "Been a long day, Abe. A long day, indeed."

Abe noted the use of his first name by the director. "That is an understatement," he said, climbing into bed. "Was there something you needed?"

Kautsch turned, nodded. "Wanted to see how you were feeling."

"I suppose I'll survive."

"Will you be well enough to come to work on Monday?"

"I think so."

"Good, because we've got lots of work to do." He rubbed his neck. "In fact, I would say that your career just got a jump-start today."

"Doug MacBrayne?"

"No, I'll be handling Doug's case. But you're about to make mental health history and have the opportunity to document it every step of the way."

The blood drained from Abe's face. "Sabey."

"He's all ours—yours, really—until death him departs."

Abe pulled the blanket to his chin as Kautsch left. He glanced out the window. All the stars seemed to be laughing at him. He wouldn't have minded, but their laughter sounded exactly like Sabey's.

A terrible response to an evil joke.

Chapter Sixteen

Thursdays meant lunch at the Crystal Cafe. Dorothy checked her watch and pulled away from the sanitarium at a brisk pace. Every Thursday, Leon went to Trenton to report on the facility's progress. Since it was so new, the program was still on probation and Leon personally appeared before the accreditation board rather than trust the report to a subordinate. Besides, he liked rubbing elbows with the politicos. Leon loved power and people with power. Look at his friendship with Peter MacBrayne.

She sighed. It's a strange world when two of a woman's lovers become bosom buddies. It was a match made in hell: Leon, who would do anything to get power, and Peter, who had all the power he needed but didn't know how to use it.

Otherwise he might still have his son at home with him.

Power can buy only so much silence, but a near tragedy is nowhere nearly so sexy as the real thing. Dorothy Slimson had watched with a newcomer's awe while the town of Douglasville closed ranks around the wounded leader of its primary industry and biggest employer. The national media, already aware of the town due to the Scorpio Slasher, tried to penetrate the mystery of the briefly-reported, then vanishing story of the wedding party that had been poisoned.

Dorothy was relieved that no one had died. Not even the smallest of the wedding guests, snuggled into the pouch of her mother's womb, was injured in the end. The hook was gone, the media fish-of-the-moment had swum away, taking with it the satellite trucks and smooth-talking Midwestern accents.

But the problem still remained. There was a sense of unreality about the whole situation. The police took their normal tack, followed the obvious evidence, then returned to Dunkin' Donuts. Had Peter resisted or stood by his son's plea of innocence, they might have investigated more closely. But he was stunned, embarrassed and hid behind the official version.

Dorothy watched Doug from the secret crows nest of her job. The powerless often resort to silence as their last bastion of safety in a loud world that has used them for its purposes. Her heart sank as she saw Doug realize that his protestations of innocence would be ignored, that the frame on the wedding portrait had been chosen, accepted and paid for by him. From that moment, he had refused to speak of it, or of anything.

She followed his days in the Douglasville Sanitarium, which passed slowly, quietly. Kautsch had him brought to his office daily, during the first two months. She knew from typing the reports, that Doug sat, arms folded, gaze steady and spoke not a word, no matter the threat or cajole.

Rather than just give in to Doug's silence, Kautsch forced him to sit and watch him work, to listen to phone calls to the outside world. Doug watched stoically as Kautsch dictated letters and therapeutic advice. At the end of each appointed hour, a psych tech came to lead Doug to his dayroom.

By the beginning of the third month, there were three other young people sharing the East Wing of the sanitarium. Another four arrived by the end of the sixth month of Doug's incarceration. They called him "The Silent One," but not as a joke or putdown. Rather out of respect for his quietude. Because whenever one of them fell, it was Doug who quietly righted him and sent him on his way. If sadness overwhelmed, it was Doug who comforted. When the confinement or anger became more than one could contain, it was Doug who approached silently and helped him regain his self-control.

Dorothy Slimson observed and understood the silence. She maintained it herself as she watched him, day-after-day, keeping her own diary of the boy's quiet ways. She learned to read the hushed murmurings, subtle communications that flowed from his eyes. Cautious messages of momentary pain, brief flashes of joy.

When he began his silence, she knew he would eventually need one avenue of expression, one person with whom he could share the news of day, even if unspoken. So she learned to read the grammar of his eyes.

There were the usual bad days. His face would be clouded, his demeanor bent against some inner storm. On those days she made sure to touch him—a hand on the shoulder, a casual squeeze of his elbow. Any contact to keep him tethered to the earth, connected to the world of people, instead of spirits.

Good or bad moments, he was learning through them all. That much she knew. There was a little more knowledge every day. Something deep and unfathomable to others was forming in his mind. About six weeks into the silence, she had asked him if he wanted a journal to write his thoughts. He shook his head. Words were too dangerous, written or otherwise.

"You just make sure you remember all this, Doug," she said. "All that's going on in your head. Okay?"

He nodded.

"Good. Because some day this is all going to be over and I expect you to tell me all about it."

He crossed his heart.

She smiled as she pulled her car into the empty slot in front of the cafe. Sometimes she thought Grumpy must put a spell on the spot on Thursdays, because it was invariably open. When she stepped out of the car, she heard her name and turned. Clint and Mandy Sharpe were walking toward her. Mandy walked as if her water might break at any moment.

"Clint, Mandy." She waved.

"Miss Slimson," Clint said, his arm around Mandy's waist.

"From the look of things, you should be at the hospital instead of walking up and down the street."

Mandy's smile was tight. "Couldn't spend another afternoon alone at home with my feet up. So I made Clint bring me here."

"Job interview." Clint explained.

"What about your thesis?"

"Almost finished. I'm not happy with some of my conclusions. But in the meantime, got to find a way to put food on the table."

"Have you applied at the sanitarium?"

"Don't think I'm qualified."

"You're a teacher, right?"

"Yes."

"Well, the state hires tutors all the time."

Clint held the door open for the two women. "I might just do that, Miss Slimson. Thank you."

Grumpy and Fiona met the trio just inside. There was a flurry of hugs and hellos and they were led to her regular table. The salad was already waiting for her and Kim was bringing a bowl of soup from the kitchen.

Dorothy thanked her, sat and began to tell Fiona of Doug's week. She stopped for a moment, to gaze at the faces before her, all full of love and friendship. A warm glow started in her chest and she smiled, blinking several times. Let her old lovers go after all the power they wanted. These friends were plenty. More than plenty.

❣

Peter glanced at the blueprints, then up again at the workmen crawling among the maze of pipes and machinery. He traced a line on the page, then measured the distance between his thumb and forefinger.

"Are you sure that bleed-off valve is large enough?"

The engineer studied the drawing, then looked at the construction. "Plenty, Mr. MacBrayne. If anything, it's larger than specified. Just to be sure."

Peter's head bobbed, he chewed his lip. "There's a lot riding on this, you know."

"Yes, sir."

"Okay then."

He handed the drawings to the man, then walked over to the office complex. He both hated and loved new projects. He loved the sense of growth, of expansion, but hated all the time it took to accomplish it. He knew the industry was watching and waiting. The stock had reached a plateau. The market waited only for the first news of successful production to zoom again.

He was grateful Dan had talked him into bankrolling the new facility with a loan, using his own holdings as collateral. The construction was right on schedule. Knapp was unusually enthusiastic about the new results. In only a week, the first batch of UltraLeather would roll off the production line and head for the marketplace.

Let someone try to take him over then. Peter took a deep breath of fresh air, then went inside. Grace met him in the hallway.

"Mr. MacBrayne, I was just coming to get you."

"What is it?"

"Dr. Kautsch is here. Says he must speak with you, immediately."

Peter thanked her and hurried to his office. Kautsch was studying an ancient picture of Sarah Douglas.

"Leon, how are you?" Peter said, extending his hand.

"Fine, thanks." He accepted Peter's handshake, pointed to the picture. "Your grandmother must have been quite a character."

"She was." Peter stood next to him. "Wacky as all get-out, but lucky as hell also."

"Lucky?"

"Well, she used some pretty unorthodox methods to keep Douglas Industries afloat during the depression. Never missed, as far as I can tell. Of course, that was long before the first MBA showed up."

"Of course." Kautsch continued to stare at the picture.

"You didn't came here to ask me about my grandmother."

"No, she just caught my eye." Kautsch chuckled. "I actually came to talk to you about Doug."

"Anything wrong?"

"Not really. He's still not talking yet and that troubles me."

"Me too, isn't there anything you can do?"

"Well, it's my feeling that his silence has gone on long enough. He's shown remarkable will. He's angry, though he rarely shows it, and there's still no sign that he's accepted the fact that he seriously endangered all those people at the reception. No remorse. And of course he's frustrated at being confined."

"Nobody's happy about that, but does he realize the alternative? Does he really think he'd be better off in a juvenile facility?"

"It's hard to say what he thinks. Not speaking and all." Kautsch pulled out a cigar, motioned permission to light it. Peter nodded. "You see, Peter, there's a certain turning point, after such a long period of time, when the patient retreats so far into themselves that only radical treatment can bring them out. I've resisted that so far, because I wanted him to come to his senses on his own. It doesn't look like that's going to happen."

"What are you suggesting? Electro-shock therapy? I don't know—"

"That would be the last resort." Kautsch blew a plume of blue smoke toward the ceiling. "There are drugs—"

"Just don't tell me sodium pentothal."

"No." Kautsch shook his head grimly. "That might break down his resistance right after administration, but wouldn't help us during the course of the day. There is a drug, Habilimyacin, that has been used successfully to soften resistance. It tends to stabilize the emotional state, make the patient more malleable, less moody."

"Is it addictive?"

Kautsch smiled. "Not in the least. Though I would venture that some psychiatrists are addicted to prescribing it."

"It's that effective?"

"Yes. What we'll try to do is gradually bend him away from this resistant state. As he loosens up, begins to talk and communicate, then we can advance his treatment. The sooner this happens, the sooner he might see the outside again."

"He is aware that his silence is part of what is keeping him there."

"Possibly. Psychiatrists are trained to listen to what patients say and gauge their state through their words. The therapy becomes less exact when we have to guess."

Peter studied his hand for several moments. He spoke without looking up. "You didn't have to tell me this, did you, Leon? I mean, you could have just gone ahead and done this, right?"

"Yes, I could have, Peter. But that would have gone against the spirit of our relationship. You and I have gone through a lot with Doug, kind of like partners. I would never do anything without consulting you beforehand."

"You have no idea how much I appreciate that, Leon."

"Well, then do I have your consent to go forward?"

"Anything you deem necessary to speed Doug's progress, so he can get the hell out of there, is okay by me."

Kautsch left and Peter walked up to Sarah's picture. She had always been nice to Peter. Crazy as an old coot, as his mother used to say, but always managed to rise out of her eccentricities and be a grandmother to her grandson. Now she seemed to be reproaching him.

He turned away from the picture. Maybe it was time to have the office redecorated.

Kautsch chewed on his cigar furiously on the way to his car. Step one completed. That was easy. The other steps might not be so. But if state accreditation board wanted action on Doug's case, they'd get it. How dare they impose a time limit on a sick person's mental health? Everything would have been fine if only Doug had responded like any normal kid to the situation.

Shit, those kids had played their roles perfectly. Jimmy had taken the bait—hook, line and sinker. Leon had almost blown the whole deal by walking into his office on Saturday. He could still hear Jimmy's breathing behind the sofa. And the hole in the wall with the missing vent? Did he think the doctor was blind? How well they had all played their parts, never realizing that the new facility would need one star patient, someone crazy enough to attract attention to the need for the sanitarium.

Leon had known that one of the two boys would fit the bill. Doug was his first choice, given the hook into the father, but Jimmy would have done just as well. He had to give Jimmy credit. The little con man had pulled off the perfect frame-up.

Of course, as it turned out, with Sabey now being assigned to them, the need for one of the boys became secondary, but hell, funding was funding—no, it was Everything.

Now everything was in jeopardy, because Doug wouldn't talk. Kautsch knew he had to show some form of therapeutic progress, or the temporary accreditation might be lifted. Kautsch understood the politics at the state level perfectly well. There were plenty of other facilities that would love to have a cash-cow-loony like Sabey.

Kautsch climbed into his car, slammed the door shut and revved the engine. Goddamn it, Doug was going to talk if Kautsch had to stick his hand up the kid's ass and do a ventriloquist act.

Abe put down his pen and rubbed his eyes. They were getting nowhere. Sabey either had some kind of block today, or wasn't concentrating. Not that he had to anymore, since the trial was over. As far as he was concerned, he had nothing but time from now on.

Abe resisted the temptation to walk to the window and see what had captured Sabey's attention.

"What are you looking at, Cameron?"

Sabey spoke without taking his eyes from the window. "That kid out there, the one that never talks. Who is he?"

"Just a kid with a problem."

"Lots of those. What's he in for?"

"To be cured of his problem."

Sabey's smile contorted his bland features. "Good answer." He shuffled to his chair, adjusted the chain and sat. "Since you won't tell me that, how 'bout telling me something else?"

"Perhaps. Depends on the question."

"Always does, Doc."

Abe tapped his pencil on the desk. "What's the question?"

"Well, seems to me, Doc." Sabey shifted in his chair, found a comfortable position. "Seems to me that you're different since we come over here. Like you got this little bitty bug up your ass about something, but can't say it."

"I don't know what you mean."

"Oh, yes you do." Sabey's eyes took on that laser pierce. "You know something you ain't saying. And I think I know what it is."

"Oh really?"

"Yeah. You figured it all out. You figured out that I was talking the truth. About dying at a certain time. And you know what?"

"What, Cameron?"

"You knew during the trial, but didn't say."

"And how did you figure this out, even if it were true, which it isn't?"

Oh, it's true, all right, Doc. Wanna know how I know?"

"I'm all ears." Abe tried to keep his face impassive. But a bead of sweat dribbled down his eyebrow and cheek.

Sabey saw it, grinned, opened his hands, palms out. "I've touched death with these hands, Doc. There's this moment, see, when death is right there, right within my fingers—it makes the hand hum—glow, kinda. There's something else there besides death at the instant. Truth is there too, see? Death and truth, they ain't so far apart. They come real close together and when you feel it in your hands, you can feel it for the rest of your life. Don't need to be close to the person, when you've held as much death as I have. It's something you can smell all the way across the room."

"Cameron, do you honestly expect me to tell you I perjured myself?"

·Sabey laughed. "Naw, Doc. I just wanted to let you know I knew. Hell, I don't give a shit. You did your job—the rest is up to me now."

"What are you talking about?" A cold hand clamped onto Abe's heart.

Sabey rose, ambled to the window. He stood for three or four minutes, gazing out. His bland, impassive face showed no expression.

"You fucked up, Dr. Avisson. You were studying me so hard, you missed the obvious. It's been there the whole time."

"Cameron—"

"See, time is the real judge and jury. And I'm the executioner." He giggled. "Yeah, I'm the executioner."

"What are you talking about now, Cameron?"

"You play your part. I play mine. And the victims play theirs. You check. You'll see." His voice was wistful, even-toned. But when Sabey turned, his eyes were black. All the blue had left them. Sky-blue had turned to dark, dark night. "Pure and simple, Doc. Orders of the Universe."

❦

Doug felt someone looking at him. He glanced around the exercise yard: empty except for the completely bald-headed psych tech who was leaning against the far wall, smoking a cigarette. He searched the windows, but saw only the shadow of a face from the West wing.

The vibrations hovered. Doug quickly walked over to the Tech, motioned that he wished to go inside. The Tech nodded, flung his half-smoked cigarette away. Doug felt the color leaving his face. The Tech responded immediately, supported Doug and hurried him down the hallway. Inside his room, the man laid him down gently and arranged his legs on the bed.

Doug barely heard the door close, before it started in full.

The hot, spicy meat burned James Davidson's tongue. He reached for the wineskin and drank deeply. Gemilla tried to hush her brothers, but they laughed.

"If you Englishers can't even take a little spice, how do you expect to defeat the Sultan's army?" Jamal, the younger brother said in Arabic.

Davidson recovered his breath. "Your stomachs may be armored, but that will not protect you from the steel tip of the archer's arrows."

This produced more laughter.

"Please, do not laugh." Davidson looked to Gemilla for help. She shrugged. "You must flee. They will be here in another day, two at the most."

"Do you not betray your brothers by telling us this?" asked Khalid, the other brother. "Are you not afraid that your God will strike you down for even eating with us in our tent?"

"I do not claim to understand the mysteries of my god, or any god, for that matter. If Gemilla had not found me after the sandstorm, I would surely have perished." He gazed at her. She lowered her eyes. "And it is only your kindness that allows me to warn you, to help you escape, so you may survive what is coming."

"Others have come, Englisher Davidson," Khalid said. "But they forgot that the desert is our father. Many armies have come from all directions to the desert to defeat us. Occasionally they win battles, but they cannot defeat the desert. Our father always wins. And we survive because we honor our father. He sends the wind and the sand into the eyes of our enemies, or he drives them mad with thirst. Our father is clever, the way he hides his water. We thank you for this warning, but we will let Allah guide us and the father desert will protect us."

Sick with misery, Davidson put down the lamb and wiped his mouth. "I thank you for this food and for your generosity." He rose and walked out of the tent.

Gemilla caught him ten yards away.

"Where do you go, Davidson?"

"I must think, Gemilla. And pray."

"Pray for what?"

He lowered his head. "There are so many things I don't understand. When I left England, my country, I swore that I would kill fifty infidels."

Her eyes widened with horror. "But why so many?"

"There was an accident—my horse—a child was killed. It was my fault."

"You would kill fifty of my people, for a child's life?"

"Yes." He could not look at her. "At least I thought so at the time. Now, I am not so sure."

"But if you are not sure, perhaps the others in your army, maybe they will think differently as well."

"No, they will not."

"But your heart has changed, has it not?"

"Yes."

"Then perhaps you can tell them, change their hearts."

"Gemilla." He took her hands in his own. "If you and your brothers will not leave, I don't know if I can save you. You must talk to them. This army that approaches is the largest ever assembled for a crusade. Nothing will stop them."

"My brothers will not leave."

"Then you come with me. We'll leave here. Come with me to England."

"Davidson. Would you stay here with me, if I asked you to?"

He shook his head. "I could not. I have sworn allegiance to the king."

"And I am a daughter of the desert. You told me your country is green, like an oasis that stretches for thousands of hectares. What would I do when the cold and rain comes? This snow you tell me of, that makes your bones shake? How long would I survive? I am a daughter of the desert as you are a son of the rain and green."

"But you would survive. I would make certain that you were warm."

She smiled, caressed his cheek. "You are beautiful to the women of your land, are you not?"

He blushed, fingered the swollen red mark, behind his ear, the mark that had been his embarrassment throughout his life. "I would not know that."

"Ah, but I do. I see it. You wear their pleasing looks like a burnoose."

"What does that have to do with what I am saying?"

"A beautiful man, just as a beautiful woman, belongs to his people, to his women. They would spit at me for stealing you away from them."

"I would kill anyone who spit at you."

She laughed. "Then you would be killing for the rest of our lives." Then she grew serious. "Davidson, your god sent you here, just as Allah decreed that my brothers and I should be born here. Your god dictated that you should meet us. You have a choice. If you tell me you will stay, I will convince my brothers that what you say of the army is true and we will hide. I can convince them that only a man who tells the truth would make such a sacrifice."

"I must think and pray, dear Gemilla. I will tell you in the morning.

And so she left him.

That night, he found no comfort on the skins that were between him and the sand. His dreams were shallow, filled with alternating cries from the mother of the dead child Willum, and Margaret's painful goodbye. In the midst of the dream, he felt Gemilla come and lay beside him. She cooled his fevered brow with kisses, warmed his chill flesh with her own.

When he awoke in the morning, she was gone. As sleep left his senses, he heard English voices. The sound of horses hooves stomping the ground. He rose quickly, hurried to the opening of the small tent. To his horror, he saw Gemilla and her brothers bound, hand and foot.

Damien Arbuthnot stood before them. He turned when one of the men shouted Davidson's name.

"Ah, brother, we were afraid you were lost in the storm."

"I was. These people rescued me."

Arbuthnot sneered. "An act of Christian charity, rare in the desert."

"But one that deserves a reward, wouldn't you agree?"

Arbuthnot's eyes became slits. He studied Davidson for several moments. Nodded. "Normally, I would agree. But there is a problem."

"And what is that?"

"You see, James, these are the first infidels we have encountered. There is no doubt their act of charity will serve them well in heaven, but they are infidels nonetheless. If I spare them, it will slow the pace of our crusade. Our soldiers may hesitate with the next group we encounter, ask if they too, are capable of Christian charity. This I cannot abide. No, we must begin properly."

"You're just going to kill them?"

"No, James. You are going to kill them."

Davidson panicked. Looked around, saw the standard bearing the cross and the lion. "What if they were willing to convert to Christianity, accept our Lord into their hearts. Might that not save them?"

Arbuthnot pondered the suggestion. "I do not believe they would do so."

"I will talk to them. Akmed taught me their language. I can assure you—"

Arbuthnot silenced him. "I will allow this, but you must prove it to my satisfaction."

"Anything."

"I will let them live, on the condition that they indeed convert, but as proof of their conversion, they will give us their right ear."

Davidson blanched at the idea, but realized that Arbuthnot would not be swayed. He walked slowly to the three and spoke softly in Arabic. The two brothers resisted at first, but James chided them, reminding them that they might go to Allah, but the only way to save Gemilla's life was to agree to the terms. Jamal and Khalid spoke too rapidly for Davidson to understand, then agreed.

Gemilla grew pale when she heard the terms but agreed after seeking her brothers' consent with words in a dialect Davidson could not follow.

"We will do this, but only if we may keep our pride."

"How?"

"I will remove my brothers' ears myself."

Davidson translated the condition. Arbuthnot looked with respect on Gemilla, then nodded his consent. One of the guards untied her and handed her a knife, then stepped away.

She walked up to Jamal, kissed him on the cheek, then drove the knife into his heart. In a flash, she turned and kissed Khalid quickly, killing him similarly. Then she turned to Davidson, the knife held high.

"I told you, I am a daughter of the desert."

"Gemilla, don't!"

She plunged the knife into her own heart.

Davidson fell to his knees, weeping. Arbuthnot lifted him by his collar.

"You fool!" The man cried, his face red with rage. "You knew she would do this."

Davidson could not speak. He stared at Arbuthnot, transfixed, as the man's penetrating, bright blue eyes turned dark as night. He barely heard the sword being drawn, did not even feel the blade on his neck.

Doug awoke with a start. His throat felt raw, sore. He went to the door, looked out the small window to the dayroom. All was quiet. He had missed supper. He returned to his bed and lay with his hands laced behind his head. He felt as if another piece of the puzzle had just fallen into place. But he still couldn't see the whole picture, and that frightened him. Would he find out in time?

If it were as important as it felt, he could break his silence. But what if he spoke to the wrong person? All would be lost. Perhaps it was, anyway.

He closed his eyes, not to sleep, but to drive the questions away. If only there were someone he could talk to about this. But who?

There was a tap at the door and then it opened. Doug sat up. The bald-headed psych tech entered. He carried a tray with a small carton of milk and a sandwich.

Doug started to say, "Gee, thanks," but stopped himself.

The tech nodded, put the tray down and left, quietly. Doug chewed the sandwich eagerly. He started to giggle in mid-bite. The man looked just like the genie from Aladdin's lamp. The idea struck him as so funny he didn't stop giggling until he realized there were tears streaming down his face.

He couldn't remember the last time he'd actually laughed. His arms went tight around his waist. He felt as if he might explode. He sobbed and sobbed as he hadn't since he arrived. He missed everyone so much, Nanny, Dad, Sally, even Jimmy. What he wouldn't give to see Jimmy, have him pull some mean trick. He could even take that now.

Just when he was sure he was going to fly apart, he felt a warm glow above him. He looked up, but it was just the light fixture, covered with strong metal mesh. The sense of warmth continued to grow, taking the chill from his insides, almost drying his tears.

Somewhere in his astonishment, the pain had slipped away. He was as trapped as ever, but the pain was gone.

There was another tap at the door. He wiped his eyes, sniffled once, then drank the last gulp of milk in the carton. The bald man entered, raised his eyebrows to ask if Doug was finished. Doug nodded, stood and handed him the tray. The man took the tray, turned to leave.

"Thank you," Doug whispered.

The man nodded without turning around.

Sally turned the music up to block the sounds of the argument downstairs. She glanced at the snapshot Talia had taken of her and Doug at the wedding, then unconsciously grasped the pendant that hung around her neck and closed her eyes. A wave of pain and loneliness engulfed her.

Doug was crying.

In her mind, she pictured him in a small room, sitting on a bed, his arms around his waist, rocking and sobbing. She concentrated, exactly as Janina had taught her, started by lighting a small candle in her own heart. As the light grew, she created a bright halo to hover just above his head. Then she sent the light down through the halo to him first, then eventually to fill the room. As she focused, the sounds of the argument below faded.

Then there was nothing but light. Before she realized it, her hand was on her tarot deck. She didn't pull the cards to any particular spread, Janina had told her to occasionally just look at the cards, one after another, and let them tell the story. She saw the Knight of Wands, that would be Doug, followed by the Nine of Swords, the dreamer, weeping in bed. Next came the King of Pentacles. Doug's father, followed by the Five of Pentacles, a boy on crutches following his impoverished mother. Then the Four of Pentacles, the miser card. Enter the Trickster, the Seven of Swords. Then in fast succession, the Devil, the Tower, and the Death card. Her hand shook as she pulled the Empress. That was her. What task though?

The Three of Pentacles: The secret ceremony. She studied the card. A young man and woman standing in a dark chapel with a gray priest. Followed by the Hermit, a shrouded man holding a lantern. And finally, the Judgment card. Young children, colorless, reaching up to an angel blowing a trumpet, answering its call.

Her eyes drifted across the row of cards. She saw the flow of events, some past, some waiting, but what was the task?

In a corner of her mind, she heard Janina's whisper. "Don't try to see what the cards mean. Remember, everything that will come to pass has already happened. And everything that has happened will come to pass. Remember."

She stared at the Secret Ceremony. Remember? Then it hit her. She grabbed a sweater and opened her door a crack. The argument was over. Her father must have gone to the bar, and her mother had retreated to their bedroom.

She tiptoed down the stairs, slipped out the kitchen door and hopped on her bike.

As she rode, she went over the cards in her mind. Doug, his father, Jimmy the Trickster, Kautsch the Devil....The Tower meant a terrible collapse. But who did the Death card represent? She was the Empress, Janina had assigned that card to her.

After several minutes of furious pumping, she arrived at the MacBrayne estate. She stowed her bike alongside one of the overgrown bushes. She shook her head when she remembered the first time she came here. How astonished she had been that the cast of Peter Pan was carved into what Doug had called Topiary. She smiled. How she missed him in school—his funny, clever way with words.

Now the bush-figures were overgrown and their tale sadly obscured. She made her way slowly to the cemetery. There was just enough light from the half moon to see. The place felt lonely more than creepy. The hulking, burned-out shell of the chapel, rose ominously in the dark. She hurried between the headstones, minding her footing as best she could.

What was his name? She searched her memory, tried to listen for Doug's voice.

"Hello?" She called out softly. "Are you there, Fester?"

An owl hooted. She jumped. Her armpits were wet with worry.

"Come on, man," she called out again. "We need your help here, dammit."

Still nothing. She thought she heard a dog bark from the house, but it could have come from the other way.

"Nestor? Are you around?"

She reached for her pendant. It was warm to the touch.

"Please, Doug needs your help, Chester."

A cool breeze rose behind her. She turned. A tall figure moved among the shadows. The man's handsome face shone beneath the shock of thick, reddish hair and the white rim of the clerical collar, barely exposed above a long, flowing black cassock.

"Oh, my God." Sally gulped.

"The name is Hector, if you please." He bowed stiffly. "How may I be of service?"

Abe pounded on the apartment door. He stopped when he heard "Coming," from inside. Grumpy opened the door wearing a robe.

"Abe? What the hell?"

"We have to talk, Grump."

"But it's nearly eleven."

"That's just it. It's eleven, and going on twelve."

Grumpy pulled him inside. Fiona called from the bedroom. "Who is it?"

"It's Abe, dear. I'll talk to him."

"Is everything all right?"

"Yes. I'll be in when we're Wnished."

She emerged from the bedroom, tying the sash to her robe. "Abe comes here at eleven o'clock. Everything is not all right." She bustled past to the kitchen. "I'll put on the kettle."

Grumpy led Abe to the living room and sat him in an overstuVed chair. "Now, you catch your breath and tell me what this is all about."

Abe nodded, waited for his breathing to settle. He glanced over at Fiona standing in the kitchen doorway, arms folded.

"I just Wnished going over everything: the interviews, the trial notes, the police reports."

"Why?"

"Something Sabey said today."

"And?"

"He was taunting me. Said he knew that I knew, that I lied in court. You know, about his dying at the right moment."

"You're worried about him turning you in? I don't think—"

"He doesn't care about that," Abe said harshly. "The man is a monster, I tell you."

"Yes, he's certainly a monster," Grumpy agreed. "But what else?"

"Well, he made this vague threat. Not really a threat, a kind of a promise, but I didn't know what he was talking about. He said I had missed the most important part."

"I don't see what you could have missed. I mean—"

"But I did. I just found it."

The tea kettle whistled. Abe held his head in his hands, listening to the clink of china in the kitchen.

"What did you miss?" Grumpy glanced over as Fiona entered with a tray.

"The most important part. He was right, dammit. It was there the whole time."

"Here," Fiona said. "Drink some tea and tell us."

Abe's hand shook as he accepted the cup. His voice was Wlled with misery. "There were eleven victims."

"That's right."

"Yes, that's right. But that's where I was so stupid." Abe reached and put a lump of sugar in his tea, stirred it. "It really was there the whole time."

"What, Abe?" Fiona's voice was tight. "What was there?"

"Each of the victims represented a diVerent astrological sign. I ran charts on all of them. Each one indicated the possibility of a violent death."

Grumpy shook his head. "What does that mean, Abe?"

"Nothing, except Sabey keeps talking about Orders of the Universe. That he is just following the Orders of the Universe. Over and over again."

"Does that mean he's any less crazy?" Fiona asked.

Abe looked up through bloodshot eyes. "No, not at all. He's just as crazy, but also just as dangerous."

"That's why he's locked up. What harm can he do to the public there?"

"To the public?" Abe sighed. "To the public, nothing. It's the patients I'm worried about. One patient in particular."

Grumpy put his cup down. "The twelfth sign."

Abe nodded.

"What sign is that?" Fiona asked slowly, then anxiously as Abe didn't answer right away. "What sign, Abe?"

"Aquarius."

Fiona moaned. "February 10. That's Aquarius, right?"

"Yes."

The three sat in silence for several minutes. Finally, Grumpy put his hands on his knees and stood.

"Well, it seems we have only two choices."

"What's that?" Abe asked.

"One, we get Doug the hell out of that place. He should have never been in there, anyway."

"Agreed," Abe said. "What's the second choice?"

Grumpy looked at Abe, avoiding Fiona's eyes entirely. "We make sure that Sabey never hurts anyone—ever again."

Before anyone could speak, there was a light tapping at the door. Fiona went and looked through the small, square window. She opened it quickly.

"Sally? What are you doing out so late?"

"Sorry, Fiona. I—I didn't know where else to go."

Fiona led Sally inside. She gasped as soon as she could see the girl's face in the light. "My goodness. You're white as a sheet. You look like you've seen a ghost."

"I *have* just seen a ghost." Sally smiled weakly. "His name is Father Hector."

"Oh Lord, not him, again," Fiona said, then hurried into the kitchen. She returned a moment later with a bottle of brandy.

"Fiona," Grumpy said. "You can't give Sally brandy."

Fiona looked up, unscrewed the bottle, and poured it into her own tea.

Chapter Seventeen

When she arrived Monday morning, Dorothy was surprised to see Leon already in his office. The coffee pot was full and he was actually humming. She tapped the jamb of his open door.

"You're here early."

He looked up. Grinned. "Come on in, Slim."

She winced at the old nickname. "I should collect the weekend reports."

"Already done." He beamed a Cheshire smile, nested his hands on the desktop.

She sat in the chair across from him. "Okay, I'll bite. What's up?"

"Big week ahead of us. I'm going to need your help."

"I work here. That's part of my job description."

"Uh, yes, sure. But this week is different. I've got a special project for you."

She pulled out her notepad. "Go ahead."

"You won't need notes. It's very simple. We have probably three weeks, a month at the most, to get Doug talking and back on track."

She slowly lowered her pencil. "What?"

"That's right. Otherwise our little Lord Fauntleroy goes to another facility."

"But—"

"No buts. The State has spoken."

"Then why are you so happy?"

"I have a plan."

"Not surprising." For a moment she was afraid he would react to her sarcasm. He didn't.

"We are admitting a new patient this afternoon. I'm going to have Doug take her under his wing. Put him in charge of showing her the ropes."

"I see. That's going to be a little difficult for him, isn't it? Given that he's not talking."

"Really?" He smirked. "I hadn't considered that part of it."

She closed her notepad, started to rise. "Well, it's an interesting plan."

"But," Leon said. "That's not all of it."

"Ah." She sat down.

"Yes, there's more. You see, if he doesn't snap out of it by Friday, we're going to start drug therapy."

She covered her concern. "And just what therapy might that be?"

"Habilimyacin."

She felt sick. The side effects of Habilimyacin could be justified for autism and other severe disorders, but not for someone so stable as Doug. She nodded.

"Don't like the idea, do you, Slim?"

"I—uh, I just think it's a little radical."

"Radical. Hm. And do you think having him sent to another facility a good idea?" He rose. "Get one thing straight, Nurse Slimson, we've coddled this boy long enough and from what I can see, it hasn't helped one bit."

She allowed no expression to cross her face.

"And Doug needs to know that there are even more radical treatments beyond Habilimyacin." He walked over and turned on the lamp, turned it off again. "Do I make myself clear?"

"Yes, Doctor."

Her mind raced. There had to be a way to get Doug talking without tricking him into it.

"Slim." His voice turned gentle. "It's very clear. Black and white. No gray areas. He either moves forward with treatment or moves on. Are you going to help?"

"Yes, black and white." she mused softly. Glanced up quickly. "Leon?"

Kautsch started at her use of his first name. "Yes?"

"What if there were another way, that might be just as effective, uh, in bringing him out of his shell."

He sat, spread his palms. "I'm all ears."

"Why don't we hire a tutor."

"A speech therapist, I could understand. But a tutor? If there's one area where he's not deficient, it's in his schoolwork."

"Well, not exactly a tutor then, but a teacher. Someone he knows."

Leon's gaze sharpened. "And I suppose you have someone in mind?"

"Well, I ran into Doug's counselor from the camp last summer and he's job-hunting."

Kautsch looked confused. The light went on. "The black guy, Sharpe?"

"That's him. Doug really liked him, as I remember. It would also help with our minority-hiring quota."

He tapped his finger against his chin, started to reach for a cigar, stopped. "No. I don't think so."

"Why not?"

"Think, Slim. Doug has this guy laced all through his hallucinogenic mythology. Doug was also responsible for nearly killing the man's unborn child. Who knows what kind of episodes Sharpe's presence might trigger?"

"True, but I thought the goal was to get him talking. Chicken and egg, Leon."

He considered her proposal for several moments, clapped his hands together. "All right, you got it, Slim."

She sighed, relieved.

"Call him. Have him come in for an interview."

"As soon as I get to my desk."

She started for the door, he was beside her, his arm on her shoulder. "Just like the good old days, eh, Slim?"

"Yeah, Leon. Just like 'em."

"One thing," he stopped her at the hall. "If this doesn't work, we start him on the Habilimyacin."

"I understand."

"Good. It's important that you understand, Slim." His hand slipped down and caressed her buttock. "Very important."

She resisted the urge to slap him, gave him a wan smile and went to her desk. She picked up the phone, while he continued to leer at her.

"Give me information for Clint Sharpe. In Douglasville. That's Sharpe with a 'e' on the end. Thank you."

❦

Sally watched Jimmy while he painted and realized that he had improved over the past year, if that was possible. The style was definitely classical, or so it seemed, from the introductory art classes she had taken. A Madonna-like woman sat on a bench outside the facade of what appeared to be a modern office complex. She was holding a miniature Christ-figure, nailed to a crucifix. She wore the garb of an ancient, but Reeboks were apparent under the folds of her cloak.

"Very nice," she said quietly.

He jumped. "Geez, Sally. Give a guy some warning, would you?"

"I didn't want to disturb you."

"Next time disturb me. Better than having the shit scared out of me."

"Sorry." She walked closer, leaned to look at the small Christ-figure. It was perfectly rendered as far as she could tell. "How you been, Jimmy?"

"Same old, same old." He took a tube of paint, squirted bright yellow on his palette and mixed it with another color. "What do you want?"

"Nothing, just thought I'd see how you were doing."

"Yeah, right." He dabbed paint on the canvas. "You hardly talk to me for nearly a year now and you expect me to believe you just happened by?"

"Yeah, well there is one little thing."

"Which is?"

"I want you to meet somebody."

"Don't tell me." He stepped away from the easel. "You want to fix me up on a blind date, what? Got some ugly cousin coming in from out of town?"

She laughed. "Nothing like that at all."

"That's good. I don't do blind dates. Blonde dates, maybe." Another laugh.

"Okay, who do you want me to meet?"

"It's a surprise. Can you get out at night?"

He snorted. "Does the Pope speak with an accent? Sure. When?"

"Tonight. Got a bike?"

"What no limousine?" He frowned, relented. "Yeah, I can get a bike. Where we going?"

"You'll find out tonight."

He looked at her, shrugged. "Yeah, why not?"

She started away.

"Hey, Sal."

She turned. "Yeah?"

"It better be good."

She smiled. "Don't worry, it will be."

❦

Doug sat in the dayroom leafing through his world history text. He was amazed at how the plague had spread through Europe in the middle-teenth centuries. There was a slight hum in the back of his head, but he resisted it. So many times when he read about the past, the hum would arrive. He was about to turn the page, when he heard Doctor Kautsch.

"Doug?"

He looked up.

Kautsch approached him, a young girl in tow. She looked to be about twelve or thirteen, though her haircut made her look older.

"Ah, there you are." Kautsch stood in front of him. "I'd like to introduce you to Abilene Winter. She's new here, so I thought you'd kind of take her under your wing, help her get adjusted to the place."

Doug's eyebrows raised in query.

"Abilene, this is Doug MacBrayne. Just stick with him and you'll get accustomed to the routine here in no time."

Kautsch walked away. The girl put her hands on her hips.

"So, what are you in for?"

Doug shook his head.

She leaned over, peered into his face, formed her words slowly. "I said, what-are-you-in-for?"

He tapped his mouth.

"Oh, great." She rolled her eyes. "My first day here and they assign me to some dummy. God, what's next, bedpan patrol?"

Doug smirked, a giggle escaped.

"Hey, noise. Hell, that's a start." She looked at his book. "World history? Man, oh man. Borrrring."

She flopped on the sofa next to him, spread her arms out to either side. Doug opened his book again, she reached over and slammed it shut.

"Look, Dougie-pooh. Let's get a couple things straight. You're supposed to show me the ropes. I don't see any ropes." She cackled. "The inmates would probably just use them to hang themselves, anyway, from the look of this bunch."

He snorted.

"Good. We got some real communication goin' on here now." She leaned over, fiddled with the hair on the back of his neck, whispered seductively. "And another thing, Dougie-pooh, you call me Abilene, and you won't get nowhere with me. Understand?"

He didn't. When he tried to scoot away from her, she slid with him.

"So, if you want to get anywhere at all, you just call me by my real name."

He raised his eyebrows. She smiled, puckered seductively, then leaned toward him.

"My real close friends—and I do mean *real* close, Dougie-pooh." She assumed an air of utter boredom. "My real friends call me Belle."

Doug's eyes widened. This, was the hellcat he'd met during his first visit to Kautsch's office. It seemed decades ago. Before the shock wore off, he spotted Miss Slimson watching from the nurse's station. She held her finger to her lips and mouthed the word "Later."

He nodded.

☙

Grumpy hung up the phone and sighed. Fiona wiped her hands behind the counter and moved next to him. She glanced at several people idly searching through the bookshelves.

"What's the matter?"

"That was Dorothy. Kautsch is planning to put Doug on drugs to make him start talking."

"What?"

He nodded grimly. "She couldn't really talk about it, but she said he's got this whole game plan devised. If Doug doesn't start communicating soon, he may be transferred to another facility."

She sat wearily at a table. "I don't understand it."

"What, dear?"

"It seems like, from the moment he was born, nothing but trouble has surrounded Doug." She looked up. "What did he do to deserve this? He's the nicest boy I've ever met."

"I know." Grumpy put his hand on her shoulder. "All I can tell you is that he must be destined for great things."

"But this is all so strange." She breathed deeply. "Horoscopes, serial killers, ghosts. It would be bad enough with the ordinary troubles he has, but all this other stuff makes my head swim. I can't imagine what it must be like for him."

"When he told you about Father Hector the first time, did he seem upset or confused?"

She thought for a moment. "No, not really."

"And those vibrations episodes, was he upset by them?"

"Not as far as I could tell. They bothered me a lot more than him."

"See? This is just Doug's life. Sarah used to say that the universe made us with just enough stuff to live our lives. The challenges were always just a little beyond our abilities so we had to stretch, to grow to meet them." He sat across from her. "Doug is an extraordinary boy, you've said that yourself a hundred times. He understands all this, in ways we never could."

"Maybe so," Fiona said. "But when does he get to start living his life? When does he get to start being happy?"

"He was happy with you."

A large tear formed in her right eye, rolled down her cheek. Grumpy cursed himself for saying it, even if it had been meant to help. He realized that he had made the same mistake as had everyone else who'd thought of Fiona as Doug's nanny. She was more his mother than most natural mothers were to their children. There was nothing theoretical or objective about her care for his grandson. When he had been away, when Peter had been busy with the company, Fiona had been there every minute with Doug. Loving and caring for the boy with vigilance, wisdom and love that far surpassed ordinary biological maternity.

"I'm sorry, Fiona."

"For what?" she murmured softly.

"For lots of things. Mostly for not being around to help when you needed it."

This brought a different light to her eye. She took his hand across the table and squeezed it.

"Don't you know, you—you—" Her smile was odd, a new one he'd never seen. "You showed up exactly when I needed you."

A tear now formed in his eye, for he recognized the new light, the new smile.

She had said it many times, shown it in many ways. But for the first time he understood, and better than that, he believed.

The light he saw in her face was real love.

"Fiona, my dear wife—" He lowered his voice so only she could hear. "I make you this vow: Before that lunatic Kautsch can give Doug one dose of his drugs, I will spring the boy myself, even if I have to go into that place with the cavalry, swords held high and pistols blazing."

She smiled. "I believe you, all except for the part about the cavalry."

"You don't think I could raise some cavalry if I had to?"

Before she could answer, the door opened and Clint burst in.

"Grumpy, Fiona." He raised his hands in a victory sign. "I've got a job."

Fiona turned. "That's lovely, Clint. Where?"

Clint grinned. "I'll be tutoring at the Douglasville Sanitarium. Full time, with benefits."

Fiona gave Grumpy a sidelong glance. He spread his hands innocently.

"Don't look at me."

"That's wonderful, Clint. When do you start?"

"Tomorrow. Old Freud-face Kautsch hired me on the spot."

Grumpy stood and clapped Clint on the shoulder. "Congratulations. That calls for a cup of coffee, on the house."

"I'd love to, but I have to get home and tell Mandy."

"Give us five minutes, Clint. There's something I need to talk to you about."

"Well—"

Grumpy pushed him down into the chair he had just vacated. "Five minutes only, I promise."

Clint sat while Grumpy poured him a cup of coffee. He put it down in front of him and smiled.

"Clint, have you ever ridden a horse?"

Clint looked at Fiona. She smiled sweetly.

"Uh, once or twice."

"Good, then you qualify."

"For what?"

"You just joined my cavalry." Grumpy winked at Fiona. "See how easy that was?"

❦

Doug stood by the nurse's station for a minute to regain his equilibrium after his talk with Miss Slimson. She had been blunt with him. If he didn't start talking soon, he was going to have to start taking a drug that would make him talk, and worse—there might be side-effects that could permanently damage his thinking.

He glanced across the room. Belle was chattering to some of the other kids. Once she had gotten over the fact that he wasn't going to talk, she carried on as if it didn't matter. He actually didn't mind her constant flow of conversation. Time had actually flown by.

But he didn't want to dive into the river of her talk just yet. He needed to think. Miss Slimson had said it was up to him, his decision. If he started talking just to keep off the drugs, Kautsch would take that as a sign that he had won. And Doug wasn't sure that was such a good thing. He certainly didn't want his brain chemistry altered, but he hadn't started this battle to end up losing by default.

She said he would have until Friday to make up his mind.

Suddenly, there was a loud slap, and a wail. Doug raced over where Belle held her hand to her cheek, tears streaming down her face. One of the other children skulked away to the far corner.

He put his arm around her but she tried to shrug it off. Her body trembled and she cursed under her breath. He caressed her hair, trying to soothe her. She looked up at him through her tears.

"Why are you doing that?"

He smiled, tried to put as much warmth into his eyes as he could.

"Just stop, okay? I hate it when anyone touches my hair."

He nodded, started to walk away. She grabbed his hand, clung to his arm.

"I'm sorry. Please, don't leave me, okay? You can touch my hair. Really." In her new desperation, she put his hand on her head. "See, it's okay. You can do that. Okay?"

Doug blushed, realized that others in the room were watching. He stroked her hair several more times, then led her to the sofa and sat her down. She stayed glued to his side.

"Everyone hits me. I don't understand. What do I do? I try to be nice, talk to everyone. Then they hit me?" She looked up at him. "Promise me you'll never hit me, okay?"

Silently, Doug agreed not to.

"I wish you had been my brother," she said wistfully. "If I had a brother—" She stopped, curled up, her legs crossed, arms tight around her waist. Then she began to emit a low growl.

Doug looked around wildly. He caught the eye of the bald tech who hurried over and knelt before them.

Grunting and growling, Belle began to thrash her arms and legs. The tech caught her and lifted her off the sofa, carried her into her room. Miss Slimson and another nurse rushed through the dayroom to assist.

He followed, watched as they secured her to the bed with leather straps. She kicked and screamed, then howled when her arms and legs were firmly restrained. Doug stood, staring at the writhing figure. Her feet looked so small, so delicate, so perfectly formed.

The vibrations washed over him suddenly. He staggered to his room and curled on the bed.

❦

Only when he reached the door did Lin Feng realize his dilemma. To appear at the wedding might embarrass his new brother-in-law. To stay away could hurt his sister's feelings. Perhaps if he spoke to her alone, it would help solve the problem.

He pushed the door open. There was no one in the kitchen. He heard voices in the front room, so he slipped down the familiar, rear corridor to the children's wing, hesitating when he reached her door. He tapped softly.

"Who is it?" The voice was that of an imperious young woman.

"I have come to rub your legs."

"What?" She opened the door.

She wore the headdress of a bride, the veil obscured her face. The silk wrap went all the way to the floor.

"Yes?"

He bowed. When he looked up, her eyes were confused. A knowing and not knowing at the same time.

"Brother?"

"Little sister."

Her hand started toward him, then retracted.

"I was not sure you would come."

"You are my sister." He smiled. "I would like to share your joy."

Her shoulders sagged. The beautiful dress and resplendent headpiece dimmed with the gesture.

"My joy—" She walked over to the mirror. Lin Feng followed her. On the dresser was his old abacus. His heart jumped. She had kept it as a reminder of him.

"Lift the veil, Mei Li, so I may see your face."

She shook her head.

"Please."

She turned, her fingers shaking as she caught the edges of the sheer fabric that covered her face and lifted.

Lin Feng had indeed been in the monastery for ten years, but even he knew a pretty face when he saw one. He cocked his head.

"You have grown into a very beautiful woman."

Again the shoulders sagged, tears formed in her eyes. She reached for a silk handkerchief to dab them.

"I'm sorry, did I say something wrong?" He started toward her. "I am not good with words. We rarely speak at the monastery."

She shook her head. "What good is a beautiful face—" She lifted the hem of her dress. "—when I am cursed with these."

Lin Feng gazed at what appeared to be the most perfectly formed feet he had ever seen.

"What on earth is the matter with them?"

"Even the strongest silk could not stop them from growing." She sobbed and dropped the hem. "Father says they belong to a horse."

"Are the size of one's feet more important than the depth of one's heart?"

Mei Li glared at him. "Oh, it's so easy to spout such words when you live among monks. But I have shamed our family."

Lin Feng searched his mind for some lesson from the master that might help. He found nothing.

"And now I am to be married to a pig of a man." She threw herself on the bed, sobbing.

He knelt beside her.

What could he say or do to help her resolve this predicament? Should he admit that his childish act of kindness was the reason her feet had grown so normally—and large?

"There are many truths that pervade each act, whether kind or evil," The master said. "A thin veil separates the viewer from every act and how the viewer decorates the veil determines whether it is evil or kind in that person's mind. Do not judge by decoration. Instead attempt to push the veil away and see the act clearly for what it is."

Lin closed his eyes and remembered. He felt the shame of his own deformity, his birthmark, especially when he looked upon his sister's perfect face. She should have been grateful for her beauty, but instead she had been arrogant and selfish—throwing tantrums when she didn't get her way, flying into a rage and blindly striking out with whatever was at hand.

"Sister."

"Yes?"

"Do you not want to marry this man?"

Her shoulders slumped. "I have no choice."

"If you had the choice, would you rather marry this man or be alone for the rest of your life?" His forceful tone surprised even him.

"Don't play games with me."

"What if I can stop the marriage? Would you rather marry him or live alone?"

She thought for several moments. "I would rather live alone—even in a cave."

Lin bowed his head. He then leaned over and kissed her foot. She pulled it away.

"What are you doing?"

"It is an act of contrition."

He tried to kiss the other foot but she jerked it out of reach.

"Brother, are you crazy?"

"Please forgive me, it is my fault your feet are so large."

She sat upright on the bed. "What?"

"I loosened your bindings at night. I knew they hurt you."

"You—you did this to me?"

He nodded. "I beg your forgiveness."

"Why? Why should I forgive you?" She ripped the headdress off. "Why did you do it?"

He reached again for her foot, she kicked at him.

"I could not stand your pain. It was too much for me. I swear."

"You stupid, hateful—because of you, I am consigned to a pig for a husband. You ruined my life."

She leaped from the bed and began throwing everything within reach at him: a small hand mirror, porcelain makeup pots, combs and brushes. He bent from the fury of her assault and staggered toward the doorway.

"Son of a turtle's egg, I hate you."

More articles rained against his back and the wall around him. He moved into the hallway with her in hot pursuit, beating him with his abacus. Voices rose in the main room and Lin headed toward them, where he stumbled and fell, at the feet of his father and the prospective groom.

Her last blow with the abacus opened a deep gash in the back of his head. He could feel the blood pump out with force. He looked up to see the groom's horrified expression. Even a greedy pig would not marry a madwoman who would beat a holy man. Mei Li would get her wish and escape the marriage.

Lin Feng's eyes swam with red, his ears filled with her curses which grew faint as he lost consciousness.

When his eyes opened, the bald tech was sitting on the chair next to his bed. Doug sat up quickly, but blood rushed to his head and he felt woozy. The man stood, motioned Doug to follow. He slowly put his feet over the side of the bed and followed the man. They walked to Belle's room. The man peeked in through the window, nodded for Doug to do the same.

She was sleeping soundly, still secured to the bed by the leather restraints.

Doug looked to the tech for understanding.

"From before. Before." the tech whispered slowly and carefully.

Doug still didn't get it.

"You will remember."

Doug looked through the window again. The dinner bell chimed and when he turned again, the tech was gone.

"Where the hell are we going, Sal?" Jimmy puffed on the bike a few yards behind her.

"You'll see."

"You'll see. You'll see." He mimicked.

They swooped over a hill and he skidded to a stop when the lights of the MacBrayne mansion came into view. Sally stopped, straddled her bike and looked at him.

"What's the matter?"

"I'm not going there."

"Why not?"

"Why should I?"

"You'll see."

"Will you cut it out? You tell me now, or I'll turn around and go back."

She rolled her eyes and straddle-walked the bike to his side. "There's someone there I want you to meet, I told you."

"Who, old man MacBrayne? I don't think so."

"No, someone else."

"Who, some long lost cousin of Doug's? Don't you get it? I don't want nothing to do with that family, or their big, fucking house."

"We're not going to the house. We're going to the cemetery."

"The cemetery." He wheeled his bike around. "That's it. I'm outta here."

"Jimmy!" Sally grabbed his handlebar.

"What?" He asked without turning around.

"You scared? Is that it? Big bad Jimmy Lyden afraid of a cemetery in the dark."

"I ain't scared."

"Then prove it. Come on." She wheeled toward the old chapel.

"Shit." Jimmy rode after her.

They stashed the bikes and slipped past the old chapel to the cemetery. Jimmy stubbed his toe and cried out.

"Shh!" Sally whispered. "They'll hear you."

"Well, it hurt."

"Good. Maybe you'll pay more attention."

She hunched over and made her way to the mausoleum at the edge of the yard, then pushed the door open and motioned Jimmy to follow. He looked up at the moon.

"If I don't come out in five minutes, you come get me, okay?"

"Jimmy," came from inside.

He followed her into the dark, dank mausoleum, bumping into her.

"Yikes!" he cried out.
"Will you stop?"
"Shit, Sal—"
"There's no need to swear," came from the corner.
Jimmy clutched Sally's arm. "W—who—w—what the hell was that?"
Sally struck a match. The candle she was holding sputtered at first, then flared. She placed it on a granite slab in the middle of the room. Golden light filled the room.
"James Lyden, I'd like to introduce you to Father Hector."
The speaker from the dark corner moved into the light on the other side of the slab.
"Shit," Jimmy said. "For a minute there I thought you were a ghost."
The red-haired figure smiled.
"Jimmy," Sally said. "He is a ghost."
"Yeah, right." Jimmy smirked. "And I'm the President of Bulgaria."
Father Hector's smile grew larger as he waded right through the slab and approached them. "I've always wanted to meet the President of Bulgaria."
"F-fuck me," Jimmy said, his eyes rolling in his head.
"Hold on there, Jimmy-boy," Sally said, supporting him. "Don't bail out on me yet, we need your help."

Cameron Sabey's eyes sprang open. He sat up in bed and tiptoed, barefoot, to the door. He looked through the barred window. Down the dark hallway, the guard dozed at his desk.
Sabey smiled and knelt beside the chair that was anchored to the floor. He felt along the inside of a leg and came away with a thin piece of metal. He checked the guard again and slowly began to sharpen the metal strip on the bed frame. He sang under his breath as he worked, a song from his youth.
"Any day now, we'll be together, darling. Any day now, you're gonna be mine."
Over and over again, his whispering song covered the soft, deadly music of his work.

Chapter Eighteen

Peter found Dan Downey in the lab with Jim Knapp. The young scientist was talking excitedly and Downey appeared to be trying to calm him with a hand on his shoulder. Peter couldn't help but smile. Dan was the perfect right-hand man, always had his wits about him. Where Peter tended to lose his cool in such animated discussions, Dan maintained his equilibrium.

"Lovers' quarrel?" Peter said nonchalantly.

"Unbelievable. Just unbelievable." Knapp repeated over and over.

Downey's smile never wavered.

"What's unbelievable?"

"Jim doesn't like the idea of CNN airing our first day of UltraLeather production."

"It's crazy, Mr. MacBrayne," Knapp insisted. "There's a hundred and one things that can go wrong. We'll be adjusting the process for weeks until it's perfect."

"CNN?" Peter asked.

"Yeah, their Weekly Business Journal is featuring us this week. It was either now or six months from now. They had an opening in their schedule."

"I'd go for six months from now, Mr. MacBrayne." The young scientist had a long green stain down the side of his lab coat.

"Jim, this is a shot at national television that may not come along again." Dan maintained his smile, but his voice was firm. "They say they could come back in six months, but network presidents, anchors and producers, come and go, all too often. We're news this week, maybe not, six months from now."

"But live coverage?" Knapp looked as if Dan were about to break his test tubes. "If they taped it, at least we'd have a shot at editing out any serious problems."

"Must it be live?" Peter glanced at Dan.

"It's our only shot, Peter. They contacted our marketing department, this morning.

"They called us?"

Dan nodded. "That's right. They saw the article in the Wall Street Journal and followed up. With a suggestion from our marketing department, of course."

"That's amazing," Peter said, still stunned.

"These are live organisms. We know what they will do in a small, controlled environment." Knapp picked up a beaker, filled with greenish goop. "But there's just no telling what adjustments we'll have to make to the formula when the proportions change. I've told you that."

"Yes you have, Jim." Downey took the beaker, held it up to the light. "And Peter put his ass on the line to provide you with the best facility money could buy to take this product to the next level. That level is production. We have a strict time line for return on our investment That means we have to seize every possible opportunity to market UltraLeather. This shot at national coverage will save us a million dollars in advertising. Do you know how many buyers for major retailers watch the Weekly Business Journal? If we had five hundred telemarketers working for a year, we couldn't cover the same territory."

"Marketing." Knapp's face turned sour.

Downey turned to Peter. "The decision is yours, boss. But I'll have to call them this morning and tell them to hold off six months."

Peter walked over to a side table, picked up a sample. He rubbed it against his cheek, smiled.

"Jim, there is a moment in every company's development when you have to take a great risk to realize a great reward. This is one of those moments." He held up the sample. "I have faith in your work and in Dan's business sense. My grandmother bet the whole company on plastics, when no one believed it them. I'm willing to bet on you."

"I appreciate your faith in me, Mr. MacBrayne, believe me," Jim said glumly, "but your grandmother had a crystal ball."

"That's right, she did." Peter put his arm around Downey's shoulder. "And I've got the best MBA ever to come out of Rutgers."

"Aw, gee, thanks boss."

Downey seemed to be kidding, but Peter was pleased to see that his financial hawk still had the capacity to blush.

Belle sulked when told that she couldn't accompany Doug to meet his new instructor. Her morning, non-stop stream of conversation had included a complete recital on the virtues of seasonal color-coordination in both attire and make-up.

"Now you, Doug, you would be what would be called a spring. Whereas I am more a winter." She pointed to the bald tech. "He is a Fall and that head nurse—Miss Slim-a-ma-bob, she's a summer."

Doug tried to follow for a while, but gave up and just nodded occasionally. Belle would stop talking when he wasn't paying strict attention, establish eye contact, then merrily roll along with another idea that was interesting to Doug only because of her animated delivery.

The bald attendant ushered Doug into the small classroom. The new instructor had his back to Doug, but when he turned, Doug's face lit up.

"Hello, Doug," Mr. Sharpe said. "Nice to see you again."

Doug nodded, happily.

"Come on in. Apparently we have a lot to discuss."

The tech closed the door. Doug walked over and shook Mr. Sharpe's hand. His eyes burned into the man. So many questions.

"Well, we're supposed to start with a survey of your curriculum to date, but I have something to show you." He pulled out a photograph of Mandy.

Doug giggled, pantomimed her round stomach.

"Yes, any day now."

Doug acted out rubbing his stomach, giving a questioning 'okay' sign."

"Just fine, Doug. It was touch and go right after the—" Sharpe paused. "—after the wedding. But they don't think it hurt the baby at all."

Doug ran his palm across his forehead in relief.

Sharpe smiled. "Me too."

There was a moment of silence. Sharpe searched Doug's face, nodded. "You should know, I told them I knew you couldn't have done it."

Doug shook his head furiously.

More nodding. "Yeah, well. Doesn't seem to be much we can do about that, except make the best of it." Sharpe glanced at a piece of paper with a typed list. "Says here you're way ahead in all subjects."

Doug agreed silently.

"Since you're so far ahead, academically—" Sharpe glanced around. "Is this room bugged?"

Doug shrugged, nodded.

"Yeah, well, we won't plot any revolutions then." He reached into his briefcase and pulled out a sheaf of papers. "I happened to bring along our boy Milton—you remember him?"

Doug chuckled.

"Good. Well, I'm finishing my Ph.D. thesis on 'Paradise Lost' and I thought we might look over some things together. It's not strictly on your curriculum list, but it is taught in a few high schools. That okay with you?"

Doug reached for the folder, weighed it. Then he whistled.

"Yeah, Doug. Heavy stuff." Sharpe leafed through the pages, stopped and pointed. "Here is a problem area, as I see it." Then he whispered, "You have any more of those Milton dreams?"

Doug nodded.

"Man, oh, man." Sharpe kept his voice low. "When this is all over, will you promise to tell me all about them?"

Doug couldn't keep the pain from showing in his eyes, but he nodded. He realized that people were much more interested in what he thought and felt since he stopped talking. He heard Belle's voice outside the door. Funny, the more a person talks, the less others listen and apparently vice versa.

He pointed to the page Sharpe had removed and raised his eyebrows.

"Oh, yeah." He took the book out and opened to a marked place. "In the early part, see, Milton seems to waffle a bit on the question of free will, then he comes on strong near the end. What I can't figure out is why he shifted, or what caused him to change his mind."

Doug smiled, walked over to the blackboard and wrote: "Aeropagitica."

"Okay, what about it?"

Doug felt the hum of the vibrations accompanying his trying to remember. He took up the chalk again and wrote, "Just as self-discipline can never be imposed by the State—could God be any less wise?" Doug paused a moment, then continued. "How can man ever hope to cultivate his own virtues if God constantly imposes them on him?"

Sharpe stared at the blackboard, reading the words softly to himself.

"Jumping Jehosephat. That's it, Doug." He chuckled in wonder. "In one swell foop you just gave me the key to this damn thesis and I've been working on it for seven years."

He grew quiet, caught by emotion. He turned away, wiped his eyes. Finally, he spoke. "It has to be true, I mean, that you were there. No boy—nobody—could know of this, otherwise."

Doug looked him square in the eye and nodded, seriously.

"And you being in here, what's that mean? How does this all figure in the grand scheme?"

Doug desperately wanted to tell his former counselor and now teacher what he had come to know over the past six months, but he realized that it wasn't time. He had no argument with Mr. Sharpe but the real battle wasn't over.

He put his finger to his lips, then winked.

❦

"Thank God, this is the last one." Grumpy was halfway through the door with a box of books when Fiona waved him over.

"Telephone for you."

"Who is it?"

"Your stockbroker."

"Jeez, he must be lonely." Grumpy put the books down. "He knows I don't have any spare money to invest."

He walked behind the counter, took the phone.

"Hi, Dale, Grumpy here."

"Hey, Grumpy. Got a hot tip for you."

"Anything more expensive than a paper clip and I'll have to pass." Grumpy waited for the obligatory laughter to stop on the other end. Dale either had a great sense of humor, or business must be terrible. "What's your tip, Dale?"

"Well, you told me to keep an eye out for a chunk of active Douglas Industries stock."

"I did."

"Well, a private investor has just made a very large offering available."

"How much?"

Dale gave him the figure. Grumpy whistled.

"Is it Peter? Is he trying to raise more capital?"

"Well, I can't tell you who it is, except it isn't your son. Most of his stock is tied up with bank loans, from what I hear." Dale cleared his throat. "Do you want any of the action?"

"The only thing I could do would be to convert my second class stock, which would probably give me one for four at best."

"True, but with the Douglas Industries being touted all over CNN, I would grab this now, before the price goes any higher."

"CNN?"

"God, you are retired, aren't you?"

"Oh, I've really become a man of leisure all right." Grumpy glanced around the bookstore, wiped the sweat from his brow for having carried in the loads of books. "What about CNN?"

"I just got a call that Douglas Industries is going to be featured on Weekly Business Journal. They're going to be running commercials about this show for the next few days. Grump, this stock won't be here long."

"Can I ask you a question, Dale?"

"Shoot."

"Is it one of the board members who's selling?"

"No, that much I can tell you."

"Okay, I'll get back to you tomorrow morning with an answer."

"Before closing today would be better."

"I know, but I have to do some figuring."

"All right, Grump. Just remember, I offered it to you first."

"Thanks, Dale."

Grumpy replaced the receiver, walked over and leaned on the coffee counter.

"Good news?" Fiona handed him a cup of tea.

"Not sure." He sipped, gagged. "My God, what's this?"

"It's good for you."

He scrunched up his face. "It's awful."

"Drink it. It's echinacea tea. Helps the immune system."

He looked at it, winced. "Why does everything that is supposed to be good for you always taste so terrible?"

"Maybe to see if you're really serious about your health." She wiped a glass and put it on the shelf. "Now you drink that down."

"Isn't there another way to take this?"

She eagle-eyed him. "Yes, but I don't think you want to hear about it."

He held his nose, drank as fast as he could, sputtered at the bottom of the cup and slammed it down on the counter. "There, I've proved I'm serious about my health. Happy?"

"Yes, dear." She grinned.

He eyed her. "You drink this stuff?"

"My immune system is perfectly fine."

"I don't believe it," he said aloud to the customers. "My wife made me drink something she wouldn't touch with a ten-foot pole."

A woman sitting at one of the tables looked wistfully at the couple at the counter. "Maybe she loves you more than she loves herself."

He started to retort, looked at Fiona and stammered that he had more boxes to bring in from the car.

"I thought that was the last one."

"It was," he said over his shoulder.

"Then what are you getting?"

He stopped at the door. "My manual for how to survive marriage to a conniving Scot."

He closed the door on their laughter and took a deep breath of air. It didn't help. Then he noticed, across the way, a bald man looking at the store. He started to wave but when the man saw him, he quickly headed the other way.

Grumpy shrugged and closed the trunk to his car. He glanced again at the retreating figure. The gait was familiar but he didn't recognize the man.

He leaned against the fender, pulled out a cigar and lit it. The smoke mingled disagreeably with the aftertaste of the tea, so he stubbed out the cigar. A young woman entered the store and he thought about Sally's ghostly arrival the night before. She had asked what he thought her random tarot reading might mean. At the time, he felt the cards for Peter had indicated a kind of spiritual bankruptcy, but after what happened to his own holdings and with this seemingly innocent information from Dale, he wasn't sure.

A car honked as it passed and Grumpy waved at the driver, one of his regular customers. He wandered inside.

"Finish your cigar already, dear?" Fiona asked without looking up from a small ring-bound booklet.

"You know good and well your tea ruined the taste of it."

"Ach, I'm so sorry to hear that." She leaned her elbows on the counter. "I know how much you enjoy your cigars."

"My last vice," he said wistfully.

"Oh, really?" The woman at the table said with an arched brow. "Pity."

Grumpy looked at Fiona, who blushed to her roots as she faked pouring over the small book. He grinned, felt a bit warm in the neck, himself.

"What are you looking at, dear?" He asked.

"Talia's photos from the wedding." She sighed. "I think she did a better job than that professional we hired."

Sally came in without saying a word, slumped into a chair off to one side. After spending the summer with a houseful of women, he had learned to not ask innocently the reason for their mood, lest he invite a PMS reply that would singe a bishop's frock.

Fiona had no such reservations. "What's the matter, Sally?"

"I don't want to talk about it."

Grumpy looked to the ceiling, mouthed "Thank you."

But Fiona wouldn't be put off. "Come on, dear. Tea? Or is it coffee today?"

"Got any brandy?"

Fiona walked over. "Yes, but you can't have any for at least five years."

"It'll be too late by then."

Fiona looked to Grumpy for help. He shook his head and opened the first box of books.

"Well, I've got something here that might cheer you up."

"What's that?"

"Talia's picture book of the wedding."

"Hey," Grumpy called out. "I haven't even seen it yet."

Fiona gave him a look and he dove into the book stacks. He listened as Fiona gave a running commentary on each picture, as if Sally hadn't been there herself. Three quarters of the way through the book, Sally stopped her.

"That's it. Damn it, that's what I've been looking for."

"Sally," Fiona chided.

"Sorry, Fiona. Can I borrow this picture, please? I promise to bring it back."

"I guess. But why?"

"I can't tell you right now, but I will."

There was a loud screech of the plastic overlay being removed. Sally stuffed the picture into her bag, kissed Fiona on the cheek, ran past Grumpy and out the door.

"What was that all about?" Grumpy asked.

"I have no idea."

"Well, what picture did she take?" Grumpy looked at the empty page.

"It was of Jimmy, standing behind the counter."

Grumpy pulled at his whiskers. "Maybe she's going to blackmail him."

"Blackmail?"

Grumpy grinned. "For wearing a tie."

Fiona ordered him to finish unpacking the books. Grumpy rang up a customer's bill, then sat down and doodled idly on a pad of paper. He really missed having Jimmy around the cafe. If only he had told the boy the truth from the get-go, they might have had a chance at a relationship. On the other hand, if he had been more of a man, when he was involved with Molly, Jimmy might have been his son. Or Molly might have at least kept her job and health benefits.

He looked down at his doodling: James Ulysses Lyden, over and over again. Then just J-U-L. Then J-U-Ly-den. He glanced guiltily at Fiona, wondered for a moment if remembering a past lover could be considered cheating on a current one. Not a question to ask a new bride. No, sir.

He looked down again. Molly had always been so funny with her cryptic notes and messages. Nothing was ever straight with Molly, always a bend or a twist. Like naming Jimmy the way she had. In one of their quiet and wistful moments, she had told Grumpy that if she ever had a baby boy she would name him Adam, after her favorite palindrome: "Madam I'm Adam," which was spelled the same forward and backwards.

He studied the initials again. J-U-L. Deep in thought, he didn't hear his name being called. He broke his reverie, looked up. Abe was standing at the coffee counter. He and Fiona were laughing.

"What's so funny?"

"I think it's time for that hearing aid, Grump. I said 'hello' three times."

"Sorry, I was thinking."

Abe and Fiona traded, "I'll bet" looks.

Grumpy walked over slowly, still pondering the answer to the question that wouldn't quite surface.

"Abe, is there a way to tell someone's astrological sign if you don't know their birthdate?"

"Sure," he said, blew on his coffee to cool it. "I've known some astrologers who have studied ancient medieval texts extensively. They were pretty uncanny at spotting someone's basic chart properties just by looking at them."

"Hm."

"Thinking of anyone in particular?"

"Jimmy Lyden."

"What's his birthdate?"

Grumpy looked at him. "If I tell you that, it would ruin what I'm trying to find out."

"Oh, yes." Abe sipped thoughtfully. "If I had to guess, which apparently I do, I would say he's a classic Leo."

"Really? Why?"

"Well, first-of all, he takes exceptionally good care of his nails and teeth. Almost out of character, wouldn't you say?"

"Why, yes." said Grumpy.

"And he can't stand anyone messing with his hair. Typical Leonine, feline characteristics: Teeth are teeth, but hair is mane and as for fingernails, read claws—" Avisson thought a minute, continued, "Then there's his art, his ego. The way he takes over groups, takes command, that sort of thing."

"Not a Scorpio?"

Abe considered this. "Well, could be, I suppose, with the right rising-signs. His secrecy and all, but that could come from his conditioning, being orphaned."

"But if you had to guess."

"I'd say Leo, definitely."

Grumpy walked over, picked up the phone. He could feel Fiona's eyes on him, but resisted turning to look at her. He dialed, waited a few seconds.

"Dorothy Slimson, please." The sense of Fiona's eyes on him increased, but he still didn't turn around. "Dorothy, Peter, Jr., here. Can you talk? Great. Listen, can you look at Jimmy Lyden's records and tell me where he was born. Yes, I can hold."

He hummed, pretended to study an invoice. Dorothy came back on.

"Great. Listen, one other thing. What was the name of that nurse who worked at Camp Shambala with you last summer? Prudence Peabody? She works at the hospital here, right? Thanks."

He hung up the phone. Fiona was standing right behind him.

"What's going on, Grumpy?"

"One more call. Then I'll tell you."

He dialed, waded through the labyrinth of protocol, finally got Prudence on the line. He introduced himself.

"Can you do me a big favor? Does the hospital keep daily logs on such things as maternities, operations, and that sort of thing?"

"Yes."

"Well, I'd like to check a log from 1969—the month of July. Is that possible?"

"Yes. Though I'll need authorization from a doctor."

Grumpy looked at Abe. Smiled. "I think I can arrange that."

"Wouldn't it be just as easy to check the birth certificate?"

"Might be, but I believe there may be a discrepancy. I'd like to check that against the log."

"Ah, I get it."

"So, if I get you a doctor's OK, you can get the records?"

"Sure."

"Where do I send it?"

"Where are you?"

"I'm at the Crystal Cafe."

"I know the place. You're the owner?"

"Yes."

"Tell you what. Have the doctor call in the authorization, I'll drop by the copies if the records are still available. And you can buy me a double latte."

Grumpy smiled. "I think we can arrange that."

"Make it a double hazelnut latte, with a biscotti on the side."

Grumpy laughed. "It's a deal."

He hung up the phone, motioned Abe to come over.

"Do I want any part of this?" Abe asked.

"You don't have a choice."

"Why not?"

Grumpy smiled at Fiona. "Because you're part of the cavalry. And the cavalry always obeys their leader."

Abe's eyes narrowed. He spoke out of the side of his mouth to Fiona. "Get out the butterfly net, boys, Grumpy thinks he's Teddy Roosevelt."

She didn't laugh. "Grumpy, are you going to tell us what this is all about?"

He sat them down at a table and told them the story of his quirky relationship with Molly Lyden, her love of puzzles and games. Also of the name she said she would give a son, if she ever had one.

"I see what you're driving at," Abe said. "But why would she alter Jimmy's birth certificate?"

"Well, think of the bind she was in. I had run away. She might have intuitively sensed even then, that she was ill. I was gone. She had no idea if I'd ever return. That meant Jimmy would be helpless. Grumpy took a deep breath. "If the richest and most powerful man in town hated you, hated the very thought of your existence, what might he do to a child who could have an almost equal claim to any estate, because of who his father is—namely, me?"

He shook his head. "I hate to say it, but Peter is the most selfish, vindictive person I've ever met. If he thought there was a brother around, even a half-brother, there's no telling what he might do. Look what he did to Molly. I was the guilty one, but he still took his anger out on her."

"That's a bit of a long shot, wouldn't you say, Grump?" Abe said.

"Yes, it is. But it is also just like Molly. You just said Jimmy seemed definitely more of a Leo than a Scorpio. There's only one way to find out."

Abe groaned, walked over and called the hospital. He covered the phone after a moment. "What was that nurse's name again?"

"Peabody. Prudence Peabody."

Abe repeated the name, thanked the clerk, and returned to the table.

"Mission accomplished, Mr. Roosevelt. Any other hills you'd like taken?"

"No, you can dismount now, thank you."

Grumpy stood, rubbed his eyes and sighed. When he opened them, Fiona was looking at him.

He anticipated the question in her eyes. "What am I going to do if it turns out he is my son, right?"

"Something like that," she said.

"Well, if it happened the way I think, then the next step will be up to him." He paused, looked at his hands. "And you, Fiona."

"Me?"

"Yes," he said softly. "Seems to me that we became true partners the day we got married. I'm not going to do anything you don't agree to, beforehand."

"But if it turns out that he really is your son, of course I'd have to—"

"Partners, remember?" Grumpy shook his head. "If and when we find that out, then we decide together what we do about it."

"Uh, there is one other little consideration here, folks," Abe interjected.

"What's that?"

"The State of New Jersey: It's representative in all matters regarding the care and welfare of James Ulysses Lyden—" He paused. "—is our esteemed Dr. Leon D. Kautsch."

"Ouch—Dr. Kautsch.," Grumpy murmured.

"And then there's Doug." Fiona said. "The two boys aren't exactly the best of friends. What's he going to think when he discovers that his sworn enemy all through school, turns out to be his one and only 'Uncle Jimmy'?"

Grumpy rose slowly and started walking to the rear of the cafe.

"Where are you going?" Fiona asked.

He pointed to the crystal ball. "Thought I'd find out what Sarah and Janina think of all this."

※

After school was the best time in the art room. Miss Stipple understood he couldn't paint at the orphanage anymore so she had made arrangements for him to have a key to the outside door, though the inside one was locked. This gave him access to his paintings, but not to the rest of the school—at least so they thought. It made Jimmy smile.

He put the new canvas on the easel and took several steps back. He liked the pure white emptiness of the space, the innocence waiting to be altered. His painting started, as they all did, with a piece of light in his mind. The candle in the mausoleum, on the slab of granite.

He liked the fact that Father Hector had red hair. Color made the difference in such a dark scene. The walls of the mausoleum were caked with dust and dirt from years of quiet waiting. No sunlight got in as long as the door was closed, so perhaps he would paint it with the door open a crack, a silver moon just visible. One peek at the outside world was enough to get the point across.

He chuckled as he considered the various characters he might use to portray Sally. An angel? Naw, too corny. A nurse would mean a white uniform and that would bring too much light to the painting.

He considered her wild proposal, which of course he flatly turned down. Why would he, of all people, risk his neck to smuggle that ghost into the loony bin? They couldn't even tell him why, only that it was important.

"If you can walk through that slab," Jimmy had said, "Why don't you just fly over to the sanitarium?"

"It doesn't work that way," Hector said. "There are, uh, limitations to where I can go. I have to stay in contact with certain earthbound materials to keep from being sent back."

"Sent back where?"

"To the light, Jimmy," Sally said. "Come on, you know you can do it."

He shook his head. "Not that easy. The orphanage and the fence, those are easy. But the sanitarium has a whole different layout."

Hector had stared at him. Jimmy wasn't quite sure what kind of powers ghosts had. Could they tell when somebody was lying?

"Well, will you at least think about it?"

"What do I get out of it?"

"Forgiveness," Hector said softly. "That's worth a lot."

"Maybe to you," Jimmy said, feeling slightly embarrassed. "Otherwise, you wouldn't be scared to go back."

"We all have to go back sometime, Jimmy." Sally said.

"Yeah, well I haven't done anything that needs forgiving. So you can drop that idea right now."

"Okay," Sally said. "Then what would it take to get you to do it?"

He really had given her question serious consideration. But there just wasn't anything he wanted so badly that he would help MacBrayne to get it.

"Nothing, Sal. Sorry." And he had meant it.

They left, but he couldn't get the look in Hector's eyes out of his mind. Terror and longing. That was it. He'd just figured it out.

Jimmy dabbed the brush on his palette and approached the canvas. A painting always has one aspect that launches it, like busting a bottle of champagne to christen a new ship. He had just finished the outline of the ghost's eyes when he heard a tap on the outside door. He went to see who it was.

Sally stood outside. She waved. He let her in.

"Hi, Jimmy."

"Sal."

She glanced at the easel. "Starting a new painting?"

"Yeah."

"Great." Her voice didn't sound happy.

"Look, Sal, it's nice to see you, but I only have so much time before I have to be back."

"Okay." She walked over and looked at the outline of the eyes on the canvas. "Doing a portrait?"

"You can see it when it's further along."

"Okay." She inspected his easel.

He sighed. "Okay, Sal. What do you want?"

"I figured out what I can give you in return for sneaking Father Hector into the sanitarium."

"Yeah, what's that?"

She reached into her bag and pulled out a photograph, held it up. He couldn't see it from where he stood.

"I don't think a picture's going to do the trick, Sal."

"Not just any picture, Jim. This one is special. It has something you cherish very much in it."

"What's that?"

"Your freedom, Jim. That's all."

He walked toward her, saw himself standing at the coffee counter, joining in the toast. He looked closer. She was right. There it was, plain as the nose on his face—or the red of the Coke can at his mouth.

He sighed. "Shit. When do you want me to do it?"

"He has to have it by Saturday, so Friday night at the latest."

"Okay, but you have to come with me to the cemetery. I'm not doing this all by myself."

"I'll meet you there. Eight o'clock?"

Jimmy walked slowly to the canvas, picked up his brush.

"I'll see you in school tomorrow."

He nodded. She was just about to the door when he called after her. "Will I get that photo after we get Hector to Doug?"

"I don't know. I promised Fiona I'd give it back. But, think about it. People might be more suspicious, if I say I lost it than if I give it back."

"Yeah, well, I will think about it. It's my ass."

"Okay."

She stood at the door. "You know, Father Hector might have been right after all."

"How's that?"

"Maybe forgiveness is worth a lot more than you think."

He didn't answer. She left, closing the door quietly behind her. He studied the few lines he had already started. Maybe he had been wrong about starting with Hector's eyes. Now they were going to stare at him through the whole painting.

Terror. Longing. And now, "I told you so."

☙

Sabey's stillness disturbed Abe. The man answered his questions, directly, no embellishments, his voice flat. When Abe tried to hypnotize him, Sabey never went into the deep state, so the voices might emerge. It was as if the man had completely evened out. No emotion. No passion. No threat.

Abe went over the tapes, listening for any hint, any nuance that might explain the shift. There was nothing. He re-examined the police records. Victim by victim, Abe analyzed each astrological chart, noting the emergence of all the crisis points, as indicated by the intersecting karmic retrogrades.

But where was Sabey in all this? There were no crisis points in Sabey's astrological chart for the killings. Nothing at all to indicate when the man was about to strike.

Abe closed his eyes. His head throbbed. Was it possible that the monster really was acting on Orders of the Universe? Could each death have been fated, a karmic balancing act? After all, what instinct had caused Sabey to select those exact people, at those precise moments? Maybe if he had a year or two, to study the data, he might be able to come up with an answer. Pity he'd already had his sabbatical at the Cayce Institute. He chuckled. Hell, even that had been a mistake. If Margaret hadn't typed up the wrong notes, he would never had been selected. The whole thing had been just plain crazy.

Abe sat up suddenly. He spun in his chair and reached for a book on Karmic Astrology. He skimmed down the opening page. "There is nothing in the universe that doesn't have magnetic qualities." Further down. "Each individual has his own magnetic energies based entirely upon how the makeup of his planetary horoscope arrangement is used."

Then, "When a person is experiencing a great deal of energy, beyond what he needs at the time, most of his planets act as radiators and he becomes a giver to others. In the opposite condition, when a person is experiencing less energy than he needs to function, his planets become absorbers, drawing from others the energy he is lacking."

Finally, and most important to Abe, he read: "Man has the ability from moment to moment actually to control his own magnetic field."

He slammed the book shut, kissed the cover. He spread the charts out on the long table at the side of his office and checked retrograde aspects against the points of high energy. In each case, Sabey was in a subtle retrograde—Uranus each time, but tuned exactly to the corresponding rise in energy of the victims. But the energy rise masked deeper concerns of self-worth. Like eleven kaleidoscopes, each of the victims had been transmitting, in their own way, self-hate and a wish to escape their lives.

Sabey was nothing more than a dousing rod that sought out self-annihilation, instead of water.

And the man was crazy. The influences that he interpreted as orders of the Universe were nothing more than a deep-rooted, self-hate of his own, which was transferred to the vibrations he received from his victims when he encountered them. Had he been more stable, or had a different psychological make-up, Sabey might have been a great healer of the mind, a Freud or Jung, who could sense the deep rhythms that were pulling people at particular periods in their lives.

But Sabey was crazy. His mind perverted each victim's subconscious, almost spiritual call for help, as a desire to leave the planet. The calls for help triggered his own protective ego, masked his own sense of worthlessness and projected it onto the victims.

He was too proud to kill himself, so he killed others who mirrored his emotional state. Sabey wasn't suffering from astrological distress. His problems were purely psychological.

And that meant he could be treated.

The thought dropped Abe into his chair. He turned from the chart-table. Past lives, Karma, astrology—all were energy, potential magnetizing forces that operated most powerfully at the soul-level, but all still had to answer to the body and thus the brain. Or at least the left brain—the part that processed rational decisions.

The right side, which processed emotions, art and spirit, was being overridden by Sabey's fears of inadequacy and ego. He supplanted the right brain's spiritual possibilities by creating an overlay he called "Orders from the Universe." That left his left brain free to control him and take the powerful influences he was experiencing and translate them into his murderous actions. Though he rationalized it away, Sabey had had a choice, each and every time.

Abe's gaze drifted across a memo from Kautsch. Was it possible that the man had been correct all along? At the edge of his desk lay Doug's chart. He glanced at it. The crisis point was on its way, but there was a very singular influence missing. Doug was the most self-possessed, positive boy Abe had ever encountered. Even after being incarcerated, he kept his pluck.

If there was one person in the world who radiated life-force and the will to live, it was Doug. Aquarian or not, there was no way Sabey would choose him.

❧

Clint was about to call out when he noticed Mandy asleep on the sofa. He knelt beside her and just looked into her beautiful face. He was brimming with news. His one-sided conversation with Doug had produced even more invaluable information. Doug had shown him parts of Paradise Lost where Milton had stumbled and the scrivener, Phineas, had showed him the way through via some of the great poet's other works.

But perhaps even more importantly, Clint had discovered something else during his day of teaching: There were other children in the facility. None as bright as Doug, but they still needed Clint.

That was what he was so eager to tell her. After the many years of despising the teaching profession since Candy's death, he'd realized that what was missing within him was the sense of being needed. He had something to offer those children they couldn't get from anyone else.

And it had been Mandy who had triggered this within him. For he now understood how much she needed him and how much she had needed him before. But he had been too wrapped up in his own drama to understand that.

He let his hand hover above her stomach, so full of his baby. The series of sonograms made necessary after the wedding fiasco, showed that the baby was indeed a girl, indeed the Canditu, they had wished for.

A wave of sadness overcame him for a moment, as Candy's smiling face drifted into view. He let it pass through him and away. She was okay, he was sure of that now. Again, thanks to Doug.

What must it be like, to remember the kinds of things Doug remembered? How confusing and at the same time how exhilarating life must be for the boy, to be able to see a path that stretched through so many years. To see the long purpose in such short lifetimes, to see the connections between them, the opportunities for improvement and progress.

"Who have you been before, little one?" he whispered. "What have you seen? Where did you come from?"

Mandy's eyes fluttered open. She saw Clint and a dreamy smile crossed her features.

"Who you talking to?"

"Our daughter," he said, then kissed her gently on the lips.

"Did she answer you?"

"Yeah," Clint put his head against Mandy's stomach. "She said she was glad she has you as a mama."

"That's nice," Mandy's voice drifted away.

"Nice for me too," Clint whispered. "Nice for me, too."

Belle had another tantrum after dinner when the techs tried to separate her from Doug and take her to her room. She kicked and screamed, wailing that she had to stay with Doug. Three techs and a nurse finally subdued her, carried her into her room, and placed the restraints on her wrists and ankles.

When Doug left her doorway to return to his own room, Kautsch was standing in his way. He nodded.

Kautsch glowered. "One word from you and she wouldn't have acted that way."

Doug bit his lip.

"Don't give me that shit." He noticed several other patients observing and shooed them into their rooms. He took Doug by the shoulder and led him into his room, sat him on the bed, pacing before him.

"You think it's all about you, don't you?" Kautsch balled his fists. "Did you ever think what this is doing to your father? And what about your precious nanny? You think she doesn't hear that you are getting worse and worse every day?"

Doug remained impassive on the bed.

"You've had it your way the whole time." Kautsch's face was dark with fury. "You've got your old camp counselor here. Like that do you? Well, here's a little clue, young man. His wife is pregnant and you almost cost them their baby with your wedding-reception stunt."

Doug shook his head.

"Yeah, right. I know." Kautsch leaned over. "Well, here's a little news for you. That man desperately needs this job. I thought he was going to kiss my hand when I told him he could start right away. You know how much it costs to take care of a baby nowadays? Well, if you don't start talking, guess who's out on his ass?"

Doug looked up, astonished at the doctor's undisguised blackmail.

"And don't think I won't do it." He laughed. "And that's just the beginning. After I fire Mr. Sharpe, you're going to start swallowing a little pill every six hours. Habilimyacin. After watching your utter lack of concern for that little girl—who happens to idolize you, for whatever twisted reason—I'm tempted to start you on the drug tonight."

Doug covered his mouth.

Kautsch picked up the novel Doug had been reading before going to bed each night. He shook it in Doug's face.

"You like reading? Well, once you're on Habilimyacin, you won't be able to focus. The words will swim in front of your eyes. He poked Doug in the forehead. You'll be able to see them, but you won't understand them. How's that for a side-effect, eh, buck-o?"

Terrified, Doug shrank toward the wall.

"God, you make me sick, you little creep." He strode toward the door, stopped with his hand on the knob. "You and all your 'past lives' crap. Did you ever take a good look at them, Doug? Study just how much good you did the people in them? They're all dead. Not one of them survived knowing you. You're bad luck. Shit, kid, you burned down your family chapel, humiliated your father, got your nanny nearly banished, then poisoned—and that little girl is in restraints every night. That's what comes from caring about Peter Douglas-MacBrayne the IV."

He slammed the door. Doug could hear him shouting angry instructions at the techs and nurses. As his voice receded, the vibrations began.

Ashna hobbled along the wide trail left by the others. They dragged their belongings and tent materials on splints. Ashna blessed the gods for making the going slow for his people. Otherwise a rain might come and wash their path away before his eyes.

He wondered what effect the new cave drawings had been on Tehuti. He had made one drawing, showing the four-leg stepping on Tehuti's foot, causing him to limp badly. He had laughed when he finished it.

Next, he painted the bow that Tehuti used with such killing accuracy. He placed a small nick in the deer-gut. Would it break when the fierce leader draw it back with an arrow? Ashna was not sure if the magic would work on the bow, because he had only envisioned live creatures in the past.

Finally, he painted himself and Huva riding away in the firelight on the four-leg. Behind them, the rest of the camp in a deep sleep, marked by a magic elk-skin dyed dark blue, like the night sky. He had no idea if the four-leg would even let them on its back, but he knew it was the only way to escape.

To fail meant death for them both.

Ten days after he began his search, he finally saw the smoke from the evening meal, rising above the horizon. Weak from hunger, he sat in sight of the camp and waited.

When Tehuti went to stake the four-leg's lead to the ground, the horse suddenly reared and stepped on his foot. Tehuti screamed in pain. Then, furious with the creature, he began to beat it with a stick. After several minutes, Tehuti threw the stick to the ground and limped to his tent, carrying a large jar that held his fermented honey-water. Ashna smiled. While Tehuti killed the pain in his foot, he would also deaden his normally sharp senses.

Ashna searched for Huva but did not see her. Night descended quickly. He hobbled slowly down the hill toward them, careful not to upset the dogs. He was glad he had always been kind to them because they recognized his scent as he approached.

As he had painted, the moon slept. The only light came from the dying fires. He walked among the skin tents, then stopped when he heard muted moaning coming from one of them. He peeked inside and barely made out Huva. His sharp eyes soon saw her hands, securely tied behind her. Two tethers held her captive: One attached to a stake in the ground at the back of the tent; the other secured her firmly to Tehuti's ankle.

For a moment he thought he should just kill Tehuti, but wasn't sure he had the courage or the strength. One of the camp dogs whimpered softly behind him.

Huva looked up and shivered with fright when she saw him, but he motioned her to continue her soft moaning. She did. Moving with utmost care, he cut a long, narrow strip from a drying deerskin and tied it around the whimpering dog's neck.

He led the dog quietly inside the tent, quickly severed the thongs that bound Huva's wrists; then showed her how to keep pressure on the tether to Tehuti's ankle. Ashna deftly cut the tether. Tehuti gargled and snorted, rolled over, nearly pulling Huva off-balance. While Huva held the tether taut, Ashna tied it to the strip of hide around the dog's neck, then cut her loose from the stake. They held their breath for several moments, but the leader just snored in his dreams.

Thankfully, the dog continued whimpering softly, as they edged out of the tent. Once outside, he led her to the four-leg and began to lift her onto its back. She shook her head, eyes wide with fear. Forcibly, he pushed her up. The four-leg quivered but did not buck. Tehuti's beating had broken his spell over the beast. Ashna untied the lead and tried to climb on too, but he couldn't do it.

A sudden commotion arose from the tent they had just left. Ashna almost panicked, but spotted a small boulder nearby and quickly led the four-leg to it. He climbed atop the rock, then scrambled up onto the four-leg, holding tight to the lead and to Huva in front of him.

Tehuti came roaring from the tent, his bow in one hand. He reached for an arrow with the other. Ashna urged the four-leg forward, as he had seen Tehuti do. The horse started, nearly toppling them from its back.

Ashna looked over his shoulder to see Tehuti fit the arrow and draw the bowstring back to his ear. Ashna closed his eyes, sure he would soon feel the arrow's sting.

But he felt nothing. Heard Tehuti scream with rage. He looked back to see Tehuti stomping on his bow.

The string had snapped.

The four-leg ran like the wind. Ashna and Huva held on for dear life. They galloped across the night plain, finally made it to the foothills and rested before starting again. When they reached the site of the old camp, Ashna released the four-leg, who ran on into the wilds. Then he and Huva climbed up the hill to the secret cave.

They passed the first week quietly, storing berries, wild vegetables and grains. They both knew Tehuti would come looking for them and hoped he would follow the four-leg's trail. But if need be, they could hide in the cave for several moons.

Every time they filled bladders with water from the stream in the rear of the cave, Huva took extra time to wash between her legs. At night she would cry herself to sleep like a child in Ashna's arms. He waited patiently for Huva to make the sign of man-woman but she didn't. During the second week he made the sign himself but she shrank from him in fear.

Only then did he understand that Tehuti had used her. He did not make the sign again, though his heart was heavy.

Once their preparations were complete, Ashna began to explore deeper into the cave. He stumbled upon a small opening partially obscured by a large boulder. Painfully, he crawled through, using his stone lamp to light the way. The passage led to another chamber, half the size of the one they had filled with provisions.

He showed Huva his discovery and they moved some of the provisions into the smaller chamber. Ashna piled larger rocks near the opening, to block the passage from view.

Now that the preparations were truly complete, Ashna started painting again. He knew that he and Huva would not long be able to survive alone. They might make it through the warm moons, but when the cold came, they would not have enough grains and berries to see them through. He must find a way to hunt.

Before he painted, he sat and let himself drift into a dream-state. He needed the old knowledge: how his people used to hunt before they became skilled with weapons. When he awoke, he painted a large pit covered with long branches. Beyond the pit, he drew Huva and himself waving their arms and hurrying after a herd of deer, driving them toward the pit. Then he made another painting of a deer falling into it.

When he finished, he showed Huva. She laughed at the drawing and pretended to be chasing the deer. They rejoiced together.

That night, while he held her just before sleep, she turned to him in the flickering light of the stone oil lamp and made the sign of man-woman.

Later, Ashna slept with a smile on his crooked face. Huva was his again. All traces of Tehuti had been washed from within her.

Gathering berries the next afternoon, they heard voices. They hurried up the hill to the cave and huddled at the entrance, hidden by bushes. But Tehuti had found their trail.

They scurried into the secret chamber and Ashna quickly piled his store of rocks in the opening. They did not light the oil lamp for fear it would be detected. They sat in the dark, arms around each other, listening to Tehuti's angry shouts. Closer, closer, the dreaded voice approached their hideaway.

Then the shouting stopped. Only to be replaced by a more terrible sound. Rock hitting against rock, the sound became more and more muffled. Ashna's heart sank, when he realized what was happening: Tehuti and his men were sealing them inside alive.

Then there was no sound.

❦

Doug awoke with a start to a terrible darkness. He felt as if he couldn't breathe. He scrambled out of bed to the door. It was locked. He looked through the little window, but the lights were out.

He staggered to his bed, sat with his head in his hands. Dr. Kautsch had been right. Every past life he remembered was terrible. Everyone he had loved, suffered. His Chinese sister had led a miserable, unfulfilled life because of his misplaced sympathy. Fionnaghal, Gemilla—and now Huva—had all died terrible deaths because of him.

And what of this life? His mother had died, giving him birth. His father was ashamed of him. Nanny cried herself to sleep every night and now, poor Belle, who loved him so desperately, had to be strapped to her bed.

The dark in the night-ward could not match the darkness that flooded him, destroying all the light from his heart. What good was he to the world if every time he lived, those who came to know him suffered so?

There was only one answer, only one way to save them from the terrible pain and ugliness that he had brought to them.

Chapter Nineteen

Peter arrived at the plant late, having searched for his favorite suit, then discovered it was at the cleaners. At first, the clerk couldn't find it on the rack. Peter nearly screamed at the young man's incompetence as he searched helter-skelter until he finally found it.

His anger melted when he saw the CNN satellite-truck parked in front of the new building. He checked his bowtie in the mirror and hurried inside.

What looked to be a mile of thick cable stretched out the doors. Strangers wandered around inside, shouting orders, placing lights and equipment.

Jim Knapp, who obviously hadn't slept much, hurried up to Peter.

"Jim, you need to see the make-up person, otherwise the viewers are going to think UltraLeather was invented by Dracula."

"Not funny, Mr. MacBrayne."

Peter put a hand on the man's shoulder. "It'll all be over in an hour."

"God, I hope so." Knapp looked around, dazed. "They got here before I could run the final test-samples."

"Yesterday, you said everything looked fine."

"It did, but the last twelve hours are the most critical. That's when we see the real results."

"Have you seen Dan?"

"No." Knapp muttered. "He'll probably show up fresh as a daisy, just before the cameras start rolling."

"Well, that's his job."

"Hey, be careful over there," Knapp shouted and hurried to shoo a video-technician away from a piece of machinery.

"But we need lights here," the man complained.

"Oh, all right." Knapp turned to Peter and made a choking sign.

Peter smiled, then was approached by a young man with a clipboard.

"Excuse me, can you tell me where I can find Peter MacBrayne?"

"You're looking at him."

"Great, listen." The man ran down a checklist as if speaking to a janitor, instead of the owner of the corporation. "Oh, and one other thing, who's going to brief Hathaway on the manufacturing process?"

"Hathaway?"

"Yeah, he's the reporter. Who have you assigned from your company to work with him?"

"I don't know. Didn't Dan Downey set all that up?"

The man looked at the checklist again. "No Downey here."

"But he's head of Marketing. Surely—"

"Look, Mr. MacBrayne, we're live in a little over half an hour. If your people make Hathaway look stupid, that's going to make your product look stupid. Capiche? Bad television equals bad exposure. I suggest you get somebody with Mr. Hathaway and quickly."

Stunned by the young man's effrontery, Peter nodded and headed toward the Administration complex. He raced into his office, turned on the overhead lights, reached for the telephone.

An envelope on his desk. Addressed to him and marked 'Personal'. He ripped it open and read it.

Dear Peter Douglas-MacBrayne:

I am hereby resigning my position as Vice President and Director of Marketing for Douglas Industries. As you know, my dream has always been to return to aviation. Such an opportunity has just arisen. I wish you nothing but luck with UltraLeather. I am proud of the job I did for Douglas Industries, but could not pass up the opportunity that awaits me.

I apologize for writing a letter instead of speaking to you personally, but leaving is difficult enough, after so many years together—and this kind of clean break seems best.

I'll be watching this morning and know you will do just fine without me.

Yours sincerely,
Dan Downey

P.S. In case you're wondering, I sold my stock this week. The proceeds helped me take a majority position in my new company. Thanks again.

Peter's bowtie flapped out of control as he dropped the letter on his desk. Loud voices echoed through the building. He limped out in the hall and saw a man with a towel draped over his shoulders, followed by a make-up woman dabbing at his face.

"You MacBrayne?"

"Y-yes." Peter recognized the man's face from his hard-hitting reportage. He gave the appearance on television of being a no-nonsense, seasoned veteran. He was no less in person.

"Where's the script?" Hathaway glared at Peter.

"Excuse me?"

"The fucking script, man. We were told it would be waiting for us this morning. We're here, all set up, but no script."

"I-uh, don't know." Peter hurried into the office, rummaged around and pulled out an UltraLeather fact sheet.

"Will this help?"

"This is bullshit." Hathaway tossed it to the floor. "I don't do off-the-cuff, unless I'm crucifying somebody."

"My Marketing Director just resigned," Peter said. "And he was in charge of this whole—"

"Jesus Christ!" Hathaway roared, pushing the make-up girl out of the way. "Did you start this company?"

"No, my grandmother did."

"Where's she?"

"Dead."

"Pity, because you are, too, unless I get a fucking script in ten minutes."

The intercom buzzed. "Excuse me for a moment, Mr. Hathaway." Peter hit the button. "Yes?"

"Mr. MacBrayne, Knapp here. We've got a big problem."

"What!"

"It's the batch. The organisms didn't take in the larger environment. All we're getting is mush and there are cameramen here, recording the whole fucking thing."

Hathaway's eyebrows arched. "God, I love television." He smiled wickedly, tore off the towel and hurried out.

Stunned, Peter slumped into his desk-chair and fingered the resignation letter. "You set me up, Dan. I don't know why, but you did."

He tossed the letter on the floor next to the discarded UltraLeather fact sheet and turned to look out the window.

❦

Grumpy turned off the television and walked slowly downstairs, to the cafe. Fiona looked up from the espresso machine.

"How did it go?"

"Well, after today, I should be able to afford to buy all the Douglas Industries stock I want."

"How's that?"

"The television coverage of UltraLeather's introduction to the world was a total disaster." Grumpy sat heavily at a table. "The reporter even suggested the possibility of insider stock-manipulation and called for an SEC investigation."

"Good Lord. Poor Peter."

"Yes, well, feel sorry for the town. A lot of people depend on Douglas Industries for their livelihood."

"So what, if the new product doesn't work? That doesn't effect the quality of existing products, does it?"

"No. But in purchasing agents' minds, if Douglas Industries becomes the laughing stock of the industry, nobody's going to want their products. In one moment of incompetence, Peter has jeopardized two generations of work."

"Maybe you should call him."

Grumpy shook his head. "He'd just think I was gloating."

Fiona wiped her hands and walked over to the table. "If you don't call, he'll think you're gloating. If you call and offer to help in anyway you can, then you show concern. If he takes it wrong, that's his problem. But you will have done your part."

A reluctant schoolboy, Grumpy got up, walked to the phone. He held it to his ear, dialed slowly.

"Peter MacBrayne, please."

"I'm sorry, he's not taking calls this morning."

"Put me through to Grace."

He waited a moment while insipid music played in the background.

"This is Mr. MacBrayne's office. I'm sorry—"

"Grace, this is his father, put me through to him, please."

"Oh, I'm sorry, Mr. MacBrayne. He isn't taking calls."

"I understand that. Please let me talk to him."

"I—I can't. He's not in the office."

"Where did he go?"

"He's on the grounds, probably down by the lake. This really isn't a good time—"

"Okay, thanks, Grace."

He replaced the receiver. Of course, that's where he would be. When Peter was a boy, almost every time Grumpy had brought him to the office, they would spend a few minutes down by the small lake that decorated the far end of the complex.

Grumpy started out the door.
"Is he going to see you?" Fiona called after him.
"Yes, but he doesn't know it."
"Good luck."

As he pulled out of the lot, he saw a woman driving a small Japanese car pull into the space next to where he just left. He glanced in his rearview mirror. She wore a white nurse's uniform. For a moment he considered turning around to see if it was Prudence Peabody, but whatever information she might have would just have to wait a couple more hours.

Fiona was glad the cafe was empty for the moment. She had known from the moment she had been awakened by a sharp tug in her gut that something was up with Doug. The feeling had stayed with her all morning, but she kept pushing it away. It wasn't psychic; it was maternal instinct. She wiped the cups again just to keep her hands busy.

When the nurse walked in, Fiona smiled weakly, regretting the end of her solitude.

"Is Mr. MacBrayne here?"

"Grumpy?"

"I suppose so, Dr. Avisson said I should—"

"Oh, you must be Prudence Peabody."

"Yes." She blushed.

"Is something the matter?"

"No, it's just—oh, never mind. Silly really."

"What is it?"

Prudence looked down at her shoes. "All my life people have been calling me 'Prudence Peabody.' They never just call me Prudence, or Pru."

"What would you like to be called?"

Another blush. "Aggie."

Fiona laughed. "Now that, I would have never guessed."

"My middle name is Agatha. But I seldom tell anyone."

"Then I'm honored, Aggie. But why not?"

"Can you imagine what the kids would have said about me if they learned my initials were P-A-P?"

It took a moment, then Fiona laughed, shaking her head. "My goodness. You Americans."

Prudence sat on a stool at the counter. "Is Mr. MacBrayne here? I've got a hair-appointment before I report for work."

"Sorry, he just left on an errand."

"Damn, and I was looking forward to a hazelnut latte."

Fiona looked at the large envelope in the woman's hand. "I think we can arrange that, Aggie." Fiona tapped espresso grounds into the holder. "By the way, I'm Fiona McLean. Grumpy's wife."

"Ah." Prudence smiled. "You decided not to take his name?"

"No, dear. And I certainly wasn't going to hyphenate it either. Might have been worse than your initials."

"Fiona McLean-MacBrayne." Prudence chuckled. "Kind of musical. Rhymes too."

Fiona steamed the milk, poured the mixture in layers, then handed Prudence her drink. She sipped, closed her eyes.

"Heaven. Pure heaven."

"I don't suppose we could peek at what's in the envelope."

Prudence thought a minute. "Well, the deal was the envelope for a latte. And I am drinking it, so—" She handed it to Fiona.

"You know, I've always wanted to do this, but never had an opportunity."

"Do what?"

Fiona took the envelope, held it under the steamer until the glue softened. She carefully pulled out several sheets of paper. She looked over the July, 1969 log, compared it with Jimmy's birth certificate. "Well, I'll be darned."

"Good news?".

Fiona shook her head. "Lately it seems every bit of news is good and bad at the same time."

Fiona gulped, replaced the papers, took a glue stick from the drawer and applied it to the flap. Then she put the envelope upright on the computer keyboard.

"There. I'll just have to pretend being surprised when Grumpy comes back."

Prudence giggled. "Why do you call him Grumpy? The couple of times I've been in here, he seemed really nice."

"He is, dear. He just likes strangers to think otherwise. MacBraynes are funny that way."

"He's related to Doug MacBrayne, isn't he?"

"Grandfather. Why, how well do you know Doug?"

Prudence nodded in mid-sip. "Well, as I said, I met him at camp this summer and I was there when he was born. Nothing more than that."

"So you were there when Felicity—his mother died?"

"Yes. Did you know her?"

"Briefly. I've been Doug's nanny since he was born."

Prudence's eyes widened. "Oh, so that was you across the lake."

"How did you know about that?"

"Your nanny-camp is famous in town. People all over town want their daughters to attend next summer."

"I don't know if we're going to do it again."

"Oh, but you must." Prudence nearly spilled her drink, caught it just in time. "Word is that you turned the toughest gang of girls in town into a bunch of civilized young ladies. Talia's mother works with me at the hospital. She says the work you did with Talia saved her sanity."

"I wish I could take the credit. There was another woman who was the real miracle-worker."

"Wouldn't she help?"

"She can't." Fiona checked a sudden rush of emotion. "She died."

"Gosh, that's terrible."

"Yes, in some ways." Fiona visualized Janina's red, flaming hair, the gnarled fingers, the radiant smile. "But to tell the truth, I still talk to her, just—I don't know. I guess when you encounter amazing people in your life, you can have them with you whether they're still around our not."

Prudence smiled. "You know, it's funny. When this cafe first opened, people were all up in arms. There were a lot of rumors flying around the hospital, the whole town really. But now—I don't know. You all seem so normal. Especially you."

Fiona laughed. "Well, thank you. As a matter of fact, I never could have imagined that I would wind up in a place like this."

"But I thought all this was part of your culture, you know, leprechauns and everything."

"That's the Irish who believe in faeries, dear." Fiona smiled. "We Scots prefer thrift."

The phone rang. Fiona excused herself. After a brief and excited conversation, she untied her apron.

"Pru-uh, Aggie, I've got to go. A friend is having a baby and she can't get ahold of her husband to take her to the hospital so I'll have to do it."

"Why don't I follow you, make sure everything's all right? She's coming to my department, after all. My hair appointment can wait."

Fiona hurried out the door, around to the side of the cafe where her small car was parked. She gunned the engine and backed out quickly, nearly hitting another car that had come around the corner. The driver honked and shook his fist.

"Sorry." Fiona called out the window as she slammed the gear into drive. "Nanny emergency!"

She looked behind her once, to make sure Prudence was there, then concentrated intently on the road ahead as she sped toward the Sharpe's house. The knot in her stomach that had been mollified by the conversation with Prudence had intensified. Not because of the baby, that part seemed easy, but more because Mandy couldn't get through to her husband. That bothered her. Just what was going on at the sanitarium that Clint couldn't be reached?

"One thing at a time, Fiona girl." She whispered under her breath to the dashboard. "One thing at a time."

※

Dorothy glanced into the room and saw Clint still holding Doug's hand. Belle's screams of anguish and anger reverberated through the hallway. Each piercing cry seemed to send Doug deeper into himself, his fingernails dug into Clint's hand but he didn't pull away. Though he did look to Dorothy for support.

"It's going to be okay, Doug," Dorothy said, trying to keep her voice even. "Dr. Kautsch is on his way here now."

The boy's legs curled tighter and his head slipped onto Clint's shoulder.

Dorothy moved down the hall. Doug's strange behavior had the entire ward in a frenzy. The young ones were accustomed to Doug being the steadying influence. When they realized he was in distress, they panicked. All the techs were busy trying to put out the emotional forest fire that had spread through the ward. She wished that Rocky, the bald tech, was on duty. He was quiet, but the kids responded to him positively.

She heard someone call her name and turned to see the receptionist waving at the glass door. She walked over, opened it.

"There's some people out front, Miss Slimson. They're asking for Dr. Kautsch."

"Tell them he's not here."

"Can you talk to them?"

"Not really. We have a really bad situation here."

"I think you should."

"And why is that?"

"They say they're from the State, Miss Slimson. Something about a surprise inspection."

Dorothy put her hand to her head, took two deep breaths and nodded. "Of course. Of course they would pick today. What other day would they come?"

"What should I tell them?"

"Nothing. I'll take over."

Her mind worked furiously as she followed the woman down the hall. If she directed them to the administrative offices first, it would buy some time. By then, Leon might have arrived and he could take over.

Dorothy pasted on a bright, professional smile and pushed through the double doors to the reception area. A team of four bureaucrats, two men and two women—all wearing appropriate attire, stood by the desk.

"Hello, I'm Dorothy Slimson, Dr. Kautsch's personal assistant. How may I help you?"

"We're here to inspect the facility, Miss Slimson," one of the men said, opening his briefcase and withdrawing a sheaf of paper. "Can you tell us where Dr. Kautsch is?"

"He had an important meeting this morning. He'll be here shortly." She motioned them to follow her. "We can start in the Administrative offices."

"We'd rather start in the wards, Miss Slimson."

"Well, since Dr. Kautsch isn't here yet, I thought you might want to check our paperwork, then accompany him to the wards."

"The purpose of this inspection is to check procedures and patient care—especially when the head of the facility is out. We'd like to see the wards, now, Miss Slimson."

"I see." She motioned them to follow. "All right, we'll start in the West Wing." She heard paper rustle behind her. "It's our top-security wing. Right now we have only one patient, the serial murderer, Cameron Sabey."

She breathed a sigh of relief that there were no objections, glanced at the clock as they passed. Good. It was eleven. That meant Sabey would be in session with Dr. Avisson.

❧

"What, no hypnosis today, Doc?" Sabey leered from across the room, where he was stretched out on the sofa.

Avisson shook his head. "No, today I thought we'd talk. Just you and me."

"You tired of meeting all my friends already?" Sabey grinned.

"On the contrary, I look forward to meeting them again, very soon. But I wanted to talk to you about some reading I've been doing. I think it throws important light on your situation, the things you believe about yourself."

Sabey's eyes narrowed. "What reading would that be, Doc?"

Avisson leaned on his desk, looked at his notes. "Well, to begin with, have you ever heard of something called 'retrograde'? It's an astrological term?"

"No."

"Ah, well, to put it simply, there are certain periods when the astral influences, uh, alignments, appear to be going in reverse—retrograde."

"Fucks things up, right?"

"Yes. People are like magnets, Cameron. There are times when we send out positive forces that radiate to others. We don't need anything from them at those times. We have more than enough within ourselves to live our lives."

"Yeah, okay."

"Then there are times when we are influenced by retrograde conditions, when we feel empty, need something, anything, from anybody who comes along. If you turn the magnet around, it pulls things toward it."

"Yeah, yeah, yeah. What of it?"

"Well, I did some extensive checking last night. I looked at the charts of the people you killed, your victims. In each case, they were at incredibly low points, emotionally and spiritually. When I examined your chart, it seems that at precisely those same times, you were experiencing high points, except for a retrograde Uranus, which runs throughout your chart."

"I have no idea what you're talking about, Doc."

"People who have Uranus in retrograde see themselves as rebels who are liberating those around them, freeing them to find better lives. Depending on their emotional stability, they can either bring great change to the world, or great pain."

"That's me, Doc. The great rebel." He laughed.

"Yes, I suppose you are." Avisson turned the paper over, laced his fingers together and stretched. A casual gesture to hide the excitement he felt. "But I have come to believe that the orders you have been following aren't coming from the Universe."

"No?" Sabey's voice was guarded. "Where they coming from?"

"Inside you, Cameron." Avisson moved his hand close to the guard button. "I believe you are a product of astrological forces, as are we all—but everyone has freedom of choice in his life. He can choose to act on impulses, react to influences. There may be a hundred people in the world with the same kinds of feelings, Cameron. But only you acted on them. Those orders were psychological, not universal."

Cameron closed his eyes. He was quiet for a long time. A small smile played at his lips but he remained still. "You can take your finger off the button, Doc. You ain't on the list."

Caught, Avisson relaxed his hand. Now it was his turn to wait in silence for Cameron's reaction. The man started slowly, his voice flat, unemotional.

"You're good, Doc. Didn't think you'd ever see it." He pointed to the ceiling. "When it's all done, we belong to up there, out there, wherever it is. Doesn't matter. What we do down here belongs to us. We come. We go. We live. We die. All very simple. It only seems complicated, because we're paying attention to down here instead of up there."

Avisson murmured assent.

"We crazy ones, we're like bad weather: tornadoes, earthquakes. We're a virus that kills. Them that survive us, they become stronger. Them that don't, don't." Sabey shifted, rolled over to face Avisson. "I didn't ask you to heal me, Doc. Or find a way to absolve me of my sins, or even set me free. I don't want to be normal, Doc. Shit, normal sucks. But people have to do what they are. Some are lucky. They're born, knowing what they gotta do. Writers write. Painters paint. Dancers dance."

"And killers kill?" Avisson watched Sabey closely.

Sabey smiled, nodded. They stared at each other for several moments.

"You ever heal anybody, Doc? I mean, really?"

Now it was Avisson's turn to smile, with chagrin. "Not really."

"Well I have. Eleven people. All their pain is gone." He held up his hands. "All their pain went right into these here."

"And how does that pain feel, in there?"

"It feels good, Doc. Real good."

"This feeling,—" Avisson turned in his chair to find the words. "—is it better than the pain that was there before you ever killed?"

Avisson heard the rustle, thought it was Sabey turning over on the sofa. He barely felt the hands around his neck, looked up wildly to see the killer's contorted face.

"You think this is some little game, Doc? Does it feel like a game now?"

Avisson shook his head. Tried to speak but the words were clogged by Sabey's grip.

"That's right, it ain't a game. You had your chance in court. If you had told them what you knew, you might have saved this whole fucking deal, but you had your stupid principles, didn't you, Doc?"

Avisson tried to pull the man's hands away. They were locked around his neck.

"Principles won't do you no good now, Doc. You fucked up."

"The list," Avisson squeaked.

"It's my list, remember, Doc? You said I had a choice. Well, maybe I choose you."

He applied more pressure. The room spun, a rainbow of light revolved before Avisson's eyes.

The door opened. Avisson dimly heard a woman's voice.

"This is Doctor Avisson's office. He's working with—my God! What are you—?"

Then he passed out.

🌱

Fiona and Prudence opened the door when they heard Mandy's screams inside. They found her on the floor beside the sofa, tears streaming down her face, her legs akimbo.

"Thank God," she panted after the scream. "My water's broke. I—argh!"

Prudence quickly went to her, instructing Fiona to immediately call 9-1-1.

"You just hang on, girl," Prudence said. "We're going to get you to the hospital in a jiffy."

"Just came on all the sudden. You know—ahhhh."

"Don't talk," Prudence looked up when Fiona reentered the room.

"They said the ambulance from our district has another call. They're sending one from the hospital. But it'll be a few minutes."

"Damn it," Prudence took a deep breath. "Okay, Fiona. We'll have to do it here. Boil some water in a big pot, then grab all the clean towels you can find."

"Right."

"This is bad," Mandy whispered. "Something bad's happening."

"I've been doing this for fifteen years, Mandy—" Prudence stroked her head, moved a stray hair back from Mandy's mouth. "—and I haven't lost a baby yet. Don't you worry about a thing."

"What about the mothers?" Mandy gasped as another contraction hit. "You ever lost any mothers?"

Half way between the kitchen and the linen closet, Prudence caught Fiona's eye. She smiled, caressed Mandy's forehead, "Not a one, darling, not a one."

🌱

Grumpy felt a tug in his heart when he finally spotted his son sitting by the lake. A flock of ducks had congregated nearby, waiting for the handouts human beings normally provided. He opened his palms as if to say, "Sorry, fellas. Nothing today."

Grumpy coughed lightly as he approached. Peter turned, scowled, looked away.

"How's it going, Peter?" Grumpy asked softly.

No answer.

Grumpy reached into his pocket, pulled out bag of seeds he'd purchased at the concession stand. "Here, give them a treat."

Peter didn't move at first, then stretched out his hand and took the seeds. He opened the package and scattered a handful. The ducks fought over the offering.

They watched for nearly a minute. Peter sighed. "You saw it on TV?"

"Yes, I did."

"Was it as bad as I think it was?"

"Probably worse."

Peter nodded. He sent another handful of seeds onto the water. The quacking ducks lunged and splashed.

"It was Downey, wasn't it?" Grumpy said.

Peter nodded. "How'd you know?"

"Stockbroker called a couple of days ago, said there was a large offering of stock from an insider. I didn't put two-and-two together until I saw the show."

"His letter of resignation said he was buying into an aviation firm." Out went more seeds. "He could have left without doing this."

"Seems to me he wanted to hurt you for something."

"Well, it's a complete mystery to me. He's been with us for fifteen years. This company gave him everything he has. I don't get it."

"Maybe we'll find out someday." Grumpy risked putting his hand on Peter's shoulder. He squeezed it once. "In the meantime, there's work to do."

"Work? You know what this kind of coverage does to a company? We're screwed, Dad."

The word hit Grumpy hard. His eyes watered. He touched Peter's shoulder again. "No, we're not. The people of this town have depended on this company for two generations. And for the past sixteen years—on you."

"Yeah, and I let them down."

"There was no way you could have foreseen this." Grumpy smiled. "I don't think even Sarah could have seen this one coming, even in her crystal ball."

Peter's face twisted for a second, then relaxed. "Well, I wish I knew how to use the damn thing, because I don't have a clue what to do next."

Grumpy rose, lifted Peter by the elbow. "To tell the truth, neither do I. But we're going to do something. And one way or the other, we're going to fight our way out of this jam."

"We?"

"Yes, son. We are." Grumpy motioned. "Come on."

"Why?" Peter stood still. "Why would you want to help after all the things I've done to you? After all the things I said."

Grumpy nodded. "I won't say that what you did and said didn't hurt me. But I know I hurt you when you were young. A hundred Dan Downeys can come along and that wouldn't change the fact that, in the end, you're my son and I'm your father."

"It's that simple?"

Grumpy laughed. "No. It's very complicated. But one thing has become very clear to me in all this and I'm actually grateful to Dan for giving me this opportunity."

"What opportunity is that?"

"To tell you that I realized something today that I should have said a long time ago." He paused, squinted as he looked into Peter's pain-filled face. "To tell you that I love you."

Peter didn't answer. Grumpy took the bag and scatted the remaining seeds for the ducks. He turned and smiled, silently led Peter to the complex. "Come on, son," he said softly. "We've got a company to save."

꽃

An ambulance roared away just as Kautsch arrived at the sanitarium. He asked the guard what was going on, but the man just shrugged.

"Somebody got hurt."

Kautsch rolled his eyes, hurried inside. He found Slim talking to four people in the lobby. They looked up as he approached. Slim hurried to him.

"Dr. Kautsch, so glad you're here." Her face said *Be careful*.

"Uh, who are these people, Slim?" Kautsch whispered.

"State Inspectors, surprise inspection."

Kautsch immediately went into "public relations mode" as he walked over. "Dr. Leon D. Kautsch. Director of this facility."

The group introduced themselves. Fell silent.

"Uh, I take it Nurse Slimson has shown you the fine work we're doing here. What have they seen so far, Miss Slimson?"

Before she could answer, one of the women spoke. "So far, we have seen one of your doctors attacked by a dangerous patient he was interviewing in his office. Without the proper restraints for a man with his history of violent behavior, I might add."

He looked to Slim. She nodded.

"Sabey. Dr. Avisson's been taken to the hospital."

"Is he all right?" Kautsch asked.

"We got him out of there in time. His throat is bruised, but he was well enough to ask if they had a fresh pear."

"Good." Kautsch turned to the inspectors. "Surely you know that such episodes are always possible when dealing with the criminally insane."

"Not if state guidelines are followed correctly."

"Yes, well. Then we shall have to make adjustments." To Slim he said, "And what's next on the itinerary?"

"We've just been to your juvenile ward, Dr. Kautsch," one of the men said. "And quite frankly, I have never seen a worse-managed caseload in my twenty-five years experience."

"What?"

"There were some problems with Doug MacBrayne this morning." Slim looked at the inspectors as she spoke. "I tried to explain how important Doug has been to the others. A model patient in many respects."

"Until today," the inspector said sarcastically.

"Well, yes."

"This is the patient the Board expressed concerns about last week, if memory serves me correctly," the other woman said. "The patient who doesn't speak."

"Well, no."

"And you have taken no action to remedy that situation?"

"He was informed this week that he needed to start, uh, communicating or we would begin drug therapy to ease his resistance."

"I see," the second man said. "Is it part of your regular modus operandi to ask patients' permission before taking obvious steps to treat them? Is this some radical new therapy? I don't believe your temporary accreditation application included the words 'experimental.' Or am I mistaken?"

"Yes. Uh, no."

"And just where were you this morning, Dr. Kautsch, when your facility was falling to pieces under Miss Slimson's direction?"

"I was at a, uh, meeting."

The receptionist called out from her desk. "Dr. Kautsch."

"Yes," he replied, irritated by the intrusion. "What is it?"

"The golf-pro at the country club said you left your clubs in the dressing room, that they would be in his office when you need them next."

Kautsch closed his eyes. Nodded, his head bobbing up and down.

"And were the results of your meeting above par, Dr. Kautsch?" the woman asked.

"Way above par," he said, quietly.

❧

Clint wove quickly in and out of traffic, cursing the cars that blocked his progress at one intersection. He thought of driving on the sidewalk, but noticed a police car around the corner. He decided to pound his steering wheel instead. The light turned green and as soon as he was clear, he hit the accelerator again.

He had already been shaken by Doug's condition at the sanitarium that morning, but even worse so, when he finally received the call that Mandy was in labor. Doug had clung to him for a moment, then pulled him even closer.

"Goodbye, Clint," he whispered, so no one else would notice. If it had been any other situation than Mandy's delivery, Clint would have never left the boy. The words hovered in his mind like Candy's saying 'I'll be back,' only this was even less hopeful. In fact, it was the very hopelessness, the depth of the sound in it that tore at Clint's heart.

Things had quieted down with Dr. Kautsch's arrival. The man had been in a foul mood and seemed to will the young patients into submission. All except Doug, who was so deep in his private darkness that nothing Kautsch said or did had any effect.

Clint swerved around the corner, spotted an ambulance in front of his house. He slammed into the curb and jumped out.

He was met at the door by the paramedics carrying a stretcher. Mandy's eyes were closed, lifeless.

"Excuse us, sir." A woman paramedic said.

"Is she?"

"She's had a tough go. We have to get her to the hospital."

"Can I—?"

"It'd be better if you followed us."

He nodded. "The baby?"

Prudence Peabody appeared in the doorway after the paramedics were through. She was carrying a bundle in her arms.

"Hello, Clint."

His eyes went wide. He blinked, went closer. "Is it—is she—"

"She's going to be fine. Both mother and daughter."

"Can I—?" He took another step.

Prudence pulled the blanket away. Clint bent over, looked into the baby's face.

"Canditu, is it really you?" He asked softly.

The baby stirred, opened her eyes, then closed them.

"Seems she already knows her name," Prudence said. "She's going to be a smart one."

"Like her mother," Clint said. "And sweet as brown sugar."

The paramedics waved Prudence to bring the baby to the ambulance. Clint looked at the front door, then at the ambulance. He couldn't decide what to do next.

"How about a cup of tea?" Fiona said, wiping her hands on a towel. "Then I'll drive you to the hospital."

Clint just stared at her. She laughed, took him by the arm and led him inside. "Mandy's going to be out for a couple of hours at least. They had to give her a strong painkiller. I've got everything just about back to normal in here, but I could use a spot of tea, if you don't mind."

He nodded his head, allowed himself to be lead inside. "I'm a father again."

"That you are, laddie. That you are."

Sally paced up and down in front of the overgrown bushes at the MacBrayne estate, cursing Jimmy—until she heard a bike pedaling her way.

"Where the hell have you been?" she whispered harshly as he dismounted. "I've been here a half hour."

"Shit, Sal, sneaking out of the orphanage isn't as simple as just climbing out your bedroom window, you know?"

"Yeah, well—"

"Come on, let's just do it."

They stashed their bikes and walked toward the cemetery, stopped when they heard muffled barking from the house. They waited a moment, then continued their skulk.

"Why are we doing this?" Jimmy asked as they reached the headstones.

"I don't know."

"You don't know? I'm supposed to risk my neck and you don't know why?"

"This is Hector's show. That's—"

"Hello, children," came from their left.

They both jumped.

"Yeow—" Jimmy started to shout, but Sally clamped her hand over his mouth.

"Sh, damn it."

He pulled her hand off. "Yeah, well, tell Lurch there not to sneak up on people."

"Lurch?" Hector asked.

"Never mind." Sally walked over. "So, what's the deal?"

"Nice to see you too, Sally." His voice was light, but strained. "Jimmy."

"H-Hector." Jimmy shuddered, licked his palm and tried to flatten his hair.

"The deal involves several artifacts that you must bring from the chapel."

"Oh, man. I'm not going in there in the dark. I might trip and break my neck."

"You didn't trip last time, Jimmy," said Hector.

"What d'ya mean?" Jimmy said quickly.

Sally eyed him derisively, shrugged. "What artifacts, Father?"

"By the altar you will find a small steel flask of holy water."

"Wasn't it burned in the fire?" Jimmy had his arms around his chest.

"It's there."

"Well, why didn't you have all this ready for us?"

"Because, my petulant young friend, I can't carry heavy things. I can move through them, but I usually can't pick them up."

"That makes sense," Sally said. "What else?"

"There is a small cross. Did you bring the canvas sack?"

"Ah, gee, Hec. I forgot that. Guess we'll have to do it another night." Jimmy threw up his hands in mock disappointment.

"I have it," Sally said.

"Good." Hector started walking toward the chapel. "Follow me, then."

They walked, Jimmy grumbling under his breath. Hector moved through the chainlink fence around the burned chapel, but Jimmy and Sally had to climb over. Sally produced a small penlight and they used the narrow beam to pick their way through the rubble. Five minutes of searching led to the discovery of the small cross, but not the flask. Jimmy again protested that they wouldn't be able to complete the assignment, when Sally whispered, "Got it! Now what?"

"We need some dirt from near the front steps."

"Dirt?" Jimmy asked. "Geez, do we need a toad and some bat wings, too?"

Hector smiled. "They went out in the eighteenth century."

At the front of the chapel, Sally put several handfuls of dirt in the canvas bag. Hector closed his eyes, then indicated she should put more inside. She did.

"Now put the cross and the flask in, as well," Hector said.

She did as she was told.

"Anything else?" Jimmy snorted. "Why don't I try and drag a pew into Doug's room. That'll be as easy as lugging this in."

"We have enough. Now we can go."

"Wait. Tell us why?" Jimmy had his arms folded at his chest.

"You'll understand everything tomorrow, I promise."

"You promise?" He laughed. "Hear that, Sally? A ghost made me a promise. That's ripe."

"Let's just go, okay?" Sally started toward the bikes.

"Okay, okay."

They walked slowly toward the bushes where the bikes lay. There was more barking from the house, but the outside lights remained off.

Sally straddled her bike. "Will you call me tomorrow?"

"Yeah, from prison." Jimmy righted his bike, turned to Father Hector who stared at it. "What's the matter? You comin', or what?"

"How does one ride on such a machine?"

"Hell, Hec, it's easy. Just like riding a horse."

Hector's pale face grew white. He looked back at the mausoleum, gulped, then swung his leg over the back.

"Good luck, Father Hector."

"Thank you, Sally." He paused. "Sally, would you do me a favor?"

"Sure."

"Would you light a candle for me on my birthday?"

"Yeah, I could do that. When's your birthday?"

"Valentine's Day."

"Okay, I can remember that."

"Can we just go?" Jimmy pushed the pedal.

"Good bye, Father Hector," Sally called.

"Good bye, Sally."

She watched them go. Boy and priest. They disappeared quickly into the darkness. She heard Father Hector cry out and Jimmy laugh. Then she laughed. He'd probably popped a wheelie. She looked up at the stars.

"I hope I did the right thing, Janina."

The stars just twinkled, silently.

Grumpy was surprised to see the cafe dark. He glanced up but there were no lights on in the apartment either. He unlocked the door, flipped the switch and was even more surprised to see the coffee machines still running. He shook his head, not knowing who to call, when a pair of headlights flashed in the front window, then went out. He walked to the door.

Fiona climbed out of her car and waved.

"Where were you?" He asked when she reached the door.

"Delivering a baby." She pecked him on the cheek. "And how was your day?"

"A baby?"

She grinned. "You know, forty years of nannying and I never saw one come into the world." She sighed. "Amazing. Truly amazing."

"Clint's?"

She frowned. "Well, Mandy actually gave birth. Though I think Clint'll pull through."

She explained the emergency call, while they shut down the machines. Grumpy then told her about his talk with Peter, how they spent the afternoon and on into the evening working out a plan to try to repair the damage.

"It's going to take time and it may not work," he smiled wearily, "But I have to tell you, Peter is one fine businessman. He rolled up his sleeves, put his embarrassment behind him, got all the employees together and said that with their help, he would make sure they survived. I don't think I've ever been so proud of him as I was today."

"Really? Not even before his mother died?"

"I realized that I never really got a good look at him, before today. I was looking through an alcoholic haze. Grumpy shook his head. "Peter is a born businessman. Hard to believe he's my son."

"No, it isn't."

"Well, thank you."

"Speaking of sons—" Fiona pointed to the envelope propped on the computer keyboard. "You may want to take a look at that."

Grumpy was confused for a moment, then realized what the envelope contained. He walked slowly to it, picked it up with a shaking hand.

"I feel like I'm about to win an Academy Award."

Fiona remained quiet. He tore open the flap, pulled out the sheets of paper. He studied them for several moments, then sighed and handed them to her.

"I already read them this afternoon."

Grumpy looked confused.

She grinned. "Always wanted to steam open an envelope."

"So what do we do, now?"

"When I first read it, I wasn't sure what I wanted to see. But after seeing that baby born today, I guess I realized something, myself." She opened her hands. "When we were fighting to get that baby out of Mandy, all I wanted was for the little thing to be okay. To have the chance to breathe and come out into the world. Mandy didn't have any choice. If that baby didn't come out, she was going to be in serious trouble, maybe even die. Then, when the little one finally made it and started screaming for her mother, I realized I was going to want to know that little girl for the rest of my life. I had touched her at the moment she arrived. She was born out of my friends' love—our friends. That baby belongs to me, too. The same way Doug did that day at the hospital when Felicity gave her life so he could be born."

Grumpy held up the envelope. "So, what do we do?"

"I say we go to the orphanage tonight and see if we can talk to Jimmy—our son."

"You're sure?"

"He's waited too long, Grumpy." She walked over and took his hand. "And so have you."

Dorothy sat sprawled in the chair, her eyes closed, her head down. Across the desk, Kautsch slammed down the phone.

"I can't believe those bastards. One unfortunate day and they threaten to pull our accreditation."

"Right now, that sounds just fine to me," she murmured.

"What?" Kautsch sat up straight. "Are you crazy? After we worked so hard?"

"Connived, Leon. You cheated, schemed and snookered this place into existence. And you know it."

"I can't believe you're saying that, Slim."

"And don't call me Slim. My name is Dorothy, god damn it."

"What is this, mutiny?"

"Call it what you like. I'm finished, Leon. Kaput, finito."

"What about your son?" He sneered. "Where you going to get a job like this? Especially with the recommendation I'm not going to give you if you leave like this."

"Blackmail, is it?" She moved to the edge of her seat. "Take care, Leon. Blackmail goes both ways."

"Jesus Christ, you are serious, aren't you, Slim—er, Dorothy?"

"You bet I am, Leon." She rose, straightened her wrinkled uniform. "You were an amazingly talented doctor. I once watched you work with children the way I would watch a great magician on stage. I was proud to work for you then. Hell, that's why I fell in love with you."

"You did?"

Her shoulders dropped in defeat. "Jesus, Leon. Did you think I made love to you as part of my job?"

"I—I wasn't sure."

"So you are an idiot." She started toward the door, stopped. "I loved you. Then you started worrying about getting this facility instead of treating the kids. You smelled the money, or the power—I don't know which." She whirled. "And you know what makes me sick? I helped you. With all your plots and deceptions. I just hope the people around here can forgive me, someday."

"What's to forgive?"

She arched an eyebrow. "You really don't know, do you?"

There was a brief flicker in his eye, but it extinguished.

"Okay, you go, if you must. I'll write you a good recommendation, I promise. But I'm not giving up this place, not for anything."

There was a tap at the door. Dorothy opened it to find Miss Groebnick.

"Yes?"

"There's some people here that want to talk to Jimmy Lyden. I'm not sure what to do."

Kautsch looked at his watch. "At this hour? What do they want?"

"I don't know," the woman wrung her hands. "They say they're his parents."

"What?" Kautsch strode to the door. "Jesus Christ, orphans don't have parents!"

The door swung open the rest of the way. Grumpy and Fiona walked into the office.

"Maybe most orphans don't, Dr. Kautsch," He held up the envelope. "but Jimmy Lyden does—now. And I have the proof right here."

❦

Doug lay with his face to the wall. He tried to sleep but it would not come. He stared at the emptiness. There was no way out now. Through the dark fog of the night before, then the long day of emotional agony, he now saw there would be no way to escape Dr. Kautsch and the terrible drugs.

Kautsch had said so, in so many words. No, in exactly those words. "You are going on medication tomorrow, young man. And then we'll see how smart you are."

Doug knew it was wrong to be proud of being so smart. But it hadn't been his idea. He had been born that way. It was fun playing with words. He tried to smile, thinking of the Scrabble game against Massah Sharpe. That wonderful moment, when the word arrived and he won. No matter that he had played the game only to keep Allie near him, he had to admit he enjoyed winning.

Funny, maybe he was more like his father than he thought.

There was a slight scrape at the door. Doug sat up in bed. Then another. The handle turned.

"Who's there?" Doug asked lightly through the dark.

"Sh. It's me."

Doug jumped out of bed. "Jimmy? What are you—?"

"And me."

Doug's eyes widened. "F-father Hector?"

They entered and closed the door, without locking it behind them.

"What are you guys doing here?" He blinked and his voice raised an octave. "Father Hector?"

"Ask the ghost," Jimmy thumbed in Hector's direction. "He's in charge of this mission."

"You have to leave, Doug," Hector said softly. "You must get out of here, tonight."

"What?" Both Jimmy and Doug said at the same time.

"That's right. Jimmy's going to show you the way out. We have to leave Douglasville."

"But—"

"No way, Hec. I signed on to bring you in here, not to get him out."

"I can't leave," Doug said. "Where would I go?"

"We'll discuss that once we're out of here."

Doug sat on the bed. He looked up. "Wait a minute. I thought you said you had to stay at the family chapel. You had to guard it or something."

Hector pointed to the canvas bag in Jimmy's hand. "My job is to protect the family. You're part of the family and you're in danger. Now we have to go, and quickly before that man returns from his errand."

"What man?"

"The one who works here."

"The bald guy," Jimmy said. "He got a phone call and went out. That's how we slipped in, without being seen."

"Shall we go?"

"I don't know."

Jimmy shook his head, exasperated. "Look, MacBrayne-less, I'm leaving. You want to stay, you and the ghost can duke it out. I'm not getting in trouble over something as stupid as this."

He went to the door. Doug looked at Hector. The priest nodded.

"What the hell," Doug said standing quickly. "They were going to screw me up tomorrow, anyway."

"Good," Hector said. "Though I wish you wouldn't use that term."

"What?" Doug asked, slipped on a sweater.

"Hell. It gives me the shivers."

"Ha," Jimmy whispered, peeking out the door. "A ghost with shivers. Now I've heard everything." He waved them to follow. "Let's hit the bricks."

Sabey used his pillow and some clothes to create an effigy beneath the bed covers. Then he reached along the leg of the chair and removed his sharpened piece of metal. He groaned loudly.

"Guard? Oh, God, my stomach."

He tiptoed to the hinge side of the door and knelt. "Oh, God. It hurts."

He heard footsteps, then a light shone through the window. Putting his hand to his mouth to deflect the sound, he groaned again.

The guard opened the door, started in.

Sabey was on him in a flash. He put a choke hold on and held it until the man fainted. Then whispered in his ear. "I'd kill you, but you're not the right sign."

He chuckled, let the man drop, then peeked out the door.

"I can feel you, so close, my lovely Aquarian. It's me, your destiny's coming."

He reached down and took the keys off the guard's belt. Tossed them in the air.

"What a bunch of rubes," he murmured, then headed down the corridor.

"I shouldn't be doing this, you know," Kautsch said as they walked across the drive to the old building. "But I want to see Jimmy's face when you give him your big news."

"Don't you think he has a right to know?" Grumpy asked.

Kautsch paused at the front door. "Oh, I most certainly think he does, but I believe he's bitter enough to spit in your face and tell you to go—excuse me, to tell you off."

He unlocked the door and led them down the hall. Mrs. Groebnick pointed to Jimmy's door and Kautsch tapped lightly.

"Jimmy, are you up? Finished with your homework?" He turned, flashed an evil grin at Grumpy. "He's a model student, you know."

There was no response from inside.

Kautsch knocked more firmly. "Open up, Jimmy. Papa and Mama Bear have brought your porridge."

Still no answer. Kautsch tried the knob, twisted it and opened the door. The room was dark. He switched on the light.

Empty.

"My goodness," Mrs. Groebnick said, "where can he be?"

"Probably robbing gas stations, given his genes." Kautsch shook his head. "Mrs. Groebnick, I want you to wait here. When Jimmy comes in, tell him he's got a meeting with me first thing in the morning."

"But Doctor, he has school."

Kautsch snorted. "School? He can finish his precious paintings some other day. Tomorrow morning, nine o'clock sharp, Mrs. Groebnick."

"Yes, sir."

Kautsch turned to guide Grumpy and Fiona down the hall. "I'm afraid your tearful reunion will have to wait until tomorrow. Pity."

"When can we see him tomorrow?"

"Well, let's see. How about nine thirty. That should give me time to prepare him psychologically."

"Yes, I bet it will, Kautsch," Grumpy said, harshly.

Doug was two paces behind Jimmy. He brushed the canvas bag against a bush alongside the sidewalk and Jimmy stopped.

"For Christ sake, MacBrayne," he whispered sharply. "You wanna get caught, or what?"

"Sorry," Doug whispered back.

Jimmy glanced around cautiously, then waved them on. Doug looked for Father Hector. He was right behind him.

They reached the limit of the east wing and heard voices coming from the parking lot. Jimmy motioned them away toward the west wing. They scurried around two pools of light that dripped down from the rooftop. They reached the dark wall of the west wing and Jimmy leaned against it.

"Man, that was close," he whispered.

"How do we get over the fence?" Doug asked.

"We don't. Hec here, walks through it and you toss the bag over the fence and climb. That's how I get out, all the time."

"You do?" Doug asked, surprised.

"Geez." Jimmy shook his head. "MacBrayne, you are unbelievable."

Doug blushed.

"Okay," Jimmy said. "Just head for the fence and get going."

Doug stuck out his hand, shyly. "Thanks, Jimmy. I know you didn't have to do this."

"Yes I did."

"Why?"

"Ask Sally, if you see her."

Doug kept his hand outstretched. Jimmy slapped it a low five. "Just go, before you get me caught."

Doug looked to Hector who nodded and they sprinted for the fence. He had gone only ten feet or so, when he was caught by his collar and lifted off the ground.

"Hey!" He cried.

"Sh. Don't cry, my little one." The voice was ugly, dark. "You're my ticket home."

"Help!" Doug cried out.

A blade glinted. Doug saw it moving toward him.

"Say goodnight, Gracie."

There was a thud and Doug was wrapped in an even larger embrace. Grunts and shouts filled the air. He was pinned to the ground beneath two bodies. He heard Hector's voice through the melee. Arms, legs, torsos rolled and swatted the air. He was hit in the head, then had the air knocked out of him.

At one point, the darkness seemed to lighten. He thought he saw Hector praying, his lips moving quickly. Then Doug was swallowed up in the fight again. After a century of moments, everything went still. Doug lay on the ground, gasping for breath. He felt himself being lifted. He looked down and saw a still form lying on the ground.

"Come. We go," said whoever was carrying him. Light reflected from the bald head.

"You?" Doug said. Then looked back. "I can't. I have to—the bag— Father Hector."

The man smiled, pointed. Hector was leaning over the prone figure, administering last rites.

"Father Hector, what are you doing?"

Hector's face shown as he smiled. "I'm doing what I was trained to do, Doug. You go on ahead."

"But the bag. How will you get back to the chapel?"

"I'm not going to the chapel."

"You're not?"

Hector shook his head. "Someone has to guide this poor soul to the light. He's suffered enough, with probably more to come."

"Are you sure you want to do this?"

"No." He looked up at the sky. "But in a funny way, I feel as if I just finished my ride on that horse tonight. Only it was a bike, with Jimmy."

"But, Father Hector, you never finished telling me the story of my family."

"It's all inside you. It's in your blood, in your eyes and in the shape of your mouth." Hector rose. "In your soul—You are the real history of your family, Doug."

"And you're truly not afraid, this time?"

He tilted his head, looked down at Sabey. "Next to this one, I'm going to look like a saint."

Footsteps sounded to their left and the tech pulled Doug in the opposite direction. "Come now."

Doug followed, glancing over his shoulder several times. The last time he looked, Hector had gone.

The tech guided Doug through a gap in the chain link, then to a car nestled in a clump of trees. Once inside, the man reached out, to turn the ignition.

"Wait," Doug stopped him. "Y-you saved my life. You were nice to me inside there the whole time. But I don't even know your name."

The man smiled, turned the key. "My name in there was Rocky."

"Gosh, you sure fight like a guy named Rocky. Is that your real name?"

He shook his head, pushed the gas pedal and slipped the car into gear. Once they were off the grass and onto the small gravel road, he flicked on the lights. The interior lights gave his face a green glow. As soon as they hit pavement, the man released a pent-up sigh.

"Where are we going?"

"Away. It is no safe here."

"That's sure true, now. I'm an escaped mental patient, and you— I guess they're going to want you for murder, huh?"

The man shook his head. "That man who try to kill you, he was the murderer. No one will mourn him."

Doug slumped, his side ached and his chin felt bruised. He rolled down the window and put his face to the rush of cool air.

"It smells different out here."

Rocky nodded. "That is freedom. Where I come from, people have not smelled it for years. But soon."

"Where do you come from?"

"Maybe you see, some day."

Doug fell silent. After two minutes, Rocky turned to him. "You quiet."

"Are you taking me to your homeland?"

"Maybe." Rocky hummed a little tune. "Is that where you want go?"

"I don't know. I've hardly ever been out of Douglasville. Is it nice there?"

Rocky shook his head. "No. Will be war there, soon."

"Then I don't think I want to go there."

"Maybe we find a better place."

They drove in silence. Doug glanced at Rocky out of the corner of his eye. He thought about Father Hector and stuck his head out the window to looked up at the sky.

"God bless you, Father Hector."

The stars glowed a little brighter, at least so it seemed to Doug. Maybe it was because he was free again.

He wasn't sure.

Grumpy and Fiona drove in silence. They heard sirens approach. Then two squad cars passed them going at least ninety, their lights flashing. Fiona jerked her head around and followed their progress, then settled in the seat.

"Tired?" Grumpy asked.

"Exhausted."

"Me too."

"Guess we're kind of old for all this excitement."

He laughed. "I think today would have tired me out, even if I were only twenty."

She reached across to pat his hand. "Me too."

They arrived at the cafe, started up the steps. A car pulled into the lot. Grumpy stopped, waved. "Sorry, we're closed."

The driver leaned out. "Closed? The night, she is young."

Then the passenger door opened and someone came running toward Fiona.

"Doug!"

"Nanny!" He threw his arms around her. "I'm so glad to see you."

Grumpy watched the driver of the car get out, his bald head reflecting light from the street lamp. The man walked up to Grumpy, smiled.

"Is good to see you again, brother."

Grumpy peered into the hairless face. "Valka?"

"You grow hair to hide. I shave it off, for same reason." He started up the steps. "Come, we must hurry. There is much to discuss."

Fiona pushed Doug away to look at the face she loved so dearly. He smiled shyly. She looked closer, realized his eyes were different, deeper, full of new knowledge. And suddenly she understood why he had been kept away from her for all these months. He *had* to leave, not just because the law would look for him, but because he was going out to find the world, fulfill more of his destiny.

Tears welled in her eyes. He reached out and caught one on the end of his fingertip, held it up to the moon, then touched it to his heart.

"Why did you do that?" She asked with a sniffle.

"Wherever I go, Nanny, no matter where you are, all I will have to do is look at the moon and touch my heart—and you will know."

"Know what?"

"That you will always be as close as my own heart."

"Then you have to promise to take good care of that heart, since I won't be there to do it for you."

"I will." He put his arm around her waist and they slowly walked up the steps.

She stopped at the door. "You know, I don't know if I'll be able to let you go. I can't imagine how to say goodbye to you."

He smiled, those new eyes sparking with humor. "Then don't say goodbye. Just practice what you'll say the next time we see each other."

"And what might that be?"

"Well, you could say, 'Why, hello, Doug. Fancy meeting you, again.'"

"Just like that?"

He nodded, serious face, laughing eyes. "Just like that."

Epilogue

Father Hector rose toward the light. All that was heavy within him lessened and began to fall away. He felt the dark pull behind him, the resistance of the one called Sabey. Father Hector's own fears faded and became images projected on an opaque tapestry of events and faces he recognized but could no longer keep close, as he swam nearer to the emanating center of something that no longer appeared as light. It was crystalline one moment, empty and full of everything the next.

"Will they hurt me?" came a quivering whisper behind him.

Father Hector extended a comforting hand and clasped the other's. "This is not a time for pain. Here, we rest."

There was a long comet tail of a sigh that he knew would not end until Sabey released his earthly concerns and surrendered himself to the Light.

Hector looked down, through the diminishing lens of his voyage. They were all still there, the ones he had protected while fearfully guarding his own being.

The grandfather, now aligned with a new mate of soul was being offered a fresh glimpse of the lessons that only love can bring to the weary and the confused. The son, whose pride had been punctured and awaited repair.

And the grandson, the child who had arrived with Cosmic knowledge. His time of real learning was just now upon him. The brilliant promise of his birth had been spun into a careful cocoon and he stood at the prow of a new ship, awaiting his new season of travel, of learning. The winds of life would carry him far beyond even his effervescent imagination. For life is the real adventure of each soul—no matter how mighty, humble, well-founded or utterly lost—it might be.

The others flashed their own cosmic kaleidoscope of momentary colors, turned once, to bring blue skies and clear hope. Another adjustment, for red eyes and the illuminated map of pain that leads to the treasure of the real heart. Child, wife, good man or sinner. All swimming in the thick twilight of earthbound existence, struggling against the pain of the long journey to reach this shining, illumined shore.

Hector's eyes met what felt like rain and his own pain fell away as surely as he felt the same quick release from the spirit of Sabey. Then he heard one last sound that contained all the promise and hurt of true nature: the long, lonely howl of a dog baying, begging the moon to return its master.

For a moment he was utterly alone, and then he was with them, with many who had mourned his passing, about a hundred years before. All waiting, their arms of light opened wide, to embrace him and welcome him home.

All below was gone, because the Light had now become All. Though he knew the tangled tales would continue on Earth, as they have time, after time, after time.

Birthmark

The collaboration between Bill Rowe and Peter Cooper has developed into a relationship far beyond the writing into one of father and son, brothers, and friends. Rowe, originally from Cincinnati and now living in Florida and Scotland, is a successful businessman, photographer and researcher. He began work on the book during the 1980's after reading about experiments to measure the weight of the soul in patients at the moment of death. Cooper, an editor and writer who lives in the Catskill Mountains of New York, joined the project in 1993.

OTHER FINE BOOKS FROM VIVISPHERE PUBLISHING:

A Death in Brooklyn
by Terry Quinn

Footprints of the Garden Snake
by Vivian Allison

Gold Marilyn
by Lia Skidmore

I, Grace Note
by J. Schwartzman

Mattie & Frank
by Katherine Anne Dieter

Adventures in Contentment
by David Grayson

The Confessions of Artemus Quibble
by Arthur Train

The Man Who Lived in a Shoe
by Henry James Forman

Nomads of the North
by James Oliver Curwood

Titles are always available at:
http://www.vivisphere.com/